THE EMPEROR WALTZ

THE
EMPEROR
WALTZ
PHILIP
HENSHER

FOURTH ESTATE • *London*

Fourth Estate
An imprint of HarperCollins*Publishers*
77–85 Fulham Palace Road
London W6 8JB
4thestate.co.uk

First published in Great Britain by Fourth Estate in 2014

1 3 5 7 9 8 6 4 2

A catalogue record for this book is available from the British Library.

ISBN 978-0-00-745957-5

Typeset by Palimpsest Book Production Ltd, Falkirk, Stirlingshire

Printed and bound in Great Britain by Clays Ltd, St Ives plc

For Thomas Adès
An E-flat sonata movement
standing at an augmented fourth to the universe.

CONTENTS

BOOK 1
1922

1.

'You will have brought your own towels and bedlinen,' Frau Scherbatsky said, in her lowered, attractive, half-humming voice, 'as I instructed, as I suggested, Herr Vogt, in my telegram. Other things I can supply, should you not have them for the moment. Soap, should you wish to wash yourself before tea, of which we shall partake in the drawing room in half an hour. Should you wish for hot water, Maria will supply you with some, if you ask her, on this occasion, since you have just arrived and had a tiring journey. I know all about trains, their effects on the traveller.'

She turned, smiling graciously, making a generous but unspecific wave of the hand.

'Shaving soap,' she carried on, continuing across the hall, 'I can stretch to. My husband and boys, my two boys, were killed in the war, and I have their things, their possessions and bathroom necessities, which I have no undue sentimental attachment to, if you do not feel ghoulish at the prospect of shaving with the soap of a dead man, or three dead men, rather. It is better in these days that things should be used, and not preserved. We have all lost too much to retain the conventions of our fathers. Don't you agree, Herr Vogt?'

'That is very kind of you,' the young man said. 'But I only need soap to wash after my journey, thank you so much.' He had the appearance of someone who needed to shave once weekly, and perhaps had not started to shave at all. Too young

3

to have known the war at first hand, blond and fresh-faced, his eyes wide open, eager to please, slight and alert. He walked behind Frau Scherbatsky, across the hallway to the heavy wooden stairs of her Weimar villa, dark-panelled and velvet-trimmed, like the interior of a ransacked jewel-box. His stance was lopsided and ungainly; his suitcase, a borrowed old paternal one, leather and scarred with journey-labels torn off, was full and heavy. He was here for three months at least.

'It was my husband's house,' Frau Scherbatsky said, proceeding in her mole-coloured tea-gown with a neat black apron over the top. 'He thought of it for many years, considering how many coat hooks should be placed in the downstairs cloakroom. "Your house is perfect, Frau Scherbatsky," Herr Architect Neddermeyer said. Everything so well considered – and reconsidered – you know. Do you know Goethe's house in the marketplace? No? You must go. Goethe's study, surrounded by a corridor and an anteroom, so that he could hear the servants coming and not be unduly disturbed. And we have just the same arrangement here. Herr Neddermeyer's bedroom, now. Necessity called, on both of us, let us say. The house –' she continued up the stairs, stately, walking, turning at the half-landing, but not looking at Vogt exactly, giving a general smile in the direction of the English stained glass of an angel with a lily, illuminating the stairwell with sanctity '– the house was finished and built by my husband to his exact specifications in 1912, and we had three most happy years here. Two years and seven months. This is your room. I hope you like it. It has a view over the park, as you see. You cannot quite see the Gartenhaus of Goethe – that is only from the corner bedroom. In current circumstances, I cannot specify the exact rent from month to month, but I will not take advantage of you, Herr Vogt, I can promise you that. And I think you said you were a student of art?'

'I am just about to start my studies,' Christian Vogt said, setting his case down. 'I begin on Monday, in three days' time.'

'And you allowed yourself three days to settle in, most wise,'

Frau Scherbatsky said. 'Those long train journeys are immeasurably exhausting. You would wish to do yourself justice. If I could only ask that, should you decide to paint in your room, you place on the floor, and especially over this rug, some newspaper. You are a painter, I hope – I do hope those are a painter's sensitive fingers. Just remember, Herr Vogt, the newspaper over floor and rug. That would be so kind. And no models, please, no models, that I must ask you. And ...'

Frau Scherbatsky looked at him with one eyebrow cocked. Christian did not at once know what she meant. But then he recalled the agreement that his father and she had reached about the payment for the accommodation, and took the old gold watch of Great-grandfather from his waistcoat pocket. He handed it over. Frau Scherbatsky, almost unnoticeably, ran her thumb and forefinger along the gold chain and bar. She placed it safely, and with due carefulness, in her apron. That would cover the costs for the three months (at least) and then they could enter into more negotiations, his father and Frau Scherbatsky. 'But does the room suit you?' she said.

'It's charming, Frau Scherbatsky,' Christian Vogt said, not wanting to commit himself in speech to being a painter, or anything in particular, just yet. Something of her stately, half-generous manner had got into his way of talking. The room was plain, but well lit, through the diamond-leaded windows the light from the north, illuminated warmly by the last of the summer greenery in garden and park. On the bed was a practical counterpane of woollen stars in primary colours, knitted together; two stained oak wardrobes built into the wall; a dark green English pattern of wallpaper and, over the bed, a small oil copy of *The Isle of the Dead*, almost expertly done.

'And here is Maria, with some hot water,' Frau Scherbatsky said. The maid came in; she poured her pewter pitcher of hot water into the washbowl with minute attention, her hand trembling slightly in the steam with the weight. Her face was freckled; her uncovered hair was gingery, smoothed back in a practical

5

bun. Maria, watched benevolently by Frau Scherbatsky, finished pouring. She transferred the pitcher from one hand to the other and, with a curious gesture, drew the back of her right hand across her smooth hair. The maid caught Christian Vogt's eye; she gave a cryptic, inward smile with the movement of her hand across the gloss of her ginger hair. 'We will see you downstairs in half an hour, Herr Vogt,' Frau Scherbatsky said. 'Welcome to Weimar.' And they withdrew, Maria closing the door behind her, not turning as she went.

As the door shut, Christian Vogt was made aware of the sound of birdsong, close at hand, in either parkland or garden, in Frau Scherbatsky's bereaved garden or Weimar's long, quiet land-scapes. It was a blackbird, and if he closed his eyes, he could see the bird's open yellow bill and shining black eye, the angle of its neck as it sat in a tree and sang to the empty air in pleasure.

'I am an artist,' Christian said, experimentally, to the empty room.

2.

He had been an artist since the eleventh of May that year. Christian Vogt lived with his father and brother in a second-floor apartment in Charlottenburg, in Berlin. White plaster dragons and Atlases held up the entrance to their block, a polished dark oak door in between, and Frau Miller, the concierge, behind her door with a series of notes explaining her absence or place, to be put up with drawing pins according to need. The apartment was serviced and kept going by their cook, Martha, and Alfred, the manservant. Since their mother had died, the spring before, Herr Vogt had decided that it was not necessary to keep a maid as well, that Alfred was quite capable – Christian could remember Alfred's departure for the war, years before. He had been a big boy, limber and grinning. When he returned from the army, he still had a sort of smile on his face, but a skinny, bony, pulled-apart one. His father had offered him his old job back. 'I could do nothing else,' he said, and let the maid go a few weeks later without complaining. There was no way of doing without the cook, however. When Christian's mother had still been alive, there had been a succession of varied dishes, and complaints if the food, even in the depths of war, had sunk into monotony and repetition. His mother had made things so much nicer. Now there was more food to be had in the markets, but the cook had settled into a routine, and plain grilled lamb chops alternated with veal – sometimes flounder, and sometimes even horse, done plainly. Nobody seemed to notice.

Egon would drive the motor, if it were needed, but it was rarely needed. There were large changes in the household since his mother's death in the epidemic, the year before. One of the smaller changes, which had also gone unattended, was that Christian's future was no longer a matter of concern. Among the large and heavy furniture, Christian and his brother Dolphus went, wearing the clothes they had had for two years, filling the time as best they could between meals. His father went to the office, or he stayed at home, working in his study. Dolphus went to school under his own steam. Christian, who had finished at the Gymnasium in the springtime, spent his days quietly and without much sense that anything was expected of him.

His days were matters of outings and explorations, running outwards from U-Bahn stop or tram-route. It was in the course of one of these explorations that, under a railway arch in Friedrichstrasse, far from home, he saw a poster advertising a new school for the arts in Weimar. It had opened the year before. Students were sought. The look of the poster appealed to him: the letters without eyebrows, shouting in a new sort of way. They might have been speaking to him.

Christian had always liked to paint and to draw. When he was younger, he had been able to lie on his bed and imagine the paintings he would produce: of a girl stretched at full length in a bare tree, a greyhound looking up into the branches, forlorn and spiky with his nude mistress. A sun rising over an alp, but a matter of geometry, not sublimity, the mountains rendered as a series of overlapping triangles. A face in a forest, no more than that, the dim chiaroscuro of the rippling foliage absorbing the cloak of the man, the woman, the ambiguous figure. You could paint a picture that was nothing much but a line and a square and another line and a rainbow – people in Russia had done that: he had seen it in the magazines an art master had shown them. A portrait of his family, the four faces, then the three, floating in the darkness of the apartment. Sometimes he thought them through as far as conceiving of a medium. It could change abruptly: sometimes an oil four-part portrait could suddenly decide to become a polished wooden relief with the word 'UNTERGANG' carved in tendril-like letters – no, in modern brash American newspaper-headline letters, much better. He would lie like that, conceiving his works of art. Sometimes he would get up and, with charcoal on the rough paper he had saved up for and kept in a stack under his bed, he would attempt to draw what he had thought of. He had learnt some things in art classes at the Gymnasium, but art there did not matter, was only brought to their attention because gentlemen needed to be acquainted with the collectible, needed to be warned of what artists in Russia were laying waste to. He learnt most at home, on his own. Nobody except Dolphus had ever seen anything he had done, except the drawings he had produced, stiffly and awkwardly and without merit, in the drawing classes at school. Those had been praised by the master and by his classmates. Christian did not know how you would show anyone you knew the drawings of an imagined nude woman in a tree, or explain what you had meant by it. Christian had been intended to be a lawyer. Nothing had been mentioned about any of that since his mother had died. Sometimes Christian wondered whether all arrangements had been made by his father without consulting him.

The poster in Friedrichstrasse, under the dank, sopping

railway bridge, struck Christian like a recruiting poster. Around him, the dry-rot smell of Berlin crowds rose, as the short, dark, cross Berliners pushed their way about him, banging him with their bags and possessions. An older woman, like one of his father's elder sisters, raised a lorgnon and inspected him: a thin, blond boy, his head almost shaven as if after an illness, wearing a soft, loose-fitting suit of an indeterminate brown, like the suits of English cloth the young had worn before the war. The poster said that makers of the new were invited to Weimar, where everything would alter, there, for the better. It was the eleventh of May. In the boulevards, the lime trees that gave them their names were opening, showing their fresh leaves, perfuming the wide way. The weather in Berlin was, at last, beginning to improve, to soften, to give out some warmth to the cold ornament of the city.

3.

That evening, his father's sister from the town of Brandenburg came to dinner. She was a twice-yearly visitor who turned up in the city to make sure of her affairs, which her brother handled, and in the last year, to ensure that her brother and nephews were continuing to live in a respectable way at home, despite her sister-in-law's death from influenza. She was a small, beady woman, full of news of Brandenburg life. Her brother had moved away from Brandenburg thirty-five years before, to the opportunities offered by a university education, a long apprenticeship, a marriage in middle age, children and a solid apartment in Charlottenburg.

'And Herr Dietmahler sold his house in the Kleiststrasse to his cousin Horst Dietmahler, the younger brother of his father the corn-merchant, his son, whose wife had twins last year. His business is suffering and he no longer needed a house on that scale,' Aunt Luise continued. The ivory-handled spoon, from the set that came out for guests, rose and fell from the grey potato soup. Occasionally her small hand, beaded with black rings and a triple jet bracelet, reached out and tore at the bread rolls. Between mouthfuls, she spoke in a tired, mechanical way of her town. 'There was a Frenchman who came to visit last week, who stayed with the Enzelmanns in Magdeburgerstrasse, you remember the beautiful house, the big beautiful house that the Enzelmanns always had, the Frenchman came after writing, he wanted to look at some furniture that Grandfather Enzelmann had brought back from Paris in the 1870 war, you remember, Cousin Ludwig, the beautiful chair and the commode and the looking-glass with the stork and the swan in gold in the drawing room, and the Frenchman came to inspect it, and pretended to admire it before he said it had been stolen from his family. And Minna von Tunzel ...'

Kind-hearted Dolphus in his sailor suit stared and listened, wide-eyed. He felt sorry for her, he had told Christian on her last visit: two sons killed in the war, both on the same day, or perhaps one day after the other, thousands of miles apart, and the telegrams making their separate way to Brandenburg, and Uncle Joachim dead of an apoplexy six months later. But Christian could remember how Aunt Luise had been before the war, and her two big, cruel sons too, and perspiring fat Uncle Joachim. His father was nodding decorously as Aunt Luise reached Minna von Tunzel's parlourmaid's baby, giving a signal to Alfred to bring in the whiting, in a circle with their tails in their mouths in a grey sauce, as they always were when a guest came. Christian was thinking about the decision he had made that morning, in Friedrichstrasse.

'Father,' he said, when the fish had been taken away and Aunt Luise was fumbling in her reticule for a handkerchief. 'We must talk about what I am to do.'

'What you are to do, dear boy?' his father said. He had had a long afternoon with Luise, trying to explain what had happened to her investments and her bonds. He never looked forward to

her visits, and this had been a very trying one. 'Is this an important conversation?'

'Father, I've decided what I want to do after school,' Christian
said, summoning his courage.

'I thought all that was decided,' Aunt Luise said nastily, placing
her knife and fork on the plate, inspecting, pulling the fork back
a tenth of a point so that they would be exactly next to each
other. 'I thought the elder was to be a lawyer and the younger
an engineer. The elder boy to study in Nuremberg; the younger
to take himself off to London, where the best engineering schools
are.'

'I don't want to be a lawyer, Father,' Christian said, not
addressing Aunt Luise. To his surprise, there was something like
a grey smile in his father's eyes, something between the two of
them. His father did not often engage him with a look: he found
it easier to look somewhere else, as if not paying attention. He
wondered whether his father had been waiting for him to start
this conversation for the last year. 'I want to go to an art school
in Weimar. I would be a very good artist, I know it. It's all I
want to do.'

'Want to do?' his father said. 'I never wanted to be a lawyer,
either, but I did, and I was very glad of it in the end.'

'Karin Burgerlicher's second-youngest boy—' Aunt Luise
began.

'You can always paint in your spare time, on Sundays and on
holidays, in the Alps,' his father said. 'Lawyers often do. But I
never heard of an artist who drew up wills and contracts on
Sundays and holidays. You could never be any sort of lawyer,
you know, if you went to an art school. Wittenberg, you said?'

'Weimar,' Christian muttered.

'Ah, Weimar, a beautiful town also,' his father said, in a full,
satisfied tone. The fish had been taken away, and now, the sour
beef was brought in. They sat in silence. Aunt Luise was
pretending to be occupied with something in her lap, with handkerchief and pill box. Dolphus gazed at his brother in undisguised

wonder. It was not clear to Christian whether his father had reached some conclusion, or whether he now thought that everyone agreed that Christian's future was as it had always been, had never needed discussion, that the discussion was now over.

'Father,' Christian said, when the beef was served and Alfred had left the room.

'Well, I don't see why not,' his father said. 'The world is changing so much. And if it all fails, you can at least become a town clerk or something of that kind. Or start again. Nothing much would be lost, by your year at an art school. I suppose that your brother Dolphus can still go to London, to become an engineer.'

'Brother,' Aunt Luise said in wonderment, dropping her fork in the beef. It was the first time Christian had ever heard his father say anything worth wondering at, the first time he had surprised anyone other than by remaining silent when he might speak. His choice of wife had been the daughter of a judge; his choice of dwelling had been between two other lawyers; his choice of children might have remained as it had been – the elder a lawyer, the younger an engineer. Christian was not surprised that his sister, even though she had known him from the nursery, stared and gasped, and in protest dropped her fork in her sour beef.

'Thank you, Father,' Christian said. 'I would be a very bad lawyer, I know it. And I can be a very good artist.' He wanted to say that he could be a great artist. But at his father's dinner table, with greyish well-ironed and patched linen, the greying velvet drapes, the Moritz von Schwind Alpine landscape, the encrusted silver candlesticks on the table and the hissing curlicue of the gas jets on the wall, the words did not come out.

'One thing I must insist on,' his father said. 'There are to be no models lounging about the place of any sort. Now, Luise. Let me help you to what passes for spinach these days.'

Aunt Luise began to tell them about what had happened to Karin Burgerlicher's younger brother in Rome in the 1890s.

4.

In Weimar, Christian came downstairs from his room, not changed from the Norfolk jacket he had travelled in, but washed and refreshed. He stood for a moment in the hallway with the illuminated light falling through the stairway, then entered the room with the door slightly ajar. In there was a man standing at the window, looking out at the parkland. His head was severe in expression, with large, round glasses, and his hair cut in an abrupt round manner that had nothing to do with the shape of his cranium, as if a bowl had been placed on his head before the scissors had been run about. The room was light and comfortable, with a pair of sofas and an upholstered window-seat where the man stood, and some chairs about the table where tea sat. A number of wasps were buzzing about the room.

'Good afternoon,' the man said, in a strong Leipzig accent. 'You must be our new arrival.'

'How do you do?' Christian said, and introduced himself.

'I am Franz Neddermeyer,' the man said. 'Also a guest of Frau Scherbatsky. How do you find your room?'

'Very nice,' Christian said. 'I am from Berlin.'

'I did not ask you that, although I am pleased to know it,' Herr Neddermeyer said. 'This is my house, and also Frau Scherbatsky's house, although we are not connected through marriage or otherwise and only one of us owns it. How do you make that out?'

'I think Frau Scherbatsky told me that you are the architect of the house,' Christian said. 'Although both the owner and the tenant of a house could talk about it being their house, so that is also a possibility.'

'Ah,' Neddermeyer said. He seemed disappointed at the failure of his conundrum. He walked away from the window, where he had left a book lying face down on the window-seat, and about the room, running his finger over the piano keyboard, covered with a crocheted shawl, the top of a bookcase, the wooden back of one of the sofas. As he came up to the chairs at the tea table, he minutely but decisively shifted one a couple of degrees; stepped back; inspected the change; shifted it back again. Christian thought of Aunt Luise as he looked at the middle-aged man – no, the old man: his skin was crêpy and drawn in a diagonal underneath his chin.

'I had always lived in the house my father built,' Neddermeyer said. 'He, too, was an architect, here in Weimar. How do you come to know Frau Scherbatsky?'

'I do not know her,' Christian said. 'My father is a lawyer, and he made enquiries about lodgings in Weimar from a professional associate here, and the professional associate came back with Frau Scherbatsky as a suggestion. His name was Anhalt.'

'Ah, Lawyer Anhalt,' Neddermeyer said. 'His recommendation – well, he is a friend of old of our "landlady".' The word was rendered in a comic tone, as if he was amused by the idea that anyone would offer Frau Scherbatsky money to sleep in a part of her property. 'Would you care for some tea? I don't know what has happened to Frau Scherbatsky. Herr Wolff, the other guest here, is on business of some sort in Erfurt today, I know.'

This seemed to put an end to Neddermeyer's curiosity about Christian's life, and while he was busying himself with the tea, Christian went about the room. On the bookshelf was a small porcelain or perhaps enamel model of an exotic vegetable, an aubergine. Christian picked it up, and just as he did so, a wasp came buzzing at him. He raised one hand to flap it away, and somehow tipped the aubergine to one side. The stalk and cap of the aubergine actually formed the lid of what it was, a jar, and as Christian tipped it sideways, it fell to the polished wooden flooring and broke. Neddermeyer looked up from the teapot.

'Oh dear,' he said.

Christian was crimson – he looked at Neddermeyer with horror. 'I didn't realize—' he said. 'I didn't realize it had a lid. I just turned it to one side.'

'Well, that is unfortunate,' Neddermeyer said. 'Let me see.' He put the teapot down and came over. Without its stalk and cap, the aubergine hardly looked like an aubergine any longer, just a bulbous purple vase. It, clearly, would not do. 'That really is unfortunate.'

Neddermeyer was, in fact, rather enjoying this humiliation. 'Please help me, Herr Neddermeyer,' Christian said. 'It can't be the first thing I do when I arrive in poor Frau Scherbatsky's house, start smashing her things about.'

'No,' Neddermeyer said. 'Although, you must admit, it is the thing which you have started by doing.' He picked up the lid from the floor. 'It is really not as bad as all that. A very clean break. And here is our hostess.'

Frau Scherbatsky came in, smiling. 'I hope you have not been waiting – the tea must be quite cold. I had to finish a letter to my daughter in Dresden. Now—'

'Frau Scherbatsky,' Christian began.

'A terrible thing has happened,' Neddermeyer said. 'I was brushing past the bookcase when my sleeve unfortunately caught your very ugly jar here; it fell; the lid has smashed. But there is good news! It is not so badly broken. It can be mended and riveted very easily.'

'Oh dear,' Frau Scherbatsky said. 'Is it so very ugly? I never really thought of it. I don't suppose it is even any use in the marketplace – no one would barter anything for it, I am certain. By all means, take it and mend it if it salves your conscience, Herr Neddermeyer.'

Christian, full of silent gratitude for the saving of the situation, tried to engage Neddermeyer's eye, but he quizzically raised an eyebrow without looking in more than Christian's general direction. 'Here is some orange cake,' he said, sitting down. 'My favourite.'

The orange cake was dry, perhaps a day or two past its best, and flavoured artificially rather than with peel and juice. Christian took a bite just as Frau Scherbatsky said, 'You are here to study, Herr Vogt, you were saying?' He could not for the moment speak: his mouth was full of dry cake and his eyes, at once, began to fill with tears of shame at his vandalism. Instead of going on talking – she had asked only for the benefit of Neddermeyer – Frau Scherbatsky waited with a courteous half-smile as Christian took a great gulp of tea to wash it down. He felt like a brutal animal invited to tea with two clever, immaculate dolls, and to finish off the toy-like impression of beauty of Frau Scherbatsky's house, he now saw, as he prepared to speak, that the teapot from which she had poured was ingeniously shaped in the form of a cauliflower, and the teacup from which he was about to drink was a circle of cauliflower leaves. He swallowed, shook his head.

'You are a student of what, Herr Vogt?' Neddermeyer said.

'I am about to begin the study of art,' Christian said.

'Ah, excellent,' Neddermeyer said. 'An art historian. That is excellent. At the university here?'

'No, Herr Neddermeyer,' Christian said. 'I am studying to become an artist.'

'At my old school, then,' Neddermeyer said. 'Is it still in existence? I came here myself to study there, here in Weimar, when I was no more than nineteen, and I have never left. Thirty-eight years ago this autumn. We architecture students had little to do with the fellows on the painting and drawing side. I expect things are just the same now – one half thinks the other flib-bertigibbets, and the other thinks them dull, money-grubbing fellows. Artists never change.'

'You put it so well, Herr Neddermeyer,' Frau Scherbatsky said. 'But is the art school that you are thinking of still in exist-ence, Herr Neddermeyer, even?'

'I am enrolled at the Bauhaus,' Christian said. 'It is only just opening now.'

'The Bauhaus,' Neddermeyer said. There was a perceptible chilling; he set down his tea and tipped his head back slightly, inspecting Christian over the top of his glasses. 'The Bauhaus.'

Christian had the distinct impression that Neddermeyer was now about to change his mind about his previous brotherliness and to tell their landlady that, after all, it had been Christian who had smashed the aubergine pot.

'I know the Bauhaus,' Neddermeyer said. 'There is wild talk in the town, both about them and, I must say, by them. When you are as old as I am, you have seen plenty of young men who hope to change the world by shocking their elders. And as time goes on, the shock fades away – the shock and the desire to shock. You hope only to make things as well as your ancestors made them. That may prove difficult enough. The Bauhaus. Well. They wish to make things new, I believe, and turn our lives upside down; to ask us to sit on tetrahedrons, and to live in houses made of glass, like tomatoes. I have seen plenty of wild young men, wanting to change the world by shocking their elders. I may have been one of them myself, once upon a time.'

Christian inspected the cauliflower teapot; the inglenook fire-place; the padded window-seat. He did not object.

'Young people will not like the same things as old people,' Frau Scherbatsky said, smiling. 'You must admit that if no new opinions ever came along we should be living in the houses of Augustus the Strong.'

'I don't think anyone wants to shock,' Christian said. 'I think we only want to start by making new things. But I haven't been there yet. I am sure you know more about it than I do.'

Neddermeyer had got up and, holding his leaf-shaped teacup, had gone over to the window, perhaps to hide his emotions. It seemed as if the mention of the Bauhaus struck some chord with him. 'They seem very little interested in Weimar, where they are,' he said. 'I don't believe they recruited any teaching staff from the town, though, Heaven knows, there are enough talents and experience to power a—'

'Herr Neddermeyer feels strongly,' Frau Scherbatsky said confidentially but audibly, leaning her whole body towards Christian from her chair. 'He was very unfortunately—'

'And here they come,' Neddermeyer said, his voice raising gleefully as he looked out of the window. 'I don't know whether you have seen your colleagues and masters yet? They come this way every day, around this time, for their exercise. I promise you, I did not ask them to appear to prove any kind of a point.'

5.

In the park, three hundred metres away, a small group of people was approaching. They had shaven heads that shone in the sun like wet pebbles by the lakeside. There were eight or nine of them; their smiles, too, shone in the light. It was their clothing that seemed most extraordinary. An elderly woman in a fur-collared overcoat was just now pausing, thirty metres from them, and watching them with open fascination. They wore floor-length robes in purple, flapping as they moved; home-made and evidently not well fitting. The robes looked very much like the garb of a wizard Christian had seen in a childhood pantomime. The tallest of the group, a man in his late twenties or early thirties, wore also a metal collar, like a pewter platter with the middle excised. The group surged around him; their combined movement was uniform, rippling, wavelike and unnervingly joyous. Christian felt that if he left the house and went towards this group he would be brought in; he would experience their joy, cut off from the delights and sorrows of the world about him. And yet he did not want to go towards them. The single, jogging, up-and-down rhythm of their heads, like a string ensemble approaching a climax, was unnatural and fruitless. What were they doing? They seemed to be going for a walk, but they were pressed together too tightly for that; they might have been a single body. Their smiles and joyous movements suggested that someone in there was talking, but you could not see that they were anything but silent as they walked. They moved to some music, audible only to themselves. With a shock, Christian saw that they were men and women mixed, brought into a uniformity of appearance by their heads being shaved.

As they passed, their attention seemed forward-facing. But one of them – a woman, it looked like – must have felt the gaze of Frau Scherbatsky, Herr Neddermeyer and Christian upon her from the leaded window of the house. She turned, alone, as if rebelling against the will of the group and, with a habitual but pointless gesture, made a movement over her shaved head. Her wide and empty smile – her mouth was, he could see, too large for her little face – did not alter; he could not see whether she had, in fact, engaged with his look or seen the three of them through the window at all. He felt ashamed. In a moment the girl in her loose Biblical robe of purple turned away again, and the tightly knit procession, like a performance, moved on away from them.

'They come every day, around this time,' Frau Scherbatsky said. 'I couldn't tell you what it is all about. My neighbours are fascinated by it.'

'I think it is some kind of newly invented religion,' Neddermeyer said.

'Oh, surely not,' Frau Scherbatsky said. 'At first we believed that it was some sort of advertisement for a children's play, something of that sort – the seven noble wizards, you know, Herr Vogt.'

'Do you know where they come from?' Christian said. They resumed their seats; Neddermeyer continued to stand at the window, entranced.

'Yes, indeed,' Frau Scherbatsky said. 'They come from the Bauhaus.'

'The one at the front,' Neddermeyer said. 'Did you see? The one at the front, taller and older than the rest, he is actually a member of the teaching staff. I have heard that he has, indeed,

19

invented a new religion, which he requires his students to follow. We were quite safe up here, but if you come close to them, seeing them by chance in the street, they emit an overpowering scent of garlic. I have heard that one of the tenets of the religion is that nothing else may be eaten. A sort of purge.'

'Very inconsiderate to the rest of us,' Frau Scherbatsky said.

'If, when I was a student of architecture all those years ago, I had been told that my professor wished me to wear violet robes in public, to shave my head, to eat nothing but garlic, and to follow a new religion of his devising ...' Neddermeyer started to say.

Frau Scherbatsky nodded, perhaps embarrassed on behalf of Christian. 'Where is Herr Wolff, Herr Neddermeyer? Did he tell you?'

'I believe he is in Erfurt this afternoon, on business,' Neddermeyer said. 'His usual business. He said he was unsure whether he would return this evening.'

'Really,' Frau Scherbatsky said. 'That, too, is inconsiderate. He might have told me before he went away.'

6.

In a room not so very far away, with a similar view of the park, a man and a twelve-year-old boy sat. The room was hung with paintings; in each of them, an animal, a form, an arrangement of lines, an exclamation mark, the heads of people as drawn by children could be seen. On the easel, a square canvas with blotches and stains in ochre, violet and umber. The boy and the man sat at the tea table, set with a cloth and an old, dented silver tea service. The man fixed the boy with his gaze; the boy's eyes were huge. The man took a small cardboard box from his pocket, opened it and took out a sugar cube, delicately, with his thin fingers on which paint had dried and dirt been allowed to accumulate beneath his nails. With the tips of his fingers, his eyes never leaving the boy's face, he lifted the silver lid of the sugar bowl, and dropped the sugar cube among other, nearly indistinguishable sugar cubes. He lowered the lid, and replaced the cardboard box in his pocket. His hands were paint-stained, but his clothes were immaculately clean; Klee liked to take off his painting smock before he had his tea in the afternoon. The boy's eyes filled with premonitory laughter. Underneath the table on a Turkish leather cushion, a cat slept in its favourite place, curled with its face into its belly, its feet about its face, and paid no attention to anything that was happening.

There seemed nothing more to say. Klee sat back and took out the cigarette he liked to smoke before tea. In one of their shared rituals, Felix got up and went about the studio until he found the place where his father had last left his matches. This time it was by the window-seat, where he often liked to prowl and stand before the view while thinking about his next move on a painting. Not exactly looking at the view, more a matter of letting the world flood in without seeing it, his father had once said. For a second, as he picked up the matches, Felix tried the trick. But it was no good. He could not help actually looking at the world; at the pack of shaved-head wizards moving off into the distance following Johannes Itten, the trees in the park, a blackbird sitting on the branch nearest to the house, and his mother almost at the gate of the house, returning from her walk and already unbuttoning her coat in her eagerness for her tea. He took the matches over to his father and, as he was allowed to, struck one, holding it up to his father's cigarette.

'Mother is here,' Felix said. 'I saw her just coming up the road.'

His voice trembled with his terrible amusement, thinking of the sugar cube. His father sucked at the end of the cigarette and said nothing. His face was mask-like in its skin; Gropius's wife had once asked his father whether it didn't hurt, having a face like that, so tight like a drum, and his father's face had grown still more mask-like, pulling back into a world of squareness. Felix had twelve tasks in the house, and they were added to every year, at an unspecified date; they included lighting his father's cigarettes, turning the pages at the piano, announcing dinner when guests came and, most recently, cleaning his own boots. Today his task was to remain normal until the sugar cube turned into what it would turn into.

For weeks now, his father had been constructing a false sugar cube with a shock inside it. First, he had carved a dreadful-looking beetle with goggling eyes and cruel buck teeth out of balsa wood – not even a centimetre long, but you could see its cruelty and ugliness. Then he had stained it black, leaving it to dry under a piece of newspaper, in case Felix's mother should stumble in. Then he had dipped it in sugar solution, again and again, and finally coated it with table sugar until it closely resembled a sugar cube. Felix had watched all the procedure. His father had not explained what he had been doing. He had merely let Felix watch the preparations and manufacture of the beetle and its encasement in sugar, as if it were a natural part of existence, which Felix would understand if he watched the process. What the purpose of the beetle in the cube was, Klee would not need to explain. It was a practical joke, and therefore not in need of any explanation.

They were sitting side by side, Klee taking occasional puffs and Felix trying not to fix his attention too much on the sugar cube, when Lily wheezed up the stairs. The cat, hearing her, roused itself; stretched and yawned, arched its back, and went to the door of the studio just as Lily opened it. It curled itself about her boots as she walked in; it largely ignored or put up with Klee and Felix's embraces and gestures of love, but Lily, who only ever gave it a gruff, impatient shake about the head and neck, the cat adored Lily. 'Am I late?' she said, dropping her coat on the sofa and coming over to the tea table. 'It was so lovely a day I felt I had to go a little further than usual. Not cold?' She felt the tea urn. 'Good, good. I saw Itten and his children in the park. Gracious heavens, they look so very extraordinary, and their painting, I know, must be simply awful. And I thought I saw Feininger at a distance, queuing with a lot of other Feininger-like beings, but it turned out to be a grove of trees. When is Frau Gropius coming, Paul – do you remember? Ah, tea! "In this world there's nothing finer/than the tea that comes from China."'

'This tea comes from India, however,' Klee said. As long as Felix could remember, his mother had always poured her cup of tea with the words of what he thought might be an advertising slogan from her childhood; just as long, his father had responded, drily, with the information that this tea, however, came from India. He did not trust himself to speak; he was not looking, with agonizing force of will, at the sugar bowl.

'Itten saw me, but made no attempt to greet me,' Lily said. 'Gracious heavens, he should be ashamed of himself, dressing in such a way, like ...' She paused, contemplating what Itten and his disciples might resemble, and as she thought, she lifted the lid of the sugar bowl and took what must be the false sugar cube, dropping it into her tea from between her fat thumb and forefinger. Felix had thought, with agony, that she might take the wrong one, and delay the catastrophe until tomorrow or even the day after that. But she had taken the sugar cube today. '. . . like Mazdaznan, is all you can say,' she went on. 'If a child of mine were in Itten's care, all I can say is—' And then she shrieked, gratifyingly. The black beetle had floated to the top of her tea and was rotating gently in the English cup. 'Ah, Paul, you will be the death of me.'

Klee said nothing, but his eyes were full of amusement. Felix was gulping back his laughter. His father was devoted to practical jokes, but exercised them with rigour: he never, as far as Felix knew, played a trick on anyone outside the family, and he only ever played tricks that he could make and invent himself. Only once, in Felix's memory, had he resorted to a purchased trick; it had been a small rubber bubble that was placed beneath a tablecloth before inflating itself and moving like a mysterious animal about the dinner things. Felix and his mother had adored it, but Klee had shaken his head, half smiling, as if deprecating his own enjoyment in something that anyone could purchase. Since then, there had been carved wooden fruit in the fruit bowl and small amounts of gunpowder buried halfway down one of his mother's cigarettes, but no more purchased tricks.

'The beetle!' Lily said. 'The beetle!'

Klee slightly smiled. Felix could see his hand under the table had yielded to one of its habits: it was running up and down a musical scale. He knew what this meant: his father wanted to return to work. When music came into appearance – some sound of humming, the gestures of a hand running up and down a piano keyboard or a violin – it did not mean that Klee was about to start practising on the violin, which sat in the corner of the studio on a shelf. It more usually meant that he was thinking of his painting, and wanting to return to it. Presently Klee finished his tea, poured another cup and finished that, quickly, too; Lily finished her story about seeing a woman who looked really very much like Frau Gropius outside the Elephant Hotel, but who had turned out to be someone quite different; Felix slid off the chair, with its uncomfortable oil-slippery seating; and they left Klee to his work.

'Do you have the black beetle, Mamma?' Felix said, as they went down the stairs together.

Lily felt in the pocket of her skirt. 'No – how awful. Now the thing will only turn up somewhere else and make me scream all over again. Do you have mathematics homework? Do you want to work in the kitchen, or in your bedroom?'

But Felix had the black beetle; he had asked knowing where it was; it was for him, now, to decide where it should turn up, and whom it should make scream. Outside, in the quiet street, the lamplighter was beginning to make his patient rounds, still wearing his white summer overall.

7.

The next day, Christian had decided to go out soon after breakfast, and to find the school building at least. He had always had a desire to place himself within cities; not to spend more time than necessary wandering without a notion, and not to put up with living in a city in a state of ignorance about its quarters. He slept well – once, in the night, he woke up and was unsure where he was until he heard an owl calling in the park, and what must be the creak of a roof adjusting as the night cooled. He had never slept anywhere other than with a family above, and a family below; he had never slept in a room with a sloping wall, like this one, underneath a long roof of tiles, and he looked forward to being woken in the night by the rattle of rain or hail. The pillow was warm, and he raised his head and turned it to the cool side. There was a faint smell of fresh laundry about the sheets, the smell that linen had after being dried in the open air. He felt, as he drowsily moved his hands from one side of the tight-wrapped bed to the other, that there was something restless about being in the same house and sharing the same sleep as people he had never met before yesterday, whose Christian names he did not know, who were not related to him or to each other in any way. They were brought together by force and by money, he sleepily said to himself, force and money, Neddermeyer and Scherbatsky, Scherbatsky and Neddermeyer, and the third one, whose name was … whose name was … But Herr Wolff's name did not come to him in the night; it came to him only with a satisfying abruptness when he was washing his face and torso at the washbasin in the morning. Wolff. He wondered if he had returned from Erfurt last night after they had all gone to bed.

'I shall not be in for lunch, Frau Scherbatsky,' Christian said, when he had finished breakfast.

'If only,' Frau Scherbatsky said. 'If only all my guests were so considerate!'

Neddermeyer, reading the *Morgenblatt*, lowered it and shook his head sympathetically.

'I'm sure he has important business in Erfurt,' Frau Scherbatsky said. 'Still, Maria grows very testy at the uncertainty.'

'Cook a nice rabbit stew,' Neddermeyer said. 'And keep everyone happy, however many you find yourself entertaining.'

Frau Scherbatsky clapped her hands. 'What an excellent idea! My mother – you know, Herr Vogt, I am quite a country lass – my mother always said that she would prefer a well-made rabbit stew to any fricassee or ragout. My father was always very pleased at shooting a brace because rabbits are a dreadful pest in the wrong place, which of course rabbits always are, in the wrong place, I mean. Yes, a rabbit stew it shall be, tonight, with some very nice little turnips from the garden.'

Christian left the house after breakfast, and walked along the road, still a rough lane, that led along the side of the park. He felt, in his loose jacket and short tie, like a man who belonged in this famous town. The houses here, like Frau Scherbatsky's, were substantial and artistically made. Outside one, with a steep-pitched red roof and a yellow door, a pair of green-painted benches were placed in the lane for the rest of the weary traveller, or so the painted motto from Goethe stated on the wall. Another had a flat roof, of southern inspiration, and others had friezes of angels and devils painted along the walls, under the roofs. There was a pleasant smell of coffee being made from one of the houses, and the sound of eggs being fried; the clatter of knives came out of the open window of one kitchen. '"Alfred, Alfred, you'll be the death of me,"' the song of last year, burst out; a scullery-maid came out of one kitchen door singing; she threw her bowlful of eggshells, peelings and muddy vegetable water over the compost heap, scattering the half-dozen white chickens who were picking over it with squawks and flappings. Dashingly, Christian reached up and plucked a pear from a tree overhanging the lane; he put it into his pocket for later. At the end of the lane, the main road out of Weimar into the country, he waited as a lumbering famer's cart went by, as heavy and groaning as if made of lead, and after it, the watering cart of the district, pulled by two huge and shaggy horses. The farmer raised his

26

fat fingertips lightly to the brim of his broad and grubby straw hat; Christian, smiling, nodded.

It was still early when Christian reached the central square of the town, and the Saturday market was still presenting an orderly and fresh appearance. Although he had just finished Frau Scherbatsky's breakfast, he took the pear from his pocket and ate it as he went round the market. He had thought that the art school was on the other side of the square, but quickly found himself in a quiet residential street. He turned back and tried another side of the square; this time he found himself facing a statue that proved to be of Goethe and Schiller and, behind that, a grand pillared theatre. A gaggle of white geese, intelligent and imperious, was making its way through the square in the direction of the market, driven by a freckled boy of fifteen or so; a man at the wheel of a black car, his vehicle shiny and bright in the sun, waited for them to pass. Christian sat down on the steps of the Goethe statue to feel in his pocket for the small map he had cut out of the guide to the city; it was not there. He remembered now taking it out of his bag, and placing it on the dressing-table ready to take out, but not taking it out.

A shabby figure was in front of him. 'Do you know what you are sitting upon?' he said, in a brusque, military manner.

'I think so,' Christian said. He observed the man: he was wearing a cheap blue suit made out of some dyed military material. It fitted him so badly that, when the man made a strong chopping gesture with his arm, a lecturer's decisive gesture, it appeared to move a second or so behind the man, as if it had its own stiff ideas of movement to follow. 'Goethe and Schiller.'

The man made an impatient movement, flinging his arm to one side and tipping his head back to look down his nose at Christian, sitting on the stone steps of the monument. 'Great poets and thinkers,' he said.

'Yes,' Christian said. 'Can you help me? Could you tell me where the Bauhaus is?'

'The –' the man said '– the— What did you call it?'

'The Bauhaus,' Christian said. He had an irrational feeling that this stranger was, in fact, Frau Scherbatsky's other lodger, the unreliable Herr Wolff. The man stood in front of him with his legs apart, building up to some sort of rage. He was wearing what seemed to be military medals, although he did not seem dressed in other ways for a funeral or other ceremony.

'He means the art school,' a woman who had been taking an interest now butted in to say.

'Yes,' the man said. 'It used to be a respectable art school, but now it calls itself the Bauhaus. So you're one of those, are you? No wonder you sit on the steps of Germany's monuments, insulting its greatness. Communists and garlic-eaters and free-love practitioners! Go off to Moscow or Paris, why don't you?'

Among the small crowd that was now gathering to enjoy the abuse, there was a girl who was grinning broadly. She was at the front of the gathering. Her clothes were simple and rustic, perhaps home-made; they were dark green, straight up and straight down, with a gathering at the neck of blue ribbon, simply tied. Her hat, impatiently shoved on her head, was a coal scuttle made out of brown felt. Her grin was empty and her mouth was too large for her small head. With some shock, Christian saw that her head under the hat must be shaved; he saw the stubble above her ear. The smile and the cock of the head towards him was of indefinable familiarity; it was the smile of a friend not yet recognized. It's me, the smile said. Come on, it's only me.

'Yes, we know what they get up to over there,' the man went on. 'Four bare legs in a bed. Klimt. Anarchy. We don't want that in the city of Goethe and Schiller. "This tree's leaf, that from the east—"'

'Oh, do shut up,' the girl said, calling loudly as soon as the man started to throw his arm out and quote Goethe at them. Her voice was hoarse but educated, with some Bavarian musicality to it.

'Don't tell me to shut up,' the man said. 'Who told me to shut up?'

'I did,' the girl said, still grinning, and raising her hand like a schoolchild. 'Don't talk rubbish about what you don't know. Do you want to know where the Bauhaus is?'

Christian did not realize for a moment that she was speaking to him.

'Hello! You wanted to know where the Bauhaus was. Come with me.'

'In this city ...' the man began, unconvincingly, but he had missed his moment, and as the girl took Christian by the wrist and led him roughly off, the little group of onlookers dispersed. On the ground, a drunk man lay on one side, clawing at the air with his left hand and cycling at nothing with his legs, like an upturned cow waiting to be righted.

8.

'Why are you looking for the Bauhaus?' the girl said fiercely, as they walked away from the Goethe-statue square.

'I'm starting there on Monday,' Christian said. 'They sent me directions but I left them behind, at my lodgings.'

'But what I can't understand, what I can't understand at all, not one bit,' the girl said, as if they had been having a conversation for days, for weeks, which had not reached a conclusion, 'is why someone who doesn't look like a complete idiot and buffoon and twit, not really, anyway, why someone quite normal should want to go and find the Bauhaus on a Saturday when he doesn't have to go there until the Monday. That I don't know if I can understand.'

'You only have to push me in the right direction,' Christian said.

'Because when you get to the Bauhaus for the first time,' the girl said, 'oho, oho, that is when it all goes wrong. You hear about lines and essences and energy in a point and the hidden cross-weave and the drain a colour can make in the middle of a form. And how yellow can be yellow or it can be a completely different thing. Look at that yellow.'

The girl grabbed Christian's arm with both hands, and forcibly made him point at the yellow wall of a palace. He felt they must be conspicuous, but the people of Weimar were apparently used to gestures of this sort. 'That is what you call yellow,' she said. 'Isn't it?'

'It is a yellow,' Christian said, being specific in the way he had heard an art master once attempt.

'And there,' the girl said, pulling him round and making him point again, at a different palace, this time in a deep rustic red, 'that, too, that is what you would call A YELLOW, is it not.'

'No, that's red!' Christian said, forgetting to be specific.

'Ah,' the girl said. 'You see, that is just a matter of context. That yellow only looks red because it lies between two contrasting greens, and the greens have their counter energy, which they project onto the underlying yellow, and there it is, red but only perceived as red. Not real red. You see?'

The wall was still, undeniably, red. The girl, a head shorter than him, came up close to his face. She smelt, curiously, not unattractively, of fresh sweat and of garlic. He remembered what his landlady had said about the diet of the Bauhaus students.

'And that is the sort of thing which the Bauhaus will draw you into, and make you believe, and make you accost strangers and explain, and turn you into a raving madman before it turns you into an artist. But let us go on. Look, beauties to the right, beauties to the left. An important library built by a duchess for her thirty-four children straight ahead of us, and directly behind – don't turn – an elephant house in the Gothic Revival style, 1674, three stars in your guidebook. What is your name?'

'Christian Vogt. I come from Berlin.'

'I did not ask all that. I come from Breitenberg. My name is Elsa Winteregger. What sort of maker are you?'

'What sort of—'

'What do you make? If you are coming to the Bauhaus, then what is it that you make?'

And now they were standing in a shady square, irregular in shape, with a poster pillar at its centre. The weathervane on top of the poster pillar swung indecisively from left to directly away from them and back again. Christian remembered his decisive belief.

'I am a painter,' he said. It was the first time he had said it in front of anyone at all. Elsa Winteregger was the person he had chosen to hear his decision.

'Oh, yes,' she said. She thought for a moment; looked him up and looked him down; she placed her hands on her hips. 'And when did you arrive in Weimar?'

'Yesterday afternoon,' he said.

'And you come out without your book, your paper, your charcoal and your pencils to draw the beautiful city of Weimar?'

Christian crimsoned. Of course that was the first thing he should have done. It had not occurred to him. Of course a real artist would have loved to take the opportunity to go outside with pencil and paper to sketch a new, a beautiful and interesting city. Christian's sketchbook was still in his suitcase. He had done nothing, and it had not occurred to him among the most urgent possibilities, last night or this morning. The question of whether he was an artist at all, whether he was deluding himself, presented itself painfully.

'Or you might be the sort of painter who never goes outside with his *easel*,' the word pronounced sarcastically, 'and his *paint-brushes*, and his *oil paints* to paint. You might stay inside the studio painting canvases of something that is almost-but-not-quite a black square superimposed on a red triangle. Don't you think red is the most important journey you can take as a painter? Who is the greatest painter?'

31

'I think the Spaniard Picasso,' Christian said, priding himself on producing so up-to-date a name.

'No, it is El Greco,' Elsa said, 'or if we are talking about the living, there is no one more wonderful, wonderful, wonderful, than Malevich. Have you discovered what he has to say about black?'

Christian shook his head. He felt defeated before he had even started. Elsa flung her face to the sky, and shouted, in the quiet Weimar square, '"As the tortoise draws its limbs into its shell at need, so the artist reserves his scientific principles when working intuitively."'

A window was flung open, and a voice responded. '"But would it be better for the tortoise to have no legs?"'

'Who is that?' Elsa shouted angrily. 'Who is that?'

'It's me,' the voice came. A head poked out of the window; neat-groomed, *en brosse*, a nice snub nose. His shoulders were bare. 'I heard someone quoting Itten, I thought I would finish it off.'

'I wasn't quoting Itten,' Elsa said. 'I was quoting Malevich.'

'You were quoting Itten, you idiot, you just don't know it,' the man at the window said. 'Who is your friend?'

Christian said, 'My name is Christian Vogt.'

'This is not my friend,' Elsa said again. 'It is a boy I found in the street. He was being harangued by a local mob. I discovered that he was trying to find the Bauhaus. The Bauhaus, the Bauhaus, the Bauhaus ...' Elsa's voice trailed off into song; she lowered her shoulders and, apelike, swung her arms to and fro in an enchanted manner. Her eyes slid back into her skull.

'I see,' the man said. 'Goodbye, Elsa. Goodbye, whatever your name might be, I didn't hear.'

'Christian Vogt,' Christian said, but the window was already closed. 'Goodbye, then,' he said to the girl in the brown cloche hat, her eyes shut as she crooned. He felt quite put out, as if a friend who had been walking with him had turned aside for someone more interesting. But Elsa was only standing, alone in

32

the square, singing 'The Bauhaus, the Bauhaus, the Bauhaus,' to herself in half-tones, with a wide open smile of pure uninterruptible joy. Christian was a hundred paces away before he knew he should have said, 'Kandinsky,' to Elsa's question.

9.

Fritz Lohse withdrew his head from the outside and back into the room. It was a pleasant room, painted pale green, with a dressing-table, an upright old leather armchair, a Turkey rug on the floor and an awkward-shaped, almost square old rustic bed painted yellow. There were twenty sheets of paper, drawn-on, pinned to the walls above the bed and to the ceiling, so that Fritz could see his best ideas immediately on waking. On the dressing-table, by the oil lamp, there sat the remains of last night's supper: some black bread and two soup pots, alongside the bones of two small game birds. There was an octagonal table, in size between a card table and a dining table; its undecidable size had perhaps led Frau Mauthner, the owner of the building and Fritz's landlady, to expel it upstairs to her lodger's room with all the other furniture. On the table there were five objects, just as there had been for the past three weeks.

Fritz observed, with admiration, the ripe curves of his girl Katharina. She was all pink and white above the rumpled bedding; she lay face down. Her back was a deep hollow, rising to her magnificent wide bottom, her thighs slightly marked with the quiver and dimple that fat under skin makes. He imagined striding across the room and taking a deep bite, a spoonful of a bite, out of her thighs. How she would shriek! Katharina was a shrieker, as well as a snorer at night, and, in times of unoccupation, a singer; it was a real trial to her to keep silent during their nights for the sake of Frau Mauthner She was still lying in the bed, hugging a bolster to her as she liked to. She was face down upon it; it ran from her chin between her breasts, under her belly and between her legs; it pushed her rump upwards and emerged between her knees. Fritz often wondered why she did not hug him at nights, but she said she preferred something long, cold, hairless and squashy. She was not asleep; she was just enjoying the bed, and the pleasure of lying there naked in the morning, far too late.

'What was all that rumpus?' Katharina said softly, into the mattress. But Fritz was used to the sort of things that Katharina said.

'It was only Elsa Winteregger,' Fritz said. 'She was making a spectacle of herself, as usual. She was giving out Mazdaznan proverbs.'

'Which one? The one you told me about breathing steadily and praising the Lord?'

Katharina was not an artist. She was a waitress in a restaurant, a good one, in the centre of Weimar. Fritz had met her a year or more ago; his people had taken him there to feed him, to make sure he had at least one hot meal inside him. Katharina had served their table. She had lowered her eyes respectfully, handing about the roast potatoes and pouring the gravy, one hand held in the small of her back. For the next days Fritz had hung about at the back, by the kitchen, waiting for her to emerge, like a stage-door johnny behind a theatre. She did not pretend, she said, to understand the sort of things they got up to at her Fritz's Bauhaus. But she liked to listen to Mazdaznan proverbs. Sometimes he made one up, too impossible to be true.

'No,' Fritz said. 'It was the one about the tortoise and the artist and his scientific principles.'

'I wondered why you were mentioning a tortoise. I've never heard that one.'

Fritz repeated it, raising his arm solemnly. He finished. He lowered his hand. He scratched his bare chest thoughtfully. 'That's only what Itten says of his own initiative.'

'Is she still there?'

Fritz moved to the window. Elsa Winteregger was in the

34

middle of the square, but alone now; she seemed to be hugging herself and chanting. Fritz reached into his trouser pocket for his cigarettes, but they were in the cigarette case on the table, with the four other objects; he reached into his shirt pocket for his matches, but he had no shirt on, as well as being barefoot. He did not know where the matches could be at all. A small snore escaped Katharina; she loved to sleep, and her question now went unanswered.

At present Frau Mauthner was moving about downstairs. Her normal departure from the house was no later than nine o'clock. It was now nearly ten to ten, and the sound of her movements had a stealthy, suspicious air. It was not at all unlikely that Frau Mauthner knew perfectly well that Katharina was in Fritz's room, as she had been for four of the last ten nights. She could have found this out in many ways, although the most likely was that her maid Sophie had told her. Fritz had been obliged to take Sophie into his confidence after an encounter on the stairs in the morning. Frau Mauthner was moving about directly below, in the dining room she barely used; she seemed to be changing the position of some furniture, but so slowly. Fritz was sure she was moving about and listening, establishing her evidence for some future confrontation. He shifted his attention from Frau Mauthner's stealthy tread to the five objects on the table. They had been there for weeks now.

These objects were for Fritz's non-representative found-object sculpture. It was a task in class. He had found five objects, with the intention of using four, but he could not decide which to leave out. There was the long, thin blade of a saw, slightly rusting along its flat edge, like the hackles of a cornered fox. This was a fierce object. There was a square of steel wool, pocketed from Frau Mauthner's kitchen when no one was looking. This was a Protestant object. There was a very old piece of black bread, now curling up at the edges slightly. This object, Fritz could not decide what it represented. Some days it was a nursery object, some days it was funereal, like the feast at a crow's wake.

There was a block of cedarwood, the size of two clenched fists together, and that was a virtuous object, but virtuous in an admirable way, not virtuous in a way you felt lectured at by it. And there was a piece of beautiful red glass, lovely vivid red glass, changing the world as you looked through it, making it warm and strange. The piece of red glass was the fall of Austria-Hungary. He had found it on the street. Where it had come from, and what its original purpose was, Fritz did not know and could not guess. Why it was the fall of Austria-Hungary Fritz did not understand. But it had presented itself to him in the way that a woman might introduce herself and say, 'I am an only child', and you thought, Yes, you are, indeed you are. The piece of red glass looked like a pane from a piece of church stained glass, but that was impossible. It had once occurred to Fritz that it might be a discarded fragment of another student's non-representative found-object sculpture. He did not like to think of that.

They would not go together, no matter which of the five he omitted. Now he moved over to the table and picked up the piece of red glass. The other four things – the bread, the cedarwood block, the saw, the steel wool – he moved about in an undecided way. Now the bread sat upon the cedarwood, which was coiled about by the flexible saw – but the bread looked stupid, and what to do with the steel wool? It had an undecided, irrelevant air. He started again, resting the saw on the bread and the steel wool at either end. They could be made to stand upright. But what to do with the cedarwood? The same as the other things, and that was no good. It had been growing in Fritz for some time that he had made a terrible mistake when he first chose the objects of his sculpture. He had concentrated entirely on contrasts in texture – the luminous smoothness of the glass, the rusty saw, the fibrous wood, the knitted piece of steel wool, and the miniature honeycomb of the bread – and forgotten altogether about the shapes. He had thought that some kind of arabesque could be made out of the saw to counteract the prevailing squareness of the other three, or four. But the square-ness seemed to dominate and to bring everything down, even the lovely piece of red glass. He could change all his objects and start again. But he had been contemplating these objects for weeks now. As Itten had instructed, he had penetrated the essence of these five objects by long observation. But he had come to understand through observation that they did not like each other and did not live in the same world.

In a dejected way, Fritz raised the piece of square red glass to his eye, closed the other, and prepared to see the world through Austria-Hungary and its fall.

At first it was merely red. There was nothing distinct about the entities in the room. But then the forms began to emerge. There were square forms, and lines, darker and blacker than the air. The air had a flexible form that would take up the space allotted to it by the solid forms. When the world was seen, red, through the eyes of Austria-Hungary, the eye was drawn to the naked body of Katharina, lying face down on the bed.

But the eye was not drawn to a naked body when it looked through a red filter. It did not look at her bottom and rounded shoulders, the tress of hair falling across her face-down head. What it looked at were pleasing curves and lines: a convex and a concave arch, and then another, longer, deeper, arch. There was no lechery, or love, or any sentimentalizing psychological structure.

'Stop staring at me,' Katharina said. 'Stop it. It makes me shiver.'

He took no notice of what It had said. The lines and volumes had weight, and movement, and an innate direction and energy, but they did not have sound or speech. It was a fascinating phenomenon to find in the room he had rented from Frau Mauthner. He looked for a second above the form at the line drawings, if that is what they are when viewed through a red square. They had retreated into the insignificant, along with the smells, the sounds of the room, and the bad metallic taste in his mouth that came from a broken tooth he could not afford to have removed. He lowered the red square from his eye. The hierarchies disappeared. Without the help of Austria-Hungary, Katharina was Katharina again. Her hair was blonde and her body was rumpled and warm and delicious, a bread smell in the morning, and she was sleepy and open and a little disgruntled. He made an effort, without the red filter. The lines started to re-emerge; the arc; the concave form; you did not have to see the animal confusion that filled them.

Fritz stood up. He dropped the square of red glass onto the floor; it fell harmlessly on his white shirt, where he had left it when he had undressed the night before. He went to the oil lamp, and quickly removed the glass form that protected the lit flame from wind and draught. It was straight, circular from above, and towards the bottom bulged out like a brandy glass. It contained air in a form. With steady concentrated fury, he took the glass; inside it he fastened the thin saw, with a dab of glue, which would be good enough for the moment; he made a spiral. Working quickly, he tore apart the square of steel wool until it looked like wild morning hair, and attached it to the end of the saw. The piece of black bread remained where it was, at the end of the piece. The cedarwood would stand behind, supporting it. Anyone could see what a sentry it was. In fifteen minutes the piece was done. Fritz walked back, critically. He picked up the piece of red glass from the shirt where he had dropped it. He raised it to his eye. It was no longer Austria-Hungary. It was just a red filter. On the other side of the filter, the room had changed. It now had two important sets of curves, lines and volumes in it. There was the Form on the bed. There was a new Form. It filled the room.

'You have been busy,' Katharina said admiringly. 'All that grunting and pulling and sticking things together. I don't know why you can't do things in a normal way like normal people. Now I want to go and have something to eat.'

'You're so …' Fritz said. He wanted to tell her how she was. But language would not stretch to it.

'I *know*,' Katharina said, putting an immense weight on the word. She was so pleased to be so … 'I want sausage, burnt, and cold cabbage, and mustard with it, and a whole basin of cold potato salad, a huge whole basin. I am *so hungry* I could eat what the wolves brought back. Is the old cow gone out yet?'

'"When China speaks with one voice,"' Fritz said, in a lust-thickened voice, '"then the ear of Europe rings."'

'You and your Mazdaznan,' Katharina said.

10.

That afternoon, Christian took his portfolio out and his charcoals, newly bought with a single gold piece from Grandfather's hoard. A true student of art would not wait until the first day of instruction before starting.

He had rarely drawn in public before, and even more rarely set out on his own like this, and never in a strange town. Three or four times, the art master at the Gymnasium had announced that they would be going out for this purpose. The eight senior pupils would follow the master onto the overground train, behaving in a subdued way. There was nothing Bohemian about the art class.

Christian thought, too, that their generation was a subdued one. He had been twelve when the war broke out, and at fourteen it sat heavily on their minds. There seemed to be no future, nothing worth studying for, except a short adult life of a few grey days commanding troops on the eastern front, running at the end towards a bank of guns. It was important to put one's life's energies into the duties of school and labour, when the eastern front awaited.

During these trips, Christian would place himself before a masterpiece in the art gallery. He liked a landscape; he admired

Philips Wouwerman, and he liked the simple arabesque, the invented backgrounds behind the Italian madonnas. How could you tell that those simple valleys with a river curving through them had been invented, whereas Wouwerman had really sat and really observed? From time to time, he raised his pencil and closed one eye; he measured the distance of each part of the landscape, and set it down on his own sheet of paper, making amends as the master made his round, commenting and correcting. Sometimes a lady or a gentleman, visiting the art gallery on a quiet weekday morning, would pause behind him, and observe what he was doing; sometimes they would know what they were looking at, and pass on without comment; sometimes a bundled and smelly individual, dripping from clothes and nose, would express extravagant admiration, call Christian or one of his classmates 'a little Raphael'. The art gallery was still quiet and warm, in 1916, in January; every class of person came there, sometimes in the love of art and sometimes in refuge from the first Berlin winter of war.

After one of these class outings, it came to Christian that artists did not only proceed by copying famous works of art, warmly in the gallery. He had developed a passion for Menzel, whose painting of clouds of steam in a factory had made him stand and stare. His mother had stood with him in front of a beach scene by the Frenchman Monet, and she had shown him that Monet had painted it on the spot. How can you know that, Mamma? Painters may sketch the composition with charcoal and pencil on the spot, but they have studios to produce the finished work. Look, Mamma had said. Look, you can see if you get close – we are going to be reprimanded, so let us be quick – look, some grains of sand, there, in the paint. And there it is, Mamma said. He did it all there on the beach, because there are lots of things that you can't set down with charcoal and pencil.

And there it was. They suffered from boredom so terribly then, in the war, in 1916 and 1917; life could not be constructed so entirely of dread and hectoring. Mamma was so thin and pretty, with warm red hair; sometimes, when he was small, and he had been very good, she would let him pull out any white hairs that he could find. He could find only a very few. Perhaps one at a time. He would pull it out, and she would wince, and say thank you, and then she would finish getting dressed.

He was forgetting now what Mamma looked like. The photographs did not get her quite right. The drawing he had made of her did not get her right, either – she had died when he was still not a good artist, did not get things right. He could summon her, just about, by thinking of Dolphus's nose, and trying to add some thick dark eyebrows, which were like his own in the mirror, and then some dark blue eyes, almost purple. The labour of keeping his mother's last-days' face from his memory was hard, too. But then, after some time of holding it in his thoughts, the real face would leap out, effortlessly, in full health, as she had been any morning at the breakfast table, a white silk hat shading her tender and shy expression, and he would wonder that he struggled to think what she had looked like.

There had been outings, after the Monet moment, to draw in the open air. Dolphus had come, to be company. But Christian was shy about his art, and he did not want to be seen drawing in public. There were quiet corners of parks, but they had a tendency to yield large and vulgar families from Pankow on a day's outing. The country was too far. The street was interesting, but you could not set up in the middle of the pavement in Friedrichstrasse. Dolphus was easy and tractable; he came not just because he enjoyed the outing, but because sometimes the artist needs a figure to add to a scene, and the figure needs to be observed at length. Dolphus rarely minded being told to stand by a tree, or to crouch over a stream. Christian's drawings were often of an unspecific male figure, leaning against a tree, or crouching as if holding a home-made fishing rod over a tree. They looked like bucolic scenes, but that was only because Christian had grown shy, and the details of the scene had been

41

sketchy, since they could be done later. Mamma had been kind, and had even had one framed for her dressing room, where it still hung, dusted and cared for by Egon, like all her possessions. But anyone could have seen that it was, in reality, a corner of the Zoological Garden, yards from where carriages and motors, unrecorded by Christian, stood in steaming queues.

In Weimar, without Dolphus to wait for him patiently and perform a useful task, there was too much burden of expectation. He had produced only three or four rapid and embarrassed sketches when the time came to return to Frau Scherbatsky's house. The market was emptying now; the stall-holders were calling to each other, and packing up what remained of their stock in boxes, pallets, packing with straw, berating their boys for getting under the feet. In the window of the coffee house two men sat, one with an amused, superior face, one with a clever, screwed-up expression. Towards Christian, a group came: five soldiers, or former soldiers, in uniform. One was in a bath chair, although it was not possible to see how he was injured. It needed only one comrade to push the bath chair, but all four of the standing soldiers had some kind of hold on it and were walking together. Two held a handle each, one was placing a blanket over the knees of the invalid and fussing, and the last, unable to find a particular task, was demonstratively letting a hand trail at the back of the chair, as if claiming territory. They were all young; perhaps no more than three or four years older than Christian. As they passed, he saw that on their arms was a band, and on the band was some sort of motif. They had the picturesque appearance of veterans, the five of them, crumpled, sincere and careworn.

11.

'Did you see that?' Kandinsky said. 'Klee, did you see that? That group of soldiers, there, with the wheeling chair in the middle?'

They had just sat down in a coffee house. Kandinsky liked to sit in the window where he could see life. Klee did not object. Sometimes he looked inside the coffee house, sometimes he looked outside. In the back of the coffee house, although it was daylight, the yellow lights were on in the card room, in an acknowledgement of the usual evening time for gambling. That did not interest Klee. His gaze disconcerted people. He gave the impression of recognizing strangers, of knowing exactly what a friend had been doing before the meeting, of looking levelly at a waiter and sharing a silent joke with him, without the requirement of comment. Kandinsky was used to it, and used, too, to Klee speaking only when he had something to say.

The group moved away, past a boy with blond, very short hair, holding an artist's portfolio – probably a student, although neither of them knew him. They dissolved into the late-afternoon sauntering of Weimar.

'The old brigade,' Kandinsky said. 'They are everywhere. The war was never lost, those responsible should be shot, the Kaiser should return.'

'They had a line,' Klee said. 'You could make a picture out of them, a picture of old, old black crows on a bench in a park in Lucerne. Or of five kittens in a basket. Are they young, or are they old? The last one, in the chair, they were saying goodbye to him. Or they were just born and discovering the way that they could live together. The one in the chair, they were welcoming him to life.'

The waitress had been standing there, not ignored by Klee, exactly, but nearly included in his comment. At some point, she lowered her notebook and pencil; at some point, she stopped waiting for him to finish speaking so she could take their order, and began to listen with curiosity and interest. Her apron was clean, but much washed and greying; her white pie-crust collar was torn at the side and had been mended in a hurry; there were things about her that were coming apart, and she looked tired and hungry. When Klee finished, she stood there, her pencil and notebook lowered, in pensive silence. The two gentleman were not different in size, but one seemed to be tall and thin, the other short and square – the talkative one and the one who had spoken. The one who seemed to be short and square stopped talking. He had a measured, tuneful Swiss voice, and his silence, too, was measured, tuneful and Swiss. Then he looked at her, with a sympathetic amusement – the half-smile of someone who knows that you will find the same thing funny, and then you will laugh at it together. She came to. All her aches and concerns returned to her face in a moment.

'Two coffees, only,' Kandinsky said.

'Yes,' the waitress said. 'That will be two hundred thousand marks today. Or what else do you have to pay with?'

'With money. Is that two hundred thousand each?' Kandinsky said. 'I see. Thank you. Have they gone, those soldiers?'

He had addressed himself to Klee, but Klee stayed silent, and the waitress had lingered. 'The colonel?' she said. 'You mean the colonel?'

'The colonel?' Kandinsky said, puzzled. But the waitress had slipped away and was saying something to an upright man of middle age, an elaborate moustache, the red streaming eyes of the alcoholic and a Bavarian coat. He was sitting with a plump woman in a white fur-trimmed coat; her hair was newly marcelled, with a fringe in the centre over her face like the tassels of a shawl. He stood up after the word from the waitress, leaving the woman and the two glasses of schnapps on the table. His right leg was amputated, and his stump rested on a wooden leg – it was the cheap sort, where the leather was padded with horsehair – and a neatly folded handkerchief.

'I was not told there would be two of you,' the colonel, if that was who it was, said. A little gust of sour smells came from him: of old schnapps on the breath, of ancient clothes, not washed, of some kind of brutal disinfectant liquid, not intended in the first instance for personal application. 'May I sit down?'

'By all means,' Kandinsky said. 'But I think there is some mistake. We were not here to meet anyone.'

'I was waiting,' the colonel said. He bared his teeth in an attempt at warmth; his teeth were brown and broken. 'I was waiting for a business associate.'

'Who was to ask for the colonel, I quite understand.'

'It is all the same,' the colonel said and, without waiting further, pulled out a chair. He nodded, sharply, not quite saluting. He might have brought his heel together with the end of his wooden leg, but the gesture would have lacked assurance. With a swivelling movement, he sat down on the sideways chair. 'My business associate is late,' he said. 'He may not come. Things have been difficult, gentlemen, you understand.'

'Things are difficult for everyone,' Kandinsky said, sharply, but with a tinge of resignation. This happened in coffee houses. It was their own fault for being apologetic.

'Difficult, yes, difficult,' the colonel said, emphasizing the roll of the word. 'I lost my leg in battle. Twenty-five years or more I was in the cavalry of His Majesty. And then there was no His Majesty, and no cavalry, as far as I know. And my leg lies in the mud at Verdun. I gave thanks for the escape then, but now I wish they had made an end of me at Verdun, and I would not have seen what I have seen.'

'Why,' Klee said. 'What have you seen.'

He asked it in a plain way, but the colonel turned on him. 'What have I seen? I have seen the politicians call back the army before they could win. And they dismissed His Majesty. And they declared that we had lost the war, and would not listen to disagreement. We did not lose. We were not defeated by the enemy. We were stabbed in the back. Gentlemen,' and his harsh voice turned in on itself, remembering that he was there for a purpose, that his voice should be soft and agreeable, 'gentlemen, I don't know if you are interested in a very interesting business proposition, but I have property to sell, a very interesting and well-made volume of clothing. I don't know if you have any means to sell it among your circle, shirts, beautifully made white cotton shirts, and boots, as solid as anyone could desire, truly excellent, and body-linen, stockings, anything you could require, and very reasonable, I know how the cost of things is going, Lord knows how we all know that ...'

At the other table, the colonel's companion raised her glass of schnapps to her lips, shaking slightly. She was tranquil, much powdered, patient and bemused. She had spent so many afternoons at this table, sipping a schnapps while the colonel made his appeal to strangers and contacts. The colonel's patriotism ran down like a half-wound clockwork engine; the colonel's offer to sell army property took over. Kandinsky and Klee said nothing. The two cups of coffee arrived. The colonel looked at them. He fell silent. His eyes rested on the table; it might have been shame. Abruptly he pushed the chair backwards, and got to his feet with diagonal thrusts and jabs.

'Fifty million marks would be a help to me, in the position in which I find myself,' he said. His red eyes brimmed. He must have seen that Klee and Kandinsky were looking at him intently, in different ways, but both with nothing more than interest, not sympathy or encouragement.

'Good day to you,' Kandinsky said.

'I am sorry,' the man finished, with a touch of parade-ground sarcasm, 'to have disturbed you, gentlemen, in your important discussions.'

They watched him go. He sat down heavily in his chair, three tables away. His companion raised her eyes slowly, as if pulling them up with great effort. The movement continued: she raised her eyebrows in question. He gave a brief, decisive shake of the head, only a degree or two, dismissing the possibility. They both took up their glasses, clinked them, and took a sip. And in a moment, as if Klee and Kandinsky had been the bad luck that the colonel needed to expunge, a quite ordinary-looking man, no more than twenty-seven, in an ordinary black overcoat and a bowler hat, slid without invitation into the third chair at the colonel's table and started to talk.

'"To one of the nation's heroes,"' Klee said, repeating the words neutrally. And the man must have been desperate to accept money, to be unable to barter his possessions for anything else. Klee liked to repeat phrases, trying them out. A week or a month or a year later, Kandinsky knew he would enter Klee's studio to ask what he had been achieving lately, and he would be handed a drawing, led up to a painting on an easel, of a giant figure, smudged with oil transfer lines, and underneath would be written 'To one of the nation's heroes', and a neat, cryptic entry in Klee's numbering system, 1922/109.

'And two more cups of coffee,' Klee said to the waitress, arriving with a pen.

'That will be five hundred thousand marks,' the waitress said.

'No, four hundred thousand,' Kandinsky said. 'You said two hundred thousand each, for the cups of coffee.'

'It was four hundred thousand when you ordered the first two cups of coffee,' the waitress said. 'The new price for two cups of coffee is five hundred thousand.'

'No, no, how can that be,' Klee said. 'Two hundred thousand is monstrous already – how can that be the price of a cup of coffee, even here, even in expensive Weimar – but five hundred thousand, half a million for two, how can the price change in an hour, how can that be?'

'The price now, at seventeen minutes past four o'clock, is five hundred thousand marks for two cups of coffee,' the waitress said. Her enchantment with Klee had disappeared. 'If we continue this discussion for long enough, the price of two cups of coffee will be six hundred thousand marks. It is entirely up to you, gentlemen.'

Outside the coffee house, the soldiers were assembling. The group they had seen before had reappeared. There seemed to be a protest or march in the making. They laid their hands protectively on the handles as if the touch would make sense of everything. About their arms, each had a cloth armband, not part of their uniform originally. On it was some kind of device or symbol, a red shape of some kind. By the door of the coffee house, the colonel, leaning on his crutch, shook the hand of the businessman, full of smiles. The colonel's lady stood five paces off, looking at the soldiers, swaying confusedly to and fro.

12.

Christian had discovered a short-cut through the park to Frau Scherbatsky's house, after the baroque sandstone bridge across the stream. He was ridiculously pleased with this insight, and came to the door of the house where he lived with a proud feeling of starting to belong in the town. The doorbell was not immediately responded to; he had to ring again before Maria, the red-haired maid, answered. She looked at him as if his face had not registered; she had a confused and perhaps even an embarrassed expression, but she stood back and let him through, with his portfolio of drawings.

There was no one else to be seen, but when he was in his room, and taking the drawings of marketplace, ducal palace, standing figures and park out of the portfolio, Christian was startled by some noise in the quiet house. It was a muffled shriek; then the sound of a woman giggling; then a shriek again, and soon, from only two or three rooms away in the house, transmitted by pipe and panelling, Christian realized that he was listening to the sounds of Frau Scherbatsky in bed with someone, in the afternoon. He did not want to listen, but there seemed no way of not listening. Her shrieks and downward glissandos of joy grew, and then they were joined by a man's noises: a grunt and a few murmured words of encouragement, though it was not possible to understand what was said. Christian went to the window, and opened it, trying to concentrate on the sounds of the park. But the noises grew and were joined by the sound of wooden furniture banging against the wall. Christian felt himself beginning to blush. He had never heard such a thing in his family circle. He was a virgin himself, if that shameful and dishonourable visit to the brothel with two schoolfriends in the last Easter at the Gymnasium were not counted. Now a phrase was heard more clearly, spoken by a man. The window of the other room must be open, too, and by opening his window, he had allowed himself to hear more clearly. The student lodger had gone out, and Frau Scherbatsky and Herr Neddermeyer had taken advantage. The phrase he had heard, whatever it was, had been spoken in a strong Leipzig accent. The maid must have known that he would hear the noises she was used to, and understood that he had breached the unspoken conditions of lodging.

Christian became worldly and calm. 'I say!' he remarked, in an undertone to the empty room. 'What beasts! Good for Neddermeyer – I hope I still have it in me when I am as old as that! And the Scherbatsky! Fine woman – and a woman has needs that an architect-lodger can fulfil. A well-known fact.' He was practising for an anecdote. But who he would tell the anecdote to, he did not know. With a large sigh and a bestial sound, the encounter seemed to come to an end. Christian realized that they were in what must be Neddermeyer's room, not Frau Scherbatsky's, which was on the other side, next door to his room. And in the meantime, an awkwardness was arising: he would need to visit the lavatory quite soon, to cross the landing to the shared bathroom. To leave the room now would risk meeting Frau Scherbatsky in dressing gown, négligé or similar intimate apparel, making her dishevelled way back to her room to prepare her appearance for supper. He looked under the bed, but this was a modern house and there was no pot. He waited.

There was the sound of a door being opened, of footsteps, the unsynchronized clatter of footsole against slipper. The sound went past Christian's door; the door of Frau Scherbatsky's door was opened and closed. He breathed out. He must keep quiet in his movements. Frau Scherbatsky and Herr Neddermeyer had only permitted themselves this licence because they believed that Christian – and, presumably, still, the tantalizing Herr Wolff – were not in the house.

He opened the door silently and, shoeless, walked across to the bathroom. The modern flush of the lavatory made a noise, and when Christian stepped out of the bathroom, he saw, to his horror, that Herr Neddermeyer's door was now standing open – it had been opened in the previous minute. 'Herr Vogt?' Neddermeyer's voice called. 'Is that you? Do come in.'

Christian stood in the door of Neddermeyer's room, twisting his hands about, one in the other. The room was attractive and immaculate. The bed was made, under a white counterpane. On the walls were views of Roman and other classical ruins; in the bow window stood a substantial octagonal table in mahogany with a central supporting pillar. The table bore a thick pile of papers, weighed down at four corners by a bronze Japanese fisherman, a millefiori paperweight, a grotesquely shaped stone, mounted in silver, and a bust of Brahms in alabaster. On the table, too, were an architect's drawing tools of pencil and compasses, squares and protractors, in an open walnut case lined with worn black leather. Neddermeyer gestured towards one of the two armchairs in yellow velvet. Unexpectedly, his appearance gave no indication of the rumpus he had just been through: he was groomed and of normal colour, his clothes not suggesting that they had been flung to the floor and picked up some time afterwards. There was nothing of the debauch about him, or about his room.

'Welcome to my home – my lair, one could say,' Neddermeyer said. 'I can offer you some coffee – nothing elaborate, nothing extensive, but I do insist on having coffee-making as a possibility in my room.'

'That is very kind,' Christian said.

'I cannot always be calling on Maria to bring me cups from the kitchen,' Neddermeyer said, going over and opening a small cupboard and beginning to fiddle with its contents. 'My one remaining vice. So, Herr Vogt, I saw you venturing out this afternoon with your sketchbook. You found some subjects worthy of your pencil? Good, good. I am sure that the Bauhaus will chase the love of beauty out of you very quickly, and replace it with a love of steel and sharp corners. I saw a soup plate that one of them had made. It was square. The absurdity!'

'Why so, Herr Neddermeyer?'

'They had not considered,' Neddermeyer said, 'that a square has angles and a circle has none. A maidservant, presenting a soup plate, presents it at the eye level of her master. The master's attention is drawn to something on his right; he turns sharply. The plate is a square one, however, as designed by the bright fellows at the Bauhaus, and the eye is thrust against a sharp corner of a hard material. The master, who has bought a daring novelty and flatters himself that he has an original eye, has, from now on, exactly that: an original eye. Only one.' Neddermeyer tittered in a genteel, practised, taut way.

Neddermeyer was talking amiably, swivelling and smiling from his post at the coffee cupboard, and now he turned and brought over the cups of coffee. They were tiny, gold and green, with a small medallion of flowers painted on the side. Despite the smile, Neddermeyer's voice had been growing tense, and he was not looking, exactly, at Christian as he handed it over. He placed his own on the small table by the other armchair, and removed a spotted red handkerchief from the inside pocket of his Bavarian jacket. He wiped his hands clean.

'I think Frau Scherbatsky said you are an architect?' Christian said. The coffee, despite coming from a small cupboard, was delicious, with no taint of chicory or acorn.

'I was an architect,' Neddermeyer said. 'I do not think I will ever build again.'

'Do you have drawings of your work?' Christian said. 'I would so like to see them.'

Neddermeyer did not exactly brighten, but he grew business-like, as if he had been expecting Christian to say exactly that.

Perhaps he had called Christian in for this exact purpose, to show his drawings. Christian reflected that after the pleasures which Neddermeyer and Frau Scherbatsky had indulged in, the ego was never satisfied; it was at that point, the day after his schoolfriends had visited a brothel, that they were most apt to show classmates their best marks, the most flattering comments made on their work by masters, or, at the very least, to treat the fellows at a coffee shop, pulling out their marks with a profligate air. Neddermeyer wanted someone to see what a marvellous fellow he was.

'I do indeed,' Neddermeyer said. 'Perhaps you noticed my drawings over there, on the table. There are some photographs, too, of some projects that came to life. A very civil young man, before the war, came to see me and spent six months visiting what I had designed and built, and wrote a very flattering article about my work in an architectural review. After that article, I had letters from architects in America, even. Of course, that was in 1905. People are not interested now.'

'Did you always build in Weimar?'

'Weimar and surroundings,' Neddermeyer said carelessly, waving his hand at the window as if to suggest that he might have built all of it. 'I could have gone to America. Interest in my work was very high there, as I said. But as I told my apprentices, my thinking, such as it is, was formed in an age where people climbed to the top floor if that was where they wanted to go. I was too old to change, to think how a tower of thirty floors could be ornamented. A mistake, no doubt. Now. Where were we.'

Neddermeyer stood, and walked over in a vague, uncommitted way to the table, as if hardly engaged.

'Well, here they are!' he said. 'There is no purpose, really, in continuing to work, but the imagination continues to thrive. Sometimes I am playing at the pianoforte and I will be seized with an idea, quite a new idea, for a suspended balcony at the front of a royal palace, or for some rolling bookshelves to simplify storage and display in a library. Now, this is an idea I had for a triumphal arch ...'

Neddermeyer's fantasy work was neatly drawn, exquisitely finished, ornamented and made human with decorative touches of trees and figures. They were a credit to the tools in the open walnut case. He began to turn over the sheets, lovingly, murmuring words of explanation, like an ambassador introducing great dignitaries. Here was an idea he had for a state library; for a permanent circus on the classical model; for an English cottage; for a nobleman's country house, refined and yet rustic; an idea for the Emperor's military barracks; a new cathedral for Berlin ('I was so disappointed, Herr Vogt, with the one His Majesty built, until I did not see why I should not put my own thoughts on paper'); a monument to the dead of the war; a bridge over a country stream and the same bridge, on a larger scale, bearing the traffic of the town; and a royal palace, eighty windows long on its front façade. Christian turned the sheets one after another. The plans were rich in ornament and fantasy; they specialized in pendentives and arches, in caryatids and classical columns, in portes-cochères heavy with mythological figures, in windows leaning out far over the street like orchards, in stucco ornament in their interiors and stone ornament on their exteriors. They specialized in the heavy imagination of the old Emperor, and Christian turned the pages with fascinated absorption. The moment for gargoyles, he thought, looking at the design for the Berlin cathedral, was gone.

'You see, Herr Vogt,' Neddermeyer said. 'What architecture needs is imagination, and variety. The eye craves richness, and finds ornament restful. Now, for one of your teachers at the Bauhaus, a new cathedral in Weimar would be a simple matter.' Neddermeyer was pulling a sketchbook towards him, a spiral-bound orange book, and now leant over the table to pluck a pencil from its place. 'It would look just like –' he began to draw '– you see, just like – ah, yes, that is that problem solved. You see?'

He turned the sketchbook around for Christian to see. On the page, he had drawn nothing more than a rectangle, then filled it in roughly with a grid. He took it back, and drew a line underneath it and, with a couple of scribbles, placed some stick figures on the ground. 'You see, Herr Vogt, I remember there was a great scandal in Vienna when the leader of the school built something opposite the Emperor's house. The Emperor had not been consulted, and when he saw the building, he said, "Who has built that house with no eyebrows, just there?" A very ugly building, still, and a gross insult to the Emperor. That is the sort of place you are going to, Herr Vogt. I am sorry for you.'

'Your buildings are very interesting, Herr Neddermeyer,' Christian said. 'I look forward to talking with you a great deal more. But I am hoping to become an artist, not an architect.'

Neddermeyer was now as flushed and excited as Christian had expected to find him. 'You see, I lost everything,' he said. 'It all went – family and business and home and everything.'

'I am sorry,' Christian said formally. He wondered whether now was the time to offer to show Neddermeyer the drawings he had done that morning. He decided that now was not the time. 'Thank you so much for the coffee, Herr Neddermeyer.'

'I believe that Herr Wolff will be joining us for dinner,' Neddermeyer said wretchedly. 'So the topic for tonight will be politics.'

'I look forward to that, too,' Christian said, letting himself out with what he felt was an expert smile, like a doctor leaving a patient in pain, a patient midway through a fit of raving.

13.

Before supper, Christian wrote a letter to his brother Dolphus.

It is not very much like being a student of art in the opera, living at Frau Scherbatsky's house. I do not think I could bring mistresses with tuberculosis to die in the attic – like in *La Bohème*.

(No attic, too.) It is a large, dull, ugly villa, built not ten years ago by a local architect. He also lives here, the architect, so it is important to compliment the beauty of the house, the convenience of the rooms, and so on, very regularly. I thought at first he was living here as a lodger, because he had fallen on hard times after the war. Actually, he has formed a connection with Frau Scherbatsky. They keep up appearances, but their connection is an intimate one. There is another lodger, a man named Wolff, who has been away, but who I have seen since starting this letter, walking in the garden smoking a cigar. I can only describe him from what I have seen – a small, well-built man, with very short grey hair, carrying a cane and wearing plus-fours. He appears alert and fit – he was whacking the side of his legs with his cane as he walked, quite vigorously. He may be younger than my landlady and her architect friend. He was accosted by Neddermeyer, as the architect of the house is called, who came out to exchange some friendly words with him, but he responded briefly and continued walking briskly from one side of the lawn to the other. Neddermeyer tried to keep up with him, but after a while he gave up and sat down on the bench under the oak tree, limiting himself to saying something when Wolff happened to pass him directly. He seemed to be taking exercise, or perhaps pacing because he had something to think through – you know how Papa does. What do they think of me? They deplore all students of the Bauhaus, I believe, but have not come out into the open on the subject. Luckily, because I can hardly defend it as yet. I have met only one student, a woman who introduced herself to me in the street, who I cannot believe is typical, and I have seen another, a man, through an open window. But I have already been shouted at by a stranger, an inhabitant of Weimar, who disapproved of art students indiscriminately, even of a polite fellow like your brother. (That is why I was spoken to by the woman student who introduced herself in the street – she was defending me. I think I may need a good deal of defending.)

Give my love to Papa and my best to the fellows. If there is anything in this letter which you would like to share with them, then you have my permission. I do hope you will come very soon to visit your brother – I have a good-sized room, and you would be very welcome to rough it for three or four days, and I can show you what an art student's life is like. Do steer clear of wild company – do not drink or play cards or stay out late, now that you have no guide in life. And take care that Papa makes conversation at dinner. He is growing silent as he grows older. That is not good. The weather here is excellent and set to continue fine.

Your loving brother

C. S. T. Vogt.

And then Christian ornamented the remaining blank half-page of his writing paper by drawing a picture with his fountain pen, which he knew Dolphus would enjoy: an Alpine landscape with a path in the foreground, and two gentlemanly snails with Alpine hats on, one smoking a pipe, rising up and greeting each other with a little bow. When he got to the second one, the idea of getting it to remove its hat politely with one of the stalks it had on its head occurred to him. It was hard to draw, but satisfying. He finished it off with a few Alpine bouquets at the foot, put the letter into an envelope, sealed it and addressed it. The gong for supper was sounding softly downstairs.

'There were Communist protesters, however,' the man who must be Wolff was saying, as Christian came into the dining room and took his seat with a brief apology. 'Or Spartacists. I do not know the exact colour of the beast. They were a small but violent group, throwing bottles. We did not respond – a brother in the movement had his head split open, blood running down his face, but still we did not respond, Frau Scherbatsky. We made our point, and we were very much applauded by the ordinary people of Erfurt. Do you know Erfurt, Herr Neddermeyer? A fine town, I believe.'

'Herr Wolff, I do not think,' Frau Scherbatsky said, 'that you have met our new guest, Herr Vogt.'

'How do you do?' Wolff said, unsmiling and closing his eyes as he turned to Christian and nodded. 'You are most welcome.'

'Herr Vogt is the son of one of my husband's oldest friends – no, not his son, but the son of a business associate of that most old friend,' Frau Scherbatsky said.

Wolff nodded in acknowledgement, again turning to Christian but closing his eyes as he did so. He had something shining in his lapel, something attached. It seemed to Christian that all the discussions about his being a student at the Bauhaus had been gone over and expurgated before he had arrived. There had been something wary, alert and savage about Wolff's demeanour when he had entered the room, like one dog when introduced to another. Christian resolved to be polite and warm.

'I was passing the time in the train with the fellows,' Wolff said, 'counting the number of places we have assembled at this year. Do you know, we have already had twenty meetings and demonstrations, and this only September? Last year, we mounted only twelve, the whole length of the year. We have really already been the length and breadth of the kingdom.'

'Which town has the best food in Germany, would you say, Herr Wolff, from your exhaustive travels?' Frau Scherbatsky said.

'My dear lady,' Wolff said, beaming, 'I can hardly say – you know, we are so busy from the moment we arrive to the moment we depart, sometimes running from missiles. We were not always so very popular in the first days. Meeting, arranging, discussing, making speeches. We often have to settle for something simple to eat. Only very occasionally do the local group leaders arrange for the principal speakers to dine. I cannot say that the food was uppermost in my mind.'

'I always think the best food in Germany is in Bavaria,' Neddermeyer said. 'Those knuckles! Those white sausages! The fried veal slices!'

'And the most beautiful towns,' Frau Scherbatsky said. 'And the country, of course. There can be no doubt about that. Surely you found time to raise your head and admire the beauty of a town in the course of your travels, Herr Wolff?'

Maria came in with soup bowls on a small trolley with dragon's head ornamentation, setting the soup down before the four of them. As she set one down before Frau Scherbatsky, she caught Christian's eye. He did not lower his: he engaged her gaze as she murmured in her mistress's ear. She made her way round the table, taking the bowls from the trolley, and he watched her, boldly. She reached him, placed a bowl in front of him, and lowered her face to murmur in his ear as she offered him a basket of bread. There was an attractive smell of sweat and of clean skin under soap, mixing with the soup's sour odours. He had thought she was going to share a moment's comment with him, but she said only, 'Liver dumpling soup', raised her head, gave the table a single, surveying glance, and removed herself with the empty trolley.

'You get good numbers in Bavaria,' Wolff said. 'When we were just beginning, in the months after the war, we were sometimes only ten or a dozen, and greeted with savage violence. You recall, Frau Scherbatsky – ah, no, it was before I was living here, it was when I was at Fräulein Schlink's, before she took exception to me—'

'How could anyone take exception to our dear Herr Wolff!' Frau Scherbatsky cried.

'Dear lady,' Wolff said absently. 'They broke my finger then – it was in Jena. But in the last year, the numbers have grown so wonderfully! For me, the beauties of Bavaria are tied up with the support and understanding the movement is gaining there.'

'What is your movement, Herr Wolff?' Christian asked.

Again, that creaking movement of the head; again, the inspection with quite closed eyes of the art student, the revolutionary, the boy of violence, anarchy and square glass-walled houses. 'It is a small group of associates who stand for what is right,' Wolff said, in a voice that seemed to have had its patience tried. 'That is all.'

'I see,' Christian said.

'There were secret forces that led us defeated out of the war, defeated and shamed, and sold us to people who have long planned for our downfall. Every week, more and more people understand what it is that lies behind. We work hard to help people to understand. In Erfurt, they lined the streets, cheering. The crowd was two deep in places. You can only rely on Germans, now. More and more people understand that, since the war. That was' – and Wolff did not lower his voice, continued to shout as he moved into compliment and said – 'a delicious soup, Frau Scherbatsky.'

Maria took away the soup, and brought in a white fricassee of what must be the promised rabbit, with rice alongside.

'And did you see your wizards today, Frau Scherbatsky?' Christian said, with an attempt at lightness.

'My wizards, Herr Vogt?' She seemed genuinely puzzled.

He immediately wished he had not started it, but persevered. 'I think you said that the eccentric people we saw yesterday – the people in purple robes – I think you said that they pass every day.'

'Oh,' Frau Scherbatsky said. 'I think I know what you mean. No, I do not think I have seen those people today.' She made a minute gesture towards Wolff, as if to indicate that such talk was not for his dignity. But it was too late.

'What eccentric people are these?' Wolff said, mixing his rabbit fricassee with the rice in an uncommitted manner.

'Oh, you know, Herr Wolff,' Neddermeyer said. He was evidently enjoying his food. 'You must have seen them – an invented religion, I believe, with disciples in purple robes and shaved heads, and a special diet. They seem to be growing in number, too.'

'I should be most surprised,' Frau Scherbatsky said. 'Is the stew not to your taste, Herr Wolff?'

'Oh, perfectly,' Wolff said. 'It may be a little dry for me, but I am an old soldier. I ask for nothing in the way of luxuries or especially delicious food, you know. And they come from? It seems a strange conception, to conceive of or invent a religion from the beginning.'

'Well, it may be an Oriental religion, brought to Weimar, taking root here,' Neddermeyer said. 'I believe they are based at the new art school, under the direction of one of the masters – now, his name ...'

But then it was clear to Christian that all three had agreed, in the interests of peace and civility, that the Bauhaus and its madness were not to be mentioned before or raised by Wolff, since the conversation was now abruptly turned to a bridge at Erfurt, one filled with shops, one older and longer and more beautiful than the one in Florence that people talked of so. Christian had been trying, without success, to see what the object in Wolff's lapel was. It was a silver insignia or motif of some sort. He could not quite make it out.

14.

Around Weimar, the Masters of the Bauhaus took their leisure.

Kandinsky sat in a deep armchair, an ashtray precariously balanced on its arm, and sucked on a cigar. His dinner was finished, and a fug of smoke hung heavily over his head. His wife was opposite him, darning a pair of his socks and listening to him talk.

'I saw Klee this afternoon,' Kandinsky said. 'He made such a fuss, oh, such a fuss, about the price of a cup of coffee. You would have thought it was the end of the world.'

'How much was the sum, Vassily Vassilyevich?' Nina said.

'It was two thousand marks. Or three thousand. Yes, first it was two thousand and then it was three thousand. The price of the coffee went up between us ordering the first cup and us ordering the second cup. What would have happened if we had not had the extra thousand marks on us. But we did, so all was well. People fuss so about small things. No – what am I saying. I said two thousand marks, I meant two hundred thousand. You could not buy a cup of anything for a thousand marks.'

'But a thousand marks is a thousand marks,' Nina said sensibly. 'Before the war, you could have bought a sofa, a table, one of my Vassily Vassilyevich's paintings for a thousand marks. And now it is nothing times a hundredfold, the difference between a cup of coffee one moment and the next.'

'That is so,' Kandinsky said, ruminating over a puff of smoke. 'Klee could not restrain himself. On the subject of money, he becomes a Swiss businessman – not a very good Swiss businessman. His one idea is not to spend any of it. He was telling me that his new idea is to paint his pictures on newspaper – he said the day was approaching when he could not afford to paint on paper or canvas. I told him that there was no need to make such savings – he should simply spend what he had on materials now, and in a year's time he would be glad of it.'

'And what did Klee respond?' Nina asked.

'Klee?' Kandinsky said. 'He cannot bear any outlay. Of course, he paints a painting every day, and none of them can be sold, so the blame lies with him, truly. Nina Nikolayevna, where is the bronze of the horse that used to stand there, on the table?'

'And there I am – finished,' Nina said, laying the socks and the needle and thread down with relief. 'What did you say?'

Kandinsky repeated himself.

'It must be travelling slowly from Russia with the other things,' Nina said. 'If it has not been robbed and destroyed. One day they will all arrive, all your things, and we will be at home here.'

'The Constructivists have taken it,' Kandinsky said. 'And melted it down for one of their towers. We will never see my little horse again.'

'Soon there will be a revolution in Germany,' Nina said. 'And we will all be shot. So nothing will matter very much any more.'

'Yes, that's so,' Kandinsky said. He sucked meditatively on his cigar.

Two streets away, Klee lifted his violin from its case. They had eaten well. On Saturday night, Klee liked to choose the dinner, and to cook it himself. He liked the inner organs of beasts, bitter, rubbery, softly textureless, perfumed with bodily waste in a way only the practised would enjoy, and Felix had grown up finding these things ordinary and even pleasant; Lily had got used to them, and now took the Saturday dinner as part of how Paul was. Klee divided food into blond and brunette; he could cook sweetbreads in either way, dark or light. Tonight the food had been the heart of an ox, a monstrous thing. Klee had cleaned and stuffed it with meat, turnip, carrot and potato, and a herb of his own discovery, which had given the whole thing an odd flavour of liquorice. It had been a little heavy. Lily sat at the piano, ready to play, but evidently slightly uncomfortable: she burped gently from time to time. Felix sat on the sofa, the sole member of the audience. Paul took the violin from its case, unhooked the bow and, without hurry, gave the bow a good coating of rosin.

This evening it was to be the Kreutzer sonata. Klee was feeling ambitious. When he felt bold, incapable of restraint, on the verge of great and exciting things, he cooked the heart of an ox for dinner and he played the Kreutzer sonata afterwards. He often played it as something to live up to, before embarking on great enterprises. Lily often concluded that a great change was in the offing when she heard, from the studio, the sound of the first chords of the Kreutzer sonata being played once, twice, a third time; meditatively, trying it out, softly, then with dramatic force. That first chord, four notes at once on the violin, would be heard again and again, as Klee tried to get the sound exactly right; then a pause on one of the middle notes, a doodle, a trill, a thoughtful and slow attempt at the tune in the slow movement, as if Klee were taking it apart from the inside. This morning, the chord was sounded in some kind of announcement: he took the top note towards quite a different place; a dotted rhythm, a gay and yet monumental tune it took Lily a few moments to place, though she knew it as well as she knew her own face. Klee was enjoying himself by playing the little prelude to the *Emperor Waltz*. A few notes of it, only. And then silence: he had returned to work. For a week now, the Kreutzer sonata had been sounding from the studio at unexpected times, and Lily had taken the hint, and practised the piano part while her husband had gone out for his daily walks or to meet with Kandinsky. Was the larger endeavour a change in Klee's art, or was it just to announce the beginning of a new term at the art school? But for days he had been practising in his own systematic way, and tonight they were going to attempt the Kreutzer. The outbreak of gaiety in those few notes of the waltz was a sign of it: he felt liberated today.

Klee raised the violin to his face. He looked, sober, at Lily, who beamed and raised her hands to the keyboard. Klee's eyes shone intently, like those of the villain in a melodrama. He hung the bow above the strings; with a single gesture, he brought it down. The chord sang out; a cloud of rosin puffed from the bow, its dust glittering in the light from the lamp. Felix sat forward on the sofa, his loose, comfortable brown plus-fours bunching up and his green stockings falling down to his ankles. He clasped his hands in his lap. The beginning of the Kreutzer sonata was the most inexpressibly exciting thing he ever heard. It was like drawing back the curtains at seven thirty in the morning and seeing the lake on the first day of holiday, like the colour of the middle of the yolk of a fried egg in the country, that exact yellow of A major. It was almost better than those other things, because it would soon turn to fury and thunder and blackness, before it went all the way round and found its way back. It was a joy to hear Papa play it and call up a summer morning here, in this dull curtained room filled with things, smelling a little bit of the ox's heart from dinner.

'Klee is really too much,' Kandinsky said in his own room, leaning backwards. 'I am fond of the dear fellow, but ...'

'He is a Swiss businessman, a quite unsuccessful one,' Nina said. 'Too concerned with money, just enough to make him frightened about it, not enough to paint to earn it. The Swiss ...'

'Is he Swiss?' Kandinsky said. 'I am fond of him. But I sometimes wonder – can he be a Jew? He has all that race's enthusiasm for pelf, for lucre, for the pile of gold. How his eyes light up!'

Nina laughed heartily, waving the comment away. 'Vassily Vassilyevich,' she said affectionately, as she always did when he said something to her that he would not say to everybody.

In another room, a large, empty one, the disciples of Mazdaznan gathered. The hall was at the back of a church, loaned to political groups, societies, choirs and amateur gatherings of a centrist-to-left disposition. One of the two Weimar Wagner societies, the one with an anti-monarchist bent, met here on Tuesdays, and on Fridays the town's Communist watercolour society. Itten's Mazdaznan group met in classrooms at the Bauhaus, but on Saturday nights the building was closed, and it was good to have a weekly meeting to which everyone came.

There were forty people in the room. Most had had their heads shaved, and some were in their formal purple robes, made by themselves, or by adept clothes designers and makers. Elsa Winteregger was talking. 'And then there's new people. Oh, there's always new people. New ideas, new images, new thinking. Do you know? I saw a man, a boy, a new one today, and I took him up, and he was so full of new life, I don't know where he came from or what he was doing, but he said he wanted to find the Bauhaus, and I helped him, and then I don't know what happened to him. It was *so* exciting. And tomorrow there's going to be so many of them, not tomorrow, the day after tomorrow, and there's going to be so many wise new young heads, all of them full of new ideas, and they'll put us to shame, we've been trodden over and made conventional in life, but them, not them, it's for us to learn from them, us and the Masters, too ...'

She went on gabbling. People about her came and went,

listening and not interrupting and then going away again. Sometimes they turned to each other and began to talk, and drifted off. Her speech had started somewhere else and it was going to be finished somewhere else. And now she was talking about her sister, who was staying with her.

'. . . only for a few days, only until Sunday, not tomorrow, a week tomorrow, she came yesterday and was so exhausted, she lay in bed until lunchtime, afterwards, easily, and she said, Elsa, what has happened to your hair, so we laughed about that, and I think she is quite used to it, quite used now, she lives where we grew up, in Breitenberg, so she is used to almost anything now. She is so dear, I could not live without her, I promised her to bring her to the Bauhaus on Monday morning, to see us all, all us oddities, but she says that only I am enough, only I am oddity enough for her ...'

The room fell silent, and Elsa too, last of all. Itten had come in, with his head slightly downwards, as if ducking a hit from a low lintel. He was wearing his purple silk robe with a red ruff about his neck. There was a gathering and a shuffling. Itten stood there. His presence commanded attention. He raised his arms to either side and closed his eyes. His chest swelled as he took a great breath in, and held it. The forty people in the room did the same, moving at an angle, not to get in a confusion of arms; they closed their eyes and breathed in, and held it in. For a second there was silence; outside in the street, the shout of two boys, something about the money one owed the other. It was the racket of two voices with no control over their breathing and no sense of the intimate and huge connection between the lungs and the world. Outside, a can of some sort was kicked against a wall, and a shout of complaint; the Mazdaznan breathed out, humming as they did so, expelling the world and its violence; a warm note filled the room, rose, fell, subsided into a satisfied breath in. Itten opened his huge wise eyes; his arms fell limply to his sides. 'The word is spreading,' he said. 'Today we are three dozen. Next week we are fifty. We spread, like breath.'

And in the room of their house, Klee slowed, and his face rose a little, and the sad reflective little tune that came just before the end seemed to fill his features. There was an expression on Papa's face you never saw at other times. The tune went its way; Mamma and Papa seemed separated by the music, diversely thinking their way through. And then they came together again; there was a little rush and a clatter of fury; and the first movement of the sonata was done. Felix sat on his hands. He knew not to applaud until the whole sonata was finished. Papa would set down his violin and smile in a brief way. But before that there was the slow movement and the joy of the tarantella. Felix could hardly bear the prospect of it.

'I am so happy to have you here,' Frau Scherbatsky said to Christian, as he was going upstairs. Her face was warm and beaming; underneath her blonde helmet of hair, she shone. 'It is so good to have a young person in the house again. I do hope you will be happy here.'

'I think I shall be, Frau Scherbatsky,' Christian said. 'I am very comfortable in my room – I feel very grateful.'

'Oh, I am so pleased,' Frau Scherbatsky said. In the drawing room, the men were discussing affairs of state; a conversation that had been an energetic exchange of views was turning into a manly argument. 'You mustn't –' she said, lowering her voice and placing her hand on the forearm of Christian's Norfolk jacket '– you mustn't mind Herr Wolff too much. I know he seems very serious and angry about things.'

'He seems …' Christian thought. He prided himself on finding the right word, when it was required. 'He seems very – decided.'

'Very decided,' Frau Scherbatsky said. 'Yes, indeed. He is. But, please, I do hope you will find some patience with him. It has been so hard for so many people of our generation. You must have seen it in Berlin, but I know that young people can find it difficult to understand, to be patient. You see, Herr Vogt, it has been so difficult to realize what, all this time, has been working to destroy our lives. We were so naïve, all of us, and we only understood now that it is only other Germans whom we can really trust. You see, Herr Vogt,' she went on confidingly, 'we let the Jews go on living among us. We had no idea. They destroyed us, and humiliated us, and are now destroying our money. And Herr Wolff understands this. Does he not have a right to be angry? I would just ask you, please, Herr Vogt, you are an understanding, a kind person, I can see, just to be patient and to listen to Herr Wolff, even when he grows – how can I put it? – loud.'

Christian bowed; he had not expected Frau Scherbatsky to say any of this. The voices in the drawing room were, indeed, growing loud. He flushed, and turned, and with brisk steps went upstairs. There were Jews living underneath his father in Charlottenburg; every day his father greeted Frau Rosenthal with a raise of his hat and a smile; Arnold Rosenthal, the elder of the two boys, had been three years older than Christian, had served bravely in the war, had returned unscathed. He was not working against anyone. He had fought for the Kaiser. Christian bowed at the turn of the stairs again, as Frau Scherbatsky beamed, her eyes following him upstairs sentimentally, as she perhaps thought of one of her dead sons. Tomorrow, Christian thought, he would take steps to find somewhere else to live. The arrangements were that he would live here for three months. However, he would move tomorrow. He said this to himself, but he already knew he would not, not because he disagreed with something his landlady had said. He already despised himself for his own cowardice. He already knew that that was the easiest path for the mind to take.

15.

On Monday Christian went to the Bauhaus for the first time. In the evening he came home. He went upstairs in Frau Scherbatsky's house, leaving his hat on the pale oak hatstand in the hall, greeting Herr Neddermeyer shortly. In his room, he took out the laid writing paper and his pen, sitting at the desk. He filled the pen with ink. He began to write. 'Dearest Dolphus,' he wrote. 'I must write to you. Today, at 9.15, in the city of Weimar, I saw a girl whose name is Adele Winteregger. My life begins.'

BOOK 2
1979

1.

There was an unusual group of people approaching the lounge from the other side of the glass wall and the door that opened into it. The waiting area by the gate was full, and had been for some time. The largely Sicilian crowd had been fanning themselves – the air-conditioning at the airport in Catania was proving inadequate, even in early June. They had been getting up to remonstrate with the employees of the airline company about the lack of information, the heat, the delay of the aircraft. Voices had been raised; hands had gestured; fury had been apparently entered upon before the Sicilian storm of complaint quickly blew itself out and the complainer went back to his seat with every air of contentment. The men above a certain age were in blue shirts and pale brown trousers; the women, some of whom were even in widows' black, fanned themselves. The sexes sat apart. Now an unexpected and interesting group of people was approaching from the other side of the glass wall, and the attention of the lounge was drawn to it.

At the centre there was a tall, blond, distinguished-looking man with a large nose and a large-boned face. There was something donkey-like about his features and their big teeth; he looked Scandinavian, perhaps Danish. He wore a neatly pressed white short-sleeved shirt with a dark blue tie and a pair of crisp blue trousers; and his neat turn-out was a surprise, because he was blind. In one hand he held a white cane, folded up and, for the moment, unused. About him were six men. They were

Sicilians, perhaps employees of the airport; dark, serious-looking and short. Two held him by either arm, guiding him briskly; another held a piece of cabin baggage, evidently the passenger's; another, the youngest, walked behind him, giving him an occasional push, perhaps to show what he could do, given the chance. The two remaining walked in front of the blind man; the more distinguished, who seemed to be in charge of the whole operation, was talking to him as they went, the other occupied himself by walking alongside the chief as if ready to take notes. But that was not this last one's only occupation. He held, it could be seen, the passenger's passport and his boarding card.

The lounge watched, fascinated. The group came to the other side of the glass wall of the lounge. The blind man was handed his cabin luggage and, by the chief's right-hand man, the passport and boarding card. His hand was shaken by all six men. They looked for guidance to the chief, who briskly shook down his jacket as if he had passed through detritus, and walked away. The lounge watched the blind man as he waved the folded-up white stick, and it went in a moment into its full length. He had been left by the group on the other side of the glass wall, about four metres from the open glass door. The blind Scandinavian waved in the direction of the wall, but it was solid. He waved to one side, then to the other. Like a blond insect, he went to his left, to his right, not finding the opening, patiently feeling, then less patiently, then tapping with rich fury, his head turning round and calling to people who were no longer there. The lounge watched with sincere interest. They had wanted to know what would happen if a blind man were deposited before a glass wall and told to find his way to the one door through it. Perhaps the guiding party had wondered this too – but, no, they had not waited to watch the consequences.

Duncan watched, too, but with less open amusement. His book, a novel by Andrew Holleran that he had read before, rested in his lap. He thought in a moment he would get up and ask the woman at the desk at the entrance to help the blind passenger through. At the moment she was sitting on her swivel stool, smoking, not paying any attention to that passenger or any other. Duncan was used to Sicilians and their cruelty, the way that dogs would be kicked and chained. In restaurants, he had seen parents pinching the noses of their small children when they refused good food, tipping their heads back forcibly and ladling the milk pudding down their little throats and over their faces. He had watched a carabiniero, a lucky pick-up, sit naked at his kitchen table at the little borrowed flat off the via Merulana, take a breakfast knife to the torso of a wasp that was absorbedly feeding on the edge of a dish of plum jam, and sever the wasp in two. He no longer felt the need to intervene when the savagery or inattention of Sicilians resulted in anyone being hurt. The only time he had intervened, after eight months on the island, was when two Sicilians new to each other started discussing, in his company, the tragedy of Sicily and its national character. That he couldn't bear: it ruined an evening like a solitary drunkard in company. So he watched the battering of the blind Scandinavian on the other side of the glass wall with mild interest, like everyone else. In time he would discover where the door was.

2.

The man next to Duncan asked him if he had a light, but Duncan did not; he asked if he was French, returning home, but Duncan explained that he was English, going back to London. Why not go back directly? The man was handsome, one of those good-looking Sicilians who peak, to the world's gratitude, at twenty-two, then lose their hair, grow papery and dry; he was in his middle twenties, and his hair was beautifully thinning. There are flights, directly, now, to London from Catania. Was the gentleman not advised properly?

'Duncan,' Duncan introduced himself. 'Yes, I know about the direct flights, but I had to return at very short notice. This was the only flight today that could take me. I needed to get back as soon as possible.'

'A holiday?' the gentleman asked. But Duncan had seen that while he had been speaking the man's eyes had gone towards the daughter of a large family, a girl in a short skirt and a tight blouse, and had run up and down her appreciatively. He was just passing the time in a neutral way in talking to Duncan – not that Duncan knew what could result from their conversation. Duncan simply said that, no, he had been working here. He had been teaching English as a foreign language to schoolchildren, and had been living in a small flat in the centre of the city. He liked Catania, yes, he did, and the food, and he had seen the fish market and had gone to Taormina to see the beauties of the island, which, yes, was the most beautiful place in the world, and he agreed that Sicilians were really very lucky to have been born in such a place, even given all its terrible troubles, which made you think you would have been better being born in the shit with no arms and no legs, sometimes, but then the sun shone and the sea was beautiful, and the women, the women of Sicily.

Duncan had been in Sicily for eleven months. He could keep this sort of conversation going with only one ear on its content. He had heard its contradictions, its flow and counterflow, many times. The other, more active, ear was busy keeping an interested and acute ear attending to the difficulties of Italian as he went. Was that an idiom the man had used – in the shit with no arms and no legs? Or just his own way of talking? He did not know.

He had come to Sicily for no reason in particular – or no good reason, not one that you could tell anyone of any serious-ness. He had been working for the government in London. His job had been in an unemployment office in Kilburn, interviewing the out-of-work and granting them the dole. There were mothers, hard cases, alcoholics, but also students and people who did not really need anything. Duncan did not engage with them, in the shabby office behind the solid stone walls. He knew that, if he thought about it, he would probably take the short step that existed between his state, as a poor employee of the government, and the most desperate of the subjects who came through the door.

One day he could no longer stand it. It was a hot day in early summer and he had, as it were, fooled himself into coming to work. All the way from his second-floor flat in Brondesbury, he had told himself what a beautiful morning it was, how lucky he was to be walking in the sun, what a joy London could be on these days. He admired the boys in their shorts and vests; they might have been on their way to the Heath or to an open-air swimming pool, and Duncan might have been going with them. He had performed this mental trick before, pushing what he did not want to think about to the back of his mind – his father, Christmas, what Mr Mansfield his supervisor had said to him the day before. He had performed the trick with his job as he did now, putting it quite out of his mind and letting his feet trace a route without thinking what was at the end of it. In his bag was a Tupperware box of lunch, in his pocket a Baldwin novel: he might have been saving the two for a read under a tree with a picnic, not an hour in the staff room at lunchtime. It was only when he was in the street of the unemployment office, almost before the staff door, which was to the side of the locked public door, that he remembered he was not going to the Heath, not going to swim, not going to take his clothes off with the boys of London today. He was going to sit in his neat white short-sleeved shirt and tie with his suit trousers on, and listen to the failures of society asking for more money.

'Did you see that programme on last night?' Marion was saying, as she puffed up behind him. She was a colleague at the same level as him. She had been there longer – it had been a mysterious amount longer for some time – and had a tendency to explain ordinary things to him, where the coffee money was kept, where the better sandwich shop was at lunchtime, how it was important to stay calm and not raise your voice even when they deserved killing, really. He had in the end discovered that she had started working there three months and two weeks before him. Some still older hands probably regarded the pair of them as having the same sort of newness. He could see it happening when, as time passed, still newer colleagues, processors and analysts and form-fillers, arrived in batches.

'I don't think I did,' Duncan said. 'I was catching up with some ironing I should have done at the weekend. Terrible, really.' He held the door open for her.

'Oh, it was incredible,' Marion said, coming in and removing her headscarf. Her hair stuck to her scalp. 'I couldn't believe it. It was a programme about nudists, all over the world. All of them, all on holiday, like that, like the day they were born. Hello, Frank.'

On the stone steps just inside the unemployment office, Duncan made up his mind without intending to. The steps were just the same as they had been at his grammar school. They spoke institution. He was smiling and trying to show an interest in a forty-year-old woman watching a television documentary about nudists and saying hello politely to a man with a scruffy beard who commuted every day from St Albans. The man looked at him in return with painful disapproval, hardly greeting him. The man's name he had always believed to be Fred and perhaps he really was called Fred, since Marion never listened to anything she was told. Duncan had been the subject of institutions before, and now, as he easily absorbed himself into the flow of the institution before the locked doors opened, he felt himself to be the easy agent of those institutions. And that would not do. It was as if he had become a schoolteacher, but without the power of doing good in the world. He would spend a glorious sunny day inside, looking at high windows through which the light fell, looking down at men who smelt, at women who had slept in their clothes, at people begging for money just to feed their kiddies because they were desperate and they didn't know where the next meal was coming from. There would be students coming in soon, pretending to be interested in getting a job between their summer and their autumn terms. There would be people who had been sacked and people who could not work through injury not their fault. He would sit in the sad, echoing hall on the other side of his desk. He thought of all those people and he really did not give a shit about any of them.

Going into his office he realized that there was no reason why he should not resign from his job and go to work in Sicily. Teaching English. It could hardly be any worse than here. And why Sicily? It was cheap, Duncan knew; it spoke Italian, which he had a smattering of. But mostly Duncan thought of Sicily because he had, the week before, picked up an off-duty Sicilian waiter in a gay pub on St Martin's Lane, and the island, now, for him, was a land full of lemons, oranges and waiters called Salvatore. By half past ten he had told an overweight woman looking for employment in the legal field that she was wasting everyone's time and should aim much, much lower. By eleven he had gone to see his supervisor, and had told him that he wanted to resign at the end of the month. By six thirty he was in the same gay pub on St Martin's Lane – he had phoned up everyone he could think of on their office numbers – and he was telling a thrilled group of twenty men with moustaches, almost all with checked shirts on, just what he had done and where he was going to go.

'You've got some nerve,' Paul said, coming back from the bar with a half of lager and lime and a pint of bitter for Duncan. 'I wish I had your nerve, even a bit of your nerve.'

'If you only had a *bit* of his nerve,' Simon said, 'that'd only get you to the Isle of Wight, not much of a life-change, that, I don't think.'

'Cheek!' Paul said.

Even Andrew had come, though it was his night for his men's group, and he never liked to miss that. Or was it revolutionary politics? 'I'll come to that some time,' Paul said. 'Sounds like a right laugh.' Anyway, it was a fantastic turn-out, and they were still there at closing time, most of them. Why Sicily? Why not.

3.

Sicily had spoken to him on the fourth day, exactly as he had known it would. He had gone to see his father in his falling-down old house in Harrow the day before he left, to tell him – after he had left the unemployment job – that he was going to the other side of Europe. He had dreaded it, but it wasn't, in the end, so bad. His father was not what he had been. His shoulders had narrowed, and surely he had grown shorter. His hair fell in a solid lump away from his forehead, not washed for some days. As always, he had immediately started talking about himself. 'When I started work in the insurance company,' he said, 'there was a man there who was a great friend of mine. He admired me immensely. "I just don't know how you manage to get through all the work you do," he used to say. When I managed to get out of going into the army, he was drafted in. And he –' his father reached for a handkerchief, sitting in a damp crumple on the walnut card table by the side of his habitual mustardy winged armchair '– he went into Sicily. The first wave of the liberation. He never spoke about it to me when he came back. By then I had made myself useful in all sorts of ways, and I was his superior by a good distance when he returned to his post, but I always let him call me by my Christian name, if no one was around, and I think he appreciated that a great deal. My father always said to me – your grandfather – he said, "Treat your subordinates with courtesy, and they will treat you with respect." And I believe I've always done precisely that.'

Duncan waited to hear something about Sicily. There in his father's mind, there was an irritating fly, buzzing about, a tiny fly, not visible, but audible, and introduced into the normal furniture and spaces of the mind without warning. The name of the fly – what was it? It was Sicily. But in time it proved to go quite harmoniously with all the furniture that was already in the room, and could really safely be ignored.

'Your mother always wanted to go to Italy,' his father continued. He stroked the arm of the chair; it was bald from this repeated gesture, carried out all the time, all day long, while his father gave the impression of thought. 'Not Sicily, I don't think. She wanted to go to Rome, and Florence, and Venice, I believe. But I looked into it, and I found that Rome was a dangerous sort of place. It would not suit us. The food, too, would not suit. The best food in Europe is the food in southern Germany, where the salads are clean and the vegetables are well prepared. I explained all this to your mother. It was only a whim on her part. In the end I decided to surprise her, and we took a holiday on Lake Como, and she enjoyed it a lot. She said, "Samuel, I thought I wanted to go to Rome, but this was a lovely idea of yours, and I don't think anything in Italy could improve on this." All the Italians go for their holidays to Lake Como, you know. You don't catch Italians going to Rome for their summer holidays. That was really a clever wheeze of mine, I always think.'

On the way out of the house, Duncan noticed the long greasy mark, like the drag of a mop, about five feet up along the old floral wallpaper in the hall. He had noticed it before. 'Let me come with you,' his father said, walking in a tired old way out of the sitting room at the back of the house. Duncan said there was no need, and with surprise his father agreed there was no need – he wasn't proposing to walk him to the bus stop. 'I've got to go out to post a letter,' his father said. 'To your aunt Rachel. She will keep on writing. "Dear Samuel …"' Duncan's father made a derisory imitation of a woman speaking his name, as if it were an obviously stupid thing to write, even at the beginning of a letter. He refused an offer of Duncan's to post his own letter for him. Then he leant his head against the wall, just above the shoe-rack in the hall, and took his slippers off before putting on his brown shoes, much mended and soft with much polishing. He moved his head along the wall as he did so, just there, where the dark streak of grease had formed.

'And you'll be off shortly, I expect,' his father said. 'I suppose all the duties of dropping in and seeing how I am are going to fall on your sister now. If you had come yesterday, I could have put all this news in my letter to your aunt Rachel, but I'm not going to waste a good envelope now it's sealed.'

'And the stamp,' Duncan said, opening the door with the stained-glass window. The glass porch at the front was hot and dry; in it, a rubber plant was yellow, dying, withered. That was not the place for it, but his father had given up watering it.

'Oh, you can detach and reattach stamps to a new envelope,' his father said, putting his raincoat on and feeling in his pocket for his keys. 'Sometimes a letter arrives and the lazy so-and-sos at the GPO haven't franked it. No, I wouldn't trust you to remember to post my letter, and then I've got your aunt Rachel to deal with.'

It was only four days after arriving in Sicily that Duncan woke up not in the cheap hotel in the centre he had settled in but in a bright bedroom at the top of an old palazzo, and just remembering the exchange of glances, the small nod, the turn and the falling into simple conversation on the street the night before. He just remembered the sequence that had followed the delicious greasy almondy dinner, the fish swimming in oil and eaten at dangerous room temperature, and the way the two of them had piled up the four flights of stairs with their hands and mouths all over each other in the hot stairwell; just remembered the man's face as he turned his head and found the warm tangle of unkempt black hair and the grand Arab nose in the dark sleeping face. His own arm, just flushed with red after wandering around the blazing city for three days, made a sharp contrast against the man's conker-coloured chest. He had heard that there were blond people in the city, descendants of what, Normans? Englishmen? His father's colleague and subordinate? But they were not like him, and he saw his desirability as something exotic. That was the day Sicily spoke to him, and it spoke when the man, whose name was Salvatore, as always, left him in bed and returned with what he called breakfast, a brioche each, with chocolate granita in one, lemon granita in the other. There was a shop just underneath. 'It's my breakfast every day, beginning May, till September,' this Salvatore said. The hot brioche and the stab of ice made Duncan's face ache; the pain of eating iced food too fast spread across his sinuses, and Salvatore rubbed his face with his big hands. Later, when they were done, they were both showered, the dog, a noble Irish setter called Pippo, had been admitted to the bedroom and praised, and it was time for Duncan to go, he commented on Salvatore getting dressed. 'You don't wear underwear,' he said.

'Again, from May to September, never,' Salvatore said, spraying his bare chest with cologne. 'Do you not know? No Sicilian will wear underwear for five months. It is just too hot. Oh, the day in September when you have to put on your underwear!'

'But the day in May when you are allowed to take it off?' Duncan said. Salvatore laughed and laughed, warmly, ecstatically, half with Duncan and half in exact memory of that annual private festival. And Sicily had spoken to Duncan. He never saw that particular Salvatore again, not even in passing in the street. He welcomed the introduction of a new rule of Italian life. Most of the rules seemed to be concerned with food, of not having cappuccino after eleven in the morning, of never eating cheese with fish, of not combining a fish course with a meat course – this was theoretical to Duncan, who had to find some means of earning a living within, he calculated, three weeks. Later he discovered rules about behaviour, of what to call people, of who you should stand up in front of. Those were all public rules, which strangers on buses would share with you.

But the rules of clothes, the rule that said you should not wear short socks or a tie with a suit, that you should not wear

81

a pair of shorts in town, and that on the first of May all Sicilian men left their underwear off until autumn, those were rules that were passed on exactly like this one, first thing in the morning in a strange bedroom or, once Duncan had found the loan of a pretty little flat off the via Merulana from another teacher, all wooden furniture and cool dark red tiles underfoot, in his own bedroom. Duncan would walk down the street and see the men passing, and think not only, They're none of them wearing any underwear, but It's the rule that they don't have to wear underwear, and they all – all of them – they all know that none of the rest of them are. Not one of them. Sicily had spoken to him, on the fourth day.

4.

'Yes,' he said to the man in the departure lounge at Catania airport. 'Yes, I like Sicily a lot. I've got to go back to England now, though. My father's dying.'

The man made a formal gesture of regret, and the conversation was over. On the other side of the glass wall, the blind man battered on and on, his face turning from side to side, as he called for help.

5.

The house in Harrow had once looked like its neighbours – a substantial Edwardian house, with gables and a bay window at the front. But it had been added to, and now was pointed out, and people shook their heads over it. A garage had come first, in the 1930s, a square box with a wooden double door, once painted blue; an old red Volvo, seventeen years old, hardly used, wallowed in there. But Duncan's father had done the rest. A sun terrace at the back, pushing the house further out into the garden; a square block of a kitchen at the side, in a sort of black tarpaulin material covering brickwork, the sort of material that covered flat roofs in this part of the world; a glass porch before the old Edwardian front door, now with a dead houseplant in it and a pile of unopened letters on the windowshelf. There was a square attic conversion at the top, a bald cube in peeling white planks and a square empty window cutting out of the dormer roof; there was another extension, which had been made on the first floor, resting on top of the garage. The original house was in there somewhere, impossible to imagine among all those black geometries, all that contrived asymmetry for the sake of an extra room here and there.

Samuel, Duncan's father, had kept the builders of Harrow busy, and the property lawyers, too: he meticulously applied for planning permission for every small change and every extension, resubmitting when he was turned down, discussing details every which way with the builder – he would not employ an architect when, as he said, the builder had to build it, and he knew very well what was needed. It was Duncan's memory of his childhood, to be banished with his sister Domenica to a spare room or other while a part of the house was rendered uninhabitable for months – the dining room with no wall, the kitchen huddled and stripped without cupboards, the builders sitting on the ground smoking where the sun lounge was going to go. There were only the four of them; their parents were in the future going to need less space, not more. In the end, he concluded that it was his father's hobby, like the law suit his father brought with gusto against a builder when one extension, to the dining room, proved to let in rain in torrents.

In the streets of Harrow, people pointed out the house as a disaster, as something extended and pulled beyond what anything could reasonably take. They pointed it out now. Upstairs, the curtains were drawn in the master bedroom, where Samuel lay dying. He was sleeping at the moment. A nurse had sat with him overnight, now that he was in no position to argue with the expense, or with the fact that she was Trinidadian. She was speaking in low tones to the day nurse, who had just arrived in her little beige Morris Marina and was taking off her thin summer coat in the hall.

In the summer terrace, the glass-covered extension at the back of the house, three women sat. They were Duncan's aunts, his father's three sisters. They had been there in pairs, or all three of them, for days. They were Aunt Rachel, Aunt Ruth and Aunt Rebecca. A grandfather had named them after Biblical figures, not foreseeing that, for ever afterwards in north London, people would ask them and their brother Samuel which synagogue they went to, creating a hostility they saw no reason to diminish. Samuel's children were called Duncan and Domenica; the children of Ruth and Rebecca were called Amanda, Raymond, Richard and Caroline. Normal names, Ruth would say, meaning what she meant by that. Rachel had no children, but if she had, she would have named them away from the scriptures too; she had a black parrot, however, named Ezekiah. Ruth and Rachel were already in black, as if preparing for the day of their brother's death; Rebecca, a plump woman, was wearing a practical tweed, her hat still on. They were talking about their niece and nephew.

'She's no use,' Rachel said. 'No use at all. I phoned her and she hardly seemed to understand what I was asking of her. I don't think we'll see her until the weekend.'

'Oh, but surely,' Rebecca said.

'She simply doesn't care,' Ruth said.

'Possibly,' Rachel said. 'I think she's a little bit simple, sometimes. I don't think she understands what's going on. She said to me that she'd wait until her brother got here.'

'Her brother!' Rebecca said.

'I don't know what she was thinking of,' Rachel said. 'Waiting for her brother.'

'She loves her brother,' Ruth said. 'At least, everyone always said so. Even when she was a little girl, she would follow him round, holding something to give him, a toy or something of that nature. Her little brother ...'

'Oh, what people do, what people justify, in the name of love,' Rebecca said. '"I *love* him." Fancy. So she's waiting until her brother gets here, is she?'

'She'll be waiting for a good long time, then,' Rachel said. 'Is it me or is it hot in here?'

'No,' Ruth said. 'It is hot, it isn't you. The brother, too – at least Samuel saw some sense over that one. Giving everything up and going to be a hippie in Italy. There's no sign of that one, is there?'

'I am so glad Samuel listened to what we suggested,' Rebecca said. 'The estate couldn't just go to someone like that. He'd just – yes, thank you so much, Nurse Macdowell, thank you.'

'Are you coming tonight, Nurse Macdowell?' Rachel asked, but Nurse Macdowell was not. 'Do have a cup of coffee – you know where the kitchen is. No?'

'Such a Scottish name, Macdowell,' Ruth said when the nurse was gone. 'You wonder where they acquire them from. Coloured people.'

'The owners of plantations,' Rebecca said. 'That would have been the Scottish one, and they pass their name on to the slaves, passed, rather, I should say. They would have thought it quite an honour to be named after the owner of the plantation, all over the Caribbean.'

Rachel and Ruth exchanged a glance: their big sister Rebecca had always been the swot, held up to the twins, three years behind in school, as a scholastic ideal when in reality she had been willing only to put her own ideas of the truth forward in firm ways. And now she was seventy-four, and stout, and wearing a good tweed with a summer umbrella underneath the chair, because you really never knew, and still putting forward her ideas of the truth in a manner that required no contribution or disagreement.

'It'll be a shock to the son,' Ruth said. 'He'll be under the impression that it's going to be him, him and the sister, who are going to get everything.'

'This beautiful house,' Rachel said. 'They would only sell it and pocket the money. And poor Samuel's savings and shares, too. Neither of them married, or any sign of it.'

There was a shriek from the end of the room. Rachel had brought her black parrot, Ezekiah, promising he would be no trouble but he liked to have some company around him. The room smelt faintly of bird, and he had a look in his eye, a wizened, assessing, timing look; Ruth and Rebecca went nowhere near him, and he sat on the backs of what chairs he chose, his claws like wrinkled grey tools.

'The son – he was always a nasty little boy,' Rebecca said. 'I never thought much of him. Crying into his mother's skirts, never wanting to come out and say hello. Scared of everything. Just the same now, I imagine.'

'I found his address in Italy,' Rachel said. 'He had written to Samuel to tell him where he lived. I sent the telegram. More than that I cannot do. You know what he is?'

'Oh, yes,' Ruth said. 'One of them.'

'One of them?' Rebecca said. 'Oh, not a marrying type. How dreadful for Samuel. I expect he will turn up once poor Samuel has died, wanting to spend Samuel's money on cushions, lipstick and a sex-change operation.' Rebecca made a gesture; a feminine gesture but not a feminine gesture a woman would make, rather the extension and admiration of her finger-ends, which were a gardener's hands, trimmed and painted with red polish. She made a curdling *moue*, a pout; she meant not to be a woman or to suggest one, but to show what Duncan might be like. 'Lop it off, Doctor,' she said.

'But there isn't going to be as much money as he thought,' Rachel said, smiling sadly and shaking her head. 'Samuel handled that all very well. I am so glad we explained everything to him so well while he was still not in too much pain.'

'It was such a good idea, getting one of those easy forms

from Smith's,' Ruth said. 'It saved all the bother and expense of going to the solicitor. That was a very good idea of yours, Rachel.'

'But there is a virtue in having a family solicitor for years,' Rebecca said. 'I always said so. And Mr Brooke is such a friend.'

'Samuel saw the point, didn't he?' Ruth said. 'We didn't talk him into anything, nobody would be able to say that. I am so glad that Rachel got the will, and did everything, and got it witnessed, and took it to Mr Brooke for safekeeping. That was very good of Rachel.'

'That was very good of Rachel,' Rebecca said. 'Of course we didn't talk Samuel into anything. If the son got hold of the house, he would only sell it immediately and pocket the money. We wouldn't have any say in the matter at all. He would probably sell it to the Jews. They buy everything for cash. They don't trust the banks.'

'They must trust some of the banks,' Ruth said. She beat the floor with her walking stick emphatically. 'They run a lot of them – *behind the scenes*.'

'That's true,' Rebecca said thoughtfully. 'If it's not the Jews in Harrow, it's the Pakistanis. Over the road, the house that used to be lived in by the Harrises, when we were girls, that's owned by a family called – well, I don't know, but they're a Pakistani family and they fill it to the rafters. Soon there won't be an English family left in the avenue at all.'

Out in the garden, on the low brick wall that surrounded the knee-high flowerbeds on the terrace, a blackbird sat; it cocked its head, and sang, and inspected the three women inside. Or perhaps it was just drawn to the reflection of sun on the large windows. They flashed in the morning light. Rachel was looking out of the window. She was not looking at her sisters at all, even as they praised her sense.

'Poor Samuel,' Ruth said. 'There was really nothing more that any of us could have done in that direction. We wrote to the son, and we wrote to the daughter. Where are they? Thank goodness he doesn't know what's going on around him any more.'

6.

Upstairs, in a darkened room, Samuel found himself. He felt odd, and then he remembered that he was ill. The curtains were drawn, but it must be time to get up. Behind the curtains there was a hot day already. He could feel it. The curtains were brown but behind them the sun was bright and making everything red. Yesterday he had been able to jump out of bed and draw the curtains across and the rabbits had been eating in the garden, a dozen of them. He had wanted to go and get his gun and pick them off from the window, but Nanny had not let him. 'Not on a Sunday,' Nanny had said. That had been yesterday. But then it seemed to him that that had been a very long time ago, when he was a small boy, and then it seemed to him that it had not happened at all.

The pillow and the sheet were creased and uncomfortable, and he could smell something – a sour smell, physical and not his own smell. But perhaps it was his own smell now. The temperature seemed wrong. His feet and legs were cold, but his head sweltered. No – his feet and legs were not cold, but they were numb. Samuel had always prided himself on getting the exact right word, and the word for his lower body was 'numb', not 'cold'. And yet the sensations in his head and neck were more alert than they should have been, as well as hotter. There was a great heat spreading from the seams and rucks of the cotton sheets into his face, and he turned his head restlessly. There was a woman in his bedroom. There had not been a woman sitting in his bedroom since – he struggled for her name and could not remember the name of the wife he had been married to for decades – since Helen died. For a moment he thought it must be Death. Her face was covered by shade from where he looked. In her lap, a strip of light fell on a book. She read on, and in a moment passed her hand over her hair in an unconscious grooming gesture. Her hair was a vivid ginger, and neatly tied back. It needed no grooming, but the hand passed over it in reassurance. When Samuel saw the hair of the woman, he said to himself immediately 'At least it's not the coloured one,' and then he remembered immediately. She was one of his nurses, the daytime one, who was sitting with him and doing things for him. If she was here, it was not early morning, when the coloured one sat with him. It would be the afternoon. He had slept most of the day, then. He congratulated himself on the continuing liveliness of his own mind, when he concentrated. Her name would come to him, but it was not important.

'Nurse,' he tried to say, and then again, 'Nurse.' The nurse looked up from her book. 'The sheets need changing,' he said.

'What's that, Mr Flannery?' she said, rising and placing her hand, unsmilingly, on his forehead. He tried again.

The nurse smoothed them out underneath him, and promised to change them when her other colleague arrived for the evening. 'I'm not sure who that's going to be, to tell you the truth, Mr Flannery, but I know it's going to be just an hour or two, if you can put up with it a little longer.'

'I don't think I can,' Samuel said meekly. 'They're really twisted and damp and I feel hot. Can I change my pyjamas?'

'That I can do,' the nurse said. 'I'll just clean you up and pop you in the chair, Mr Flannery, and then I'll change your sheets as well, straight away. How do you feel in general?'

'What was that shriek, that scream? I heard a woman screaming.'

'It was your sister's parrot,' the nurse said. 'He's downstairs. He shouldn't be here at all, in point of fact. It has a strange name, that bird.'

'I remember,' Samuel said, and was about to say the bird's name, but it had gone, and there had been a woman shrieking about it, screaming, really, not ten feet from his ear. He hope that terrible screaming would stop soon. 'I feel terrible. Terrible,' Samuel said. 'I don't think I can sit in a chair. It all hurts so much and I don't know where I am sometimes.' Then a thought came to him. He remembered very well where he was and what was happening. 'You could ask one of my sisters to help to change. They're here. They're the three women sitting in the kitchen. They used to be girls but they're old women now. You know the ones I mean.'

'Oh, Samuel,' the nurse said. 'Mr Flannery, I mean. You are a card.'

He was puzzling over what she meant, but then he felt quite suddenly very sleepy and he closed his eyes and when he opened them again it was night-time and there was a different nurse.

'Would you,' he said, 'would you ...' but he couldn't get any further.

'Hello, Mr Flannery,' the other nurse said. She stood up in a quiet but decisive way. She was the one called Balls. Nurse Balls. He remembered that one. Not all of the nurses remembered they weren't to call him Samuel, but she did. She didn't have ginger hair. It was hard to say what colour her hair was.

'Would you,' he said, then stopped again, puzzled. He was not quite sure what he wanted to ask for.

'Water?' the nurse said. 'Is it water that you're saying, Mr Flannery?'

And then Samuel smiled – did he smile on his face or was he just smiling inside? He was probably smiling inside. His face hurt so much. But he smiled because he had said, 'Would you,' and she had thought he said, 'Water'; perhaps there was some-thing wrong with her ears or perhaps he had spoken indistinctly, having just woken up, and in fact he had forgotten what he was going to ask for but it was right: it had been water he had wanted. That was strange. He tried to say, 'Would you bring me some water?' but it grew complicated, his tongue in his mouth. It seemed to have grown and grown. He shut his eyes, and he found himself in the same dream of illness he had always had, since he was a small boy, whenever he had fever. He was floating in a colourless space with no features, just a grid of small dots, when the small dots began to swell and grow inside. One of them had got inside his mouth, and it grew and grew, swelling until it forced his mouth open, and inside his mouth there was nothing but a great hard stone. He opened his eyes. The taste of the stone was still there. He did not know whether he had slept or not. The woman who was standing there, he did not know her. She was wearing a coat, or a white dress, or a uniform of some sort; it rucked up tightly around her thighs and bottom. What was she doing there? It was his room and he was being ill in it. She was not his wife and she was not his sister, any of them. Then he remembered he had a daughter but she was not her either.

'Would you like some water, Mr Flannery?' the woman said, and then he remembered what she was. She was a nurse. He nodded and she went over to the dresser where a glass jug stood covered with a plate. She removed it and poured water into one of the large tumblers from downstairs. It was really a whisky tumbler, engraved, but he took it and drank from it. I'll drink whisky again, he thought, but only when I feel a good deal better.

'Where is Helen?' he said, passing the glass back. 'I want to see Helen.'

'I think she's downstairs,' the nurse said. 'That's one of the ladies downstairs, is she not?'

Samuel nodded. 'And I want to see Duncan,' he said. 'I don't know where Duncan can be. I haven't seen him since he was – oh, fifteen or sixteen. He ran away to sea, you know. He ended up in Italy. He's there to this very day. I want to see him now, because I don't want to die without seeing him. Am I dying? I know I am.' And his eyes filled with tears. He pitied himself so much for what he was having to go through. Nobody else had ever gone through this. He had asked a question, but the nurse

91

was moving around the room, settling things and returning the water jug to its place. She had not heard any of what he had said. It was typical. But then he thought that perhaps he had not said any of that out loud. 'I don't want to have to go to Sicily,' he said.

But this he had said out loud, because the nurse said, 'If you don't want to, you don't have to, Mr Flannery,' quite comfortably.

'Is Duncan coming?' Samuel tried to ask. His tongue fell back in his mouth. His head turned to one side. It seemed all so normal.

7.

There were pubs in Camden, which would never be touched, and streets, too. The Queen's Arms in Goldborne Street sat at the corner of two converging Victorian terraces, its corner rounded and sailing out into the junction like an ocean liner. It had recently been painted in dark green and white. The landlord had decided to place only one hanging basket at the front, rather than the usual seven or eight of London landlords – Tarquin thought it was a waste and a demand on labour. He did not discover until too late that it is as much a waste and a demand on anyone's time to have to water one hanging basket daily during the summer as it is to water a dozen. The Queen's Arms was one of those pubs that must have been constructed in anticipation of a great crowd of drinkers. Its downstairs rooms, the saloon and the snug, were both gigantic under low ceilings of rosettes and plaster ornamentation. But the crowds that would have filled it never arrived. Perhaps it was in an awkward position, tucked away between residential streets. Perhaps the adventurous young middle-class people who were the only people who bought houses in these two or three streets were not great pub-goers, or not Tarquin's sort of pub-goers.

There were generally a few groups, perhaps only three or four, of slow old drinkers scattered around the place, not making much money for Tarquin. He had refused all the stratagems of other pubs in the neighbourhood; there were no cabaret nights with singers at microphones at the Queen's Arms, and he would not stoop to strippers at lunchtime like the Dog and Crown – that would scare away his loyal old Regent's Park ladies, who dropped in twice a week for their Dubonnets.

The pub, inside, had a curious smell, more like a laundry than a public house. No one who entered would be able to tell where it came from. Tarquin sometimes caught his own expression in the mirror, superior and unenthusiastic, when a customer came in, or observed Nora's way, when a customer was trying to attract attention with a pound note, of lowering her eyes and sorting out the drying cloths rather than attend to him straight away. He tried to remember why it was that he and Nora had thought, ten years before, that running a pub was a good business proposition for them, or why the brewery had gone along with them, either.

The one thing about the pub that was a success and had some kind of use was the upper room. It must have been some kind of club room when the pub was built, and still had a giant dining table there and an assorted mismatch of chairs, dining chairs with yellow velvet seats as well as swivelling captain's chairs, more recent in manufacture, and odd painted kitchen chairs. There were hunting scenes on the walls, and a tired, torn wallpaper with floral relief, which he must ask Tom to get round to replacing one of these days. (Tom was their son, recently left home; he had gone into the painting and decorating trade, which kept him busy.) Five years ago, a man, a student-type in a neckerchief, with long hair and purple bags, had come into the pub just before the afternoon closing and asked if they had rooms that they hired out for meetings. Tarquin had shown him the upper room, then piled high with lumber and old broken things, and had said it could be cleared out easily if this was going to be a regular thing. It was – Jones and his group of revolutionaries met every Wednesday night, paid five pounds for the privilege and managed to sink a few drinks downstairs once their meeting was over. The revolution didn't come, during which Tarquin and Nora, Nora observed sardonically, would probably have been strung up as bloodsuckers by Jones's group. Instead, Jones's group kept coming, every Wednesday night, the same eight or nine of them, give or take a few.

The word spread. These days, there were four weekly groups and three that met once a fortnight or once a month, all shelling out eight pounds each, now that the costs had gone up so much, as regular and uncomplaining as clockwork. Nora thought they should raise the cost of hire again, but Tarquin thought they'd jib at ten pounds. 'They'll pay up,' Nora said. 'They always feel more passionately about revolution when there's a Tory government. They don't like *her*, you see. They talk about women's rights, but they don't like it when there's a woman in charge.'

He didn't really know what they were all up to. They were all lefties, he supposed, but you got that, living in Camden Town, these days. The biggest one was CND – he knew what they were, all right. It was so popular; the group that met here was only the West Camden division, and still forty people came every week. They brought their own film projector, quite often, and liked to sit in darkness, watching old films about nuclear war. It took all sorts to make a world. There was one that might be something to do with vivisection or vegetarians, judging by their strange shoes. But they paid their eight pounds like anyone else. 'I draw the line only at nudists,' Tarquin said sagely to his son, Tom, who shook his head. Tom had voted for Mrs Thatcher in May.

Tonight was one of the fortnightly ones. They were all men, coming in ones and the occasional pair, but not talking loudly or, most of them, even greeting Tarquin. They just ducked their heads and moved through the quiet pub as quickly as possible. They wore, most of them, checked lumberjack shirts and denim trousers or, until the weather really hotted up, leather trousers; one or two, now that it had hotted up, some bright-coloured shorts, like the ones the teenagers wore, though these daft Herberts were verging on middle age. 'I know what they are,' Nora had said tonight, but Tarquin didn't respond. He didn't care, so long as they were just talking upstairs. One of the first to arrive had asked if he could pin up a sign, on the brown-painted doorframe by the side of the bar, directing 'anyone new,' he said hopefully. On it, now, pinned neatly with two drawing pins was a piece of paper reading 'CHE meeting – this way!' There was another on the door of the pub outside – he hoped that wouldn't lead to trouble, he said to the main one. But he didn't think it would. For whatever reason, Tarquin thought that they weren't a revolutionary group calling for executions in the streets. Whatever CHE meant. It was the exclamation mark, or perhaps the heart underneath, or perhaps just because the notice had been written by the daft Herberts in purple felt-tip pen.

8.

They had hardly started when the door to the upper room was opened abruptly. There was an unfamiliar face, a big bearded fellow and a slim girl with limp blonde hair behind him. 'Is this the Central and South American group?' he said. 'I was told it met on Fridays.'

'It might well do,' Christopher said, turning round impatiently. 'This isn't it. We're nothing to do with Central or South America.'

'I saw your sign,' the man said. 'So they meet on Fridays still? We want to come to that.'

'I've no idea when they meet,' Christopher said. 'It might well be Friday. But it's not today. We're here today and we've got nothing to do with Central or South America.'

The man and his girl withdrew; she had been holding a bottle of some kind of clear spirits, only two-thirds full. She waved it in obscure greeting, or farewell, walking backwards down the stairs.

'Do you think they'd been drinking that in the street, out of the bottle?' Nat said, when they had gone.

'Oh, no,' Alan said. 'They're very strait-laced, those revolutionary types. They look scary, but they're like pussycats, really. They'll have brought that from home, or from their mum and dad's, probably. They won't be drinking out of a bottle in the street. You know, that's not the first time that's happened.'

'What, the confusion with the South American struggle?' Andrew said. Andrew was the most revolutionary of them or, really, the only one.

'It's being called CHE that does it,' Nat said. 'They think it's something to do with that man they all like so much, the one with the beard and the gaze upwards, you know, Che Guevara. That's the third time we've had that. We should really spell out what we are on the poster, write Campaign for Homosexual Equality, then they wouldn't come upstairs by mistake.'

'I don't know,' Simon said. 'I don't mind them coming upstairs. One was quite nice. I was sorry to see him go, to be honest. That one I wasn't so bothered about.'

'People talk about anal sex as though it's the be-all and end-all of gay identity,' Christopher said. He had been trying to revert to what he had been saying before the bearded man came in. 'And for me it was very important. But I understand if people don't want to assert it as important. For me—'

'I don't think we can really write Campaign for Homosexual Equality on the poster,' Alan said. 'The landlord might have views about that.'

'Well, we've got nothing to be ashamed of. Honestly!' Nat said. 'I thought the point of all of this was to be proud and public. I don't see anything proud and public about hiding behind initials, in case the landlord doesn't like it.'

'He'll get his windows smashed,' Alan said. 'And we'd be beaten up.'

'For me, anal sex was always very important,' Christopher intoned.

There was a noise on the stairs, and the noise of a homosexual talking to himself. 'The cheek of it,' he was saying. 'Now, where did I put my wallet? Not that pocket, not this pocket, not— Oh, here it is. You'd lose,' he said, as he came into the room, 'your head if it wasn't attached to your shoulders. Hello, hello, hello, hello, Christopher, hello, Nat, hello, all. Am I late? Have you started?'

'Yes, Paul,' they said. 'Yes, you're late, we've started, it doesn't matter, you're late.'

'Well,' Paul said. He was always late for CHE meetings. He was wearing, like the rest of them, a lumberjack shirt, but it was oddly assorted with a pair of tiny denim shorts, and he had tied the tails of the shirt somewhat above the waist of the shorts to leave his midriff bare. He had blond hair with highlights, and a glossy moustache; just to the left of his mouth was a beauty spot, which some thought was applied with the end of the same mascara brush that gave his eyelashes such length and curl. 'You'll never guess why I'm late. I was just on the way out—'

'Have a seat,' Andrew said. He was eyeing Paul from head to foot with a faint air of disapproval; his hairy arms were folded across his stomach and his voice was deep and emphatic; he had his revolutionary scowl on.

'I *will*,' Paul said, and sat down. From his bag, he extracted a quarter-bottle of supermarket vodka, a glass filled with ice and a slice of lemon from the bar downstairs, and finally a small open bottle of tonic. 'I was just on the way out when the phone goes, and I think, Oh, drat, that's going to make me late, *definitely* going to make me late for my gay men's group. So I could have ignored it, but you know me, I can't ignore a ringing phone. For the rest of the night I'd have been thinking, Who's that phoning me, who was that. Worst thing that can happen, you say to yourself, I'll ignore it, then after ten rings you say, I can't stand it *any more* and make a dive for it just as it stops ringing. And you'll never know who it was who was calling you – it might have been the love of your life for all you know. So—'

'You're not *that* late,' Nat said – Paul's stories could go on for some time if not curbed.

'So, anyway, this time I go to myself, I'm not going to be strong and ignore it, I'm going to be pathetic and answer it. And you know what, I'm glad I did. Do you know who it was? Go on, have a guess, you'll never guess.' The others showed no sign of making a guess. Christopher shook his head, his lips pursed. 'Well. It was only Duncan. I thought he must be calling from abroad – you remember my friend Duncan, you know him, don't you, Nat, but I'm not sure he knows *you*, Andrew, because I asked him if he knew you and he wasn't sure. Listen, he says, I'm calling from the airport – I just landed. So I just shrieked. Ethel – you know, the clone who lives in the flat opposite – Ethel he came in and said, What are you shrieking at, you silly mare? Duncan says he's at the airport, he's just landed, and he wants to see everyone now, tonight, and so I said I'd tell everyone to go off to the Embassy tonight, and we'll all be there, and then I said, So have you come back for good, why are you here, and he says he's only got two two-pence pieces, he's had them at the bottom of the suitcase since he went to Sicily, so they'll cut him off in a moment, and then he's about to tell me why he's come back and, sure enough, the telephone cuts him off before he can tell me, just as he said it was going to, which I think as I said to Ethel is really a bit ironic if you think about it.'

'That's not ironic, my dear,' Alan said. 'That's just Duncan running out of money for the telephone. Don't sit over there all on your own. Come and sit down by me. I want to hear all about it.'

'So I wasn't going to come, but now I have come, though I can't stay, because I've got to go on to tell everyone I can find in Earls Court, but you've all got to come to the Embassy later. Duncan's back!' Paul said, waving his hands like Al Jolson, taking the vodka and tonic and downing it in one, then getting up and, instead of going over to Alan, trotting off down the stairs. For some reason, Nat and Alan got up and went to the window; they watched him walk down the street in his shorts, with his bag over the crook of the arm. Outside the window hung two small Union Jacks; they had been there since the Silver Jubilee, two years before, and the landlord saw no reason to remove them. The sensibilities of his radical customers, who rented the upstairs room once a week or once a fortnight, did not worry him.

'I don't think,' Christopher said, 'I ever met Paul's friend Duncan.'

So then they all told him about Duncan.

9.

'Who is that coming up the path?' Aunt Rachel said, peering out of the window.

'It's some man,' Aunt Rebecca said. 'He is probably selling something from his little bag. Silk stockings and shoe brushes. How dark he is!'

'I know who it is,' Aunt Ruth said with a note of triumph. 'He is that horrid little boy.'

Duncan had been delayed: the plane to Paris had been an hour late, and he had just missed his connection; the next plane from Paris had been four hours later; his luggage had been lost or mislaid in the confusion, and he had had to fill in a lot of forms at Heathrow. All his clothes were somewhere between Catania and London – they could be anywhere in Europe. The only clothes he had were in a suitcase somewhere under his sister's bed in Clapham, and the ones in his hand luggage, the tiny shorts and T-shirt he had changed out of at the airport. He had meant to get to his father's house before lunchtime, but it was now nearly night. He was ravenous.

All the way up the hill, he had been thinking of food – he wanted solid, dry English cheese and perhaps, if there was some leftover cold mashed potato in a bowl, that fried with some peas. Sicilian potatoes didn't go into any kind of mash – too waxy, or something. Even the sight of his father's ramshackle house hadn't shifted his thoughts. But when he rang the doorbell, and it had its familiar, inexplicable half-second delay before sounding, its four-note Big Ben call, which had been there for twenty years at least, Duncan remembered where he was and how much of his life had been there. The house bell was so jaunty, and so little of the life within was jaunty. The sound of the doorbell could always bring him and Dommie to their feet, racing downstairs to open it to whoever it was – usually the postman or the meter reader, nothing more exciting than that. It was the things you put out of your mind that could come back into it, with force.

Aunt Rebecca opened the door. She had put on some weight since he had last seen her, seven years ago at Christmas. She was pretending not to know who he was, but overdoing it in an amateurish way. She peered into his face, screwing up her eyebrows and forehead. 'Yes?' she said, hooting rather. 'Can I help you?'

Duncan wished he had insisted when he left home that he had kept a key. But his father had said he couldn't have sets of keys being mislaid all over London, and he'd always be there to let Duncan in – or if he weren't, then he didn't want Duncan going all over the house in his absence. Dommie had done better and insisted; Duncan had been weak and now, with his father dying upstairs, was at the mercy of his aunt.

'It's me,' he said. 'Duncan. How are you, Rebecca?'

'Aunt Rebecca, you used to call me,' she said. 'How extraordinary. I thought you were in Italy.'

'I was in Italy,' Duncan said. 'But I had a telegram saying that my dad wasn't very well.'

'Ha!' Rebecca said. 'That is an understatement. He's very ill indeed.'

'So I came,' Duncan said. 'I came as fast as I could. Can I come in?'

Rebecca had been leaning with her arm heavily against the doorjamb, guarding; the word 'dragon' came into Duncan's mind. It was her weight and awkwardness; but she was blocking Duncan's way all the same. She gave him a thorough look. 'Of course,' she said. 'I don't know whether your father can see you. He has been *very uncomfortable* the last two days.' Duncan felt accused by her expression, as if he had been the cause of the discomfort, even though he had not even been in the country. 'He is only sleeping in fits and starts, so I won't wake him if he's asleep. You could come back tomorrow.'

'He might be asleep when I come tomorrow,' Duncan said, putting his little bag down in the hall by the hatstand. All the doors in the hall were closed, as if in the central lobby of some office. They had never been closed like that before; doors had stood open or closed as they happened to be. In the panelled hallway, closed off, with nothing but the wooden stair rising upwards to the death chamber, Duncan found himself in an unfamiliar and formal house. 'I'll wait until he wakes up.'

'Oh, very well,' Rebecca said. She retreated into the sitting room; she opened the door and there was the sight of a woman reading in the gloom. The lights had not been switched on; there was only a small table lamp by the side of her, and she peered in a pool of light downwards, not looking up as Rebecca entered. It was either Ruth or Rachel; he could not see. They must have heard him coming in, perhaps even discussed who should answer the door. There was something territorial about her, something relaxed and confident about her ownership. She was saving her own electricity bill, not her brother's, by reading in the dark; she was not greeting him because he was there to perform a function, like a meter reader or a Gas Board employee. She might as well have been counting the silver spoons. And now, as if from nowhere, a shape leapt onto the back of her chair; not a cat, but an animal of burst and flutter. It took a strut into the small pool of light, and Duncan saw that it was a parrot, quite black. The parrot tipped its head on one side; it looked in Duncan's direction; it raised a foot and began to groom itself, quite uninterested in the new arrival. Presently the aunt reached up behind her. She had taken something – a nut or a seed – from her lap, and the bird snatched it. All this Duncan watched remotely, as if it were a drama on a television screen. And then an unknown force seemed to push the door behind Rebecca, and it closed, leaving him alone with the staircase.

The stairs creaked. He felt like a burglar. And upstairs the bedroom doors were also closed. For the first time, Duncan saw the box-like construction of the hall downstairs, the landing upstairs; the distinguished shape that the house had once had, and still had at its core. The panelling continued upstairs, and a threadbare green and blue carpet. This was where Samuel had hung his less successful acquisitions in the way of paintings, including the 'Constable', signed extravagantly, from which he had hoped to make a fortune until he was laughed out of Sotheby's – a red-jacketed farm boy on a wagon in the middle of a dark wood. Samuel's bedroom was in the middle. Duncan gave a very gentle knock, and in a moment there was a small crisp bustle and the door was opened by what must be a nurse. She came out, closing the door softly behind her.

'Are you Duncan?' she said. 'I'm Sister Balls. We've been having a slightly restless couple of days, and sometimes he doesn't make the best sense, but I don't think he's in pain any more. He's falling asleep and waking up and falling asleep again, but he'll be very happy to see you.'

'I don't think so,' Duncan said. 'It's kind of you to say so, though.'

'Now why would you say that?' Sister Balls said. 'He's asleep, but he's been asking after you a lot, saying, When is he going to get here? I'll be all right when Duncan gets here. It's been very nice to listen to and to be able to say that you were definitely coming today.'

'Shall I wait downstairs?' Duncan said.

'Oh, no,' the nurse said. 'No, that's not necessary. Just come in quietly and hold his hand, and he'll wake up when he's ready, and then I'll go and leave you two in peace for a bit. Don't tire him out, I'm sure you won't.'

Duncan felt a kind of gratitude to Aunt Rebecca for being so abrupt, to the other two aunts for being so rude as not to come out to greet him. He felt tenderized. Talking to Sister Balls, he had been admitted to a caring space, concealed and protected. Then the nurse opened the door to the dark room, and he remembered that inside that space, his father lay.

There was the smell of an enclosed hot room, and something alongside, unexpected. Oh, he thought, that's the smell of a deathbed. But it wasn't unpleasant, or particularly human, apart from its warmth; it smelt of something unfamiliar, something welcome, and some blocking agents on top, floral and medical and antiseptic. His father's room had its own smell, too, a masculine one of wood and shoe polish. Duncan went in, closing the door behind him softly. The room was very dim. But he didn't want to turn the light on and startle his father. He groped around the room, to the side of his father's head, and in a moment he banged against the winged armchair that had always been on the landing until now, in case anyone tired themselves out climbing the stairs. He felt on the seat to make sure there was no medical equipment – he had a dread of syringes and containers, of cardboard bedpans – and sat down cautiously. He could hear his father's breathing. Not dead yet. He sat for a few minutes, and shortly his eyes got used to the dim light, as his nose got used to the room's lingering odours of illness and cure. His father's profile was sharp and drawn; his hands were under the counterpane, making a pulling gesture. Duncan waited. There might be no need to remain. He had seen his father now. He would wait

103

only fifteen minutes more. But just then, his father gave a deep, rasping breath, as if choking, and woke. His eyes were still closed, but there was a change in his being and his breathing. He gave the impression of being disappointed to wake and find himself still alive.

'Who's there,' his father said. 'I can't see.'

'It's me,' Duncan said. Then there was a pause, a lingering silent question, and Duncan had to say, 'It's Duncan, Daddy.'

'Oh, Duncan,' his father said. 'I thought you were in Italy. Well, better late than never.'

'I came as fast as I could,' Duncan said. 'I only heard two days ago, and the earliest flight I could get was last night and today. I had to change in Paris – there was no direct flight.'

'Heard what,' his father said. 'That's what I'd like to know.'

'Just heard,' Duncan said. 'I came over as quickly as I could.'

'Always in a great rush,' his father said. 'Always not doing things properly because of something that's turned up in an emergency. You were the same as a little boy.'

'Oh, I don't know,' Duncan said, finding himself unable to think of what he should have done to preserve his father's sense of the right thing to do, while simultaneously coming as soon as possible. 'I do my best.'

'Have you seen your sister?' Samuel said. 'I was expecting to see her, as well.'

'Are you sure she hasn't been?' Duncan said. 'I'm sure she's been to see you. Hasn't she?'

'What do you think I am?' his father said. His voice was dry and rasping; the heat in his throat, its pain, tangible. His eyes were still closed; the annoyance of his existence, his ways as if a headmaster, surviving until his last moments. Duncan reflected that anyone else, he would pass him a glass of water without a request. His father would demand one, and then expect the person to put up with being called an idiot for not having one poured out ready. He waited. 'Do you think I can't remember if Domenica has been or not? I'm ill, not stupid.'

'Sometimes you're not quite sure of things when you're as ill as this,' Duncan said.

'She hasn't been,' Samuel said. 'I don't suppose it's important to her.'

And then, to Duncan's horror, his father raised his hands to his face in a gesture of self-benediction, his palms over his eyes, and began to sob, juddering. 'My life's been for nothing,' his father said. 'My life, and my children can't wait for me to die.'

'You don't need to think that,' Duncan said. 'Don't say things like that.'

His father's noise of weeping would soon bring the nurse into the room or, worse, his sisters. But then downstairs a harsh call came; a barbaric yawp and shriek. It seemed to interest or divert his father, and, just as a child's tantrum can be pushed to one side by an entertainment, so his father paused in his fit, just gave one more shudder, and lowered his hands. 'I keep hearing that noise,' he said. 'I don't know what it is. It's like an animal crying.'

'It's a parrot,' Duncan said. 'It's a black parrot that Ruth brought. Or Rachel. I don't know which one.'

'It would be Rachel,' Samuel said. 'She has a parrot, a black one. Why has she brought it here? I don't want it here. I don't want that noise downstairs.'

'I don't know,' Duncan said. 'I thought she must have asked you. I'll tell her to take it home again.'

'Oh, she won't do that,' Samuel said. Then all at once he fell asleep; so instantly that Duncan thought it must be a coma or even a final collapse. He went about the room moving things, putting off the moment when he must go outside and say that his father seemed to have taken a turn for the worse. In curiosity rather than anything else, he turned on the bedside lamp. It was the same pink fringed one his mother had always had. The light showed an old, unshaven man, the cheeks sunk in deep under the cheekbones and the eye sockets like a skull's, falling profoundly into worlds of darkness. The skin was yellow and slack, as if its possessor had slept long under bridges, living on methylated spirits. Only the cleanliness of the dark blue pyjamas with white piping, and the neatness of the sheets, suggested anything but the derelict. It was as if an old tramp had been taken from his streetside cardboard box by a benevolent, given a bath and set down within clean linen to die. Duncan resisted the temptation to run his hand down the side of his father's face. There was no temptation to kiss it. But the thought came to mind like this: what would it be like to have a father who, on his deathbed, you wanted to kiss? The light had disturbed Samuel in his sudden sleep, and now he woke, raising his fists to his eyes and rubbing them, yawning like a cat, turning about to see what the disturbance was.

'Oh, it's you again,' Samuel said. 'I didn't know if it was really you. I keep thinking people are here. You should have stayed in Spain. No, in Italy, that's where you've been.'

'I've come back,' Duncan said. 'I'm not going to tire you out. I'll come back tomorrow.'

'Yes, perhaps that's best,' Samuel said.

(And downstairs Rachel was turning to her sisters and saying what she should have said hours, or days ago; saying that she had, in fact, not got round to taking anything to the solicitor's, that she was rather afraid that the will was upstairs still, in poor Samuel's keeping. 'But he won't know about that, the son, will he?' she was saying plaintively, and Ruth was shaking her head, and Rebecca was shaking her head, too.)

Samuel looked around conspiratorially. 'I'll tell you something important tomorrow, if you come back.'

'You can tell me now, if you like,' Duncan said. 'I don't mind listening.'

'It's not a question of whether you want to listen or not,' Samuel said. 'It's whether I want to tell you. It's my business.'

'Well, you can tell me or not tell me,' Duncan said. 'But if I were you, I wouldn't put anything much off until tomorrow that you want people to know.'

'You wouldn't, wouldn't you?' Samuel said. But doubt set in, and he started saying 'You wouldn't, would you – would, would, wouldn't, should,' until he could no longer decide what it was normal to say, and he fell silent.

'You know,' Duncan said, quite calmly, 'it's very bad luck, getting lung cancer like that. Not smoking, ever, and then you get lung cancer. I don't know that that's supposed to happen.'

'I did smoke,' Samuel said. 'But before you were born. Before I met your mother, even. It was when I was at school, and when I had my first job. I was a clerk in the office of – of – of – they were Jews. That's right, they were Jews, the first people I worked for. I smoked because they didn't, none of them. But it didn't do me any good. I gave up just before I met your mother and before I went to another job. That was when I realized that I was never going to be promoted in that place. They only promoted their own type.'

'That must have been fifty years ago,' Duncan said. He wondered that he did not know that his father had ever smoked. His mother, he was sure, never had. 'I don't think you get lung cancer from that, decades later.'

'They don't know,' Samuel said. 'Doctors never know. I'm glad I'm not in hospital. I'm glad they're letting me stay here.'

'Do you remember,' Duncan said, and Samuel, for the first time, turned his head towards him, and almost smiled. 'Do you remember that day when you and Mummy and Dommie and I, we went out for the day? I think it must have been for Dommie's birthday.'

'I think so,' Samuel said. His lips were dry and flaking; he was running his tongue over them.

'Where did we go? Did we go to Whipsnade, or some other zoo, or Box Hill, or was it to the theatre? It would have been a special treat. I don't know that Whipsnade was open then, come to think of it, so maybe not there. And did you ask Dommie if she'd like to bring ten friends with her? I wish I could remember what her special treat was.'

Samuel turned his head away. 'When it gets worse,' he said,

'they'll take me into hospital, but I hope I'm not going to know about any of that.'

'Oh, you're not going to get any worse than this,' Duncan said lightly. 'This is probably it. I wouldn't have thought you had long to go. About Dommie's birthday. What was it that we all did together? I think I remember now. She was going to be nine, and you told her that you thought she was too old to have a party, and she couldn't ask her friends round because it would cost too much and it would be too much noise and trouble. But since you ask, you're not going to get any worse. You're probably going to die quite soon.'

Samuel turned his face to Duncan in disbelief. His hollows and unshaven angles said only this: it's your obligation to do whatever I say. It was not for Duncan to do anything but to give way.

'So,' Duncan said. 'Are you comfortable? Can I do anything for you, in your last hours? Or do you just want me to go away so that you can sit with Rebecca and Ruth and Rachel? I don't really care.'

'Oh, you think you're so clever,' Samuel said, breathing deeply, the air juddering within. He raised his thin hand to his hairy, bony chest in the gap in his pyjama jacket. 'That's what you were always like, showing off. Let me do my dance – I made it up, Mummy. Look, Aunty Rachel, look, Uncle Harold, look at the dolly I made, isn't it pretty. Oh, yes. I can see you came back to show off and tell me to bugger off before I die. But I can show you one thing.'

There was a long pause; Samuel's breath guttered and shuddered; he twisted in pain; he pulled at the bedsheets. Duncan waited. He did not want to help his father. He wanted to see how long it would take him to return to the point where he could speak again, or sleep. He watched with interest. In less than five minutes, his father had calmed. Outside the door, a chair scraped against the parquet. Sister Balls must have returned, and be sitting outside. He did not have a lot of time.

'It hurts to talk,' Samuel said. 'There's one thing I want you to see. In that box, there, on the dressing-table.'

Duncan went over and drew it out. It was a document; a pre-printed form filled in in Samuel's wavering looping hand, a will. 'I don't want to see this,' Duncan said.

'Look at it,' Samuel said.

Duncan did. There was what looked like a duplicate underneath. In a moment he read that his father was leaving his whole estate in equal parts to his two children, his three sisters, his five nephews and nieces, and seven named charities and educational institutions, including the Harrow rugby club, and Harrow School, which neither Duncan nor his father had attended. 'I see,' Duncan said. The will, which was to give him, what, a seventeenth part of this ugly house and the bank balance, was dated from two months ago. It was witnessed by a Corinna Balls, and another woman, whose handwriting made Duncan think she was another nurse.

'You didn't ask Aunt Rebecca or Aunt Ruth to witness it,' he said.

'No, you stupid boy,' Samuel said. 'You can't get people to witness something they're going to—' He broke down in coughing.

'Going to benefit from,' Duncan said. 'They're not going to benefit very much, though, are they?'

'I think,' Samuel said. 'I think – I'm going to cross Domenica out. She hasn't been to see me. So you'll get a little bit more. That'll be nice, won't it.'

'And a lawyer's drawn this up, has he?' Duncan said. Samuel looked withdrawn and serene. 'Oh, I see – it's just something you've bought from the newsagent and filled in. Got Sister Balls to get from the newsagent. Something for everyone to discover after you die? I see. You just want people to know that they don't deserve anything from you.'

Duncan looked at his father. He knew perfectly well that Duncan would take this document and destroy it. It could have no effect on what happened to Samuel's estate. But before Samuel died, he wanted to make clear to Duncan what he thought of him.

'The thing is,' Duncan said, 'I don't think that Domenica would take your money anyway. I think she'd probably take however much it was, and hand it over to the NSPCC. Do you think she wants anything to do with you?'

'I'm her father,' Samuel said.

'There was an afternoon, wasn't there,' Duncan said, 'when you said, Let's all go out swimming, the children and I. Which was odd, because you never suggested anything like that for the children's pleasure. You know, don't you, that because Dommie never had any parties after she was eight years old, no one ever thought to ask her to theirs? I don't suppose you ever thought of that. You only ever wanted to do your own thing. And Dommie said that she couldn't swim, she didn't know how, and you said that didn't matter. You'd gone to the effort of buying her a swimming costume. She didn't have one. She was only six. And when we all got to the swimming pool, you said to her, This is the way to swim, you know, and you picked her up by her arms and legs and threw her into the deep end, with no floats or anything, and just stood there. The lifeguard jumped in and rescued her. He gave you what for, you horrible old man, asking you what you thought you were doing. Don't you remember?'

Samuel shook his head demurely. He looked like such a small person, a small entrapped dwarf in a fairytale with a secret.

'I remember. Even in the 1950s, you didn't just throw small children into the deep end of swimming pools and wait to see if they drowned or not.'

'Oh, once,' Samuel said, shaking his head.

'Every week,' Duncan said. 'Making her wait at the table to eat mutton fat. Making her walk all the way back to school in the dark in January to make her find a pencil case she had dropped. Do you know, you've never once given me any help or advice – you've never done anything for me, except once. Mummy made you explain to me how to shave. You couldn't get out of that. That was it. I'm glad you're dying. It won't make the slightest difference to anyone. And what's this rubbish?' He held up the will. In the light it was a sad object: the hand-written parts were shaky and full of uneven gaps and holes. 'No one's going to pay any attention to that. I'm surprised Balls didn't tell you not to be so stupid. Shall I burn it or shall I just tear it up?'

'You do whatever you want to,' Samuel said, crying. 'The last wishes of a dying man. The last wishes of your dying father.'

'The last wishes of my dying father are about as good as the wishes he had during his lifetime,' Duncan said. 'I'll get rid of this, somehow. My conscience is going to deal with it. And it's all going to come to me and Dommie, your money. You bet. A hundred quid to Balls and another to the other one. They won't remember they'd ever signed anything. If you've told your sisters, do you think anyone's ever going to believe them? And do you know what I'm going to do with my money? All that lovely money? Because you saved quite a lot from the insurance racket, Daddy. And this horrible house? Not enough to go round seventeen, but plenty for two. Me? I'm going to open a book-shop. I'm going to open the first gay bookshop in London. There are so many good books written by homosexuals. And lesbians. You know what they are. And there's going to be a bookshop where you'll be able to buy their books, if they're dead or foreign or not available, and a place where you can come if you're a homosexual or a lesbian and spend all day there, buying books and meeting people like you. That's what your money's going to do. That's what you were working towards, all your life, without knowing it, Sam – you were working towards a bookshop celebrating sexual perversion. You know me – you know I'm a sexual pervert, too? My God, the men I've had in Sicily. It would make your eyes pop out of their sockets. Oh, I look forward to entertaining your ghost there, in my gay bookshop. We're going to hang up a picture of you by the front door to say thank you, Sam, for making all of this possible. You thought you were buggering me up, and Dommie, too, and it made you laugh. But you were actually saving up, and giving us the chance to get out from under your stone. So thank you so much. And –' Duncan took the two wills – 'I'll take care of these. Thanks. And 'bye. I won't be seeing you again, Daddy.'

'I'll,' Sam said. 'I'll. Write. It.' His chest was torn open with coughing. Duncan waited and counted. He would not start caring now. He would not remember his father's lifelong actions – he could not: most of it was neglect and a sneer. 'Send. Nurse. Out.'

'You stupid old man,' Duncan said. 'You can't write it again. Don't you know? You're dying. You're going to die tonight. You might last until tomorrow morning. You can't write any more. But at least I saw you before you died. Remember that. Oh – I'm sorry. It's us that will be remembering you, not the other way round. 'Bye then. I'll send the nurse in.'

Duncan got up, and turned the bedside light off. He folded the two stationers' wills – they were only a couple of pages each – and put them into his jacket pocket. He stroked his father's forehead – it was damp and hot, and writhed under the touch. His father cried out, an inarticulate noise, and his arms came up, as if to hit Duncan. The door opened, and the nurse whose name was Balls stood there, her stance inclined and concerned.

'I'm just leaving,' Duncan said quietly, going over to her. 'I think he's in a little pain, but we've managed to talk. I think it meant a lot to him. Thank you for everything, Sister.'

'It's my job – you don't need to thank me. I'll give him some morphine for the pain,' Sister Balls said. 'He does seem bad. It'll help him to get some rest.'

'And Daddy,' Duncan said, raising his voice over the calls of pain, 'I'm really looking forward to tomorrow.'

But there was no articulate response. Sister Balls switched the light back on, and went to her case on the chest of drawers for the morphine. Duncan left the room and walked downstairs. From the sitting room came a violent shriek, the parrot's *yayayayaya*. He ignored the aunts and their clawed familiar, and left the house with the sense of a burden lifting, or about to lift. Somewhere, a knotted little Clapham presence, a girl in a one-bedroom rented flat surrounded by her favourite objects, intensely waited. He could feel Dommie's northward gaze on him. She knew he was back in her city, and had gone where she would not go. He saw her, in the safety of her room, surrounded by animals in plush on the bed, animals in glass and porcelain on the windowsill. In her frozen menagerie, she was expecting him.

10.

'Thank God he's gone,' Rachel said. 'I'm going to go upstairs and get the will – the real one, the last one. And then tomorrow I'm going to put it in a very, very safe place.'

But Rebecca and Ruth just shook their heads. Rachel's parrot raised his head, and looked around from the back of the chair where he prowled and surveyed, and gave one reprimanding, minatory, regretful shriek. He was thirty-four years old, a great age for a parrot. Despite that, his voice was what it had always been, and his plumage as black, and he looked about him with triumph. He enjoyed it when he shrieked, and made the women leap.

11.

It was later than Duncan thought, and the train back into town was almost empty. He stepped into the carriage, its slatted wooden floor and its damp-smelling upholstery familiar but not thought of for months. At the far end of the carriage, a middle-aged black man sat, reading his book. Duncan put his bag on the seat opposite, and opened it. The Embassy would just be opening now. There was no reason not to go. It would be good to spend his first night back in London with a stranger; to get fucked by someone whose name he couldn't quite remember at the exact moment his father was dying. The suitcases would turn up tomorrow – something else to look forward to. But in the meantime he had the clothes he had been wearing that morning in Sicily, changed out of in the toilets at Charles de Gaulle; a satin pair of shorts and a tight black T-shirt with an American flag on it. He was glad he'd taken the trouble to fold them neatly. He took off his jacket, there in the carriage, and then his white shirt; he pulled his jeans over his trainers, and folded everything. At the end of the carriage, the man had abandoned his book: he was staring, astonished, at the thin man with a shock of blond hair who had got onto the train and quickly stripped to his underpants. Duncan gave a mock curtsy to the man, whose attention quickly focused on the book again. The rackety bopping of the train's wheels was going all disco in Duncan's mind; the music on the dance-floor was in his thoughts. He could hardly wait. And then he wriggled into the shorts, glad that he had put on white socks with the trainers; he unfolded the T-shirt, and slipped into it. In his mind was the pump and funk of the two a.m. sweat machine, and the hot grind of jaw and hip after speed; and thirty boys he hadn't seen for months. To the rhythm of the train's wheels, he gave an unseen little pirouette, a twist, a shake, a small punch of the fist upwards, just there in the train carriage. And tomorrow he would call Dommie, as soon as he felt up to it.

BOOK 3
Next Year

1.

'I don't know why we've got to come here,' Nick said.

'Allow it. Always the fucking same,' Nathan said. 'We were all right where we were. Then they say to you, you can't stay here, you've got to come with us. So we come with them—'

'Yeah, we come with them,' Nick said.

'And when we get there, it's long, man. They say us, you can't stay here,' Nathan said.

'Not downstairs, no way, is it,' Nick said.

'You've got to go upstairs,' Nathan said. 'That's for you, is it?'

'They don't say that,' Nick said. 'They pretend it's a treat, like it's what they're doing it for, like it's total nang.'

'Skeen. And we're like wagwarn, having to eat all that food and make out you're liking it, like,' Nathan said.

'Leastways,' Nick said, 'leastways we don't have to be eating that food and shit. That looked rank, man.'

'Don't laugh at the food, man,' Nathan said. 'She said she was bringing us up some food in ten and it ain't gonna be Claridges.'

'Oh, man,' Nick said. 'I'm glad you bring that bottle of poppers, bro.'

The first speaker was a boy of thirteen, with dark blond hair in curls and thick, adult eyebrows. The second was his identical twin. Both of them had newly deep, grating voices; their faces had grown in large, unexpected directions recently, giving them big noses and angular Adam's apples. They talked at each other, not looking into each other's faces, rapidly and with London accents. The room they were in was a large study, with a picnic table set up in the middle with a cloth cast over it. The leather-topped desk had four drawers on either side, and a long drawer under the green leather surface, topped with gold inlay. One drawer to the left was locked, as was the long drawer. The others were all open, but contained nothing interesting: plastic pens, papers of no interest, a ball of string. On the desk sat a small hi-fi system; on it, a man was speaking over the sound of strings playing slowly.

Nick sat in the executive chair at the desk; from time to time he swivelled violently. His twin lay at full length on the green leather sofa to the side of the room, kicking at the underneath of the suspended bookshelves above him, which contained nothing but two dozen boring-sounding books about law.

'I ain't eating what they're eating,' Nick said.

'That's right,' Nathan said. 'I'm going to sniff poppers all night, I'm going to get so high, and I ain't eating that food they're eating. Did you see that shit?'

'Who's coming, apart from us?' Nick said.

'There's that sket whose husband left her,' Nathan said. 'She's got a kid who's coming.'

'Who the fuck's that?' Nick said.

'I don't fucking know,' Nathan said. 'She's that sket with the fat arse down the street.'

'That why her husband left her?' Nick said. ''Cause her husband's left her, is it? Was it 'cause she's so fucking fat, he couldn't stand it?'

'Yeah, fat but no tits,' Nathan said. 'That's bad luck in life, man, that's bad luck. You're a sket who's fat, but you've got no tits.'

'Not like Andrew Barley, then,' Nick said. They convulsed at the thought of Andrew Barley, a boy in their class who was last to be chosen, whom they'd beaten with a torn-off branch from one side of the playground to the other, who'd produced a note from his mum saying that he might be late for chemistry because it was on the other side of school and he couldn't run because of his weight – it had actually said that, because of his weight. 'Andrew Barley and his gigantic tits.'

'Yeah, she's like that,' Nick said. 'She's coming because they feel sorry for her, is it? And her little boy, we've to be looking after him and he's going to be sent up here.'

'I look forward to that,' Nathan said, using a sarcastic phrase they'd heard, with admiration, from Mr Andropoulos next door whenever he'd been told about something really boring or unpleasant about to happen, like the Notting Hill Carnival and Mrs Barley promising to make him her Facebook friend and his garden being bought up to make room for Crossrail and shit.

'Yeah, I look forward to that too, all right,' Nick said. 'And their daughter's coming in here in a bit, Mrs Khan said. She said she was coming back from something, from orchestra or something, and she'd come and sit with us and have dinner and play cards and that.'

'Fuck me, Anita Khan,' Nathan said. 'I'd forgotten about Anita fucking Khan. She's fucking mental.'

'She jezzy,' Nick said. 'She's never gone to orchestra with her flute – she's out being fucked by the gangsters all the afternoon. She's just told her dad she's gone to orchestra.'

'Poor old Mr Khan,' Nathan said. 'She's piff, but I wouldn't fuck her. She takes after her mother in that.'

'Shut your mouth, wallad, she mother coming,' Nathan said.

There was a noise on the stairs that Nathan had heard, a creak and a clink of glasses. The twins made huge eyes at each other; Nick dug his heels into the carpet to stop his chair and Nathan sat up on the sofa, pulling the bottom of his jeans down. The door to the study opened, and Mrs Khan came in, pushing it backwards and carrying a tray. Behind her came a much smaller woman, carrying another tray. Nick leapt up and held the door open – 'Oh, thank you so much, you are kind,' Mrs Khan said. Bina, the housekeeper, set her tray down and left. Mrs Khan set her tray down, also on the desk, but stayed. She was a thin woman with a streak of white in her black hair; her dress was a mauve raw silk with an octagonal neckline showing a slightly wrinkled bosom. She was a sex-bomb, the twins had heard their father say, in a jocular manner, and their mother respond that she was a very good sort all round. Which she was, they hadn't decided on just yet. She was sket, but the twins described every woman they knew as sket.

'Hello, boys,' Mrs Khan said.

'Hello, Mrs Khan,' Nathan said, and Nick echoed him.

'Is Anita not in here yet?' Mrs Khan said, setting the tray down on the desk. 'I'm sorry to be leaving you without anything or anyone to entertain you, boys.'

'That's all right, Mrs Khan,' Nick said. 'You don't need to make any special effort to entertain us.'

'We were just chatting,' Nathan said.

'It's so nice to see brothers who get on so well. You could put the television on, you know. I brought it in here because I thought you might like it.'

'Thanks, Mrs Khan,' Nick said, 'but we're all right, we're happy just chatting.'

'How's Mr Khan?' Nathan said. 'Is he well?'

'Yes, thank you, very well,' Mrs Khan said, eyeing them strangely. 'He'll be up to say hello in a while.'

'There's no need for that, Mrs Khan,' Nathan said. 'I wouldn't want to disturb him. We saw him only last week, at the garden centre.'

'At the garden centre?' Mrs Khan said. She was fitting a cigarette into a cigarette holder. 'Are you sure? It might have been someone who just looked like Mr Khan. Don't worry, I'm not going to light this one in here. I know all about you young people not liking passive smoking.'

'Last Friday afternoon, it would have been, Mrs Khan,' Nick said. 'It was definitely Mr Khan. He was looking at shrubs with … It would have been his secretary, maybe – she was blonde and in a short skirt, a pretty girl it was, Mrs Khan.'

'Well, then, it certainly wasn't Mr Khan,' Mrs Khan said. 'His secretary is fifty and very fat – I don't think she would go out in a short skirt. And actually last Friday—'

'Maybe it wasn't his secretary, then,' Nathan said disconsolately.

'Last Friday I called for Mr Khan at lunchtime and we spent the afternoon together, so it must have been someone else you saw. Now – these are chicken samosas, and this is what we call chaat, and these are pakoras, vegetable pakoras, and these are just little fritters. They are Indian, but there's nothing to be frightened of. I'm sure you'll like them. And this is salad, you'd make me so proud if you ate even some of it. Lemon squash, Coke – the television? You're sure? There's a pack of cards on Mr Khan's desk if you want to play whist – Anita will teach you if you don't know.'

'Thanks for everything, Mrs Khan,' Nathan said, as she walked out. There was a click, the noise of a cigarette lighter striking. 'You've been very kind, thank you very much. Man, that sket is bare long.'

'I thought she'd never shut it and fuck off. I was going to call the feds,' Nick said.

'Yeah, and she call the feds on you, wallad,' Nathan said. 'Wagwarn with Mr Khan and the jezz at the *garden centre*? Oh, she blonde, she hot, she short-skirt sket. You know you trouble? You say too much detail when you tell lie, is it. Friday afternoon, blond secretary – she know, Mrs Khan, she know what her man doing Friday afternoon. You leave it vague and imprecise, fool, you plant seed of doubt in Mrs Khan mind.'

'Yeah, I do better next time,' Nick said. 'I buy packet of seeds at garden centre – packet of seeds of doubt and plant them in Mrs Khan mind.'

Nathan and Nick looked at each other, and burst out laughing.

The door opened again. There was Anita Khan. She stood against the jamb, kicking it gently, looking from Nick to Nathan. She ran her fingers through her hair, pulling it out, letting it drop again. 'You're Nick,' she said, 'and you're like Nathan.'

'Yeah, that's right,' Nick said. 'You're good. Most people can't tell the difference.'

'I can't tell the difference,' she said. 'I was just guessing in like a totally random way, you know, and in my random way I was right? I could have said the other way round, easy. I'm supposed to like entertain you. How old are you anyway?'

'I'm thirteen,' Nathan said.

'Oh, kay,' she said. 'And how old are you, little boy?'

'We're twins, man,' Nick said. 'That means we are like exactly the same age, only by minutes. That's what twins means.'

'Wow, is that the case?' Anita said, coming in and letting the door slam behind her. 'I never knew that. I was always hearing about twins, you know, but I never believed they like really existed? I was like they're, like unicorns and shit, mythical beasts, yeah? But here you are. And you're like the same age, the exact same age, and you have the same birthday, you know what I mean? Wow. Cool. Anyway.'

'Oh, come on, Anita,' Nathan said. 'You know you got to stay in here with us to make sure we don't trash the place.'

'Whatever. That's the best time I ever heard of,' Anita said. She ran her fingers through her hair. 'Like, spending a whole evening in a room with two thirteen-year-old boys. That sounds like incredible?'

'There's an eleven-year-old boy coming as well,' Nathan said. 'And they be thirteen-year-olds in the ghetto in Chicago done be killing they third man, so you don't be treating us like kindergarten, you feel me, Anita. Ain't they told you that one, about the eleven-year-old? His mum's coming on her own – she's that sket where the husband he left her, and she's wondering why. You get me? She lives down there, ten doors down, is it, and she's fat but no tits, you know the one.'

The doorbell rang downstairs; a four-toned chime.

'That's her,' Nick said. 'That's her with her eleven-year-old we got to entertain.'

'O-kay,' Anita said. 'That sounds fabulous. I'm like running a crèche here, you know what I mean. Are we going to watch CBBC, I hear *In the Night Garden*'s like on – that's going to keep them all quiet?'

'No, it's *X Factor*, is it. But that's dutty. We ain't seeing that.'

'That Louis Walsh, he badman, is it.'

The twins laughed. Anita went over to the table where her mother had deposited the tray.

'Oh, my God,' she said, running her fingers through her hair. 'This is like – have you seen this food, it's like a million calories in like every bite, I'm not touching that. My mother, she's crazy? She thinks she's got to feed me up every chance, you know what I mean? You've got to eat twice as much or she'll think I'm anorexic and shit. This food is like so random. This shit, it reminds me, it was like this one time at my friend's house, like once, it was incredible?'

'Hey, Anita,' Nathan said.

'Yes, Nick,' Anita said.

'No, I'm Nathan,' Nathan said. 'You got my name right a minute back.'

'I've like forgotten already,' Anita said. 'So, Nathan. What were you saying?'

'Are you going to tell about this one time at your friend's house, because it was like incredible?' Nathan said.

'Oh, fuck you,' Anita said.

'I was *saying*,' Nick said, 'that

2.

'I just couldn't believe it,' Mr Carraway was saying, drink in hand. 'I had a phone call from Simon Wu about the Middlesbrough plant, this is four thirty on a Friday afternoon, an aspect of the sale we hadn't considered, and could I draw up a memorandum for Helen Barclay's office, which I did – it was a whole weekend, dawn till dusk – and got it to Simon Wu first thing on Monday morning. It was a piece of work, I can tell you – it was really one of my proudest moments, turning something like that round in, what, forty-eight hours? Next thing I know—'

'This is amazing, this,' Mrs Carraway said, confidentially, leaning forward to Mr Khan. 'Amazing.'

'The next thing I know, Shabnam, is a furious phone call from Helen Barclay's office. On my mobile – I was in Birmingham in a meeting on a completely different project that Monday morning, I had to leave to take the call – and it couldn't wait. What did I think I was doing? I'd sent the report to Simon Wu and cc'd Helen Barclay's office. They'd have me know that next time I should send it to Helen Barclay's office and cc Simon Wu. They were in the lead and I should be writing to them.'

'Doesn't matter that they would have got the report in the same way, exactly the same way,' Mrs Carraway said, in the same confidential manner. 'Can you imagine, Michael?'

Michael Khan shook his head. 'It's all about ownership,' he said. 'People believe that they own a project and should be addressed first. I've met this before. People are so concerned about who comes first in these situations. The main person and the cc is just a part of those questions of hierarchy.'

'And women,' Shabnam Khan said. 'It's just so typical of a woman in this situation, that a woman like—'

'Well, I don't know about that,' Mr Carraway said.

'Another drink, Caroline?' Michael said.

'Well, I don't mind if

3.

we can have some fun up here,' Nathan said. 'You get me? Anita, you like poppers?'

'Poppers?' Anita said. 'Are you like seriously asking me if I like poppers?'

'Ah, come on, Anita,' Nick said. 'We're having a bit of banter with you, man. We know you ain't been to orchestra practice this afternoon like your mum says.'

'Oh, yeah,' Anita said. 'So I've been like where, then?'

'You've been doing it with some badman all afternoon, ain't that the truth?' Nick said. 'You've been lying there, and saying to him, go on, do me, do me.'

'Whatever. Go away, little boy,' Anita said. 'You're wrong in the head. I went to orchestra practice, you know? I took my violin, and my dad drove me, and I like rehearsed Dvořák's like Eighth Symphony, and then at seven my dad came to pick me up. So where was I supposed to be *doing it* you know with some *badman,* do you think?'

'Ah, come on, Anita, we know you like it, we know you sket deep down,' Nathan said.

'And we brought you some poppers,' Nick said. 'You like poppers, Anita?'

Out of his back pocket in his falling-down, underpants-showing jeans, Nick pulled a small brown bottle. Anita leant over and examined it. The label said Jungle Juice.

'That's Jungle Juice,' Anita said. 'That's poppers, is it?'

'I love poppers,' Nathan said, putting it back in his pocket. 'Oh, we love poppers. You just take one sniff, Anita, and it's amazing, you're falling over. One time, right, we were in IT and we were just passing it around, because our IT teacher, Mr Brandon, he never notices anything, you can just show him your screen and he's lost in space, and the whole class was just high, and, Anita, listen, Mr Brandon just never noticed.'

'Yeah, Brandon, he wallad,' Nick said.

'He what?' Anita said.

'He wallad, I said,' Nick said, thrusting his chin out and shrugging.

'I have no idea what that means,' Anita said. 'I can't understand half the things you say. Wallad?'

'Yeah, man, everyone knows wallad,' Nathan said.

'I'm like so –' she made a face of horror and despair, a mask of tragedy and abandonment '– when I even like listen to you, you know what I mean? It was like this one time, at my friend's house, you know, it was just like ...'

'You don't have to like listen,' Nick said.

'Yeah, but I can't help it, you know, I'm stuck in here.'

The door opened, and there was the eleven-year-old. He had been dressed by his mummy. He wore an ironed white short-sleeved shirt and blue trousers; his shoes were black lace-ups. He himself wore a cheerful, open expression, his black hair cut short at the back and sides, sticking up somewhat on top. Behind him was Mrs Khan, smoking.

'Hi, kids,' she said. 'Having a good time? This is Basil. That's Anita, and that's ...'

'Nick,' said Nick, and 'Nathan,' said Nathan.

'That's right. You know Mrs Osborne, don't you? Have you met Basil before? He's not in your school yet, are you, Basil?'

'No, Mrs Khan,' Basil said. 'But I'm in the same orchestra as Anita. She plays the violin and I play the cello, though I'm only in the seventh desk back. We're rehearsing Dvořák's Eighth Symphony and the *Emperor Waltz* at the moment. The cello's not really my main instrument, though. My main instrument's the organ, but you can't play that in orchestras apart from a few pieces. For instance, did you know Mahler's Eighth Symphony has a part for an organ?'

'I never knew that,' Mrs Khan said, puffing on her cigarette. 'That you were in the same orchestra as Anita. We must have a word with your mum, and then we can pick you up together rather than both turning out every week. That would save a lot of effort.'

'Oh, it's not an effort for Mummy,' Basil said. 'She says she enjoys the drive and I'm happy to be with her as much as possible, since the divorce, you know.'

Nick and Nathan exchanged incredulous glances of joy.

'Oh, yes,' Mrs Khan said, with an air of distaste. 'Of course.

126

Well, I must be getting back downstairs. There's lots of food there, on the tray, look – my daughter and these two haven't started it yet. I'm happy to see she has some manners still. If there's anything else you need, just come downstairs. Bina's cooking in the kitchen and she'll help you out, help you to find anything. There's some dessert, which she'll bring up when you want it, it's her special dessert, you'll love it. You'd make everyone so happy if you ate the salad, too, kids. Well, I live in hope. See you all later.'

She left, closing the door.

'Is this your father's study?' Basil Osborne said. He went round the room, looking in particular at all the books. 'What do you think of the *Emperor Waltz*, Anita? It's hard, isn't it, harder than you think it's going to be, but it's satisfying when you get it right. I didn't think I knew it, but I'd heard it before, somewhere. I know you, I've seen you a lot, but we've never said hello or anything like that.'

Anita was looking at him with disbelief.

'So, Basil,' Nick said heavily. 'You play the organ.'

'Yes, that's right,' Basil said. 'I don't have one at home, of course! I have to go and practise it in St Leonard's Church, you know, the one up by the bus terminus. They let me come in on Tuesdays and Thursdays after school. Shall I sit here?'

'Is it a big organ?' Nathan said. 'Do you like a big organ, Basil?'

'Well, I've seen bigger organs, perhaps in cathedrals,' said Basil. 'But I've never played a really big one, I've only played on quite medium-sized organs, like the one in St Leonard's. Is that food for us? Golly. It looks delish. Can we start on it or are we waiting for someone?'

'Does it give you a lot of pleasure,' Nick said 'When you sit on a really big organ.'

'Well, I don't know that the size of the organ makes all that much difference,' Basil said. 'But I wouldn't know. It's true that even a moderate-sized one, when it's going at full tilt, can be really exciting.'

'So when you see a big organ,' Nathan said, 'I bet you can't wait to sit on it.'

'I don't know that that's really what organists think,' Basil said, puzzled.

'Oh, shut up,' Anita said. 'They're being horrible, don't pay any attention. Do you want some food? There's plenty. That's like lemon squash or you can have some Coke. There's some like orange juice as well.'

Basil scrambled up from the beanbag and started filling his plate with food. It was as if he were in a race and might end without enough.

'Take your time, man, take your time. Ain't no ting,' Nathan said.

'You talk like black people do,' Basil said gleefully, with an air of discovery. 'There's a boy in my class called Silas who comes from Jamaica, at least his parents do, he was born here, and sometimes he talks like his grandmother talks and he sounds just like you do. This looks really good, I like everything here. It was nice of your mother to make all this food specially for us.'

'Yes, she knew how to make food that appeals to people who talk like a boy called Silas's grandmother,' Anita said. 'Ah, Basil, you make me laugh, you really do.'

'That ain't true,' Nick said. 'Do I look I'm laughing, man?'

'True that,' Anita said, in Nick and Nathan's style. Then she went into hostess mode. 'Take your plate and sit down, Basil – there's plenty of food, you can go back for more later. And some squash? Or Coke? There's more downstairs if we finish this bottle.'

'Like I say, man, take your time, ain't no ting,' Nick said.

'Skeen, man,' Nathan said. 'Is it time to get wavey, man?'

'Because Anita, that OJ, that Coke, that lemon squash and shit, well, I look forward to that, but there is something that you can put into those things to make them a less long, alie?' Nick said.

'I have literally less than no idea what you're talking about,' Anita said. 'Anyway.'

'Anita,' Nick said. 'Have you got any vodka that we can maybe put into the OJ?'

Anita looked from one to the other; she did not look at Basil, who had a samosa in hand and was, frozen, examining them all with interest. 'Have I got any vodka?' she said.

'Vodka, yeah,' Nathan said. 'I know you do, girl.'

'Is there anything else with your banter? Some like rum for the Coke or some gin for the lemon squash and shit or anything else completely random, you know what I mean?'

'Oh, man, who's the fool now, bro?' Nathan said.

'Well, I don't know about that,' Basil said. 'I don't think it's a very good idea if your parents come upstairs at the end of the night and you're all stinking of booze and can't get up because you're so drunk. They'll smell it on you straight away. I could always tell when my daddy had been drinking because you could smell it on him, even the next morning, and he always said, Never again.'

'And I suppose he did, though?' Anita said.

'Yes, he certainly did, sometimes in the same evening as the morning when he'd said, Never again or sometimes the next day. That was certainly a pie-crust promise.'

'That was what are you even saying?' Nick said.

'That was a pie-crust promise, I said,' Basil said.

'What the fuck is a pricrust promise?' Nathan said.

'Not pricrust, pie-crust,' Basil said. 'It's like the crust of a pie. Easily made, easily broken. Have you never heard that before?'

'No, I ain't never heard nothing like that before, man,' Nick said. 'Did you hear it when you were sitting on some massive organ, you might have misheard somewhat, man.'

'Yeah, you so pricrust,' Nathan said to Nick. 'Easy to break, you are.'

'So, boys,' Anita said. 'I'm not going to give you rum, because, you know, he's right, it smells when the parents like come upstairs at the end of the evening? And gin less so but still it smells in the room and they're definitely going to come in in some like totally random way and they're going to like smell it? But vodka, that's cool, we can put a little Mr V in our Mrs OJ and they won't smell that. I've done that before? Like this one time at like my friend's house, this is my friend Alice, we got like so wasted, and no one could tell, though her mum, the next day …We can do that, sure.'

'I've never had vodka,' Basil said, with the air of a reminiscing old colonel. 'I've had a glass of champagne at my uncle's wedding, when he got married to Carol, that's his second wife, and once Polly, who's my daddy's girlfriend, she let me taste a bit of her margarita –' and as Anita left the room, he turned to Nathan to go on '– because she likes making herself cocktails before dinner and I was there one night on a Saturday and my mummy was supposed to pick me up, only she thought that my daddy was supposed to bring me over, and I was still there when Polly had made her margarita and was putting their dinner in the oven – they get readymeals from Marks & Spencer, my daddy says Polly can't cook and they like different things. I didn't know,' Basil went on confidingly, turning from Nathan to Nick, as Nathan, open-mouthed with disgust, got to his stockinged feet and followed Anita out, 'I didn't know about the margarita, whether I liked it or not, it was really strange. I don't know what was in that, it was more of a mixture. But I've never had vodka. Oh, and once this boy in our class brought a can of beer to school and we all had a taste, I really don't know why people like that, it was horrible.'

'Yeah, you talking to yourself, man,' Nick said. 'I don't know why you think anyone in this room even listening to what you

4.

'Well, that is kind of you,' Vivienne Osborne was saying. 'Just a very weak one. I've been so looking forward to this, I can't tell you – I've had such a week at work.'

'I do like your blouse,' Shabnam Khan said.

'It's new, actually,' Vivienne said. 'I bought it only yesterday in

Marks & Spencer – I shouldn't say, but we all do, don't we? It's such good quality, and much better than it used to be, I mean from the point of view of fashion. You really wouldn't know sometimes that it wasn't from some Italian designer in Bond Street.'

'What do you do, Vivienne?' Charles Carraway said.

'Me? I teach economics at one of the London colleges – you won't have heard of it, I won't even embarrass you by asking you.'

'Try me,' Charles Carraway said drily.

'Oh, I shall, I shall,' Vivienne said, with a lowering of her head, a glance upwards with her eyes that dated her to the early 1980s. She had seemed, initially, confused and unprepared as she had come in, handing coat and umbrella and glimpsed son over to Shabnam as if she had thought that Shabnam might be the housekeeper named Bina. Now she appeared to have resources of flirtatiousness, directed for the moment at Charles Carraway. 'It's called London Cosmopolitan University – people say it sounds like a cocktail. So you haven't heard of it and now we can move on.'

'I think I do know the name,' Charles said. 'Is it in Bethnal Green?'

'Close,' Vivienne said. 'Oh, thank you so much, a lovely weak gin and tonic. Perfect. No, we're in Fulham, actually. But I'm thrilled that you've heard of it. Thank you so much –' she gestured with her drink, which spilt a little '– for asking me. I've just recently been going through the dreaded breakdown-and-separation-and-divorce from my husband,' she explained, turning to Caroline Carraway and making quotation marks in the air, 'though, Heaven knows, there wasn't much to dread about that, it was really quite a relief in the end. We had a long period of not getting on, then of him moving into the spare bedroom, then of spending time avoiding each other in the house, I think he ate at the Chiswick Pizza Express every night for a month, and then his girlfriend, who I wasn't supposed to know about, moved to a slightly larger place and he decided to move out. It was really not just a relief but a real pleasure for Basil and I when my husband moved out. That would have been two years ago. But nobody asks a divorced woman with a great lump of a son out for dinner. This is so kind of you – I mean to make the most of it. And you must come round to mine for dinner too! Very soon. Single women can entertain and make a success of it, I mean to show you. You have a son, don't you, Caroline?'

'They're upstairs,' Caroline said. 'Actually, there are two. They're twins. Do you like it, there, at the Cosmopolitan University?'

She had tried, apparently, to say the name of the university without altering her tone; she had almost succeeded.

'It is a silly name, I know,' Vivienne said. 'But they decided when they turned into a university to appeal to Asian students, students from Asia I mean, which was very forward-thinking of them, and now we're all quite used to the name and hardly notice how silly it is any more. Well, it would be nicer if my ex-husband, soon-to-be-ex husband, no, really ex-husband now, of course, didn't also work there, so I see him all the time and occasionally have to deal with him. He's the registrar. So I'm looking for another job, somewhere else.'

'It shouldn't be hard,' Michael Khan said. 'Economists must be so in demand everywhere, these days, with things in the shape they're in.'

'Oh, thank you, thank you, but I'm not really that sort of economist,' Vivienne said. 'But it's nice of you to say so. The thing is, after my husband left, it was really an immense relief. For Basil, too – Basil's my son, Shabnam – Shabnam? It is Shabnam, isn't it? You get good at names in my trade. Now, you know, this is an awfully unfashionable thing to say, but I really am enjoying being single, for the first time in years, decades, since I was fifteen perhaps, maybe ever! Anyway. Basil, too. Well, that is kind of you – I will have another drink, a very weak one, though, please, Michael.'

'And an olive?' Caroline said, passing over a ceramic bowl.

She herself would not touch olives, death to the digestion, straight to the hips.

'Thank you,' Vivienne said, hovering and then judiciously taking one, as if she were judging produce in the market. 'The truth of the matter is that

5.

'Give it me in my Coke,' Nathan said. 'I don't like that OJ, I drink Coke, me.'

'Oh, my God.' Anita took her half-full bottle of Stolichnaya vodka and poured an inch into a glass. 'Vodka and Coke, that's a terrible drink, that's a really like thirteen-year-old's drink when you'll drink anything? Oh, I forgot, you are thirteen. And you, Nathan, what do you want?'

'I'm Nick,' Nick said. 'That's Nathan. Can't you tell us apart?'

'No, I can't remember,' Anita said. 'What do you want?'

'I'm going to have some vodka with OJ,' Nick said. 'That's how you drink vodka, fool.'

'I'm drinking vodka how I like it,' Nathan said. 'Fool.'

'And you, Basil?' Anita said. 'Do you want to try some?'

'It's not horrible, is it?' Basil said. 'But just a little bit, so I know what the taste of it is like. I don't want to become addicted or an alcoholic. But just a little bit and mostly orange juice. It won't taste horrible, will it, Anita? Promise?'

'Promise,' Anita said. She poured an inch or so into Basil's glass; she dropped ice cubes into his drink; she took a slice of lemon from a plate where it had been sliced into half moons; she filled the glass with orange juice from the cardboard carton. She handed it to him, and Basil drank immediately from it, as if getting the drinking of poison over with.

'Steady, mate,' Nick said.

'Mummy always said that I ought to be given the taste of alcohol when I was younger, like Granny giving me a glass of champagne to make sure what it tasted like, because she said if I did – if I did I would get used to it and never have a problem with it. But Mummy said that Granny had done the same with Daddy. My daddy does drink a bit too much, I think, and when he's been drinking, he has a tendency to light a cigarette or two, and that I just don't understand one bit. You know what? I really quite like this. You can't taste the vodka, though I don't know what vodka tastes like, it just makes the orange juice taste really orangey. I could drink this all night. Does it do the same for your Coke, Nathan?'

'I'm Nathan, fool,' Nathan said.

'Yes, I know,' Basil said, puzzled. 'That's what I called you.'

Nick brought his knees almost to his chest with laughing. 'Ah, he got you, man,' he said, punching himself on the breast-bone. 'He got you. He said does it do the same for your Coke, Nathan, and you said I'm Nathan, fool, though he'd said Nathan, and you weren't listening, man, you just know everyone's going to call you Nick when they mean Nathan, you don't own your name, man, this wallad, he owned you, wallad.'

'The fuck up,' Nathan said. 'Ain't amusing, wallad.'

'That was pretty funny,' Anita said. 'He was so like cross, too? Do it again, do something funny, Basil.'

'Well, I can do this,' Basil said, and he pulled a face, his long lower lip out and his hands to his ears. But they looked at him and did not laugh. 'Most people think that's awfully funny, it's my best face. I can't be funny to order. I didn't know I was being funny when I called him Nathan, because that's his name anyway. Mostly it isn't funny when you call somebody by their right name, so I don't know why it was funny then. I like this drink, Anita, can I have another one?'

'Take it steady, wallad, take it steady,' Nick said. 'That stuff is lethal, man. You going end crunk in five minutes you take it like that. Wavey, man, wavey.'

'This ain't bad,' Nathan said. 'Vodka/Coke, it's sick, man. But I want something better, me, I want me a safe ting.'

'Happz, man?' Nick said, and made that gesture with his hands, a casting down of a viscous liquid, like Spiderman throwing jizz to the floor.

'Alie,' Nathan said. 'I want me a safe ting.' He wailed upwards as if in song.

'Oh, my God,' Anita said. 'Keep it down or my dad'll be up and he'll like know you've been drinking, it was like at my friend's house once, this is my friend Alice, I was just saying, we brought in this bottle of voddie and asked her mum just for a couple of cartons of Tropicana, and we like just, this is like four of us, me and Alice and Katie and Alice, the other Alice who we don't really like that much, you know what I mean, but we were like getting out of it, and making all this like noise, you know what I mean, and suddenly there's this amazing noise on the stairs, like a herd of buffalo coming upstairs, and it's like Alice's dad telling us to keep it down, but we managed to like shove the bottle under the bed just before he came in so that was just about OK.'

'I want me a safe ting,' Nathan said, still crooning what he had said, but more quietly.

'Here it is,' Nick said, standing up. His jeans hung down below his buttocks, showing a pair of red 2XL underpants; he reached down and from his back pocket extracted the small bottle labelled Jungle Juice.

'Well, you're not going to get at all drunk on a tiny bottle of that,' Basil said, in a mature, scoffing voice.

'You don't be drinking it, man,' Nathan said. 'You watch and learn, my friend, watch and learn.'

'I can't believe that you've brought some poppers out with you. It's like we're in a gay disco *circa* 1996,' Anita said. 'Where did you get that, your boyfriend?'

'Fuck you, man,' Nick said, giving it to Nathan. 'Ain't no gay ting.'

'That is like so gay,' Anita said.

'It's safe, man,' Nathan said. He grinned; he unscrewed the lid of the bottle. He placed one forefinger against one nostril,

135

and put the bottle to the other where he sniffed noisily. He put another forefinger to the other nostril, and sniffed in the other nostril. He clamped his thumb to the top of the bottle, and handed it to his twin. Nick did exactly the same, going from right nostril to left.

'That stuff smells awful,' Basil said. 'It smells like disgusting old socks or something. Why would you want to smell that to enjoy yourself?'

'I'm going to have to open the fucking window now,' Anita said. 'My God, I can't believe it.'

'But it just smells so awful,' Basil said.

'Safe, man,' Nick said, smiling in a watery, wobbly way to Nathan. They raised their fists and, with some care, managed to bring them together.

'You'll like it when you get old enough to try it,' Nathan said to Basil.

'I look forward to that,' Nick said. He was quite serious, but Nathan shook his head and laughed.

'I look forward to that. Man,' he said. 'This stuff is the stuff.'

'Yeah, the gay stuff,' Anita said. 'You have literally no idea how gay you look, passing that stuff between you.'

'It gets you high, man,' Nick said. 'It ain't no gay ting.'

'Don't you know what it does?' Anita said. 'It's a gay sex thing, you sniff it and it makes you want anal sex. That's why gays always sniff it like the whole time. You get it in gay sex shops.'

'Yeah, that's it, my girlfriend, she always wants to sniff it before we have anal sex,' Nick said. 'She can't get enough of that gay anal sex, man.'

'Yeah, mine too,' Nathan said. 'She's like I wanna sniff that and then I want it up my backdoor pussy, Nathan, yeah, I don't know if I can take it, it's too big, man, oh, yeah, I love that gay anal sex, man.'

'She loves anal sex once she's had some poppers, you see,' Nick explained.

'What in the world is anal sex?' Basil said. 'I've never heard of anal sex. I know all about sex, we had that in class last year, but we all knew about it anyway – I heard about it from Mummy when I was maybe seven or eight, and then some boys in the playground tried to tell me, but they got some of it wrong. But I've never heard of something called anal sex.'

Nathan went through it, his head lolling back and forward. When he had finished Basil said nothing.

'That was like a horror story,' Anita said. 'You'd never guess in like a million years that anyone did that because they thought they would enjoy it.'

'Yeah, you've done it, I know you have,' Nathan said. 'Yeah, like Basil here, sitting on a massive organ and loving it.'

'That is none of your business, little boy,' Anita said. 'What Marco and I do in the context of a mature loving relationship is really none of your like business.'

'Yeah, she's done it a million times, the sket,' Nick said. 'Yeah, 'cause you don't get babies if he jets his beans up your curry-chute, is it. Hey, Anita, have a sniff on it, it's good stuff, it goes with your Mr V and Mrs OJ.' He made an unkind imitation of her voice.

'Oh, I can tell,' Anita said, 'that I'm just not going to have any peace until I have some of your awful drugs. You know what my friend Alice says, the other Alice, the one who lives in Crimond Road? She says that if these drugs are legal, they're basically random, they're bound to be rubbish, even if you buy them in like a gay sex shop. The only good drugs are illegal drugs, according to Alice, you know what I mean?'

'We didn't buy this in a fucking gay sex shop,' Nick said. 'We got it off Chris Garry's older brother Kevin, he gets it off the internet and sells it to us.'

'So what do I do?' Anita said, taking the bottle from Nathan. 'I have a sniff here –' she made a ladylike little noise '– and a sniff–' and another one. 'Ow,' she said. 'That stings,' and holding one hand up to her eyes, she held the bottle out. 'Put the lid on quickly, it smells awful.'

137

But Nick held back: he let Basil reach out and take the bottle, and in a quick, puzzled way, he sniffed too, first with one nostril, then the other.

'Wagwarn!' said Nathan.

'Wagwarn!' said Nick.

'Wagwarn!' said Nathan.

'Wagwarn!' said Nick.

'Safe, man,' Nathan said, taking the bottle from Basil and capping it. 'Basil, my man, you did it, man. You is the bossman, Basil, respect.'

'Oh, that is strange,' Basil said. 'I feel all wavey now.'

'Wavey, man, he said wavey,' Nick said, laughing.

'No, I really do, I feel wavey,' Basil said, 'my hands are almost wobbly, I don't know why. But I don't feel that this is like being drunk would be, well, maybe a little, but I feel wobbly, I don't know why.'

'I can't believe you just like gave—'

'I know why you is feeling a little bit wavey,' Nathan said, 'it is because ten seconds ago you had a massive snort off the poppers. Now give me

6.

'and in the end I suppose I spent about forty-eight hours on it,' Carraway was saying. 'It was a whole weekend, dawn till dusk, and in the end,' he burped sadly, and looked down at his plate, smeared with rice and gravy, looked down at it with the sad realization that he had in fact told this story before, told it earlier in the same evening to the same people, wondered only whether he had told it when the fat divorced woman had been there, drawing some comfort, anyway, from the thought that one person round the table hadn't heard it before, if he had told it before, which he wasn't one hundred per cent sure of, 'in the end, I was really proud of it as a piece of work.'

'He's an odd boy in some ways,' Vivienne was saying on the other side of the table, not listening to Carraway at all, 'I would say rather old-fashioned. I don't know who he takes after. He has hobbies in the way that children, these days, don't seem to have hobbies, real, old-fashioned hobbies. Do your boys have hobbies?'

'Hobbies?' Caroline Carraway said, with a sharpness in her voice. 'What do you mean, hobbies?'

'Oh, things to pass the time, hobbies, you know,' Vivienne said. 'My son has half a dozen, and a strange couple of collections, too. It seems so old-fashioned nowadays – he plays the cello and the organ, he keeps a record of the morning temperature, he's done that for years now, since he was seven. He did all the usual things that children do, like getting obsessed with dinosaurs, only with him it was cactuses, cacti I should say, he always corrects me.'

'No,' Charles Carraway said heavily. 'I don't think Nick or Nathan do any of that, actually.'

'Can Bina take your plate away, Vivienne?' Shabnam Khan said.

'This was truly delicious, Shabnam, delicious – thank you – thank you! Well, children are all so

7.

'time we were at my friend's house, my friend Alice, it was amazing,' Anita was saying.

'I don't know,' Nathan was saying. 'I don't know what that means.'

'This is this one time when her boyfriend Jonah wasn't there, because he's like always there, he and she, they're like always all over each other with tongues and shit.'

'I don't know what you said,' Nathan said. He was insistent. 'What did you say?'

'What you saying, wallad?' Nick said.

'What did you say?' Nathan said. 'You said something like, This shit is booky, man.'

'Yeah, man, I said this shit is booky, man,' Nick said.

'Oh, yeah, cool,' Nathan said.

'Am I just like talking to myself, or whatever?' Anita said.

'You don't know what booky means!' Nick said.

'Yeah, I do, man, I invented it, wallad,' Nathan said.

'Yeah, well, what's it mean then, you feel me,' Nick said.

'I ain't dealing with you and you foolishness,' Nathan said.

'What's it mean?' Nick said.

'Fuck you,' Nathan said.

'What's it mean!' Nick said, and launched himself at Nathan with a chicken samosa in either hand, grinding them into Nathan's face. They had disintegrated by the time Nick finished.

'Fuck you,' Nathan said, brushing the food from his T-shirt and trousers.

'It means like when you ain't sure what's going on,' said Nick, 'you think there's like a conspiracy, you think it's gonna lead to something bad, then you're like This shit is booky, man, that's what it means. I ain't believe you don't know what booky means, man.'

'I know what it means, man,' Nathan said with disgust.

'This shit is booky, man,' Basil said experimentally.

'Poor little boys,' Anita said. 'I know where you can find something better than that poppers, though.'

'Ah, fuck you, Anita, with your no more vodka and your Indian Cornish pasty or whatever,' Nick said.

'No, seriously,' Anita said. 'Look at this. My dad would go spare if he knew I knew about this.'

She raised herself from the floor, and went over to the desk. She pulled out the second highest drawer on the left, and awkwardly felt under the bottom of the top drawer. She tugged, and came away holding a small key attached to a strip of Sellotape. She made a mock curtsy.

'Yeah, what's that, the key to your mum's sewing box?' Nathan said.

'No, little boy,' Anita said. 'It's the key to the top drawer. My dad thinks I don't know where he hides it.'

'So what the fuck's in the fucking top drawer?' Nick said.

'Oh, you wait and see,' Anita said. 'You just wait and see.'

'I don't think you should be doing that, Anita,' Basil said. 'I just don't think so. If your daddy hid the key like that, he really doesn't want you to be using it or knowing that it's there even.'

She took no notice, and put the key in the lock and turned. She gave a little cry of triumph. She pulled something out, pushed the drawer to, and locked it again. She turned round. In her hand there was a small plastic sachet, half filled with some white powder.

'Oh, my days,' Nick said. 'The fuck is that. That is never your dad's, I don't fucking believe it.'

'He thinks my mum doesn't know about it,' Anita said. 'He gets it and then he likes to have a little snort off it sometimes in the evenings when we all think he's working up here. I saw what he looks at on the computer, and it's all like lesbian porn – he has a snort of this stuff, and then he switches on his computer and watches these like whores going at it, and my mum's like going don't disturb your dad and shit, he's working so hard at the moment, and I'm like trying not to piss myself like laughing.'

'Man that shit is nang,' Nathan said. 'Yeah, this is like the best evening ever, turning into.'

'Turning into, man, turning into,' Nick said, and they bumped their fists together. 'We is going to watch us some of that lesbian porn and get high. You ever see lesbian porn, Basil, my man?'

'But what on earth is that stuff?' Basil said. 'I've never seen anything like that. What on earth is Mr Khan doing hiding it in his top drawer?'

'Ah, well,' Nathan said. 'We is going to show you just how

excellent a ting can be, and you is going to have yourself a good time.'

8.

'We've just stayed too late for the children,' Vivienne was saying, helping Basil into his overcoat at the end of the evening. 'Basil gets so tired, he sort of stops making sense altogether.'

'Poor little boy,' Michael Khan said. 'I hope you all had a good time, children.'

'Yes, thank you, Mr Khan,' Nathan – or was it Nick? – said. The three others were in a line on the stairs, Anita's head in a shadow from the upstairs landing. 'We had a smashing time.'

'Come back soon,' Anita's disembodied voice said. Michael Khan gave her a glance, a suspicious glance. What had happened? he seemed to be asking himself; but then his head clarified, and he smiled again.

'Come on, you,' Vivienne said to Basil. 'It's time you were in bed, really.'

'Time, yeah,' Basil said, his head lolling from side to side with tiredness. 'That is just so wrong.'

'Poor little boy,' Shabnam Khan said, laughing a little. 'Your car's not blocked in, is it, Vivienne? It was lovely to see you, too, Charles – Caroline. I guess the next time we see you, we'll have been to Washington State, we'll have lots of lovely boring whale stories to tell you.'

'We look forward to that,' Charles Carraway said. 'Come on, boys. Had a good time, did you?'

'Peak, man,' Nathan said.

'Yeah, peak,' Basil said.

His mother gave him a startled glance. And then, without any intervening time, Basil was apparently being driven away. He felt drowsy but full of ideas. It had been very nice, he had told his mummy. The others had been fun. It had been a nice evening.

And she had had a nice evening too. He wasn't going to tell her everything! About the vodka, no fear. She didn't need to know about that. And the other stuff, that came later, the poppers, he wasn't going to mention that. There would be a fearful row if he mentioned that, or if she found out about it somehow, she or Daddy. It had been strange and he wasn't sure at first he liked it. But he had liked it, it had been fun to feel all wobbly and wavey for five minutes. The other stuff, the stuff that Anita had given them from her daddy's secret drawer, the white stuff called cocaine, he didn't think that was so good. She had said that he might feel frightened and he hadn't felt frightened exactly, but he'd wanted to talk a lot and he was worried afterwards, and it made his nose hurt, and it felt really strange, the idea of doing that. He wouldn't be doing that again, no fear. But it was interesting to have tried all those things and to have found out about that thing called anal sex, which Basil had never heard of before and then to have seen it even later on, that had been really quite a coincidence and Basil felt quite grown-up to know about all these things. Basil remembered that those twins had said that they had bought the poppers from a boy called Kevin or a brother called Chris and their name was Garry. He was fairly sure that there was another brother at his school, a boy called Adam Garry, and on Monday he would surprise him by telling him that he would like him to get some of those poppers for Basil, too. There was the Christmas money which he would spend on it. And then there were plenty of people at school who would be interested to try it. You could charge 50p for every time someone sniffed it. He couldn't wait to tell people how nice and strange it was, and they carried on journeying the short distance into the night.

BOOK 4
1979

1.

There was something about the shop across the street. It never did well. Andy had been here five years, and in that time, he'd seen businesses come and go. There had been a florist's, which had been on the point of failing when he got there. He didn't think that had been there long. There had been a sort of health-food shop, selling beans out of old sacks – Andy could have told them that would fail. The sight of the sunflower painted on the window, that had sent Andy's sale of bacon sandwiches across the road through the roof. It had been the making of him, that vegetarian bean shop. And then, till four months ago, there had been a luxury rug shop, which Andy didn't believe had sold more than one rug a month throughout its existence, which added up to maybe four rugs in total. Nice bloke: no idea. Andy had watched the nice blokes come and go.

Like farming land, some patches of retail were just barren, would yield no crop. Other patches, perhaps very close, were fertile ground. Nobody could tell you why definitely. If you had selling in your blood, from generations, you could tell whether a site for a shop would work or not, as a farmer could tell good land from barren by picking up a fistful and sniffing it. It might be just the way the sun hit the front of your shop in the morning. It might be on the road that people naturally walked down to get to the tube station, and preferably on the other side of the road to their path, so they would get a good look at your shop rather than walking straight by it, head down.

Nobody really knew. But everyone knew that there were some sites, some shops, which never did anything, a tenth of an acre of barren land where no seed would grow, where it was not worth hoeing or labouring, because nothing would come of it. That shop opposite was one of those. Andy could have told them that from the start.

Heatherwick Street, in general, was a good little street, tucked away but near a tube. If you knew it, and you lived within a mile, you would probably do your shopping there. There were plenty of people who made a good living there – not just Andy's sandwich and coffee shop, but the hardware, the suitcase shop, the greengrocer's, the fishmonger's, the specialist Airfix model shop and the newsagent and sweet shop. That spot between the fishmonger's and the barber's: its windows were dark – was that it? Hard to say. Next to the shabby blue door to the flats above, it did seem to send custom away rather than bring it in. 'Course,' Andy would say, to his assistant Reggie and his son Chris, 'if the right business settles anywhere, then they'll make a success of it. We're just waiting for the right business. When I came here from Cyprus five years ago, me and Chris and Chris's mum, we looked around and Heatherwick Street needed a coffee-and-sandwiches. Phwoar, you should have seen this place when I took it – in a right state, it was. Look at it now. But then I saw the potential. I'd never have taken the shop opposite. Not even a good business can make a success if the site is total shit.'

Andy's conversation was like that: a monologue that took up two different positions and got them both wrong.

You never knew, but the people who were doing up the shop opposite might make a success of it. He didn't think so. There were a lot of them; they were friends of the new tenant; they dropped in, did a day or two painting, then went off again. That didn't seem too promising. Chris had gone over with a tray of mugs of tea to welcome them to the neighbourhood, and had come back with the information that it was a bookshop – 'The bloke said "a community bookshop", Dad.' That explained the shelves all round the inside of the shop that two carpenters had spent a week putting up. Community, bollocks, whatever that meant. Andy's dad went to the Cypriot community centre twice a week to say *kali mera* to the old ladies and lose small sums at skat, the German card game he liked to play. That lot, they didn't need a bookshop; they didn't really need a community centre, but the local council had given them one. Over the road, there were professionals, in Andy's view, like the electricians who did the lights, but the others were friends of the new tenant. They only had one pair of proper overalls to paint in, and the rest just in their old clothes – jeans and denim dungarees. They didn't have a plaster-embedded radio playing Radio 1, like proper workmen. Andy, he liked to have some classical music playing in the kitchen. It was educated, but mostly he just liked it, making sandwiches to ... the *Emperor Waltz*, it had been this morning.

Over the road some days there were twelve of them, all doing the same bit of painting; some days there were just one or two. 'If you rely on your friends turning up to do the work for nothing,' Andy said, 'you haven't really thought it through, now, have you?' But they seemed nice enough, though obviously not used to hard work. One day they brought along a hired floor sander. The bloke operating it, in bright yellow dungarees, had approached it gingerly – Andy had gone to the open door to watch, saying, 'This'll be good,' to the customers. It had started with a roar, and the bloke had screamed, really screamed, a girl's big shriek, and jumped back. 'I don't suppose he's handled one of those things before,' Andy said generously.

The tenant was a nice bloke called Duncan. He'd come across to introduce himself the day after Andy had taken over the tea, and to get rounds of sandwiches for their lunch. He'd come into some money when a relative had died, and had always wanted to open a bookshop. He looked forward to finding out all about the business side of things. Andy didn't think much of that. Business was in his family's blood, his father's restaurant, his grandfather's cobbler's shop and his great-grandfather's as well. People didn't just wander into it and make a success of it. For a start, the bloke seemed to think a place between the barber and the fishmonger was perfect for a bookshop. For the kind of instinct that would see through that, you needed generations of restaurant-owners and cobblers in your family, Andy reckoned. Still, Andy wished him well, and he'd been in every day to get rounds of sandwiches for them all, and buying his paper at the newsagent and fruit from Denny the greengrocer, which was a good sign. Two days ago, he'd said that they'd recognized their limits when it came to painting, and though they'd managed all right painting the inside of the shop a nice neutral cream, they wouldn't be attempting to do the sign themselves. A sign painter was coming in to do that.

The sign painter came, in a professional white overall, a van and two ladders with planks running across. He was at it all morning, painting something white on a dark blue background. Andy himself never went inside bookshops. He didn't know what they were called. They were just blank spaces in streets to him, not useful, not interesting, like a pub to a teetotaller or a William Hill to someone who didn't bet. 'Jesus Christ,' Chris said, towards the end of the morning. 'Do you see that, Dad?' Andy came to the window. The sign painter was two-thirds of the way through, and what he had painted, in neat Roman capitals, was 'The Big Gay Bo'.

'They can't call it that,' Andy said. 'They don't know what it means. Gay. Not everyone understands what it means, these days.'

'They know all right,' Reggie said, doubling up laughing. And as if to prove it, out of the door came the tenant, followed by the bloke in the yellow dungarees and the fat woman who sometimes came, and they stood on the pavement and looked upwards at the sign, raising their hands to shade their eyes, and the one in the yellow dungarees suddenly started applauding with his hands at the same position, not crossing each other, like a small girl; and the tenant turned to him and the two of them, they gave a kiss, just there in the street.

'The big gay bo,' Chris said. 'Bookshop, that's going to say. The evil fucking bastards. Gay fucking books. Fucking each other on the pavement in Heatherwick Street.'

'Mind your language, son,' Andy said.

2.

People had volunteered to help out almost from the start. Duncan was really astonished. There were the old gang, of course, but there were people from Paul's men's group who Duncan just didn't know at all. They had just turned up each morning, saying they were volunteering to do anything that Duncan wanted them to do. Paul came first, on the very first morning Duncan started work on the place. He'd come in in his yellow dungarees with nothing underneath – with Paul it was either that or the Andy Pandy ones, blue-and-white striped, these days. Duncan had been standing at the back of the shop, just measuring the space, making a list of what needed to be done. The builders had said they were coming that morning, but hadn't turned up yet. Paul had called from the open door, 'Coo-ee!' They'd sat down, Paul on the floor, Duncan on the cherrywood counter where the rug-shop man had kept his account books and order forms – it had been too grand to have a till as such. No wonder they had gone under. Duncan was so pleased to see Paul: after half an hour they were laughing together about everything that needed to be done before the bookshop could open in a month's time. Duncan would have had to laugh on his own otherwise.

'The worst of it is,' Duncan said, 'that I'm paying rent anyway, while I'm turning it into the shop of my dreams.'

'The shop of my dreams too,' Paul said sententiously. He looked about in the empty shop for a mirror; he found none, and satisfied himself with licking his canine tooth as if to clear it of spinach. 'I've always wanted a big gay bookshop to buy my filth from.'

'No filth,' Duncan said. 'I insist – no filth.'

'What?' Paul said, but Duncan was convinced of that, and tried to explain. There were plenty of places in Soho for that. What there wasn't was somewhere that stocked novels about gay life, books about what it was like to be gay, a place where gay people could come and meet ...

'There's the Salisbury,' Paul said.

'We got thrown out of there last week,' Duncan said. 'There's a new landlord. I heard from Andrew that he's put up a sign saying "This pub is for couples only", meaning breeders.'

'The ingratitude!' Paul said.

'It's a total disgrace,' Duncan said. 'They can come here and meet instead.'

'You're dreaming, dear,' Paul said. 'I'll come, but I don't think the Dilly boys are going to make it all the way up here. There's still the Coleherne, I suppose.'

'The ingratitude of that man!' Duncan said. 'When you think of the number of drinks we've poured down our necks at the Salisbury over the years. I hope it goes bust.'

There was a pause; a contemplation of the Salisbury, its gilt and theatrical flourishes, its sour and watchful bar staff, the throwings out and the goings on. They would care less about the Salisbury's future if there was much in the way of an alternative. As it was, you had to invest your hopes in what was there.

'I wouldn't have thought there was much likelihood of the Coleherne going straight, there's a consolation,' Paul said. 'Now, enough of messing about. What needs to be done? I put my third-worst dungarees on, so don't be afraid of being the cause of my broken fingernails. I'm in a butch mood.'

They went round the shop with pliers and screwdrivers, wrenching the little shelves from the walls, tearing down the artistic William Morris wallpaper. 'It's not too bad, the counter,'

Paul said. 'It must have cost— That's solid wood. It's a shame to get rid of it.'

'It's in exactly the wrong place,' Duncan said. 'Do you think my Sicilian tan is fading?'

'Well, it'll do that over time,' Paul said. 'But the counter?'

'It's in *exactly* the wrong place, as I said,' Duncan said. 'Do you know? I think that might have been why no one ever came in here to buy a rug. Do me a favour, Paul – just go outside and *walk past*.'

Duncan half crouched behind the counter, facing the door. There were no chairs. Paul went out, to the left, leaving the door open. He then walked past briskly.

'No, no!' Duncan called. 'Look in.'

'I did look in,' Paul said. 'Not very hard. I could just see you *glowering* like a madman at the door.'

'And would you have come in?'

'Well, you wouldn't be glowering in future, and there'd be lots of lovely things to come in and rifle through even if you hadn't thought of buying, but, yes, you might have a point. The cash till directly facing the door is a bit *off-putting*. Shall I make a cup of tea?'

'There's no tea,' Duncan said. 'Or kettle. Or cups. You could go over the road and make friends with that fat bald bloke who runs the café. Got to blend in with the local community, you know.'

'Blend in!' Paul said. 'Blend in!'

Paul was wearing a pair of sunshine-yellow dungarees; his hair was cut upwards, like a cockatoo's comb; he had a diamond earring in his left ear; it could not be sworn that there was no mascara on his eyelashes. He had a point in pouring scorn on the idea of blending in. Paul, Duncan supposed, was his best friend. 'You're the best friend I ever had who I've *never* been to bed with,' Paul had once said to Duncan. Duncan hadn't believed it. 'Come on, besties?' they would say to each other, after a row or a bicker, and besties they were.

They had known each other for seven or eight years. One day at work, Duncan had been sitting at his desk between unemployed when his supervisor at the time, a woman called Karen, approached, followed by a willowy figure. His movements were strange and interesting: Karen was walking decisively forward; the new boy was havering from side to side, like a candle caught in a side wind. Mysteriously, they seemed to be progressing at the same speed.

Karen introduced Paul, and placed him down at the desk – really, just a table – next to him. Paul had just joined them, she said, and she wanted him to watch what Duncan did. 'He's one of our old hands,' she said. 'Been here years. Longer than me. He knows the ropes. If you need anything, Duncan will show you. Everything all right?'

Off she went. 'I've been on a *training programme*,' the new boy began. 'And it was *marvellous*. I did think it wonderfully well *thought through*.'

'Oh, there's not so very much to master,' Duncan said. 'Ninety-five per cent of the people we see are completely straightforward to deal with.'

'*That*,' Paul said, 'is so true of life. If only people told one that at the very beginning! That ninety-five per cent of all people, everywhere in the world, are completely straightforward to deal with. But that is because ninety-five per cent of people, *everywhere*, don't really exist. Tell me, Duncan – Duncan, it is Duncan, isn't it? Tell me, Duncan, has it ever struck you that ninety-five per cent of people *everywhere* –' there was a smooth, slow movement of the hands apart from each other, gesturing towards the room, the civil servants, the unhappy unemployed, like the opening gesture in a stage musical '– simply don't have any real existence? Illusions. None of them real. Tell me, Duncan—'

At this point a long-term unemployed came up, wearing a Sherlock Holmes hat in orange tweed. Duncan told her to take a number and wait her turn, which the woman did.

'Tell me, Duncan,' Paul continued. 'Have you ever found

154

yourself in bed with a stranger, or at dinner with someone you've never been sure what their name was, and then suddenly found yourself wondering this – *are you real?* Does this person really exist, or is the universe providing me with a three-dimensional model of a human being to keep me quiet and fill the time?'

'Well, that's a big philosophical issue,' Duncan said briskly. 'But we're quite busy this morning. Let me take a few people to sign on and you'll see what it's all about.'

'Oh, piffle,' Paul said. 'You just go ahead and take the tiny few people you need to take in order to keep Karen out of your hair, and I'll just carry on keeping you entertained with camp old metaphysical *speculations* as we go. How does that sound?'

'Let's keep it professional,' Duncan said, but Paul continued anyway, once asking a bedraggled fat woman in a purple coat why she believed in money when it seemed to do her no good at all. That was Paul's induction, but at the end of the day, told by Duncan that he could have his own desk tomorrow and carry out his own interviews so long as Duncan sat in and helped out, he said, 'Whoopee. Will it be that desk? Can I *enliven* it with my own personal touch? Is it there to contain important files and information or just to provide a *barrier* against the angry hordes of the *workless many*? Do you know the Salisbury?'

'The Salisbury?' Duncan said.

'It's a gay old pub down on the St Martin's Lane. You like a drink or two after work, I can tell – you look the sort, I must say. Come on, it's part of my *induction* and *training*.'

Much later in the evening, when they were sitting in the Salisbury in a corner, a Spanish waiter by Duncan's side, pawing at his thigh under the table, Paul continued as if nothing was happening, Carlos had not appeared, and none of the nine vodka-and-tonics had been drunk in the previous four hours. 'And then,' Paul said, 'my friend Derek told me that I couldn't stay in his house one second longer because he couldn't bear my *mannerisms. My* mannerisms! I can tell you, Duncan, it was *his* mannerisms that were truly the more marked. He just would not accept it. Another drink?'

'Your friend,' Carlos said. 'Your friend, I think he is really a twat. Why don't he go home and leave us to have our time together? You tell him, or I tell him.'

'He's not my friend,' Duncan said. 'I only met him today. He works with me.'

'OK, well, you tell him now. And that really your third vodka I see now, and I don't think that first vodka you were drinking when I come over, I don't think that was your first either, so I don't know how much you drink and I want to make sure you give me a nice rough sexy time?'

'My friend Derek,' Paul said, returning with the drinks – two vodka tonics and a tonic water for Carlos in the half-pint dimpled mugs with handles that the Salisbury always used, 'well, the thing was that we'd been going together for two years, maybe nearly two years and a half. But he'd never, ever, once said to me, Would you like to be my boyfriend, or anything nice like that. I was never allowed to stay over two nights running, and never allowed to leave anything like toothbrush or toothpaste in his bathroom, and as for a spare pair of *underwear*— And then I found out that he'd taken another boy home – this is on a night after a night I'd stayed over, he'd told me I couldn't stay and sure enough he nipped out to the Coleherne and picked up this leather boy. The place, I can tell you, *stank* of poppers when I went round there the next day. Purely by chance I went round, I hadn't arranged to go there. I asked him what he thought he was doing. Paul, he says to me. Paul. I could understand you throwing plates at my head if we'd sworn to be faithful to each other. But we're not even boyfriends, we're not going out together, so I don't know why you should mind in the slightest if I'm seeing someone else. Seeing someone else, is it? I say. I thought it was a yield to temptation that you couldn't resist and that you regretted seriously afterwards, and now it's you're seeing someone. That, he said, is none of your business and please stop throwing plates. Well, I can tell you, he wasn't seeing anyone else, that was all my eye made up to make me feel jealous, but he would never say to me You're my boyfriend or, Heaven forbid, I love you, or ...'

Coming to the words 'I love you', Paul had opened his mouth wide and spoken the words without sound.

'You see, Carlo,' he said, turning to the Spanish waiter, 'cheers, down the hatch, you see, Carlo, the important thing in life is to say to people what they mean to you. Not to wait until it's too late to tell people that they love you. You see, Carlo, people just can't get it into—'

'My name is Carlos,' Carlos said, raising his voice. 'Carlosssss. You don't call me by some other wop's name, you stupid queen. Carlosssss. We sick of you and your friend Derek, no one interested round here, you finish your drink and go, leave us in peace, OK?'

'I'm so sorry to have forced my presence on you when it was so evidently unwelcome,' Paul said, and got up, with a great deal of poised and dignified handling of bags and a brushing down of the jacket as he left. Duncan watched his immaculate deportment going out of the door. There seemed no point in rescuing the situation. He would see Paul tomorrow at work and they would take it from there.

He had never seen Carlos again – those Spanish waiters had a tendency to appear and disappear. But Paul was in his life for ever. Even after he had been given the opportunity to leave the Unemployment, as he put it, a year later, Paul had stayed in touch with Duncan. 'Been given the opportunity' was one way of putting it: being strongly suspected of pilfering from the Christmas fund kept in Mr Khan's office another. Paul went straight away into a job as waiter in a West End restaurant of theatrical tendencies, and in six months was working as front of house, meeting and greeting and kissing the most distinguished, or almost the most distinguished, of the actor-patrons.

'You see,' Paul confided, over a cocktail at Peter Harper's, as the theatrical restaurant was called, underneath a red-papered wall of near-identical caricatures, some signed, some with a loving kiss, 'you see, some of us just find our niches somehow. And I'm sure that you will, too. Mother was saying that it seems such a waste that someone of your talents and charms should be so wasted down there in that dreary office. She's quite right, you know.'

'I don't know what your mother knows about it,' Duncan said. 'She's never met me.'

'Oh, believe you me,' Paul said, 'she knows a lot about you. When someone's a real human being, like you, or like Mother, you don't have to meet them to understand what makes them go. These people aren't real – she's not, and he's not, and this one behind the bar who calls herself Doris, she's certainly *not* a real person.'

'Oh, not this again,' said the moustachioed barman, polishing a cocktail glass with a cloth. 'I get this three times a week – Doris, you're not a real person, you're just a … What was it last time? A kim-rar, whatever that may be. And don't call me Doris if you don't think I'm real.'

'There, you see,' Paul said. 'And it's *chi*-me-ra, you uneducated lout. Almost the only proof that another person is a real person is the evidence of an erection. That, I insist on. When I go to bed with a man, Duncan, I insist – I simply insist – on an erection from the *moment of nudity onwards*. Anything less – the slightest hint of flaccidity – I regard as a personal insult, and probably evidence of them *not* being a real person at all. How is that Carlossss of yours, darling?'

'I haven't seen him in an age,' Duncan said. 'I only saw him that one time, actually. There's been a phalanx of Spaniards since. I've felt like I've been standing at the top of the stairs with a white coat and half-moon glasses, looking at my clipboard and going, Next, please. Shouldn't you be working? There's a lot of lost-looking people over there.'

'Oh, fuck them,' Paul said. 'I'll go over in a moment.'

On the other side of the bar, there were seven people of provincial appearance, between forty and seventy, smiling and attempting to ingratiate themselves with whoever there was to be helpful. It was a matinée crowd. Their relations were unclear but their optimism at being admitted to Peter Harper's, where the stars flourished, was radiant. This was where the magic happened, nightly, after eleven. At twelve midday, one of the slots reserved for unknown names, there was nobody in the restaurant apart from Marti Caine, knocking back the vodkas at a corner table in company with three elderly rabbis.

'They'll find their own way to a table, I should say,' the barman called Doris said. 'Have another drink, Duncan, love, it's on the house.'

'Oh, I'd better go over,' Paul said. 'You'll be all right for twenty minutes?'

'I've got my book,' Duncan said, hoicking an old Gore Vidal paperback out of his pocket.

'And then he asked me if I would shit on his head if he gave me fifty quid,' Marti Caine said, at top volume, to the three enraptured rabbis. The waiting women of the matinée party fixed their smiles, and moved their tan handbags from one hand to the other.

'Thank Heaven, he's gone,' the barman said. 'You can talk to me now.'

'No, I really was going to get on with some reading,' Duncan said. 'It wasn't a prop or anything.'

3.

The sales reps started arriving long before the shop was at all ready for business. The first of them came through the door on the second day. The carpenters were still measuring up; the floor had only just been cleared of detritus, and Paul had gone over the road for a cup of coffee. A small man, pale and rodent-like, with a sharp nose and beaky teeth, was poking his face around the open door. In his hand was a hard black plastic briefcase, thicker than normal briefcases; he wore, however, a brown tweed jacket and a yellow shirt. His blond hair was combed down in a neat, divided helmet. 'Hello?' he called. 'Hello? Anyone at home?'

The carpenters looked over; one made a gesture with his head in Duncan's direction.

'Hello there,' the man said, advancing in a self-consciously confident way, his hand already held out. 'We're delighted to see a new customer, a new sales outlet. I'm Roland Inscape. Ardabil and Cowper. I think you spoke on the telephone to one of my colleagues, a week or two back. About stock.'

Duncan remembered: he was not sure how to acquire stock, and in a fit of enthusiasm had gone round his bookshelves, writing down the names of every publisher he could find, and then looked in the *Yellow Pages*, and phoned up the head office of all of them. He had been redirected and talked to patiently; they had agreed to send out sales reps to talk to him and supply him with material. Roland Inscape of Ardabil and Cowper was the first to arrive.

'So, general stock, general interest, a few children's books, perhaps some of our reference lines. We have some very interesting novels coming out this autumn, which I'm sure I could get you a proof to see what your customers would enjoy. A history of exploration in the South Seas ...' and by now Roland Inscape was opening his briefcase, extracting a loose-leaf glossy folder and opening it on the cherrywood counter to show a mock-up of a cover displaying a Gauguin girl and the title in bold, sinuous lettering. 'And a life of Gluck. Very fashionable, the composer Gluck, and Stephen McGiver, the biographer, he's always had a passion for Gluck, and we expect it to do at least as well as Stephen's life of Emmeline Pankhurst, which you may remember from two years ago, twenty-two thousand in hardback and three times that in paperback to date and still selling strongly, no one can say that the Edwardians have lost their appeal to the discerning readership and we expect there to be a lot of coverage of the Gluck biography too, not an Edwardian, of course, but Stephen has a good loyal readership. A real word-of-mouth author, you might say. Shall I put you down for—'

'Is he gay?' Duncan said.

'Is he ...'

'Is he homosexual?' Duncan said. 'The biographer. Stephen –' he peered '– McGiver.'

'What?'

'I'm just asking,' Duncan said.

'He's only *asking*,' Paul said, coming back through the door behind the sales rep with a cup of coffee. 'Hello.'

The carpenters were greatly enjoying this; they were only pretending to confer now.

'Well, I really don't know,' Roland Inscape said. 'I really don't think it's any of our ...'

'Or Gluck,' Duncan said. 'At a pinch. I ought to know, I know. Gluck, he was some sort of composer before Mozart, wasn't he?'

'No, she was a lesbian,' Paul said. 'A pre-war sort of lesbian. And there's Robert Gluck who's a queen in San Francisco who we really ought to stock but I don't think you can be talking about him.'

'The Mozart one,' Roland Inscape said.

'I really ought to know,' Duncan said. 'I'm so glad I was thinking of the right Gluck, the Mozart one. Was he – I know ...'

Roland Inscape was staring at them, his hands frozen over his folder, looking wildly from Paul to Duncan and back again, as Paul began to sing: '"*Che faro* ..."'

'We're not really a general bookshop,' Duncan said kindly.

'You're not a general bookshop,' Roland said.

'No,' Duncan said. 'We're a gay bookshop. We stock books

about gay people and by gay people. Or we're going to. Children's books, no. Or not yet. Homosexuals,' he clarified. 'And lesbians.'

Roland Inscape came to life. He seized Duncan's hand, and shook it firmly. 'Well, what an interesting idea,' he said. 'What a very interesting idea. Like that bookshop that only stocks science fiction, won't look at anything else. How very interesting. Let me think. I'm sure there are some things we publish that would interest your customers. You see, when we saw the name of your bookshop, we did wonder, we wondered whether you quite ... but Go Gay.'

'Go Gay?' Paul said.

'Go Gay,' Roland said. 'It's a laundry in Parsons Green. I live in Parsons Green. My wife and children. They think it's terribly funny. I explain to them, it's nothing to do with ... It's been called that for ever, since it was an innocent, a sort of ...'

Roland Inscape's bluster ran out. He looked from one to the other, and his expression was almost pitiable. 'Let me think,' he said. 'We had a great success last year with a life of Ethel Smyth. Very popular, those lady Edwardians. It might appeal to ...'

'We'll take one,' Duncan said. 'Perhaps if you leave us your catalogue?'

'Just one?' Roland said, but Duncan could not be swayed. He would confirm the order when he had had a chance to look through the catalogue; the bookshop would open in six weeks, so there was no particular reason to panic, he told Roland. They shook hands; Roland went; he cast a curious eye at the carpenters as he went, appearing to wonder how it was that two carpenters endured the company of Paul and Duncan. The carpenters watched him go, stumbling over his briefcase in his hurry.

'You can't open a bookshop with just one book on the shelf,' Paul said. 'A life of Ethel Smyth. Who was Ethel Smyth?'

'Lady Edwardian,' Duncan said, in a veiled way. 'Very popular with ...'

'Are you planning to be popular with …?' Paul said. 'I think the word he couldn't say was *Lesbians*. That'll make our fortune. Lesbians and their disposable income, it's a well-known phenomenon.'

'Oh, don't you worry,' Duncan said. 'We'll fill the bookshop with lovely gay stock. I'm full of ideas.'

'I'm sure you are,' Paul said. 'Your dad left you a million quid or something, too, which helps with the *ideas*, I expect.'

'And what's with the our?' Duncan said, a moment too late. 'Less of the our.'

4.

There was just so much to do. Duncan put on a brave face to Paul during the day. But in the evening he had to sit and watch the television in his new flat in Notting Hill, a glass of whisky in his hand, and try not to think about how much needed doing, and what needed to be done next. *Blankety Blank* could not bring his thoughts away from the carpenters, the electrician who had come to fix the lights and declared that the whole place needed rewiring, the people to install a kitchenette at the back, the accountant, the plasterer who had been found necessary, the signwriter, the decorators, the stock ordering, the post office for the telephone account, the paperwork; the stuff, Duncan thought. He had just wanted a place where people could come and buy books about people like them, and people could write a book knowing that somewhere would stock it and appreciate it, where people could meet and talk to each other. What had any of that to do with electricians and accountants? It had been a mistake to buy and renovate this flat at the same time as starting the shop up; he had two sets of carpenters, two of electricians and decorators to deal with, not always knowing who it was who had left the message on the flat's telephone, since they always began, 'Hello there, it's Brian the electrician here.' Confusion followed, and expenditure; his mind went from the new people in his life to an escalation of figures, which was already cutting into what had seemed a colossal amount of money, six months before, after his father's death.

There was some pleasure in deciding on the interior of the shop. The bookcases were an ingenious, lavish design, with a floating case on wheels that you could push to and fro before the stock in the back shelves; it added half as much shelving space again to the shop, though puzzling to the carpenters who had to put it together and make it move smoothly. There would be a display case for community magazines, mock-splendid with Grecian terminations and flourishes. The pretend-tasteful William Morris wallpaper had gone on day one, Paul and he ripping it off with yelps of joy. The floor would be sanded down to the wood, then repainted black; Duncan had it in mind to seek out the previous tenant and buy a couple of Turkey carpets from him. There was some gesture of goodwill in this that he didn't quite manage to make sense of, even to himself. Paul had turned up with a chandelier and, when this had proved a success, had returned the next day with a stuffed pheasant in a glass case, mounted against a miniature Scots backdrop of moss and heather. 'You thought that what the shop really needed was a *big cock*,' Duncan said, beating Paul to his own joke. 'No, I'm not having it.'

'I think I've shown restraint,' Paul said. 'You should have seen the capercaillie, darling.' And since Paul had bought it, out of his own money, on the Portobello Road and since it was marvellous, the sort of thing your grandchildren would love again if you were going to have grandchildren, which, thank the Lord, they weren't, Duncan gave way. For the moment the bird was staying, sitting with a beady, quizzical air on the cherrywood counter. Duncan would find the moment to get rid of it after the shop had opened.

There were invitations to be printed for the opening-night party. Not the very opening night, but two or three weeks in, just to make sure everything was all right, and things always overran so with builders. There was the community to consider, not just your friends. (Though there were your friends, too – astonishing how friends, and friends of friends, quickly amounted to three hundred names and addresses.) There was a nice man and a cross girl from *Gay News*, who had promised them a big spread. 'Nothing like this has ever happened before,' the man had said, almost before he was through the door. 'We're so excited.'

'But there's always Prinz Eisenherz in Berlin,' the cross girl had interjected. 'Do you really think you can be as good a bookshop in London as they are?'

'Let me get you a cup of coffee from Andy over the road,' Duncan had said. 'And then we can start the interview, if you like.'

There was Francis King and Paul Bailey and Maureen Duffy and Angus Wilson and Brigid Brophy and any number of famous great gays; there were painters too, who might as well come if they were in the country, which Maggi Hambling was and David Hockney wasn't, more's the pity. There was *Gay News* and the men's group magazines that might run something. Then a man turned up from *Zipper* and *Vulcan* – God knows how he had heard about it. *Zipper* and *Vulcan* were porn mags, run from the same flat in Islington by the same bloke; he got most of his 'models' from the steam room at the baths in Bethnal Green, he told Duncan, putting them in *Zipper* if they were over twenty-five or had hair, in *Vulcan* if they were under, hairless and 'just looked a little bit nervous, a little bit scared-like, in front of the camera,' the man had said, and laughed wheezily, lighting another cigarette, the seventh of nine, in Duncan's shop. (The shop that would never, ever, stock *Zipper* or *Vulcan*, but Duncan wasn't going to tell the man that.) The man came back two days later with a sample of each, and Duncan liked the *Photographer's World* naffness of the props and the studio lighting, and some strange engagement with the laws that meant all the models had erections, but they were held down by the thigh to point down-wards in the photographs. Would it be the enthusiasts for hair – that one turned out to be *Zipper* – or the proto-paedophiles who would read the piece and run to the bookshop? The bloke would make a decision when he'd written the piece, he'd said. Well, he had to be invited to the party, too, Duncan supposed, dropping the terrible porn in the dustbin behind the shop.

There were the other traders in Heatherwick Street to ask, as well. Duncan had been doing the rounds, buying his fruit from the greengrocer, his morning coffee from Andy opposite and his lunchtime sandwich. He'd made a point of dropping in to buy some rawlplugs from the hardware shop, some fish from the fishmonger, and where there was nothing to buy – you couldn't expect him to drop ten pounds at the suitcase shop just to make friends – he called in and introduced himself anyway. There was a limit to what could be achieved. The hard, distasteful stare of the old sod in the hardware shop as he had handed over the rawlplugs – that didn't suggest someone who was going to be welcoming them. Gay people needed lightbulbs too, and they'd be buying them somewhere else. But Andy seemed perfectly cheerful, and the fishmonger had said it would be nice to see a bookshop in the street, though he wasn't one for reading himself, before handing over some startlingly orange smoked haddock. Duncan hadn't quite caught his name. All in all, there were about five hundred people on the list, and a week after compiling it, Duncan woke with a start in the middle of the night and remem-bered that he hadn't thought to invite a single politician or public administrator.

5.

Paul was the first to turn up, and he came almost every day from then on. The next person to turn up to offer his help, or condolences, was Freddie Sempill. Paul and Duncan had been going over the shop, and had settled down behind the counter, where the kitchenette and discussion table were going to go. Outside the window a short figure was standing, his legs astride, his fists on his hips.

'You won't want to come in,' Duncan called. 'It's a gay bookshop, called the Gay Bookshop. An old closet case like you, it's not for you, sweetie.'

Freddie Sempill looked from side to side. There was nobody outside except Andy, standing as usual at the door of his sandwich shop, and two old ladies in tweed coats and hats with a little dog yapping at their feet: respectable old ladies, washed up in this corner of London and left there to maintain a standard of behaviour no one else had cared about for many years. One was indicating the bookshop to the other; it was unlikely that they were about to beat up Freddie Sempill.

'Oh, do come in,' Paul said. 'Look at the silly queen, he's not going to come in unless someone goes and brings him in. Just look. I was saying,' as he opened the door, 'I suppose we've got to come and fetch you in. Silly old closet-case queen, honestly.' Freddie Sempill followed him in breathlessly.

'All right, mate?' Freddie Sempill said.

'What?' Duncan said. 'What did you say?'

'I said, all right, mate? Are you all right? How are things going?'

'Oh, you were asking after us,' Duncan said. 'Nobody would have guessed –'

'Thanks, mate,' Freddie Sempill said.

'– would have guessed that your father was quite an important civil servant, they really wouldn't. You sounded almost exactly like a Cockney barrow boy.'

'Almost, but interestingly, not quite like,' Paul said. 'How are you, my darling old closet case?'

'I'm not a closet case,' Freddie Sempill said. 'Most people think I'm straight, that's all. It's not the same as being a closet case.'

'Your mother doesn't think you're straight,' Paul said. 'Come to think of it, I can't think of a single person who does.'

'Ah, well, the squaddie the other night thought I was,' Freddie Sempill said triumphantly. 'He said so. You wouldn't have heard about him, though, I expect.'

'Where did you meet him?'

'That pub by the Knightsbridge barracks. You should have seen him. Shaved head, fat lip from a fight and a black eye, blond—'

'How do you know he was blond if he had a shaved head?'

'It was sort of glinting blond on his scalp, do you know what I mean? Amazing. And we had a drink, and I told him I was a plumber—'

'Oh, pur-lease,' Paul said, because Freddie Sempill worked as a manager on the menswear floor in Simpson's on Piccadilly, ordering in lovely spring modes for the gentleman with the fuller figure.

'It was just like two lads having a beer or two together. There was no reason for him to think I was anything but straight. It would have ruined the evening. But then at closing time he said he was in the mood for another drink, and I said, come back to mine, it's not far—'

'You're in Fulham, still, aren't you?' Duncan said, but Freddie Sempill ignored this.

'And he came back, and one thing led to another, and we ended up fooling around, if you know what I mean, and he said at one point, I've never wanted to do anything like this before, it must be being with another straight lad like you, you'd never tell anyone, would you? And he went off in the morning saying what no one knows doesn't hurt anyone. He was perfect.'

'He left in the morning?' Paul said.

'Yes, he stayed all night,' Freddie Sempill said.

'And he still thought you were straight after the whole night of kissing and cuddling and doing all sorts of awful gay-sex things?' Duncan said.

'That wasn't my point,' Paul said. 'He's supposed to be a soldier, and he stayed all night. Don't they have to spend the night in the barracks, or whatever?'

'He was on leave,' Freddie Sempill said promptly.

'And he was staying in his barracks anyway,' Paul said. 'You stupid queen, you've picked up another queen like you, pretending to be a soldier like you were pretending to be a plumber. Anyway. What are you doing here? Just passing? You won't be coming in once we put the sign up that says "Big Gay Bookshop".'

Freddie Sempill rolled his eyes; he put his hands to his throat; he laughed boldly. Then he remembered that most people in the world thought he was straight, and he made a straight man's shrugging gesture. 'You aren't seriously going to call it that, mate?' he said in the end. 'Not seriously.'

'They are going to call it that,' one of the carpenters called from the front, coming in after their cigarette break. 'You're behind the times, mate. That's what all shops are going to be called these days. The Big Gay Grocer's. The Big Gay Furniture Shop. The Big Gay Menswear Shop. The –'

'It's here. It's called Simpson's, sweety,' Paul said. He had a warm relationship with the carpenters, who thought him a card.

'– Big Gay Bookshop and the Big Gay Butcher's.'

'Butcher and butcher,' Paul said. 'Now, I can see you're torn, Miss Sempill. You don't want to stay in a big gay shop in case people think there's something wrong with you. But you can see we're about to do something manly and you want to join in, though you're not quite sure what the manly thing is. Let me enlighten you. We're going to paint the back wall a nice shade of terracotta.'

'Looks orange to me,' Freddie Sempill said, with an attempt at manliness, trying to impress the carpenters.

'Well, it's terracotta,' Duncan said briskly.

Freddie Sempill was one of those queens whom every queen knew: his attempt at being perceived as straight saw to that. He made a point of only going to bed with straight men, or those he believed to be straight. It was surprising, at first, that he had come at all to the Big Gay Bookshop. They had thought that, as Paul remarked to Duncan afterwards, he was only going to come before they put the sign up, before anyone could have seen what he was visiting. Once that had gone up, they wouldn't see him for dust.

'So what needs doing?' he said now. 'Painting? I can do a bit of that.'

'If you feel like it,' Paul said. 'Roll your sleeves up. We've got some overalls somewhere – there, that pile of what looks like rags at the back of the shop. Pop those on and get busy. We'll start you on the ceiling – we'll see how you do with that.'

'I'm going to get a tattoo one of these days,' Freddie Sempill said. 'One of those that sailors used to have, on the forearm, saying Mum. Don't you think?'

'Don't you ever have to roll your sleeves up in Simpson's?' Paul said. 'When it gets hot? No, I don't suppose you do.'

6.

'And then he made such a hash of the ceiling, I can't tell you,' Paul said later on, at the CHE meeting. 'We're going to have to repaint it all tomorrow. We thought he couldn't do much harm – we haven't touched the bookcases, which are all in now, or the walls, and the floor was all covered up so, no matter how much he spilt all over the place, he couldn't do much harm. But *paint* in his *hair* and *hair* in the *paint* on the ceiling. And then he was about to fall off the ladder and he put his hand in the bit he'd just painted and then he leant immediately on one of the bookcases and there was a sort of smeared handprint on it. Duncan went all tight-lipped, you know how he does when he's seriously annoyed.'

They were in the upstairs room at the pub in Camden. They

were supposed to discuss the likelihood of extending Gay Pride outside London, maybe to Birmingham or Manchester to start with. On the other side of the table to Paul and Alan, the discussion was coming to an end with a long story, told by Christopher, about a man he had met at Gay Pride the year before last, who had come down from Newcastle, and he had said that there was quite a good scene in Newcastle now, and they'd had a good time marching, but Christopher had lost his phone number the next morning and he supposed that the man had lost his too, since he hadn't been in touch. But Christopher was going to Manchester only next week.

'I thought you said he was from Newcastle?' Simon said, draining the last of his pint of bitter. 'I wish you'd get these things right when you tell a story.'

'Yes. He was from Newcastle,' Christopher finished decisively. Simon and Christopher had had years of turning up at the same meetings and saying 'hello' to each other when they met over a conference table in Whitehall. There had often been a professional tinge to the way they spoke to each other at the CHE meetings, a sense of mild mutual deference, but there was a petty sharpness about the way Simon was speaking to Christopher tonight – he had told Christopher to 'get on with it' earlier when he was explaining, as an account of personal growth, how he had gone to gay rights meetings for the first time in America.

'And I don't even know how Freddie Sempill came to hear about Duncan's bookshop in the first place,' Paul said to Alan, not paying any attention to Christopher's story.

The landlord came in without knocking. There was, as always, a faint stiffening at this: he was never openly hostile, unlike his wife, but they had in the past wondered whether he had known what they were, and what they did; the general consensus was that he hadn't known at the start, but when he had found out had decided to be bonhomous, at least to their faces. His name was Tarquin: nobody had discovered what his wife's name was. 'Everything all right?' Tarquin now said, going round the table

171

and collecting what pint glasses there were. 'Don't mean to be rude, gents, but ...'

'It's about time for another one,' Simon said dutifully, after he had collected everyone's money – CHE was not the sort of place where they bought rounds for each other. Some of them thought they shouldn't be drinking: they were really there to talk serious things over and decide on the future. Some of them (Christopher) said this every time they met, but he went along with it and bought a soft drink. 'I do wish there was a gay pub with an upstairs room,' Simon said, leaving the room. 'There's that one in Romford we talked about.'

'No one's going to go to Romford,' Nat said, as Simon left. 'We can't plot the next stage in the sexual revolution from there. It's not even a gay pub, or only every other second Thursday of the month. The only place we can go to is the cellar at the King's Head. We've been through this before, it's not used on Tuesdays.'

'I'm not going to sit in the King's Head cellar,' Alan said, getting up and going to the uncurtained window. Outside, it was raining heavily; a woman under a black umbrella was making an unsteady progress down the street, her personal black dome glistening in the yellow streetlights. 'I'm not, and that's final. It might not be used for anything on Tuesdays, but it's too well used on Mondays and Wednesdays, and Thursdays, Fridays, Saturdays and especially Sundays.'

'I saw a man being weed on there one Sunday,' Nat said. 'I really did.'

'Well, there you are,' Alan said. 'I really don't think the King's Head cellar would be an improvement.'

'So why was Freddie Sempill there in any case?' Christopher said.

'I don't know why they don't get on, but they just don't,' Paul said. 'But he turned up – he'd turn up at anything where workmen were hammering and sawing. After he'd made such a mess of the ceiling and we told him for Heaven's sake to stop, he started asking the carpenters where they went for a pint, these days, but they made short work of him, I can tell you.'

'A pint of bitter, a lemonade for Christopher, a half of lager and lime, another pint of bitter, and a peppermint cordial with a dash of rum in it, here you go, Nat,' Simon said, coming back and shouldering the door open, turning round carefully with a laden tray. It sloped dangerously as he turned. 'And a half of bitter for me and that's going to be my lot.' He set the tray down, sat down heavily, and passed the drinks to left and right.

'I can't wait for the bookshop to open,' Christopher said, 'and then at least we won't have to come here any more.'

They stared at him.

'Well, it's a community resource, isn't it?' Christopher said. 'I thought that was the whole point of it. We'll just start meeting at the bookshop after closing time. Of course, we won't be able to buy alcoholic drinks, but Paul said they were putting in a kitchenette, so we can make cups of instant coffee and tea, and perhaps even a cheese toastie if we get hungry and the discussion seems to be going on fruitfully. And there's probably a "pub" on the same street or not too far, I don't really know about these things, but there often is in London, I know, for anyone who feels after the meeting that they need an alcoholic drink, I mean feels they can't go for one evening without one.'

'Well, I don't know,' Paul said. 'I suppose that would be a good idea. But you'd have to ask him. Go round tomorrow.'

'I can't go round tomorrow,' Christopher said. 'I've got meetings about North Sea oil all day long. It's interesting, but it takes up your time. I don't know whether you can go, Simon?'

'No, naturally I can't, Christopher, I don't know why you even ask,' Simon said. Nat and Paul exchanged meaning glances.

'But it would be a good thing if we all buttered Duncan up by volunteering to do something or other in the next week,' Christopher said.

'Rather than just turning up to the party,' Alan said. 'You have a point there. I can go tomorrow. I don't know what I can do. I'm really as hopeless with my hands as Freddie Sempill. The only thing I can do is find little treasures in country antiques shops. I was only seven when I came home with my first little treasure. Mother complimented me on it and said I had an eye. That was when I was seven,' he went on, turning in his seat to Nat, 'the war hadn't even started. That was the golden age of treasure-hunting in country junk shops, you know. It was never the same after the war. Do you know, we still have that first little treasure, in the spare bedroom at Tregunter Road, a real little treasure, but of course ...'

So then, of course, they all knew that at some point in the last three weeks, perhaps over a conference table in Whitehall about North Sea oil, where Christopher was representing the Treasury and Simon was representing the President of the Board of Trade, they had shuffled their papers at the end of all that technical talk, and had let their eyes meet, and Christopher had said, 'Do you fancy a drink?', no, 'a cup of tea' from Christopher, and perhaps over a smooth and oval and shining conference table in Whitehall the two of them had let their formal front fall away, as Simon did when he came to CHE meetings but Christopher never did. Paul and Nat were saying all this very quickly as they hurried away under their umbrellas, dashing away saying they had to get home, but in fact wanting to find a quiet corner of a different pub to talk over this deeply interesting development.

So Paul dared say that probably they had just seen each other as if for the very first time, no one knows what causes these things, maybe just there was one last pink wafer biscuit on the civil-service plate, one of those pink wafer biscuits that are such a temptation even to the joyless civil-service palate, one last biscuit between Christopher in his pinstriped suit and Simon in his blue serge with the waistcoat, and they both reached for it, and Christopher said, 'No, you have it,' and Simon looked at him and smiled and took the last one, and gave him such a flirtatious look as he put the little pink thing in his mouth ...

Nat burst out laughing; they entered the second pub, shaking their umbrellas at the door, like black herons opening their wings and shutting them after a fishing plunge; the pub was crowded, and they stood at the bar to carry on, Nat buying the drinks, a brandy for Paul, a third pint of bitter for Nat. 'I don't suppose it was exactly like that,' Paul said. 'I can absolutely see the look in Christopher's eyes when he realized that he was going to get an offer from Simon, though.' So then the pair of them had gone out, and they found themselves, entranced, walking in the same direction, and pretty soon they were in the public toilets in St James's Park because they couldn't bear to wait until they were home together, and first Christopher said to Simon, no, Simon to Christopher, please, just do it to me, now, hard ...

A girl wearing an Afghan coat beside Paul now turned and stared at them, Nat laughing so hard he had to rest his hand on Paul so as not to fall off his stool. She smelt of patchouli oil. 'Do you mind?' she said, in a quick, drawling, upper-middle class voice.

'Oh, fuck off,' Nat said. 'Honestly.'

'Yes, fuck off back to ... Catford,' Paul said.

'I'm not from Catford, actually,' the girl said. 'I'm from Hereford actually.'

'Well, fuck off back to Hereford actually then wherever that is,' Nat said. The girl turned back to her friend, another student-type girl, with a flounce of the shoulders, observing with a loud voice that they were all the same and her father would have had them all shot at birth. 'But,' Nat went on, paying no attention, 'how did we know? That they're having it off? Simon and Christopher? They weren't feeling each other under the table, were they?'

'Those two? *No*,' Paul said. 'What an *extraordinarily* horrible thought. No. I know exactly what it was. They were being so *unkind* to each other. Christopher telling Simon he drank too much. Simon telling Christopher he didn't know what he was talking about and to shut up for a change. They might have been married for years.'

'It won't last,' Nat said. 'They'll be looking round for new partners to keep things going. Honestly.'

'Discussing whether or not they should have an open relationship.'

'Spicing up their marriage by having the occasional threesome.'

'Yes,' said Paul, finishing his brandy in one gulp and holding up his glass to the gormless-looking spiky-haired student behind the bar with one finger raised. 'Of course there's *one thing* that Christopher's got going for him.'

'Oh, yes?'

'Didn't you guess? That borderline-bewildered air of Christopher's? Could only mean *one thing*. I know for a *fact* that he's got,' Paul said, 'a *truly enormous* cock. One more double brandy, *if* you please. And another pint of "bitter" for you, my darling?'

7.

All it needed was persuasion, one person after another, that it was not so bad, that you could live your life openly. And then you would persuade people who saw you, one after the other, as if turning to the sun, that life did not need to be like that. They truly believed it. They had no choice in the matter.

On Sunday Duncan left the flat in Notting Hill. He had moved out only for two weeks, while the new bathroom and the new kitchen were put in – the old lady who had lived there for forty years, on the first floor of a once grand stucco villa, had lived with the same ones all her life. The top of the bathroom walls had been green with mould: the kitchen cabinets had hung precariously off the wall, dragging the rawlplugs with them. She had gone into a home only two months before she died; it had killed her. Her family, consisting of two sons and their children, living in Enfield and Ealing, had thought themselves lucky to sell the flat to Duncan for £60,000 in its current state.

He had been glad to pay that. The rooms were huge, and the ceilings were grandly remote; you could see, from the patterns of stains on the carpet, where the old lady had huddled in corners and moved slowly from point to point in the rooms. She had not carved up the space with hardboard partitions, like a lot of flats he had looked at; she hadn't needed to, and her boys, they told Duncan, had shared the second bedroom until they had married and left home. There were probably disasters to be uncovered underneath the plaster; there were probably disagreeable and difficult neighbours to overcome. Duncan loved his new flat. He was making a kitchen out of, and around, a huge slab of light oak, and a bathroom out of white fittings, a rolltop bath, a stained-glass window instead of the suburban rippled glass the fitters obviously thought more appropriate. They had discovered blue asbestos in the floor; they had found that the mortar between the bricks in the back wall had dried, crumbled, trickled down and disappeared; they had found rats' nests and a boiler that broke all up-to-date safety rules and could kill Duncan at any moment. They had discovered the extent of the damp that had stained the wallpaper in the bathroom, and expressed wonder that the house was still standing.

Every day, for some time, there had been more and more horrible discoveries, and Duncan had been escaping the nightmares at home only to go to the nightmares in his shop. His father had left him hundreds of thousands of pounds, against his will at the end. It was pouring down the gullet of workmen in one place or another. Still, Duncan did not doubt for one second that he was doing the right thing. To put a sum of money into a shop was not to submit to the nature of London, where money melts like a wine gum in the mouth, but to transform expenditure into investment, which will grow and grow, and make a man rich.

On the other hand, Duncan had serious doubts about the

Notting Hill flat. He associated builders with madness, ugliness, vanity and absurdity. It was only his sense of the height of the Notting Hill ceilings and the beautiful walk to the shop in the summertime that kept him going, carrying on enriching the richest tradesmen in London.

He shut the front door and locked it – even the clunk of the new lock in the new, steel-framed front door was a satisfaction to him, a proof of new ownership. Outside, the sky was casting a wet springtime pall over the creamy stucco of the street. The front door of his neighbours stood open: from the house of Hubert St George there came an intense perfumed smell, almost delicious, almost a baker's advertising smell. It was only mid-morning on a Sunday: Hubert St George and his friends and cronies must have been smoking quietly all night. One of these days Hubert St George's landlord was going to notice what the houses round here were fetching and would evict Hubert, who would have to go and live in King's Cross, Kentish Town or some still more alarming place. When Duncan had looked round the house and up and down the street, Hubert St George had seemed like an appealing guarantee of life, not like a lot of people doing up their houses. Now, Duncan rather longed for Hubert to notice, in his drug-stewed way, that the street wasn't there for him any more, and for him to move out. This was particularly the case since one of Hubert St George's friends had called him something amusingly insulting when he was just talking to the builders on the pavement outside. Duncan hadn't understood the word, but its specificity about Duncan's favourite sexual act was unmistakable, and disconcerting in its accuracy. 'That's a quaint old-fashioned remark I haven't heard for a long time,' he had said at the time, however. There was something to be said for knocking through and doing up, of tarting up and making over, for the reformation that people like Duncan were shaping across London.

The tube was quiet: on a Sunday morning only three or four people stood on Notting Hill platform. One was a young dad with a pushchair, a small child with an Afro and a striped burglar's sweater asleep in it, a bunch of flowers tucked into the handle. Was the father on his way to see his wife? Duncan liked to think she might have just given birth, and they were going to see the child's little brother or sister. And a heavy, drooping, depressed woman in a weighty old coat, on her way to her job, and a young couple, laughing, on their way to an early day out. Duncan took out his book and for a couple of minutes was lost in Dawn Powell.

He was getting used to this trip; the Circle Line down to Embankment, the change to the Northern Line, the six stops southwards, and Dommie at the end of it. She had moved to Clapham years ago. It was as far from her father in Harrow as she could manage, and she felt safe with the weight of the river and the whole expanse of the city between her and him. But he was dead now, and his money had gone to Dommie as well. One of these days, she was fond of saying, I'm going to do what you've done, Duncan; I'm going to buy a bigger place, and I'm going to use the money to set up a business, leave Carter, Gershon and Carter, they can find a new contracts person and good luck to them, and I'll have my life sorted out. She had said that a number of times now.

At Clapham Common, after the half-hour journey and the change of lines, a completely different young father and child got off; this time Indian, not black, this time holding his daughter's hand in her pink party dress. He left the station. The homeless congregated here, in a small fenced-off square of land, already drinking, and the handsome eighteenth-century church with a steely, frowning gable could have done with a reroofing and a repainting. Wesley must have preached there once. He followed the road round, past the bad butcher and the good butcher, the newsagent and the hairdresser. There was an Asian grocer with displays of old-looking fruit, and just there, by the display, Duncan noticed something lying on the floor. It was a lady's fat purse, green and crocodile-skin in effect. He hesitated and looked around, but there was nobody in sight. He put it into his pocket to investigate later, and in a moment got to the turn-off for Dommie's square.

All the way, almost since waking up that morning, he had felt quite clearly that a particular gaze was fixed on him, approaching from Notting Hill. He had always known this, that Dommie's life was addressed towards her brother in adoration and responsibility. And as if to confirm this, when he rang the doorbell – one of six in the tall stucco house in Granby Square – which had Dommie's name by it, reading 'Dommie' in her fat, feminine, poignant writing, with a circle over the *i*, the buzzer to let him in rang immediately. Dommie's flat was not large: it had been what she could afford; but it was Dommie's way to place her armchair flat by the entry buzzer, perhaps from the moment she dressed, waiting to hurl herself at the button.

Duncan walked up the communal stairs, a mad steel spiral arrangement that defeated the deliverers of furniture. In his bag there was the copy of Dawn Powell's book, some papers he wanted to show Dommie, a bottle of Vacqueyras, which someone else had brought to a dinner, or to a party, or just to say thank you for something years before – Duncan had no idea how good it was, but he hadn't paid for it and was going to drink half of it, so it didn't matter. Above, on the third floor, as high as it got, there was the noise of the door to the flat opening. Plump, in a black dress with a nameless stain on her breast, a turquoise and purple silk scarf tied around her neck and a bracelet of pearls on her wrist, Dommie held the door open with her foot. He was glad to see the bracelet of pearls: it was new, he thought. She was spending some of the money.

'I didn't know whether I should come to you,' Dommie said. 'I can't wait to see what's happened in the flat this week.'

'Oh, more disasters,' Duncan said. He handed over the bottle, which Dommie took and they went together into the kitchen, an untouched desecration of today's cooking and yesterday's eating. 'You don't want to hear about the stuff that's happening with builders, though, surely.'

'Like hearing about other people's children,' Dommie said. 'Probably lovely if you have some of your own.'

'No children, no builders …'

'What were we thinking of?' Dommie said.

'I had such a lovely letter from Aunt Rebecca,' Duncan said, as Dommie poked hopefully in a pan – it might be a stew, or it might be some sort of meat sauce she was planning to turn into some kind of made dish, it was impossible to guess. 'I almost wrote back.'

Dommie shuddered, closing her eyes and putting her hands up as if to ward off a leaping hound. 'Don't,' she said. 'Don't. It's too early to hear about anything like that. Horrible Rebecca. I thought we never needed to hear from her ever again.'

'It's about once a month she writes,' Duncan said. 'I used to put them on one side and not open them for a day or two. But now I open them quite calmly and I read them straight away. I thought I might have got to the point where I could throw them away without reading them.'

'I would do that, I must say,' Dommie said.

'Well, you might do it once – I did do it once,' Duncan said. 'But it tormented me for days, weeks afterwards. I found I wanted to see what she said. It was only the same as every other letter, I expect. How could I do this. Don't think that she didn't know what I'd got up to. Don't think that my father's wishes could be flouted on his deathbed with impunity. Look forward to hearing from her solicitors very shortly with an arraignment. Does she mean arraignment?'

'I couldn't really guess at the meaning of Rebecca's letters. I tell you what, though,' Dommie said, wiping her hands on a tea towel. 'I don't know why she isn't writing to me. I almost regret it. I almost take it personally.'

'She thinks I'm flaunting the money,' Duncan said. 'What

with leaving my job and opening a shop and buying an expensive flat where my father would have been shocked to find any of his family living. You haven't done anything with yours, you're just where you've always been.'

'Tell her I've given it to charity, the fat beast,' Dommie said. 'Do you have it? Let's see it. Just one moment, though – we need a stiff drink before we face Rebecca's worst.'

It was only twenty to twelve, but Duncan felt that Dommie had a point. He accepted a vodka and tonic from her, and together they went through to the sitting room where, side by side on the sofa, they went over Rebecca's letter, phrase by phrase, setting it down and huffing, shaking their heads, commenting, dismissing, and once laughing. 'I wish I knew where she got it from,' Dommie said. 'She seems so pleased to be writing like this. You should save them up and publish them. And the shop? How's that going?'

'Don't ask,' Duncan said.

Towards the end of their time together, the terrible lunch finished and laughed over, they went out for a walk in the sunshine. They were halfway down the stairs when a wail was heard from the flat on the ground floor, and a bedraggled, long-haired woman's face peered through the gap.

'Oh, Domenica, thank heavens,' she said.

'Not now, Margery, I'm just going out,' Dommie said decisively. Margery's doings and her habit of imposing obligations with tragic little gifts irritated Dommie more than anything, she often said.

'Oh, but everyone's gone out. I just don't know what to do,' Margery said. Her hands opened and closed somewhere around her face. 'I went to the newsagent's for my paper, as usual, and I don't know why, but there was something on the front cover of the *Sunday Telegraph*, which is *not* my usual paper ...'

'Margery, we're in a very great hurry here – you remember my brother?'

'Yes, I do! And this awful thing – somehow and somewhere

I lost my purse, and it has so many important little things in it. I don't know what I can do, and on the back of my bank card I wrote down my machine number, you know, the number you punch in to get out money, which of course I never use, but now anyone can take money from my account and the bank's not open until tomorrow, it's too awful.'

Duncan remembered. He reached into his bag, and the woman's purse was still there. He brought it out. 'Is this it? I didn't have a chance to take it to the police.'

'Well, yes, it is,' Margery said. Her panic seemed to dissolve; her hands calmed and took the purse from Duncan.

'There you are,' Dommie said. 'All's well that ends well. Now, we really must be going.'

Neither Dommie nor the neighbour seemed the slightest bit surprised that Duncan had in his possession the exact thing that the neighbour had lost. On the other hand, Duncan thought that in ten minutes she was going to start suspecting him of trying to thieve her purse. The neighbour was probably one of those egotists who thought that the world ought to labour on her behalf, and was not surprised when things worked out, elaborately, in her favour. But Dommie, Duncan knew, was not surprised because her brother had always been going to set the world right. No wonder she believed in the bookshop so.

8.

The previous time Duncan had seen Dommie had been two weeks before. She had cooked for him – a roast chicken – and they had talked about the shop, and about Dommie's job, and about the flat, and about what Dommie might do with her two weeks' holiday. And afterwards, as it had been nice, they had gone for a walk on the common and had an ice-cream each from a van.

That sort of thing. They had had a nice time. And the time

before that, it had been two weeks before, and much the same sort of thing had happened then. The time before that, and that, and that, and that, and that, perhaps ten or fifteen times – a terrible lunch with which something had gone wrong, and catching up with the fortnight, and a walk on the common if it was nice and not if it was not.

But the time before that …

(This is going back a good couple of years now, going backwards into Dommie and Duncan.)

Duncan had arrived without warning at Dommie's office in the City, a grey marble lobby with a man behind a desk who didn't think much of Duncan in his scrap of a red tie and a scruffy tweed jacket, and the remains of a big night out on his face. Dommie had come down straight away, and they had flung themselves into each other's arms. 'You should have told me you were coming,' Dommie had said. 'I knew you were on your way. I didn't know when you were arriving.' Then he had led her out of the building and to a coffee shop in a side street, still quiet at eleven forty, and had told her that he had seen their father last night when he had arrived back from Sicily, and this morning had telephoned the house to be told by Aunt Rachel that he had died quietly in the night. Dommie had cried; he had held her hand. 'I don't know why I'm crying,' she said after a while. 'I wouldn't go to see him, I wouldn't be made to care.'

'It's over now,' Duncan said.

They agreed that Duncan, who was staying with a friend, would come over for Sunday lunch at Dommie's place in Clapham. 'We could make a thing of it,' Dommie said.

And the time before that, it had been a year before, they had seen a film, Dommie not wanting to make a big thing of saying goodbye when Duncan went to Sicily – Dommie had suggested *Heaven Can Wait* but it was full, surprisingly, and they had settled for *California Suite*. She hadn't cried then, but they'd deliberately just said goodbye casually. It would be hard for Dommie. He wondered who her friends were, apart from the loyal pair of Katy and Bella, girls whom Dommie had known in her first job in the City.

The time before that, they had had the sense of getting back to normal after a long period of remoteness.

Because the time before that they had met by arrangement, a bit stiffly, and had dinner in much too formal a restaurant. It wasn't their place: the waiters, on the plush ground floor of a block of mansion flats in Swiss Cottage, had murmured the specials of the day and hovered with vast leather-clad menus and wine lists. Duncan had chosen it as a place to make things up, to force her to see what an effort he was making, and in the end, though it had cost him an arm and a leg, it had been worthwhile. 'I'm sorry I said those things,' Duncan said. 'Lucien was really quite a nice man. I shouldn't have said those things. I can see what you saw in him.'

'No, he was dreadful,' Dommie had said. 'He was really awful. You were quite right. I lent him money, five hundred pounds, and he's gone and I'm not going to see any of that again, I know.' And then it was all right, over the strudel and the schnitzel and a strange sort of fish cocktail to start with, smoked oysters in mayonnaise, and a bottle of German wine in a blue bottle.

Because the time before that had been terrible, simply terrible, a year and a half before. It had just been by chance in the street, and Duncan had said that he knew she hadn't been to see their father in an age, and she had said she wasn't going to see him any more, not ever again. 'So it's all down to me, I suppose,' Duncan said, and Dommie had looked scared but determined, and had said, yes, she supposed that it was. And then before they knew it they were onto Dommie's French boyfriend Lucien, and was she going to support him for ever and, oh, there on the pavement in Regent Street, they had had such a blazing row, and in five minutes she had told him that she didn't want to see him any more, either, that from that moment onwards she had no family but Lucien. She had walked away with her neck stiff and her face upwards, away into the September crowds. Duncan had turned and walked in the direction of Piccadilly Circus. His face was burning. He had said what Dommie needed to be told.

The time before that had been six months; it must have been her birthday. There was Lucien, grumpy and refusing all the food in the restaurant Dommie had suggested, and there was Bella and the other one, Katy, Dommie's friends. He had left early.

And then the time before that had been at their mother's funeral. For some reason Dommie had got dressed up to an appalling degree, and was wearing Bianca Jagger sunglasses with an old-fashioned black dress and a black shawl of some kind. She had turned up at the crematorium, and had refused to come back to the house. Lucien was wearing sunglasses too, and what was evidently a new suit, bought for the occasion. She seemed harder, less open, guarded like a film star, smiling faintly when Duncan came over to say something to her. He had looked pointedly at Lucien, but Lucien had stayed by her side, looking out – it was hard to see, but he appeared to be gazing into the remote distance. 'And you, Duncan,' Lucien said eventually. 'You don't have a kind friend, a boyfriend, who comes with you to your mother's funeral? You don't go home on your own, I hope.'

'No,' Duncan said. 'It's quite all right.'

The time before that had been in Harrow, where their mother was dying. It must have been the last time Dommie had ever gone to the house in Harrow. She didn't stay; she said goodbye; she hardly exchanged a word with her father.

And the times before that were in Dommie's new flat in Clapham. She had loved it then; she had told Duncan that he really needed to buy something, not go on sharing a flat with those boys. Duncan had agreed for a peaceful life; then, at the end of one evening, he had told her that he was going to give up his job and go and work in Sicily. 'I don't see the point of a career that makes you so unhappy,' he said. 'And this country is finished. You might as well go to work somewhere where the sun shines.' That had been four years before he left, and every time they saw each other, he had told her that his mind was made up. It took so long to organize.

And the time before that, and the time before that ... There had never been a moment when he had sat her down and told her that he was gay, that he liked men rather than women. She knew and the whole thing was all right. And then there had been the pair of them, living in the monstrous house in Harrow, her father dismissive and hurtful and contemptuous at mealtimes. She would leave home, she said, as they sat upstairs in her bedroom, and she would come back for exactly one Christmas, for her mother's sake.

She said these things when he was there but not for his benefit. When a friend came round – was her name Tricia, the main one? – they had sat in her bedroom and talked incessantly. Duncan liked to sidle in and listen. He so admired this line of talk Dommie had. She was going to triumph in the world, and their father was going to regret it, would observe it from far off. She and Tricia, putting their faces up against the mirror, the pink-framed one in the blue bedroom, trying on eyeshadow and then lipstick, making efforts with the blusher, first placing it in a round spot on the cheeks, then learning to brush it lightly over the cheekbones to enhance the bone structure, Tricia with her ripple of spots underneath the foundation and Dommie with her lovely skin being covered up. They would bare their teeth to make sure there was no lipstick on them, not in a smile. That was a long time ago. Dommie could make herself into anything, once she got out of Harrow.

But it was not as long ago as those times before, when Dommie was his big sister, and in charge of him; ignoring him after school yet keeping an eye on him in a way he couldn't define. In the playground on the first day, standing with the cardboard-stiff new blazer cutting into his neck, clutching the regulation brown leather satchel with nothing as yet in it, he was in two worlds; in one, he was talking to, then running around with, the other boys; in the second world, invisible and unfelt by all the others, he was subjected to the gaze and concerned, intense speculation of his sister Dommie. She was in the girls' school next door to his. In the junior school, before, they had been in the same school and she had ignored him in just the same way. But he knew it didn't mean anything. He could feel her gaze on him.

And then at the same time, there was that time when their father had said to Dommie …

And then before that, there was that time when Dommie was just walking along and Father came up to her and …

And then there was that time when Dommie had come in and gone straight to her room and after a whole evening without Dommie his father had grown crosser and crosser and finally he had said to his mother and to him that she could …

And then there were all those other times around that time a long time ago when Father …

No. He would not think of that. That was not what had forged their relationship.

But how could he feel that gaze on him? How could he be so sure of the safety his sister offered, her sense that he was in every way going to do well because she was looking out for him and believed in him? There was no safe and tucked-in feeling from Daddy, and there was only a dutiful attendance from Mummy at bedtime and mealtimes. You felt with them that they were not quite sure whether they had done the right thing, and were busy. Mummy smiled with her mouth when she saw you do something for her benefit, but she did not smile with her eyes, and soon the mouth-smile went. There was that feeling of safety with Dommie, though she said, 'Go away, horrid boy,' and ignored him altogether when she was with her friends. You knew she would stand up for you. It went back to a time when she went out to school and he did not, he was so tiny. Watching Mummy make pastry with the radio on, playing with his toy cars on the kitchen floor. And then Dommie coming home and playing too. The feeling went back all the way to the moment when he had just had Mummy and Daddy and Dommie and they had always been there and he lived in the room where he lived and that was the way things were. Dommie said she could remember him being born. He was born at home, in Mummy's bed – second children often were, back in the late 1940s, to save on hospitals. And he was born when there was snow outside the little house in Harrow, the semi-detached, frowning, 1930s house with lead in the windows and Tudor gabling in the roof. His father had had to walk out to the telephone box at the corner of the road. The midwife set off at once, but still had only just arrived in time, having to walk up Harrow Hill without her bicycle. It was so easy that he just arrived, and there was a sound of a baby crying, and the midwife cleaned him off and put Mummy in a new nightie and dressing gown, and then Daddy and Dommie were allowed to come in, with Duncan only just born in Mummy's arms, in swaddling and a soft white blanket, light and open and crocheted. It was the nicest moment Dommie could ever remember, she always said afterwards, him with his squashed little face and any amount of black hair. Knowing that he was always going to be her little brother and she would always look out for him.

So that was how Dommie and Duncan came to be sitting in a sitting room in Clapham, talking about the gay bookshop that Duncan was in the process of opening up.

9.

'Thank you,' Duncan said, coming down into the shop. Behind him was a tow-haired man with a flush of pink cheek, a smooth complexion and a big smile. There was nothing upstairs except a room that had been used for storage by the previous tenants; there was no plan to make anything more of it in the near future. The man picked up his briefcase, which had been by the cherrywood counter. Andrew and Simon, who had dropped in to help out twenty minutes before, had been warned by the plumber that Duncan was in a meeting upstairs, that he had said not to disturb him. There was nowhere to have a meeting upstairs; Duncan always had his meetings downstairs. Then Duncan came down with this English country face in a suit, like the cheerful half of an A. E. Housman poem, the part before the ploughman gets sent off to be killed in the trenches. The man said goodbye buoyantly; he gave Simon and the plumber a look, before exchanging a different sort of look with Duncan, and off he went, as if about to whistle.

'You didn't,' Simon said to Duncan.

'Oh, I thought I would, just this once,' Duncan said.

The word had got out among the sales reps. It became clear to Duncan that their stock would rest on all the classics anyone could think of, a lot of single copies of academic books and the entire list of four publishing houses. There was Gay Men's Press, there was Brilliance Books, Onlywomen Press and there was the classics list of Virago. There was a list of US publishers who specialized – some of it was porn, but Duncan had come to the view that printed porn, porn in the written word, might as well be stocked. It was images that would be the problem. The mainstream publishers were sending their reps to persuade Duncan to stock all sorts of absurd things that, they said, would be of interest to gay readers, including one hopeful man who tried to talk him into stocking every children's pony novel written by the three Pullein-Thompson sisters. The shop could be stocked with second-hand classics – he himself proposed to start things off by emptying his shelves at home and asking for a pound a copy, three pounds for first editions. Christopher and Alan, both great readers, had promised to go over their bookshelves, and to keep an eye open for stuff when they went to second-hand bookshops. There were, too, the radical producers of radical magazines. But was there enough out there? Would people sacrifice their precious libraries? Duncan's line was that when you looked away from the traditional sort of publisher, there was lots of stuff out there that people just didn't know about, that they'd be so happy to be pointed towards. In reality, he just didn't know. He had a vision of the shop opening with half of its shelves empty, or filled with the traditional publishers' biographies of Gluck and Ethel Smyth. As if they knew all about Duncan's self-doubt, the traditional sort of publishers kept on sending their traditional sort of sales reps, and Duncan kept taking a book or two from them, in self-doubt and pity. These books were often about the Blooms-bury Group. They were a popular diversion, these meetings, now that friends had taken to dropping in regularly to help out.

The sales rep that Duncan had taken upstairs to shag was an unexpected turn-up for the books. He had been greeted by Duncan, and announced himself as a rep from Sachs. Duncan made him a cup of coffee.

'And we have great hopes for this,' the rep had said, opening his book of samples. 'Charming. I couldn't get through it myself. Writing at the height of her powers – we all know what that means.'

'Not for us,' Duncan said bravely, running his fingers over the embossed gold cover of the latest novel by the widow of the department-store owner; the rep, whose name was Rupert, let their hands touch as he took it away.

'You're hard to satisfy,' Rupert said, inspecting Duncan with his round blue gaze. 'Well, there's always this – no? – and this, but what I really want to recommend to you, the thing which we think you'll do very well with ...'

It was not a familiar name to Duncan, but the author photo-graph, taken in a Victorian cemetery by a mourning cherub, black-and-white and deep in shadows, showed a hollow-cheeked prodigy who seemed familiar; then he realized that it was just a familiar type. The book was called *The Garden King*, and the cover image was of a Roman torso in sunlight.

'It's his first novel,' Rupert said. 'We love Stuart, we think he's got a marvellous future. It's a brave novel, in lots of ways, but we know it'll appeal a lot to your customers. It's a very romantic love story. Between men. Italy, between the wars. Shall I leave this with you?' Rupert reached into his bag, and pulled out a proof with the title in Sachs's generic print, bound in suede-like paper in a neutral pale brown. 'You're going to love it,' he said. 'Shall I call back in a week for your numbers?'

But Duncan was surprising even himself this morning. 'No need,' he said. 'I think we'll take two hundred and fifty. Can the author come in to sign copies, perhaps do a reading?'

'Two hundred ...' Rupert was saying smoothly, writing it down, evidently hiding any gesture of shock, as if bookshops of Duncan's size ordered first novels in this quantity every day of the week '. . . and ... fifty. Well, I'm sure you'll do very well with it. It'll go on selling for years, a modern classic, you might say. I don't know about a reading – I'll have to pass that request on to the publicity department. He's very shy, I understand. But he'll definitely come in to sign some copies. I like your shirt.'

'Thank you,' Duncan said. 'It's an old favourite, really. I like your bag, if I can say so.'

Rupert reached up and fingered the soft collar of Duncan's purple-and-green striped shirt. 'It's lovely and soft,' Rupert said. 'I like that faded thing. Are you going to be running the shop with your boyfriend?'

'No, no,' Duncan said. 'No boyfriend. We might run to an assistant, in time, but ...'

'I can't believe that,' Rupert said, lowering his voice. Duncan could have laughed. And in five minutes, Rupert had raised his voice and was telling Duncan that he would like him to 'show me the premises'.

'I'm astonished,' Simon said later. 'But impressed. He was cute.'

'Yeah, he bought two hundred and fifty copies of a book off

him and all,' the plumber said. 'That was before he showed him the premises, mind. The boiler's dead, mate, you know that? You're going to need a new one.'

'He's told me that three times,' Duncan said to Simon. 'About the boiler.'

'I don't know much about these things,' Simon said. 'But two hundred and fifty copies – really? That sounds like a lot of copies of one book. Something famous? *The Joy of Gay Sex*?'

'Or radical?' Andrew said. 'There's a lot of people that want radical gay-liberation texts, of course.'

'No,' Duncan said. 'It's a first novel. But I've got a very good feeling about it. I think it's going to be huge, and I want everyone to come and buy a copy from us. They will. It'll be the making of us. And the author's promised to come in and sign them all when they arrive.'

'Two hundred and fifty, though?' Andrew said. 'Of a book nobody's heard of until now?'

'Probably won't, ever,' the plumber said cheerfully. 'I wouldn't lose any sleep over it. You can always send them back. Not like in my game.'

'To be honest,' Simon said, 'I think we need to have a word about cashflow.'

'Oh, I expect you're right,' Duncan said. 'It probably won't work. It's no way to run a business, I know.'

But now Andrew was gaping at him. 'To run a business?' he said. 'Are you running a business here now, then?'

'Sorry?' Duncan said.

'This isn't a business,' Andrew said. 'We never thought this was going to be a business. It's a community opportunity, isn't it? You're not here to make money out of the community, are you? You're here to bring the community together.'

'No one ever got rich from running a bookshop,' Duncan said. 'You don't need to worry about that.'

'But you called it a business?' Andrew said.

'Well, there are business-like aspects to it,' Duncan said. 'As well as some not very business-like ones. Don't lose any sleep over it, darling.'

10.

Andy, across the road in the sandwich shop, opened up much earlier than anyone else in Heatherwick Street. There were always people who wanted a bacon sandwich at seven. He lived off the Seven Sisters Road, and picked up Chris in the yellow Saab at six thirty. Chris lived with his English girlfriend Sammy a couple of streets away, but there was no point in telling him to be at his dad's house by six fifteen or else: you had to go round and ring on the doorbell, be his alarm clock. He'd given Chris the deposit on the white-painted brick house with the blue door and the red flowers in the window box two years ago. There weren't many twenty-five-year-olds paying the mortgage on a two-bedroom house in central London, Greek central London. Andy's granddad would have been proud of him. Well, no, probably not: he'd have said what his dad always said, which was 'You could have done better.'

They were arriving at the shop at ten to seven, as usual. It was a beautiful day, the sun shining almost horizontally into the car. Andy had put on a cassette and was singing along; Chris had yawned and rubbed his eyes and complained – he'd lost the taste for Greek music. Over the road, that bookshop was nearing its opening time. The inside was painted and finished; there were boxes all over the floor, which Andy supposed were boxes of books, stock, property. The window was decorated – they'd put in some fake grass for some reason, which was odd. You didn't think of grass and books together; it looked more like an old-fashioned butcher's shop with mince packs sitting on plastic grass. That was a sign that they didn't know what they were doing, like the health-food shop before them that had painted a sunflower on the window. And there was the shop sign, finished and brazen. In Roman letters on dark blue, it read 'The Big Gay Bookshop'. It got worse: there was a painting of a kind of naked bloke on the left, reading a book, and another one on the right, reading another. Andy knew he should have said something about the naked blokes to the one who ran the place and came over looking very pleased with himself every day to get a sandwich for lunch, or a round of sandwiches. But he hadn't. It was too late now. Already, someone had passed a remark to him about it – 'Oh, I see you're facing the Big Gay Bookshop, it's your shop that's in Heatherwick Street, isn't it?' And that was someone who hadn't even come into the shop, had just seen it while driving through. The customers who came into the shop had had a lot to say about it.

Andy and Chris parked the car round the corner, and walked to the shop. In the tree in the street, a blackbird was singing, as loud as it could. There was a bundle in the doorway of the bookshop, a bundle of blankets with an outcrop of hair at one end, when they went over to investigate. Heatherwick Street was not usually their hang-out.

'Oi,' Andy said, nudging the bundle with the toe of his shoe. 'Oi. Oi. You can't sleep here. What's your game? What are you doing here?'

'I'm waiting,' a voice came from the blankets. 'I'm waiting for shop to open.' Then he put his head outside the blankets. He was a teenager, very white in the face, with a home-made dye job; his newly black hair, too evenly coloured to be natural, was spiked, with both sleep and gel. Around his chin and neck were fat red spots, and under his head was a knapsack. He looked from Andy to Chris and then back again. 'It's not you who run shop, is it?'

'Us? No, mate, not us,' Andy said. 'Don't be a berk. No, they'll be along in another couple of hours. We're just the sandwich over the road.'

'You don't want to sleep in this doorway, mate,' Chris said, yawning and rubbing his eyes with his fists. 'You don't want that. You don't know how they'll wake you up when they get here. Didn't you see the name of the shop, son?'

Andy looked at the boy. He had been a runaway, too, he reckoned. Well, he'd had to run away from Cyprus, like all the rest of the Greeks. Sometimes people ended up sleeping where they didn't want to sleep because of circumstances beyond their control. His mum and dad had left their house in such a hurry that they hadn't had time to clear up the table from lunch. It was a source of shame to his mother that they had left like that, and ever since, she had sometimes said that those Turks, they would be able to come in and see the lamb dish festooned with mould and maggots and flies and making the whole place stink, and be able to say that those Greeks, by God, they were dirty people. So Andy knew that sometimes you had to leave the place where you'd lived for years, that sometimes people would treat you with not much respect because of the way you'd had to go or the way you'd had to leave things. There was a lamb dish abandoned, somewhere, by this boy; not a real lamb dish, but something he'd had to leave that would make people talk about him in a bad way when he was gone.

So because of all that, Andy turned to Chris and said, 'Shut your mouth,' before telling the boy that he could come over to the shop and they'd give him a bacon sandwich and a cup of tea.

'Are we going to give him a sandwich?' Chris said.

'Yes, Chris,' Andy said, with a warning look. 'We're going to give him a sandwich.'

11.

The phone had rung at seven – the earliest possible time anyone could ring anyone else, even a brother to a sister. A catastrophe had happened, had struck both shop and flat simultaneously. 'I don't know what I'm going to do,' Duncan had said to Dommie.

She calmed him down, and it turned out that the boiler in the flat and the boiler in the shop had broken down simultaneously. He had been warned. He was going to replace the one in the shop, but the one in the flat had seemed to be working perfectly well. It was all my eye about it needing to go altogether, just another way of making some money out of a customer, Duncan had thought at the time. Then the water had had to be switched off for a couple of days while the bathroom had been fitted, and when they had switched it back on, water was just pouring out of the boiler. God knew how. They'd told Duncan, he said, they told me that a washer was perished and only holding together because normally it was damp and flexible and then they turned it off and it dried out and then it broke and when someone switched it back on again …

Dommie could not quite follow everything, but it seemed as if he needed to stay at home while the boiler was being fixed, and someone else needed to be in the shop to let the workmen in to install the new boiler there.

'When is he coming, the boiler man? I can come over so long as I leave by twelve,' she said.

'Oh, Dommie, that is kind of you,' said Duncan. 'I don't know what I'd do without you.'

So Dommie decided to call in sick, saying she had a headache and sometimes these things cleared up by lunchtime but sometimes they didn't. She had a key to the shop for exactly these emergencies, though she had not been inside it on her own. She had been three times, every time when Duncan was there. She came in: she sat while Duncan's friends did some handiwork, talking amusingly all the while. Sometimes they knew who she was, but sometimes they overlooked her. The professional handymen were more interested once they knew she was Duncan's sister. The sign painter, who of course knew what the shop was to be called and what sort of customers they were going to have, found it extraordinary that Duncan was in touch with his family, even. There was an awful man called Freddie Sempill, who talked in a false and unconvincing way to her, which she could not understand; then she realized that he was putting on a performance for the benefit of the electrician. There was Christopher, who was a stiff old thing, old beyond his years, talking carefully in sentences and holding himself rigidly upright. There was Paul, who she'd met before, who was, he said, Duncan's best friend; she quite liked him once she realized that his performance was the most sincere of all of them. It was interesting to sit and watch a business taking shape in such a physical way. But all the time she had longed to be alone in the shop, to take charge.

She was at the shop by eight thirty, with a sense of joy at putting things right. She did not turn on the lights. She liked the dim mercantile shadow; the clean smell of shaved wood and new paint, the kitchenette with its cupboards and sink still in part wrapped in coloured cellophane. The sound of birdsong filled the shadowy interior. The troublesome boiler was in the middle of all that kitchen newness and, looking at it, Dommie wondered why Duncan hadn't decided to have a new one from the start. The floor was filled with boxes of stock; there would be a stockroom upstairs in time, but this stock would fill the shelves, and her brother's stock boxes stood filled with promise.

She had always wanted to play shops when she was little, and she had always wanted to have her own shop when she was older. Perhaps a dress shop for glamorous older women, but her thoughts hadn't really got that far. She saw herself placing a book in a paper bag, saying, 'I do hope you enjoy it,' to the customer, a distinguished silvery fellow a touch too perfectly dressed; taking his money; putting it in the till; and saying, 'Goodbye, then,' and listening to the shop-door bell ring. It would be simply perfect.

There was a shape at the window, peering in. It was not the boiler man, but the sandwich man from across the street. With him was someone unfamiliar, a teenage boy with a sullen, inexpressive face and a rucksack. Dommie turned on the lights as if she had been about to do that all the time and, smiling, opened the door.

'This young man wants a word,' the sandwich man said. 'This lady can help you. Now off you go. And remember, your parents are the most important people in your life, and they're not going to be there for ever.'

The sandwich man turned round and crossed the road. The boy, outside the shop, looked at Dommie, and Dommie, inside the shop, looked at him.

'I thought you were gay men,' the boy said. He had a northern accent. 'I thought you'd all be gay men. Are you a lesbian?'

'Indeed no,' Dommie said. 'It's my brother's shop. I'm just here this morning to let the man in to mend the boiler. You wanted a word, did he say?'

'I'm Arthur,' the boy said. He reflected, looked about with his long neck and jutting chin and nose; he looked Dommie up and down, and then about him at the street. 'You've not got anything in your window yet.'

'I don't think he's quite got round to it,' Dommie said. 'That probably comes last. There are still a few things to get right.'

'I've run away from home,' the boy said. 'Can I come in?'

'Well, I don't see why not,' Dommie said. 'No, you don't need to take your shoes off. This is only a shop. But the ruck-sack by the door, please.'

12.

When Duncan turned up at the shop at half past eleven, he was in a much better mood. The boiler man had looked, and said that the old boiler in the flat didn't need replacing: if he put together half a dozen parts, it would be good for a couple of years yet. That was a relief. Duncan had left him to it. Now for the boiler in the shop.

He arrived, and inside the shop, there were Dommie and Paul

and, at the back of the shop working, another boiler man. With them was a boy Duncan didn't know. They were sitting on chairs around the table, which had arrived yesterday, the table for group discussions: large, polished and round, it would hold twelve, fifteen at a pinch.

'This is Arthur,' Dommie said. 'He's come about a job.'

'A job?' Duncan said, pulling up a chair and sitting down. 'A job in the bookshop?'

'I told you,' Paul said to the boy. 'I told you he's not taking on help.'

'You've got to take me on,' Arthur said. 'You've just got to.'

'How did you hear about the shop?' Duncan said. 'We aren't opening for another week or ten days.'

'If it's ten days,' Paul said, 'we won't be open before the party.'

'It was yesterday,' Arthur said. 'I was in newsagent near the City Hall where I buy my *Gay News*. I'm from Sheffield, this is in Sheffield. It's the only newsagent I know of in town that sells *Gay News*, it's the fourth time I've bought it. And I was reading it on bus home. I don't buy it and then hide it in a newspaper, I read it on bus, I don't care, me. And there was this article about you. You've seen article?'

'No, what article?' Duncan said. 'I knew she was going to write something, but I haven't seen it. She was supposed to send me a copy when the magazine came out. When did it come out?'

'It's only just out,' Arthur said. 'It's supposed to be out on the fourth of month, but I start looking for it on third – it sometimes comes a day early. Don't you get it early in London? It's published here, we're always miles behind in Sheffield. Look, it's here – I was showing your sister and your friend.'

Arthur reached into his pocket, and handed over the magazine. On the cover an interview was flagged up with a Broadway legend, who perhaps did not know what she was letting herself in for, and features about types of lesbian, amyl nitrate, 'Is Earls Court's Day Over?' and 'Does London Really Need a Gay

Bookshop?' The magazine, much-handled, was folded down the middle, its ink smeared by Arthur's hot hands.

'Cheeky cow,' Duncan said. 'Why write about it if you don't think London needs one?'

'It's better than it sounds,' Arthur said. 'I read it and I wanted to come to London to find you straight away.'

'I want to read this,' Duncan said, turning the pages – there were adverts for bum-douches under the slogan 'For That Big Night Out', and for bed-and-breakfasts in Blackpool, and a fashion spread, which seemed to have been shot against a backdrop of foil by a photographer's stand-in. The types-of-lesbian article was illustrated with cartoons of 'Gay Woman', 'Lesbian', 'Butch', 'Dyke' and 'Gay Lady', this last one sitting on a bar stool wearing a fedora. Over the page was Duncan. The photograph was simply terrible, in dim light and with Duncan standing bolt upright, looking startled. He was sure he had managed to smile at one point, at least, during the session. The headline was 'Read All About It! We investigate the opening of London's first gay bookshop and talk to its manager Duncan.'

'"There's nothing better than curling up with a good book,"' Duncan read out loud. 'Oh my God. "Unless you count curling up with a good bookshop owner. When GAY NEWS heard that Duncan Flannery, thirty-three, was planning to open a gay book-shop in London's King's Cross –"'

'We're not in King's Cross here,' Dommie said. 'This is prac-tically what I would call Marylebone.'

'"– London's King's Cross,"' Duncan went on, '"we thought, What a good idea! So we minced on down to Canning Street in the West End, to ask its manager and owner Duncan Flannery what plans he has for this shop. "I've always loved reading," Duncan said, "and men. So I thought I would put my two passions together."' She said that. She said to me when I said, "I love reading," she said, "And men, too," and I thought that was embarrassing, but I sort of agreed. I never said that.'

'Oh, go on,' Paul said. 'We don't care if it's *accurate*, just if it's *sensational*. Shame she got the street wrong, even.'

'No, she got it right later on – "Heatherwick Street seems not quite sure yet about its new addition," blah blah. I'm not going to go on,' Duncan said. 'I'll curl up with it later. Like a good book. Oh, God.'

'So I saw this article,' Arthur said, in a faintly aggrieved tone. 'It was on bus back home. And I thought immediately, I love men, I love books, I can't get enough of them. I've taken *Maurice* out of the central library about ten times almost. That's a fantastic book. I love it when Scudder says to Maurice, when he says, well, when he says anything, really. They should make a film out of that, it would be magic. And I hate it at school, I really hate it. When did you know you were gay? I knew when I was *nine*, the first time I heard of it, I knew that was me all right. But them – they've all known I was gay since I was fifteen, and this boy came over one Saturday, we got drunk on gin and vodka and the boy said he had to stay the night because his mum couldn't see him like that, and we slept in my mum and dad's bed, they were away, and I said I thought everyone was really bisexual—'

'Heavens above, are they still using that old chestnut?' Paul said. 'Everyone's really bisexual? It *doesn't work*, child. It's never worked. If they're going to have sex with you, they'll have sex with you. There's no point in bringing in the mirror stage and the Wolf Man and Uncle Sigmund's ideas. It won't work.'

'How do you know about the Wolf Man?' Dommie said. 'You're full of surprises.'

'I wasn't landed the last time the wind blew from the east, darling,' Paul said. 'I am an *educated* queen, if you please.'

'It didn't work, you're right,' Arthur said. 'He looked at me as if I was just talking rubbish, which I was. But he kissed me and he felt my cock and I felt his cock, and we were both really hard. But then on Monday it turned out that he'd told everyone and that I'd told him I was gay and then had tried to force myself on him and he'd had to go home. Which wasn't true, he'd stayed and had breakfast and everything, he asked if I'd cook him bacon, but we didn't have bacon in. I thought that was a bit cheeky. But I didn't know where to run away to, until I read this article about your bookshop. And then I knew. It's going to change world, your bookshop.'

'Oh, yes,' Duncan said, looking up from the article. 'No trouble.' The tone of irony in his voice could not be shed.

'I love, love, love, books,' the boy said. 'Please let me stay. I won't be any trouble. I'd cook you bacon, any day.'

'"We asked Duncan what he would save from his stock, if his shop caught on fire. What are the five books he couldn't live without?"' Duncan read out loud. 'This is really the most boring interview. I can't imagine anyone coming to the bookshop after reading this.'

'I came,' Arthur said simply. 'I went to wrong street and then right one. And you aren't even open yet. If I came all the way from Sheffield, there are loads of people who are going to come from all over England – all over world, probably. I read your five favourite books. I think they're amazing. You've got to give me a job.'

'Oh, God. You're going straight back to Sheffield,' Duncan said. 'I haven't got any money to pay anyone with, and I don't know that I ever will. Don't start going on about bacon. It's not going to work on me. I can't employ every runaway.'

'Oh, I don't want paying,' Arthur said. 'I'd work here for nothing, if you could just find somewhere I could live for nothing. I could live in stockroom, even. If there were just a bed in there. I would wash in little kitchen and make myself things to eat. I'd manage somehow. I can't go back to Sheffield. You see, I went back home with my copy of *Gay News*, and my stepfather, Donald, who's married to my mother, he said he was sick of me making a spectacle of myself. And I said it weren't me who were making people stare. And he goes, well, who the hell is it then? And I go if they don't want to stare they shouldn't

203

stare. That's their decision and I'm only carrying a magazine, they don't have to read magazine theirselves. Then he goes it's not just the magazine, it's your clothes and way you walk and way you talk, and he goes say "decision" again. And I say "decision", and he says no, "decision", and I say yes, "decision", and he's about to hit me.'

'What?' said Paul. 'I can't understand *what* you're saying. It all sounds *terribly thrilling*, but why did your stepfather make you say "decision"?'

'Because of my lisp, I've got a bit of a lisp, my stepfather's always on about it, I can't say "decision" and it drives him up wall. So he's saying say "decision" and I'm trying to say "decision", and my mum's coming out of kitchen and she says no, Don, don't do it, it's just a phase he's going through. And he stops and he looks at his hand, and then a right mean look comes over his face and he belts me one, with the back of his hand, across my face.'

He was telling it as an exciting story, his cheeks flushed and his voice fast. But now he saw Paul's face, and Duncan's, and Dommie's, and he slowed down.

'So I went upstairs and threw some things into a knapsack. And then I came down with it, and I went straight back down to town. By now it's nearly nine o'clock. I know where Donald keeps his money, and I'd taken all of it, three hundred and fifty pounds, it's illegal cash payments, he's a builder, so I'm not worried about being pursued by police. I buy myself a ticket to London, and I say to myself, I don't care, I'm going to that bookshop and they're going to give me a job. And I catch last train to London, and I get here about half past midnight. I don't know why I thought you'd be here. I came here anyway and I slept in doorway, it wasn't so cold last night. Then that man over road came and gave me a cup of coffee and a bacon sandwich. Then he brought me over and she were here –' nodding at Dommie '– so I told her the story, then he came –' nodding at Paul '– so I told the story again, and now you're here and it's the third time she's heard the story and the second time him.'

Duncan waited for a pause. It seemed to have come. Dommie got up and went to the back kitchen. There, she filled the new kettle from the new tap. Duncan watched her. There were five mugs back there; for the moment, they matched, but in five years' time they would have been smashed, and replaced, and would be a jumble, a mismatch, witnesses to passing moments. For now they were five in different pastel shades, all the same size. There was a new jar of Nescafé, which Dommie was unscrewing, then puncturing with one of the new teaspoons. There was a delicious smell, the first thing out of a new jar of instant coffee, though perhaps in time they would stretch to a percolator and proper coffee. Dommie was measuring out the coffee into the mugs; she was asking the boiler man if he wanted one; she was opening the bookshop's new fridge and taking out the single object inside it, a pint of milk, which the milkman must have brought that morning for the first time. There was even a little bowl of sugar in the kitchen cupboards for Dommie's sake, and anyone else who still took sugar in their coffee. One day – perhaps soon – there would be biscuits, two sorts of biscuits, and customers reading, absorbed. Dommie handed the green mug to the boiler man; she placed the other four on the ceramic tray with a view of the Taj Mahal; she brought them and gave them to her brother, to Paul, to Arthur, to herself, the pink, the white, the blue, the purple. Duncan contemplated his business decision. There was no doubt that Arthur would cost money. He had worked out that he could get to London and live rent-free, but what was he going to eat? How was he going to use the launderette? What would he wash with and eat off and sleep on? It was all a very bad idea. He was the one new human in the shop.

'You've got no experience,' Duncan said.

'I'm very experienced!' Arthur said.

'In retail,' Duncan clarified.

'He's not asking you how many men you've had sex with,' Paul said. 'That's not a useful qualification for working in a bookshop.'

'Oh. No. I haven't, really.'

'And you've never stuck at anything.'

'Well, I would stick at this!'

'And your parents don't trust you.'

'No, but they're evil, they're horrible, you wouldn't want to take their word on anything, you wouldn't.'

'All right,' Duncan said. 'You can stay. I'll get some kind of bed for the stockroom upstairs. I'll pay you twenty-five pounds a week.'

'Mind,' Paul chipped in, glaring at Duncan, 'there's to be no hanky-panky upstairs, no mucking around. No boys. You meet a boy, you go to his place. You're not letting people in to steal the stock.'

'Never, never, never,' Arthur said. 'Now I never need to see my mum and stepfather ever again. You don't know what this means.'

The boiler man sauntered over. 'It's got to go,' he said, and pushed his pencil back behind his ear in a solitary, assured, assessing manner. 'There's no two ways about it. You can't carry on with that boiler. It's illegal for one thing.' Then he took a look at Arthur, whose eyes were moist with tears. 'You lot,' he said. 'You lot. It's always drama with you lot, isn't it? Can't you just get from one end of a day to the other without the water-works and the kissing and making up? What's wrong with him?'

'Tell us about the boiler,' Duncan said, standing up.

13.

Two days later, it was the day of the party. The stock was on the shelves, shining and new and glossy as racehorses; there was a nice little corner with books that had been much loved and read repeatedly, priced up by Dommie in a more or less random way. The two hundred and fifty copies of the new novel, it turned out, would fill an entire bookcase, which wasn't reasonable. The author had come in yesterday, announcing himself in a diffident way. He'd had a dreadful cough, and was painfully thin in the face. He spoke in an undertone, saying that it was exciting, he supposed, to have a book out, but he just felt so tired all the time, 'like an old man, and I'm only thirty'. He signed slowly, scrupulously, taking nearly two and a half hours to get through the two hundred and fifty books – he had to have three breaks in between. Arthur had turned the pages and held the book open as he signed. It was his first task in the bookshop, and he did it with nervous care.

'We love your book,' Duncan said, as he was going, quite truthfully. 'I hope you're writing something new.'

'There won't be another one,' the author said. 'I don't think there'll be another one.'

'I hope that's not true,' Duncan said, smiling. 'And will you come to our party, tomorrow night?'

'I'll do my best,' the author said, holding on to the door. Then he glanced at Duncan with dark, shadowed eyes. He looked very ill. Duncan wondered what was wrong with him. His eyes dropped, and he went like a wraith in a black PVC raincoat.

The invitations had gone out to the whole of the street, as well as to everyone else. The leader of the GLC had replied, and Angus Wilson, and Derek Jarman, and Maureen Duffy, and John Schlesinger, and Maggi Hambling, and half a dozen actors, asking if they could bring friends. But the fishmonger had not replied, or the hardware shop – didn't expect him to – or the suitcase man, the greengrocer, the bookmaker, the newsagent or the butcher. Some of those, Duncan thought, would probably come round when they realized what sort of business the Big Gay Bookshop was – just an ordinary bookshop, no trouble to anyone. He felt that when the wife of the suitcase man, Mrs Dasgupta, had sidled out behind her husband and looked in a frightened but not hostile way at Duncan, the one time he had dropped in and told them about the shop he was on the verge of opening and he hoped they would come to the party to open it, he had felt that she was in her own way a little bit interested. Those Indian women were often steely; they made a pretence of being downtrodden and not speaking up before their men, but they ran the show when they thought no one outside the family was looking. It took only one person to change their mind, one person at a time. It had to be done like that, in fact.

But he was disappointed that Andy, the Greek sandwich man, hadn't responded, or his son, though Duncan had been careful to specify both wife and girlfriend on the invitation. Duncan had religiously gone every morning to get the coffees – the day Arthur had turned up was the first day they had moved to instant coffee from their own kitchen – and every lunchtime to get sandwiches for him and whoever had turned up to help, Paul or Andrew or Freddie Sempill that one time. They'd been good customers of Andy over the last two months, and Andy had seemed quite cheerful to see them, not hostile like the hardware man or the underage lunchtime drinkers at the corner pub. (Arthur had reported, in recent days, that the abuse from the drinkers in that pub grew worse in the evenings.)

'Maybe he'll come,' Duncan said to Dommie. 'It would be too bad if nobody from Heatherwick Street came, not one person.'

'Well, you could ask him,' Dommie said. 'Why don't you ask him directly? You could phrase it as a reminder.'

It was a hard thing to ask. Duncan put it off and put it off. And then it was the day of the party, and everything was complete. The shop was painted; the shelves were filled; the carpet was down; Thomas, the florist four streets away, and perhaps the nearest sympathetic neighbour, had donated four big bouquets and loaned some vases; there was a record player on the cherrywood table, and Nat had promised to put a ball-gown on and play Dusty Springfield all night; the white wine was in the fridge or in the bathtub; Arthur had been talked into a white shirt and black trousers, and to walk round filling glasses. The stuffed pheasant and the chandelier looked eccentric but not insane. Duncan had actually come to be rather attached to the pheasant, though not to the point of giving it a name. The bookshop smelt so good, with books, and paint, and flowers, and a big round of Brie and salami and baguettes. Duncan had fretted over what to wear, and in the end had bought a bold red shirt and some drainpipes, and had decided to give himself a rockabilly look with gel and a quiff. He had achieved it all. The only two things left to do were to sell perhaps one book, to one paying customer, and to be bold, say to Andy that he was really looking forward to seeing him and his wife, and Chris and his girlfriend, later that evening.

At twelve thirty, he went over, a little earlier than usual.

'Looking good, Mr Duncan,' Reggie, the black junior sandwich-maker, said.

'Thanks, Reggie,' Duncan said. 'It's finally there, I reckon. Big opening tonight.'

'What can I do for you?' Andy said, rubbing his big knife clean with a dishcloth. 'Same as usual for you? And is your sister ready for her lunch?'

'Same as usual for me,' Duncan said. 'Roast beef and tomatoes on granary and extra mayonnaise. My sister's not in today – she's had to go to work herself. She's been taking too much time off, I told her to go in and just come this evening, to the party. That reminds me – I do hope ...'

'What can I get you?' Andy said, turning his attention to the customer behind Duncan, a black workman from the council in navy boilersuit and fudgy, concrete-encrusted boots. 'Coronation chicken, is it, Dave, my son?'

The order was taken; Duncan still stood there, foolishly.

'I do hope,' he said, in a moment, 'I do hope that you and your wife are going to be able to drop in to help christen the shop. At the party tonight.'

Andy made the gesture that people make, not when they have forgotten and remembered something, but when they want to make it clear that they have forgotten and now been reminded of something. He struck his forehead with the palm of his fat, heavy hand; he shook his head, he rolled his eyes, he let out a sound resembling 'K-chuh'; he turned back to Duncan. 'Not tonight, is it?' he said. 'Not tonight? My wife'll kill me. She's only gone and asked her sister to come over with her kids to dinner. Tonight, Mr Duncan – I'm very sorry, but there's been a terrible mix-up.'

'Oh, that's all right,' Duncan said limply.

'Now, it was a roast beef on granary, tomatoes, extra mayonnaise,' he said. 'Let me go back and see to that myself.'

Andy went into the little back kitchen; there was nobody there but Chris, slicing and cutting. The workman waited patiently. Reggie, behind the counter, made a faint smile and nodded, as if singing along to some imaginary music – one of those Viennese waltzes Chris always had on in the shop. He moved to one side, and started rearranging the bottles of ketchup and mustard for something to do. There had been something amused and supercilious about Andy's response. For some reason, it made Duncan want to look into the kitchen. He walked about the shop in a casual way, inspecting the drinks and the cans and the posters of Greece and Switzerland, and ended up in an unplanned way where you could see right into the kitchen. At that moment, in the back room, Andy was holding up the top slice of granary bread; his son Chris was bending over, silently spitting onto the beef and tomato and mayonnaise. They shuddered with silent laughter. Duncan moved back, quickly, behind the counter, not showing to Reggie that he had seen anything, just smiling and nodding. It was not the first time that they had done this. That was obviously the case. And in a moment Andy came out with the sandwich, wrapped in grease-proof paper, placed it in a bag, twirled the bag about to close it. 'That'll be sixty pence, Mr Duncan,' he said. 'I'm sure your party will be a great success. Me and the wife – we're not great party people. Not your sort of party people. You wouldn't miss us.'

'That's quite all right,' Duncan said wretchedly. He handed over a pound note. He took the sandwich, feeling that everyone – Andy, Chris, even Reggie, even the workman called Dave – was watching him go with silent suppression of laughter, their shoulders going like Edward Heath, and the whole street, and the whole of London, all laughing hatefully and wanting them all to fail, and die, and eat a lot of sputum without knowing it, and pay the full whack. He opened the door of his shop. By the side of the cherrywood desk there was a bin, and Duncan dropped the sandwich into it. Tomorrow he would bring his own lunch from home. He had known all this was going to happen. He had been prepared. It was ready to begin. In his wallet, he remembered, he had written down the number of a neighbourhood glazier, for the first time the shop window would be smashed with a thrown brick. He must remember to give the number to Arthur.

BOOK 5
1922
(and a little before)

1.

The gardener's boy was already hard at work, weeding the English flowerbeds, when Christian Vogt left the house, that first morning. He was tugging, twisting, laying aside in a wicker basket; he was kneeling on a small wooden footstool. From his perspiration, he must have been at work in the front part of the garden for some time. Christian nodded to him and, in his carefully chosen limp crêpe suit, with its pattern of dogstooth, turned right into the lane. It was five to nine in the morning. He had learnt that the Bauhaus, unlike schools, did not start until mid-morning, and even on the first day of registration, there was no need to be there before half past nine. Unlike a school, too, when he approached the Bauhaus, the noise of conversation from the waiting students was mellifluous, continuous, like a crowded room of intelligent people. The street wound about, opening into a half-square with a lime tree at its centre; a window was opened, and a bolster case flapped three or four times in the clean air; the sound of people talking grew stronger, and then, with a turn and a lump in his throat, there he was. Behind the lawn and the line of trees, the Bauhaus rose with its huge windows, its sliding pitched roof. The fifty or so people were sitting or standing at the double door to the building, smoking and, one or two, eating. Their clothes were smart and undecided; some had done the same as Christian, and put on a fashionable suit; others were wearing what looked like country farmers' clothes, with thick boots and heavy trousers. The women had short and square haircuts, and many were wearing trousers with weighty, probably self-knitted, sweaters. Perhaps Christian hesitated somewhat; a woman glanced over and saw him pause. She had a basket at her feet; her head craned out, searching for something in the crowd. She looked away again.

Afterwards, he could only know that this moment had happened. He had no memory of first seeing Adele Winteregger, or of beginning a conversation with her. How could he begin a conversation with someone his life had always been waiting for? They were in mid-conversation before his convulsive senses registered and recorded the moment.

'Are you beginning this year?'

'No,' the girl said. 'I am not a student here. I am only here to visit my sister.'

'Where do you come from?'

There was a pause. From a thousand miles away, Christian heard voices exchanging remarks, the squeal of a tram some-where near by, the melody of a violin from the upper floors of a house.

'My name is Adele Winteregger. But why do you ask these questions?' the girl said. When she spoke it was as if a consoling hiss of silence fell around her, as if a seashell had been placed to his ear.

'I want to know everything about you.'

He looked at her. It was with a shock and a delight. Her face was smooth and neat, a little button nose, trim eyebrows and neatly pulled-back hair. Something extraordinary about her eyes, only; a tiny-pupilled deep blue, a kind of blankness in the expression. When he looked at her, it was like the moment before the shutters in a room opposite were drawn. Years ago, when he was young and did not even understand, the newly married couple in the apartment facing theirs across the street came home; they were in their bedroom; behind them was an oil lamp that lit up their shapes and their bold embrace as a coat, a dress was undone, and, without the embrace being interrupted, placed by the side of them. A wolf whistle from the street, years ago; a sudden start, a jumping apart, and the man came to the window and closed the shutters. Here, too, the thrill he felt in his neck, his arms, that too foreshadowed a closing of the shutters. No point was to be served by delay or dissemblance, and he said what he had to say, not knowing what he was going to say before he said it.

'One day I am going to paint you.'

'My father said that the art students would be like this. But my sister has to come here, to be qualified. She is so good at art! After this, I think she is going to become a teacher of art, in a school. That would make my father so happy. What is your name?'

'My name is Christian Vogt.'

Around them, the people were moving slowly into the Bauhaus; the clock had chimed the half-hour, and the doors had been found to be open the whole time.

'I must go,' Adele Winteregger said. 'I came to make sure my sister arrived safely and on time, and now I must go to buy some food for our dinner.'

'But how long are you here for? What are you doing here? Not just cooking your sister's dinner?'

'Our father asked me to come and make sure that Elsa was quite settled in, and then travel back home again, as cheaply as possible. I do not know. I have a job as a dressmaker and seamstress. I make sure that the work of the others is good enough. I am lucky to have the job, and would not like to lose it through being away. They are so kind! They offered me three weeks' holiday, unpaid, in order to settle my sister in. And my sister is here for her second year. She does not truly need me.'

'One day I am going to paint you,' Christian said. The girl looked at him; she wrinkled her nose, she turned away slightly.

'Here is my sister,' she said. Christian heard, as if for the first time, her saying that she had come to make sure Elsa was quite settled in. He saw the girl from Saturday, her shaved head, her waving manner. She came directly up to them, and dropped her broad canvas portfolio at his feet.

'You!' she said. 'Are you talking to my sister? She went on ahead, I don't know why. She wanted to be at the Bauhaus door before me, to make sure that I was coming. Why shouldn't I come? What are you doing here? I don't need you, and this boy doesn't want to meet you.'

'I only made sure that you were here, that you were going to your class on time,' Adele Winteregger said. 'And now I've seen you in, and I can go and do what needs to be done.'

'Yes, go away, go away, we are quite all right now,' Elsa said.

Adele Winteregger picked up her basket and, with a neat, satisfied walk, walked away from them. Just at the point where the path between trees turned into the road, she turned, and gave a smile in their direction. She was used to being spoken to like that by her sister, it was clear. And some of that smile might have been intended for Christian. He watched her go, her little shape passing between trees, and across the road where a blind soldier in a bath chair waited, an oil can on the floor in front of him, waiting for contributions. Adele Winteregger reached into her basket and dropped a folded-up banknote into the man's receptacle.

'That is your sister,' Christian said, to make sure.

'Your first day at the Bauhaus!' Elsa said. 'You must be terrified. I was terrified. Everyone I know in my year was terrified. I'm still terrified.'

'That is your sister,' Christian said. 'I would like to meet her again.'

'You could go to Breitenberg,' Elsa said. 'That is where she comes from, where we come from. She is going back there, very soon. Martin!' she said, calling out to a man with a shaved head and a hunting jacket on. 'Martin! Martin!'

'But where is Breitenberg?' Christian said, now speaking alone, to himself.

2.

In the north of Bavaria, where a town called Breitenberg sits perched, black-and-white, stone, plaster and wood, over a gushing river, there lived a puppet-maker and his two daughters, one lovely, one clever.

The town had known patches of prosperity, and these had left their mark in the shape of energetic building. Half a millennium ago, the merchants of the city had knocked down everything they could, and replaced it all with broad, winding streets and handsome, tall-faced buildings of black wood and plaster, black-and-white and top-heavy. Some time later, another burst of prosperity had led the town to put up grand stone palaces, heavy and laden with cornucopia and fruit flourishes in the local yellowish stone. One of these spanned the river, with a strange back-house of wood and plaster, like a compromise between old and new; another formed a tall gate-house, and a third was a three-spired cathedral whose roots and cellars, beneath the extravagance, were said to date back to the three-digit centuries. Since then, not much had been built. The town remained as it had been. From time to time, a visitor appeared to admire or register its backwater charm. Once, recently, a photographer from Berlin had arrived, and had set up his equipment in the street, promising to document the whole of this interesting and picturesque town. It had once been considered as the capital of the Holy Roman Empire, before being passed over; it had been considered for a railway in the 1840s, before being passed over in favour of Bamberg; it had been considered again in the 1870s, before being passed over; and finally had been connected to the rest of the world in the 1880s, the largest German town at that date not to possess a railway station. The town's accent was considered amusing (by Bavarians), baffling (by most Germans) and interesting by philologists, who noted some archaic vowel structures and some unique habits of elision. Breitenberg had its own beer and its own cake; the Breitenbergerkuche was a friable confection of up to ten thin meringue circles held together with whipped cream and raspberries. It was made by three patissiers in the town, who said that they guarded the recipe closely, although it was a recipe that a child of ten could have worked out. The Breitenberg beer was a more specialized taste, which demanded the smoking of the hops at the earliest stage of the brewing process; some people described the beer that resulted as 'ham-like' or, sometimes, reminiscent of a liquid cigar. It was famous throughout Germany, a thousand years old, and not much liked even by the hardened drinkers of Breitenberg. The brewery, which emitted a strong smell of tarry sweetness several days a month, was owned by the dukes of Breitenberg, as it always had been, and was situated two miles away, in a forest-lined valley, by the side of the river running down from the mountains that circled the town. Only when the wind came from the south-west did the brewery's smell bother the town.

As well as the beer and the cake, Breitenberg was known for a puppet maker called Winteregger. His father had made puppets, and his father's father, and his father's father's father. The puppets were beautifully made, hanging from strings, and were taken about the country by Franz Winteregger himself. Winteregger went to Christmas fairs throughout the German-speaking world, and was known even to historians of folk art and to the great makers of toys. His puppets were sold in the best toyshops in Berlin, Prague, Cologne and Vienna, and hung in the best nurseries in Budapest, Sarajevo, Trieste and Lübeck. Winteregger's puppets were uncanny, both in stillness, on a hook, and in movement, in the little marionette theatre his father had built at the back of the family house. In stillness, their faces were expressive and human, often persuading buyers that they depicted someone that they knew – someone whose features were just out of memory's reach. In movement, they were transformed. Winteregger often made four or five separate heads with different expressions for his performing marionettes, so that the sad-faced puppet of the first act would be able to marry the heroine in the last with a face of joy. It was their movement, however, that transfigured them. A simple arc of the puppeteer's arm, a straight line, uncannily transformed itself into the fluid sweep of the puppet's body. The awkward and conscious gesture of the puppeteer's arm, re-enacted by inanimate matter, became a lovely arabesque of grace and flirtation. The puppet knew things that the puppeteer could never grasp. That was the statement Franz Winteregger lived by: you can never know what you put in motion. They had no need of the ground; they grazed it only lightly, for appearance's sake. At the end of the string, they had shed the self-consciousness that prevented the puppeteers, at the other end, from moving as if in a dance. Winteregger's studio worked as it had in his father's day, and his grandfather's, and his grandfather's father. He had four craftsmen working there, one of whom was his nephew – his sister's boy Joseph. In the puppet theatre, there were two puppeteers, a married couple called Schwind. Joseph would inherit the business. Franz Winteregger had only two daughters, one clever, one beautiful, and since his wife had died in 1905, he would have no more children, unless he remarried, as Breitenberg hoped he would.

The daughters were a spectacle in Breitenberg. The elder, by two years, was clever but awkward. Her voice shrieked; her movements were jerky and undecided; her hair flew out from under her hat; her clothes were curious and assorted incoherently. She showed the lack of a mother who would have told her to lower her voice and not say such things, to make sure of her tidy appearance, to make certain to wear *this* with *this*. She was clever and would become shocking, in the small town of Breitenberg.

The second was the younger by two years. She was beautiful. Her hair fell in a smooth fillet across her forehead; she liked to wear a black ribbon with her mother's portrait in a miniature medallion; her clothes were simple but lovely. She was still, and did not fidget. Her sister had taken up all the energy and restless fury that two sisters may possess. She was not clever, but the depth of her blue eyes, fixed entirely on the person speaking to her without movement or change, had convinced many people that her talk did not reflect her thoughts. People had been saying that she was deep since she was three years old, since it was too banal and obvious to say that she was beautiful. They would go on saying it all her life.

The elder of the two sisters was called Elsa Winteregger. The younger of the two sisters (by two years) was called Adele Winteregger. In 1914 they were sixteen and fourteen years old.

3.

On a Saturday morning in May in the year 1914, the two sisters were returning from the Saturday market. A mist had risen from the river Alster and the pool beneath the town, and had not cleared by nine. There were signs of brightness made tangible in the solid white air. The sisters were of different shapes. Adele, perfect, small, and smooth in all her surfaces, her plaits neatly tied in circles behind her blonde head, her nose a button, her mouth a little kiss for Papa. She wore a striped skirt in black-and-white ticking underneath her blue household apron; she had made it herself, with the help of Rosa the kitchen-maid, and it was perfect in every way. She wore sage-coloured stockings and smelt of thyme soap; the household keys jingled in the pocket of her apron as she walked. Despite being younger than her sister, she was the keeper of the household keys and, to some extent, of the household accounts.

The elder was talking, making strides of different lengths – scramble, pause, turn, a little step and another scramble. Her arms rose and fell as she talked, like an orator or a priest on an important walk. Her fingers spread and shut with the movements. Elsa's family had long given up on her hair; its doglike qualities of curl and spring with the texture of terrier, of mattress ticking, could have been tamed, but would never have been tamed by an Elsa. She carried the empty basket, which flung about wildly as she gestured. As they passed underneath the stone gate into the marketplace, Elsa's voice multiplied and echoed before being lost in the noise of the stall-holders. She was talking quickly, in her harsh adult voice, about the meal she would like to make for their father.

'And one day we could make a dinner all in yellow, in lovely yellow, with a fish covered in saffron mayonnaise, and yellow beans, and potatoes, too, with saffron, and a flower to the side, not to be eaten but to be admired, and perhaps a fresh banana, unpeeled, with a strong custard, and to go with it a glass of the yellowest, yellowest wine we could find, a beautiful, beautiful Italian wine, and all the same yellow, not variations on yellow, but exactly the same, because you could make a mayonnaise and colour potatoes to exactly the right yellow a banana has with saffron, I know you could, and I could serve it on a beautiful, beautiful yellow plate, no, on a colour completely different, on a violet plate, yes, the opposite and different colour! Yes, that would be astounding, a meal that Papa would never forget, a meal of yellow on violet, indigo plates. This week ...'

'That would not do,' Adele said. 'Because we need to buy food which will make for another dinner tomorrow, and soup on Monday, and perhaps cold meat to serve at breakfast tomorrow after church, and fish will not do for that. Besides, we do not have any violet plates and it would be a waste of money to buy a flower just to place on a plate, and perhaps dangerous, as some flowers are poisonous and none is good to eat.' She reached out and took the basket from Elsa, who gave it up willingly.

'Unless you are a bee!' Elsa said, and her arms flung up about her head as her mouth opened wide and spittle flew out. 'We could be bees for the day, bzz, bzz, bzz, and eat nothing but honey, and snoffle at flowers on our plates, and do a little dance with our bottoms when we are finished, like this.'

There, by Frau Grawemeyer's cheese stall, in her stained blue frock with the bow half tied, half untied, Elsa gave a waggle with her bottom and a double movement with her elbows. 'Bzz, bzz, bzz,' she said.

'Good morning, the sisters Winteregger,' Frau Grawemeyer called. 'A foggy day.'

'I am trying my hardest to buzz it away,' Elsa almost shrieked.

'Elsa, behave yourself,' Adele said. 'Good morning, Frau Grawemeyer.'

'And this week, I made a painting, and it was all it was, it was a half of orange, the boldest, biggest, most angry orange you ever did see, and that was in the upper half, and in the lower half there was nothing but a half, a block, of pure green-blue-turquoise-teal, a colour with no name, a lovely, lovely colour, but how it did hurt your eyes to look at it, the line where the orange and the violet did meet, and the master came to me and he looked over my shoulder at what I had done, and he said, he said, what is all this, and I said …'

'Good morning, Herr van Olst,' Adele said.

'Good morning, Fräulein,' Herr van Olst said. He was a tall, saturnine individual, red in hands and at the end of his nose; his meat lay in beautiful neat piles, carved and shaped and put in pink pyramids. 'I will just be finishing with Frau Steuer, and then I will be with you.'

'A beautiful raw pink dish, a lovely dish of pink food, of cherries and raw pork and a strawberry shape …'

'I think it hurts her to stop talking,' Adele said confidingly.

'But she must stop talking to sleep and sometimes when she goes to church,' Frau Steuer said. She was a young widow of thirty-two, trim and smiling, black-haired and blue-eyed. Her cook was by her side with a frank, assessing gaze over her kitchen notebook, a licked stub of pencil in her white, blood-drained hand. Frau Steuer lived in a tall old house in a winding street, half-timbered outside, and inside full of sinuous Belgian and Viennese furniture; she had married an old man when she was seventeen, and had seen him out and his money come in. Her coffee cups were square silver blocks, and her sugar bowl and spoons bore a round amethyst each. 'Thank you, Herr van Olst.'

'I have heard her stop talking when she lies in bed, sometimes,' Adele said, confiding in Frau Steuer. 'But she only starts talking again once she has gone to sleep. The only time she ever stops talking is in front of Papa's marionette plays, or sometimes when she is making something, one of her strange things that she makes.'

'Ah, your papa's marionette plays,' Frau Steuer said. 'How I loved the Faust play he did last year! The Gretchen, she broke your heart, hardly possible to believe that she was wood and paint and string and those strange screws with the circular head. Tell me, what is he doing this year? What play, I mean?'

'Thank you, Herr van Olst,' Adele said. 'How is the pork today? Is it bled and hung and good to eat?'

'As always, Fräulein,' van Olst said stiffly.

'And the beef? Beef for *sauerbraten*?'

'Not for today's dinner, Adele,' Frau Steuer said, alarmed. 'If you want to make *sauerbraten* ...'

'Not for today,' Adele said, shaking her head. 'For the end of the week. And for today a chicken, Herr van Olst, plucked and ready, if you please.'

'The marionette play!' Elsa said, actually plucking at Frau Steuer's sleeve. 'You asked what marionette play Papa is putting on. There is going to be a new marionette play, and it is about a woman like the devil, with black, black hair, who kills her old husband and settles in a town and tries to befriend her neighbour's children, two girls, and then she plans to marry him, and steal his money, because he is not rich but a toymaker, not just puppets, but he makes puppets as well, and it is so so beautiful,

225

beautiful, you will see, and the wicked widow gets her comeuppance, you will see, and the puppetmaker and his daughters, before the end, they, they, they …'

'Thank you, Adele,' Frau Steuer said. 'If you want any help with the *sauerbraten*, my cook will be very happy to come over and explain things to you.'

She departed, with no sign of having heard anything that Elsa had said.

'I don't believe that Papa's marionette play is anything like the story you told,' Adele said. 'I don't think it is like that at all. And you know it is not, Elsa. You know it is not, because you are painting the scenery, I know you are.'

'That is the play I would write and put on, if I were Papa,' Elsa said. 'The story of how to scare away a wicked widow and how a man can live very happily with his two daughters without a new wife, particularly a very, very evil new wife.'

4.

In his workshop, Franz Winteregger sat at the bench. The apprentices were working to either side, under the leaded window; light fell on them as they planed and chiselled at the body parts, making a rough shape out of limewood that could be rounded and painted later. They did not speak. In the workshop there was a warm smell of limewood burning and of linseed oil, which neither Franz nor the apprentices noticed any more. In the corner of the workshop was a blue-and-white ceiling-height oven; in front of each of the three of them was an array of tools, held in each case by a canvas roll-up bag, each chisel, hammer and miniature saw in its own pocket. The puppet-master insisted on neatness, and his apprentices supplied it. There were no piles of shavings on the floor in this workshop: every half an hour, one of the apprentices got up and swept the floor with brush and pan, emptying the shavings into the Dutch oven.

Franz Winteregger was turning a puppet over slowly. It was unfinished; the features were sketched out on roughly planed wood. But the weight was nearly right, and he had taken the opportunity to fix the limbs together, to see how it would move. It was a new departure. Most of Franz's puppets were variations on well-established types; the size of the limbs, their thickness, the proportion of body to head were the same in any number of puppets. They were distinguished only by the paint, and by the features the puppet-master chose to give them. But this was a new puppet. Franz had woken one morning with the idea of a puppet, a witch, a sinister reaching puppet with too many joints in its arms. The arms would not fold, but would roll up; eight joints would have the effect of a boneless arm, reaching across in a sinister loose way to embrace the witch's victims. The arms were twice as long as usual; the legs, in a perverse decision, had no joints at all. Franz had an idea for the puppet's hair and face; the face should be green and orange, the hair black and furious, like a witch, like his clever daughter Elsa with her dog hair. The new puppet needed to have its weight tested, its centre of gravity established. Franz was not sure where that lay. He passed it from hand to hand. He held it from above, by the strings, and with a small straight gesture of the hand let the witch fly freely, tracing an arc. There was something wrong about the way the puppet swung; some delay or overshoot that came from an excess of weight somewhere, perhaps only a couple of shavings of wood, perhaps needing to be corrected with a small weight of dentist's silver, moulded onto the other side, wherever it was. He swung the puppet again. It moved well, but the weight felt wrong, its centre of gravity too low. He took it up and began methodically passing the limbs from hand to hand. The apprentices, their heads lowered and apparently concentrating on their work, watched him carefully.

The workshop stood at a right angle to the house, and though it would have been a simple matter to knock a hole in the wall for an internal door, Winteregger had preferred to keep the single door on the outside, so that to walk from the house into the workshop, it was necessary to walk a few steps across the court-yard. He did not want the apprentices to get into the habit of walking through his kitchen in a familiar way, and perhaps exchanging banter with his daughters as they went. He also wanted to know when someone was approaching before they opened the workshop door. Now, at almost exactly noon, the kitchen door gave its usual squeal, and Franz set down the puppet, now trimmed of some weight on one side, given some extra weight on the other. 'I think that must be the end of the week's work,' he said kindly to the apprentices, who started to wipe and put away their tools in their canvas holdalls just as the door opened and Adele, the puppet-maker's pretty daughter, came in with a blue apron over her black-and-white striped ticking dress.

'Frau Steuer is here,' Adele said. 'She said she wanted to have a word with you, Papa.'

'I see,' Franz said. There was a pause. He raised his hand solidly once, twice, in different directions. It was almost a gesture of benediction, but he was actually saying goodbye to the two apprentices, who could now leave with their tools in the canvas holdalls, go to their lodgings in the Herderstrasse above the stationers' shop, and spruce up before their evenings with their cronies and friends and barmaid allies at the Blue Elephant beer hall. Sometimes they would sit in the Platz and eat yellow ice-cream outside off white marble tables, with girls or friends, from little cut-glass bowls with crisp wafer fans. They said goodbye with murmured, respectful noises.

'Did you ask her to have dinner with us?' Adele said, when the door was closed.

'This puppet,' Franz said, raising it meditatively, swinging it to the left, and swinging it to the right. 'This puppet. I am not quite sure about it.'

'Frau Steuer,' Adele said.

'Oh, yes,' Franz said. 'Yes. There must be enough food on

the table. I am sure you have made enough food for us, and for Frau Steuer too, if she would like to stay and take her dinner with us.'

'That is not what I meant,' Adele said. 'That is not what I meant at all. Don't forget to wash your hands and to change your shirt before you join us.'

But she said it with a smile, and left her father still swinging the witch-puppet to and fro, feeling the weight of its movement, following slightly behind the movement of the hands, like a thing flying that was never meant to fly. He ran his fingers along the ordinary white bands that the puppets used. All at once he saw that the thing for the witch-puppet was to hang it from violet ribbons, violet ribbons in shining perfect silk. He saw them moving, taut, through the lit theatre, like promises, with a witch on the end.

Franz Winteregger was the object of interest in Breitenberg, and his daughters did their best to deal with the interest. He was young to be a widower, only thirty-seven, and his wife was not sharply remembered, her memory paid tribute to rather than cherished. His dark hair curled tight against his skull, the cause of the bulk that gave his elder daughter such problems; his eyes were the vivid blue that was so beautiful in his younger daughter, and so beautiful in him. There was a word for him, and the word was 'boyish'; he had been a puzzled widower with two small girls in black at twenty-eight, and the puzzlement had frozen him in time. The women of the town had shown an interest within a year, almost before he was out of mourning, and had gone on showing an interest. There was, too, his business, which did well, and which because of its natural curiosity raised Franz from the circles where he might have been expected to find a new wife. People felt that, just as the inanimate pieces of wood were given a grace and an intrinsic propensity to dance through the air by the unseen puppeteer, so Franz, who might have been considered a variety of carpenter, was raised into the spiritual, even the philosophical, by the obscure dignity of his

229

calling. He gave life to what he made; he remained modestly unseen in the execution of his art; his physical beauty could be matched by his unspoken, spiritual exercise. He had married well the first time, as, indeed, his father had, somewhat above the levels that their income might have attained alone. He seemed to possess no awareness of any of this, and not to value his own qualities; he had said, to anyone who asked, that his elder daughter was clever, and he hoped she would pursue a profession, and become a teacher of some sort. There was no son to take on the workshop, and that would go to a nephew.

The widows came; the old maids; the daughters, even, of women who were not much older than Franz and had established visiting rights. They came with lowered eyes, or with the propensity to laugh Franz out of his humour and into marriage. They had started coming a year or two after Gertrud's son had been born dead, and a day or two later, Gertrud herself was dead. The girls had still been in black, at seven and five years old, and Franz too. It was hard to know when the visits had stopped being in respect, and had started to take on a besieging aspect.

'Don't you think,' Elsa would ask of one old maid, 'that if a lady has received not one offer of marriage by the age of thirty that it would be a good idea to accept that it will not and probably should not happen, not ever?'

'Don't you think,' of the seventeen-year-old daughter of a lawyer, 'that marriage between young and old is unfair?'

'Unfair on whom?' the lawyer's wife would say.

'On all concerned,' Elsa would reply.

'Don't you think,' she would ask a widow, 'that this is really a very good painting for a child of twelve to have produced? Don't you think? Don't you think?'

Nothing had come of any of these visits. Some had settled into a regular habit of visiting, some even forgetting over time that they had begun by considering Franz a possible husband for themselves or others. These had become friends. Some, on the other hand, had continued to bring gifts of cake and special, pretty things for the girls, saying that they knew what girls liked, and that they were sure Herr Winteregger never gave such things a moment's consideration. Adele had put these gifts, whether of cake or of trinkets, away in a special place and, according to the visitor, had either eaten the cake and used the trinket, or, in one case, had disposed of it uneaten and unused, as if it were cursed.

It was Adele whom the greater number of the visitors found more offputting in the end. Elsa's questions and behaviour could be safely ignored, as her family ignored them: she lived in a narrow field of perceptions of the world about her, of colour and form and shape, of seeing how the world could be made into an object or a painting. Her perceptions of the world's behaviour and manners, on the other hand, did not exist. That had its advantages: nobody would much care what Elsa thought of an eventual marriage, and she would carry on in much the same way as before. Adele, on the other hand, made so efficient a housekeeper, with her keys and her apron, her sharp ways with market stall-holders and grocers, her prompt paying of bills and her constant querying of accounts, that more than one of the Breitenberg widows had decided that she would not be at all likely to relinquish her tasks. More than one widow had fallen at the first hurdle of Adele remarking calmly that she was not at all likely to marry; that Papa was her entire concern, and she loved living in Breitenberg and seeing that everything ran so smoothly; innocently, she seemed to mean exactly what she said, and was happy that things were ordered so. There were two daughters of the puppet-maker Winteregger, one beautiful, one clever, and they lived together in the town of Breitenberg.

5.

'But why do you want to marry me?' Adele Winteregger said, much later, in Weimar, to the strange man who had accosted her in the street, and had later turned up outside the house where she was staying with Elsa. 'Why would you stand outside the house for four hours, from five in the morning to nine in the morning, until I left the house, and then insist on walking with me like this through the streets, and telling me that I should come with you into the park and along the river and into the trees to listen to the songs of birds? And you only met me once, and only spoke to me once, not thirty words. I cannot understand why you now say that you want to marry me. I have never heard of anyone saying to a stranger, I want to marry you, then being accepted and any good coming of it.'

'Listen to that bird,' Christian Vogt said. He laid his hand on Adele Winteregger's sleeve where her arm carried the basket. His hand, lying on the coarse texture of the clean brown cloth with cuff and neat blue buttonhole, thrilled and tensed at being nearly in contact with Adele. 'It is a nightingale, singing for you.'

'That is not a nightingale,' Adele said. 'I do not know very much about birds, but I can see that it is a blackbird. There is not a lot of point in talking to me about nightingales and expecting me to marry you because it is a romantic thing to say. Nothing is romantic if it is untrue. Perhaps truthful things are not very romantic either, but it is important not to say that things are nightingales if they are not nightingales.'

'It is a beautiful song, and the bird is sitting in a beautiful tree, and I am walking here with you,' Christian Vogt said. 'I don't know what else I can say to you to convince you of my sincerity.'

'I do not disbelieve you,' Adele Winteregger said. 'I only think that your feelings at this moment cannot strongly influence my actions, and should not influence yours. There was a lady called Frau Steuer who was very much convinced that she should persuade my father to marry her. She came round to our house every month, sometimes twice a month, and always issued an invitation to her house to have dinner and afterwards a cup of coffee and perhaps a piece of coffee cake, but my father said that it would mean dressing up in his most uncomfortable clothes and polishing his boots, so we did not go to her house more than once a year. When she came to our house, she always brought something she had noticed that we did not own, or something to replace an old object. That showed she loved our papa without her having to say so.'

'It doesn't sound very romantic,' Christian Vogt said. 'If I brought you a gift, it would be something that had no necessary meaning or use, just a beautiful object that you could live with, so beautifully, you and it.'

'That is what many people think,' Adele said. 'And many people would be wrong. Anybody can buy a useless piece of floral arrangement, or chocolates, or a painting, or something of that sort. But if you notice that the person you visited last week and are visiting this week as well has only a nutcracker with a loose screw and tarnish at the joint, and you buy a good replacement, that is a good gift, which shows love and attention.'

'Did that ever happen?' Christian Vogt said.

'Yes, that happened,' Adele said. 'We had for many years a nutcracker that had a loose screw, and every time we cracked a nut, Papa would comment on it, and afterwards take it to the workshop and tighten it. But it was always the same the next time. I think the screw had gone. We did not eat nuts every day. But then one day Frau Steuer arrived with a new nutcracker, beautifully made, which opened and closed so smoothly, and never creaked. Papa still uses it whenever he wants to crack a nut, which is not every day, as I said. It still works perfectly. Look!'

Adele was indicating through a window; they had reached the borders of the park, and in the lower rooms at the back of an office building, there was a telephonist at work; at the brown telephone switchboard she moved steadily and surely, before the tangle of jacks and the web of wires, green, red or blue-striped. 'Look!' Adele said. 'How busy and interesting!'

'I want to know everything about you,' Christian Vogt said,

turning away impatiently. He had seen telephonists before; he knew, from his father's office, how they efficiently plugged in lines and let the tiny shutters fall down, like eyelids. 'I want to know even about the nutcrackers you owned and the names of the girls in your class at the Gymnasium and—'

'The nutcracker is not a romantic gift,' Adele said. 'But it is very much to the point. That is my idea of a very good gift, not a box of chocolates, which you could not eat at once and which would have to be shared with people you did not even like very much. That is not a very considerate gift.'

'But did your father marry Frau Steuer in the end?' Christian Vogt said. They were crossing the ornamental bridge over the river that wound through the ducal park – crossing it for the second time. He ran his fingers through his hair; he felt wild and sprawling next to this patient, neat, tidy woman, explaining about her family with no need, apparently, to wave her hands as she talked.

'No, he did not,' Adele said. 'But he was very glad of the nutcracker.' She stopped dead in the middle of the path; she looked up at the autumn sun, squinting and screwing up her little nose. 'Now I must be about my business. You should be getting back to your art classes. My sister would never skip a class. She is going to become a teacher, she knows she must not. I do not know what someone like you will become. I have to go now. Thank you for the walk in the sunshine. I enjoyed it.'

'But you didn't answer me!' Christian Vogt said. 'You didn't give me an answer!'

'Oh, that,' Adele Winteregger said, and he was exultant that she had, after all, been thinking about it, that she had borne the question in mind at least. 'No, Herr Vogt, I am not going to marry you. I have my father to look after, and perhaps, afterwards, my sister too. Goodbye. Thank you for the walk in the sunshine. I enjoyed it.'

Adele's father Franz had been lucky: he had been buried in rubble on the battlefield only six months after the start of the war, and had been returned to his daughters, like unsatisfactory goods, smelling of hospitals, iron, iodine, the Red Cross and railways. His eardrum had burst: he carried a strange serpent of an instrument, an ear trumpet, in the upper pocket of his old jacket. Adele would look after him. Later, she might marry her cousin, the Friedrich. If this man persisted, she would be obliged to tell him why her life would run in such a way.

6.

The days of Adele Winteregger in Weimar followed a routine. She looked at her sister's existence, and did not know how she could be happy and productive without knowing what she should be doing today, and what she would be doing at this time tomorrow. Elsa had the timetable for her studies, which Adele strongly suspected her of not following to the letter. But apart from that, she did things on whim and for spectacle. She did not even go to bed at the same time each night.

Adele had been in Weimar for six days, settling Elsa in, and was to be there for another week. She did not propose to take advantage of the full three weeks that her employer, the Jew, had offered her. Already she had established herself a routine. She woke before Elsa, and washed herself quickly in the wash-bowl with a damp sponge. She dressed, making plenty of noise to wake Elsa, and made coffee in the little metal pot with the coffee-and-acorn mix that worked out more cheaply, and with it, a bread roll each, bought at the end of the day from the baker in the street below. Then she would walk with Elsa to the school, and make sure that she was there for her first lesson, at least; she would return to the market, and see what was good for dinner. This took most of the morning. The prices were so sharply rising that you could find a difference between one stall and another very easily. The least perishable items, like potatoes and cheese, Adele had bought a good quantity of when they had arrived from Breitenberg. It had seemed like a large outlay of their money, but when she looked at what a sack of potatoes had cost five days before, and what it cost today, she was glad of what had seemed extravagance. She knew the faces of the stall-holders and some of their names; some of them now knew hers. She would return to the little room above the bookshop that Elsa was living in, and where they shared a bed for the time being. She would prepare the food, paring the potatoes and roots and, if it were a meat day, putting the pig's trotter into the pot after trimming it. When it was done, Adele took the pot down to the baker below, and he would put it into the oven for her, where it took up no space. Elsa came home at twelve thirty, usually, and they ate their dinner together, Elsa sitting on the bed and talking in the way she had about what she had done and what she had made that morning, bouncing up and down; Adele sat on the one wicker chair and listened, encouragingly. In the afternoon, Adele mended clothes, and cleaned the room, and was happy to make and mend clothes belonging to the baker's wife, or the kitchenware-shop owner's wife opposite, or the clothes belonging to the wife of the man who kept the accounts in the bookshop three doors down. She was kept busy, and one of them had returned and asked her if she could make her a dress, so the work must have been satisfactory. At five o'clock, she gave in and put her hat on, and walked out of the house to tell the boy Christian Vogt that she would take a walk with him for an hour, when Elsa would return from her studies. In the evening Adele and Elsa ate soup and Adele read ten pages of her book. She would tell Elsa of the latest absurd things that the boy Christian Vogt had said to her, and Elsa would act them out, striding about the little room and laughing. They went to bed at nine thirty, and she slept easily. If you held Elsa, she did not turn in the narrow bed as often and as violently as she otherwise would. Adele was not clever like Elsa, she knew, but she made herself a useful day and she lived in it.

She lived an orderly and reliable life, and it made her happy.

What made it impossible was the lack of order and sense shown by money. Before the war, in Breitenberg, she had gone to the market each day with the money her father had given her, and had bought what they needed. They had even eaten veal or chicken every day. It had cost the same on Friday as it had on Monday. Adele thought of that with astonishment, so used was she now to discovering that a potato bought for a million, a thousand million marks at ten in the morning would cost ten thousand million by noon, and nobody could say what Monday's potato would cost on Tuesday. Adele stuck obstinately with her routine, but it seemed to her that money was behaving like a Bauhaus student, like Elsa; it had wild hair or a shaved head, it leapt up, it shrieked madly and ran through the streets, rending its garments, it arrived or it did not arrive, it disappeared altogether when it was most expected and most relied upon. It spoke words in the marketplace that nobody had heard before the war, and that nobody should have to listen to now; words that shocked and appalled, words that only men in their most private circumstances should be allowed to speak. Words for panelled rooms and the shut door were now bandied around for children to overhear, to learn, to repeat. Words like 'billion'. She had bartered in Breitenberg, swapped Dresden figures for a necessary sack of flour; she had given the labour of a week not for money but for a hand of pork. She suspected that her father was doing the same. There was nothing to do in response to the behaviour of money but to establish a routine, and discover what, in the end, was of worth. If Elsa made anything worth selling, she could live on that. But the market in Weimar for tapestry and carpet and ornamental textiles was limited, and dealt with a glut. Adele hoped that Elsa would manage on the twice-weekly supply of money they sent through the post. It had once been, not so very long ago, a million-mark note. It was hard to imagine now the day when that had seemed a large sum of money. But Adele was not clever, she knew, and she had long ago stopped trying to understand what could not be understood.

Against the harmonious working of Adele's Weimar routine, too, there was the routine of the boy Christian Vogt. Adele could not understand it. At some point during Adele and Elsa's morning walk to the school, Christian Vogt would pop out from a side-street. He would pretend to be preoccupied, and only when he was upon them would he give a start of surprise and say, 'Good morning.' You would have to be a child of five to think that this happened every day by chance. Then he would walk them to the school and go in with Elsa. He would cast a sorrowing look as he entered the building. Adele did not think he appreciated the opportunity he was being given. Between one and two in the afternoon, he would appear at the wall opposite, like a loafer, or a pickpocket waiting his chance. He would make a pretence of reading the newspapers that had been pasted to the wall. But in reality he was just waiting for Adele to come out. She watched him from the upper window. He was always there by two, but she could never leave the house before five. He waited in his best clothes, a limp patterned suit, an American hat in his hand, his shoes polished to a shine. Adele did not give up before five; then she gave up. She left the house and told Christian Vogt that her work was done for the moment, and she would be grateful for some fresh air. If she insisted on a solitary walk, she knew that she would have Christian Vogt dogging her footsteps, his eyes on her back, trying to see through, to see her heart. She could have told him that a heart was just a fat organ with tubes, probably best when trimmed and stuffed, but very nutritious and, because it was not very widely esteemed, very cheap and easy to obtain by anyone who made a small effort.

'Do you not have a timetable?' she asked him. 'Did they not hand you a piece of paper, marked out into squares, that you are to fill in with the names of your classes and their times? Do you not stick to it?'

'Yes,' Christian said, gazing at her as she pulled the white muslin scarf around her neck and fastened it with a little cameo brooch. He had been standing outside the house for three hours, his figure a recognizable one in the neighbourhood by now. The baker downstairs had rudely called across, some hours ago, that if he was going to be as long as yesterday, why not buy a cake to keep him going, as it would be more expensive by the time Adele came out. His thin shape, his upward cock's crest of hair, his modest and fearful eyes made an impression on all the neighbours. Adele ignored him until she was ready to leave.

'Yes, what?' Adele said. She could feel that a garter was already coming loose. The elastic was frayed and would have to be replaced somehow. She hoped it would not fall down altogether. She would prefer not to have to adjust it underneath her skirt; it looked so like an indelicate itching to other people.

'Yes, I do have a school timetable,' Christian said. 'I have nothing to do this afternoon.'

'You should be working,' Adele said, as they set off. 'I know that not everything that is done in an art school is done during the lesson hours. My sister is hard at work in the textile studio. She is making a large tapestry of her own design. Now, why are you not in the studio, developing your own work? This is no good, waiting for someone you do not know.'

'I only want to be in Weimar because you are here,' Christian said. 'There is no other reason.'

'Well, I am going back to Breitenberg in a few days,' Adele said. 'So you will have to find another reason to stay in Weimar. Elsa knows why she is in Weimar. She is learning to make beautiful objects, taught by the best masters. And when she has a diploma, she will be able to take it and teach in the best schools in the country. It is absurd, a shame to say that the only reason you have to stay in Weimar is because a little dressmaker is here on holiday.'

'If the teachers are talking to me, I just hear Adele, Adele, Adele. I do not think I have learnt anything since I arrived here. Nothing but your face, and your walk. And now you want to scare away people who want to marry you. It is not very good, the way you have made a profession of scaring people away.'

'That's so,' said Adele, considering. She had scared away a good number of women who had come bearing gifts, their arms open. She could not see how it was that anyone should change their mind, and tell a man that his offer was acceptable. But sometimes a man must be told that his offer was acceptable, or the human race could hardly continue.

'A man,' Christian Vogt said, 'must sometimes be told that his offer is acceptable. If that never happened, then the human race would die out altogether. And that does not seem to be happening.'

'That's so,' Adele said, her heart pumping. She had not seen that her thoughts were going to be captured and expressed by this man she hardly knew. 'I was very good at discouraging the widows, laying siege. But no one has laid siege to me, until now. It has all been to Papa.'

'So tell me the story of how you got rid of all those suitors, suitoresses – is that a word?'

'I have never heard of such a word,' Adele said. 'We used to call them the Weed Bed. There was nothing you could do about them. They came up in bundles. They were attractive, sometimes, on their own, just as a flowerbed with weeds can be shown to have even some pretty flowers, like bindweed. But to leave them be – Papa would not have been happy.'

'How can you just – get rid of a tiresome person?'

'Well, once – this would have been during the war …'

7.

The faces in the room were in a circle, each holding a deal board with paper pinned to it; the paper was not good paper, as they were going to get through a lot of it. They were turned to the man at the apex of the circle. The circle does not have an apex, but this circle did have an apex. The man at the apex had been talking for some time, and the faces around the circle, thirteen of them, were puzzled, serene, scared or excited. The man's face was broad and mask-like, the skin stretched tight over the bones. Klee had seen this class earlier in the week for the first time. He liked the beginning classes, and the sound of ingrained thoughts being erased; sometimes easily, sometimes with painful, incomplete grindings, like a motor running on empty. He had been talking about the line; all the things a line could do, once conceived of. It could make a fish; it could make the water a fish swam in; it could make a man or a point, or a pattern of lines and other lines. He looked at the class and saw that he had not made himself clear.

'I want you to do an exercise,' he said finally. 'You have your pencil, not too soft, not too hard. Take your pencil, and draw a single straight line, one that goes from one edge of the paper to another.'

The students all did this, some looking from one side to another in case they had done something wrong. Klee saw with interest that the boy who never said anything, the one who appeared to be dreaming about something entirely different, bored and openly drifting – that boy had drawn a line from the top edge of the paper to the bottom edge. All the rest had drawn a horizontal line, somewhere between halfway and three-quarters down the paper. Klee examined his own instructions. It was right: he had not indicated the direction of the line. The boy had seen the line in his own way, top to bottom of the paper. Klee pondered this, and why he had thought of a horizontal line, and why a vertical line seemed already so original. He came to no conclusions.

The class looked at him expectantly. Klee's mind returned to the room. Outside the window of the room on the first floor, there was a tree, just turned yellow, and in the tree, there were three, perhaps four, birds singing loudly. It was like a machine with three, perhaps four, parts moving in different ways, apparently independently, but in fact connected remotely, like a piano and a violin playing together, separated by space. The students were looking at him.

'You have drawn a straight line,' Klee said. 'Now, I want you to think hard, and then draw a second line; one that negates the first line. You should think about the line that has nothing of the first line in it, which wants to be completely indifferent to the first line and have nothing whatsoever in common with the first line. Can you draw that line?'

The students looked at him still. Klee loved the first-year students. They had had no chance to be influenced by the students who had arrived in the year before, or the students in the year before that, having only just arrived. And yet they were very much the same as those students. They wore simple clothes, some of them, almost like the clothes of agricultural workers; or they wore the clothes their mamma had thought appropriate for them, a soft suit with a pattern on it and a red rag of a tie; others wore clothes that were neat, practical and efficient; one had paint stains already on his old jacket, which was torn – looking at this last one, Klee felt the torn lining in the inside of his jacket, the trouser pocket he must remember not to put anything in, as there was a hole in it after he had absent-mindedly thrust a paintbrush in, sharp end first. And there were three advanced students who had already found each other through dress and appearance, and were now sitting together. There was a girl who had an abrupt, angular bob to her hair and a slash of red lipstick; there was a girl who was wearing men's trousers, a cap and a pair of workmen's braces; and there was a boy who had found his way to Itten, and to Mazdaznan, and had already shaved his head. The mamma's boy, the one in the neat soft suit and the red rag of a tie who never said anything, he was the one who had surprisingly drawn the vertical line. He was now sitting gazing forward, thinking, his pencil at an angle between third and fourth finger. The advanced figures, on the other hand, had set to work straight away, their mouths pursed. The boy with the shaved head, the early Mazdaznan recruit, had closed his eyes and was humming as he moved his hand across the paper. Klee looked, unamused. He could see what the result would be; a movement of scribble and a cloud. He wanted a line, as usual. Today he would fulfil the task in his own way, in a different way from yesterday. What seemed interesting to him today was the quality of thin-ness in a straight line. His second line, should he make one, would fight against that quality. It would struggle to be as fat as possible. He considered this possibility.

One student after another set their pencil to paper. They drew swiftly, or scrupulously; they raised their pencils, and looked up. Only the mamma's boy, whose name, Klee saw, was Chris-tian Vogt, did not start work. Only after four or five minutes did he start; he made one mark on the paper, then another; he set his pencil down, and smiled, in a tender, satisfied, confident way. The others had smiled, too, but had smiled at each other, shown each other what they had done. Christian Vogt had smiled at the paper and at the line he had made. Klee recognized that smile.

'Let us see,' Klee said, and they had all done what he had thought they might do. The Mazdaznan boy had made a line that meandered so much it turned into a cloud. Others had made an arabesque with no straight line. Some of the neat-dressed girls had made another straight line, which crossed the first at an unpredictable angle. Klee nodded, and made encouraging noises. But then he came to Christian Vogt, and there was no second line on his paper, but just two little crosses, five inches apart. Klee looked at the page, and looked at Christian Vogt, an enquiry in his eyes.

'I thought,' Christian Vogt said, in his careful voice, which few in the class had heard much, 'that the first line was so solid and substantial. It looked so fat after I had been looking at it. Like a road or a vein or a pipe, full of something. It looked as if it would be so hard to change, once it was made.

The second line should not be hard to move. It should be something you could imagine, and then imagine somewhere else, moving in a different way. So there is just a line between these two places that you can make if you think hard about it. That is my line.'

'I see,' Klee said.

'But it is the artist's job to decide what sort of line should go on the paper,' one of the clever, advanced women students said, the one in men's braces. 'It is not the artist's job to say to the observer, you should make up your mind.'

'No,' Christian Vogt said. 'But the observer will make up his mind, whether the artist instructs him to or not.'

Then it was as if he had said enough. Klee looked at the piece of paper again. It was true. He had envisaged a line that went directly between the two points marked by little crosses. It was a line that existed only in his mind, and not on the paper. And yet the artist had drawn that line and made him think of it. He could not remember a student making an invisible line before.

'Today,' he said, 'your task is to make a drawing with a single line, and the line is not permitted to leave the paper, or to cross itself, or to touch itself at an earlier point in its journey. Bring that to class on Thursday.'

8.

'We have designed a new banknote today,' Kandinsky said to Klee, as they walked away from the Bauhaus building.

'Yes?' Klee said. 'I am not asked to design banknotes. I drew an invitation to the student ball in the summer. But I think I would like to draw a banknote. Perhaps a very large one, and then be allowed to keep it, and perhaps even spend it, afterwards. It would be good to draw something that could be exchanged for the sum of money you said it was worth.'

'We are not allowed to do exactly that,' Kandinsky said. 'And all banknotes are very large ones, nowadays. I have banknotes for ten million marks in my wallet that are now worth nothing. I overlooked them for a few hours and then they would not buy a box of matches. We are making designs for the one thousand billion banknote for the Thuringian State Bank. Young Bayer designed it, and we came along to discuss it.'

'What does such a thing look like?' Klee said, bringing his leather case up to his chest and shivering slightly. They paused at the edge of the road; a farm-cart, nearly empty of all but a few husks of corn and straw, went past, pulled by a heavy white horse. They watched it go with different creative impressions: a sagging line, a large sad eye, a series of green slashes against the white-painted floor of the cart. 'How would you decide on the colour of a thousand billion marks? The mind would shrink from the responsibility.'

'It is like the colour of money always,' Kandinsky said, as they continued walking. 'It is not something one person can decide on. It is never you who decides what the colour of the money you hold will be.'

'But somebody must decide on what colour money must be,' Klee said, and he reached into his pocket and extracted a ten-thousand-mark note from some time ago. He dropped it into the upturned hat of a begging veteran sitting on the street. The hat was positioned just where his right knee would have been. 'It does not grow. Someone must decide, other than God.'

'Today I think it was Gropius who decided,' Kandinsky said. 'He said he was very proud that the Bauhaus was making the designs for banknotes, though I think he meant only himself. He has told Bayer that the ten thousand billion marks should bear a thick red stripe at the bottom, and otherwise be black printing on white. Bayer has made it sans serif. It shouts.'

'A red stripe at the bottom,' Klee said, and turned his expressionless broad face away. He made with his hands a small gesture, as if trying out a new piano; Kandinsky had got to know this movement as a warding-off gesture. He could not imagine what was bad luck, or impossible, or evil, about a thick stripe of red on a banknote. 'That is what the Bauhaus is doing, is it? Making banknotes with a thick stripe of red at the bottom, for thousands and millions and billions?'

'Yes,' Kandinsky said simply. 'We are up in our studios, making beautiful objects for the bourgeoisie, founding religions, talking mysticism, and Gropius cannot believe that there will be a place for us in the new Bauhaus, in the new Germany. He wants to make chairs and tables and banknotes and cutlery that works better than any cutlery before.'

'Did he ask you about the design of the banknote?' Klee asked. 'Was he concerned about what young Bayer's banknote looked like, and did he want you to make it more beautiful?'

'No,' Kandinsky said. 'He was speaking to me because he wanted to discover my experience using red ink for printing purposes. But the red ink in the prints lasts very well because it is looked after, and it is not screwed up like a banknote.'

'But could you help him? It is a shame that you could not help him,' Klee said. 'Shall we walk through the park today? It is still so nice. The trees are so beautiful, all in that red and yellow, just for the moment. Trees are red, as well as money.'

'But why?' Kandinsky said, as they stepped through the elaborate ducal gate that led into the ducal park, closing its ironwork behind him. Klee was right to want to come this way. Here, it was impossible to believe that anyone was poor. A nanny was wending her way home with her two charges, one in pale blue with a swansdown hood, the other, still smaller, tottering along with a toy dog on wheels, wearing a tiny sailor suit. 'I really could not have answered his questions. He would not listen. He is the man who decides on the colour of money, you know.'

'I want him to give me twenty banknotes of ten thousand billion marks, out of gratitude,' Klee said simply. 'I want to make his money so beautiful that he returns a lot of it to me.'

9.

Christian Vogt entered the hallway of the Weimar villa. It still reminded him of the inside of a jewellery box, all velvet and panel; its smell was still as it had been; but the strangeness had gone. He hardly saw it, and he was aware that his response to it was all verbal; it was 'the place I live in', 'This hall's like a jewellery box' and 'Frau Scherbatsky's house, or Frau Scherbatsky's husband's house, as she always says'. Expressed in conversation or in his own thoughts, these seemed to be enough. He had no urge now, as he had had two or three weeks ago, to sit down and draw the interior of the hall. That urge had gone, leaving only a faint tinge of duty and the belief that he might have said something along those lines to Frau Scherbatsky, and really ought to get it over with to please her.

As if to strengthen this guilt, Christian found himself closing the front door of the house behind him at the exact moment that Frau Scherbatsky came out of the sitting room to the right. She appeared to have been waiting for him. Her expression, normally one of warm delight, had withdrawn into one of tightly smiling forbearance. Christian had seen this expression on the faces of schoolmasters. Before she said anything, he knew he had once been admitted to the company of the grown-ups; now, he was going to be ticked off, like a child.

'Herr Vogt,' Frau Scherbatsky said. 'How very nice to see you.'

Then Christian knew exactly what it was about. She gestured, and he followed her, in a hangdog style, into the sitting room, depositing his portfolio by the hall table where the vase of white tulips sat. He shut the door behind him.

'I was concerned, I must admit,' Frau Scherbatsky said, 'not to see you at supper last night. Herr Wolff thought you might be ill, and I sent Maria up after supper with a bowl of beef broth. But she said you were not at home, and had not been at home all day. I was woken up, in fact, when you did finally come home – it must have been nearly midnight.'

'I think that must be true,' Christian said. He knew it was true. He had walked and walked with Adele Winteregger, from the afternoon into the evening. And then, when she had said, 'This is too bad – I must go back inside. Elsa hates to come home and not find me there – I must, I really must,' he had leant down and had kissed her, and she had not moved. There was some resistance in the lips, he could feel, but it was melting as his mouth touched hers, and she had not moved back; she had stood there simply and let him kiss her. Her lips; her skin against his; the smell of her clean hair. She had let him walk her the short distance to the house where she and Elsa lodged, and had darted inside without saying goodbye or looking back. He had stood there outside her windows for a long time, watching the light of the oil lamp come on at her hand; watching, or imagining the warmth inside as she moved about, lifting and tidying, then seeing her shape against the oil-lamp's glow, beginning to peel the vegetables. He had gone on standing there in the street even after Adele had come to the window and closed the shutters. And after some time, when her own glow had finally left the street where he stood, he could not go to Frau Scherbatsky's place and talk about the cost of living and the future of Germany with her and Wolff and Neddermeyer. He had walked and walked, first through the city, then out through new suburbs, and finally when he walked between fields and heard the movement of animals and their night calls in the dark, he knew he had walked enough, and turned homewards.

'I had hoped to mention it to you this morning,' Frau Scherbatsky said. 'But you were not at breakfast either. I don't think you have been at breakfast very often this week.'

'No, I think that must be true,' Christian said.

'I am very sorry to say that I am going to have to go on charging you for meals, even if you miss them, you know,' Frau Scherbatsky said. 'But it is only considerate to inform me whether you will be there. This is not exactly a boarding house, you know, Herr Vogt – I would naturally prefer to have a guest and friend who favours us with his company in general. I understand that Herr Wolff cannot always be here because of his political commitments. But he always tells me well in advance, so I do not delay the serving of dinner, as happened last night on your account.'

'I am so sorry, Frau Scherbatsky,' Christian said. 'The fact of the matter is –'

Frau Scherbatsky held up the palm of her hand as if halting traffic. 'You do not need to explain,' she said. 'I know that art students get up to all sorts of tricks that it is better not to know about in detail. But in future, Herr Vogt, if you could make your plans known to me? And you are dining with us tonight, I hope?'

Later, in his room, Christian wrote a letter to his brother Dolphus. He wrote on the heavy cream paper of Frau Scherbatsky, in the same brown ink that compositors and printers used. It was his habit to keep his brother's letters before him on the desk, addressing point after point in response, and adding a few independent observations and anecdotes as he went. Today he did not trouble to look at what his brother had written last time: he had too much to tell him.

Dear Dolphus [he wrote],

Today an important thing happened between me and Adele. I will tell you about it later. But first there was something that happened in class. I do not know quite what it meant, but it seemed important to me. We were told to draw a line, and then a different line – a line as different as could be from the first one.

I drew a line that was only in my head, and that was only to be seen when you closed your eyes. You see, I saw the first line, the solid one with a single direction, as like Adele – she is reliable, and always there, and you could always trust her. But the other line, that was like me. It was like the line that was completely different whenever anyone else looked at it. Now that I have met Adele, I see that I made no sense in the world until she looked at me and saw what I was. When she is impatient with me, that is because I am not worth anything. When she endures my presence and listens to what I have to say, that is because I have become a good and valuable person.

I felt that I was like a line that could go in any direction, according to who placed their gaze upon me.

I am so happy, Dolphus. Yesterday I kissed my Adele, and today I saw her again. She would not kiss me, but I had drawn my two lines in class, and I know when I give her the drawing of the two lines, the straight line that you can see, and the invisible line that could go in any direction, she will understand what we mean to each other. The gaze of love, altering what it falls upon.

This is the most wonderful thing that has happened to me, and perhaps to anyone who has ever lived. I truly feel that. I send you my fraternal greetings. I am so changed you would not know me.

Your brother, C. S. T. Vogt

Christian's handwriting was so large and swooping, with the modern loops and French shapes he had acquired in the art room at school, that he had used up four of Frau Scherbatsky's writing sheets. He had the sense that he had written absurdly, with some suggestion of madness, perhaps making his brother think that he had been drunk when he wrote it. He and Dolphus had never spoken like this when they were together, but Christian believed that there was nobody else in the world who would understand what had happened to him. He placed the sheets in an envelope; addressed it in a neater, more compact hand than before; sealed it, and placed it on his bedside table to post in the morning.

10.

At that moment there was a soft knock at Christian's bedroom door. He threw an automatic glance at the letter, as if, even sealed, it could betray him. 'Come in,' he said.

The door opened; it was Neddermeyer. 'I am sorry to disturb you,' he said. 'But there is a young woman here who wants to see you.'

'Here?' Christian said.

'She is waiting in the hall. A young woman,' Neddermeyer said, in his precise way, placing the visitor. 'She said she knows you.'

Christian got up and followed Neddermeyer out, taking the letter with him. Downstairs, sitting in one of the large hallway chairs, her feet not quite touching the floor, her little white hands resting on the wooden arms too far apart for comfort, was Adele. She had come dressed for a call, although it was nearly nine o'clock; her dark green skirt was in a sort of slippery oilcloth, its folds sticking out stiffly at her knees; her tidy umbrella was at her feet. She looked up as Christian came downstairs, watched from the top of the stairs by Neddermeyer. 'Good evening,' she said.

'Hello, Adele,' Christian said, placing the letter on the table for posting. She seemed in this house a quite different part of his life. Her expression was defiant, her mouth firm; he wondered if it was difficult for her to come to a house like this, and demand admission at nine at night. Then he recalled the widows of Breitenberg. 'I thought you had to stay at home with Elsa, always.'

'Elsa went to her Maza– her Mazadazana – I can never get the name right. Her spiritual group. She wanted me to go, too,

251

but I don't think it would suit me.' There was the noise from upstairs of Neddermeyer softly closing his door.

'I don't know what it is,' Christian said. 'I know that a lot of people belong to it, and they sometimes shave their heads and wear odd clothes and eat nothing but garlic. Does Elsa not eat garlic?'

Adele waved her hand in dismissal. Christian observed that the door to the sitting room was somewhat open. He could hear the voice of Frau Scherbatsky and, after a moment, the harsher, more grating one of Herr Wolff. Their voices had an artificial tone, though he could not hear what they were saying. They were talking in order to disguise the fact that they were listening to Christian and Adele. Christian sat down in the other chair; it was identical to the one Adele was perched on, and placed on the other side of the fire, facing in the same direction.

'It's nice to see you here,' Christian said.

'I can't talk like this,' Adele said. It was true. Seated on the chairs, it was impossible to carry on a conversation with the other person, facing rigidly in the same direction, ten feet to the left. Christian attempted to move his chair round, but it was too heavy to move, or perhaps even fixed to the floor. 'I don't know what to do,' he said. 'I could sit on the floor.'

'Is there nowhere else we can go?' Adele said. 'In a big house like this.'

There was the dining room, but that was now set for break-fast, the next morning; the study, which was full of Frau Scherbat-sky's private papers, and into which he had never gone alone, and which was very much her territory; and then there was the conservatory at the back, which would need special measures to light up, mastered only by Maria with a taper. There were other rooms, but they had not been shown to Christian, and he did not care to wander. Christian stood up and walked awkwardly over to the door to the offices and kitchen, where a small three-legged stool sat, more for ornament than use. He put that down and sat on it, his legs crossed, almost seated on the floor. At least he was facing Adele now.

'This is a strange house,' Adele said. 'Nothing in it seems designed to make things more comfortable. Do you like it here?'

Adele had a penetrating voice, now you came to hear it in unexpected circumstances. Had he ever talked to Adele inside? Their meetings had been outside, walking, waiting outside houses. He had hardly seen her without her coat, and did not know how her voice would sound in an enclosed space. 'Yes,' he said. 'It's very spacious, and I do find it comfortable. I was lucky to find something so very nice.'

'I had to ask three people where you lived,' Adele said.

'I would have told you tomorrow,' Christian said. But he braced himself; it was wonderful that Adele had changed her mind about him and had come to find him in his home. It made, surely, a new bond between them.

'I have been thinking about what you said,' Adele said. She looked at him, and a new quality of tenderness, of pity, entered her face. 'And tonight seemed a good night to come and tell you, when I was in no hurry and Elsa was busy on her own account.'

'Tell me what?' Christian said.

'Well, you asked me if I would marry you,' Adele said. 'And I have been thinking, and I have decided to accept, and so we shall be married.'

'Oh, Adele,' Christian said. His mind went over things. It was true that he had asked her to marry him. At the time, it had seemed the most important thing in the world. He had proposed to her in the belief that she would not, could not accept him; that it was a beautiful idea that would never come to pass. As Adele spoke, she answered only a romantic statement that she would listen to, be touched and amused by, that she would say no to. But she had said yes. His eyes were full of her: her steady gaze; her steady practical decision. At once he saw the line of women who would have come after this first lesson in love. For one crazed moment he considered saying, 'I didn't mean it,' or 'I think I've changed my mind.' But it was impossible. After a few seconds, his terror and shock began to ebb away, and what was left behind was the sure knowledge that he did, after all, love this girl. He had held onto it for so many days, and now it was going to be here for him, for ever. With a little difficulty, he pushed himself up off the tiny stool, and stood over Adele. He could embrace her now; but she did not stand up.

'You don't say anything,' Adele said. She smoothed down her oilcloth skirt with one hand; it made an odd noise, like a yacht's sail moving under a breeze. She cocked an eyebrow, turning her head slightly away.

'I don't know what to say,' Christian said. 'There is so much to decide, now.'

'We can marry here, in the spring,' Adele said. 'Of course it will not be a large wedding. But I will want my father to come, and your parents will come, too.'

'There is only Father,' Christian said. 'My mother died. Like your mother, I think.'

'Yes, that's true,' Adele said, extending her hand and looking at her nails. 'I don't know if you mentioned that. Do you have any more family? Well, they can come as well, so long as it is not hundreds of people.'

'This is so sudden,' Christian said, and felt a huge urge to laugh; he could have raised his hand to his throat in a maidenly movement. 'We have so much to find out about each other.'

'I can't discuss all this in a hallway,' Adele said. 'And your landlady is listening, I have no doubt.'

'Have you discussed any of this with your sister?' Christian said.

'It was something that Elsa said. But she did not know she was saying it. I took my own meaning from it. And now I have changed my mind, and we are to get married, as you wanted. Goodbye, then, Christian. You may call for me tomorrow. I must go back now – Elsa comes from her spiritual sessions at ten o'clock, or a little afterwards.'

She wriggled from the chair. Again, her stiff oiled skirt made a slithering sound, a faint watery hiss. It was an outdoors noise of tent and sail. She smiled tightly at Christian, and stood there; he remembered with an outburst of politeness that he had kissed her, and perhaps now might kiss her again, as he would every night and every morning from now on. He kissed her. After a few seconds, she took him by the shoulders, and ended the kiss in a practical, rational way. 'There is no need to walk me home,' she said. 'I know the way very well, it is quite safe. But I shall see you tomorrow. I will not tell Elsa our news just yet.'

Christian watched her go. As the door shut, Frau Scherbatsky came out of the sitting room. She performed a small cut, but of the most friendly variety; she pretended that she had not seen Christian at all, and headed for her study in an absent-minded way, clucking slightly at the newspaper she held. 'Frau Scherbatsky,' Christian said, raising his voice.

Frau Scherbatsky turned, in a larger than normal way, as if Christian's presence in the hallway were the most extraordinary thing imaginable. 'Ah! Herr Vogt!' she said. Then, with a gesture of vagueness, a wave of the hands in the air denoting that she was deeply occupied by mental concerns and, perhaps, by slight irritation, she continued on her way. He did not know why he had hailed her. He had nothing that he needed to say to her.

At the evening of the next day, there was a telegram waiting for him on the hall table. It was from Dolphus, his brother: 'COMING WEIMAR FRIDAY FIVE DAYS STOP ARRANGE BED STOP YOUR BROTHER ADOLPHUS'. Christian could not imagine why his brother was coming to Weimar. Then he remembered that he had written to him, the previous evening, before Adele had come round to accept his proposal of marriage. What had been in it was enough for Dolphus to decide to come immediately. Christian could not recall what he had written. It was so long ago.

11.

On a very cold and dark Friday afternoon, a young man sat in a halted train carriage somewhere in Thuringia. The sky outside was dark with snowclouds, a heavy descending grey, like a face held too close. In the last five minutes, since the train had been standing there, fat flakes of snow had begun to fall. It was as if the train had had foresight, and had stopped even before the snowfall began. At another point in the carriage, the voices of two women were talking about the snow, about how they would manage if their husbands were unable to come home. Dolphus had seen them getting on at Jena, and making their way past his compartment, puffing and complaining that there did not seem to be a compartment free. They had been dressed in slippery silk dresses, their fat knees shining, one in blue, one in green; their coats had fur trimmings. They had been making the same observations for five minutes now, drifting through the wall of the compartment, or along the corridor; but I don't know how we will cope; he is so vague about the house; the children are better than he is, more practical, more reliable, but they are only seven and nine; I don't know how long this is going to last, I really could not say. In a compartment next to the one where the two women sat, one in green silk, one in blue, sat Dolphus Vogt. He did not quite have the courage to shut the door and draw the curtains. He merely shrank into the corner.

Dolphus was a young man. He had the appearance of someone of fifteen or sixteen or seventeen at most. This was his first train journey alone, and he had been offered the company of a manservant. He had rejected the offer, and his father had looked at him with an odd, proud, decisive gesture. But now he was travelling on his own, and Dolphus was an anxious boy who could not understand the urge for adventures. He wanted things to stay as they were, and had been rather despatched to Weimar to visit his brother than suggested the journey. His mouth moved, soundlessly. He was practising what he would say when the waiter from the restaurant car came to ask if he would be taking lunch, when the ticket collector arrived. Thank you, his lips silently said, here is my ticket; and his hands quietly went to the outside of his jacket pocket, pressing and establishing that the small rectangle of card was still there since the last time of checking. He wore a green tweed suit with knee-length wool trousers, tightly bound, and bright red woollen socks; over his head in the luggage rack was a brown leather suitcase, quite new, with brass at its corners, Dolphus's initials, A.F.T.V., embossed in gold on the front.

The train began to move again. Dolphus pressed his face against the window; it was snowing heavily now. He could feel the cold, draining force of the weather outside, and the steely metallic smell of the air when snow came to transform the world. He closed his eyes. The pressure of the cold glass and the daylight darkness outside together sucked the sensible feeling from his cheek.

Dolphus knew he was not clever. His father's insistence that he become an engineer bore heavily upon him, and the reports he brought home from school were burdensome, too. He admired his brother more than he could say, but he had under-stood as soon as Christian had announced that he was to be an artist and not a lawyer, that his own obligation to follow the plan set out for him since birth could not be shirked. He had always been a hero-worshipper; people had always said to him, quite gently, 'And if Christian jumped off the top of a building, would you do so too?' His hero-worship subsequently took the form not of imitating a course of action, but of admiring a fellow, perhaps his brother, perhaps an older schoolmate, then telling himself that there was one path of achievement and excellence now shut off to him. He believed that Christian's pencil drawings were so clever, of landscapes and imaginary girls, of extraordinary scenarios in which impossible figures were stretched out in impossible interiors or miniature landscapes, that they would astonish Weimar. No one, surely, had ever made such images in the history of the world. Dolphus knew that he could not now set pencil to paper. The lectures of the art master at school, carried out on the top floor with the high, sloping windows forming half of the roof, piled thick with fallen leaves from the Tiergarten behind, were torment to Dolphus; he was always reminded with a shake of the head what his brother was capable of, as if that was a cause of emulation and not of proscription. When Christian renounced the planned career of lawyer, too, he did not leave it open for Dolphus: he made it completely impossible, as if he had cast aside a girl. Dolphus sometimes thought that the law would suit him: he liked getting small things right, and checking things, and making sure of stuff at his own leisurely pace. But he could no longer think of that, any more than he could of taking a girl from his brother's protection. When the time came, he would go to London to study engineering, just as his father had always wanted. He wondered if Christian would go through his life erasing large possibilities in other lives by his unthinking, free actions.

There was a small cough from the other side of the compartment. In the corner there now sat a small man with his English bowler hat in his hand, a neat and very clean pair of white leather gloves, a black overcoat and, most impressively, a beautiful and very pure white moustache over a tiny pink mouth. Dolphus had heard nobody come in while he had been resting his eyes. He realized, a second later, that there had been no cough. What had drawn his attention was the sudden silence in the carriage; he could no longer hear the conversation from the women in the next compartment. The door had been closed. The advent of silence had seemed like a cough.

'I hope you do not mind if I join you,' the man said.

'Not at all,' Dolphus said nervously. 'I didn't realize that we had stopped.'

'Stopped?' the man said. 'No, no, we did not stop. I got on some time ago. In fact, I got on when the train started, in Berlin. I think you did, too. I have just changed compartments. To tell you the truth, I grew very weary of the conversation of the two other gentlemen in the compartment where I had been seated.'

Dolphus made a general sort of noise.

'Are you travelling alone?' the man said. 'You are young to be travelling alone.'

'I am seventeen,' Dolphus said. 'My brother has just begun to study in Weimar, and I am going to visit him. I have never been to Weimar, and I am greatly looking forward to it.'

'A beautiful city,' the man said. 'The girls there are said to be beautiful. Are you excited about that possibility, too?'

'Sir,' Dolphus said.

There was a moment's awkward silence before the man seemed to relax, and smile encouragingly, as if to say that Dolphus's comment was of no importance, that he would overlook the little social blunder. 'Are you –' he seemed to brighten, not just in his eyes, but in his skin and his moustache, too '– are you close to your brother, in general?'

The man had struck Dolphus as elderly at first, because of his white moustache and his pure white hair. There was, too, his lack of any idea of what someone Dolphus's age would think of going to a city to see beautiful women; it had suggested to Dolphus that the man's own youth had been over many years before. Now, however, he realized that the man was only in early middle age, perhaps thirty-two or -three. He was fresh and pink in his skin. His hair had bleached prematurely, and bleached totally. Such things were known, since the war.

'My brother is a beautiful artist,' Dolphus said. 'I am so proud of him.'

'An artistic family,' the man said, and before Dolphus could deny this, he had half raised himself to his feet and had slipped across the compartment. His movement was fluid, even graceful, rather than the stiff way his moustache suggested he would move; he moved like the young man he had so recently been. So like a movement of fainting had his movement been, Dolphus almost believed that he had been taken ill in some way. He seemed not in control of the movements that would make him slip himself next to Dolphus with a fearful and yet warm and sincere smile. 'How lovely, to be in an artistic family, my dear,' the man said. Dolphus looked down; a gloved hand, a surprisingly large and square hand, had been placed on his knee.

Dolphus got up rapidly, pushing the man away from him. 'Get off me,' he said briskly, for once knowing exactly the right words to say. 'Get out,' he said, and then, with a sense of acting rightly and decently, he drew back his fist and hit the man hard in the face. The man looked humbly astonished; he raised his hand to his nose, and his hair hung in a cowlick above his eyes, dislodged by the blow. 'I really am most terribly sorry,' the man started to say, but blood was running from his nose into his white moustache. He reached for the white handkerchief in his jacket pocket, and dabbed ineffectually.

'You'd better get that seen to,' Dolphus said efficiently. He felt himself shaking now; but he had taken control of the situation. He had heard of such things occurring in railway compartments, and had rejected approaches of this nature in other settings on two or three occasions. Never before had he hit someone, however full of filth and dirt their minds had shown themselves to be. It was a medical failing, he knew, which could be cured, but for the rest of it ordinary decent citizens had the right to defend themselves. He had heard, too, that such tastes had spread in the conditions that the war had been fought in, and this man was the right age to have gone through it. 'There is a tap for drinking water at the end of the carriage. I'm sure you can clear yourself up with that and your handkerchief. Good day to you, sir.'

'I made a terrible mistake,' the man said, departing swiftly.

He cast a look of fear and supplication at Dolphus. 'I hope you will forget all about it.'

Dolphus was trembling as the door shut, and waited, his hands clenched on his knees in protection. The man did not return after leaving the compartment, however. In time, Dolphus's attention turned to the country outside. The train had slowed. Thuringia, in its picturebook way, must be unfolding: forests, and what might be woodcutters' cottages, just by the line; rolling hills, with dense layers of trees and crested with castles. Outside, the snow continued to fall, and there was nothing to see but a dense whirl of white in grey, grey in black. Dolphus closed his eyes. He hoped that the train would reach the next station, at the very least.

12.

All at once, there was a banging on the window. Dolphus opened his eyes. There was a bustle of passengers and luggage in the corridor along the train, and outside, up against the glass, was a human face, wrapped in black scarves and grinning. Behind, the snowing world was lit with gas-lamps. The face belonged, he realized in a second, to his brother Christian. 'Get up! Come on down!' Christian was shouting. 'This is Weimar. Were you asleep?' Dolphus jumped up, pulling on his coat and mufflers, his hat and gloves, trying to pull down his case from the luggage rack, all at the same time.

'Were you asleep?' Christian said, as they shook hands, as brothers do, with warmth and relief. 'The train – they must have turned up the oil heating to full blast, you are so red in the face. It is so strange. I thought it would be an hour late, at least, and here you are, almost exactly on time. The snow had no effect at all on you. Here, let me take that.'

'It was hot in the train,' Dolphus said. 'I put my head against the window, once, and it was almost burning with the cold outside. It made me so—' and here he yawned immensely. 'Oh, I'm so sorry, I'm still sleepy and confused. I don't know where I am.'

'We can walk,' Christian said. 'You don't mind a walk in the snow, do you? Gloves and hat and scarves and all? And you are in Weimar, by the way. There are no cabs to be had for love or money. Not that I have any money.'

'No, a walk in the snow is nice,' Dolphus said. 'It is better if the walk begins after the snow stops falling, but a walk in the snow is nice.'

'Give that to me!' Christian said, and hauled the bag from Dolphus's grip. 'I want you to be my special guest while you are here – I don't want you to make the smallest effort. You are only here until Tuesday. You should be on holiday, do nothing, raise not the slightest finger.'

'I was intended to be here only until Tuesday,' Dolphus said, giving up his bag. 'But this snow looks terrible.'

On the station platform, like a nightmare of punishment and retribution, the man who had forced himself upon Dolphus was being led from the train by two guards. There was a police officer on the station platform and, sheltering from the snow inside, three or four shabby men, taking an interest. The man had his head bowed; he was expecting some kind of violence, immediate or long drawn-out.

'Wait,' Christian said, and he set down his brother's bag. He bent to retie the laces of his boots, which had come undone. Against the snow on the platform, a leaf had fallen; an oak leaf, a fat hand's print against the solid, stained frozen heap. Dolphus pressed his foot against it. Around, men and women had greeted each other and were leading each other off.

'This is Weimar,' Dolphus said. 'I always wanted to know how it was. Do people read poetry here? Are the women of the town notably beautiful?'

'Are the women of the town notably beautiful?' Christian said. 'Dolphus, what has happened to you?'

Dolphus hit his brother gently on the shoulder, laughing. He would explain the joke later, when there was a moment to mention the stranger on the train in a harmless and funny way. 'Well,' Christian said, 'I dare say you will find out about the women of the town very shortly.' He wound his muffler around his neck. They set off. 'But Weimar? No, people worry about money, and food, and the cost of living, and perhaps then, a long way later, about art and poetry and things of that sort. There are no grand dukes any more, or none that pay for poetry.'

'And the weather,' Dolphus said. 'They are concerned with the weather, I'm sure.'

'It is snowing again,' Christian said. 'Are you going to be able to walk? About twenty minutes, I think. It is not so very bad.'

It was early in the year for snow. It fell in fat globes, swiftly, weightlessly, making the sky a small room full of collapse. The substance filled the air as if in revolution, a device ceaselessly turning. They walked away from the railway station, along a boulevard whose other side could not be seen, muffled against the snow. The fresh fall on the ground was crisp, and underneath the new surface, the snow was already hard-packed and thick. It was not slippery underfoot, but solid. Out of the whirling substance, lit in patches and flurries, figures came, faceless dark bundles with no shape or character. As they went further, the streets narrowed, and a wall was thrown up to one side or another, and occasionally a shop window, bright-lit or shuttered. Sometimes, as they went, Christian made a comment on what they were passing.

'That was Klee,' he said, when a bundled figure banged against them with the case of a musical instrument. He howled to make himself understood. 'He is a Master at the Bauhaus.' But Dolphus could not see how he could be identified. 'And this is the Markt-platz. We can cross it directly, from this corner to the opposite one.' A little later: 'Those were Mazdaznan. Are you cold? You don't say anything. Is that your teeth chattering? It is so cold!'

'What is Mazdaznan?' Dolphus said, for something to say. He had nothing to observe but some people, perhaps four or five, who had brushed past him. He had felt, strangely, a texture of silk, like a ballgown without structure, like a loose robe, and then nothing else but a body underneath it. The people must have been insufferably cold. Mazdaznan explained nothing, but then he remembered that the word had come up in one of his brother's letters somehow. The word, alone, had registered and had come to his mind when he heard it spoken.

'Oh, I forgot,' Christian said. 'You don't know Mazdaznan. I'll explain when we get home.' Then he seemed to say, 'We live such lives of cat and elephant in this wise—' the snow and the muffler and a horse somewhere nearby, whinnying, it seemed in Dolphus's ear, all combining to mangle what his brother said. Then there was silence again, and the silent tumult of falling snow.

Four figures came at them, now in some kind of uniform. Christian took Dolphus's arm, and they moved sharply to one side. 'And those were friends of Herr Wolff,' Christian said. Dolphus had the impression of raw red faces, a military cap, a band on the arm bearing some kind of insignia, a determination of purpose, and a sharp smell of cheap soap and old beer on the breath. He had seen such men before, outside the U-Bahn in Friedrichstrasse in Berlin. He did not know whether 'friends of Herr Wolff' was meant literally. He remembered that Wolff was a name of one of his brother's friends, or of something similar, here in Weimar, that he had been written about in letters. 'And some more,' Christian said, bringing his face close to Dolphus's ear. Three men now, similarly dressed, but moving more slowly; one in an invalid carriage with an oiled hood folded over him, but an amputated leg sticking out, and two behind him, injured permanently in some way Dolphus could not grasp until they were quite by him, and then he saw how their faces were marred and torn, one with an eye a socket. 'More friends of Herr Wolff. You remember I told you about Wolff. He is the political genius in the house.'

'When am I going to meet Adele?' Dolphus shouted.

'Adele?' Christian called back. 'Adele?'

'Your sweetheart,' Dolphus said. He had been practising this expression for ten minutes, his mouth moving silently. It seemed to him to contain the right measure of engagement and sympathy and interest. There was a short busy silence between them, as they stepped over a body at full length on the road, perhaps fallen on ice, perhaps a more permanent collapse. Dolphus had the impression of a bottle grasped, a face gripped tight against the snowfall, an end awaited.

'Down there,' Christian said, indicating with a well-wrapped arm. 'If you follow that lane down there and take the second right, that leads to the Bauhaus itself. From now on it is my walk home. I can do it in my sleep.'

'Adele,' Dolphus said, reminding him. The fallen man or woman was still there, disappearing now as he turned to look, disappearing in the bright-lit obscurity of the blizzard.

'You will meet her,' Christian said. 'But she goes back to Breitenberg very soon, perhaps tomorrow, perhaps the day after. We will try to meet, but I think it may not be this time. There are so many people for you to meet. I am going to marry her. Did I tell you?'

Dolphus wondered if he had heard correctly. He found this passing on inexplicable. But his brother's ways had often been potentially inexplicable to him, obscure as a heavy falling snow. In the past, he remembered his brother taking on a passionate and talkative enthusiasm about drawing in pastels, and him explaining at all times about the ability he now had to capture warmth and flesh; he had talked about it at the dinner table, on the walk home from the Gymnasium, at all times. He had called his brother into his room, and explained, and shown. Then one day he had stopped, all at once. He had stopped talking about it, and Dolphus had thought for a day or two that he had lost interest. But he had not lost interest. He still drew with pastels, perhaps more than ever, and Dolphus came across him in a corner of the kitchen, drawing the scullery-maid with what Dolphus was sure were pastels. Christian had just decided to stop talking about it, or had been told by their father – it was possible – to find another topic of conversation for the sake of all of them. Sometimes, however, he had stopped talking about something of burning interest because of exactly that, a loss of interest. Christian's fervent enthusiasms and abrupt worldly silences were so hard to interpret; muffled, in the extreme weather, embarrassment could not be interpreted confidently.

'You are going to be married, you and Adele?' Dolphus said.

'Yes, that's right. I asked her to marry me, and in the end she said yes. That is the way things go, you know. This is the old library, the duchess's old library,' Christian said, giving a pale blue wall a firm slap with his gloved hand, like an ostler greeting a favourite horse. 'You will want to come to see that. Every tourist comes to the duchess's library, like the house of Goethe and the duke's palace, none of which I have been in, myself. The duke's palace should be over there. Perhaps you can see the tower. No. Too dark, too much snow falling. And now we cross the road – you are quite all right still? Not too cold? We are going to take a short-cut across the park. Don't worry. I can do this in my sleep. I'll tell you everything when we are warmed up and have eaten something. You must be so hungry.'

Dolphus, freezing, feeling the weight of the fallen snow on his shoulders and the crown of his cap, just nodded. They stamped their feet on the side of the empty road, and moved off, side by side, into the dark and thick-wooded park. In the silent muffled fury of the falling snow, no birds sang.

13.

'My dear young men,' a middle-aged woman cried, coming out from the open door of a sitting room. 'Stand and shake – stand and shake – there, stay there. No galoshes! Your feet must be soaked through. The electric light has failed, but we hope that it will be merely temporary.' Dolphus had the impression of a large, warm cigar box of a house. It was dark and flickering; light came from two candelabra on tables in the hallway, more candles from inside the open door, and the high-piled fires in hall and sitting room. The two of them stood and stamped, shaking the snow from their shoulders; they looked like winter buffalo, hunched and white. 'At least it is warm. You must be Herr Vogt's brother Adolphus – a great pleasure to have you. Maria will take your bags up to your room. There is a truckle bed prepared for you there, and you will want to get into some dry clothes. Your splendid red socks, Herr Adolphus! Come down and there will be coffee and something warming for you. And, Herr Vogt – a letter, a note was brought for you. Take a candle each, or you will fall over in the dark. I am so sorry for this. The electricity has never failed before.'

Dolphus and Christian were struggling with gloveless hands to unhook their boots. A maid – presumable Maria – appeared from behind another door and, ignoring protests, took Dolphus's bag, leading them in their socks up the stairs with a candle. Christian picked the letter up with a smooth, rapid gesture. The girl had vivid red hair, tidy under a cap; she turned at each corner with a small superior smile, raising her hand to her smooth hair.

'Frau Scherbatsky is a good sort,' Christian said, when they were alone. 'The house is her pride and joy, so don't be knocking your pipe out against her skirting boards, or using her curtains to clean your boots.'

'She seems a good sort,' Dolphus said, trying the expression out – it appeared a new one on Christian's lips. 'Who is the letter from?'

'Oh, from Adele,' Christian said. 'I think one of the other lodgers was there in the dark – it was probably Neddermeyer. He was the architect of the house. He lives here rent-free, I reckon, and he and Scherbatsky are more than landlady and lodger to each other. I don't think anyone is supposed to know

267

that, though. He is a good sort, a bit of an old woman, but a good sort.'

'Aren't you going to read the letter from your sweetheart?' Dolphus said. He proffered his candle in an absurd way.

Christian took it, placing it on the table. He looked at the letter's outside. 'Yes, it is from Adele,' he said. Then he took a kind of decision and tore it open. He held it next to the candle flame, and read it with some attention. 'You can read it if you like,' he said, handing it over. 'There is nothing private in it.'

Dolphus took it. It was written in an old-fashioned hand, a Gothic script that few people he knew in Berlin still used, and those all middle-aged or older. He saw that the letter had been written first in pencil, painfully, then traced over in ink, with much use of abbreviations and lines over the script to indicate longer words. The paper was thick and flocculent, a piece of paper for drawing on, and Dolphus remembered that Adele's sister was an artist with Christian at the Bauhaus. The letter was an invitation, formally phrased and directed at both Christian and Dolphus, to come to an address in Weimar to take a cup of coffee the next day at a specified time in the morning. 'My sister and I' had sent the invitation. Dolphus thought of handing it back and saying, 'She seems awfully nice,' but there was nothing to cause the comment. He wondered if Adele was sixty years old; then he remembered that she came from the country, or from the south, or from something else that explained her formality. On the other side, in thick pencil, scribbled rather than written in the careful old-fashioned hand of the rest of the letter, someone had added, 'I add my name to my sister's invitation. E. W.' Some pressure had been brought here on the writer; its unwillingness was clear in the almost legal precision of the wording. It could be brought up as evidence much later, as proof that she had not always fought against her sister's young man.

'Well, that is polite of her,' Dolphus said. 'I'm looking forward to meeting her.'

'You won't meet her for long,' Christian said. 'She's going

back to Breitenberg on Sunday morning. Now – are you dry? Old Scherbatsky was right – we ought to have worn galoshes in the snow. Change your knickerbockers and socks, you'll be quite all right. The food here is good, hearty stuff, solid great piles of meat, just the thing for a night like tonight. I don't know how she manages it – no sausage meat and sawdust for her.'

'I'll meet her for longer in the future,' Dolphus said. 'Adele. When you make your life together, I mean.'

'Oh, yes, that's so,' Christian said. 'When we make our life together. It sounds so odd. I thought you were talking about old Scherbatsky for a moment there.'

Outside the warm and fire-lit room, the snow was falling without cease, an obscure and complex movement in the dark beyond the candle's light. Dolphus wiped the condensation from the glass, but nothing could be seen. The night, despite the fury of the snowfall, had a quality of silence about it. There seemed no sign of the snow diminishing or slowing. He wondered if the trains would continue to run.

14.

It was possible to make a cake out of parsnips and brown flour, if you sieved the flour carefully. Sometimes, too, honey was cheaper than sugar of any sort, not just the refined white sort. Eggs were a problem, but Adele knew the baker's wife, and she had told her of the women in Weimar who kept chickens, and with some persuasion, Adele had extracted four eggs from four separate housewives over the previous days. The cake was made, and glazed with a sort of fruit jam. There was still the question of coffee, however; Adele could only hope that the Vogt boys had grown as accustomed as anyone else to the opaque and sour mixtures of chicory, acorn and root vegetables that usually made do for coffee in these days. She was not convinced, however. The house in which Christian Vogt lived, which had taken her an hour to find, smelt to her of real coffee and good cuts of meat, of comfort and warmth and hot water on demand; it smelt to her like profit and black marketeering.

'I have never seen such snow so early in the year,' Adele said, peering through the window in their room. The beds were made, and covered with a crochet counterpane; cushions were placed neatly to left, right and in the centre, and the table at which they ate had been cleared of the breakfast things and laid with plates, napkins and the parsnip cake. Outside, the snow was falling, as it had fallen most of the day before, and all of the night; it heaped up against the walls of the house opposite, and down this street, only three or four brave people had forced their way. 'I don't know if they will be able to come. But I am sure they will do their best.'

'I don't want them to come,' Elsa said. She was hunched in an armchair, her overcoat on. It was true that it was cold in the room. Adele would light the fire shortly before the Vogt boys were due to arrive. As Elsa spoke, a little cloud of vapour emerged from her mouth. 'I don't want to know them, and I don't know why they have to come. I don't know why you are doing this. I hate him, I hate him. I think it's all so stupid.'

'You promised you would be polite to him, and to his brother,' Adele said.

'I promise,' Elsa said. She paused, pensively. 'You don't have to do this. There will be someone else, or there will be just us.'

'I know there will be,' Adele said. 'But, all the same, I am doing this. It will be for the best all round.'

'I can't even draw anything,' Elsa said. 'I tried to draw something this morning, but I couldn't see anything. There was nothing my pencil wanted to draw. Everything was just …' She made a sideways gesture, an erasing gesture. 'When are they coming? Can't you stop them coming?'

'No, Elsa,' Adele said. 'They will be here in an hour. You liked Christian when you met him, remember? Before you knew he was going to marry me? And he is still the same person. They

270

come from a very good family, from Berlin, and I should be proud that one of them wanted to marry me. I can't go on explaining.'

'I don't want you to go,' Elsa said. She lowered her hands; her voice had a quality of inspiration about it. 'I don't want you to go back to Breitenberg, I want you to stay and get to know this boy Vogt, and you'll realize how awful he is, how he's just come to take you away from us, how he doesn't like anyone, he's not even human, he's just a Berlin lawyer who's playing at painting for a year and then he'll go back and make money, like all his family, and you won't marry him.'

Adele made no response. And since the boys were to arrive in an hour or a little more, she now went over to the fireplace with the newspaper of two days ago. She took the sheets, one by one, and rolled them before tying them into a knot and placing them in the hearth; they burnt longer that way. Then there was some wood, donated by the baker from his backyard stores; she piled the logs up carefully, not too tightly, allowing air between them; and twelve precious lumps of coal, resting in a doleful, well-spaced way in the brass coal scuttle. Those had had to be bought – she did not like to think about it. She placed four on the top of the pile with the coal tongs, wiped her hands on her apron, and took a match from the box on the mantelpiece. The fire caught first time, and the first rush of flame started to consume the knotted paper.

'I think you should stay,' Elsa said again. 'You can find out all about him, and he can find out about you.'

'Well, I may have to stay,' Adele said. She took the apron off and folded it tidily, in two, four, eight, sixteen, a small square of green cloth; looking out of the window, and not at Elsa, she hugged it to her chest, perhaps in cold. 'I don't believe that the trains will be running today in this snowstorm, and there doesn't seem to be any prospect of it slowing down. They may not come, of course, and we will have to eat the cake on our own.'

271

'Oh, they will come,' Elsa said, wailing. Her fists pumped up and down. 'I can hear them, they are coming in now.'

'No, I would have seen them,' Adele said, but she was wrong: downstairs there was the noise of the door being opened and rapidly closed, of feet stamping and male voices. The wife of the bookshop owner, who kept an eye over the coming and going in the room over her husband's shop, had been warned and was now letting the guests in. The substance of what she was saying was not possible to catch, but the tone of reprimand and complaint was clear, as an F sharp in a crowded square would be to a musician. Clear, too, was the tone of apology and humorous deprecation from the boys. There was an unfamiliar rumble of men's boots on the wooden stair outside.

The room they lived in was bare – as they came in, Adele saw it clearly. The things they had used to make it their own were ordinary: a five-coloured crochet counterpane, and two small hard cushions in green; three books on the bedside table, and a clean but darned turquoise tablecloth; against the white-washed wall, propped up with their backs to the room, were two piles of paintings and drawings by Elsa. The air in the room was luminous, greenish, subdued with the heavy falling snow outside. It was not yet warm, but it soon would be; the little fire, now making noises of collapse and crackle, had started work on the logs, and soon on the coals. Perhaps the first edge of cold had been taken off the room, and naturally the boys, coming in out of the falling snow, would not feel the room as cold in the first minutes. Only after that, of seeing how her room looked to them, did she see them; the elder, hawkish, one, with his eyes wide-spaced and half alert, and the younger, who, she saw now, was a child, perhaps only fifteen or so, with hair that was blond and heavy, a big thin family nose he would grow into and pale skin with flushes of red at the cheekbones; he looked about him in an almost fearful way, shyly, not quite greeting his brother's fiancée with his eyes. Elsa mutinously stood up, holding the cushion to her.

'It is snowing so hard out there!' Christian said, shedding his outer garments and dropping them carelessly by the door. 'It hasn't stopped for nearly a day. The drifts in the park are simply colossal, a man's height – we had to turn back and go by the roads.'

'Don't leave your coat there,' Adele said, submitting to being kissed. 'We have hooks like Christians, there, behind the door. You should hang it up to dry.'

'And this is my brother Dolphus,' Christian said. He took a special moment to separate out this introduction from everything else; he gave the words a particular emphasis, and the shy boy put his surprisingly large flat hand out to greet Adele. She shook it. 'And Elsa, Adele's sister.'

'You should not have come!' Elsa said. 'The weather would have been its own excuse.'

'I wanted to come, very much,' Dolphus said, in his boy's grating voice as they all sat down around the table, Elsa on the bed covered with counterpane and cushions. He looked at Adele as he spoke, his eyes large and weeping a little in his frost-flushed face. 'What a lovely fire! I thought that Fräulein Winteregger was returning home tomorrow, so this would have been my only chance.'

'I don't know about that,' Adele said. 'I was supposed to be returning home, but there is really no likelihood of anyone going anywhere while this snow continues to fall. I suppose I should go up to the station to find out what the situation is. Please, call me Adele, I don't mind at all.'

'Yes, we are all going to be stuck,' Elsa said. 'You two – you could get here in one piece, without any trouble. But we are going to have to entertain you for the rest of the day, the week, the month.'

'We will manage very well,' Christian said. He looked at her, as if waiting for something – perhaps for her to invite his brother to call her, too, by her Christian name. 'How are you filling the time? It is so dull to be inside when you have to be inside.'

Adele looked at Elsa, who made a big-eyed, hands-open, incredulous gesture of denial and ignorance. The brothers both smiled, somewhat nervously. 'My sister,' Adele said. 'My sister has been keeping busy since the school closed.' She took the coffee pot while she talked, and poured the black acorny mixture into the four little cups; she hoped that it was not too bad. 'Cake, Dolphus – I may call you Dolphus, may I – it is my own cake. Elsa came home, and had nothing to do, and was disappointed. So I suggested to her that she should spend the afternoon drawing. Of course she does that very often, in any case, finding things to draw in odd moments.'

'Yes, I do that, too,' Christian said. He seemed slightly affronted.

'Of course,' Adele said. 'But yesterday, and again this morning, we made quite a game of it, pretending that Elsa had to draw a proper picture in fifteen minutes, as quickly as she could, and then she remembered a game that she had to play in class last year, a game – what was it, Elsa? No, she can't remember. But it was something to do with a single line, or not lifting the pencil from the paper. I don't understand these things, or why that might be important. My sister is the clever one, you know.'

Dolphus took a plate of cake and a small steel fork from Adele; she handed him a limp cotton napkin, very pale pink. All the time, and as he started to eat, he inspected her. She brushed her hands down her striped skirt, not quite certain what he was looking for.

'But what did you draw?' Christian said to Elsa. 'I never know what to draw. Either I see only things which have been drawn a million times before, like a sunset, or a pot of flowers. Or everything seems worth drawing. Sometimes I could draw just the corner of that table, there, with that edge of a chair and perhaps the line at the bottom of the window.'

Christian and Adele both looked at Elsa; she gave a mountainously rude shrug, and reached out herself for a piece of the parsnip cake. She began to gnaw at it without benefit of plate, napkin or fork.

'Elsa,' Adele said, but made no further attempt to discipline her. She turned back to Christian and Dolphus. 'I love it when Elsa makes a picture of something that you hardly notice yourself. When she was younger, she used to draw corners of my father's workshop, just two or three tools, or perhaps one of the apprentices. I liked that so much. Yesterday, she was drawing me at the washing-up or making the beds.'

But it was Dolphus who now leant forward and said, 'May I see? I would love to see.'

Elsa gave another shrug. Adele looked at her in a warning manner. She got up and went to the wall, where a tattered brown portfolio stood. 'These are just the drawings from yesterday and this morning,' Adele said, bringing it over. 'This is me sitting darning socks; and then again, looking out of the window; and then again, coming in from the market, covered with snow, you can see – how well she has caught that! I feel completely cold all over again, looking at it. And here, mixing a cake to take down to the baker to cook. They are so kind downstairs!'

'No, they aren't,' Elsa said. 'They aren't! How can you say that? They always complain, every single time, they always say it's hard enough to find space for people they've known for years, let alone people like us, a crazy art student and her little sister! They aren't kind! And the bookshop woman, too, the one just now, she hates us! She was laughing at me when I went out last week to Mazdaznan, she said, you, you lunatic, before the war, people like you, they were locked up. How can you say these things?'

'I suppose,' Adele said, as if Elsa's shriek had been a soft demurral, 'I suppose that they can be a little resentful. But they have a lot of requests, it is true, down there in the baker's. And they do put things into the oven for us, sometimes straight away. I think they only once refused to put something in altogether, which was really a shame. People are so good, generally, and times are so hard – I would love to be able to buy one of their beautiful cakes, but I am really afraid to ask the price, even. How does your family cope, Christian? Do they have a good baker nearby?'

'I think so,' Christian said. 'I don't think I quite know the baker that Martha uses. Martha? Oh, she's the cook. No, I know, it is that place in Friedrichstrasse, the good one further from the railway station, where everybody goes. I remember seeing their bills with the beautiful writing and the picture of the miller when I was little. I thought it was so kind of them to send in a letter with a jolly picture on it. But you said your father had a workshop that Elsa used to draw. What is your father's work-shop, please?'

'My father makes puppets,' Adele said, but she had hardly begun when Elsa flung herself forward.

'You! You're going to marry my sister! You asked her to marry her, and then you start wondering – who is her family? What does her—'

'Elsa, please,' Adele said.

'No, I will say it,' Elsa said. 'How can you say, "I love this woman and I want to marry her and I want to be a member of her family," when you don't know anything about her, you don't know anything about her family, you don't know anything because you don't care anything, you only want to be in love with someone because it will all be so wonderful?'

'Elsa, this is not helpful,' Adele said. 'You should not be so rude to Christian and Dolphus. It is not their fault that they haven't found out about Father yet.'

'Yes, he is a puppet-maker,' Elsa said. 'His puppets are beautiful, beautiful. They are hanging there, look, in the corner by the fireplace, one of them. Do you know where he comes from? We come from Breitenberg. He is famous all through Germany, our father. How could you not know? How could you not want to find out? You think we are nothing, that you are going to do everything for Adele, make her your wife and then she is never going to see her crazy sister again or her father, who is a puppet-maker, and you are going to find out some time what happened to her mother, what she died of, and then that will all be quite all right. Adele, you must not marry this man, you must not.'

'I am sorry, Fräulein Winteregger,' Christian said. He was flushed and quiet; his hands were placed firmly on his knees, gripping tightly. Dolphus had taken a large bite out of the parsnip cake; as Elsa shouted, he lowered the remains to the plate, chewing in a discreet, ruminative, secretive way, as if it might soon be wrong to eat it at all. 'I didn't mean to offend. We have so much to find out about each other.'

He spoke in a formal, slow manner, as if suppressing some other comment. He did not look at Adele or at Elsa as he spoke, but at some point between their heads, as if at the far wall. 'And it is true that I did not know what your father's profession was, and I am sure that there are many other things I did not have time to discover about your family. I am sure that Adele will say the same thing, that there are things she does not know about our family, that she wants to discover a lot of insignificant small things about us. I am sure she does not know what the profession of our father is, either.'

'Of course I know what the profession of your father is,' Adele said, astonished and, it appeared, even a little offended. 'Your father is a lawyer. Of course I knew that.'

Dolphus turned from one to another, to Adele, to Christian, to Elsa, munching and taking everything in. He turned back to Adele in wide-eyed entrancement. It was, it seemed, as good as a play to him.

15.

The effects of the snowfall, making rounded shapes of the trees in the ducal park, obscuring the town's buildings, making old men out of gabled houses, marking them with white eyebrows, was all known to the poets of the town. But the best of the poets of the town would have known what it came of. The atmospheric pressure falls, and remains low; the temperature falls to a certain point, as the sun withdraws and the earth tilts away from it; the masses of cloud are moved upwards by wind as they hit the Thuringian hills, and the conditions, very specific in their requirements, are met. The water in the clouds freezes, coagulates, forms a snow crystal, and another, and another, and their own weight, like small furry beasts come to existence in mid-air, sinks them to the ground. The low pressure remains; the temperature stays constant; the snow continues to fall. The ground freezes; the snow packs hard; the surface snow hardens, freezes, solidifies.

What can be done? Nothing. The animal life in the town and thereabouts withdraws inside, for warmth: those animals who can sit before a fire, the windows and the curtains shut tight, and eat small, toasty, pleasant things brought to them by maids. The coal stores are reckoned, and thought to be good for a few days yet. Others of the animal life in the town light smaller fires, and sit inside, swathed in blankets and mufflers, or they encourage their confused dogs to sit on their laps for once, to do the forbidden thing of leaping onto an armchair. It is astonishing how much heat a dog gives out, more than one Weimar wife will remark to her husband, sitting in small rooms with their gloves on. Other animal life retires to the stables, and makes a serious start on the winter hay; the last of the horse-drawn cabbies gives way, and there is no work to be had, and they might as well surrender until the snow finishes falling. There are people who are now out of food, and out of what little fuel they had. There is an old couple in a tiny shack, meant only as a garden shed but which was sold to them in the aftermath of the war by someone who needed a couple of hundred marks when a couple of hundred marks meant anything at all. They sit, swathed in every piece of clothing they can muster, and are still cold. They are thinking about burning the third chair, because there are only two of them and the snow must stop before long, and when it stops falling, the temperature will rise a little. They are thinking about it independently. Tomorrow one of them will raise the subject with the other, and they will argue about it a little longer before burning the last thing they can burn. They have no food to eat, hot or cold, apart from some hard black bread. There are animals in the park, huddled together in the hollows of logs, performing the lot of animals everywhere, which is waiting in terror. Somewhere outside the city boundaries – it is so hard to draw the boundaries, and the lands of snow are a mapless nation – somewhere outside the boundaries, a horse wanders blind and stumbling, lame and panicked and in pain. Its owner is somewhere about; he lies on his side in a mound of snow, his face rimed with frost, his staring eyes open, his lips drawn back in a snarl. The salt tears from his eyes are frozen to his cheeks; the saliva in his open mouth is hard-frozen ice. His animal terror is over. He will be found when the snow melts, but that will not be for many weeks. He is the water-carter of the town, and the water in his great barrel is frozen, spilt out across the country road in a small frozen lake. In her house, the water-carter's wife sits in her overstuffed parlour, a fire going, the curtains drawn, an English toasting fork bearing a slice of bread. She is well provided for by this handler of a town monopoly; he must have found himself safe quarters as the storm broke, and is probably now being looked after in great comfort by some chit of a farmer's daughter, as she observes to the maid when she comes in. There is plenty of food around. It is just getting to it that is the problem, or getting it to us, rather. She will give him what-for, when she sees him, she says. But in fact she would exchange the prospect of a future punishment for the sure knowledge that he is safe somewhere, and not lying dead, frozen, by the side of a deep-covered country road.

At home, Klee wears woollen gloves with the ends of the

fingers cut off: with a pencil, he draws. He notices that his fingers are white with the cold, and shuddering when his hand holds still, in the air. Is his violin safe? Could it crack with the chill? He sees the indeterminate but purposeful movement of his breath in the cold air of the studio, like a brushstroke of much-diluted ink on paper. It is too cold to paint. Today he is drawing. Tomorrow or the day after or the day after that, the Bauhaus will reopen. There, he will paint the wizard who brings the chill to the earth, flying through the air. He brings his thoughts back, purposefully, to the drawing in front of him. It is a drawing of a fish, an old, old fish, one that knows everything, in the bottom of the deepest lake, beyond the fall of light. It looks upwards, towards what, it does not know.

In the kitchen, Lily talks to the cook. What will they eat for dinner? Heart; there is heart still. And tomorrow? The cook does not know. They may have to eat beans. Is there anything else? Nothing; they may have to brave the snow, if the butcher's shop is open, and if the butcher's shop contains anything in the way of meat. So perhaps beans. Like the ancient Greeks, Lily remarks, with a despairing laugh. But the cook doesn't know about that.

Itten walks in the park. He is cold, and he rises above sensations of cold. Cold is a delusion and a snare, like the effects of all the senses. Last week he walked with twelve; today he walks with only one. He says these things as they walk. They cannot see far. Their eyes must be turned inwards. The world is a gift and an illusion, Itten says. He does not raise his voice above conversational level, and the words of his speech do not survive the short journey to his single disciple's shuddering head. One disciple is enough, Itten says, in kindly consolation. The disciple hears that, and tries to hold on to it against the thought that one disciple is too much, and that one disciple is hungry and colder than he has ever been in his life. Some disciples decided to stay inside by the fire and come back when the weather is better, Itten observes. Those disciples have failed, as Mazdaznan's disciple always fails, through the call and tug of animal spirits, which we try to rise above. But Mazdaznan does not fail, even if every one of us fails. Mazdaznan, without any proponents or disciples, goes on in the cosmos.

In a hall, sixty men in uniform stand and sing their song. Almost everyone came. They are red-faced and chilblained, but they came. Their animal spirits are strong; they feel like beasts and they look like doughnuts. Their song is about a hero of their movement; the speech that is to come is about the Jews. They look forward to it.

The door of the garden shack opens. It is an old man. In one hand, he holds an ancient wooden chair. In the other, he holds an axe. The time has come to burn the chair for heat. He has taken it out to slaughter it, like a well-loved animal. He places the chair on the ground; he raises his trembling arms.

16.

In the room above the bookshop, Christian observed the tiny fire with a kind of longing. It was sinking and sinking, and now was surely beyond rescue. Christian's longing was for the fire of the future, the high-banked and roaring fire that he would insist on once they were married. He observed that, in the coal scuttle, there remained only three pieces of coal. Adele gave the impression of being a good and practical housewife, but her cake was not very good, and her coffee was awful, and surely a good and practical housewife would have made a better estimate of the amount of coal she needed to bring up from the coal cellar. Adele would have to go down again once he and Dolphus had left, and bring up another load of coal to see them through the day.

They had been talking about Breitenberg, and Adele had been answering his detailed questions with detailed answers. Elsa was watching him narrowly, sometimes puffing with despair when he asked something stupid, when he felt he had been told the answer at some point earlier. He could have asked Dolphus to contribute, but his brother was just sitting, staring at the two of them who were talking in a shy, embarrassed, blank way. The English nanny had drummed it into them: you must speak in company, not sit in silence as Germans do. But Dolphus had forgotten the lesson. Christian went on asking polite, amused questions. His mind was on the fire. It had been a great mistake to take off their coats and scarves when they had arrived: the room was growing colder, and nobody seemed to be taking any steps to feed the fire.

'We must be thinking about going,' Christian said eventually. 'I expect that the train you were planning to return home on will not be running in this weather.'

'Almost certainly not,' Adele said. 'I must try to send a telegram to Father. We will just have to sit and wait, and hope for the best.'

'We will come and see you tomorrow,' Christian said. 'If there is anything we can do ...'

'That would be very pleasant,' Adele said. 'If you happen to see any eggs for sale, one can go on living on eggs for days, and somebody always has a chicken.'

Dolphus said his goodbyes, in a remote and withdrawn way, to Elsa and to Adele; Christian kissed his fiancée on the cheek. They dressed, in coats, scarves and gloves; they pulled on their galoshes. It seemed to go on for ever, with Adele standing there patiently waiting for their departure. The service he had offered, and had had in mind, was more like holding an umbrella over the pair of sisters as they walked to the railway station.

They let themselves out. The snow had slowed, and the sky was almost beginning to clear. There was a patch of intense, lucid blue between snowclouds. The cold was fierce, and they walked with their faces wrapped in scarves, in silence. The sound of their galoshes in the snow was solitary in the noiseless town. Dolphus followed his brother through the winding streets, softened and rounded with the snowfall. The shops they passed were closed, their windows covered with planks of wood; they passed through a square where the central statue – had it been of Goethe and Schiller? Christian could not remember – had been swathed in sheets of green-painted planking against the cold. What was it to guard against? Would an iron statue really shatter in the cold, and if it were cold enough, would the green-painted planking do to protect it?

They reached the park. A path across it had been cleared. A wind was parting the clouds, and an allegro suggestion of sunlight on the brilliant white – white with a suggestion of purple in its shadows, of blue, of pink, even – was transforming the landscape, as the snow had transformed it in the last days. They began to wade through the deep snow; it was laborious work. Something hit Christian on the side of his head; a block of snow. He turned, and Dolphus, whose eyes alone could be seen, alive with merriment, threw another fistful of snow. Christian bent and packed the snow into a ball, and threw it back. They ran as best they could through the deep snow, and fell, and threw snowballs, and fell again, and were covered with snow, and pulled themselves out of drifts and waded through still deeper snow, as fast as they could. The snow, apart from where they had been, was a perfect smooth surface. Nobody had been in the park for days, and if they had, their tracks had been covered.

When they arrived at Frau Scherbatsky's house, the maid Maria was watching out for them, and she must have called her mistress. Frau Scherbatsky opened the door to them as soon as they knocked.

'My dear Herr Vogt,' she cried. 'My dear Herr Dolphus. It was most unwise to go out at all – I would have insisted that you stay at home today. Look at you! Quite covered with snow. Maria will make you some bowls of hot water which you must soak your feet and hands in, immediately. You young people, you have no idea of the pains of chilblains! And then change into dry clothes and come downstairs to sit with Herr Neddermeyer and me by the fire. He has stayed at home with me all day. Very sensible. Herr Wolff has gone out, in his medals and his uniform and his heavy coat, to one of his meetings. Herr Dolphus, please, leave your coat and hat and scarves down here – they will dry much better in the cloakroom downstairs. How did they get so covered? Herr Wolff will come back in the same state, I know. Maria, is the hot water ready for Herr Vogt and his brother? Maria! Maria!'

When they were upstairs, their trousers rolled up and their reddened feet sitting in bowls of hot water, Christian allowed himself to return to Adele, with the beginnings of an apology. He did not see how he was going to be able to remove himself from the situation. He had had an opportunity to say, 'Perhaps it would be for the best,' when Elsa had pointed out in her noisy way that they knew nothing of each other, and should not marry. But he had not taken that opportunity when it came. And now the opportunity would not arise again. Adele was the daughter of a puppet-maker who had seen her chance to marry the son of a rich Berlin lawyer. He could not tell her he had changed his mind: not only honour but the law would not permit him to. He knew enough of Adele to understand that she would not permit him to, either. Her tidy mind would not leave the matter unresolved.

'I know that Adele is—' Christian began, not turning to Dolphus, but looking down into his bowl and his sore, reddened feet in it. But Dolphus interrupted him.

'I know,' he said. 'I know exactly. I can't say how much—'

'Adele?' Christian said.

'She is ...' Dolphus said. He raised his head like an animal at the first light of dawn, stretching and feeling the first rush of blood. '. . . she is wonderful. The most wonderful woman I ever met. I can see exactly why everything made such sense to you. I would marry her, too, tomorrow. If she were not spoken for, I would fall in love with her like a flash.'

'I know,' said Christian. He was sunk in perfect misery. Adele had come between him and his brother, and had made a barrier of misunderstanding. Dolphus had not noticed how cold the room had been, how the coffee had sunk to a layer of gritty, sandy acorn grindings, how pert and irritating Adele had been, how the cake had had a strange aftertaste of parsnip. Such a misunderstanding had never happened before.

'We should go down and sit by the fire with your landlady and her lover,' Dolphus said. 'I want to tell them all about Adele, too. Look!'

He held up a piece of paper, rounded and slightly crumpled. It was one of Elsa's drawings of her sister; this one of Adele making the bed. It was done in large, confident pencil strokes, thick and expressive. It was unmistakably Adele, and in the pencil strokes, there was affection. 'I stole it,' Dolphus said, with simple pride. 'I hid it in the back of my jacket, when no one was looking.'

17.

That night it did not snow again: the temperature dropped stolidly, and the ground froze. The next day began brilliantly, but towards noon the clouds moved back, and after lunch it did begin to snow again. Herr Neddermeyer observed that he had never seen such weather this early in the year, and Frau Scherbatsky agreed with him. The Vogt brothers played cards quietly in a corner of the sitting room; they would have gone out, but Dolphus had unwisely asked Frau Scherbatsky for some honey and lemon juice in a cup of hot water, and she had promptly observed that he had the beginnings of a sore throat. They sat and they played whist, a game from their English-nanny childhood: Herr Neddermeyer called out from time to time that skat was a much better game, that he would school them in that later. It was a dull afternoon. Christian would have liked to remove his boots and stretch out in his stockinged feet on the chartreuse sofa, and to sleep the dull afternoon away. But he behaved himself.

At four, Maria brought the tea in and, with it, a note that she gave to Herr Neddermeyer. How had it been delivered, across these drifts and banks of impassable snow? It was a mystery. At six, Neddermeyer's friend and colleague Grausemann would come to call. 'I have known old Grausemann for many years,' Neddermeyer said. 'His time hangs heavy on his hands now that his practice is wound up and his wife is dead. I would be very glad to see him. It is not far for him to come.' Frau Scherbatsky followed Maria out of the room.

At six precisely, an old man with an elaborately shaped, expressively styled moustache and beard was shown into the sitting room. He seemed somehow familiar; it was the gestures, which were the same as Neddermeyer's: the same experimental baring of the teeth, the same side-to-side smoothing gesture in the air. They had indeed known each other for decades.

'It may surprise you to know,' Grausemann said, 'that we have not always been in such good odour with each other. There was the case of a pupil architect, in the summer of 1892, was there not?' His eyes shone; he reached across the table for the dish of potatoes, and helped himself extensively. Wolff, who had been upstairs silently all day and had come down only for dinner, let his eyes count the potatoes as the old fool doled them out to himself.

'Young Fragewort,' Neddermeyer said. 'Indeed, young Fragewort.'

He shook his head, and Grausemann made a theatrical shrug, his shoulders half rising about his ears. They looked at each other, Neddermeyer narrowly questioning, Grausemann with eyes innocently open; and then, without any suggestion of cause or meaning, they both burst out laughing.

'That must be thirty years ago,' Grausemann said.

'Surely not,' Neddermeyer said. Wolff leant forward and

rudely took the dish of potatoes from where it stood, before Grausemann.

'Thirty years!' Grausemann said. 'The summer of 1892. That is thirty years ago and several months. Count them.'

'Thirty years!' Neddermeyer said. 'Thirty years!'

'Young Fragewort,' Grausemann said. 'And now he is …'

'Young Fragewort,' Neddermeyer said, wonderingly.

'Hardly that,' Grausemann said. 'But when you think about it?'

'Yes, astounding would be the word,' Neddermeyer said. 'He ought to be in gaol, young Fragewort.'

'And some people would say, so should you,' Grausemann said. 'So – should – you. I don't know that young Fragewort isn't in gaol. He may very well be.'

'And richly deserved,' Neddermeyer said, nodding. 'Is there more of that excellent venison stew, my dear Frau Scherbatsky?'

There was not: the addition of Grausemann had seen to that. Frau Scherbatsky had always impressed on her guests that they might ask their friends to dinner, if they were presentable and if they would amuse her. Dolphus was one extra person already, and Christian wondered whether she had meant the standing principle to apply in the middle of a snowstorm when there had been no deliveries of meat for three days. The venison stew had been presented with an unusual number of dumplings, almost piled up and obscuring the surface; the potatoes had been augmented with a large amount of noodles. Frau Scherbatsky's kindly smile was as it had always been, or almost, as she passed the water jug or the little silver and blue-glass mustard pot to her guests or her guests' guests. Herr Wolff, on the other hand, in his weekend pinstriped suit with his little political badge on his lapel, was silent, scowling, hungry and meditative.

The next day was much the same. At six, two men arrived at the house; this time, they were associates of Herr Wolff. Frau Scherbatsky greeted them with pursed mouth. They were less sociable, and their names hardly registered. Their suits were frayed at cuff and lapel; they wore, each, the same little badge that Wolff wore. Their conversation was much less sparkling even than Grausemann's. It was mostly about the Jews. When the dinner bell came, they leapt up, but not to leave. Frau Scherbatsky asked with every appearance of practised surprise if Herr Wolff had invited his friends to dinner. But Wolff was inured to this kind of treatment, and replied that it was one of the happiest memories of his time here that Frau Scherbatsky had in the past offered hospitality to friends of both – of all – her lodgers. Of course, if it were now a problem ...

It was not a problem, and, once places had been set, Wolff's two friends sat down to dinner with them, making the best of the vegetable soup, the two rabbits, and the bowl of nuts that was brought out to supplement the quark and red fruit dessert. It might have been tactful of them to stay off the subject of food shortages, and not to take such pleasure in talking about the impossibility of buying food at any price in Weimar today or yesterday, to talk about the results of the Jews' machinations bringing about the starvation of good Christian folk. Frau Scherbatsky listened, and did not contribute, other than in muttered asides to Neddermeyer; Dolphus had lost his voice, and raised and lowered his spoon in a tired, mechanical manner, wincing as the soup hit the raw back of his throat. Christian did not believe that any conspiracy was taking place to deprive anyone of food. He believed that it was the snow. The sentences followed one another as if rehearsed many times before in exactly these terms. One of the men had a strong Berlin accent and a spoilt, gaseous odour from his mouth. He made gurgling noises with his lips as he drank his soup; the other looked sharply at Neddermeyer whenever he said anything, and tried to put his arm around Maria's waist as she was taking the soup plates away.

Afterwards, when the associates of Wolff had eaten and promptly gone away, saying goodbye with a belch and a damp handshake, Frau Scherbatsky cornered Christian at the foot of the stairs.

'I am going to have to ask you,' she said, 'to make a particular point of not asking friends or colleagues of yours to dinner for the next few days. I am so sorry to be inhospitable, you know, but it is so difficult to find food even for us!'

'I'm sorry about my brother,' Christian said. 'I'm sure he wouldn't be a burden if he had any choice in the matter.'

'Herr Vogt!' Frau Scherbatsky said. 'No, I beg you – I did not mean that in the slightest. I was really referring to those who see an opportunity to feed themselves up at our expense. Herr Grausemann is a welcome guest. But those gentlemen tonight – I really am not so very sure. I will be speaking to Herr Wolff on the subject, you may be sure.' She waved her hands in an evocative, imprecise way. 'Of course, Herr Wolff's friends may be correct. There may be hoarding going on by people who do not really care about ordinary Germans. But I don't think knowing that will help any of us to eat better if this house becomes a staging post for all manner of hungry acquaintances.'

Upstairs, Dolphus was reading a book and smoking, his stock-inged feet outstretched on the truckle bed he slept on. But Christian did not think that he was concentrating on or very much absorbed in his book. The book he was reading was a school book, a tattered and much-used edition of *The Aeneid*.

'What did Frau Scherbatsky want?' Dolphus said, not raising his eyes from the page. 'Was she telling you that I've got to go? I don't think there's much more food in the house. At least there won't be, if Wolff keeps bringing people of that sort to dinner.'

'She's become very fond of you,' Christian said. 'Heavens knows why or how. I wish you wouldn't smoke in the bedroom. I never do. And you should not smoke with a sore throat at all.'

'It has an antiseptic effect, but I'll stop immediately,' Dolphus said, but rather waving his pipe round than extinguishing it.

There was a confidence about Dolphus that Christian had never observed before.

'No, she was saying that you are very welcome, but she's going to have to call a stop to any of us asking guests for dinner until she can restock the larder, or some such phrase,' Christian said. 'There is food enough for the regular guests, apparently, but not for any old wanderers or chance-takers.'

'We can't invite anyone?' Dolphus said.

'Why?' Christian said. 'Who—' and for one moment he had completely forgotten about Adele and Elsa; forgotten their existence, their life, the obligation they bore each other. Dolphus had remembered, but Christian had forgotten that he was engaged to anyone at all. 'Oh, they're quite all right, don't worry. They are in the middle of town. They can call across the street to any number of friends, Bauhaus people, innkeepers; they can make their way. It is much easier for them than for us, you know. And we will see them again when the paths are clearer.'

'If you think so,' Dolphus said, with a sidelong glance, returning to his book.

18.

Somewhere in Weimar, before a fire, a man with his feet in slippers and a pleasant warm shawl about his neck was writing on his ninth sheet of paper. He went on fluently, his pen leaping up and down like a seismograph. 'One can see how wonderfully the stock exchange Jew and the leader of the workers co-operate, how the stock exchange publications and the newspaper of the workers echo each other. They both pursue one common policy and a single aim. Moses Cohen on the one side encourages his association to refuse the workers' demands, while his brother Isaac in the factory incites the masses and shouts, "Look at them! They only want to oppress you! Shake off your fetters!" And his brother ensures that the fetters are well forged.'

He stretched out his feet, his toes separating within the slippers; he set down his pen and ran his fingers through a little stretching exercise, as if about to play the piano. He had written a lot this morning, produced a good stretch of his speech to the Association when it met next Saturday in Eisenach – if the weather had improved sufficiently by then. They were good, honest fellows, the fellows in the Association, but he wondered whether he was talking over their heads.

His wife put her head in at the door; a sweet, smiling face, twenty years younger than his own. 'Is it going well, my sweet?' she said, in her childish way.

'Very well, thank you, my love,' he said, smiling. She placed a finger to her lips and withdrew, theatrically, slowly. She amused him: that was the secret of her appeal. He picked up the pen and began to write about Moses and Isaac again. It was important to persuade people, and he remembered that it could only happen little by little, one person at a time. Every change of thought was a revolution and a turning towards the sun. It was pleasantly warm in his study. It was very agreeable to sit in these comfortable surroundings, with a fire blazing and no need to go outside, and write confident, inspiring paragraphs about the Jews.

There was no food at all in the room the Winteregger sisters lived in, except two pieces of black bread and three potatoes. That would do for their luncheon, and then they would have to try to find some more food somewhere in the town. But the town was still so heavily under snow, and no shops in the street had opened for many days. If only the boys had not eaten so much of the cake she had made! That had only lasted another day after they came. Adele thought that there might be shops elsewhere open. But she knew that the prices would have doubled or trebled. She had no idea how she might pay for anything. All around her, there were people waiting to take advantage; people who had seen the closure of the railway lines as a way of making a good deal of money. She could feel it in the crisp air.

'I will go out later this morning,' Adele said. 'There must be somewhere open where I can find a little something for us to eat. People may have some soup, or something small that they can spare. And if that doesn't succeed, then I am sure it will not kill us to do without food for an evening, and things will be different tomorrow.'

'I am so cold,' Elsa said. 'And hungry. Very, very hungry. There was not nearly enough to eat last night, or yesterday during the day.'

'I know,' Adele said. 'But at least I am here for you.'

'Can't you go out now?' Elsa said. 'I can come with you. I don't mind.'

'There is no point at all in our both getting cold and wet,' Adele said. 'I can be much quicker on my own. I am sure I know places that will be open for food and wood, and I can get there and get back before you know it, and this afternoon will be like Christmas. You wait and see.'

Out in the whitened streets of Weimar, a few people were starting to move. Julius Pringsheim had been sent out by his wife Dora; there was still some food in the house, but it would be good to see what the situation was. In their little house just outside the centre of Weimar, Dora sat with their twin boys, both two, in front of the fire – thank heavens there was a good lot of coal in the cellar. She fed them and entertained them with simple games and songs.

'Seven things are needed
For a lovely cake,
Eggs and fat!
Butter and salt!
Milk, flour and saffron makes it yellow!'

She patted the boys' hands gently; they hit hers back as hard as they could, shrieking with joy. Julius was a teacher and had often observed that there was nothing you could do to stop boys taking on their nature, setting on each other violently. 'Were you like that?' Dora would ask, since Julius was a gentle soul with three gentle sisters.

He would smile and shake his close-cropped head. 'They must learn it from their sister,' Julius would say. But that was a joke, because Lotte was a dark-haired angel who had never been a moment's trouble.

The angel was well wrapped, her fur-edged coat and muff keeping her warm as she sat on the sledge. Her father pulled her along. She was no weight. The streets were empty, but Julius thought there might be some life around the Hotel Elephant; that was where he was heading. Lotte was singing something into her muff as Julius turned, panting slightly, into the Bött-chergasse. 'What are you singing?' Julius said, turning, but Lotte was absorbed in her song, which seemed to need hand gestures. 'You'll catch a cold!' Julius said. 'Put your hands back in your muff!'

Julius had not been thinking. In the Böttchergasse there was the café he knew not to go to, the Café Harbach; it had been no trouble before the war, but now, in the last year or two, it had been taken over by the wastrels of the town. It was best to walk another way. He saw, too, that the café was actually open, a path cleared to its door and two men sitting in the well-lit window. If the Café Harbach were open, then things would be better than he thought.

In a room lined with paintings, with a violin resting on a table, with a pianoforte covered with a purple velvet cloth, Klee sat hunched before an easel. On it, there was a painting. He thought it might be of birds at dawn. He had finished it the day before, in the intense cold, thinking hard of a summer morning. There were four birds on a line. He saw now that the line was not a tree branch, as he had thought, it was the mechanical arm of a musical instrument, turned by a handle from below, to make the birds sing. He remembered the title that had come to him at dawn, as he woke, his lips almost moving with the rightness of this title. He would not write it down just yet. If the title remained in his mind tomorrow, he would write it down. He turned to the table by his side and, with paint-stained fingers, picked up a pen. It was his habit to write in notebooks when a thought came to him. He did not write the title of the painting. He wrote, 'Art does not exist to reproduce the visible. It makes visible.' He had written this before, in different circumstances. He wrote it now because that was what he had done, and what he was about to do. Every person who heard it might change their mind, and find it a new thought. You could only change the world by changing the way individuals thought, one individual at a time, as if turning towards the sun.

Fritz Leitner and Gottlob Gebhardt were the two men sitting in the window of the café. They had been pleasantly surprised to discover that it was open. The night before, they had decided that the best thing was to go to their comrade Wolff's lodgings – he lived in high style, and his landlady fed him well, they believed. The welcome had not been everything you could have hoped for, but they had fed like kings. It was good to talk over the present situation, too. But now it looked as if the town was starting to move again. The Café Harbach was open, though old Harbach was complaining that there was not enough food to run a full menu. And people were starting to move through the streets. There, a man pulling a child on a sort of sledge, there over the street.

'That's an awful Jew,' Gebhardt said.

'I know him,' Leitner said. 'He teaches at the Gymnasium. He teaches my niece mathematics, I believe. A Jew like that, teaching at the Gymnasium.'

'A disgrace,' Gebhardt said. 'Where's he going now?'

'They've seen a chance to make some money,' Harbach said, coming over in his apron to observe.

'Taking his child out, too,' Gebhardt said. 'They want their children to learn early how to make money.'

'My little son,' Leitner said, hunching up his shoulders. He lisped and whined as he talked, making what he thought of as a Jewish voice. 'Son of mine, watch how their money flows into our pockets, and stays there. Plot and plan, my son, plot and plan.'

'Most of them know better than to walk down the Bött-chergasse,' Harbach said.

'If Wolff were here, he'd be explaining about the blood and inheritance that makes the Jew stoop like that, makes him clever,' Gebhardt said. He and Leitner and Harbach were conceded to be very good fellows. But they were not very sophisticated about their understanding of the world. They understood this fact, too, and were often to be heard referring in respectful, jeering tones to the theorists of the movement, like Wolff. He had read deeply in scientists who understood the difference between the races; he understood in detail what Leitner and Gebhardt and Harbach and their kind, very decent fellows who were the life and soul of the movement grasped through instinctive revulsion.

'It's the blood of centuries, hawked around half of Europe and half of Asia, by the cosmopolites,' Leitner said. 'Look at the cosmopolite. He couldn't punch a soldier in the face. He wouldn't have gone to war. He'd have found some clever way out of it.'

'There was a Jew in our battalion, a butcher's son from Berlin,' Gebhardt said. 'How he yelled when he found out that his wife was dead! Dead of the influenza. He yelled and screamed and howled when he got the letter. But the comrades in the battalion, many of them met the same fate. Did he yell then? No. Probably working out ways to sell their uniforms back to the army.'

'You're letting that Jew get away,' Harbach said.

'It's so nice and warm in here,' Gebhardt said. 'And it is only one Jew. We could let him go on his way. Oh, very well.'

They hauled themselves to their feet and left the café. Leitner let out a hostile shout into the street, and the Jew and his child, now in their effrontery at the end of the Böttchergasse, both looked round. It was as if they were expecting to be greeted by friends who just happened to be sitting in the Café Harbach.

'We carry on walking,' Julius said to Lotte in a cheerful, ordinary voice. 'And they will grow bored and go away. On we go! We have to find bread, and milk, and eggs, and all sorts of good things to eat, to make a cake!'

But then there was a fat man in a hat in front of him. His face was red and moist with the remnants of an overheated room.

'Excuse me,' Julius said, and tried to pull the sledge around him. But it was not so easy, and there was a second man there now, a man with a gingery moustache in a shabby black overcoat; the man, despite a very recent haircut, was as shabby and worn at the edges as his overcoat. 'If you will excuse me, gentlemen,' Julius said. The sledge was hard to pull to one side; it preferred to follow the same direction, and Lotte suddenly felt quite heavy.

'Are you out on business, sir?' the fat man said. 'Most people prefer to stay at home in this weather, unless they have a good reason.'

'Yes, that is so,' Julius said. He tried again to get between the two men, but the ginger man now stepped directly in front of him. He could not move without exposing Lotte on the sledge to these two men.

'Have you had a successful morning, then, Moses?' the fat man said.

'My name is not Moses,' Julius said. Behind him, Lotte was being very good. She knew when to interrupt and when to keep absolutely quiet. This was a playground taunt. Julius had seen them in his school, and he remembered them from twenty years ago.

'Oh, I got your name wrong,' the fat man said. 'Have you had a successful morning then, Isaac? Have you been out making the blizzard pay for you?'

'My name is not Isaac, either,' Julius said. 'If I could pass, gentlemen, my business is my own.'

The gingery man now placed a hand on Julius's shoulder. Close, he smelt of old beer and the remains of some cheap cigarettes. His hand was ungloved, and was red with cold or drink.

'Please, remove that,' Julius said firmly. 'My business is no business of yours.'

The gingery man did not remove his hand. 'There are people in this town who have had nothing to eat for days,' he said. 'There are people in this town who cannot afford to buy anything to eat even when the shops are open. Why is that, Isaac? Have you done well this morning, Isaac? Have you been making a profit out of Germans, Isaac?' At the last, the man hissed, lisping the *s* in 'Isaac' as if imitating a snake.

Julius was aware that this assault was not happening unobserved. A girl – a young woman, neatly dressed and small, with sage-coloured stockings underneath her brown coat – had paused fifteen paces away, at the turn into the Böttchergasse, and was watching them.

'None of that is true,' Julius said, maintaining a light, pleasant tone. 'My daughter and I –' he indicated, thinking that perhaps a reminder that he was with a small child might turn away assault at least '– we were merely coming into Weimar to buy a few essentials.'

'Let's see what is in your pocket,' the fat man said, and the gingery man reached intimately towards Julius's neck and lapel. Julius stood back, amazed and now angry, but the man pushed him against the wall, and quickly reached into his inside pocket. In there was a bundle of notes – it could not be otherwise. The billion-mark notes were now worth so little. They had to be fastened with a pin, run through them, and it was this bundle that the gingery man now brought out.

'That's a lot of money you've made this morning,' the gingery man said.

Julius began to protest, but the gingery man was shouting now. Lotte behind – he could hear her crying.

'Look at all of this!' the man shouted. 'All this money. Making it out of our suffering, out of German surrender and humiliation. Look!' He tore the pin out, and sent a billion-mark note into the air. It fell to the snow. 'You bought goods cheap, before the snow, and now you come into Weimar, and you have sold them to the Germans, who have no alternative. Everything gone, Isaac? A good morning's work, Isaac? Have you sold everything, Isaac? Everything except one child? You're waiting for a few years for her to fetch a good price, Isaac? Or are you going to buy a little Christian girl to be her servant, a little German blond girl, Isaac?' With every five words, the man was throwing a note into the air. Julius did nothing. He knew that to scramble after money would persuade them to put their boot on the back of his neck. It was so little, the money, so little.

'You love money,' the fat man said. 'And we love our country. That is the difference. That is why we are going to win in the end. You can't live on the money that you love so much, can you? Here—' and he took the money from his comrade. He took seven or eight notes from the top, screwed them up, and now pushed them into Julius's face. He would have forced them into his mouth, but Julius would not open it. His teeth were clamped shut. That noise was the noise of Lotte crying, and calling for her mummy. But Mummy could not hear. 'There, thief,' the fat man said. He cast the money down to the ground. 'You earned it. Enjoy it while you can.'

For the moment, that seemed to be all. The two men turned away. One made a gesture at his neck, a tightening gesture, as one who goes into an important argument or as one who has won it. They walked away. They took some of the money with them, but most of it now lay about Julius and Lotte on the snow. She was crying, and he stroked her as he bent down and started to pick up the money. It was all so little. At the end of the Böttchergasse, the young woman who had stopped watched the two men going, and looked for a moment at the sight of a Jew scrabbling around in the snow for money. She had seen everything. She did not come to help. In a moment, she turned away, too, walking in the opposite direction to the men. For the moment, it had not been too bad, not too bad at all. They had not found the little gold chain in his pocket with which he was really hoping to pay for food. There was not much hope that anyone would take the billion-mark notes, but they were worth offering, just in case.

In Weimar, a few shops were open, though not the market stalls as yet. Adele went her rounds, pleasantly surprised that there was anything open. She could buy some food. It was not much, but it was better than two slices of black bread and three potatoes. They would be able to eat today. Elsa would be so proud of her! The only matter was how very expensive everything was. The prices seemed to have doubled or trebled with the coming of the snow. Her boots creaked like old wood in the snow as she walked around. She had a pair of sausages, a pair of turnips, a very little flour, some more potatoes, a very little sugar, a twist of coffee-and-acorn-and chicory, and that would be plenty for them. Tomorrow it would be better still. If only everything were not so expensive! She would love to be able to ask the Vogt boys to a proper dinner, to show how she could cook. But that would have to wait. She looked forward to being married to Christian, now that she had properly considered it. She had thought at first only to teach him a lesson. But now she thought that it would be a good thing to do. Father would be so surprised. Perhaps he would marry Frau Steuer after all!

She reached home, and climbed the stairs to their little apartment. The bookshop was still closed. People would not be in such a hurry to buy a book as they would be to buy food. Elsa sprang up with a cry of joy when she saw that Adele's wicker basket had things in it, good things to eat. Adele began at once to cook. They were so hungry! They had not admitted it to themselves, and indeed had not allowed themselves to feel hungry. But now there were sausages and potatoes cooking before them, and smelling so very good, they could admit to their hunger. It was unbearable to have to wait even for a few minutes until the sausages, so good, were ready. And in the meantime, Adele told Elsa about how things were; about how expensive everything in the shop had become, and about how some people, the Jews, were taking advantage of the storm, and were making money out of people's suffering by raising prices and selling dear what they had bought cheap and hoarded. The Jew had had his pockets stuffed full of money. She had seen people taking revenge on him. It was sad, but she had seen the Jew's money scattered all about, and him wanting to do nothing but count it up, make sure none was missing from the money he had made. 'I wonder …' Adele said, then stopped herself. She had been about to wonder what her employer in Breitenberg, the Jew, had been doing to fill the time and to make himself some money while she was away. But that was unfair. He had been good to her and not all of them had contributed to the way things were. But there it was. And now the sausages were ready.

'If only there were some mustard!' Elsa said. 'Then our happiness would be truly complete!'

From the pocket of her apron, Adele brought, as a lovely surprise, a tiny clay pot. It must be the smallest clay pot of mustard anyone had ever made. It would do for a dollop for her, a dollop for her sister. Adele smiled. It had not been truly necessary – nobody would starve without mustard. But what were sausages without mustard? And she had found she had a tiny sum left at the end of her shopping, a hundred million marks or so, no more than that, and had retraced her steps to the shop where she had seen that there was mustard.

'You are the best sister anyone ever had,' Elsa said. Together they sat in front of the fire, and they ate their sausages and potatoes with the mustard, and the world began to look as if it had a future. 'I wish that, even when the trains start running, you would stay with me in Weimar.'

'Oh, Elsa,' Adele said. But she was happy now that Elsa would be quite all right. And her fiancé Christian would look out for her. She would tell him what Elsa needed, in person, or perhaps in a letter.

BOOK 6
AD 203

1.

The town had been built in an ambitious moment. The hot wastes came up to the half-finished walls and gates of the place, and were not kept out. There was a marble meeting hall, and a marketplace, a bath-house and a temple.

There was also an amphitheatre, of some splendour. Some had thought and some still said that there might have been better uses for Rome's money. But there was no amphitheatre for far around, in any of the similar towns of the colony. Sport was not the most important thing in life. But it was clear that their desert town rose above its rivals because of the amphitheatre.

Of these buildings, a local dignitary had said two years before that he had found the town brick and had left it marble. The thought was not original. The amphitheatre, temple, meeting hall and marketplace, however, were the only marble buildings in the town. Much of the rest was not even brick, but smeared, hardened mud that the inhabitants had brought into the town from their native settlements, or it was a means of living that Rome had never known, of branches and cloth, of suspended blankets.

Sand blew constantly into the town, and sometimes rose up in a furious storm, running towards the town in a sky-high wall, making it impossible to see more than a handspan in front of the face. Sand was piled up against the walls of the few marble buildings in great drifts. The walls did not have the polish and gleam of great Rome's marble. They were starting to become pitted and rough with the constant buffeting. There had once been talk of a great project, a viaduct across the desert. But there did not seem to be as much money emerging from Rome as there once had been. The town still had a poet, but that was a poor thing to show as proof of Rome's trust.

There were few reliable amusements in town. One was to sit at the window of a house, and observe the street going by. There might be a camel-drover, a group of dirty street-urchins, the slave of a neighbour carrying a basket, the water-carrier with his cart and donkey, a beggar with a terrible facial ailment, such as the one who sat always opposite with a dark hole where his nose should be. For the fourteen-year-old daughter of one of the merchants of the town, with three elder sisters and four elder brothers, that was the limit of the permitted. Sometimes she and her slave would, semi-permitted, venture out veiled to the marketplace. Her sisters had warned her about the traders who had snatched a child and taken it off to be sold in a neighbouring town, never to be heard of again. But that had been fifty years ago. The great fat men, glistening with sweat, their heads shaved, calling out their wares to the bidding public, whether soap, fruit, meat, household goods or any other matter, were not threatening.

Sometimes, too, there was a rare and splendid entertainment. If her brothers and sisters consented, she could go with them to the amphitheatre, and watch the games. But her sisters did not always want her company, though she was old enough to marry.

There were other entertainments, and on this day, the daughter of the merchant and her slave were sitting quietly, faces veiled, to one side of the public room in the building that served as the town hall. The sand was blowing in at the window with a hot, abrasive, dry blast. Outside, there was the moan and deep grumble of a desert wind mounting in strength. The nomads of the desert would be out there, settling down, wrapping themselves in their dark blue cloths, walling their camels about them and waiting for the storm to pass over them. Here, a magistrate was getting very irritated.

'I just can't understand,' he was saying. 'I'm really trying my very best to help you. It doesn't seem a great deal to ask. All we ask is that you go to the temple and make a sacrifice – a very small sacrifice – to the Emperor. Do you understand? We are not even requiring you to abandon your rites, whatever they may be. All that we ask – all that Rome asks – is that, from time to time, you come along with the rest of us and make a very small sacrifice to the Emperor. As well as all the performance about your dead God you enjoy so much. Not instead of. *As well as.*'

There were five prisoners, an older man with a white beard and a woman who could have been his wife, then two young men who must be brothers, and a strong-jawed man. The merchant's daughter recognized this last man as a market trader. He sold oil for lamps. The younger of the two brothers was definitely very scared, and the merchant's daughter thought that the woman was, as well. But the older man with the white beard, who seemed to have some kind of authority over the others, did not even look about him to gather opinion before he spoke.

'That is not possible,' he said. 'Our Lord forbids it. We can make no sacrifice and we will not.'

'Well, bring your Lord here, and I'll persuade him,' the magistrate said, smiling somewhat. The court officials laughed at this pleasantry. They knew by now that the man they spoke of as their Lord was a dead man, the founder of their cult, but the magistrate had amused them all by pretending to forget this.

The elder man made no response.

'Now, look,' the magistrate said. He was quite a young man; he had been sent out, already balding, from Rome. His accent was of the very best, people said. Some wiser and older people wondered what he had done in Rome before Rome had decided to send him here indefinitely. He ingratiated, humoured, broke out in petulant rage, reached for recherché punishments, argued with the prisoners and the forces of the law, or joked with them. 'Now look. I am a reasonable man. I don't care to put people to death for no reason. You don't seem to perceive that I am searching for a compromise, under which the laws of the empire can be respected, and your practices can go on out of sight. I am trying to help you. Is that so hard to understand?'

'Yes,' the man said. 'We want no such help. Such help would pitch us into the eternal flames. We want no such agreement with people like you.'

'Such help would keep you alive,' the magistrate said. 'Honestly, I start to lose my patience here. Do you want to stay alive, or do you want to die? It's not a hard question.'

'No,' the man said. He made no effort to consult the others. 'It is not a hard question. We want to die, rather than accept what you call a compromise.'

'Oh, very well,' the magistrate said. 'Take them from this place and put them to death in the amphitheatre, if they absolutely insist. I just want to say that none of that was at all necessary. It really is simply maddening. And you –' he pointed at the leader '– you must make sure that your son is going to carry your business on. The whole town relies on that.'

'One day,' the older man said. 'my son will light other lamps that may not be sold in the marketplace.'

'Well, of course he will,' the magistrate said. 'You know, sometimes you Christians drive me absolutely up the wall. That will do. Take them away and have them put to death some time very soon, please.'

A shrieking broke out at the back of the hall, a noise in which there was a joyous note as well as the wailing that might have been more to the front. In it was mingled the beat of a drum, the hiss of some cymbals. The five prisoners were led away. As they left the room, roped together, the last of them turned and tried to raise his hand in greeting or farewell. It was one of the young men, the one who had not appeared scared during the proceedings.

'I would be scared, if I were them,' the merchant's daughter said to her slave, in her bright, clear voice, after commenting on this. 'I would be so scared. But then I think I wouldn't turn down that offer. Why would someone not agree to come sometimes to the temple and sacrifice some measly goat to the Emperor? No one was asking them to give anything up. They had only to do something a little bit extra.'

'The Christians are strange, madam,' the slave said. They were struggling to reach the exits; if they did not leave before the mass of people, then it would be best to stay until the end. But if they had to wait for long, then people at home would start to wonder where they had gone, and there was a sandstorm coming, too. They pushed on, the merchant's daughter holding tight to the slave's clothes, just as she had when she was a little girl.

'I would not choose death,' the merchant's daughter said. 'I would wait very patiently until it came to me.'

'You might not have to wait patiently,' the slave said, turning her head. 'None of us knows the hour of his death.'

There was a deep thrill in the slave's voice. The merchant's daughter had known her all her life. She knew when she was saying something important. She looked at the slave's eyes. It was a band of face, of wet eyes, of a dark slash of eyebrow, and a tear on the dark cheek. She was crying silently and not very conspicuously.

'If we hurry, we can reach home before the sandstorm strikes,' the merchant's daughter said sensibly. The slave agreed, and in a moment they were out of the door.

2.

That night, the merchant's daughter had a dream. In it, she was standing outside a garden, a beautiful garden, with a fountain playing and an orchard of silvery, fruit-bearing trees. The wind from the garden through the gates was exquisitely cool, and bore on it the odours of fruit and flower. (Even after she woke up, she could still smell those lovely odours amid the buffeting roar of the sandstorm. She could not remember dreaming in odours and perfumes before.) Inside the garden was a group of people, of all ages. They called to her, in a language she could not speak but which now she could understand without any effort. But how am I to come into the garden? she asked, because that had been their invitation. She did not speak with words, with her tongue, but they understood her just the same. You should come in, of course, one of them said, and another said, from the other side of the gate, But how do you ever come into a garden? You should think of pushing against the gate. She pushed; it opened, and then she was inside the garden. How had that happened? Why had she thought it was impossible? And now the group of people was running away, gracefully, in fits and starts, some turning their heads and laughing to encourage her to follow them. In the middle of the garden, there was a golden ladder. It was narrow, the ladder; it would take only one person at a time. You have to climb a ladder yourself, she said, feeling at the time that this was an enormous statement of colossal weight. It has to be done on your own. But it is not so hard. There was a joyous burst of feeling as she said to herself, But it is not so hard, a shrugging off of the weight of the world, and with that, the first of the people ran up the ladder – scrambled up it, poured himself up it, like a lizard up a wall. The merchant's daughter approached the narrow golden ladder. She placed her hand on its side, and it was cool and refreshing to the touch, just for a second before she woke up.

The perfumes of the garden from her dream were still in her mind. She could feel the cool touch of the gold, the substance of it in her hand. In the world she lived in, the night was dark, and the roar of the sandstorm was pitiless. She shook her bedclothes; a layer of yellow sand covered them. She could have woken her slave to do this – she still slept at the foot of the bed – but the slave was deep in sleep, her dark face hardly showing in the room. Only by her comforting, warm, womanly smell could her presence be deduced. The merchant's daughter thought she would allow her to sleep. The floor could be swept in the morning. She had never asked her slave about her history in detail. For the first time in her life, the merchant's daughter wondered what it would be like to be somebody else.

3.

In the morning, the storm had subsided. The merchant's daughter had thought, at one point, that the underworld had surfaced, and was mounting a great futile rage against the Christians who had chosen death. She had slept long; the sun was high in the sky. Around her, the comforting hiss and whisper of the stiff wicker broom at work. The slave was mildly commenting to herself on the amount of sand that had come into the chamber.

'Oh, I slept so well,' the merchant's daughter said, raising herself up. 'I always sleep well when there is a sandstorm. I believe I was born during one.'

'You are alone in that,' the slave said. 'It keeps the rest of us awake with its boom, boom, boom, and the shriek of it.'

'It did not keep you awake!' the merchant's daughter said. 'You snored all night. I woke once – I heard you.'

'I snored,' the slave said passively. 'I snored. Your mother was asking for you, once you are dressed and fed and awake. Do you want to send her a message?'

'No,' the merchant's daughter said. 'Let her wait. I woke up only now. You know those people? The ones in the courtroom?'

'Christians,' the slave said.

'What happens to them? Are they going to be put to death immediately?'

The slave did not reply. She made a gesture of the hand, which was one that an elder person might make to a younger person. But the slave was the same age as the merchant's daughter. She had been bought for the merchant's daughter as a child, to keep her company.

'What happens to Christians? Do you know?' the merchant's daughter asked sharply.

'I know what happens to Christians,' the slave said. Sh-sh-sh, the broom went across the floor. 'But the magistrate does not know what happens to him.'

'What do you mean?' the merchant's daughter said. 'The magistrate ordered the Christians to be put to death.'

'The magistrate, too, will die,' the slave said. Her eyes turned to the merchant's daughter's face, fearful but full of knowledge. She seemed to be inviting more enquiry and turning it away at the same time.

All that long, hot, dusty roar of a day, the merchant's daughter was slow and absent. Her tutor commented on it. They were in the Peloponnesian war, and she had not prepared the chapter. Some of the words were not familiar to her, and she was close to remarking that if the names of the different ropes of ships were to be of any use to her, she would learn them when she became an oarsman, no doubt. The tutor, an aged Greek with a blue wig that kept slipping from his bald and polished pate, was patient, but he commented on it, and remarked that those who worked hard at scholarship were the ones who found it of greatest support, all their lives. 'I, now, have read the great Thucydides twenty or thirty times, for pleasure or for these purposes. And each time I learn more about the world as it is constituted.'

'Oh, I know,' the merchant's daughter said. 'I had other matters on my mind. I was called away from the great Thucydides and had no time to prepare. Tell me: what are Christians?'

'Christians, madam?'

'Christians,' the merchant's daughter said.

But the tutor could tell her nothing. He knew that there were some who had been put to death that morning, in the amphitheatre. But he knew nothing of their beliefs or their habits. To tell the truth, he thought that very little that had happened since the great Augustus was of any interest or importance, and nothing at all that happened in this small marble city in the African desert with one poet only was worth his attention, or ever would be.

Her parents dined out that night, taking her two eldest brothers and their wives with them. There was a general in town. Her mother bathed in scented oils and had her hair elaborately curled. Her mother's chamber was filled with musk and rose-water, and even her father had had his hair cut by his manservant. The merchant's daughter retreated into alcoves with a pome-granate and a pin to get out of the way of the servants. They rushed with bowls of hot water and tiny jars of green glass the size of a thumb, with paint and knives and strigils. Her father hoped to impress the general as a supplier of goods for the army, should an army return this way. Her mother looked beautiful and smelt delicious when it was done and they mounted into the four-man palanquin to take them to the dinner. The quiet urgency had been very much like the household activity around childbirth, her eldest sister thoughtfully remarked. The child last being born had been the merchant's youngest daughter, who went back into the house; also thoughtfully.

'My sister has forgotten about my little brother,' the merchant's daughter remarked after dinner to her slave. The evening had been independently splendid. Their parents, as a gesture towards their own luxury, had not stinted on the household arrangements. The children had dined in great style, on sows' udders and little birds, on dates and even on dried fish. Afterwards, the remains of the dinner would be thrown out to the midden heap at the back of the marketplace. The family was rich, and was growing richer. Her parents had gone to dinner with a famous visiting general, and were welcomed there.

'I am sure your sister remembers your brother,' the slave said, drawing a comb through her mistress's hair.

'She forgot. She said the last time my mother had a baby, it was I. But it was not I. It was my brother, the one who died.'

'It was a slip of the tongue,' the slave said. The brother in question had been a pretty baby, with curls and a fat smile. His mouth and eyes opened wide and easily. But at two, his fat cheek had begun to swell, and then to blacken. He had had a black growth on his jaw, and his face had rotted. It was swollen, foul and deformed, his baby teeth showing through a great hole in his cheek. There was nothing that could be done. He was kept from the sight of his parents. The merchant's daughter, who was only three years older, had gone into his small and bare chamber and waited with him for death. The stench of the sick chamber had turned her stomach. It was perhaps unsafe to enter the world of the sick so lightly. But she had gone in, and spent time with her brother, whose frightened eyes and muffled cries of pain were all the speaking he could do. He had died in great pain and was often forgotten about by the elder brothers and sisters. He had been their brother, and had been born, and been the subject of rejoicing at his birth.

'Do you think the dead know about us, after they are dead?' the merchant's daughter said.

'Yes, I do,' the slave said. 'I believe that they can be helped, and that we can make offerings to reduce their sufferings.'

'But they do not suffer,' the merchant's daughter said. 'They are dead! They cannot suffer more.'

'I believe that the life of suffering can be eased during life by kindness, and after death by making offerings. I have heard that the suffering of the dead is such that they look back in longing for the suffering they lived through when they were here on the earth. But there is bliss, too, and happiness we cannot conceive of.'

'Offerings,' the merchant's daughter said. She put her hand up and halted the progress of the comb through her long hair. 'What offerings? You mean an animal sacrifice, on their behalf? You offer that at the temple?'

'No,' the slave said. 'It is just my offering, and very simple. I kneel and I make a request on behalf of the dead, and that is all. It is quite soon over.'

312

'But you make a request of whom?' the merchant's daughter said. She knew the answer. She did not know why the slave was stating the facts of the case with such clarity and fearlessness.

'I make a request of God, and of Christ,' the slave said. 'Christ who is my God. Now you know everything.'

'You were crying when those Christians were sentenced to death,' the merchant's daughter said.

'They were my brothers,' the slave said. She returned to her work with the comb.

4.

That night, the merchant's daughter had a dream. The dream was about her dead brother. He came to her, and they were in a hot, dry place. He was crying because he was so thirsty. There was a fountain of cool water playing, but the bowl of the fountain was far above his head. His face was black and disfigured and holed as it had been. About them were the sands of the desert. The merchant's daughter, in her dream, drew her veil across her face against the blast of the sand. But her brother, wailing, had no cloth to protect his mouth and his poor damaged face. He plucked at the rags that hung about his body, and he pulled at his sister.

In the dream, she did not know what to do. She was not suffering. She did not even feel the heat. If she grew thirsty, she could reach out and take the golden cup that hung from a hook in the fountain, and drink from that. There was nothing to cause her suffering or irritation in the dream, except for the small, ugly, torn and swollen figure by her. It was more like a dwarf than a child, or a moving statue, destroyed in part but still a recognizable whole. She was astonished at how much suffering and irritation this figure was causing her.

But then, as if with a cool wind, an understanding came to her. The understanding was that it was her brother, and that he was suffering more than anyone could ever suffer, now, somewhere, after his death, and that nothing could halt it except her kindness. All at once, her thoughts turned away from the annoyance she felt. She understood what her brother needed, although, in his animal suffering, he did not realize it himself. She took the gold cup and dipped it in the running water. How cool it was, both cup and water. She bent and, shielding it with her veil, she lowered it to her brother's poor mouth. She bent his head to one side, so that the water would run only into his whole cheek, and not run out at the side of the cheek with great purple-black gaps in it. She wiped his dirty face, and he looked at her, with surprise. He did not recognize her. She gave him a second drink of cool, fresh water, and this time he gave her a look of recognition and gratitude. In her dream, she stood up. Please, she said silently, not knowing to whom she was talking, please make it all right for him. He is my brother. The beautiful word *is* sang out to her. She could have said *was*.

It seemed to her that she was thirsty now, and there was an ache in her face. The light in the desert was so bright she shielded her eyes against it. There was water in her eyes. But she was looking after only herself, and she turned again to her small brother. His right cheek, where the growth had carried out its worst destruction, was now scarred but mended. His face was the face of her brother. She understood that he no longer suffered. She woke up, and the tears on her face were real tears, not tears in her dream. Her throat choked with joy. At the bottom of the bed, the slave slept. She made small snuffling noises in her sleep. The room was filled with her comforting animal odour.

5.

The next day, the nomads rode into town to kill and steal.

The tribes of nomads in the deserts sometimes came to the town on horses and rode through as if they recognized neither wall nor gate. They took from the market what they needed and paid what they wanted. Their faces were dark and they did not shave their chins. The merchant's daughter had seen them through the window of their house. Once, they had seen her and pointed her out to each other. The servants had pulled her away from the window and bundled her into an inner room. The oldest manservant of her father had made a gesture out of the window meant to ward off wickedness and evil. The nomads in their blue cloaks, on their splendid horses, rode on. Afterwards, her mother had explained to her that they had been fascinated by her red hair. They had never seen it before. She should be proud of her red hair, the result of a British princess in the family, five generations before, a grandfather who had been one of Claudius's quartermasters. Her family had always travelled. Now Rome had brought the red hair of the British princess to Africa, and the nomads in their blue cloaks had stared and pointed.

'Why do they not come on their camels?' the merchant's daughter asked.

'The camels are for long journeys in the desert,' her tutor explained. 'When they may need to escape quickly, they ride on horses, like the civilized world.'

'How long do camels live?' the merchant's daughter asked.

'Until they are killed for meat by their masters, when they are hungry,' her tutor explained. 'And their humps are filled with water so that they can continue in the desert for weeks without drinking.'

The nomads did not ride in on camels. They came in on their magnificent horses, their blue robes wrapped about their faces. They rode in with swords raised, and they fell on the faces of the townspeople. They rode into the marketplace, and slashed and thrust and seized the gold from one trader, kicking over other stalls, wheeling and roaring. They rode their horses into the temple itself, turning awkwardly, their weapons raised. They had no understanding of what the temple was for. They did not ride into the baths, which was where the Roman general was, and where he sensibly remained, flushed and naked and frowning, the whole morning. He would not have been recognized by the nomads, who had followed their white and gold splendour across the gold and white desert and recognized only that clothed splendour.

All this was told to the merchant's daughter by her slave. The merchant's daughter had been bundled away into an inner room, the only red-haired daughter in the family. The slave had watched from the windows, and had been told of what had happened in the town by others of her sort.

'I was afraid we should die,' the merchant's daughter said.

'I knew we should not,' the slave said.

'It is strange, that those Christians were put to death only yesterday,' the merchant's daughter said. 'But if they had not been discovered, the Christian whose business was in the market, he would have been there and would have been killed, only by barbarians instead of by the magistrate.'

'Yes, that is so,' the slave said placidly.

'Did anyone die that we know?'

'Your mother sent a message to the Roman general enquiring after the health of the general and of all the members of his suite. She would not forgive herself if harm came to him or to them from his visiting our humble town.'

'What happened?'

'There was a reply saying that all the members of his suite and the general himself were quite well.'

'Was it from the general himself?'

'No, the general must have been very busy.'

'That won't have pleased her one bit. She wants to be great friends with the general, and he is here only for another two days. She looked so pretty and she smelt so delicious, too.'

'It is all the same, in the end,' the slave said. It was so unusual a remark that the merchant's daughter lowered her veil. They were walking in the street. It had been forbidden them, but the merchant's daughter had veiled herself and her slave, and they had slipped out. They wanted to see the disaster. All about them, there were interesting signs of blood on the walls, and splintered wood and scattered objects, the product of undisciplined destruction of the market.

6.

The daughter of the merchant was of an age to marry. She was aware of this. There were meetings between her parents and friends and acquaintances of theirs at which she was brought in and greeted. Sometimes there was a son as well; sometimes not. Her parents were sociable creatures, but all that winter they seemed to go out every night, oiled and perfumed.

'It is because nobody wants you,' the merchant's daughter's slave said, when they were alone.

But the merchant's daughter believed that the process was protracted because her parents were being careful over her future. There were not so many families in the small marble town in the white and gold desert. Her parents would want to be sure of the right choice for her, as she was their youngest child living. The merchant's daughter could remember the last time this had happened, and her sister had been married off. That had been no more than five years before. She remembered some of the same visitors, her sister being summoned to show herself, some of the same suitors, in fact.

Her mother went out in the afternoons to the temple, to make offerings. One of the elder daughters would arrive, perhaps the second, heavily pregnant and sweating in the heat of the desert town. They would retreat into her mother's chambers and emerge some time later after nightfall, having discussed the suitors of the previous days. They would ladle themselves into the waiting palanquins by torchlight, and the pair of them would set off. The merchant's daughter was not included in these outings, and she was not supposed to know about them. On past occasions, her mother had taken her to make the offering on behalf of an elder daughter. This time, too, there would be the incense; the smell of animals' blood; the cool and gritty feel of the temple's marble floor; the banging of drums and the wail of pipes and voices; and, to one side, the malevolent presence of the temple virgins, standing veiled and observant, their eyes full of resentment and malice. When it was done, they would nod sourly, pull back their wicker baskets inside their robes and watch the merchant's wife and the merchant's daughter retreat. When her mother and her sister departed, she could reconstruct the sequence of events. She hoped that the husband who came would not be too tall; she hoped he would not be as old as her father; she hoped that he would not be one of the two men that all her sisters and half of the town had turned down over the last twenty years.

'You don't talk about your religion,' she said to her slave. The house had retreated, and was asleep or resting on their couches. Only she and the slave were awake, talking in low voices as the merchant's daughter steadily took and ate plums from the red-and-black ceramic dish. She sat on the couch; the slave knelt on the floor.

'I have talked too much about my religion,' the slave said.

'Oh, I won't tell anyone,' the merchant's daughter said. 'But is it a secret sort of religion? In caves, in the desert, sacrificing babies to their gods, and it is death to speak of the mysteries?'

'My religion is not like that,' the slave said. 'One day, it will live openly and everyone will see everything about it. It is not a religion made for darkness.'

'Why do you not live openly now?' the merchant's daughter said, but the slave had nothing but a gesture of the hands in response to that. 'I can see, you would be killed if you did. But you don't seem to mind being killed in the name of your religion. Those people, they were demanding to be put to death. If they don't fear death, why are they living secretly?'

'Some of us are not as strong as that,' the slave said. 'I fear death. I try not to fear death, but I fear death. I have hidden my light under a desert rock, and not one person has seen my light.'

'Oh, that's not true,' the merchant's daughter said. 'And even if it were, you have followed the commands of your religion, I'm sure. Would anyone see your light in the desert, in the noonday sun? Are you a sort of temple virgin?'

The slave hissed, and warded off the comparison with a bold movement of the arm, like a wounded dog touched on his sore limb. 'No,' she said eventually. 'Not like any of that. We are told not to hide our lights under a bushel, and that is what I have done. We are told to bring the good news to others. But I sit in silence and darkness and fear only death.'

The merchant's daughter tossed away the stone of the plum, sucked clean. 'It was brave of you,' she said slowly, 'to tell me anything. What was your Christ?'

'As a man, I would say that he lived and died in Judaea seven or eight generations ago.'

'And what sort of god is he?'

'He is the only God, he and his Father and the Holy Spirit.'

'That is three gods. I don't understand.'

'There is one God in three.'

'I don't understand.'

'It is not important to understand.'

'Oh,' the girl said, put off by the self-regarding formality of the maid's responses. She had not said it before: she had merely rehearsed this exchange, the first example of an exchange she had always wanted to have. 'But what sort of god is he? Does he punish, or control the weather, or pass judgement over your fortunes? He can't be that – the Christians never seem rich around here. Excuse me if I say the wrong thing.'

'He stands for love,' the slave said. 'And I am to bring that message of love to everyone, even at the cost of my own death. But I am so afraid, so terribly afraid.'

'Those people who were killed,' the merchant's daughter said.

319

'They can't bring a message of any sort to anyone any more. You could be being useful in any number of ways. They're dead. I heard they were beheaded in the amphitheatre.'

'That was their message,' the slave said. 'People will never forget their message. I am going to tell other people, as we are commanded to. And if it leads to my death, it leads to my death. It is so hard to die well, alone, but it makes no difference whether I die with terrible fear, or calmly and bravely. Listen.'

7.

Two years passed.

The merchant's daughter was married to a man. He was the younger son of the governor. It was a better marriage than the sisters' of the merchant's daughter. Afterwards, a magnificent mosaic was installed in the house of the merchant and his wife. Such a marriage made clear what the family's standing had become.

The daughter took her slave with her, and there were other slaves devoted to her appearance and her pleasure.

Her husband was a man of thirty-three. He had been married before to a girl who had proved to be barren. He had travelled a good deal, even to great Rome with his father, and liked to tell of what he had seen, in the evening, to their guests. The house they lived in was the house he had lived in for fifteen years, since his first marriage. She fitted into it, her red hair much commented on by the slaves, who had grown comfortable and confident; they listened to her suggestions about the food, and about other small matters, and sometimes took notice, and sometimes not. Her husband's first wife lived in a small villa on the outskirts of the town, well walled, surrounded by nine steady old slaves, as if in widowhood. She had grown aged in appearance, it was said.

Six months after they married, she discovered that she was to have a child. The governor and his six sons rejoiced. It was born whole and healthy, a son. In its face she could see the governor's cross and satisfied features, and her husband, a little, but herself not at all, and the sacred soul not one bit. It looked up at her and sucked angrily; the next time, she said to herself, it would be better and the child more agreeable.

Around this time, she asked her husband about the Christians. He explained to her that it was a cult of human sacrifice, like the cult of Baal Hammon. Somewhere in this continent, people still killed children to their gods, not goats and sheep. The Christians had taken it one step further, and presented themselves for sacrifice, like their god. The arena of the amphitheatre and the courtroom were as the sacrificial altar to them. And if we did not choose to sacrifice them? A town of two thousand people, not so far from here, had woken to discover that sixty citizens had self-slaughtered themselves in the night, and all of them Christians. The governor's son laughed heavily, briefly, in the courtyard of their house. His wife sat listening on the rim of the fountain, in the morning sun.

'These cults come and these cults go,' he said. He passed his hand over his forehead, wiping the sweat away. 'Why do you ask about them?'

'I heard about them somewhere,' she said. 'They sound so very strange.'

'People are drawn by the unfamiliar and the strange,' her husband said. 'There is no need to reintroduce human sacrifice. That was one of the reasons why we fought and razed Carthage.'

'I see,' the merchant's daughter said. She did not believe that her husband knew anything whatsoever about the matter.

At the end of the week, her husband came to her in her rooms. As he was washing himself afterwards, he said, 'You were speaking about the cult of Christianity. Does it interest you?'

'No, not especially,' the merchant's daughter said. It was cold tonight: a wind from the desert brought a chill into the room, as well as the ordinary grit and sand that floated there. She reached for a blanket that lay on the floor where her husband had pushed it aside. Her wrist hurt where it had been twisted and pressed. The sensitivity of the flesh was something she remembered before, and she felt that she must be pregnant again. She would not mention it for a month or two. 'It was something I heard about. I forget why I raised it with you.'

'There is a spread of it in the town, my father said. There were some executions a year or two ago. It doesn't seem to have put them off. If it came into the house?'

'I don't know,' the merchant's daughter said truthfully. 'You make it sound like the sand the wind brings in. I don't know what we should do if it did. Sweep it out, but sand always comes in again.'

'I don't know that it has come into the house,' he said. He looked at her oddly, like a dog with its ears pricked, waiting for a command. In the first days of their marriage, when she made comparisons, such as saying Christianity was like the sand of the desert, he would take the trouble to laugh at her and say that she talked nonsense. 'It may not be true, what Copreus told me.'

That was his way, to sound matters out without revealing what he knew, and when she had stated her opinion, to explain that Copreus had informed him of some state of affairs. She thought back with alarm; but she had not committed herself to there being Christianity in the house.

Her husband went on talking. There was a lot to follow about duty and standing. At the end of it, he did what he had come to do, for the second time. She submitted to it. He was a bull of a man, even at his age, even in a second marriage, his chest and shoulders like a cupboard, his bodily hair and his blood both thick and surging. She felt like a translucent piece of fish on a slab beside him. She felt that he must be able to see the child, tiny, within her translucent belly as he pushed up into her. Her pale arm under his grip was like the limb of a separate species.

She spoke to her slave about Copreus. Neither liked her husband's manservant. He had been found on a dungheap and named for it, but now was a man of pained dignity and careful pronunciation. He looked dull in the face: his eyes did not go from side to side as he walked, carefully, through the villa with his burden of clothes or food. He barely greeted anyone, except his mistress: her he greeted with a deep, even reverential salutation, his eyes on her feet. His comments were servile and elaborate and verged, no more, on the impertinent. He was very clean, pale and shining in the face, wringing his hands as he walked, face downwards. He murmured his servilities and he murmured his impertinences. She had sometimes to ask him to repeat what he said, though her husband never. He had been used to Copreus since childhood. She would not speak to her husband about Copreus as he spoke to her, derisively, humorously, about her slave. When she had been married a month, it occurred to her that Copreus's curious, mincing, precise, mangled way of talking had originated in an attempt to sound like the women of her husband's family, their clipped words, the open sounds of their voices when heard across a fountain-centred courtyard.

'He watches me,' her slave said simply. 'I think he watches you too.'

That was not an aspect that the merchant's daughter had considered.

'But he is a soul, as well,' her slave said. 'I should speak to him.'

'Don't do that,' the merchant's daughter said. 'He would not hear what you had to say.'

'He would not listen,' the slave said. 'But he would hear what I said, the words, and they would stay with him after my death.'

The merchant's daughter did not pay any attention to this. Her slave, dressing the bruises on her arm with an almond paste late that night, was often full of what she should do for her beliefs. The merchant's daughter believed that she found solace in the statement of what her Christ would have expected of her, and also in the flagellation she subjected herself to for not doing

323

any such thing. The merchant's daughter listened patiently, but she found this tiresome, as she found any situation on this earth that would never change.

At the end of the next week, she lost the child she had been bearing. There was no obvious cause. There was nothing she had eaten and no exercise she had been taking. She had not gazed upon a nomad, or upon a virgin. She had had the child only for a time and then it was gone in a flush of blood.

But she was saddened by the death of this child. She did not know why. She found herself saying to her slave that she did not know why her God allowed such things to happen. It would be better to think and feel nothing about it, like a dog that loses a puppy and then quickly forgets.

'We do not know that they forget, of course,' she said.

'We are not animals,' her slave said. 'We know that the child had a soul that is now gone to another place.'

'How can you know that?' the merchant's daughter said, then quickly forbade her to answer. She knew what the slave said to all questions of that sort. 'How does your God permit us to feel such pain and anguish when there is nothing to be gained from it?'

'Because we are not animals, and we are not the wild men in the desert, beyond feeling and beyond sympathy,' the slave said. 'Because we mean something to each other, whoever we are. We want to speak to each other, and when we cannot, what we are made of – it fails. Even Copreus is not like that. Even the wild men of the desert. They have a spark that flies upwards, too.'

The merchant's daughter did not understand, quite, but she pressed on. 'And why does your God allow such people as the wild men of the desert? Why does he not speak to them? And why the death of my child? Is it to allow myself to be strong and silent and not to speak of it?'

'One day my God will speak to the wild men of the desert,' the slave said.

The merchant's daughter had been running a comb through

her red hair. Now, with a single gesture, she smoothed it back behind her shoulders and prepared to sit while it was pinned up. She ran her palms over it again: it was quite smooth. The slave began to show her how her God permitted suffering in the world.

8.

In the dreadful wastes of the desert, far away, the camels formed a ridge. The nomads in their blue cloaks sheltered behind them out of habit, though the night was windless and cool. There was the noise of groaning and creaking somewhere far off. It was the sound of the sands, singing. The men sat in a circle and listened. Their faces were lined and blank, their eyes bright in the dusk. One of them began, without invitation or preamble, to tell the story.

'Once there was an evil king,' the storyteller said. 'And the evil king ruled over an evil kingdom and the men were slaves and they lived inside and were never permitted to see the sky. The king kept every horse in the kingdom for himself, and every camel. One day She-of-They came to the city, and she saw the great walls and the great gates, and she dismounted and beat on the gates and the gates were opened to her. The gatekeeper had never himself seen a horse like the horse She-of-They rode upon, or a camel like the camels that bore her goods and her household. She-of-They said that she would come inside and she would meet with the three sons of the evil king. And the evil king heard of this and said, "She is our enemy that would meet with my sons," and he sent word that his eldest son would meet with her in a room, in the palace. And She-of-They went to the palace, and she entered into a room full of spun gold ...'

'Ah,' his audience said, and muttered, remembering the room full of spun gold. It made the story for them.

'. . . and she waited, and in a moment a man came in and was announced as the eldest son of the evil king. But it was not the eldest son of the evil king. It was only a servant, and when She-of-They was still suspecting, he brought out his sword and he smote her head from her shoulders. But a strange thing happened. She-of-They reached down and she picked up her head, and she placed it back on her shoulders, and it was as if nothing had ever happened. The head laughed, and then it opened its mouth, and said,

> '"You can take of me my life,
> You can make of me your wife,
> But I cannot be harmed by a liar."

'And then the executioner fell down dead, because of what She-of-They had said. And the next day, She-of-They demanded to see the evil king's second son, and she was shown into a room full of beaten silver, and in came a man. But it was not the evil king's second son. It was another executioner. And he swung his axe, and he separated the head of She-of-They from her shoulders, and it fell to the floor, and he believed that she was dead. But the body reached its arms down, and it picked up the head, and she placed it on her shoulders, and it spoke. It said,

> '"You can take of me my life,
> You can make of me your wife,
> But I cannot be harmed by a liar."

'And the second executioner fell down dead, as he was a liar and had attempted the life of She-of-They.

'So the three brothers spoke with their father, the evil king, and they decided that though the eldest brother would not speak to She-of-They and the middle brother would not speak to She-of-They, the youngest brother could be spared, and he would speak to her. And the next day She-of-They, when she came to the palace, she was shown into a room made of rock, and she waited. And through the door came the evil king's youngest son.

And though he had a dagger in his hand to kill She-of-They he did not want to kill her. She came to him and she bared her throat, and she said,

> '"You may take of me my life,
> You can make of me your wife,
> Because you, alone in the kingdom, are not a liar."

'And he dropped the dagger on the floor, because he had no need of it, and because She-of-They had sacrificed herself for him, he took her and placed her in the locked rooms in the palace, and she never left again, and nobody ever saw her again, and her horses and camels were given to the youngest son. And in time the evil king died, and the eldest son and the middle son were defeated by the youngest son, who was brave and no liar, and he became a good king to his people because of the sacrifice that She-of-They had made in coming to the people who were her enemies.'

The sun had fallen below the horizon as the storyteller spoke. As he reached the end, the listeners could no longer see him in the complete darkness. They rolled away, binding themselves in their cloaks, the material about their faces. They shuffled to make a hollow in the sand below their camel's flank. Soon there was the noise of sleeping in the black desert. They dreamt of horses.

9.

The merchant's daughter and her slave left the house early one morning. Once, before her marriage, she had walked short distances, such as the trip to the marketplace or to the temple. But her husband expected her to travel in the incognito of the palanquin, now that she was married. Her parents made no comment, but they were not surprised by her appearance in state on the ordinary occasion of her visit. She took the palanquin, both she and the slave inside, she sprawling at full length, her slave kneeling. The house porters were expert, with no tossing or pitching. She liked to see the life of the street through the chinks in the curtain. On the corner, there was a familiar beggar. His face was rotted away, a sad black hole in the place where the nose would have been. She had no idea what his name was, and had never heard anyone refer to him in any way. She rapped on the wooden roof of the palanquin, painted with stars, and the porters set it down. Inside, she quickly wrapped her face and head in a veil, and held her hand out for the shawl that her slave always brought, in case of evening chills. It was a beautiful, fine, expensive shawl in a pale green; it would slip through a ring. It had been given to her by her mother, whose shawl it had originally been. Now it was folded up. She thought how uncomfortable the beggar must be, unable to veil himself from the hot wind and flung fine sand. And if he did not need it, he could sell it for food. In a moment, she slipped out of the palanquin. She was out of a world of shadows and dimness, where nothing was clearly seen, and into the world. She was veiled in the heat, but there was still much more of the world there for her, and she was standing in it among humanity. She shocked herself with the feeling of joy. She stood before the beggar, who must have seen that she was a great lady, and kept his eyes lowered as if in shame. 'Take this,' she said, and handed the beautiful green shawl to him. She did not wait to hear his thanks or gratitude. She turned quickly and slipped back into the shadowed light of the palanquin, not looking to see what the porters thought of her gift. She rapped again on the ceiling, unveiling herself. Her slave bowed her head as if expecting a beating. The palanquin was raised, and lumbered on.

10.

'The problem in the household,' her husband said one evening, 'the problem in the household is solved.'

'What problem was that?' his father said. His father and mother, a brother and his wife and a visiting administrator from Carthage with his secretary were dining. Her father-in-law the governor, especially, wanted the evening to go well. He was not in good odour, she gathered. The administrator and the secretary had spent the previous three days going through the governor's books, and had arrived at tonight's dinner without having refreshed, in a perfunctory mood. They talked mostly to each other, waving away delicacies one after another. The food had been carefully ordered – it was not always what could be wished, but tonight, she thought, it was good.

'There is a spread of Christians in the town,' her husband said.

'The Christians!' her husband's mother came in. 'They take children out to desert caves and sacrifice them. They drink their blood. It terrifies the children – my grandchildren, I should say.' She emphasized each word at the end, raising herself upright on her elbow. She was hardly looking at all with her purple-painted eyes at the visiting administrator, who was not paying attention.

'It has come into our house,' the merchant's daughter's husband said. Against cries of shock from his mother, he went on, 'My man Copreus warned me of it, and with my authority, he investigated. It is lucky, in a way. They are a secret sect, but they wish always to recruit new members. So they grow, but for the same reason, they risk always being discovered, when their persuasion falls on stony ground. Copreus found a garden-er's boy weeping in the shade, and when he asked him why, the boy said that the Christians had found him. I think he thought they would sacrifice him in time.'

'As very well he might,' the governor's wife said.

'The Emperor has passed a decree, which seems to be working well. Even here. They have been stopped in this house,' the merchant's daughter's husband said. In the room, the musicians began to play a dance of some sort, as if in celebration of his words. 'I took immediate action, this evening, when he told me what he had discovered, and the culprit has been taken away. My dear ...'

He turned to the merchant's daughter. She had known what he was about to say: she had known it since the men came into her house, and a housemaid had come to arrange her hair rather than her usual maid.

'You will just have to manage for the time being,' he said. 'It was your maid who was so hard at work. I hear from the courts that it is really occupying half of their time. These things come and these things go.'

She noticed that the visiting administrator had stopped talking to his secretary and, for a minute or two, had been paying some attention.

'What a dreadful shock,' her mother-in-law said. 'You must be dreadfully shocked, my dear. What did you do tonight? How did you manage? You look so pretty,' she went on, dropping into the undertone she always used when feminine trivialities were the subject.

'A housemaid did my hair,' the merchant's daughter said. 'It was quite all right, really. I don't suppose it is as hard as all that.'

'I think tomorrow we are going to have to talk about the cost of the marble in the forum,' the administrator said, his voice harsh and unmodulated. The governor turned to him and smiled, his head nodding as he tore a roasted blackbird with his teeth.

11.

That night, the merchant's daughter dreamt. She was alone in the desert. The light was murky and obscure, and her eyes struggled against it. Something moved, gracelessly, from side to side, coming towards her slowly. She stood and did not move. The shape approached, and it was a man; it was a great slab of an Egyptian, stripped and huge, his hands spread out against her like the seats of stools. She knew that she would have to fight him when he came to her. In a series of movements, agonizingly slow, he raised his hands to her face, and she brought her hands to him. They were so small, her hands, and white against his dark rough ones. The touch of his hands was shocking, overwhelming, crushing, and she pushed against them as one might push against a wall. There was such pain in her hands and wrists that she almost cried out. But there was nothing in her throat to cry with. She pushed again, and with a feeling of righteous rage, she pushed a third time. The mouth of the naked Egyptian gaped open, and quite suddenly they were fighting. She felt a great power falling through her like the blaze of the sun. All at once it was quite over and the Egyptian fell away from her.

She woke alone, and on her knees gave thanks for what she was about to do. The next day, early in the morning, she dressed and went to the gates of the town's prison and, after some difficulty and confusion, was admitted to the prison and to the company of four Christians, including her maid. The gates were shut and locked behind her, and in the dark, they taught her to sing. The Holy Spirit descended upon them, like a sea eagle hovering above its helpless screaming prey.

12.

The next day they were led from the prison to the marketplace. News of the trial had spread in the town, and there was a crowd in the bright light of the dusty day. It might have been the news that the daughter of an important merchant had surrendered herself willingly that had encouraged the crowds and the town's curiosity and baffled fervour. Of course the crowd would be bigger when they were torn apart by wild beasts, in the arena.

They walked, tied by ropes at the wrists, and did not look anywhere but directly ahead. A man in the group immediately before her sang as he walked, his voice quavering. It seemed to her that she had seen this scene before, to prepare her. Above her she felt the Holy Spirit. It was merciless and clawed and supervisory. It blessed them. It would descend upon them, and would descend, clawed, upon the unbelievers around them, screaming and howling. They would die and be cast into the pits of Hell. She and the others would pass through suffering and into bliss. She saw them, their faces and hands only emerging from a blaze of pitch, their faces terribly distorted with pain – her father, and husband, and mother, and sisters and brothers, and the governor and his wife, and Copreus. She saw herself looking down as if from the wall of a high garden, green and watered, a fountain playing. The Holy Spirit descended on them, shrieking, and would tear the liver from Copreus's chest once a day, like Prometheus. She saw him screaming for mercy, and she would turn her head away and smile at the angels and the blest and at God the Father.

A voice called from the crowd, and she looked. Pushing to the front, there was her father.

'What is this?' he was shouting. 'That is my daughter. What has she said? She is lying. Her husband will deal with this. Daughter –' and now he was walking alongside them, pushing the crowd and the soldiers out of the way, trying to speak to her '– daughter, how can this be?'

The words came to her, and she said that just as a water vessel could not be called under any name but what it had, and just as it could hold only water, so she could not call herself anything but what she was, a Christian, and what she now held within herself was the truth. Her father flung himself on her with rage. His fingers tore at her face, and she was glad of it. She knew now what the Egyptian in her dream was. He was pulled away from her by the guards, and the crowd laughed – shrill, joyous, animal cries.

Then she could look at the crowd. The worst had happened and she no longer needed to look ahead, seeing nothing. There she saw faces she knew; she saw, even, her husband, and his expression was inscrutable, but unsurprised. They passed on, and now all of them were singing: she was singing too. She understood that there were those in the crowd who would never forget what they saw this day, and she understood that in this blazing heat and desert dust, it was not just her who was thirsty and suffering, it was those around her who would know no relief.

13.

They were brought to the forum, and led up to a platform that had been erected before the chair of judgement. There was a sea of yelping humanity about them. They stood, tied together with ropes, and waited while the procurator ascended to his place. Below her, her father appeared again, but now he was holding a child. It was her son.

'It is not too late,' her father said. 'Think of me in my old age – the shame of this – and think of your son. Do you think that—' But he was carried away, he and his grandson, and she was not sure that she had heard what he had to say.

The procurator began to ask questions of them. They each confessed that they were Christian. At each confession, the procurator moved on, making no gesture of disgust or disapproval. He came to her. The crowd, which had been howling with disapproval at each question and answer, now quietened. The procurator made a kind of gesture at the base of the platform, and her father appeared again, holding the child. He ascended two steps and, turning to her, said, 'Have pity on the child, at any rate.' At that, he seemed to believe that he had said enough with the child in his arms, and he passed the baby to a womanservant who was standing behind him.

The procurator made a silencing gesture with his flat hand. 'For Heaven's sake, your father is old. Your child is very young. Look, just be sensible. Make some kind of sacrifice to the Emperor.'

'No,' she said. It was an easy answer.

'Very well, then,' the procurator said. 'I am going to ask you the question that I am required to ask you by the Emperor's decree. Are you a Christian?'

It was the formal question he had put to the others, which they had answered easily, though not always very resonantly. Her maid had almost shrieked the answer; the man who had begun the singing had had to be asked to repeat the answer, so quietly had he replied. 'I am,' she said.

There was a commotion from her father: he leapt forward, his arms outstretched, like those of the naked Egyptian in her dream. But the soldiers were quicker, and seized him. One soldier beat him back with a rod – the crowd roared with approval, some perhaps thinking that her father, too, was a Christian, not yet apprehended. Blood was beginning to flow from her father's face. She looked away.

'This is all madness,' the procurator said. 'I pass sentence. They will be placed in the arena with the wild beasts.'

'We return to the prison with joy in our hearts,' the man she was roped to said, as loudly as he could, with terror in his voice. She tried to feel joy. The heavens above her poured with light, and perhaps, then, as the rough rope tugged at her wrists and she was led down from the platform into the howling, spitting mob, she did begin to feel something in her heart that was joy.

14.

'You get a last feast,' the gaoler said as he pushed them into the cell. It was filthy in there, and hot. The only window was high up in the wall, and the stench of bodies, of blood and excrement was heavy in the darkness. There was nothing to sleep on but some wretched blankets.

There were five of them. The merchant's daughter knew only her slave – but she could be thought of as free, now. The older

334

man who had sung so uncertainly was a handler of grain, and he was there with his wife. They had converted separately, and without knowing it of the other. In the end, the wife had started to talk of it to her husband, convinced that she must die if she kept silent any longer, even if she died by speaking out. They clung to each other in the cell. There was the merchant's daughter. And there was a very young boy whose voice was only just broken. He seemed too young to know what he was doing, but he spoke with great certainty. He longed for martyrdom, and talked of it in detail, lovingly.

'We shall make a feast of love,' he said of the gaoler's last feast. 'We shall break bread together, like our Saviour, and pass bowls between us, and smile and laugh through happiness. They will see us, and wonder. But the next day they will see us die in the arena through sword and wild beast, still in a state of joy, and realize that they have known nothing of joy until today. They will go away, and think, and come to Jesus on their own, through our example.'

Someone paid for comfort for them, and they were moved to another cell, a larger cell, higher up. It was clean and well aired. They would live there until the time came, in three days' time. They rejoiced at that. The feast of love was announced, and they each asked as many of their family and friends as they could. Her mother came and her sisters and brothers. Her father did not come. Her slave asked her sister, and others the merchant's daughter did not know, and even Copreus, and they all came. They watched the five of them pass the bread and the meat and the mess of beans among them, laughing and talking without grief. The merchant's daughter told stories of her childhood, and how she had loved to go out into the desert, and how vain she had been of the colour of her hair. Her slave talked of the day she had first met with the Christians. Others told of when they were first allowed to hunt with falcons, or smiled and wept at the coming reunion with family members they were parted from. The grain-handler took up the corner of his coarse blue robe and wiped his wife's face lovingly. Around them, their families and friends watched, silent, with their own thoughts. At the end, the merchant's daughter went about the circle with a rough wooden bowl filled with torn-up bread, and offered it in peace and love to everyone who had come to their feast. There were no larks' tongues and sows' udders at their feast. When the guests left, they carried each of them the beat of the wings of the Holy Spirit in their hearts. Before long, they, too, would be put to death in the arena with joy and thanks.

The merchant's daughter lay down. She felt joy, she knew, but there was so much still to discover before she died. She knew about Jesus, and how he had died and how he was born, in the stable with the animals. She had read about his life, and she had heard people tell stories of him. She did not know what Mary his mother had been doing before he was born. She had asked when the world had been created, and she had been told. But it was more important to know that the world would end soon, perhaps this week, perhaps next week. She did not know what Heaven looked like. When she thought of it, she thought only of running water, and green fresh earth, and a cool wind with no sand or minerals in it, only the scent of water. But she did not know, and had felt as shy about asking as an heir about the exact sum of money that would certainly come to her. She hoped that her father and Copreus would remain deaf, and in their deaths lie in torments, the shrieking beak and claws of the Holy Spirit descending on them in vengeance for ever more.

A small hand touched her shoulder. It was the woman who was once her slave.

'They are all asleep,' she said.

'I am awake,' the merchant's daughter said.

'I cannot sleep,' the slave said. 'All my life, I have slept easily. I worked in the days, and I was tired at night, and slept. But these days, I have had nothing to do. I have rested without moving, and I have had no tiredness at night. This is the last sleep of my life, and I cannot sleep.'

'Are you afraid?' the merchant's daughter said.

'I know that God loves me,' the slave said. There was a choking sound in her voice.

'Don't be afraid,' the merchant's daughter said. 'I will be with you.'

'Will we go together?' the slave said.

'Yes, and I will hold your hand as long as I may,' the merchant's daughter said. 'It will be so short a time, and then there will be for ever. There will be a breeze blowing, and birdsong, and fresh water, and cool shade, for ever.'

'I shall eat dates in the shade, for ever, and my feet shall be cool in the running stream,' the slave murmured. Together they heard a beat in the desert air, far away.

15.

The next day they were taken to the arena. There they stood, the men apart from the women. First the wild beasts were set upon them. A leopard was freed from the cages, and approached the men. But it prowled away. The well-armoured guard prodded it with a spear, but it took no action beyond a snarl. 'It will not come until I ask it to,' one of the men said. The guard paid no attention, but poked the animal again. It turned its head and hissed at the guard. 'It will not come,' the man said again, calling across bravely, 'until I ask it to.'

'Ask it to,' the crowd called, and finally the guard nodded.

'Come,' the man said, and the leopard turned and leapt upon him. It tore his throat, and blood poured from it. A bear came from a different place, and as the young boy who had proposed the feast of love knelt and sang, he was cuffed and mauled and his face torn half off. Still he sang, as well as he could, until the bear fell on him and his soul left his body.

The merchant's daughter and her slave were next. The howls in the arena were enormous. She felt that she was in the middle of a great storm of hatred as of the wind-flung small stones of the desert, flying in the air. She prayed for them; she tried to pray for them; the words would not come. 'Holy Father,' she said, but the words would not come. By her, the woman who had been her slave was trembling in terror. 'Holy,' she began, but no words more would come. 'Holy Father,' the merchant's daughter said. The gates to the bestiary were flung open. The leopard and the bear had come out slowly, from darkness, but this time a maddened heifer ran out almost before the gates were open. 'Holy Father,' the merchant's daughter said, but then the beast was upon them. Her face was pressed against the hot dirty sand, and sand and blood were in her mouth. Then, out of sequence, it seemed to her that a great wall of flesh and sharp bone and horn was hitting her, and punching the breath out of her body and, with a broken deflation, she was flying through the air. Again that wall of force, pressing her now into the sand, and the noise of something breaking. Her bowels emptied. She could do nothing about it. There seemed to have been silence, but now a wave of shriek and chant and the noise of hatreds. She wondered where the woman who had been her slave was. It was very important now to stand up, and not to die lying there in the sand. She placed her wrist on the sand, but then blackness came upon her. A time later she came to. She had not died. This time she raised herself on her other wrist, which did not hurt. In the middle of the screaming, she could hear singing. The heifer had gone. She hoped nobody wished it ill, poor beast. Over her stood the guard who had goaded the leopard, his sword raised. She could see that it was trembling, and in his eyes she could read wonderment and terror. She tried, so hard, to smile at him. His sword was lowered. Not far away, there was a woman kneeling, her hands at her face, held together. The merchant's daughter felt that she knew who this woman was. She reached forward, and took the guard's unwilling sword by the blade. It was very sharp. She brought it towards her neck, and she looked at the guard, and smiled as best she could.

With a gesture of grooming, her good hand smoothed back her red hair, a confident, flattening gesture, and brought it away from the side of her neck for the executioner to strike more easily.

It was important that things be born amid sacrifice, marked by the biggest sacrifice anyone could offer. She opened her mouth to bless him, and as he moved the sword away for the swing, she placed her hands together, the good one with the poor broken one, to pray. The words began to pray for her. The wind of the sword's descent was the air under the wings of a great bird, descending upon her.

16.

Two thousand people saw Perpetua die.

A hundred went away thoughtful, and detesting what they had seen. They told five people, ten, twenty.

There was the gesture of the girl at the last: the way she had raised her hand and smoothed her red hair, brought it to one side, left her neck bare to be struck by the sword. They remembered that best, all the days of their lives.

One of those twenty who heard the first telling of Perpetua's death said that the Romans were no better than the wild men of the desert. They were all beasts in their appetites, their meaningless justice and reprisal.

Another of the people who went out into the town was the executioner who had brought his sword down on the neck of Perpetua, and seen her poor broken body give up the ghost. He, too, thought of that movement of the hand, pulling her hair to one side and flattening it. That day he did not join with the other soldiers in the barracks. He rose up early the next day, and on a horse rode out into the desert. After a time he slowed the horse to a walk in the early-morning light. The sky was pink, and the sands were calm, littered with small white rocks, and the stones called roses of the desert crunched under the horse's hoofs. There was a remote and resonant singing, somewhere far off: the deep noise of the sands of the desert moving, many leagues away. There was nothing but the great circular horizon and the sky. Like most of the curious town, he knew the story of Perpetua's last days. He wondered why someone should feel the need to leave everything she knew, and surrender the certain for the unknown. He had heard her called mad, but he did not think now that she had been mad. It was so hard to be virtuous. She had taken the step. In the first light of the day, so much like every other day in the desert, he saw a path like a line of steps, leading away from him towards the light. He felt with shame the acts he had carried out in his life. On the back of the horse, he stretched his arms upwards, in relief, in the empty world, like a boy stretching in the empty air.

BOOK 7
Last month

1.

When the doctors said to me, 'How did this infection happen?'
I answered, 'I cut my foot.' And this was true. But if they went
on to ask further, I started to lie. I said that I had been walking
in the kitchen in the dark one night, and a piece of glass had,
unnoticed, cut my foot, and I had only noticed it the next
morning when I saw some blood. (The comparative lack of
feeling in the feet of diabetes patients makes this plausible.) In
fact my first statement was accurate. I had cut my feet. I had
taken a pair of nail scissors and, trying to hack off some hard
skin, had cut into the flesh beneath. It had grown infected to
the point where I had had to go to hospital. Why did I not
admit to the stupid thing I had done? I wanted the medical staff
to like me, and an accident seemed to place me on their side,
whereas a stupid piece of reckless self-mutilation would place
me among the mass of incomprehensible other.

I presented myself at Accident and Emergency at St Thomas'
Hospital in London at eleven on a Wednesday night. The infection had been apparent since Sunday. I had been ignoring, or
half ignoring, the pain in my foot and the slight feeling of
delirium. This was a mistake. When I had been diagnosed as
diabetic, ten months before, one of the things that I had been
told was that I must pay attention to my feet, and especially to
any injuries. I had listened. But my blood-sugar at the time had
been raised to such a level that I was more or less incapable of
paying attention. Delirium had made me stare, incapable, at the

doctor explaining this. So I had treated the infection as a tiresome thing that would probably go away with some antiseptic cream and Elastoplast.

On the Wednesday night, I changed the dressing. Beneath the dressing, the toe's skin was angry, red and swollen up to the first joint; above that it was white, dead and swollen. There was no sensation anywhere. I got into a taxi and went to Accident and Emergency.

Somewhere, Virginia Woolf remarks on the division that exists between the well and the ill, how invalids and the unwell disappear into a world that hardly exists for the healthy. For the seriously ill, one of the most immediate of these divisions is in the distinction between him and the medical professionals confronting him. You are a patient; we are your cure.

The mass of invalidity and incapacity in a London Accident and Emergency department is uniform and repulsive, especially at night. I sat in the waiting hall to be seen by a triage nurse. About me were homeless men, a couple of students who had been assaulted in a minor way, and an unusual couple. They were Haredi Jews. One, in a wheelchair, was extraordinarily obese, his belly not just spilling onto his thighs, but actually protruding beyond his knees as he sat. His head was lolling from side to side: he was beyond communication. His companion, a thin man with ringlets and a hat, wearing the traditional black overcoat, was deep in prayer, bending his head back and forth energetically over a copy of the sacred texts. From time to time, a receptionist or a nurse would nervously approach, try to speak to the obese patient, then, on getting no response, would start to approach the devout carer. He made no response, continuing with his intricate prayer ritual; his ritual spoke to God, and not to the world. He had no interest in drawing anyone into his world of contemplation and revelation and God. His religion did not convert or persuade. It just was. The nurse or receptionist would approach, and mutter something like 'I'll come back in five minutes.' But in five minutes, the prayer was still continuing, and they went away again.

My experience of Accident and Emergency is varied. In the past, I had cycled, and had been thrown from my bicycle, been hit by cars, had fallen onto my elbow over the handlebars. On another occasion, I had sprained an ankle, which had swollen enormously, and been staggeringly painful. Then, I had been given painkillers and told to go home and rest it. Now, I was in nowhere near as much pain. Did I belong in this room? It was only an infection and an unattractive appearance.

I might have been the only person in the room, staff aside, who was sober. A woman in a bay opposite kept trying to get up, her hospital gown falling open at the back to show underwear that did not match but was clean and even expensive-looking; the bra strap was a vivid pink against her dark skin. You only ever see very incapably drunk black women in London. A man in a suit next to her, hooked up to a saline drip, was either asleep or comatose with alcohol. They were alone, but somewhere near by someone was shouting, 'You make me sick. You make me fucking sick, what you put me through, what you fucking do.'

I was conscious of not belonging to the rest of the admittances. There was a community of emergency, but I did not belong to it: I was not drunk; I needed medical treatment. From time to time a doctor or two came into the bay where I was extended on a slippery trolley. They talked to each other without introducing themselves. They were junior doctors, for the most part. They appeared frightened, probably of tonight's patients and, equally, of the senior colleague who would descend on them. I tried to talk to them as they passed through, and to the nurses, and to the senior colleague, who appeared around three. I thought of the story I would tell in the future, when I was surrounded by my friends. I wanted to heal the divide of strangeness and examination that had arisen between me and those who were tasked with curing me.

2.

We exist in society, and we make our own societies as we go. Those people who attempt solitude are rare, and often have to resort to external limitations to make a success of it – moving to an island, or taking up drugs, or ecstatic meditation, blotting out others with intoxication or God. In a society, isolation leads to eccentricity; eccentricity leads to loneliness; loneliness leads to madness. In the 1970s, a serial killer called Dennis Nilsen committed his first murder, he said, after not speaking to another human being for many days. That is one solution the soul comes to. Another is to grow inward, with one's own mannerisms and solutions. We are all egotists, but the withdrawn and isolated human can turn into an egotist with no interest in others and no understanding, either. Today I watched a man walk along the Wandsworth Road. He lived alone. His clothes indicated that. They were in simple colours between beige and blue. They were comfortable-appearing and not very well fitting. You felt that he visited the hairdresser, but the hairdresser had correctly intuited that he had nobody at home to comment on the result, or to advise him that he needed to go somewhere else to have his hair cut. As he walked he talked; his lips moved; his head shook and his face twisted from time to time in anger at some recollection. He was thinking of injustices done to him, and there was nobody in the street who could be alarmed, because nobody knew him. He was not mad, not quite, but almost, and he was definitely alone, incurably.

Out there is society, and we live in it. We think of our society as made up of people we have known for years, of our oldest friends, of people we know and trust. But it is made up of people, too, whom we see once a week or once a month, perhaps only serving them or being served by them, whose names we might know or might not know; of acquaintances and friends of friends; of people, too, whom we meet only once and with whom we exchange a word or two. Does it matter whether we get to know these people, whether we pass the time of day pleasantly or ignore them entirely? Should we be good to strangers? Are we good to strangers, not feeling any moral imperative?

There is a dilemma that economists puzzle over, which no amount of self-interest can, apparently, explain. It is called the One-off Tipper. You are in a strange town for the first time, and are about to leave. You go to a restaurant opposite the railway station. The restaurant, a large sign on the window announces, is closing down tonight at nine p.m., as the owners are going into retirement. It is now seven thirty. You order your meal; it is brought to you without much conversation; you eat your meal; and you finish it while reading a book. The bill arrives and you pay it, adding fifteen per cent as a tip, for service. You leave and you never see any of the people involved, ever again.

Economists puzzle over why you should have left a tip. For them, tips, like everything else, are self-interested investments in future existence. But why should anyone tip when there will be no future relationship? Why should you tip a waiter in a restaurant that is closing, or a taxi driver in a huge city whom you will never see again, as much as the man who cuts your hair every fortnight or the waiter in the steakhouse a hundred yards from your house who serves your dinner once a week? Is the tip a hedge against the possibility that you have left your bag or hat behind – a tipped worker will be helpful, an untipped one will have thrown it away?

But the bond is what counts. For an hour, we are in the company of strangers, and we do not want them to continue as strangers. A gesture of kindness: an unnecessary donation; a financial statement of gratitude, even if we can't say much more than 'thank you' in words: these come naturally, still. Perhaps we want to form some kind of society, to reach out, to make it plain that something human has passed between us and we might, very well, have talked.

Without that, there is discomfiture; aloneness. I felt like that the night I was admitted to Accident and Emergency. I had no connection with the other patients, and I had no connection with the professional carers.

3.

As the medical staff came and went, few of them seemed to have time for anything more than a generalized gesture of kindness. The care in the temporary ward I had been moved to, from which either I would soon be removed to a more permanent and tranquil ward or despatched home, was driven, practical, swift. It did not have the anonymous quality of the care in the Accident and Emergency department, but there was no quality of leisure about it, either. The ward sister was an Irishwoman of formidable efficiency; the doctors who dealt with me asked questions or turned to each other and discussed matters as if I were not there, in terminology that I could not completely understand.

This detached and swift quality was something I started to share. And it started to influence the attitude I had towards the infected part of my body. At one point that morning, a doctor turned to me and said, 'We're not certain. But we think the infection may have reached the bone. If it has, there is a likelihood that we will have to amputate.'

'The toe?' I asked.

'We hope it won't be more than the toe,' the doctor said. 'The good news is that it isn't gangrenous as yet, and you do have good circulation in your feet.'

At this news, I felt mildly proud – at having fended off gangrene, and having achieved good circulation. Like those participants in daytime television who demand applause from a paying public for the most routine and universal moral positions – 'Hey, I *love* my children!' – I was modestly accepting acclaim for the circulation of my blood. Had I been working behind the scenes, unknown even to myself, all those forty-seven years, to maintain a beautiful flow of blood to the feet? I felt almost tearful at the unsung commitment. The assertions of danger and the possibility of losing the toe, the foot, the leg, on the other hand, had nothing at all to do with me. I listened to these diagnoses in a detached way, as if I too were standing at the end of the bed waiting for my opinion to be sought. 'You'll be moved to Albert Ward later today, after the MRI scan,' the formidable Irish ward sister told me, around ten. I nodded sagely. It was the best thing all round for the patient. At the same time, I had a detached and interested awareness that 'gangrenous' was probably one of the worst words, even in renunciation, that one might hear when in a hospital bed.

4.

Because I had come in without any intention of staying more than the hour or two it took to prescribe me some antibiotics and patch up my wound, I had brought nothing with me. So in Accident and Emergency, I had been asked to change into a hospital gown, one of those that the drunks opposite kept failing to fasten properly so that all about saw their naked backs, their non-matching underwear. In the ward on the sixth floor, I was still, self-consciously, in this floral robe with my pants underneath. The clothes I had been wearing – jeans, shirt, an overcoat, socks and brown brogues – had been in a pile by the side of the trolley, my valuables, such as phone, keys and wallet, tucked under my side. This was at the advice of the nurses. Accident and Emergency, with its transient population, was evidently familiar with the lifting of personal property.

But upstairs, now it was clear that I was going to be staying longer, I asked the staff if there were some pyjamas I could wear. They brought some clean orange ones, a colour few people would choose. These orange pyjamas, like the uniforms at Guantánamo, had an institutional air. Their colour was meant not just to be ugly and, for white men, very unflattering – I later shared a ward with a black patient who looked magnificent in his orange jim-jams – but to distinguish the ill as a class from the many different sorts of medical caregivers. The tea-pourers, the takers of blood, the junior nurses, the senior nurses, the junior doctors in their white coats and their stethoscopes, like avant-garde necklaces of rubber and steel – they all had their uniforms. And so did the patients, in their orange pyjamas and their hospital gowns. Only the senior doctors and consultants and the administrators who walked about importantly had no uniform, and, of course, they dressed in exactly the way that consultants and hospital administrators are expected to dress by society. I felt that, as a matter of urgency, I should get hold of a pair of pyjamas from home, and some other means to detach my condition from its institutional setting. I envisaged a framed photograph on the wheeled bedside unit, a favourite book, a pen and a notepad, and some pyjamas and a dressing-gown to impress my individuality on the minds of the doctors, like a hostage to kidnappers.

Albert Ward was where I ended up. In a state of isolation, I had texted a dozen friends overnight, telling them where I was and cancelling any engagements I might have had. I was supposed to travel to Germany the next day, where I was chairing a writers' conference, and directly on to India to the Jaipur festival to promote a book. Now, in the morning, on Albert Ward, my phone was pinging with messages back – expressing horror, concern, practical help, and, from my husband, who was in Geneva, a promise that he would take the first plane over in the morning. I was surrounded not just by professional care, but by the investment of relationships, in some cases, decades old.

The ward contained six beds, separated from each other only by blue pleated curtains that could be drawn forward and across for privacy. The window at the end of the room contained a view of the long, metallic, sinuous path of the river under a morning January sun. At the far end was a vast, tattered old man, whose rasping voice, devoid of consonants, suggested the ravaged survivor of at least one stroke. In time I discovered that he had survived five: for the medical profession, he was the object of wonderment disguised as admiration. They did not seem at all curious about his success; they just came to wonder, almost in benign amusement. Opposite was a man waiting for an operation on his knee. In the middle bay was another survivor of a stroke, but mute and incapable of efficient movement on one side. He communicated with bell and gesture, indicating with his good side what he needed. He patiently nodded or frowned at suggestions from the nurses. He was called Robert. Somehow, his limited capacities allowed him to suggest that he was requesting things with polite diffidence and not expressing impatience when responses were slow or obtuse; he indicated the grey cardboard pisspot, even, with politeness and gratitude in his index finger. I could never understand how he did this. The nurses loved Robert, and spoke to him with special consideration and warmth.

The ward had, like all hospital wards, its own disinfected smell and, on top of that, a particular stew-like odour. The clean, blasted smell was overlaid at lunchtime by a rotting, organic sweetness. As the day went on and turned into evening, the smell clarified itself and grew stronger. By six, it was clear that you were smelling shit. When in the morning you went to shower and returned to the ward, the stench of human shit was overwhelming. It remained like that until its source, an Irishman called Joe, was argued into being taken for a shower by the nurses. In his absence, his bed was stripped and its mattress washed down. He would return momentarily roseate, his washed hair in a clean shock about his stunned, sideways-on head; he would lie down. In half an hour the characteristic stench would start to drift over again.

Joe had an ally in the bed opposite, another Irishman. I never discovered the other Irishman's name, because the nurses never used it, and Joe might have forgotten it. This second Irishman

351

was a cut above Joe socially, though he, too, wore the institutional orange pyjamas. His family visited and telephoned – a mark of distinction in the ward. His skin seemed to be his problem. It was red raw, and he had to be swabbed like a deck with lotions and unguents until he shone scarlet. He was a short-term inmate. Joe, on the other hand, was in for as long as he could wheedle and contrive.

At ten each morning, shortly after having to submit to being forcibly washed, Joe would begin his demands.

'Nurse,' he said. 'Nurse. Can you take me out, please, for me cigarette, one small cigarette only?'

The passing nurse might ignore this. The mornings were their busy time, and they had to be about to help the doctors making their rounds. If one stopped, she would say only, 'Not now, Joe,' and move on.

There was no risk of not discovering Joe's name. The nurses and the doctors hated him, and they used his name all the time.

'It's a fucking disgrace,' Joe would say, to his friend opposite.

'You're fucking right there for once, Joe,' his friend replied. 'A total fucking disgrace. This place is a fucking shambles.'

'It's just one fucking cigarette I'm after,' Joe said. 'Nurse. Nurse. Nurse.'

'What is it, Joe?' a nurse said. She stood there, her hands on the blood pressure trolley, her hair scraped back like that of a 1970s hostess. 'I'm very busy, Joe.'

'I just need a cigarette,' Joe said. 'That's all, I need one.'

'Not now, Joe,' the nurse said. Her name was Lucy. Joe never used it. 'Not now. We're all very busy. You know you don't get taken out until after lunch. If Mario has time, after lunch, he'll take you. You know that was what we agreed, Joe.'

'She's a fucking disgrace, that one,' Joe said, when Lucy had almost gone. 'Jesus, it's just one fucking cigarette I'm after. What a fucking shambles.'

'I'm out of this fucking shithole,' his friend remarked. 'Just as soon as I fucking can, Joe.'

'Once you're out,' Joe said, 'that'll be the last I see of you. Ah, you're all the fucking same. The few who are nice to your face – even them – they can't wait to be fucking shot of you.'

'Ah, don't you be like that,' his friend would sometimes say. 'Sure, I'll be back next week, don't you think otherwise.'

I doubted this. The morning went on. Joe took, after some time, to pressing his patient's buzzer, intended to summon a nurse. He understood that the purpose of the bell was not to reiterate a request that had already been made, and fabricated another purpose to be offered up at first.

'What is it, Joe?'

'Nurse, I need some of those pills of yours.'

'What are you talking about?'

'Those pills that get you over your withdrawal, Nurse. It's bad today. It's real bad.'

'Joe, I've told you before. You haven't had a drink for six weeks. You were brought in six weeks ago, remember? You're not suffering withdrawal symptoms. I can get you a paracetamol if you're in pain. Are you in pain, Joe?'

'Ah, Nurse, when are you taking me out for a cigarette? You promised. It's not fair. I need a cigarette. You're depriving me. You all hate me.'

'Joe, I've got to get back to my job. You'll be taken out after lunch.' Then an evil thought evidently crossed the nurse's mind. 'If someone has some time to spare.'

In the days that followed, I overheard Joe's story in bits, some repeated frequently, some brought out just once. His head was twisted grotesquely on his neck, almost horizontal to his shoulders, and only one arm appeared to work at all. Sometimes these injuries were ascribed to the experiments of the medical profession. Joe would tell a nurse or his friend that he had had not a problem, not a one, with his head or neck until the day he had come into hospital. Sometimes they would be blamed on a car that had hit him. Had this accident happened just a day or two back? Or was it impossible now to discover which of Joe's

353

enemies had been driving the car, because it had been months or years ago, and the police, everyone knew, were very good at losing clues and evidence and that when it suited them? The one detail that never changed was where the car had hit him. It was always 'just where the Kennington Road makes a big curve, you know what I'm referring to, coming into the Elephant and Castle roundabout, where you can't see the traffic coming, not for the life of you', a detail so precise and yet lacking in accord with London geography that it made me think Joe's familiarity with the world came and went at his own convenience. 'I don't know who's behind all of this,' Joe would say, his feet waving in the air as if he could summon somebody with the movement of his toes. 'But I can take a fucking guess.'

'You're right there, Joe,' his friend would say, in happy disgruntlement. 'You're right on the fucking money.'

There was a strong and inventive strain of paranoia in Joe's world, and its presiding principle was that Joe had never done anything wrong in his life. The sister who never came to visit, God knew what was behind that, the old bitch – it was only slowly apparent that she had been living in Australia for twenty years. The nursing staff who had failed to take him out for a cigarette were neglecting him out of deliberate malice, and the doctors had carried out the experiments that had left him in this sorry condition. Now they were trying to remove him to one of them hostels – but Joe knew what they were like. They were places where your money and your property were stolen by any passing little runt, and the poor innocents they got molested by them child molesters before you could say knife. That wasn't going to happen, no fucking way.

'You stick to your fucking guns,' the friend in the bed opposite remarked comfortably. 'You don't want them to be putting you in no fucking hostel. You want them to be putting you in your own fucking home.'

It was news to me that Joe had a home of his own.

'I don't want to be put in my own home,' Joe said. 'Jesus

Christ, that shithole. Look at me. Look at the fucking state of me. There's no way I can cope on my own. No, I'm staying here, where them fucking cunts can experiment on me all they like. I wasn't like this when I came in here. There was nothing wrong with me six fucking weeks ago.'

Joe's paranoia that something lay behind his current state that nobody was prepared to acknowledge or investigate was shared, to some extent, by the hospital's medical staff. It became apparent that though Joe had now dried out, and his various old injuries, his twisted spine and his abandoned-toy-soldier neck and side-ways-on head, were considered by the hospital not susceptible to treatment, there was the question of his incontinence and his catastrophic digestion. Joe and the medical profession had reached a well-constructed impasse. Every morning's doctors' rounds ran the same course. The doctors would assert that Joe's condition needed to be examined. Joe would say that there was no fucking sympathy for what he was going through. The topic and the respective positions in the argument were so well estab-lished by now that the doctors and Joe talked allusively before slipping, on both sides, into impatience. It took three days before I understood that Joe's condition couldn't be diagnosed accurately without a colonoscopy. He was steadily refusing permission for this, and insisting that the doctors were refusing to discover what was wrong with him. Without an accurate diagnosis, as Joe knew quite well, it would be hard for the hospital to discharge him. For this reason, he went on refusing the colonoscopy.

I thought long and devotedly, but skirting over the details, about the gentleman whose professional duty it was to undertake colonoscopies into incontinent alcoholic Irish tramps.

To keep out Joe's conversation, it was possible to put on earphones and listen to music on the iPad. I did that on my first morning, setting it to select things at random, and it gave me, in no predictable order Bunji Garlin, the septet from *Les Troyens*, Miss Platnum and the *Emperor Waltz*. To shut out Joe's smell, or to do anything about it, proved harder. I thought of those eighteenth-century town-dwellers who walked the street with a posy clutched to their nostrils. The nurses tried to make sure that Joe was washed by the time the consultants came round in the morning. It reflected, I suppose, on their care if the senior doctors found a patient caked in day-old shit. While Joe was gone, his Irish friend in the bed opposite tried to engage passing nurses in conversation.

'Ah, it's a relief when he's gone, even for a minute, isn't it?' he said. 'You know what's the worst of it? It's the language, I swear to God. It's disgusting, what comes out of that one's mouth. I've never heard the like. I tell you what, Nurse – there's not a chance of a cup of tea for me, would there be?'

But tea was rationed, coming round at regular intervals, or only for the relations of the dangerously sick, and he was unsmilingly told to wait until the proper time.

'Ah, I'm looking forward to getting out of this fucking shithole,' he remarked, when Joe returned from his shower, clean, startled, stunned-looking and wide-eyed, like a well-rinsed owl. 'And being able to get a cup of fucking tea when you feel like it.' A malevolent look flickered over his face; he controlled it, his fingers fluttering over the grey bedpan in his lap, and his face turned to an expression of studious blankness. 'Or something better – a couple of pints in the pub with your old mates. Just a couple, enough for a drink, make you feel you've had a fucking drink, not enough to render you incapable.'

'I don't know where my mates are,' Joe said. 'They're all fucking cunts. I never want to see them again. They can fuck off. And my fucking sister. She knows I've been here for six weeks, dying, and no sign of improvement. Where the fuck is she, my own fucking flesh and blood, the shite.'

'It's sad when you've no mates,' his friend said. 'Me, I've got hundreds. I'm like him at the end with the fucking flowers and the fucking queue of visitors.'

'Ah, him,' Joe said. 'Him with the roses. Nurse, can you take me out for a fucking cigarette, now, you're treating me like a cunt.'

'Not now, Joe,' Lucy said, walking past. The flowers were tulips, brought by my friend Richard. But otherwise Joe and his friend were right. I had been lucky in the number of visitors I had had.

5.

In the space of the ward, contact with the world was exiguous. What I remembered best about a previous three-week stay in hospital when I was fourteen was how very odd the world looked when I came out: sparkling, cold, fresh. I had had the sense of everyone moving quite gingerly through its air. On this occasion, since I didn't feel ill, I had no compunction about taking the lift down eleven floors once or twice a day to the cafés and shops that were making money out of the hospital's unclinical lobbies. In my pyjamas, slippers and dressing-gown among the crowds, but licensed in my *déshabillé*, I felt inexplicably invisible. Nobody looked at me, though to be caught in public in your night- or sick-wear is a familiar dreadful dream of conspicuous discovery. I think they were perhaps tactfully averting their eyes, since nobody wants to be caught staring at a person who is seriously ill, or just insane. The lift upstairs was a capsule returning me to an enclosed, epic and safe world. It was easy to see how a week or two would rob you of any curiosity about the world, even where your nurse had come from that morning, even about the long, laden boats sliding noiselessly over the grey-surfaced river below, with the silent pregnant greatness of the boats in Homer. For this reason, the nurses and other medical staff would be surprised and vulnerable to any genuine-sounding or interested enquiry in their circumstances. I banked on this.

The lack of curiosity about the world was strong in Joe and

his Irish friend. I put it like that, since the lack seemed a positive, even an energetic, quality of decision and the averted head. I never heard them ask a question that wasn't aimed fairly directly at extracting a favour for themselves. Their sight could have extended only three feet from the borders of their bed, taking cognizance only of what happened to blunder against them. Beyond that, there was nothing but inaccurate speculation, a world made out of rage-filled fantasy, sentimental constructions – those hundreds of imaginary mates in the pub – and a great emptiness of malice. Of the world they knew and saw and cared nothing at all, and those blundering and aim-directed objects came into their circumference from nowhere, and went on to nowhere, to do nothing further once they were detached from Joe. Joe's imagination did not fail. It had never begun to work. The ward existed in a kind of void that from time to time provided a laden trolley with tea or machinery or medicine. From time to time, the remote end of the bed would be crowded with white-coated dignitaries. They would shake their heads, metaphorically speaking – in reality, one or two would raise their heads and gaze penetratingly at nothing in particular while the rest hung their faces over their notes, hoping not to be addressed. Below, on the river, long empty boats, like yellow shoeboxes, went from right to left in the early morning's mercury-shining light; in the early evening, the same boats went from left to right, bearing ribbed burdens of iron-boxed waste, and the boats sank deep in the water with their new weight. Where did they come from, and where did they go to disgorge themselves? In the placid world of the ward, I looked down from the steel-framed window and began not to care.

Joe and his friend had forgotten all about the world, and the world had certainly forgotten about them. There were few visitors to the patients in the ward; the quintuple stroke victim had a visit from three gigantically obese people, his daughters and a grandson. A sharp-faced girl with skin as red as a scrubbed thing turned up, and spent exactly ten minutes with the other Irishman.

Outside, in the world, polemicists and activists were arguing that it was a tragedy that the physically infirm and helpless had been forgotten about, were ignored by society. Up here, the physically infirm had forgotten not only about the world, but even what to do to enquire about it. They knew their nurses' first names, since they sometimes wanted to call one to do something for them. More than that they could not venture, and would have been astonished to discover that normal people could not live in such empty boredom without enquiring about idle details. But, of course, they were normal people: that was what life made of normal people, friendless and incurious, attended only by the dutiful, who had no choice in the matter.

For the moment, I was new and in unfamiliar territory. The world outside wanted to know what was up, and my friends came to visit. Nicola was first, at nine in the morning after my admission, then, as soon as he could, my husband Zaved. Then they all came. Richard, Yusef, Renaud, Alan, Lucy, Jess, Amy, Georgia, Erin, Nicholas, Ginny, Matthew, Giles, Thomas, one after the other, in pairs and threes, so many that they had to wait or we had to decamp to the pastel-green family room or to the café downstairs. Zaved, who was there from two till eight every day, heard me tell the story of my infection and admission so many times that he started removing himself, by the fifth day, in mild annoyance. I had so many visitors that I started to feel myself *popular*, though I had only seventeen visitors in two days; I felt myself popular even when my sister Kate came to visit. I also, interestingly and very authentically, began to feel myself tired by society, like an invalid in a book. The stream of visitors to my bed infuriated Joe, who listened keenly, making abusive comments in the third person when he could hear the conversation, or complaining about people whispering when he could not. But if the numbers irritated Joe, they made a positive impact on the nurses, who seemed to show an interest and to like me more when they saw that I had, at the least, two dozen friends and a sister who got on with me and who had not moved

359

to Australia in high dudgeon, the better never to lay eyes on me again. By the end of the second day, I started to feel that I could have got the nurses to do anything I wanted.

6.

Once I wrote in a novel that sometimes we see a new friend coming from far off. He falls into step with us, companionably, and as he begins to talk, we recognize that we had a Bertie-shaped hole in our lives and affections. We didn't know about it, but it was there, and now it has been filled, by Bertie. It is hard to remember seeing him for the first time, or what our life was like before we knew him.

How do we meet friends? How do we know that the person we have just met will or may become a friend? There he is, perhaps in a slightly awkward place in a group. You are not quite sure what his name is, and you make a remark that is not quite meant for him, though it does not exclude him, and not quite general in tendency. But he says something in return that is not quite what you expect, something that makes you pause, or that echoes something you've thought yourself. You look at him; he looks back when you make some kind of response; and a friendship begins. The next time you see him, you are not quite starting from scratch.

This theory of friendship leaves too much out. Our friends are not people we happen to agree with most of the time. Only very shallow egotists *choose* their friends at all, and what basis you might decide on approving a stranger as a friend for the future is not something to be listed. We prefer to think of our friends as happy accidents – the person we have an office next to, the person we happened to be standing by at the Freshers' Drinks in a beeswax-smelling Arts and Crafts common room, and said, 'I'm really terrified – I want to go home before they find me out' to. That was thirty years ago. You saw a movie with him last night, and you offered him your popcorn without thinking. Or they were friends of friends who became friends in their own right. They were somebody we once met in a bar and took home, and the sex did not work, but you made each other laugh over breakfast, and a week later you bumped into each other in Vauxhall and you laughed again over drinks, but didn't go home together again – ten years later, you wouldn't dream even of thinking you once went to bed with your old friend. They were somebody you used to meet at parties to launch books, whom you thought of as a professional contact to be civil to. Then one day you broke your ankle falling off your bike, and the phone rang and it was the professional contact pointing out that they only lived five minutes' walk away, and it would be no trouble to get some food from Waitrose. The alternative, she said, was going in and facing a series of phone calls from fucking poets about why their work wasn't selling better. Was it embarrassing to ask her to get a bottle of white wine and the cheap shepherd's pie, which wasn't too bad at all? Well, you asked anyway, and now she's your friend.

They are happy accidents, but there are plenty of happy accidents that fail to become the beginning of a happy friendship. The man who drove into you and broke your ankle, for instance, or the appalling man you used to work with, and had to be polite to every day, but who wrote prose poetry about clowns and small girls. He might have thought you were his friend, but the day you left that job was the day after which you never spoke to him again. There were other people, too, who came round with help when you were ill, whom you, indeed, visited with the second-best shepherd's pie from Waitrose when they broke their ankle. They are not really your friends. If you saw a friend enter a crowded room of strangers, or walking unexpectedly across a crowded city street, your heart would rise at their dear flapping trousers and their church-bazaar orange-and-lime scarf wrapping itself round their face with the wind. If you saw a pseudo-friend like this, your heart would sink, inexplicably, guiltily, and you would wonder if they had seen you. The sentence, two weeks later, 'I thought I saw you on Regent Street a couple of Saturdays ago,' will fill you with terrible, unspeakable, unshareable self-flagellations, and you will promptly invite the man and his terrible wife to dinner, and cook a whole shoulder of mutton and even make both a green soup and a pink pudding from scratch, and at this dinner you and your partner will both get unforgivably, atrociously, unacceptably drunk.

Friends don't happen because you share their views, or because they are going to be useful to you. But afterwards you do find yourself sharing their views and, to your mild surprise, you are cheerfully being helpful to them; they are cheerfully glimpsed lifting a box of thrillers into their car to take on your behalf to the charity shop. They are coming to see you in hospital, and bringing you whatever you need, without you having to ask, but you don't mind asking. It could be that the appearance of friendship, in the guileful, could get strangers to do your bidding, too.

Perhaps there is a sense of the pariah, just outside the friendship. There are people whom we may agree we don't care for – Liberal Democrats, hunting folk, people who are glimpsed transfixedly picking their nose just on the other side of their car window, sitting in a traffic jam, or single-issue activists, people who say, 'A friend invited my wife and I on holiday,' and explainers over dinner of the Chechnyan conflict. More specifically, there are the fucking poets or the friends of the past who introduced you to each other, who, years later, you confess that you wouldn't care if you never saw the intermediary ever again. The pariahs cement our friendship, even if they are quite out of the room. And what are we, together? We may be holders of some special beliefs: our qualities will spread and the opinions we hold will triumph in the end, and the world will improve. Sometimes the opinions we hold, the ones that our pariahs would probably fight against, are on vegetarianism, racial equality, the purity of the Line, the importance of having a few hundred books and a nice painting or two around the place, the inferiority of certain races or of one gender, the idea that rhyming poetry and the C major chord aren't done for quite yet, the rightness in all things of the Tory party or the Communist party, the conspiracy of the paedophile establishment, a single European currency, world peace and the excellence of the films of Douglas Sirk. (We don't necessarily argue for any of this: sometimes we just embody it, and the belief gets spread just the same.) Sometimes these opinions that we jointly hold merely add up to the belief that, if we have to be in hospital at all, we should be in a small room, away from the smell of human shit, with, in ideal circumstances, a view of the Houses of Parliament there, just across the river. I was definitely going to get my way on this one.

7.

I began to work on a doctor whom, afterwards, I always referred to as Dr Arsehole. It was a childish play on his surname, which was not very much like the word Arsehole. At first he appeared to be a Vauxhall type, taking time off from a long shift at the disco coal-face. He had a shaved head and a twinkle in his eye: he was in early middle age and had a rascally quality. He was a podiatrist, not a doctor at all; he came in the first morning to examine my feet. The first thing he did was to get out a scalpel and cut off the dead skin that made up most of my toe, cut off the sodden white mass that was the previously hardened skin at the end, probed through the ulcerated segment at the end, probing down to the bone. I could feel nothing, and I watched him at work with interest and some social speculation. He was senior enough not to wear a uniform of any sort.

'You know,' I said, 'I've often wondered, in circumstances like this, what leads people to decide to specialize in one unlovely part of the body or another. Or, rather, when it dawns on you that the foot is where you want to spend the rest of your life.'

Dr Arsehole giggled. He sat down on the end of the bed in a jolly, conspiratorial way. I felt that I was probably only slightly older than him, and could easily have been his friend in other circumstances. 'Oh, I don't know. It just sort of crept up on me.'

'It can't be nice coming into work in the morning and finding that you've got to deal with something like that, after all.'

'This?' Dr Arsehole said, with amusement. 'This? Oh, this is nothing. You should see some of the things we see. They're interesting, feet, though – they really are interesting little diagnostic tools for the rest of the body. If you have problems with your feet, there'll be a problem somewhere else, often.'

'There's an awful Chinese thing, isn't there,' I said, 'where they tell you that your digestion is bad or you suffer from migraines by sensitive bits on your feet or something? Reflexology.'

'Yes, well,' Dr Arsehole said, looking long, deep and languidly into my eyes as he cut off another pad of hardened, soggy, pus-drenched skin and cast it aside. 'There's something in it, even if they take it too far. What do you do for a living?'

'I'm a novelist,' I said.

'Ooh,' Dr Arsehole said. 'What sort of novels? My wife's reading that *Fifty Shades of Grey*. Not a novel like that one, I hope.'

I hid my disappointment at the existence of Dr Arsehole's wife, and explained the sort of novels I had been writing as briefly as was compatible with civility. As always, I felt that signed-up writers of thrillers, pony-based adventures, fantasy novels about giant insects or historical romances had this particular conversation much more easily sewn up than I did, and Dr Arsehole politely said he would look out for them. 'But not much standing up required,' he said.

'What?'

'Not much standing up required in your job.'

'Oh. No. I don't suppose any, in fact, apart from performing at lecterns occasionally.'

'Now I think I want to have a look at your shoes, if they're the sort of shoes you usually wear.'

Zaved came in that afternoon, flying in from Switzerland in a concerned state. I told him about Dr Arsehole's consultation, exaggerating parts of it for his entertainment.

'And then Dr Arsehole said – get this – if they're not happy about your shoes, they think they're contributing to your poor state of foot health, then the NHS can actually have some shoes made for you. Bespoke shoes. Do you know how much that normally costs, how much if you had them made on the high street? Three thousand pounds, I reckon, minimum. So I said, I can't believe it, I've really landed on my feet here, and Oliver said, Well, that's one way of putting it, and actually, it's cheaper for us than admitting you to hospital with infections like this one, look at it this way. So I said Oliver. Look me in the eye and tell me that you're not going to make one of those terrible pairs of shoes for me, you know, those shoes for remedials, I couldn't bear that, look at my shoes, the ones I'm wearing. Those cost five hundred dollars in New York. I couldn't bear it if I had to start wearing the sort of shoes that remedials wear. But Oliver goes No, no, don't worry, don't panic, it's not like that, you can get brogues, anything, all sorts, honest. And then he started talking to me about his wife reading porn all the time.'

'Oh, come on,' Zaved said, shaking his head. He had ten years of experience of my exaggerations in conversation. 'There's a terrible smell in here. What's that smell?'

'It's Joe,' I said, my voice lowered. 'Just on the other side of the curtain. It's worse when you go out and come back in again.'

'My God,' Zaved said. 'Is that the man who shouted Nurse at me? He thought I was a nurse. How can he have thought I was a nurse? I was wearing an overcoat. Can't you ask to be moved to a room on your own?'

'No, of course not,' I said. 'Don't you ask on my behalf, either. Tea! How lovely! That is kind of you! Milk and no sugar, please. How lovely! Thank you so very, very much. I hope I'm not going to get into awful trouble for having a little bunch of tulips on my bedside table, am I?'

'Oh, well,' the ward assistant said. 'I think we can probably overlook it for now.' She went away smiling.

I had won the game with Dr Arsehole, but he was only an occasional visitor to the ward. On the second day, he finished his treatment of my foot by cosily sitting down on the end of the bed and cutting my toenails, even the ones on the toes with nothing wrong with them. He went on so long that lunch arrived – a stolid mass of fish pie with carrots and peas on the side – and he said, 'Oh, that looks delicious. It's just a sandwich down in Pret à Manger for me,' and went off, ignoring Joe's urgent calls of 'Nurse'. Ten minutes later a harassed and junior assistant, a woman with a dumpy figure and bags under her eyes, appeared at the end of my bed and rattled off my date of birth – this to prove that I was who she thought I was. 'I've come to cut your toenails,' she said.

'You're too late,' I said. 'Oliver's just done them. He's only just gone.'

'Oliver?' she said. 'Oliver the podiatrist? They sent me to cut your toenails. I'm supposed to do that.'

'Well, you can have a look if you like,' I said. Oliver seemed to have done a very neat job of cutting my toenails, as the woman orderly had to agree.

'Well, that was nice of him,' she said huffily. 'I wish they'd let me know that I'm not needed, though.'

'I'm sorry if you had a wasted walk,' I said. I was quite concerned that urgent toenail-cutting was being neglected on the other side of the hospital because of her being summoned to my bedside.

I had mastered the professionals without trouble. The nurses, however, were the ones with some control over where I could be placed, and they needed more careful handling. The doctors could be subjected to influence by worldly chatter, and not deferentially lowering my voice to address a hospital worker as 'Doctor'. The nurses, however, did not seem to care much either way whether you addressed them as 'Nurse' or 'Sophy', and they were not to be cowed by suggestions about my social life outside the hospital. I concentrated, for the moment, on being modest, thankful, cheerful, and no trouble at all. Evilly, I waited for a time when I could introduce an object of loathing and hatred into the conversation, when I could exert some influence over them by establishing a shared pariah. The identity of the pariah was never in doubt. If I could get to the point where I could talk to them about his awfulness without sounding like a whinger, and get them to talk back, then the deal would be done, and I could move happily into a private room. It needed very careful handling.

'Nurse,' called Joe. 'Nurse. Is it not fucking time for my fucking cigarette yet? You promised. You fucking promised. Ah, you cunts.'

'Not now, Joe,' a passing nurse said.

The infection in my toe was of such virulence that I needed regular, and at first constant, supplies of antibiotic delivered through a drip, and the nurses came to see me very frequently to change the bag, to take my blood sugar, blood pressure and temperature. On these visits, I concentrated on being meek and no trouble. But the antibiotics were of some strength, and after two or three bags, the passage of the liquid became unendurably painful and sore. Once a day at least, I had to call a nurse and say that the site of the cannula was now so painful that she would have to move it to a different place, and the cycle would begin again. I was always very apologetic about this, though there was really nothing else to be done. In fact, I noticed that the nurses were not at all impatient with this repeated request, and perhaps became more sympathetic towards me. Perhaps the confession of suffering, not overdone, reminded them of their vocation in a harmless way.

The nurses had a mode of existence that was quite different

from that of the doctors. They existed between an onstage and an offstage set of indicators. Within the ward, there would be a strict restriction on personal conversation between the nurses, and when they talked, they exchanged only information about the patients, and firm instructions from senior to junior. When they were outside the small ward, at the desk where 'paperwork', as they called it, was carried out and where interaction with administrators might take place, they often dropped into offstage behaviour. No patients sat there; we only passed by from time to time, and there what we overheard were exchanges about private existence, about partners and husbands, about inconveniences of travel and the doings of children. When in this mode, they relaxed; their bodies slumped; they scratched their heads with fingernail and biro; they adjusted their tight uniforms and yawned; stance and expression yielded and shifted, softened, the smiles came naturally and not professionally, and they did not use each other's names in address. We were not exactly shielded from such behaviour, or from such frank conversation, but it only seemed to be happening in spaces a patient might pass through, but not stop within.

Patients, too, behaved for the most part within onstage and offstage modes, meekly using the vocatives 'Nurse' and 'Doctor' in ways unfamiliar in the outside world – the parallels would be 'Shop assistant, will you sell me a white shirt?' 'Architect, you may have forgotten to put a staircase into the building.' They toned down their habitual diction, and assumed a facial expression of terrible sweetness when anyone professional was by. They mostly took orders, and had agreed to do everything at the time ordained for them by the hospital – I never heard a patient say, as would have been quite reasonable, 'Actually, I'm just in the middle of a phone call – can you do Dennis first?' Offstage, once the nurses had gone, the patients embarked on a more relaxed and habitual style of behaviour, saying 'fuck' and 'cunt' as they would normally do, and sharing details of their lives without any restraint.

Onstage and offstage behaviour differs greatly between professions and occupations. A contrary set of offstage indicators was made apparent to me some time after this stay in hospital, when we went on holiday to Mykonos, the predominantly gay Greek island. The beaches on Mykonos are filled with sunbeds under umbrellas, tended by extraordinarily beautiful men in skimpy shorts who bring drinks and refreshments at some expense. These men had a distinctive onstage behaviour. With the customers, they were openly flirtatious, even somewhat lewd, telling us that we had a 'nice bum' or they bet we were going to go off for a 'nice naughty walk' later, meaning that we were going to go and have sex with strangers in the dunes. This manner was formally assumed, and not very natural. When the beach boys were talking among themselves, they dropped into a natural, offstage manner; their voices grew harsh and direct and complaining; they lit cigarettes in a tough-guy mode; their stance grew less servile. Though their conversation was in Greek, it was easy to guess its content: how much money each of them had made, a subject unalluded to in onstage behaviour. It was not about sex, and certainly admitted nothing of flirtation in it; their behaviour grew direct and complaining. Although the content of their onstage and offstage behaviour was quite different from that in other professions, for instance that in the hospital, the clear division operated in precisely the same way. There was even the same useful physical indicator of the rows of beds – of patients and of sunbathers – in both cases.

The divisions of offstage and onstage behaviour between both patients and nurses was not enforced by the other group's presence, merely encouraged by it. Sometimes, late at night or at quiet times, a nurse or a patient would slip into offstage mode with each other, and the nurse would sit down on the bed and talk quite happily about informal matters, if she liked the patient enough. The patient's offstage manner was more flaunted, less rationed; he often tried to reel the nurse in with offstage confidences and even an offstage style. It seemed to me that no sharing of ideas, no persuasion could take place while either patient or nurse was in onstage mood. The only thing that could occur would be the successful appeal to aspects of the nurse's professional, onstage, duties. Only when the nurses gathered together at the administration desk of the ward could one tell another that she had seen *Django Unchained* last night, and it had been gory but very entertaining, and she recommended it; if a patient, walking past in a parallel offstage manner, had interrupted to say that he, too, had seen it and enjoyed it, but it wasn't a patch on *Jackie Brown*, which was the most underrated of all Tarantino's films, then the offstage nurses would have reacted with surprise, would have turned back into efficient, professionally kindly figures, would perhaps have seen the off-duty cinephile patient back to his bed by holding his elbow and pulling him firmly along with coos and amicable sounds of encouragement. In no case would they have admitted to enjoying the same film, in the limitless space outside the hospital's decreed tasks.

The offstage space was a dangerous one, and both nurses and patients were vulnerable to it. Its looming prospect, in anything other than well-defined areas, secured from intrusion or onstage performers like Joe, appealing for sympathy and a cigarette in accordance with agreed structures of behaviour, persuaded the nurses to retreat sharply, and take up a formal position, one arm raised in pity and sorrow like Sir Joshua Reynolds's *Tragedy*. Joe and his Irish friend failed in almost every attempt to persuade the nurses to do what they wanted them to do, because they had no means of bringing them into an offstage space. Their informalities only created a responding chilly formality, and the target replied by using the patient's name: 'I've told you before, Joe …' The only people with whom they could share an offstage space was, it appeared, each other, and they could not do each other any favours whatsoever. The dropping into a formal offstage mode, as Joe and his friend should have discovered by now, would not by itself create a reciprocal offstage mode in the interlocutor. It would be just as likely to push the target into a more rigid onstage manner.

I noticed, however, that though this was true of the nurses, the same could not be said for the doctors. I wondered if it was a function of power within the social structure. Doctors would enter the ward, still chatting to each other about the holiday they had just booked in Mali, and would discuss the patients loudly while at the end of the beds, not troubling to keep any professional, important, backstage discussions to their own space. The grander the doctor was, the more readily he would engage with a cheerful conversation about wives, husbands, bus routes, books that had just been read, films that had just opened, and other social strategies. Sometimes this clearly fell into the category of 'good bedside manner'. Sometimes, however, this was not an attempt at a good bedside manner, but simply a superior disregard for professional demands of onstage and offstage behaviour, which not only occurred within the earshot of the patient – 'Ah, Charles,' one consultant said, standing at the end of my bed, 'let's see if you can make yet another hash of this, then. How's Rebecca?' – but sometimes actually engaged him in the break from the onstage stance. This, I believed, was why it was in fact easier to influence and gain meaningful contact with the doctors. Their superior conviction that there was no need to maintain a rigid and performed onstage mode once through the ward doors left them wide open to the exercise of influence, and fertile ground for the spreading of principles. The nurses, on the other hand, were much harder to reach and to influence. Their rigid sense of onstage and offstage moments left them invulnerable to the spread of thought, and it was hard to plant a seed of consideration in this stony ground. You had to get them sitting on the edge of the bed. I concluded that the way into their thoughts was not to try to spread an idea, but to act as a calm, offstage recipient for whatever ideas and principles they wanted to spread. I waited, and I understood why they were called 'patients'.

8.

The ward sister, like many of the nurses, was Nigerian, stern and practical, and ran a tight ship. The first time I saw her, I was on my way downstairs to fetch a morning newspaper, and meekly asked permission to leave the ward. 'Very well,' she said, examining the watch hanging upside down on her breast. 'But you must be returned here in twelve minutes, exactly. That is when the consultant begins to make his rounds, and you must not miss him. He will not return for your sake. That is your responsibility. Do you understand? Twelve minutes?' She said all this not in a fierce or reproving way, just in a manner that set out the facts and left me to assume responsibility for my own actions. I said that I would wait until the consultant had seen me, and returned to my bed.

Her name was Desdemona, and I did not see her relaxing her stance in any circumstances, even with her staff. She was the person who would decide if I could be moved from my present position, directly next to the colossal shit-machine that was Joe. But why should I be moved? Somebody had to occupy that position. Why should it not be me? The solution, it appeared to me, was that Joe should be moved to a room of his own, but the reasons why that had not been undertaken were clear. Joe's demands were too much even when he was calling out to the passing nurses; if they had to respond every time he rang a bell, they would do nothing else all day long. Moreover, it was evidently a principle with the nurses not to do anything that Joe asked them to do, and that had spread into a principle not to do anything beyond the necessary that might benefit him. It was necessary, therefore, to find a way in which one could persuade those in power, without asking directly, to be moved away from Joe and ideally into a private room. The means of achieving that would be to enter Desdemona's offstage space. But she had no offstage space.

She came to see me half a dozen times a day, to take blood pressure and blood sugar – 'obs', in the hospital's terminology. I submitted cheerfully, passing a little comment each time. The first time she pricked my finger to draw a bead of blood for analysis, I heard her muttering, 'Sorry, sorry, sorry,' and I said,

'That's really quite all right – it doesn't hurt a bit.' It did not, in fact; years of playing the double bass had given me a tough pad of skin at the tip of my fingers, and a bicycle fall had deadened the sensation long ago. But she looked at me with a little surprise, and explained that in her culture saying, 'Sorry,' was not necessarily an apology, but a means of expressing empathy with whatever someone was enduring. Desdemona, with her formal offering of empathy, was going to be a hard nut to crack.

On the third day I was there, she came to my bed to take the obs, and found me in a low mood. My cannula had had to be removed in the middle of the night and replaced at a different point, it had become so very painful. Subsequently, a doctor had that morning told me again that my toe might very well need to be amputated. I had no memory of using that toe for any purpose at all, and I didn't suppose it did anything to keep me upright. Still, from adult experience of tooth extraction, I believed that once something started to be trimmed, it went on being trimmed and clipped; one toe would be followed by another, and another, and the foot. I wanted not to start on this process, and a restless night of pain had not helped me to take a positive outlook.

'Do you have a problem?' she asked, not unsympathetically.

I explained some of what the doctor had told me.

She shook her head. 'You are in the right place,' she said. 'We are keeping a very close eye on you. Nothing will go badly wrong, and we will let you go when we are happy about everything, when everything looks as if it is heading in the right direction.'

'That may be days,' I said. 'I really don't want to stay long in hospital.'

'Maybe so,' Desdemona said. 'This is the best place for you at the moment. Are you …' She seemed to be about to ask about the ward arrangements, but I had decided I would not raise that on my own: I would get them to make the offer as if from their own initiative. 'May I ask – are you a Christian?'

I could have kissed Desdemona. I knew that she was probably not allowed to do this, and as she sat on the end of my bed, and started to explain that she had found her faith of great help in dealing with suffering and difficulty, I felt all the power of the potential convert, wavering and wondering, and all the time reeling in the evangelist like a salmon on a hook. Desdemona had found English people so strange, discovering that they had no religious faith and did not, it seemed, care whether they had one or not.

'I see, I see,' I said, nodding and opening my eyes as wide as I could.

You see, Desdemona went on, her children had been raised knowing about God, and now were very fine people, with children of their own, and very good jobs, and still, they all go to church every Sunday … Her voice, deep in its offstage enchantments, wound on, her tone lowered as she explained, quite gently, not at all offensively, what religion had done for her. My eyes were firmly on a bed in a private room with, ideally, a good view of the Houses of Parliament over the river. I concentrated on appearing to accept everything she said, as if I were ever in my life going to give a moment's thought to Christianity's old rigmarole, as if its history and hopes of benevolence would ever occupy my mind for a moment.

'I see, I see,' I said, and Desdemona's voice was low and trusting, and her eyes were shining. She was about as offstage as a nurse in this busy ward would ever allow herself to get. After a few minutes, she got up from the end of my bed, and again took my blood pressure. I let her get on with it. Only when she went to make a record of it did she notice. 'I've done this already! I'm getting all in a tizzy,' she said.

'Oh, you're allowed,' I said. 'I should have said something.'

'Now, give what I've said a good thinking over,' she said. She smiled, a pleasant, kindly smile, and I was for a moment a small child in a mother's care. 'I must get on, but we'll have another talk some time. This is a good place for thinking about your life, a few days in this place.'

It was true. She went on with her chores. I waited until she left the ward, and then hopped off my bed to limp towards the bathroom. Nobody was about yet – it was the dead time between lunch, served at twelve prompt, and the arrival of visitors at two. In the ward, I caught the eye of Robert, the stroke sufferer. He had heard me attempt to listen and show the appearance of interest in Desdemona's Christian belief. He had more time for thinking about life than anyone else here, not eaten up with thoughts of injustice or neglect, unable to be anyone but himself in his mute gaze and gestures, and the nurses loved him. His mute gaze caught mine. He looked at me with rage, contempt and dismissal. I looked away.

But that afternoon I was moved from the position next to Joe to the bed by the window, without having to ask directly at all.

9.

I noticed that, as the days went by, I stopped being grateful for what was being done for me. When I took a shower in the morning, I took no trouble to keep my foot dressing dry. Instead, I returned to bed with it sopping wet, and rang the patients' bell for the nurse, explaining that it would need to be changed. The first time I did this, I said it had been an accident; the second time, I merely said that it would need to be changed. The expression of regret and human sympathy was beginning to give way to lordly demands, and after that to querulous complaint at how slowly things were being achieved, no doubt.

There was a danger that in hospital, I would start to think of human relations as a means to get things done for me. The only point of the performance of selflessness, of interest in other people, was going to be that it would serve my selfish requests. I could put up with pretending to be interested in other people, so long as it got my way. Was this all that human relations were? To spread ideas that would benefit ourselves, to create a community in order to achieve what we wanted? I had another example in front of me in hospital, between two and eight, each day.

When he arrived at two, on the dot, Zaved sat and told me what he'd been up to.

'Oh, I just watched the telly. It was *Miranda*.'

'I don't know how you can bear that rubbish,' I said. 'She's not funny at all.'

'She's so funny! I laughed so much. Come on, she's really funny.'

'Ha,' I said. 'What's in the bag today?'

'Well, I got you a new pair of pyjamas,' Zaved said. 'Three pairs isn't enough – I'm constantly washing them. It's only Marks & Spencer.'

'Show me, show me,' I said. 'I love new pyjamas. If I were a billionaire, I'd have a new pair of pyjamas every single day. That's the fourth pair you've bought – take some money from my wallet. Come on! Show me!'

'Here you are,' Zaved said, fishing them out and smiling at my appreciative mewing noise. 'They're very boring, really. And I am going to take some money from you, I definitely am. What did you have for your lunch?'

'Fish pie,' I said. 'It was gorgeous. And peas! Lovely, lovely peas. I'm loving the food in here. There's not enough, but I'm loving it. I'm going to go down for some seeds. Or nuts or something. Or chocolate.'

My husband gave me what could only be called, in an old-fashioned way, an adoring look. I knew he was matching one of mine, in the other direction. 'Phil, you know you're not allowed chocolate.'

'No, I was joking. What did you have for lunch?'

'There was some leftover biryani from last night at home. I thought I'd have some fish tonight. Why have you got so many books? That's ridiculous. You've only been here three days, and you've got twelve books on your bedside cabinet. Are you going to read them?'

'People keep bringing them,' I said. 'They know I'm not allowed grapes and they're not sure about flowers, so they bring –' I picked up the one on the top of the pile '– Tash Aw's new novel. Nicholas brought that. He's publishing it next month. It's about Shanghai. It's quite good. Did you met him at Mrs Blaikie's ever – Tash, I mean?'

'I'm reading Edmund White. It's so nice. All about Jack Holmes and his great big penis. It's like he's got a little pet in the house that he needs to take for walks sometimes, in the park. I really like it. Who's coming today?'

And so it goes on; in novels dialogue has emotional freight, and as clever readers we learn to interpret the weight of insinuation and understand what unspoken pressures of plotting, what dissatisfaction and desires lurk beneath the surface of words and gesture. Secrets bubble under the surface; one man turns the cheek, the other kisses it, full of concern. One speaks; his words do not mean what is in his heart. We watch, and read, and nod knowledgeably. But my marriage is not like that, not mostly. We live an offstage existence. There is love there, and love, really, doesn't have to be written about. At no point do we say to each other, our voices rising, a flush coming to our cheeks, 'What do you mean by that?' We know what the other means by that.

Through that offstage existence love works, and we achieve what we want to achieve, but we achieve it not for ourselves, not through manipulation, but for someone else. I spread the news of what should be done for me in a calculated and observing way through the medical staff. I planted ideas in their minds and watched them grow. I never wanted Zaved to do anything in particular. I just wanted to be with him. His mind was full of ideas that I had put there without quite knowing it. My mind was full of ideas that he had placed there, and I hardly knew whether some of them were mine or not. He had thoughts about Wagner that he had not possessed in 2000, and I had thoughts about war crimes of a similar age. Whose thoughts were they?

Well, my beloved was mine and I was his, and that is what marriage means.

10.

On the fourth day I could stand it no longer, and when Desdemona, out of genuine concern, asked me how things were, I said without hesitating that I thought Joe could do with a wash.

'I'm sorry,' she said. 'We know how difficult he is.'

'It's fine,' I said. 'I won't be here for very much longer, but you've had it for six weeks, and then there will be someone else just as bad. I'm full of admiration for what you do, and what you put up with.'

'Some of my staff find it difficult,' she said. 'Being called what he calls them.'

Just then, as if to prove the point, Joe groaned out a demand: 'Nurse. Nurse. You black cunt. Where is that black thieving cunt. I saw her a moment ago. I want my cigarette. I want my cigarette now. It's not fair.'

He subsided into muttering. Desdemona smiled, quite brightly, and cocked her head on one side. 'I think we may be able to move you,' she said. 'It should be a little bit better for you, here by the window. And after that, we'll see – I don't know, there may even be a quiet room that we can spare for you. I don't promise anything, mind you.'

I brightened. 'That would be wonderful,' I said. 'Thank you.' And by the end of the day, I was lying in a bed in a private room. I was wheeled out in my bed, and as I passed Joe's bed, he called out to me: 'You. You'll have brought your own things. You'll have brought your own pyjamas, your sheets and things. You'll have brought them all,' and then he subsided into his own world as I was wheeled towards the private room, only to glimpse him in the days to come. I was settled and secure. My visitors were astonished. Out of the window was the great sweep of the River, and the Palace of Westminster lying golden and recumbent in the January sunshine. Below, boats moved from right to left, from left to right; the tide shifted the river up and down the bridge's piers; I could watch it for long hours. I was so happy to sit, my drip attached, my nurses knocking before they entered, and my husband sitting in a chair and laughing, not minding a bit what I asked him to do, laughing again at the thought of what we would do when the people let me go. Somewhere, a long way away, an alcoholic Irishman lay in his own shit, and called out malevolently, demanding what he wanted, getting only the same response: 'Not now, Joe.'

'He'll have brought his own towels,' Joe would be calling. 'That's how you get treated special, in this world. You bring your own towels.'

As for me, I would get better; I would retreat to that quiet space where everyone is offstage, and everyone is listening.

BOOK 8
1983–1998

1.

'You will have brought your own towels and bedlinen,' the old queen said, in his lowered, theatrical, half-humming voice, 'as I think I said, I suggested, Arthur, in my advert in *Time Out*. Or was it over the phone? I forget. Some queens turn up, think I'm going to do everything, and then they do a bunk with my best Egyptian cotton, and try and get Lily Law after them. I don't think so. Other things I can supply, should you feel an urgent need for them. Soap and shampoo, there's always a bottle left behind by one of the previous, as I call them, done a bunk and left me their Vosene – left you, I should say. You're not going to do a bunk, I can tell, you're a nice young man. This is a respectable place, there's no drilling of holes in the bathroom wall to watch the tenants at their ablutions, not like some places I've heard of, and I like to keep it clean. You can have a friend back, we're only human after all, but only the one, or at the most two but don't make a habit of it, and try not to make too much noise when you're coming in. Make as much noise while you're at it as you like, my friend Bernard used to say to the new boys, I like that, he used to say, it makes me feel young again and I might even think about coming up and joining in. Gone his way, poor old Bernard, in the Charing Cross with the Gay Plague. He was the first I knew of – we gave him a lovely send-off, it was a release at the end all round. I hope you'll call me Kevin, or Kev even, everyone does. When you think of the Gay Plague, it's really for the best these days that we put on a cheerful face and get on with what queens do best, don't you think, Arthur? It was Arthur, wasn't it?'

'Yes,' Arthur said. 'That's right. I've got everything – sheets and towels and soap and shampoo, thanks, Kevin.' Arthur was aware of being only twenty-one or twenty-two at most to the assessing gaze, and Kevin, the old queen, proceeding in his stately way up the staircase of the lodging house in Islington, kept pausing to turn around, to take him in, to turn round and rearrange one of the china animal ornaments that he kept on the landing or on a shelf on the way up. It was a respectable house, he had said earlier, and he advertised in *Time Out* and not in that grubby community centre in Old Street, on that grubby notice-board they'd got. You got all sorts from there.

'I don't know why,' Kevin said, stopping halfway up the stairs, 'but you look very familiar to me. We've not met in some way, have we?'

'I don't remember,' Arthur said. He was not being unfriendly: he was out of breath from lugging the colossal brown leather suitcase up the second flight of stairs. 'We might have done. Or you might have come in the shop, I dare say.'

'What shop is that, Arthur?' Kevin said. 'I didn't know you worked in a shop. Did you mention? When we spoke? On the phone this would be?'

'It's the Big Gay Bookshop,' Arthur said. 'Do you know it? It's the gay bookshop in Marylebone. It's brilliant – I love it there. I've been there four years.'

'I didn't know it had been there four years,' Kevin said. 'I know it, I think. I've been in once or twice. It's a little bit … it's a little bit … you know … well, for me, it is, anyway. I may as well say, I'm not a great fan of that sort of thing. But I will pop in now. I dare say I wouldn't be the first you've had in, in four years. Anyway.'

The house was a succession of plywood doors, some painted, some left raw; it had been a handsome town house, once, but had been divided up with partitions and divisions. Kevin was a

384

man in his late forties, a clone; he wore the clone's uniform of checked shirt and jeans, a neat ginger moustache and clipped-short ginger-and-white hair, but as he paused in their walk upwards, his hands went theatrically to and fro, as if he were passing a silk scarf between them. Now a door on a landing opened timidly; a face came out, a pale round face.

'Timothy,' Kevin said, without enthusiasm. 'I wondered whether anyone was in, or everyone had got lucky last night and was scattered across this great metropolis of ours, like the scrubbers they are. This is Arthur. He's our new one. He's in Bruce's old room. Keep your shop-soiled hands off him, I know your sort.'

'Hello,' the face called Timothy said, looking Arthur up and down.

'Hello there,' Arthur said, and Timothy retreated into his room.

'Terrible old queen that one,' Kevin said. 'He'll ask you into his room. Don't go. Or do go. What do I know? You might be into what Timothy likes. It seems ever so unlikely. But there again, someone must be. There's someone for everyone, here in London, they always say. You're from the north, aren't you?'

'Yes, I am,' Arthur said, still wondering what Kevin wouldn't be the first of when he came next into the bookshop.

'I thought so,' Kevin said, and gave a disconcertingly broad smile. 'It'll all be very new and exciting for you, then, all of this.'

He gestured around him at the second landing, chipped china models of deer, a cat and a polar bear on the dusty window ledge and a pink glass vase full of peacock feathers and honesty. The carpet, of brown, purple and green Liberty intricacy, was less dirty than downstairs; a repainting had stopped, on the other hand, on the landing below, and up here the walls were covered with a primeval wallpaper at least twenty years old. There was a faint, persistent and familiar scent in the air up there, too.

'Well, I've been here four years, now,' Arthur said.

'Like the bookshop, you were saying,' Kevin said. He passed a hand over his scalp in a curious grooming gesture, but there was no hair long enough to smooth back, and the gesture remained theatrical. 'And here we are. The door sticks. I don't know why. It's not in the least damp, this house. I put it down to mild subsidence, which, of course, isn't your concern in the slightest. It's a lovely room, Bruce always said. Of course, Bruce was a dreadful poppers fiend – there's possibly a touch of that still in the air where he maybe spilt it on the carpet, but a few days of the window open and it'll be quite gone. Poppers evaporate, after all, that's what they're meant to do.'

The room was surprisingly large – Arthur had anticipated a narrow strip of corridor with a bed inside it. The ceiling, up here on the top floor, was low, but the room was a good size. On the other hand, someone had painted all the walls black, so it was hard to see what it would be like in normal circumstances.

'Some people blame poppers,' Kevin said. 'But I don't see how it could be, to be honest. We were cultured folk, Bernard and I, and when two years ago they said that if we were going up to the Edinburgh festival, English boys were on no account to have relations with visiting Americans, we took that very seriously. It was all too late for poor Bernard, of course, without him knowing it, but I'm all right so far, I'm happy to say.'

'Can I repaint it?' Arthur said, putting his suitcase down and gesturing at the black walls. 'The room?'

'Well,' Kevin said. 'It's true that Bruce painted it this shade – he said it was going to be purple, and I didn't mind that, and I was surprised when it turned out to be so very dark a shade of purple as this. So I don't see why not. I must insist, though, everything the same colour. Not green on this wall and orange on that and pink on that. Everything the same colour. That was the stipulation I made to Bruce so it's only fair I make the same stipulation to you.'

'I was going to paint it all white,' Arthur said.

'Well, there's no problem at all, then,' Kevin said brightly.

'Just put some sheets down. You might need more than one coat, I dare say. It'll come out grey the first coat or two. If you were ambitious, you could think about rag-rolling. Jocasta Innes. I thought I'd give it a go some time. Now – bedlinen and towels, I've done, the telephone I've done, friends and visitors I've done, what else? I said thirty-five pounds a week, didn't I? That can be monthly, we can call that a hundred and fifty a month. I mean sixty. I might come calling for the electricity bill and the gas bill from time to time – I work it out and we just split it. There's a gas fire, there's a Baby Belling, it works quite well, and there's the bed. Don't you want to try the bed out?'

Arthur went over and sat down on the bed, gingerly bouncing up and down. Kevin followed him, sat down next to him, and bounced alongside. 'It's a lovely bed, really,' he said. 'There's been lots of fun had in this bed. Lots of fun. We heard most of it, all through the house. I do hope you're going to have fun here, like the rest of us. Arthur, wasn't it?'

2.

It was a Sunday lunchtime that Arthur moved into the room in Islington. Perhaps other people would have had more stuff to move in. He just had a cardboard box and his brown suitcase, the one he had bought when the Singhs' suitcase shop over the road from the bookshop closed down, on the last day, for three pounds. It was too big for most people; the style was old-fashioned; and it had sat in the shop for years. They had been glad to sell it to him, even for three pounds. A furniture shop making sofas was there now.

Everything that Arthur owned he carried with him, and all of it was in the suitcase and the box in the hallway. Apart from the books, which were still in boxes above the shop. It was a cold and sunny April day outside; the clouds scudded across the sky. He stood there, at the window high up in the shabby house's façade, and wondered what Duncan would be doing. He knew he went to his sister's, Dommie's, for lunch most Sundays. He did not blame him for asking him to move out. As he had explained, it was only ever intended to be for a month or so, until Arthur had got himself back on his feet, and four years was too long. Besides, Duncan said apologetically, the law was after them enough, without them finding out that one of them was living illegally in the room above the shop.

There was a timid knock on the door; a faint knock followed by a louder one, as if the knocker had not quite established where the door was in relation to his fist. The door was opened slowly, and the round face from earlier appeared. 'Hello,' the face said. Arthur said hello back.

'I'm Tim,' the round face said, coming in, the body somehow following the face in a sly, tracking, unsure way, like an animal. He was blond, undecided, round in features. 'I know who you are. I've been in your shop. I'm not a great reader, I was looking at it, though, because I thought I would. Have you …' He trailed off, standing by the door, his left arm behind his back and clutching his right elbow.

'Do you want a cup of coffee?' Arthur said. 'Actually I don't have my kettle here yet. It's downstairs in a brown box, and the coffee too.'

'I was wondering what that box were,' Tim said. 'But then I realized it must be the new boy's, yours. It doesn't matter, I don't drink coffee much. It's nice up here, it's nicer than mine.'

'Have you been here long?' Arthur said.

'Oooh,' Tim said, brooding crudely. He let silence fall. 'What are you into, then?'

'What am I into?' Arthur said. Tim had gone over to the window and was peering out of it into the street, perhaps not to engage Arthur's gaze.

'Me,' Tim began, 'I'm—'

'I like all sorts, me,' Arthur said. 'I've just read *A Boy's Own Story*. Have you read that? That's ace. Everyone who's read it says so, we've sold tons in the shop. And I love, love, love Genet – do you know Genet? He wrote all his books in prison, almost, and they're all about prison. But I like all sorts, me, I'm going to have a go at Proust one of these days. Mr Bailey who came in the shop told me everyone should.'

'Oh, books,' Tim said, turning round. 'I should have said to Kevin, I want to move out, I want a bigger room. Still, I'm settled. I meant, what are ...'

Arthur let Tim's sentence trail away. 'Oh, I thought what are you into, reading, like, because of bookshop.'

'I'm into leather,' Tim said, superfluously since he was wearing leather trousers and a leather jacket, although he was in his own house. He had put the jacket on over the white Brando vest to come upstairs.

'Oh, I see,' Arthur said. 'What am I into? Let's see.'

As Tim watched closely, Arthur elucidated, ticking off what he had done and what he had enjoyed, there in the upper room above the bookshop, in the last four years, with seven boys. There had not been so many. Only one had come once and never come again. Or there had been other rooms, elsewhere in London, in shared flats, in a boarding house a bit like this one, in a neat one-bedroom in Palmers Green, miles and miles away, but he'd been sweet, that'd been a nice summer, the summer before last with him and William trailing up and down to Palmers Green and back, and once there had been that rich bloke who had seemed quite ordinary at first but had turned out to live in a huge four-storey white house off the King's Road and had been just that one-off. All but one had been customers in the first instance in the Big Gay Bookshop. You were a sitting duck, there at the till, a sitting duck by Paul's stuffed sitting pheasant, as Duncan often said sunnily. Arthur went through these now, not talking about the houses or the individuals, but about the acts they'd done together, which, in the end, were fewer even than the number of men, over those four years.

'Oh, you're vanilla,' Tim said, sitting down on the brown

wooden chair. 'Me too, really. I like a kiss and a cuddle best. In leather, a leather kiss and a cuddle, though, that's nice.'

'Oh, yeah,' Arthur said.

'Have you got a boyfriend?' Tim said. Arthur thought of producing one. But then he took pity on Tim. It was Sunday afternoon, after all, and Arthur had nothing to do except bring up the cardboard box from the hallway, and unpack his few plates, his kettle, a saucepan and three tins of food. He guessed that Tim only really wanted to do it once.

Afterwards, Tim seemed in no hurry to go. He walked around the room, occasionally turning to inspect Arthur, lying on the bare mattress – it had seemed a waste, unpacking the sheets when they'd only have to be washed again afterwards, and anyway they were in the boxes downstairs.

'Smells of poppers in here,' Tim said. 'Are you into poppers? I could have fetched mine from downstairs. You must be into them, if your room smells like this.'

'I've only just moved in,' Arthur said. 'I've not had chance to make it smell of anything else but what it smelt of before.'

'Oh, yeah,' Tim said. He paused in the little kitchen, turned the tap, let it run for a moment, turned it off again. 'That was fantastic. We should do that again.'

'Oh, yeah,' Arthur said. 'I've got to go and get washed. Or I could wash my bits in the sink.'

'Yeah, you don't want to go downstairs with no clothes on,' Tim said. 'Did Kevin show you the bathroom? You don't want to use that more than you have to. He's a bit of a pervert, that Kevin. He likes to watch, that's what he's into. I wouldn't have any more to do with him than you have to. Sometimes Bruce said to him, if I let you come and watch, will you let me off this week's rent, 'cause I'm a bit skint, and I don't think he ever let him off the rent, but that was after he'd come to watch Bruce and his trick anyway. Then there's Stuart on the ground floor. He's into role play and dressing up. Some people like that … I don't think it's for me – it takes too much effort. And next to him there's Lyndon, he's Australian, he's gorgeous, he goes to the gym, he's into worship, he'll just stand there like a statue, flexing. First floor François, he's French, from Paris, I reckon, and Tony in the room next door, he's into feet. Then, let's see—'

'I've got to get on,' Arthur said.

3.

The gay men's group had moved its meetings to the bookshop three years before. Sometimes when the weather was hot, nobody turned up on a Wednesday: people went to the pool in Covent Garden or up to the ponds in Hampstead, or just out for a gin and tonic in St Martin's Lane. Tonight, at the beginning of summer, Christopher had turned up half an hour before closing time and was downstairs with Arthur while Duncan had another look at the room upstairs. Andrew, who sort of ran the gay men's group and was sometimes on speaking terms with Duncan, sometimes not, would probably turn up after closing time with his ring-binder and cuttings book. Christopher seemed to find it easier to turn up early. Perhaps the economy was looking after itself for a change. Duncan had tried to charge the same as the old landlord of the pub had, and they had agreed to make contributions, but it hadn't stuck. Only Alan devotedly and regularly paid his subs to Duncan. The rest of them thought it was Duncan's responsibility to the community to host it, and only paid for the occasional jar of Nescafé.

Since Arthur had moved out, three months before, Duncan had thought constantly about what use he might make of the space upstairs. It was incredible to him that Arthur had managed to live there for four years. The space was full of potential, as estate agents always said. There were two big casement windows at the front, and in the back room, the remains of a stripped-out kitchen in which nothing worked. Arthur had lived there, surrounded by the two hundred and thirty-eight signed copies of *The Garden King*, which had remained downstairs for six months, a great bronze wall of reproach after the shop's opening, until Duncan and Arthur could no longer stand it and had moved all the unsaleable copies upstairs. Now that Duncan had some experience in these things, he could hardly believe that he had talked himself into buying two hundred and fifty copies of a first novel, four years before. Four copies had been sold at cover price; eight had been given away to members of the gay men's group, three of which had been returned unread; two had been lifted, or conceivably just lost by Arthur carrying a copy around London; one was still downstairs, on the fiction shelves. There had been an unpleasant scene, a year after the shop opening, when Duncan had discovered something else about the retail trade. All two hundred and fifty copies, it turned out, were unreturnable, as the rep had regretfully explained, having been signed by the author. 'Defaced,' Dommie said, with disgust. If it hadn't been for the cheque from Sir Angus, Dommie said she didn't know what they would have done. It was, all the same, Arthur's favourite novel, or so he said.

The room was hot and still, the motes moving in the afternoon light, the atmosphere entranced and blanketed with unmoving air, as if a room behind a secret panel. The noises from the street were clear, and yet detached, remote, insignificant, like sounds heard from a sick room. It was only up the stairs behind the painted plywood door. Arthur had survived up there, despite there being no proper bathroom; he had used the toilet at the back of the shop and washed in the sink in the kitchenette, twice a week going for a shower to the swimming baths in Covent Garden where people went. He had slept on an old mattress that Dommie had needed to get rid of, sitting on the floor, and neatly transferred his washing from plastic supermarket bags to the launderette, going there every Sunday afternoon. He was clean, but not immaculate; his shirts were crumpled, since he had no iron, and when he wore his one jacket, a curious urban smell of the second-hand clothes shop, the mothy, fungoid, warm

jumble sale, rose from him. He had lived on what the kitchenette could deal with, and what could be produced without too
lingering a smell. At the weekends, sometimes, Dommie had
him over for dinner on a Saturday, muttering about the dangers
of scurvy. He had suppressed his concern by telling himself that
young people could eat any old stuff – Pot Noodle, soup from
powder – and not die of malnutrition, think of (he went on to
Dommie), think of all those children that crop up in newspapers
from time to time, saying that they've eaten nothing but toast
and Marmite for three years and they look all right. Possession-
less, constantly preoccupied with washing himself, curling up
upstairs among books and boxes, living on the same foodstuffs
night after night without interest or complaint, Arthur might
have been a cat. Duncan had liked arriving in the morning to
find Arthur already by the till, reading a publisher's proof of a
new novel, a cup of instant coffee by the side of the stuffed
pheasant, smelling faintly mouldy and fresh-faced in his unironed
but clean shirt, blue, purple, white or khaki. Arthur habitually
sat in his socks in the shop, on a high stool with a book,
explaining that it hurt his feet to wear shoes all day long and
he wasn't old enough to put slippers on just yet. It had been
nice. There had also been the point that Arthur was already on
the scene when bricks were thrown through the window at
night. They had not expected him to stick it for four years, and
Duncan was still not quite clear in his mind why he had told
him to move out. 'Oh, I could see him still living like that when
he was forty,' he would say when asked, and that was certainly
part of it. Hardly any of Arthur's life seemed to have changed,
however, in the months since he had moved out into what
sounded like a terrible gay boarding house. His shirts had
remained unironed.

   There was the noise of the plywood door being opened downstairs, and Arthur's shoeless pad on the wooden stairs. Without
turning round, Duncan could hear Arthur yawning as he came
in, then scratching himself.

'I'm going senile,' Duncan said. 'I came up here for a reason, and I can't think what it was any more.'

'That's first sign, intit?' Arthur said. 'Going into a room, saying, I don't know what I've come here for. Was it to fetch stock down?'

'No, I'll do that tomorrow,' Duncan said. 'We've sold ten copies of *A Boy's Own Story* since Saturday. I've never had such a hit. Actually I was just thinking about turning this into a meeting room again. Just a table and chairs and a proper light.'

'There's probably rules and regulations about that,' Arthur said. 'Like that man from Camden who come in, said you were running a café.'

'It would just be a meeting room – they'd come and sit round a table and discuss things. You don't need to get a licence for that.'

'You don't need a licence for any of it,' Arthur said. 'Nothing but a kettle and a big jar of instant and some Rich Tea biscuits. Café, indeed.'

'It was probably the Cup a Soup you were drinking at the time that did it,' Duncan said lightly.

'Yes, or that Andy over the road, informing on us. I know which side his grandfather was on in the Second World War, down there in Greece, getting invaded. Shall I turn sign round? Christopher's downstairs, he's thrilled to bits to be in charge. Are you staying tonight?'

Duncan made a noncommittal noise. 'Well,' he said, in the end, 'I'm supposed to go and buy some queen's book collection. In Hammersmith. He died and I don't think the boyfriend reads. But I only said some time this week. I could stay, I suppose.'

It had been a while since Duncan had stayed at a gay men's group meeting. If Arthur couldn't stay, Duncan's preference was generally for going round the corner for a pint and a pie while it was going on and coming back at nine to lock up.

'Christopher says there wasn't going to be a turnout, much, and then he said Alan decided he was going to come tonight anyway, and Nat was going to visit Freddie Sempill in hospital, but apparently he's a bit better so Nat's putting it off until weekend, and that new boy, the black boy from Leicester, he might come or he might not, Paul says, and George and that Tim I live with. I don't know about Simon, Christopher didn't mention. So it's all going to be all right. Alan's coming too, did I say that?'

'Oh, good,' Duncan said. 'Is there any milk in the fridge?'

'I'll get Christopher to go out and get some from newsagent's,' Arthur said. 'And he's not taking money from till this time. The instant coffee I got Alan to buy, last jar, that hurt him, I can tell you. We're not buying milk any more, they're just taking piss with that one, every week it were, and biscuits and all we've paid for while they go on and on about gay men and oppression and why they don't know any lesbians and all that. They should go back to meeting in pub. I'm sick of the lot of them.'

'That's a new one,' said Duncan, though in fact he had had some inkling of this.

'Aye, well,' Arthur said. 'I'm thinking of going to that group that meets at Old Street. When I come to Andrew's group—'

'It's not Andrew's group,' Duncan said.

'When I come to Andrew's group,' Arthur said, 'I'm always the youngest by about ten years. Apart from the black boy from Leicester but I don't think he's coming back anyway, he only came those two times. I don't know why you don't think it's Andrew's group – he's the one keeps them all up to scratch, decides what they're going to talk about.'

'It's only Tim starting to come that's put you off,' Duncan said gleefully. 'You were quite all right till he started coming and gazing at you.'

'Oh, it's not me he's gazing at,' Arthur said. 'I can promise you that. He's had me, anyway. He's moved on to Tony on the first floor – they've lived in the same house for a year and a half but never got round to each other, Tim says he doesn't know why. He's grown a moustache now, under Tony's influence. I don't want to call them clones, but, you know …'

'Tony who's into feet?' Duncan said.

'Yes, how do you know that?' Arthur said. 'I said, I suppose. Tim says he doesn't know why he's not seen the appeal of feet till now, he's grateful to Tony for showing him a new direction. He's got a new interest in life. It's like he's retired or summat. He says you ought to have a shelf of books about it. Feet.'

'Oh, for Heaven's sake,' Duncan said. 'The day we start … Tell Tim and Tony who's into feet that we'll order any books they want to read on the subject of feet but they'll have to pay upfront for them and I'm not putting them on shelves. We're not porn barons.'

'It's only feet,' Arthur said. 'Who's that? Was that someone coming in? I'd best get down.'

4.

As Arthur went downstairs, his mind went onto sex, as it so often did, and at the forefront of his mind was an image of Tony and Tim at each other's feet. He did not really know, he realized, what was involved when someone said they were into feet. He tried various possibilities, turning the scenario round in his mind, altering it until it seemed plausible, and then trying to see if changes would make it more so. The Tony and Tim in his head picked up the foot of each other, applied it to themselves, removed it and tried something different, with a quizzical naked air. The scene changed, like an object picked up and rotated, as the figures in Arthur's mind tried one thing after another. One day there had been only one gay man in London who was into feet. But how would that one gay man find someone else in London who was into feet like him? It would be easier to convert someone who had never thought about it. So then the next day this single gay man had met another gay man, in his bed, and had asked him if he were into feet, and the other had said no, but then had allowed himself to be introduced to feet, and they had enjoyed it. The next day the both of them had gone out and met new people, and had both independently asked if the new one were into feet, and they had explained and demonstrated, and so the word had spread. On Monday, there had been only one gay man in London who was into feet, and the next day there were two, and the day after, four, and by Thursday eight, then sixteen, thirty-two, sixty-four, one hundred and twenty-eight, two hundred and fifty-six, and in ten days five hundred and twelve. What a good idea, another five hundred and twelve were saying on the eleventh day to the original five hundred and twelve, we had never thought of doing that, and now we, too, are into feet, doing with each other in bed whatever it might be that men who were into feet did with each other. Soon there would be no gay man in London who was not into feet; the question would not need to be asked, because it would be like saying are you into men or do you like kissing or do you think love is a good idea; it would be universal. But what gay men who were into feet did to each Arthur did not know. And, of course, it would not always multiply like that. Sometimes a Tony and a Tim would not go out the next day and convert new people to the pleasures of being into feet. Sometimes they would stay with each other and just do things with each other's feet, like chiropodists. Perhaps Arthur could ask Tony or Tim, one of these days, what you did with each other if you were into feet; how men who were into feet might signal to others, in a bar or a club, that that was their interest without having to say anything at all. He trembled with laughter as he walked down the stairs.

'What's so funny?' Christopher said, as he came into the shop. The man who had come in was only Alan.

'I was wondering about coloured hankies,' Arthur said. Christopher and Alan exchanged a baffled glance.

5.

'Got Aids yet?' a child shouted in at the door, and ran off like a celebrant in a street fair, followed by two or three children of the neighbourhood who paused to say, 'Fucking bummers,' before running after their friend. 'Did you hear what I ...' you could hear them calling as they ran.

Alan tutted and looked away. He was no more than fifty-five, they reckoned, from his talk of 'before the war' as a remote childhood paradise, but he dressed and presented himself like a pensioner. His hair was quite white and combed upwards into a cockatoo's crest, listing sideways; his walk was strict, his hands held firmly downwards by his hips in case they broke out into florid gesture. He lived, as he always had, in a shabby but now rather valuable house in Fulham, on the borders of Chelsea, with his mother. Nothing there had changed since 1957, when the hall wallpaper had been removed and distemper applied. 'Oh,' Nat used to say, with a despairing wave of his hand, 'Alan's really just like his house. He's so much like Tregunter Road, it's hardly true.' His clothes, too, were sourced by his mother from a west London emporium quite isolated from the 1980s, or indeed the 1970s; like a pensioner, he dressed imperviously to the heat, as if his mother had warned him to wrap up warm, it might turn nasty later. He wore a tweed jacket, with broad lapels and gold buttons, in brilliant oranges and greens; a tie was making a break in a floral direction; his shirt and trousers were different shades of man-made brown. Despite his age, both performed and real, his face was puzzled and yet eager, like a keen dull boy at the front of a maths class. It was as if he had not understood what the youths had shouted in.

'Do you want a cup of tea?' Arthur said. 'I'm just making one.'

'That is so kind of you,' Alan said. 'Milk, no sugar. Christopher?'

'Oh, tea,' Christopher said. 'I've had such a day you wouldn't believe. That Lawson! You just would not believe what he's decided to do with us.'

'Still, you got off on time,' Alan said. 'I don't see him keeping you behind at the office just yet. I was supposed to have a meeting with the deputy VC, but he'd gone off to play some golf, the weather being so nice. Just slid off.'

'The trick is, Alan,' Christopher said, 'around four twenty-five, you start ruffling your papers as if you've got a meeting at four thirty, you start checking your watch, and then – this is the clever bit – you leave your jacket over the back of your chair and just walk straight out. It's really a cinch. It does mean that you've got to be back early the next morning to bundle your jacket from yesterday into your briefcase. I've done it for years. I'd love a cup of tea, thank you, Arthur. Is this the book everyone's talking about?'

He picked up a copy of *A Boy's Own Story* from a pile of eight.

'We've done ever so well with it,' Duncan said. 'We've had to reorder four times already. Everyone's reading it.'

'Nat was telling me about it,' Alan said. 'He's not a great reader, is he? I mean, not even his best friends. But he said he couldn't put it down. He got to page twelve and he had to have a wank, and then he was a bit ashamed of himself, because it's actually about fourteen-year-olds having it off, or cornholing each other – had you ever heard of cornholing before? I said to Nat, there's no need to apologize, it's only words on a page, but he said – well. Mother read it, actually, she saw it on the coffee-table, and when I was busy in the kitchen, I was running up a little apple-and-cinnamon strudel that I'd been saving up for a quiet afternoon, I was otherwise occupied in any case, and when I came back in, all hot and bothered, she was reading it, twenty pages in, and she said straight out to me, Alan, I hope you don't go in for any of that cornholing. It sounds very ill-advised. You could have knocked me down with a feather, because you know, Mother and I, we don't talk about any of that side of my life, but she then said what an interesting way of writing the author had, and now I really think that I might have to buy another copy – she's passed the one she read on to her friend Dolly with a strong recommendation and I hadn't even finished it. Dolly's a man, by the way.'

'How was the apple-and-cinnamon strudel?' Duncan said.

'Disappointing,' Alan said. 'Very disappointing. And such a lot of work, too. There was a story on the cookery page in the magazine I got it from that you were supposed to be able to read a love letter through the pastry when it was done, which I suppose tickled me rather. I said to Mother, after I'd been slaving away at the pastry, I've got a lovely old 1890s ceramic rolling pin that only gets taken out on very special occasions, I said to Mother, come on, we'll see if we can read an old love letter through this pastry. And she said, well, I'm sure I don't want to read any of your love letters and I'm not at all convinced that I have any of your father's to hand, so we ended up attempting to read a circular from the head of German through it, not at all the same thing although I do see it maintained the Austrian theme.'

'Who's coming?' Duncan said to Christopher. 'And what's the topic tonight?'

'Socialism, gay rights, equality and lesbians,' Christopher said. 'Seems a bit much. It was Andrew's idea. Speak of the devil.'

'In any case,' Alan said, as he and Christopher took their cups of tea from Arthur, 'hello, Andrew, I was just talking about an unsuccessful apple strudel I attempted, in any case I don't believe the quantities were right. It was really unpleasantly sour. Now, I don't ask for anything too sickly sweet, I don't care for that, but this, it really made Mother and I wince. We ended up sprinkling Demerara sugar on top just to make it palatable. It's the last time I cook anything from Mother's *Family Circle*.'

Andrew stood, with a faint impatient air, barely in the door. He carried a folder of documents and, in his hand, a Sainsbury's carrier bag full of books. His beard was full, and his T-shirt carried a hand-printed message about GAY PRIDE 1977. His shorts were bright blue, tight and short, and he wore brown leather Jesus sandals. He was a hairy man – his legs and arms seemed surrounded by an aura, half an inch thick – and was sweating lightly. 'Is this everyone?' he said. 'I thought there'd be more tonight. How are you, Alan?'

'Thank you, Andrew,' Alan said. 'I'm feeling really a lot more myself, it's kind of you to ask. I've been out for two weeks now, and fingers crossed ... I never thanked you for the cake you brought into the Charing Cross. Beetroot, so original. Of course, I couldn't eat anything much, my appetite was completely shot, but it came in so handy for visitors and for the nurses, too, to tell the truth. They were shockers.'

'You've not been ill, have you, Alan?' Christopher said quickly.

'Oh, no, nothing like that, Christopher,' Alan said. 'Just gall bladder, nothing ... Well, anyway, the beetroot cake was a lovely contribution.'

'Not up to his standards,' Duncan said quietly to Arthur, as they went through the day's takings. 'Sixty, sixty-one, -two, -three and ...' he counted through the change '. . . don't disturb me, now, that's -six, -seven and ...' There was a long pause as Duncan furrowed his brow. 'That's seventy-two pounds seventeen, better than some days, not so good as a few. There was ten pounds sixty in change in the till this morning. And three cheques.'

'Excellent,' Arthur said. 'That's excellent. Three people paying with cheques, that's an improvement.' (He meant that people were not so worried about leaving their names when they paid; his thought, which Duncan followed, was about frankness and openness. Someone who wrote, 'Twelve pounds payable to The Big Gay Bookshop' – one day everyone would be like that.)

'And no bloody credit cards today, either,' Duncan said. 'That's another thirty pounds – no, twenty-nine pounds, no, thirty-one forty-nine. That's ... Where's the calculator?'

'Christopher,' Arthur called. 'We need your help.'

'No good at mental arithmetic,' Christopher said, ambling over. 'Simon's better at it than I am.'

'The nation's finances are in these fumbling hands,' Duncan

said, quite fondly – this exchange was a regular one. 'What happens when Lawson says to you, Quick, Duffy, what's last year's income tax receipts minus government expenditure minus the National Debt? How much money have we got to spend on tea and biscuits and a new bridge in Norfolk that the Ministry of Defence wants?'

'Well, I should turn very briskly to the principal who sits behind me and pass him an urgent note,' Christopher said, 'telling him to his great surprise that we've found we've got a nice lot of money left over and we don't know what to spend it on. Lawson tells everyone they can't spend money, that's his job. I can't believe you ever worked in the public service.'

'Not just me,' Duncan said. 'Paul did, too. I met him first in the unemployment office. We were dealing with the unwashed together. He didn't last long. He was even worse than me.'

'I forgot that!' Christopher said, with a brave cheerfulness. 'Paul in the civil service! What a fantastic image! They didn't sack him, though, did they? He just left, didn't he?'

'Well, I can't really remember,' Duncan said. 'It was so long ago. Well, not so long ago – it's just that stuff's happened, it's hard to think of him ever being there. They didn't send anyone to the funeral, at any rate.'

Together they thought about Paul's funeral, six months before; that cold December day, his respectable father no one had ever met, sitting for form's sake with the mother everyone knew, divorced years before. And a handicapped sister smiling at everyone. The parents had seemed numb in the Northamptonshire chapel, and about them a hundred people Northamptonshire had never seen or experienced. One boy in full Adam Ant drag with a white stripe across the face and a pirate jacket; a girl in a fluorescent pink leather catsuit; a woman in an emerald taffeta ballgown. Half the queens had been wearing their black PVC raincoats, tightly belted. If any of them had been asked, they'd have replied, 'Oh, Paul specifically asked me to wear it.' Duncan had just worn a suit and a black tie, which, he'd noticed on the train, had glitter in its material. He had tried to put on the normal one in his flat, first thing that morning. But he must have reached for the wrong one. He had cried over breakfast, and cried again in the shower. Paul had put him off and put him off, saying in a postcard, 'Oh, no, I'm fine, come when I'm out of hospital, they're not worried.' He hadn't seen him for six weeks. The last message he'd had from him was on the back of a postcard with a picture of the Duke of Edinburgh on the front, and the farewell message, handwritten in blue biro in Paul's looping, confident hand, had said, 'Suck a black man's cock for me, darling.' He had been spared blindness, then. The next he had heard was a hoarse-voiced man announcing himself as Paul's father, and Paul had died in the hospice. Paul had been thorough, however, and had made a list of everyone who should be invited to the funeral with their phone numbers. The restaurant must have closed for the day; the funeral was full of its waiters and customers, beautifully dressed and weeping in squadrons. Bonnie Langford had come, even. Over the coffin was a six-foot-by-four photograph of Paul, soft-focus and unrecognizable. The hearse was glass-sided and pulled by black-plumed horses; the coffin brought in by beautiful muscular boys in frock coats. The music was Donna Summer, at which everyone smiled, and a fat girl singing 'Va, Pensiero' with a struggling organist – he'd never had to play it before, he'd confided to Arthur, who had got his phone number anyway with an expression of big-eyed sympathy. Every detail was planned and specific, and very Paul, while at the same time not evoking him in the slightest. It was all what he would have wanted it to be. On the way back, Duncan, Andrew, Christopher, Nat, Arthur, Simon and Freddie Sempill, who had invited himself, they had got a bit drunk at the wake and got drunker on the train. They had gone parading up and down in the carriage, their funeral clothes awry, performing Paul's encounter at the dole office with the Yorkshire bricklayer in search of work. 'I can see you're firm, and if I had but a single opening I could insert you into, it would be my pleasure,'

Nat recited, and then a woman in a blue hat and a pink scarf deep in Anita Brookner had stood up and complained that there were women and children in the compartment. 'Our fucking friend's died,' Arthur said, outraged, and Nat had said, 'Honestly.' But then Duncan had stood up and in a moment of inspiration, drunk as a lord, had responded by saying the other thing Paul was famous for saying: 'When I go to bed with a man,' he had said once, and Duncan now said for the benefit of the carriage and the complaining woman, 'I expect him to maintain full erection – *full erection* – from the *moment of nudity onwards*. Do I make myself plain? The *very first* moment of nudity. Anything else – anything that falls short of that – I regard as a *personal insult*.' And then they all joined in, with laughter and applause and cheering even, and chanted, 'Anything else I regard as a personal insult,' and laughed and laughed, like football supporters on a drunken train. There were more of them, for once, than the normals. There had been people leaving the compartment. Fuck them. Two days later, Duncan had told Arthur that he'd better find somewhere else to live than the room over the bookshop.

They thought about that day of Paul's funeral. 'No,' Christopher said in the end. 'They probably wouldn't have known about it. There's such a turnover of staff in that bit of the civil service, no one would have remembered him.'

'Let's make a start,' Andrew said. 'Are you staying tonight? Arthur? Duncan? It can't just be the three of us.'

Arthur agreed with a bad grace.

'It's socialism, gay rights, lesbian feminism tonight,' Andrew said, his voice rising brightly, like a hostess offering a particularly alluring and yet healthy quiche to a weight-watching guest. 'It'll be fun.'

'So my landlord – he says to me, he's one of them, he says,' Arthur said, continuing some long-abandoned fragment of conversation. 'You know – one of *those*.'

'We're all one of them, I thought,' Christopher said.

'That's what I thought. He kept saying it,' Arthur said. 'But then he came out with it, why he didn't expect we ever saw one of his type in BGB. The thing is, Arthur,' he dropped into impersonation, cocking his head somewhat, 'I don't see any reason to hide it, I'm just a Thatcherite, and I don't see why not. I think we should all be so proud of that woman after what she achieved last year. I for one certainly intend to vote for her.'

'Oh,' Christopher said, as they sat down. 'One of them.'

Andrew made an elaborate chest-crossing gesture; Alan made a deal out of not hearing what Arthur had said, perhaps confirming what Duncan had heard him say in private, that he saw a good deal of Mother in the Prime Minister and would hardly not vote for her.

'Don't call it the BGB,' Duncan said to Arthur. 'It's the Big – Gay – Bookshop. It makes me think that you're going to talk me into hiding behind initials.'

'Anyway,' Andrew said. 'Thanks for coming. I thought we might start tonight by looking at this article I found in the radical press, about lesbian separatism.'

He started to pass pieces of paper round, purple, camphor-smelling Roneos.

'Where are the lesbians tonight, then?' Alan said. 'Why are we talking about them when they're not interested enough to come to the discussion?'

'They're separatismed,' Duncan said.

'Still,' Andrew said. 'I think their situation raises some really very interesting questions.'

6.

In the end, four more people came, apologizing for their late arrival. There were a couple of people who were irregular attenders, the guy from Leicester and Arthur's co-lodger Tim, and then Nat had come as he had promised, though George hadn't,

405

and a person whom nobody had known or recognized, who must have read about the gay men's group in *City Limits*. Like most people who had just read about it and turned up, he had sat with eyes burning and saying nothing; he might come again but probably wouldn't. The discussion came to an end, and everyone was standing up and taking their mugs to wash and continuing it with each other. Duncan went upstairs to turn the lights out and check the windows were locked. Of course, he said to himself, if it did raise interesting questions, you might wonder what the answers to those questions were, and if you couldn't think of those interesting answers, you might wonder whether those interesting questions were questions at all, or worth speaking out loud. If you wanted lesbians to come to a discussion, too, it might be better not to call your group the Gay Men's Group. He foresaw another evening-long discussion about the group's name.

Downstairs, voices were raised. He knew exactly what about.

'No,' Arthur was saying, as he came back into the shop. 'No, you can't. You can buy copies. You can't just take them.'

'Is this a community resource or not?' Andrew said. He was holding seven copies of *A Boy's Own Story*, apparently about to hand them out to the group. Only one was still on the table.

'Yes, it is,' Arthur said. 'And we want it to stay here. So if you want it to keep going, you pay for the books.'

'We've had a really interesting discussion about it,' Andrew said. 'And now you're preventing those who haven't read it from going away and reading it.'

'No, he's not,' Duncan said. 'We would be delighted if everyone read it. You just need to buy a copy first.'

'Not everyone can buy a copy,' the boy from Leicester said. 'Not everyone can afford a full-price book. Seven pounds ninety-nine – that's a lot of money to a lot of people.'

'Well, in that case, a lot of people can borrow copies from well-intentioned people who actually buy their books, once they're finished with it,' Arthur said. 'You don't borrow them from us.'

'Come on, Duncan,' Andrew said. 'You said you thought it was the most important book in years.'

'Yes, I did,' Duncan said. 'So important, you ought to pay for it, not just waltz off with it. I'm sorry. The answer's no. Do you want to buy copies? I really recommend it.'

Two of them did: five of the copies went back on the table. Sometimes Duncan really hated gay liberation. As they left, Tim was saying to the boy from Leicester that he could borrow his copy when he'd finished with it; he wouldn't be long. And after that he didn't mind lending it again. Everyone would enjoy it, he was sure, he said pointedly, as they all headed off to the not-really-gay bar near by. Suddenly Duncan realized he was really very hungry; he hadn't had any lunch.

7.

Duncan was woken by the phone, and for a moment was confused. 'My God,' he said, levering himself out of bed and reaching for the silk dressing-gown he kept on the bedside chair. It was freezing cold in the flat – he'd been warm as toast under the continental quilt and had overslept. 'My God,' he said, looking at the clock in the hallway as he picked up the phone.

'You weren't asleep?' Dommie said, at the other end of the line.

'I was, actually,' Duncan said. 'I thought I'd have a little lie-in.'

'Oh, a little lie-in?'

'No, Dommie,' Duncan said. 'Not what you seem to be suggesting. We're going to Brighton, aren't we?'

'You've really only just woken up,' Dommie said. 'I've been up for hours. Have you looked out of the window?'

Duncan pulled back the heavy brown velvet curtains and peered out. 'My God, it's snowing,' he said. 'Are we still going?'

'It says it's not too bad on the weather,' Dommie said. 'It's settled a bit, but it's not supposed to carry on. What do you reckon?'

'Oh, all right,' Duncan said. 'And Arthur's arranged for his friend Tim to come and help him out in the shop. If we get stuck in Brighton, mind ...'

'Celia will be very pleased,' Dommie said, and there was real pleasure in her voice.

'Celia won't notice or care where she is,' Duncan said, but not crossly. 'She's happy in Brighton or Tooting or wherever.' This was true. Celia, Dommie's daughter, was eighteen months old, and cheerful in temperament. There was no need to cart her across three counties to show her a good time. Today's trip, to Brighton and the Lanes so that Duncan and Dommie could buy all the Christmas presents they needed, was more of a day out for the pair of them.

Duncan couldn't understand why it was so cold in the flat, and went to turn the thermostat: it had to be turned almost to the top of the dial before the system juddered into noisy life. The bath yielded water slowly, and you had to run the hot tap for a few minutes before the temperature was raised to anything above that of the room. There was no question about it: the boiler, which should have been replaced four years ago, was now going to have to be replaced. The money was there, just about – he had managed to invest what was left of his father's after buying and doing up the shop and the flat, and it brought in enough of an income that he didn't have to panic immediately when the shop had a quiet week or two. But when he looked at it coldly, he had the same sort of income as he'd had at the unemployment exchange as a junior clerk. The only advantage he now had was that he didn't have to pay anything in rent or mortgage, since he'd bought the flat outright. But anything that needed money spending on it, like the boiler or the car, filled him with terror. Only that week, he had paid a queen in Highgate's boyfriend three hundred pounds to take away a book collection. Not quite out of kindness – there were some nice things – but he wouldn't have taken the whole collection if its owner hadn't been buried the day before. How much did a new boiler cost? Eight hundred pounds? A thousand? Two thousand? He had no idea. He knew he didn't have a thousand pounds in his current account, and it would have to come from savings.

Existence was such a drain. He felt his energy going out of him like money. He wished he did not think of his personal resources, like money, like the contents of a bank account, but there it was. Everything that was good in him spilt out, like water from a holed bucket, and he had no idea what happened to it. The shop window, ceaselessly installed, ceaselessly broken, ceaselessly replaced – and that was another bit of expenditure, since the insurance was no longer going to cover the constant shatterings and seemed to think it was the bookshop's own fault for not having a solid wooden cover, like a sex shop in Soho. Shivering in the bedroom, he dressed in his drainpipes and a favourite black poloneck; just the thing for Brighton in December.

Outside, the snow was falling but not settling, and there was a brightness in the sky that suggested it would not be falling for long. Duncan's neighbour, Hubert St George, was standing on his steps, staring vaguely upwards, confused at what the sky was now producing, though after three decades away from Trinidad, snow in London could not have been so astonishing as all that. He was wearing pyjamas, a pair of army boots and a woman's overcoat with a hand-knitted scarf wrapped round his neck a dozen times; the characteristic smell of weed and Hubert was perceptible.

'Hello, Hubert,' Duncan said, locking his front door and pulling his woollen hat on. 'Caught us all by surprise, the snow.'

Hubert St George looked around slowly, creakily. 'Oh, it you,' he said. 'Yeah, Mr Batty Bummer Bend-it Backdoor, don't you come anywhere near of me.'

'No, I certainly won't,' Duncan said. 'See you around, Hubert.'

Every day, Duncan regretted having bought an Austin Princess. Its only recommendation was that it would never be stolen, even in drug-addled Notting Hill, even by one of Hubert St George's terminally confused friends. It sat on the road, its mushroom colour veiled by a thin layer of snow, somehow smugly. You can never go wrong with a British car, his father's voice had sounded in his ear four years before. That had guided him with wallet open, knowing nothing, towards the incredulously joyful Austin Princess salesman. Paul, bless his heart, had instantly observed that the Austin Princess Duncan had come to pick him up in had the appearance of a woman looking down her nose, and not a very smart woman at that. And the back half doesn't seem to have any kind of connection with the front half, he had gone on. But beggars could not be choosers, he supposed, he had concluded, stepping as gracefully into the car as a finishing-school debutante demonstrating the art. How long could it be before he could justify getting rid of the thing in favour of something better? Something Japanese, something Korean, something tinny and deplorable from far away that would never fall apart.

'Lovely!' Dommie said, stepping out from the front door of her tiny terraced house off Clapham High Street, her daughter asleep and already strapped into a sort of car seat. Dommie could by now reconstruct a pram with one hand while holding a sleeping Celia on the crook of her elbow. 'Lovely! Bang on time. No traffic? Good. I've got everything. Madam woke me up at five forty-five, full of beans, then two hours' charging about, then breakfast, and then, like a log, whoosh, back off to sleep. I can't help thinking she hasn't made a rational assessment of her sleep needs.'

'You don't look like someone who's been deprived of sleep,' Duncan said. 'Shall I take that?'

Dommie had surprised Duncan when, two years before, she had taken him out to dinner at Ménage à Trois – a flash place for her and definitely for him. He'd at first thought she might be trimming the bill when she ordered water to drink. He hadn't believed it. The father, Dommie said, was nobody; she had just found the best-looking and healthiest specimen she could reasonably persuade to take part in the transaction, and let him go his way afterwards. He wouldn't know anything about it. Duncan had been amazed. 'After all,' Dommie said, 'I'm not getting any younger. I'm not going to hang around for a man to show up, and then years of debate about whether we had a future, and then years of trying, and then it's all too late.' Over a dinner that consisted, modishly, of two starters each, one with a kiwifruit garnish, another exploiting aubergine, she confided in her brother, 'I really wanted a child much more than I wanted a husband and a father to the child. So there you are.'

There had been other and much more difficult dinners in the past, reconciling or arguing, Dommie making herself into a new person or living up to what other people hoped to turn her into. Duncan had been the first on the scene when the child was born in St George's, Tooting – he would have stood by her side, but she'd said she really only wanted professionals, not weak-minded boys who would probably faint at the sight of where babies came from. Duncan was relieved and guilty, but had come with a great bunch of flowers, and had not gone into it too much when Dommie had said what the child was going to be called. The child had lain in her white cot in the white room, with smiling, tranquil nurses around her, in the happy part of the hospital where everyone, more or less, was well, and her face turned to the air with its flushed red cheeks and nose, her surprising scrub of very dark hair; her tiny fists flailed in the air like those of a floored tiny boxer. Duncan loved her, not knowing why. She looked nothing like their father Samuel. The father, Dommie mentioned much later in passing, had been Syrian, and beautiful.

'How's the shop?' Dommie said, when they were out of London. The snow was not quite over, and on green spaces, gardens and roofs, it was settling.

'Mostly lovely,' he said. 'We had Paul Bailey in last week signing copies of his new novel and all the old stock we could get hold of. He was charming. Told a lot of stories about actors. Oh, God, get off the sodding road if you can't be bothered to … Sorry. It's the ones wearing trilbies when they drive I can't cope with. It's like a symbol of non-driving ability, that bloody trilby.'

'But your author.'

'Oh, yes, he was charming. Bought a lot of stock as well, I mean other books, and left a box of old things for us to sell in the second-hand corner. A donation, he said. Very nice of him. We offered him a tenner for the lot, and at first he wouldn't hear of it, then he would. Perfectly reasonable of him, really.'

'I hope you didn't let him sign too many of his own books.'

'Ten of the new one, five of the last, two each of the novels before that, the ones we had, I mean. That should do us quite well. Anyway, he's only in Shepherd's Bush so he can come back and sign some more.'

'You learnt your lesson with that bloody book,' Dommie said. 'That bloody …'

'Now then,' Duncan said. 'I'll have you know I sold a copy of *The Garden King* only three months ago.'

'That was the first since when, exactly?'

'It was really good, too. I don't know why no one bought it.'

'How absolutely frightful,' Dommie said. Duncan gave her a sidelong glance. Had she always been so posh? It seemed to him that she had been getting steadily posher in the last ten years. It was catching on like the plague. He had heard Christopher and Simon saying 'simply awful' and even Nat had been known to say 'absolutely ghastly'. Soon they'd all be at it, and Arthur would be talking about the drawing room looking awfully unspeakable, or something.

'You should pack them up and send them back to – what was he called, the author?'

'He died, poor soul,' Duncan said. 'No, it's all been written off and forgotten about. They might as well sit upstairs gathering dust and selling one copy every two years. I didn't have the heart to ask his family if they had a use for two hundred and thirty-six signed copies of their son's only novel. Ah, well. Lesson learnt. Someone's catching up with some important sleep, there in the back.'

'I don't know why,' Dommie said, 'it always sends her off to sleep, the back of the car. Ah, Celia. Yes? Celia, Celia, Mummy's here.'

'I have no idea why you called her Celia,' Duncan said. 'Everything about it – before it was just her name, I kept thinking coeliac, and then someone said "Celia, Celia, Celia shits –"'

'Well, she does,' Dommie said.

'– you know, that awful poem,' Duncan said. 'I just don't understand it.'

'Well, I like it, and it suits her,' Dommie said. 'I thought I would think of the future. She looks like a Dame Celia already. Highly authoritative. Anyway.'

'Is this Brighton?' Duncan said. He thought the alternative might be that your child was run over by a lorry at fourteen, and then you would only have a child with a bewildered pink face and a strange adult name to remember. He corrected the death-filled direction of his thoughts.

'No,' Dommie said. 'It's not even Haywards Heath. We're hours off. It's thinking of snowing again, too.'

'I love snow,' Duncan said, with a burst of enthusiasm. 'And I love Christmas too. I love it now. I never used to, but I really love it now.'

'I love it too,' Dommie said remotely and casually, as if talking about nothing so very much.

8.

The snow had begun again in earnest by Brighton. They parked on the front, and for a moment Duncan and Dommie sat and looked at snow falling on the metal-green sea. As far as Duncan could remember, he had never seen snow falling on sea before. It fell; it disappeared; the sea flexed and swelled. Celia stirred in the back, waking, and they both turned. She gave them a lovely broad smile; her woollen hat had fallen off at some point in the journey, and her almost blue-black hair spilt out in curls.

'Car,' she said, with an air of delight.

'I wish anyone else felt like that about the Austin Princess,' Duncan said. 'Now. Where are we going?'

'The Lanes are just there, aren't they?' Dommie said. 'I don't know – it's so long since I've been in Brighton. I used to come here with Lucien, you know, my awful Frenchman. He had a real thing for it.'

'And now you have a thing for it, too,' Duncan said sagely.

'Well, I don't know about that,' Dommie said. 'I quite like it, I suppose. I tell you what – let's go and find a nice little tea shop and have a cup of tea and even a cake before we start on anything. I've got quite a little list of people to buy things for, not including you. Are you ready?'

They got out, and in the falling snow Dommie quickly opened the boot of the car and put the pushchair together. She opened the back door, wrapped Celia up as tightly as possible, and as the child gurgled and joyously writhed, she bundled her deftly into the seat. Brighton was quiet, and they soon found a tea shop at the entrance to the Lanes with an Australian proprietress, her hair under a scarf, and a less exuberant school-leaver taking their order laboriously on a pad. 'Quiet today,' Duncan said, with a merchant's fellow feeling, but the girl said, 'Yes, that's because it's snowing outside,' so slowly that at first he thought she must be joking. But she brought a pot of satisfying orange stewed tea, a coffee cake (for Dommie) and a toasted teacake (for Duncan) as well as some warm milk for Celia, which Dommie took the skin off and decanted into Celia's infant cup. 'She likes it, doesn't she?' Dommie said, for Celia's benefit rather than anyone else's.

'Cup!' Celia said, with ecstasy, and then 'Milk! Milk!' That was a new one, Dommie observed. She had talked of *cup* until now meaning her favourite drink, but since her favourite drink always came in her favourite cup, there was no way of separating it.

'She seems to have worked it out for herself,' Dommie said dispassionately.

'Beastly stuff,' Duncan said. 'I don't know how she can bear it.'

'Let's not sit and talk about my prodigy child managing to call milk by its proper name before she's two years old,' Dommie said. 'Let's talk like adults.'

She made her brother smile – it had always been such a thing with Dommie to talk like an adult, to spend time with the older boys, to impress her little brother with the adult conversation she could embark on and baffle him. Once it had been talk about men and professions and sex and restaurants, with her friend Tricia in front of the bedroom mirror; now it was about her professional development, and when she thought she was going to go back to work. Duncan observed that that was one worry he didn't have as an employer, maternity leave, and Dommie replied tartly that he should be aware of his responsibilities too; there was such a thing as sex discrimination when you gave people a job. It was that sort of nice, responsible, grown-up conversation, and it was watched and observed by two keen listeners, the waitress leaning against the Welsh dresser and waiting for customers to come in from the snow, and by Celia, her little hands competently around the lukewarm pink cup with rabbits on it, raising it to her face all by herself, her eyes going from Mummy to Uncle and back again, round as saucers, taking in, it seemed, every word.

'I don't suppose there's such a thing as sex discrimination when there's no one to discriminate *against*,' Duncan said.

'That wouldn't stand up for a second if someone turned up and made a claim. How many pregnant women have you employed in the last four years?'

415

'I would be simply thrilled to employ any number of pregnant women – well, I wouldn't, but for the sake of this conversation I would be simply thrilled – but the fact remains that in four years the only person who has asked me for a job and the only person I've given one to is Arthur.'

'Dear old Arthur,' Dommie said. 'What's he doing today? Is he going to be all right?'

'Oh, yes, safe as houses,' Duncan said. 'He's got his friend Tim dropping in after lunch, he said. I told him I'd give him a job title – shop manager, if he wants that. But he says it's only of any use if he had cards or anyone to give them to, or if he was going to go for another job. Shall we?'

Dommie paid – he noticed that she worked out 10 per cent exactly of the bill, and then, since that would have been 33p, she returned the coppers to her pocket and left another 40p on top. He liked the practical, exact sides to her personality that had become clear in the last few years, and especially since she'd had Celia.

Outside, the Lanes were almost absurdly picturesque in the falling snow. Duncan could not remember whether he had been there before – it seemed more familiar to him from people's mentions and stories and tales of acquisition than from direct experience. He was almost sure he had been to Brighton more than once, but perhaps he had not made up as diligently as Dommie for the lack of childhood outings. She knew exactly where she was going, and although she had declared her interest in silverware, she ignored two or three windows, like a dentist's cabinet, before turning her head and saying, 'In here,' to Duncan. It looked much like the others, but Dommie evidently knew what she needed.

'Yes,' the man said. 'Yes, I remember Lucien. I remember his girls, too. Were you one of his girls?'

The man was sitting behind a high counter on a pinewood stool; he had been reading the *Daily Mirror*, but at Dommie's introduction and the mention of Lucien, he had put his paper down. He wore a dirty old cravat tied in a knot and a shirt with a pattern of graph-paper; his eyes were hooded and knowing, his nose swollen and bulbous. He looked rheumily from Dommie to Duncan and back again.

'I haven't seen him in an age,' the old man said. 'I thought he went back to ... Toulouse, wasn't it?'

'I haven't seen him in ten years, almost,' Dommie said. 'I suppose he's somewhere. How's business?'

'Business? Oh, good, good, very good,' the man said. 'Never better. Not today, of course. I'm branching out. I used to be eighteenth-century English tableware, but everyone's at that game nowadays. You never know where this trade's going to lead you. In Chipping Camden once, at a house sale, I'd gone there for a chafing dish I'd been tipped off about and there was an Ashbee bonbonnière. Nobody else seemed to be interested in it. I looked at it and I saw what a nice piece it was, in its own terms. Not very fashionable. Very nicely made. Everyone about me was going mad for the candelabra and the chafing dish I was supposed to be there for. I got the Ashbee piece for a song, and then, I suppose I had the bit between my teeth, three or four more pieces and even a Voysey plate, though I don't suppose I'd ever bought a plate in my life.

'The next thing I know, I'm in Elsenham and there, at that little auction house they have over there, there's a nice little piece of silver, something of the same sort, and again, no one's noticed or no one cares. You see, the thing about Arts and Crafts is that it looks very plain to the untutored eye unless there's a bit of jewel or a bit of enamel on top of it. That catches the eye and suddenly you're bidding against what I call the magpies – they love a bit of tourmaline or a shiny piece of enamel. They don't care about Ashbee or the proportions or the quality of the piece, they just want a bit of shiny colour. Without that, the best pieces can look as plain as if they come from Woolworth's. Look.' And he drew out a small box, the surface rippling under the spotlight but the shape simple and pure. It looked like a pedestal, no more than that. 'Nothing to it,' the man said.

'But it looks so lovely when you put it on velvet like that,' Dommie said.

'They don't come on velvet,' the man said. 'They come in boxes any old how, dented and filthy, and no one's interested. Unless there's a scrap of garnet or tourmaline, like I saw – anyone can see that. It led me on. I haven't bought a piece of eighteenth-century silver in eighteen months. No interest. There's a bit more interest around in the Arts and Crafts now than there was. You can't clean up now like you could. At any rate it's harder. You know what I'm interested in now? It's not caught on yet, but it will. German silverware. German and Austrian. You think of that heavy stuff, you don't think of this.'

He turned behind him, opened the door of the cabinet. Dommie took the opportunity to give Duncan a look: an old-fashioned look, a sceptical look, a look that said as a parent to a child to do or not do something. Duncan found it impossible to read. The dealer turned round with a vessel of some sort – a novelty teapot, he would have said as the dealer placed it on the green cloth on the worktop. His movements were all relaxed and without the hushed reverence Duncan might have expected; he was used to handling these things, and in any case they were silverware and not china. Still, he was holding the teapot by its black wooden handle and not touching the silver body. It was a half-globe, resting on a crossed base; a spout jutted impudently upwards and a horizontal circle formed the lid. If it were not for the black wood – evidently some kind of luxury element – it might have looked like the sort of thing that hospitals and schools used. Except—

'It's not very big,' Dommie said. 'You wouldn't get a whole mug out of that.'

'Dessau,' the dealer said. 'Probably. The silverware is difficult to date definitely, but I think it's the period when the school had moved to Dessau. They started in Weimar, you know – where the Republic is named after. Beautiful town. I don't suppose this ever left Dessau, where they moved to. That's not such a beautiful town – very run-down. The school's still there. They're talking about renovating it.'

'The school?'

'The Bauhaus?' the dealer said. 'Oh, I'm sorry. Lost in my own world. The Bauhaus. They started off in Weimar, then the town council drove them out. Couldn't bear all that free love and political agitation. Dessau offered them a place. Nice town. Very quiet. Don't know that they went down any better there, either. They're both in the DDR, East Germany. I go over from time to time. There's stuff to buy, people very glad to sell it to you. Can't take out much at a time, and it can be a little bit tricky. The best idea is to pack a big picnic hamper with knives and forks and stuff, and throw the teapot in with all that stuff. It's harder with a sugar bowl – who takes a silver sugar bowl on a picnic? This is a nice little thing, though. Found it two years ago. Old lady in Dessau, said her husband had bought it sixty years ago. He was dead. She didn't know what it was. Had to buy three worthless silver photograph frames and a silver tea caddy I wouldn't necessarily have wanted to hide my tracks. "Oh," you say, "that's an unusual teapot. While I'm here …" Doesn't always work. Bauhaus. A lot of academic interest in it. Collectors only here and there – it's so difficult to find the good stuff, and people still think it's ugly, not like the Werkstätte. In twenty years, you'll be getting begging letters from museums. Feel it.'

Duncan had been growing warm towards the curious, squat, insulting object, like an angry punctuation mark. He could see himself, in four years' time, bringing out a beautiful range of Bauhaus silverware for the delectation of guests. And this, he was saying, was the little piece that started it all off, this teapot, handing it round. Without quite intending it, he was handling the teapot, picking it up, turning it over. It was heavy in his hands. Underneath, the crossed sheets of silver it stood on were soldered with a pucker, as of scarred tissue. For the rest of it, the surface was smooth, only very lightly tarnished. He looked at it, aware that he was moving his face in the simulacrum of a connoisseur. The dealer and Dommie were observing him, curiously, and Celia, quiet in her pushchair until now, began to make a small querulous noise, of boredom and request.

'It would look so beautiful in the shop,' Duncan said, and was about to say that he would think about it, that they would talk about it and come back, when Celia said something.

'See,' Celia said, quite clearly.

'It looks better at home than in the shop,' the dealer said persuasively, not understanding what Duncan had said. 'You'll want to talk about it with your wife. It's two hundred and twenty pounds, but I dare say I could do two hundred for cash, what with ... your wife being an old friend, and all that.'

'No,' Duncan said, envisaging his gracious future. But it was more than that: it was an object that he wanted to be able to pick up and hold whenever he felt like it. The solid silver teapot, too small to hold anything like a mug of tea, sat solidly and patiently, and there was a regretted absence in the house of a widow in Weimar or – where was the other place? 'No, I don't think I want to think about it. I'd love to take it.'

'You won't regret it,' the man said. 'This style is definitely coming back into fashion. To tell you the truth, I'll be a little sorry to see it go. I've grown very attached to it.'

'It's a good excuse to go back to East Germany,' Dommie said. 'Don't get arrested.'

'Oh, I have my ways,' the dealer said, mysteriously. 'Now. Cheque or cash?'

9.

Arthur was reading a book at the till, but in reality watching the two men who had come in together; watching them with what the novel in his hand – by a pulp crime novelist, an American specialist in a detective with fabulous tits and a hunky

420

sidekick called Watson and a tendency to break off for three-somes whenever you might have thought it would be better to chase after the escaping villain – would have called a beady eye. Sherlock flaming Homo, Arthur thought. It wasn't as engaging as watching these two. It was the third time in two weeks they'd been in, and they'd spent a hundred pounds this Monday, and seventy or eighty the Wednesday before. They ought to have been his favourite customers.

Another familiar sort of customer was browsing the shelves in a dim, hopeful, self-conscious way. He had walked past the bookshop three times before entering: he did not give the impression of coming to bookshops much, and had stood for a second on the mat, breathing in the atmosphere of a gay shop, not sure where to start. Arthur liked this sort of customer. He would start by looking at the picture books, hoping for a bit of smut, and then he would circle the shop, finding the Californian academic texts on gay people in the middle ages and the reconstruction of gender a little taxing. Some of them would work to left or right, picking up books in a desultory and undecided way, and would discover a novel with a man on the front – if he was lucky, an American small-press gay thriller; if he was unlucky, the paperback of *Querelle de Brest*. The speculatively acquired pile would return to Tooting or Cardiff.

Arthur regarded this particular customer with tenderness. His short-sleeved white shirt revealed quite a sexy tight torso, and his blue M & S slacks were tight round the bum. He had achieved sexiness by accident through his shopping, without knowing he had done any such thing. The queen who picked up this tow-haired hero for the first time, with his puzzled expression and untutored gratitude, wouldn't be able to believe his luck, as he spunked over that same puzzled expression and untutored gratitude, two hours later. Arthur thought he would ask him whether he'd read *A Boy's Own Story* when he came to pay.

There were other recurrent customers – there were the argumentative ones who had come to men's group nights and asked to borrow books. There were the knowledgeable literati who came with friends and boyfriends, sometimes with well-dressed women and straight men with a benevolent glitter of condescension in the eye; they would expect to be greeted by and engaged with Arthur and Duncan in conversation while the friend or boyfriend made a noisy way round the shop. The polite reference to the knowledgeable writer's most recent work would be made by Arthur or Duncan, to be batted away; a book or two would be bought with cries of excitement; the companion would promise to return to buy all their Christmas presents here; and they would depart, leaving something of a silence behind. There were teenage versions of Arthur, burning with desire to discover – what? They didn't know, but they came, and they spent or they shoplifted. There were those who came to cruise – disappointing on a Tuesday morning, and never very successful at any time of the week – and those who came to build up a library, carrying their possessions in two tattered old supermarket plastic bags. Arthur knew them all. The two men now in the shop were none of these. They were policemen in mufti. Arthur went on observing them over the top of the new *Kiss Me, Handsome* novel with keen attention.

Their clothes seemed hardly to match, or resemble, in the ways that friends' usually did. They seemed more like the clothes of straight men who had been thrown together by ill fortune, in the corner of a pub or in the queue of a service station. One was fifty, and wearing an old but quite good quality overcoat – it was early in the year to be wearing an overcoat, on this September day, and he might have been sweating. His shoes were very old-fashioned, solid and thick and black, like the shoes of someone who did a lot of urban walking. The other was more like a homosexual, but only quite like: his pastel sweater over his shoulder with arms dangling, his little leather-stringed necklace were at odds with the way he held himself and moved, and as he turned to his friend, *The Nude Male* photo book in hand and said something in lowered tones, he ran a finger round the

422

inside of the necklace; clearly an unfamiliar and skin-irritating presence. He had dressed up sedulously to come to the Big Gay Bookshop. He, too, was wearing old-fashioned solid and thick and black shoes. It was the shoes and their dissimilar quality that told Arthur what they were. If they went on buying copies of books in the hope that they might find something illegally filthy, on the budget of Her Marge's Metropolitan Police, then all well and good. He wished that he could tell the one with the necklace on, the butch one who was trying so hard, that nobody round here gave a shit what you wore: they obviously weren't gay anyway, whatever they put on.

They were causing some nervousness, some disturbance in the atmosphere; the other customer, the one with the tight clothes who had walked past the shop repeatedly before coming in, was edging away from them. He could see that something was wrong, though he probably didn't know what, exactly. 'Do you want to leave them over here?' Arthur said kindly, as by now he had a pile of six books balancing under one arm, and the man, blushing crimson at being addressed at all, came over and left them silently, but with a nervous smile. He hovered; took a step back in the direction of the shelf he had come from; indecisively looked at the two plainclothes policemen, and indecisively turned back to Arthur.

'I love this one,' Arthur said, tapping the book on the top of the pile. 'Have you read *Anglo-Saxon Attitudes*? That's brilliant, that's my favourite book ever, I reckon.'

'I'll look out for it,' the man said, in an unpractised, croaky way. Perhaps he had hoped not to have to speak at all. He had a Scottish accent, perhaps a light Edinburgh accent, and Arthur smiled brilliantly at him. It was illegal still in Scotland, wasn't it? He'd come down on the train, was buying books to keep him going through the long illegal Scottish nights, would come back in six months' time. Arthur looked at Edinburgh with some tenderness. Men were always trying to pick you up, sitting here at the till, but once a month or so, Arthur thought he could be so happy with a customer. He might never see this customer again, and like all the men Arthur could be so happy with, he paid with cash and not a cheque, from which Arthur could at least have discovered what his name was.

The Scotsman left. There was a brief exchange between the two plainclothes policemen, and the one who had made slightly more effort came up to the till while the other one loitered. He would not meet Arthur's eye as he put them down. Arthur would do all the work.

'Hello again,' Arthur said. 'Nice to see you again. You're getting to be a bit of a regular, you and your friend there. Do you come far?'

The plainclothes policeman made an assessing, official gesture at his top pocket, as if his radio might be in there, or perhaps just protecting his right nipple from sexual assault by bookshop assistants.

'You're keen readers, I can see,' Arthur went on. 'You're like me – you *get through a lot*. Oh, I like this.' He took the top one from the pile and keyed it into the till. It was a quite innocuous novel about American high-school students falling in love, which the Boston publisher had put a startlingly frank cover on. 'Four ninety-nine, and this – yes, you'll want a book about helping yourself sexually, getting to know your sexual needs, we all do, don't we, when we're coming out – eight ninety-seven – and this one – and this one – yes, and a picture book, lovely …'

Arthur could have sworn that these two policemen had bought *The Nude Male* last week. Certainly they had had two copies in stock when he'd reordered it, last Tuesday, and Duncan had commented that another one had sold the next day. They'd been in on Wednesday because Duncan had had to take another half-day off to go to another funeral. The more he thought about it, the more Arthur was sure that the policemen had already bought this one. He wasn't going to mention it, though, since they were paying with money. *The Nude Male* was published by Weidenfeld & Nicolson and was largely full of pictures of Greek vases, which hadn't been considered rude since Queen Victoria died. He thought the forces of law and order would ultimately be disappointed in their hunt for obscenity here.

'There,' Arthur said. 'That'll be sixty-one pounds eighty-three pence.'

'Is this everything?' the policeman said. He had a light, feminine voice, either put on for the occasion or the thing that had led him to be selected for the mission. Operation Bumboy Books, Arthur thought derisively. 'Is this all your stock, out here in the shop?'

'Well, mostly,' Arthur said, keeping a straight face. Policemen had asked this before. 'Was there something special you were looking for? If it's not in stock, we can order most things, and some things from abroad.'

'What sort of things do you order most?' the man said.

But his friend had been listening, and called over, 'I bet you get some unusual requests.'

Arthur didn't know who he was supposed to be responding to. He thought for a moment about reeling them in with the tale of the book about feet that Tony and Tim had got them to order from Amsterdam. It had cost thirty-eight pounds, plus shipping and ordering costs, and when it arrived it was in German, with photographs of twelve pairs of feet, some in socks, between pages 104 and 105. That had been the only time they had ordered anything 'special' from abroad, and they'd only done it for Tony and Tim. There was nothing else that hadn't gone straight on the shelves. If he could get the policemen to order a second copy of the book about feet, he would feel satisfied. But then he realized that he didn't know what the German text had said, and he had a better idea. 'We keep a little bit of stock upstairs, for special customers,' he said. 'At the moment, up there –' he looked around as if there might be someone else in the shop '– we've got quite a sexy book. Our customers are eating it up. We can't get rid of it fast enough.'

The policemen looked dubiously at the copy of *The Garden King* that Arthur returned with, its artistically misty cover in

425

blue and green, and if they had opened it up, they would have been still more dubious if they had started to read the elegant prose. But they bought a copy and off they went.

'Well, good luck to them,' Duncan said, when he came back and Arthur told him about the visit. 'They're getting to be some of our best customers.'

Then Arthur told him about the copy of *The Garden King* that he'd persuaded them to buy, and Duncan couldn't stop laughing. If the police forces of England could be made to hear about this filthy novel, which could justify prosecuting the filthy gay bookshop in London, they'd all order a copy, and extra copies for the prosecution, and then it would get into the press and normal gays would read about it, and they'd all be down here wanting a copy and …

'Won't happen,' Arthur said. 'The police aren't as stupid as that. No, they are that stupid. They wouldn't be able to get past page five, they'd just flick through it looking for if it said "cock" or "arse" and that.'

'You didn't leave them alone in the shop, did you?'

'Well, only when I went upstairs to get the book.'

'Oh, God,' Duncan said. 'That means a stock check. I know they'll have stolen something they were too embarrassed to buy. *The Joy of Gay Sex*, I'm sure of it.'

It proved to be the case.

'Dying for a cup of tea,' Duncan said to console Arthur. There was nothing to be done about policemen and Arthur shouldn't feel so guilty about it. They were always going to be there, policemen, like the weather, stones through the window, Aids.

10.

'It was January the seventh, 1987, this year, a Wednesday,' Duncan would say a few months later. 'It would have been about eleven o'clock in the morning.'

'The date and time are not in dispute,' the lawyer would say.

Over the road, Andy and Chris were observing the arrival of the police in their van.

'Not a moment too soon,' Andy said. 'Shut them down. I don't know why it was allowed in the first place.'

'That's right, Dad,' Chris said. 'Selling filth. Anyone could have gone in.'

The van disgorged the police; there were nine of them. The officer in charge counted them out, seven men and a woman police officer. There was something queer about their hands: pink and shiny. Arthur came to the door.

'What's all this?' he said. 'Are we suspected of robbing a bank or summat?'

'You're believed to be selling pornographic material both openly and in a concealed manner,' the police officer. 'In this first instance, we are not arresting you, but taking material away for examination. In there, Sergeant.'

'There's nothing pornographic in there,' Arthur said. 'I'm going to get my boss. What the hell is that?' He had seen that the police officers were wearing pink plastic gloves.

Duncan and Dommie had been going through the accounts in the little store room upstairs, the one that had been Arthur's room until four years ago. They had heard the rumpus downstairs as the policemen came into the shop.

'What's all this?' Dommie said. The police had started bundling books into black plastic bags. 'What on earth do you think you're doing?'

'They're doing us for selling dirty books,' Arthur said. 'Oy. A bit more care. That's valuable stock you're throwing into them bags.'

The police were throwing books indiscriminately into bags, or not quite indiscriminately: they had lists they were consulting, and were going to specific shelves. But they were taking dozens of books.

'If in doubt, chuck it in,' Duncan said hotly. 'Is that it? Who's in charge here?'

'I am,' the officer in charge said, coming in from the doorway. 'We've received substantive information from members of the public that your shop is selling pornographic material.'

'Rubbish,' Duncan said. 'Members of the public my foot. Those two plainclothes officers that kept coming round last summer. I'll have you know that the fourth time they came round, one of them solicited a bribe from my assistant here. Five thousand pounds they wanted, and then the whole thing would be dropped. He told your officer – he quite rightly told your bloody officer – to piss off and never come back.'

'All this and any other claims you wish to make will be aired in due course,' the officer said wearily.

'And they stole a fucking book, too, when we weren't looking. That's not pornography,' Arthur was saying to an officer ladling books into a bag. 'That's E. M. Forster's *Maurice*. Can I ask you, have you ever tried to have a wank to that? Have you? Have you?'

'I must ask you to restrain your assistant from using obscene language and/or making improper sexual approaches to my officers, if that's what the little twat is doing,' the officer in charge said, delicately turning his head away from Arthur.

'Fuck off,' Duncan said. 'Dommie, go and phone a lawyer. You're a lawyer. Phone another one.'

'They're wearing gloves,' Dommie said; she was already holding the telephone at the desk. 'What are they wearing gloves for? Officer, why are they wearing gloves? It can't be for finger-prints.'

'I have to guard my officers against all possibilities of physical danger,' the officer in charge said.

'This is a bloody bookshop,' Arthur said. 'There's no danger here, except if a copy of Proust, translated by Terence Kilmartin, falls on your foot.'

'This is standard practice when investigating non-traditional communities of drug users, Haitians, haemophiliacs and homo-sexuals, and the safety of my officers must come first,' the officer in charge said.

'Your officers are not going to catch Aids from a bloody paperback,' Dommie said.

'What? What?' Duncan said. 'You think—'

'In this area I am not permitted and not prepared to take risks and not prepared to enter into discussions about measures I have decided to take,' the officer in charge said.

Out in the street, a curious crowd of onlookers had arrived. The greengrocer had crossed the road and was talking to the Greek sandwich-makers on their step; a couple of regular old ladies who must live near by had stopped to watch, their tartan or jolly spotted shopping trolleys waiting patiently like dogs. They looked worried; it was clear that they were greatly enjoying all of this. If only the raid could have happened on a Saturday afternoon, when everything was so much busier.

'You realize that you are bringing me into disrepute with the whole of this street,' Duncan said. 'I've been here for nearly eight years now. Do you know what it's been like? Do you know how many times this front window's been smashed? Well, neither do I – I've lost count. Do you know what it's like being called a queer fucking cunt twice a week on the way to work? And now they'll think we're fucking pornographers they can catch Aids from. What a fucking disgrace. We should have paid your fucking officers that five grand and looked on it as an insurance premium.'

'I would be very grateful if you would not use foul language towards me or other officers trying to do their job,' the officer in charge said.

'Go on, piss off,' Duncan said. 'Before I bite you.' And then, to his horror, he just burst into tears. He wished Paul was still there.

It took all morning and what would normally have been lunchtime, and at the end, when the police went, anyone would have thought that the shop was proposing to shut up and close down. The bookshelves were filleted, leaving great gaps; the photography section was almost completely emptied. Stock had been dropped on the floor and left there; a policeman had trodden on a new hardback novel and torn its spine off with his boot. How long would it take? As long as it took, the officer in charge said, departing, not removing his gloves until he was safely outside on the pavement. He had touched nothing in the shop.

'I don't know how we're supposed to go on,' Duncan said. 'Just when we were starting to do all right. I just don't know.'

Together, they started putting the books back in their places. The other shopkeepers outside started dispersing, discussing, casting surprised or interested glances back towards the shop. For whatever reason, the officers had not gone into the display of books in the window, and the neat arrangement was undisturbed. Arthur had done it last week, right after New Year. It was of a summer garden with little deckchairs, a Barbie in sunglasses drinking a cocktail, and a copy of *The Joy of Gay Sex* spread-eagled downwards on some sand. (Arthur had stolen some from an open sack a builder had left a couple of streets away – that had been his inspiration, along with an old Barbie.) An old mirror was meant to be the sea. The proportions were wrong and *The Joy of Gay Sex* in Barbie's world was the size of a volleyball pitch. The police had not noticed the solitary remaining copy in the window. There must be some way to turn that to their advantage, Duncan thought.

'Go away,' he said, to the blond young man who had just poked his head through the door with a startled expression. 'We're closed.'

'No, I'm awfully sorry to have taken such a time to get here,' the man said. 'It's no distance really, but, you know—'

'Oh hello!' Dommie said brightly. 'You must be Gervase. Duncan, this is Gervase – he's going to make everything all right, aren't you, Gervase? I knew everything would be all right. As soon as I saw your face, I knew it. Now. First things first – a cup of coffee.'

11.

'I just don't know what to *wear*,' the voice came from upstairs. Clive was in the dressing room, judging from the muffled sound and by now, Stephen thought, he had spread most of his wardrobe over the bed, the available chairs in the bedroom, and into the dressing room by the side. This had happened before.

'Wear what you like,' Stephen called. 'You look lovely in anything.'

There was a muted response. Stephen himself was sitting at the desk in the drawing room, writing a postcard of thanks to Diana for last night. There was a proper study on the second floor where he kept papers and books and did proper work. This art-deco desk in silvered wood had been just the thing for the drawing room, Clive had thought, and Stephen had agreed. The desk on the second floor was not for company: it was a repro desk topped with green leather that Stephen had inherited from his father. Neither Stephen nor his father had had any taste, as Clive quite fondly observed from time to time, and thank heaven Clive had come into Stephen's life as nobody had come into his father's to put that right. Clive never had to go to the second floor: up there were briefing notes and the documentation and the framed certificates of Stephen's professional life. On the first floor all was *luxe, calme et volupté*; the ground floor was silver, sage-green, with quite daringly acute touches of neon pink, and the basement was the kitchen of Stephen's dreams, so he was told. All of that was Clive's doing. He himself was wearing an old graph-paper patterned shirt and an ancient pair of – he looked – dung-green corduroys. It was what he had flung on when he had got back from today's case in Isleworth, that interesting tax fraud, his white shirt soaked in sweat under the double-breasted pinstriped suit. He knew he was going to be made to go up and change into something better. It wouldn't take him a moment.

'The thing is,' Clive called, coming down the stairs, 'I have absolutely no idea what you're supposed to wear to something like this.'

'Something radical and chic,' Stephen said. 'Something fund-raising. Something that shows you're going to fight for the cause. I'm wearing dungarees.'

'Oh, Stephen,' Clive said, coming into the drawing room, 'I would say that you don't have a pair of dungarees, except that I'm not one hundred per cent sure about what lies in that half of the wardrobe.'

'One third of the wardrobe, at the absolute most,' Stephen said.

'Be that as it may. How do I look?'

'Perfect, my darling,' Stephen said, and he meant it, as he had almost every night for the last twenty-three years. Clive really looked nice tonight. Other people's boyfriends dressed up and followed fashion, but Clive just looked beautiful: he was wearing a white shirt and black trousers, high-waisted and with something very slightly unusual about the cut that defeated Stephen – anyway, they were not at all like the black trousers he put on in the morning. He had first seen him doing the jive, or the twist, or whatever it had been, in a basement in Notting Hill in 1963, and he had been wearing a white shirt and black trousers then, and Stephen had just known from his turn and his smile that he would be perfect, my darling, for evermore. 'You do look nice.'

'Oh, I don't know,' Clive said, but he would never go on about it once a decision had been made. 'I've left such a mess for Mrs Thing to sort out tomorrow. Everything's on the floor.'

'Well, it was well worth it,' Stephen said. 'I wish there was something better than a party in a bookshop I could be offering you. Did you go to the park again? You're lovely and brown.'

'You're not going out dressed like that, I hope,' Clive said. 'You really are the limit. The car's coming in fifteen minutes, too.'

'I'll be ready,' Stephen said. 'It's only a bookshop party.'

'It's a fundraising party,' Clive said. 'It's for their defence costs. And we all know how much that can amount to, don't we. Have you even had a shower since you came in?'

'The car can wait, darling,' Stephen said. 'There. That's done. Have you got a stamp?'

'I'm sure there's one in the top drawer,' Clive said, coming over and sitting on Stephen's knee. 'What were you up to today?'

'That interesting tax fraud,' Stephen said. 'Didn't get much further, though. Now – give me a nice big kiss, lovely husband of mine.'

All over London, rich and literary and well-intentioned men were discussing with each other, in person or over the phone, what exactly one wore to a party meant to raise funds for the defence of a gay bookshop. Something festive? Something sober? Radical? Rich? 'It's a charity event, like a ball,' Alan said to his mother, as he tied his black tie. The mirror in the sitting room was best for that – an old flatterer of a mirror, one that didn't shine up your wrinkles and blotches like the mirrors at work. 'But it's a sort of ball that you don't have to take anyone to in particular.'

'I wish someone would take me to a ball,' his mother said, pulling her blanket up about her knees. 'Now, I remember once, your father—'

'Oh, Mother,' Alan said, impatiently. 'I've got to make a move. You'll be all right then. I won't be late back.' He knew that he would be the only person in black tie, but fundraising suggested dressiness, even if it was just in a bookshop. Would there be food? Would they all go on somewhere jolly afterwards?

'You look nice,' Tony said to Tim, and Tim said the same back to Tony, in the lodging house where Arthur lived. They were matching tonight, in white vests and black leather trousers but, then, they often were. They stood by the window, and it was Tim's turn to trim Tony's moustache.

'Look at your whiskers,' Tim said. 'I wish mine grew half as fast as yours. I'll never have such a pretty moustache as yours. Ah, well.'

'But yours is so nice and blond,' Tony said. 'I'd love to have a nice blond moustache.'

'Yours is nicer, though,' Tim said. 'How was that guy last night?'

'That guy?' Tony said, his upper lip tickling as Tim, concentrating, trimmed the hair with a frown. 'Oh, that French guy. He was OK. He wanted to take me home, but I said, where do you live, Jacques, and he said he was staying with his sister in Tulse Hill and sleeping on her sofa, so I said maybe later and we did it in a cubicle. He wasn't called Jacques. I can't remember what he was called.'

'Oh, yes,' Tim said. He lowered the scissors, looked critically at his own work. 'I was as wasted as a monkey. Are we going with Arthur tonight?'

'Arthur?' Tony said, smiling as Tim's frown disappeared and he gave a small nod. 'No, he came home and changed but he went out hours ago. He said he'd got things to do at the bookshop. We ought to have a threesome with him.'

'Oh, I don't know about that,' Tim said. 'He's quite a nice boy. Vanilla, he is.'

The literary gentlemen of London were dressing, or being reminded to dress, were setting off in keen or reluctant moods, unwilling to be prised from their *Nationwide* or their Jane Austen. One had refused an invitation to dinner with Kingsley Amis for this; another had promised to take his editor, who had, in a ladylike way, said that she had always longed to see a room full of sodomites. 'You see,' she had said, 'I was brought up in Cheltenham. I only really *read* of them.' Her author admired that ladylike *of*; promised himself he would use it soon, in dialogue. Francis King was coming, and Paul Bailey, and Angus

Wilson, and Adam Mars-Jones, and ladies too, Maureen Duffy and Kay Dick and Maggi Hambling and for some reason Olivia Tempest. She had heard about it from Maureen Duffy and had phoned the bookshop in quite a rage demanding to know why she hadn't been invited. (They invited her.) They lived, these literary ladies and gentlemen, in shabby and overstuffed houses, full of books and objects and paintings, still-lifes and portraits, Staffordshire china dogs and fine Indian screens, and they lived amid dust. They were coming with a book, each of them, signed, and they were going to be auctioned off to the willing guests. It had been Arthur's idea. 'I don't know what we're going to fetch for Kay Dick's autobiography, however she signs it,' Duncan had said, but Arthur had said, very properly, that Kay Dick had her fans, too, and they would be very happy to pay to show their support for her and keep the bookshop going. Olivia Tempest was bringing a signed copy of that book that everyone had read or anyway seen on BBC2 a couple of years ago.

The gang were coming, the men's group, and the gay radicals from the old CHE days, and they were bringing their radical friends. Andrew lived in a little house in Clapham, and Nat, who lived in a little house in Kennington, was going to pick him up and drive him to Marylebone. It had not been Andrew's usual way to request a lift, and it was going in slightly the wrong direction, really, but Nat had agreed. When Andrew opened the door of his little terraced house in North Street, Clapham, Nat saw why he had asked. Andrew was wearing radical drag.

'I like your frock,' Nat said ironically. It wasn't a frock to be liked. Andrew hadn't shaved his beard, and he had applied green eyeshadow and pink lipstick with an inexpert hand. The dress was tight on him, the bosom flapping loose over his hairy chest, the cap sleeves tight on Andrew's hairy upper arms. He was wearing Dr Martens boots.

'It's a radical critique of gender roles performed in the urban space today,' Andrew said, in a perfunctory way. 'Come in.'

435

Nat cautiously followed Andrew into the hallway, making his way past the bicycle, a pile of leaflets on the floor, and surreptitiously trying to reattach a soggy piece of peeling green-and-yellow flock wallpaper that was peeling off.

'Where did you get it?' Nat said. 'Your frock.'

'Littlewoods catalogue,' Andrew said. 'They'll never stop sending me their stuff now, I know.'

'You should have gone to Evans,' Nat said. 'They've got outsize. I suppose you would be outsize for a girl.'

'Be that as it may. I'm not sure if I'm going tonight,' Andrew said. They were in Andrew's kitchen, and he opened the fridge door and poured them both a glass of wine. Nat sat down at the scrubbed-pine table. The fridge was chock full of dirty-looking vegetables, preparatory to being turned into some enormous and tasteless meatless stew, a vague orange colour. Nat's fridge in Kennington, it contained a bottle of wine, a bottle of vodka and maybe some olives and a yogurt. But he was everyone's friend; he never really cooked for himself.

'Oh, Andrew. Honestly. Why not?' Nat said.

'I've been thinking about it,' Andrew said, sitting down heavily in his frock and green eyeshadow, 'and I don't know it's what I want to support any more. Duncan – he's just in it to make money.'

'Well, it's a shop – it's got to make some money, or it won't stay a shop much longer.'

'We've been through this,' Andrew said. 'It could be a collective, and give out books to the community. A meeting place for people of all sorts, to discuss the future of society, young and old, straight and gay, male and female, working-class people of all sorts, and how to bring down this government. That's what we should be talking about. I've been thinking about it.'

'Yes, that would be simply lovely,' Nat said. 'What's this wine?'

'Parsnip,' Andrew said. 'And I don't think Duncan's really behind that. He looks as if he likes the community, as if he's there for us, but I don't think he really is. Maybe we should just let this trial run its course, see what happens to the book-shop. Afterwards, someone else could take it over.'

'Oh,' Nat said. 'Oh – really?'

'The last straw was last week,' Andrew said. 'I was in there buying – *buying* – that new anthropological book about gay weddings in the Kalahari, and there's a new poster on the wall, saying "Use Condoms Always", or something like that.'

'Yes, I saw it,' Nat said. 'You've not been in for a while – that's been up for months.'

'Tory propaganda,' Andrew said. 'It's just Tory propaganda, in what ought to be a radical bookshop. But it's being run for money, for profit, and it's putting up Tory propaganda now. I don't know that I want to support him in this case at all. Let the police prosecute him, close the place down. It was an experiment and it didn't work.'

'I don't know that those posters are Tory propaganda,' Nat said, puzzling. 'How do you work that one out? I thought they were from the Terrence Higgins Trust.'

'Tories,' Andrew said, taking a huge swig from his glass of parsnip wine. He left a pink lipstick stain on the rim. 'Don't you understand, Nat? I thought you were one of the thoughtful ones. We'd never have disagreed about this at CHE. The government's got its own moral agenda to pursue. Stop men sleeping with each other. Stop them exchanging fluids in love and fun. So there's this conspiracy, ooh, stop them, frighten them, tell them they're going to die unless they stop sleeping with other men and maybe marry Maureen next door and have two point four children and never think about how you could change society. Or at best – if you're going to have to sleep with men, you sick pervert, we'll allow you to so long as you use one of these condoms, thanks, we take credit cards, they're manufactured, these condoms, by some very good friends of ours in the pharmaceutical industry. Did you see what happened to the price of shares in the condom manufacturers, after the first time the government advert told everyone to use them, all the time, whenever anything looks like happening?'

'No, I didn't,' Nat said. He settled back in his chair. There seemed to be something underneath the cushion – he cautiously fished it out, thinking it might be a book, but it was an empty package of some sort.

'The shares – they shot up. Doubled in value. Massive profits for private enterprise, off the back of dead people,' Andrew said. 'Every dead gay man means another million in condom sales. Every one. Did you know that?'

'On the other hand,' Nat said, dropping the package on the floor, 'if you use a condom, you're probably not going to die, fingers crossed.'

'We're all going to die,' Andrew said. 'Capitalism can't stop people dying. And it can't stop the progress of progressive working-class thought. Promiscuity is a radical critique of the heteronormative structures of this society,' he went on, and thoughtfully rolled it round his tongue once more. 'Promiscuity, Nat, is a deeply – profoundly – radical critique of the heteronormative structures that keep everyone in this society in place. Surely you can understand that.'

Oh, do shut up, Nat thought. Honestly. You don't half go on, Nat thought. And it was all too clear how this one would end. He would talk and grouse and then he would say that it was important to get your point across after all, and he would get into the car with his green eyeshadow on and his flowery dress and his Doc Martens. My days, how that Andrew goes on, Nat thought, and there isn't even a drink in the house apart from parsnip wine and if you were very lucky some organic potato vodka made by Welsh lesbians, which you could have with beetroot juice. And the party would end with Andrew pawing at someone, drunk as a skunk, and still going on about capitalist structures. A bit less energy devoted to grousing, and a bit more to housework, would work miracles with Andrew.

'Did I tell you about the Brazilian I met at the Vauxhall Tavern last Friday?' Nat said, when they were finally in the car.

'No!' Andrew said, then he remembered himself. 'I suppose there was a reason why he's had to come to this country, though.'

Here we go, thought Nat.

12.

Arthur had put up a notice in the window in his neat Roman capitals, done on a sheet of pink A3 with a green marker pen, both bought especially for this purpose. The notice read 'PRIVATE PARTY – EVERYONE WELCOME'. Dommie had thought that you didn't want to have just anyone wandering in. You could get people who wanted to smash the place up. But Duncan thought they probably wouldn't want to come into a shop called the Big Gay Bookshop for a party. He did put the kibosh on Arthur's suggestion that the invitations read 'You Can't Get Aids Off A Glass Or Six Of Wine'.

'Who's coming from your house?' Duncan said.

'Tony and Tim said definitely,' Arthur said. 'There's a new boy who said he might – he's in room that Frenchman used to be in. Kevin said he might, but he's got to be up early mixing marge wi' butter, whatever that means.'

'I don't know why you stick it there,' Duncan said. 'How long's it been?'

'Three years now,' Arthur said. 'I've been working here seven.'

'Seven years,' Duncan said. 'If they get their way and close us down, we can say we gave it a good go. Bugger this, I'm going to have a glass of wine before anyone comes.'

'They're not going to close us down,' Arthur said. 'We're going to win this one. They're not going to have us up for selling dirty books when exhibit A is *The Garden King* and exhibit B is summat about Greek vases. They're honestly not.'

'Oh, I don't know,' Duncan said. 'I can always go back to working at the dole office, I suppose. It's just you I worry about – I mean, it's not like you've got any talents or anything.'

'Oh, don't you worry about me,' Arthur said, smiling and running his hands through his hair. 'I'll go back to that rich bloke who lived off King's Road, I'll be a kept boy.'

'That rich bloke who never stopped ringing, you mean?' Duncan said. 'Is that Dommie with the ice?'

But it was only the Greek sandwich-maker from over the road and his son. He paused outside the shop window, as he sometimes did on his way to his van at the end of the day, and said something to the son that they fortunately couldn't hear. He looked in with an expression of disgust; his eyes might have caught theirs, but he was standing in the light and them in the dark. The son looked in too, even raising his hands to shadow his eyes. He said something contemptuous to his dad, and they both laughed. From across the road, locking the door of their sandwich shop, came the black dogsbody whose name they couldn't remember. The Greek sandwich-maker swore at him, and held out his hand; the dogsbody dropped the keys into his palm, raised his hand weakly in farewell, and they went in their separate directions. It had been seven years since Arthur or Duncan had said anything to any of them, though they worked directly opposite.

'And music,' Arthur said. 'I've got a pile of cassettes here, but I don't know what any of them are. I thought we'd play something different to usual stuff we play during the day – I'm sick to death of Sade and Lloyd Cole and the Commotions. I don't know whether any of it's any good.'

'Where did you get it from?' Duncan said. Arthur was just slotting a tape into the shop's ghetto-blaster.

'Here you go,' he said, and the music started. They had both expected party music, but it was classical music, an orchestral piece; a sort of Toytown march with frills and trills and perky Toytown cheerfulness. 'What's this, then?'

But then it changed; a waltz started, and it was rather nice. 'I know this,' Duncan said. 'Leave it on.' Arthur thought he knew it too, and proved it by starting to sing along. But he didn't know what it was. How could you know a piece of music without

440

knowing what it was? The waltz continued, having come into their lives separately, without their judging it or deciding it or making any kind of move towards it, and they found they knew it all. 'I like this old stuff, really,' one of them said, and the other one even started moving his arms and feet as if in a one-man Viennese dance. It caught the ear, and the ear had already assented to it. It had spread from player to ear, from music to memory, and passed on and on, through fashion and neglect making its way in the world. It was so easy to pass on a piece of music, like a benevolent contagion, without requiring persuasion or argument. 'It's the *Emperor Waltz*,' Dommie somehow knew and told them as soon as she came in and found Duncan and Arthur waltzing together, Arthur's head reclining in a beautifully ballroom gesture. 'We're not having this at the party, surely.'

'Only for the auction,' Duncan said. 'It'll make them feel rich and classy.' But he was not as cynical as he made himself sound. It was sad when the *Emperor Waltz* came to an end. It carried on for a while as Duncan went round, setting out glasses; continued in his head as he hummed its best bits. 'I'm really quite nervous about the speech,' he said to Arthur as he went round. 'And the auction. I think I'll have a drink before anyone gets here.' In his head was the *Emperor Waltz*. He had no idea where he had first heard it, and how it had come to be so familiar to him. It seemed as if he heard it every day, as if from just over the road.

'And here I am,' Sir Angus Wilson said, coming in through the door with his charming friend Tony behind, carrying all the bags. 'Here I am, writer of all those big gay books, and the party can begin. Is there such a thing as a very small – a very small – glass of white wine?'

13.

'"My old mother! And another! They both said – I always, always should ..."' Nat bawled, the chorus of an old music-hall song. He was standing on the counter, hanging onto a double-bass player, who had for some reason come with his instrument and hauled it up onto the counter too, slapping and plucking it in generalized accompaniment to Nat's performance. Somewhere at the back of the heaving mass a couple of people were joining in, or were they just cheering? Anyway, Nat, who had lost his trousers somewhere along the way, did a shapely high kick or two. It was lucky he had a glamorous pair of new white boxer shorts on, and he had such good legs, everyone always said. Where was the capercaillie that usually stood here? There it was, safely on top of the lesbian bookcase.

'Look at all these people!' Duncan said. He wasn't quite clear who to. 'I can't believe I'm going to have to make a speech to them. And conduct an auction. I've never conducted an auction. I'm terrified.'

'So just – fuck off,' Maggi Hambling was saying. 'It's perfectly simple, darling. They just have to be told – very, very firmly – just fuck off, darling.'

'Where did you get that from?' the girl whose name hadn't been caught said. She couldn't gesture, as she was pressed so tightly against Maggi Hambling, but she meant the can of Special Brew being held somewhere above shoulder height.

'Brought it. Where's your drink? Your glass?'

The girl nodded downwards; there was a half-full bottle of red wine between her breasts. 'That's my glass. Thought I'd pick it up and hang on to it,' she said.

'Excellent idea.'

The man in the dinner jacket and bow-tie had seemed quite nice, and had pointed out to George that there seemed to be a bit of space over there by the bookcase that read TRAVEL on top. He'd said this after a dyke had jogged George's elbow and spilt white wine down his new shirt for the third time. George hadn't been quite sure that he would come. It was only that the new boy on the flight last week had mentioned it, and George had said he'd come along, since they were both laying off in London that day.

442

They'd met outside the tube, and almost the second they'd entered the room, the new boy had gone to get a drink and had never come back. His name was Dmitrios, but he'd said to call him Mike. This man was rather older than George usually went for, and he wasn't quite sure how they had got into conversation anyway, but he looked very distinguished in his dinner jacket. George followed him as he continued, saying, 'Excuse me – excuse me – so sorry – just making my way through – if you don't mind,' and they reached the other side in five minutes. Unfortunately, the space by the travel bookcase was illusionary: it had been created by a very drunk man who had slumped to the floor and was reading a book about Syria, George observed.

'That's nearly a coincidence,' George said. 'My family are from Cyprus, which is not far from Syria.'

'What did you say?' the man in the dinner jacket said. 'I didn't catch what you said.'

'Cyprus,' George said. 'Not far from Syria. That's where my family comes from.'

'Where what comes from?'

'My family.'

'No, I meant where were you talking about?'

'Oh, sorry, I was saying Syria, that's where my family doesn't come from, we come from Cyprus.'

The man giggled, raising the back of his hand to his mouth. 'I'm ever so tiddly,' he said. 'Have you got a friend?'

'Oh, yes, lots of friends,' George said. 'But there's always room for one more.'

'Excuse me,' the dyke said behind him, in an accusing way. She and her fat girlfriend had followed them over from the other side of the room, perhaps also thinking that there was space here. She craned over, and observed the drunk man on the floor. 'Get him to stand up, there's not room. For Christ's sake.' She turned in a disappointed way, nudging George's elbow, which spilt white wine down his new shirt for the fourth time, or possibly only the third.

'Really,' Christopher was saying to Olivia Tempest, the disgruntled lady novelist, 'anal sex was always very important to me. From almost the first, you might say.'

'I'm delighted to hear it,' Olivia Tempest was saying bravely. 'I don't know whether you've read all my books. You'd see if you did that I was really the first – almost the very first – to ...'

Duncan was talking to a man he was not quite sure he knew. It seemed possible.

'And then my father died, and he left me half the house and his money, though it was a really close thing, my aunts, they tried to keep it from me and keep it to themselves, and I thought, I know what I really want to do, I want to open a bookshop. Have you ever been to my bookshop?' Duncan said.

'I'm in it now,' the gentleman who was a friend of Christopher's said, smiling. Was he a friend of Christopher's? Or had Duncan confused something here? Christopher had introduced him, certainly. But had he met him only ten seconds before?

'Oh, I know,' Duncan said, beating the man gently on his breastbone.'But I meant before.'

'Once or twice,' the man said. They were somewhere in the middle of the room. There was such a crush! Duncan was glad he'd thought to put Paul's pheasant on top of a bookcase and his Bauhaus teapot in a locked drawer, or they would have been crushed or stolen or anything could have happened. Poor Paul! He would have loved to be here tonight, raising money for the bookshop that was probably about to close down. Duncan and this man were jammed together, their smiling faces only an inch apart. Duncan hoped he didn't have bad breath from the piece of celery and hummus he'd eaten earlier. That was the last of any food he'd seen, hours before. He hadn't recognized this man when Christopher introduced him, and now he couldn't remember his name – Raymond, or Randy, or Raphael, or Rodrigo – but Christopher's introduction had had something confidential about it, a kind of handing over of precious goods, as if the name would mean a great deal to Duncan. 'This is Raymond,' he'd said – or Randy, or Raphael – and off he'd gone, leaving Duncan to do his important task.

'Where do you live?' Duncan said.

'Victoria,' the man said. 'I've only just moved in.'

'No one lives in Victoria,' Duncan said. 'Victoria! That's just a bus station and a railway station and three theatres, or two, I forget. It's either Pimlico or Belgravia.'

'I don't believe in Belgravia,' the man said. 'I don't think you say you live in Belgravia, do you?'

'Well, I don't,' Duncan said. 'I never say that. Because I live in Notting Hill, you fool. Do you know, I'm convinced I'm going to kiss you. I don't know why! I just think it's going to happen, like looking up at clouds and saying those are rainclouds, it's going to rain today, that's what it's like.'

'I see,' the man said, not kissing Duncan, but he was amused.

'I'm so sorry. I'm just so nervous,' Duncan said. 'It's this speech I'm going to have to make, you see.'

'You need another drink,' the man said. He was positively grinning; his brilliant teeth shone in his dark face.

'Oh, how kind. What lovely manners. Where are my manners? Where do you live?' Duncan said, to improve the general tone of his thoughts.

'Victoria,' the man said, smiling. 'But I used to live in Chelsea.'

'Oh, I see,' Duncan said, realizing why Christopher had handed the man over with such ceremony. He wondered why Christopher knew such a plutocrat, if he knew him. And how much this millionaire would be prepared to sign a cheque for and if he had a boyfriend and whether it was the hummus after all that was keeping him from kissing Duncan. The hummus! Duncan thought, accepting another drink. The hummus!

The party had poured in every possible direction. The sash window at the back had been pushed up, and three boys were sitting on the ledge with their legs dangling out, passing a bottle of vodka one to another and a spliff, by the smell of it. The door upstairs to the stock room was open, and people were spilling up the stairs. Arthur, passing a bottle of cider forward, hoped there was nothing to steal up there, but then reassured himself that, apart from unopened boxes, there was nothing but a lot of copies of that unsaleable novel, and they were welcome to steal that. Against the far wall two men, either both over six foot seven in height, or both standing on a pile of lesbian magazines, were kissing furiously; underneath them, Paul Bailey was casting up amused looks, half listening to a fan telling him how much he'd loved his last book. People were drinking on the pavement, too; the party was so full that anyone who arrived late, or who went out to the off-licence to pick up some more to drink, found themselves carrying on outside, drinking from bottles and cans.

'I really don't give a fuck any more,' Freddie Sempill was saying on the pavement outside. 'Really, not one fuck. I've thought about it and I really don't give a fuck.'

'About what?' the man was saying. He had introduced himself as Rupert – he was a publisher's rep, he had said, but he thought he had a lovely relationship with the shop, so he'd come to show support. Rupert had come, he explained confidentially, in a jacket and tie; the jacket, a brilliant mauve, was somewhere inside – he'd hung it on a hook, and that was the last he'd seen of it. 'What do you not give a fuck about?'

'About any fucking thing,' Freddie Sempill was saying. He knew he looked ill. He'd been through so many scares now, and he was gaunt and yellow and frail. There was, too, the small matter of the sarcomas all over his neck and hands. You got to recognize the Aids-visitor gaze: the way that their eyes would lock onto yours and not wander to the neck, to the hands; the way that their smile would stick and not falter, the way they would hold your hand for an extra second on parting. He was visited, at his weak times, by men called Buddies. They were OK. But the whole world looked at him like men thinking of volunteering as a Buddy.

446

Rupert looked at him and started to speak. At first it was difficult for Freddie Sempill to understand all of the words. Then he wondered whether his brain had switched off for a moment and come back again in five minutes. How old was he? He could not think for a moment, then he remembered the year he was born, and the year they were in, which was nineteen eighty-six – or -seven. Or -eight.

'What year is this?' he said to Rupert.

But it came out wrong, and perhaps it was only inside his head. He took a big gulp of what was in the glass in his hand, which was white wine, and then everything that Rupert had been saying came to him out of sequence, all at once.

And Rupert had had a wife and three children, well, he still had three children but the wife was detached. 'I had an important relationship with a guy at university, I was at Christ Church, this was back in the sixties, nearly twenty years ago, and then after university ...' and then it was gone again. Freddie Sempill concentrated and then the man, whose name was Rupert, was telling not just him but a small and very tidy Indian gentleman, looking up and nodding, about the civilized way that his marriage had come to an end. 'I used to own a suitcase shop opposite,' Rupert said, with an Indian accent, but surely he was a publisher's rep. Freddie Sempill looked firmly from one to another and realized it was the Indian gentleman who was talking and explaining that he had come in from Tooting with his wife's best wishes, and that he – no, the other one, the English one – had married a woman after Oxford hoping for the best, and it had been for ten years or even twelve, but one of the things was meeting Duncan and coming to this bookshop. The two of them looked at Freddie Sempill, and he realized, swaying backwards and forwards, that it was him who had said 'Washing the car – it's just so ...' He had no idea what he was about to add to that. They were waiting for him to say something. The boy Rupert, the man, the father rather, he had said everything about his life. Freddie Sempill understood he was talking again, and in embarrassment raised his half-empty glass to his mouth. But it was fully empty. He tipped it up against his mouth; his head leant backwards; a force seemed to be pulling at him. He felt almost a little dizzy as his gaze left the party and swept up towards the summer night sky, which was blue and then black and then starry and then black.

'Someone's fallen over outside,' Tony said to Arthur, carrying two glasses. Arthur was sitting at the bottom of the stairs, doing an impersonation of Duncan losing his temper with an inept shoplifter. He was doing it for the benefit of Dommie, who had seen it before. 'Have you seen Tim? He said he was going upstairs.'

'I don't know,' Arthur said. 'Aren't you hot in all that?'

'It's like a little black dress, girlfriend,' Tony said, gesturing downwards at his leather jacket, his leather trousers and – some acceptance of the heat – a white vest. Dommie looked at him narrowly, inspecting the humour of queens rather than their lamentable wardrobes. 'It's fabulous, it's classic, it's understated. Some queen's keeled over outside with the heat.'

'Who is it?' Arthur said. 'Dommie, did you see?'

'No, I didn't, honey,' Dommie said. 'Here's Francis King. Who's fainted, Mr King?'

'Hm?' the distinguished novelist said, giving Dommie the once-over in her little black dress – really a purple cocktail dress, which might have been from Antony Price. He went onwards without explaining further.

'I'm taking this up to Tim,' Tony said. 'He'll be ever so pleased I found it.'

'Don't do anything I wouldn't do,' Arthur said.

'That doesn't leave much, girlfriend,' Tony said. 'See you later.'

'Who was that?' Dommie said, and Arthur explained about his housemates.

Gervase was here, and he knew Stephen; they were discussing the case. Just by them, on the counter, a man in his underpants had his arm round a double-bass player, swaying dangerously to and fro. The man in his underpants was singing very raucously, to what Stephen recognized as the march in the Tchaikovsky *Pathétique* symphony.

'"Why should we go to Pariiiis/When I'd much rather stay at home!"'

'Who's that man in the dress?' Gervase said.

'No idea,' Stephen said. 'He hasn't made much effort, has he? But the case.'

'I shouldn't have thought there was any question about it,' Gervase said. 'It's a perfectly absurd case for them to bring. There's no question of any of the books they seized being thought obscene. It'll be thrown out before we're halfway through.'

'Astonishing,' Stephen said. 'What were the police thinking of?'

'Well, it's not my business,' Gervase said, 'but the assistant – Arthur, he's called – said that a policeman came in a week before the raid and asked for five thousand pounds to leave them alone. Unfortunately …'

'Don't tell me,' Stephen said. 'It always happens, I believe. The upright young man told him to bugger off.'

'Either that or they bribe them, then think twice later. I know. Maddening. What one would give for just one gentleman in the porn trade who said, Yes, of course, Officer, come back tomorrow, and then had fixed up the joint with tape recorders.'

'Oh, they're wise to that one. You'd quickly find your place of meeting being changed at short notice, for some very good reason. Ow!'

'Sorry, sorry, sorry,' Nat said, bending down and giving Stephen a kiss on the top of his head, then, as he turned his face upwards, a big smacker on the lips. 'I always do that,' Nat explained, straightening up and turning to the double-bass player. 'I'm forever kicking people in the face by accident when I've had a dry sherry or two.'

'Oh, he'll be fine,' Arthur said outside. They had propped

Freddie Sempill up against the shop window and given him a glass of water.

'He doesn't look fine,' the man said. 'He really doesn't look fine, Arthur.'

Arthur hadn't recognized him. It was Rupert, the publisher's rep. 'He's fine,' Arthur said. 'Well, he's no worse than usual tonight. Just let him sit here.'

The party outside had gathered, gazed, concentrated, and was now dispersing, back to their drinks. At first, five years ago, there had been a natural habit of looking away from anyone who looked as Freddie Sempill looked. Probably that habit was still common in the rest of the world who, if they were forced to turn to a Freddie Sempill, would be apt to say to him stuff like 'But do you know who you caught it from?' and 'How long do the doctors think you have?' and other sensitive things. In this crowd, you rationally did not look away. You looked at the person as if he were a person, which of course he was. But then you looked away again in a relaxed and ordinary way. The temptation was to turn away and then turn back, one second later, for another appalled look at whatever it had been. But this crowd had had plenty of practice, and they looked away in a sociable, incurious, generally friendly way that had no specifics in it. Then the community spirit was spoilt by Simon, Christopher's boyfriend, coming up and laying a hand on his elbow and saying, with something very like enjoyment, 'Is that Freddie Sempill? I haven't seen him in three years. Is that really him? Jesus Christ.'

'Look,' Nat said, still standing on the shop counter, 'here's Duncan.'

Duncan had been coming through the party for ten minutes now, accepting congratulations and good wishes, and pushing through the crowd where he could. He didn't believe that it could grow any larger now, and the party had been going for an hour. He believed that, from this point, it could only grow argumentative, tearful, bad-tempered. They had been quite enjoying the crush. Soon there would be a shortage of drink, and people would start complaining about it. This was the point, or possibly a little after that point, of maximum goodwill towards the bookshop, and he ought to make his speech and conduct the auction now.

'Help me up,' Duncan said to Nat. He found himself poised between his old friend Nat, standing in his underpants, and rather a plump double-bass player. How did he know he was a double-bass player? Ah, that would be because the man was standing with a double bass on the counter. 'Is he going to get down?' Duncan said. 'I don't know that there's room up here for all four of us.'

Nat burst out laughing. 'Oh, that's good. Her name's Susan, he says – that thing he's holding. I don't know why she's come, though.'

'She's come because she used to bring – she used to bring – the teas – she used to bring—' Duncan started. It was all terribly funny; the best joke he would ever invent or make. But he was choking with laughter, and he was swaying backwards and forwards in quite an alarming way, up there on the shop counter. There was a great gust of *Wooooo* beneath him, and he saw the faces turning upwards in comedy or alarm. Oh, he would be fine. He just needed to get his balance.

'I was going to ask my friend here to get down so there'd be room on the counter for you, and then I was going to get down after,' Nat said. 'But thinking about it, I think we're both going to stay up here, if that's all right. I don't know where he'd put his giant instrument, anyway.'

Duncan was overcome for a moment with love for Nat. He was the nicest person he knew. How long had he known him? He had no idea. Nat with his nice blond curly hair and his way of saying 'Honestly' and the way he had of never reading a book and never saying anything about his job, but always wanting to listen to gossip and always saying funny things like, I don't know where he's going to put his instrument. He was so nice. The nicest, nicest person he knew.

451

'Nat,' Duncan said, his hand on Nat's shoulder to balance. 'How long is it we've known each other?'

'We were at school together, you silly cow,' Nat said. 'I taught you how to smoke – *behind the bicycle sheds*. Honestly.'

'I don't remember the bicycle sheds,' Duncan said.

'It's a figure of speech,' Nat said. 'I think it was actually on the bus home, on the upper deck, among other places.'

'I've known this one for *ever*,' Duncan said, turning to the double-bass player, still slapping away joyously. Sweat was gleaming on his face with the effort, and his head jerking up and down as if his neck had no bones left in it. 'He wasn't at school with us, too?' he said, turning back.

'I've only just met him this evening,' Nat said. 'I don't know who he is. I thought you were going to make a speech.'

'Oh, yes,' Duncan said. He really started to feel rather drunk.

14.

'Ladies and – ladies and – ladies and gentlemen,' Duncan began. 'They can't hear me, Nat. How do I get them to shut up and listen?'

'Quiet, please,' Nat said. 'Quiet, please. No, it doesn't seem to work.' He raised his hands to his face like a megaphone, and bellowed. Duncan had a bright idea; he took the keys from his pocket, and dropping them into his empty glass, started jangling them. The ringing noise was quite successful; at any rate, people in the front half of the shop quietened down, though not so much on the pavement or at the back.

'Hello, everybody,' Duncan said.

'He's going to make a speech,' Nat said. 'I'm not.'

There was a great gale of laughter, as at anything not actually tragic spoken at a fundraising audience.

'No,' Duncan said. 'He's *not*. Now. Where was it? I know it was here somewhere.'

'Find your speech *before* you ask for quiet,' a cross dyke in tweeds called. 'That would be a good thing.'

'Why?' Duncan said. 'Are you in a hurry or something?' The dyke started to make some principled objection – she got as far as saying 'Secondly' before those around her told her to pipe down. 'Now. I don't know what I was going to say but I can say it anyway, I believe. It was seven years ago I opened this bookshop and it was with the benefit of some money I came into. No one had ever opened a bookshop for gay people. There are bookshops for socialists and bookshops for French people and bookshops for women—'

'Yeah!' the dykes at the other end of the room shouted.

'Yes, hurrah to that,' Duncan said. 'We're not a bookshop just for women, but hurrah to that, anyway. And bookshops for music and bookshops for art and bookshops for soldiers and – and – and—'

'Is there much more of this?' Arthur called out.

'You listen patiently,' Duncan said, 'or you'll be on the dole in the morning. So there were lots of bookshops for all sorts of people but not a bookshop for gay people. And the one thing we all know gay people really want to do is ...' He made a big upward gesture with his arms, and everyone near him shouted, 'READ!'

Apart from Nat, who said, 'Screw,' apparently sincerely intended, since he covered his face with his hands, and Andrew, who was standing underneath, might have called out, 'Ferment the working-class revolution,' or possibly 'foment', and obviously didn't get that it was meant as a joke. Andrew had come wearing a dress and lipstick, but not having shaved his beard off. Now he was very drunk, like everyone, but drunk in a dress with his lipstick smeared. Duncan averted his eyes as from a road accident, as the rest of the party had been doing.

'Yes, well,' Duncan said. 'So it's thanks to Dommie, my sister, and Arthur, who turned up on the first day or maybe even a little bit before that and demanded a job. It's been fantastic.

There are other people I want to thank too, but let me just say this once. Let me just say this. I want to thank you all by name but it would take too long. So let me just say this once.'

'Just say it once,' a wit called out.

'Let me just say this once,' Duncan said.

'Oh, get on with it,' Dommie called, not bad-humouredly.

'Those people I want to thank – *you know who you are.* And then there are lots of people who aren't with us any more. I wish they could have been here today. I really wish that. But we're not here to celebrate the bookshop. We're here because nearly a year ago some policemen came in and started inspecting our stock. And then they came back, wearing gloves in case our stock might infect them or something, and they took a lot of it away. And now we're being prosecuted for selling porn, which it isn't, but never mind that. They just want to wear us down and get through what little money we've got, and then we'll close down and that'll be that. It's because we didn't – Arthur didn't, thank you, Arthur – Arthur didn't hand over five thousand pounds as a bribe to the first policemen, the ones who came in without gloves and pretended to be customers.

'I hope they didn't get Aids, anyway.'

'I hope they *did*,' Sir Angus said, in his famous tones, from the bottom of the staircase. Quite a lot of people had thought of saying it, but only Sir Angus, perhaps, could.

'Yes, well,' Duncan went on. 'The thing is, about those books, the ones they took away. Loads of people have come and bought books from here in the last seven years, and all of them, they've spread through the world, they've gone out like little candles. Sometimes someone on their own has read the book they bought, and thought, I'll lend that to my friend John. Or sometimes they've thought I've got to stop being so alone, I'll go out and I'll try to meet people like me. I'll stop being so ashamed. And sometimes they've just loved a novel and handed it to their mum or their best friend, and said, You'll love this, and the mum or the best friend, they have, and they've lent it on rather than give it back.

'Books are like that. They go into the world. They're like us. We've got to go into the world. We've got to go even though there aren't many of us and even though most of the world hates us and would put us in gaol and wants us to die of this disease. A book can go out into the world. It's like a ten-pound note, it's like a virus, it's like an idea, it's like a brilliant joke, it's like a tune, it goes from one person to another. It never stops. It goes out into the world and and it changes things a little bit even if people hate it, they don't want it, they want to go and read something better or they start thinking that it's all wrong, I'm not going to agree with any of that, and they talk to someone about what they think, and that other person listens. Do you see what I'm saying?'

He was losing his audience, he could see: they were turning to each other and speaking with low amusement. Nat and the man playing the double bass had their hands on his arms, and were holding him upright. It was so hot in here. He had forgotten how he got onto this part of his speech, and then suddenly remembered that in his jacket pocket he had the speech he had written, short and witty and full of good points. He had a feeling that he had covered some of those points, but had brought other things into the discussion that he'd only just thought of. It was too late now, surely, to reach into his jacket pocket and get out the notes and start making his speech again. Gays would start shouting, 'You've already done this bit.' What was it he'd been talking about? But then, as if by a miracle, he remembered why he'd started talking about books changing the world, mind by shining mind, and he came back. Had it been a long silence?

'The thing is, people,' Duncan said, 'the thing is that those books the policemen took away – they're the only books ever that didn't do anything, that just left here and fell to the ground. No one's ever going to engage with those books. No one's ever going to have their mind changed by those books, the physical books and what's in them. They're just Exhibit A, and that's no way to treat my lovely books. So these people – they can't be allowed to get away with it. They can't. We're a bit hard up, what with all the loss of stock and the lawyers' fees, and we're going to be more hard up if things don't go our way, which they might not. So Arthur and I and Dommie too, my sister who's been so great the last seven years, we thought we'd have an auction of wonderful donated lots from lots of wonderful people. Please give generously. Where's that box? There's two boxes, Arthur. Just the first one for the moment.'

He swayed and, for a second, thought he was going to be sick onto the heads of the people below him. Then he was all right. Life, he thought, was like that, as the crowd saw that he'd finished with what must be considered a speech, though in a not very decisive way, and parts of it began to applaud uncertainly. Life was like that: thinking you were going to be sick on someone's head, then realizing you weren't, that you were OK really. Down there, a box was being passed over the heads of half a dozen people from where it had been safely stowed. His eye caught the eye of the rich man, the one who had lived in Chelsea and now lived in Victoria. The man looked, of all things, immensely full of pride – personal pride, as if he'd had every faith in Duncan to get through his speech without falling off the counter. Duncan realized who the man must be. He must be the man who had once, years before, picked up Arthur in the shop and taken him back to his great big four-storey house off the King's Road. His name, he'd said, was Rupert. It was Randy. It was Rudolph. It was Raymond. No, it wasn't Rupert – that was the name of the publisher's rep he'd had just that one time in the stock room, the one Duncan thought he'd seen tonight, actually. This one's name was Raphael. It was Rufus. Then the man looked around, as if nervous in case anyone might glimpse him, and gave Duncan an immense smile. Another sort of man, Duncan felt, would have given him a thumbs-up, but for Ronnie, that nice smile

456

was enough. You could see him encouraging his staff in the City with a smile.

Oh, yes. That was his name. His name was Ronnie.

15.

Annunziata had managed to finish all her shopping for Mr Hayward's Christmas the day before Christmas Eve. That was a blessing. He would only be on his own on Christmas Day and the day after that, on his own and with his friend who was coming. She liked working for Mr Hayward. He was thoughtful and had said, as he always said, that she need not come after the twenty-third, that he would certainly be able to manage on his own for four or five days. But Annunziata was not so certain about that. She had worked for Mr Hayward for eight years now. She had worked for him when he lived on the other side of Sloane Square, in another white house, very much like this one, and she had come with him when he had moved. She had never left him on his own for as much as four days without arranging for someone else to come and help him out.

She had bought vegetables, potatoes and root vegetables, and had peeled and prepared them all. She looked up, from the basement of the house in Chester Terrace, at the grey weather and the occasional passer-by. But there were not very many people passing by. This was a very quiet neighbourhood normally, one of the best in London, she knew, but now at Christmas there was nobody at home. They had all gone away, all of Mr Hayward's neighbours. To the country, Mr Hayward had explained. But he was not going away this year. The carrots and potatoes and parsnips were peeled and placed in a dish and were now roasting; the smell of the garlic and the thyme was very good in the warm kitchen. That could be taken out and left for Mr Hayward to heat up tomorrow. Then there were the Brussels sprouts, only a very few; Mr Hayward had said that he did not like them, but you had to have them. And then there was the black fruit pudding, a Christmas pudding it was called. Annunziata had taken advice about that from Mr Hayward's mother, and had bought one from Waitrose – not the luxury one, Mrs Hayward had said, but only the ordinary one; it was cheaper but better. Annunziata had the utmost respect for Mrs Hayward, and her beautiful though quite frightening manners. The pudding, too, Annunziata was cooking, in a pan of water, for Mr Hayward to heat up tomorrow in the microwave. Brandy was involved in its preparation, Annunziata remembered, but Mr Hayward could see to that himself. And the duck's skin had been pierced, and she had poured boiling water over it, and the fat had run out from under the skin. Now it was only for Mr Hayward to put it in the oven at the right time, and take it out at the right time, and pour over the delicious sauce she had made for it, out of orange, and cornflour, and onion and carrot and celery, and the roasted wings of the bird, and all manner of spices. She was sure that there was something she had forgotten. It would come to her in the middle of her own Christmas morning, when there was nothing to be done.

She had bought a present for Mr Hayward, too; a small china box for sweets, a very beautiful box that she was sure he would love. He had given her a hundred pounds as a present, but she was sure, too, that he had bought her a proper present as well as the money, as he had last year. She was almost sure it was waiting in the hallway, on the little table, by the photograph of Mr Hayward's mother.

This year, Mr Hayward was having his friend for Christmas. He was a new friend. He was a very nice man, too. Mr Hayward had had different friends over the years. One had been Italian; another had been Irish. The Irishman had lasted for two years. He had not been so nice. He had accused Annunziata of having taken a ring of his from the bedside table, in front of Mr Hayward and Mr Hayward's friend Angela, and someone else, whom Annunziata could not remember. It had been while Annunziata was carrying in the soup for their supper on a Friday night, one of Mr Hayward's supper parties. The Irishman had said it mildly, as if he were saying nothing so very much, but he had said that she had stolen his valuable ring, and that she must be sacked. Mr Hayward had gone very quiet and then, when Annunziata had left the room without saying anything, had followed her into the kitchen and told her that he knew that she had not done anything of the sort, and that this was the last evening that the Irishman would spend in his house. Of course Annunziata had not thought that Mr Hayward would sack her, or anything of the sort, but she had not thought that he would so promptly and quickly decide that he would rather have Annunziata than the Irishman. He had worked in the same sort of business that Mr Hayward did, to do with money, in the City of London. Six months later, Mr Hayward had said to her that he had come across Frank, the Irishman, in the course of his work again, and he had noticed that he was wearing the ring he had said had been stolen by Annunziata. Had anything been said between them? Mr Hayward was not the sort of person to create a scene, she knew. So that was all for the best, he had said, not dabbling in people who pretended to steal their own rings. Four months after that, he had introduced Annunziata to his new friend. But the new friend was quite a different sort of person; an educated person, the owner of a bookshop.

There was a noise at the top of the steps that led down to the basement, which was called the area. The little iron gate creaked open, and a woman's, then a child's voice was heard. Annunziata peered up from where she was cutting little crosses in the bottom of the Brussels sprouts. It was a pair of plump legs, in black stockings with beautifully shiny black shoes, like only English-women knew how to wear, and what proved to be a black coat. She was ushering down the steps a very pretty little girl, in an old-fashioned sage-green coat with white piping, white woollen gloves, scarf, hat and stockings, and a blue china brooch on the lapel. Both the lady and the little girl were carrying packages in

459

festive paper. They were not people that Annunziata recognized, or was expecting, and she was always cautious on Mr Hayward's behalf, but they were not people to worry about, she could see that. It was the way the mother was concentrating, with great pleasure, on her little girl, who was talking steadily.

'. . . and then he's going to come, I know he is, but how does he get round to everyone – I mean, everyone in the whole world, everyone? And does he get a glass of sherry from everyone, does he? Mummy?'

Annunziata opened the door to the area, wiping her hands on her apron.

'Do be quiet, Celia, just for one moment,' the lady said. But she said it kindly. The little girl had no shyness at all, but gazed at Annunziata with a lot of interest, her hands clasped together in a fist at her chest, as if in supplication. She was dark, and might almost be Italian. 'You must be Annunziata,' she went on. 'I'm Dommie – Duncan's sister. And this is Celia. Do shut up, Celia – no one's interested in the slightest. You know, Ronnie's boyfriend, though he's getting too old to be anyone's boyfriend. I've heard so much about you from Ronnie.'

'Oh! How nice!' Annunziata said. It was nice that the lady did not tell her how much Mr Hayward praised her or depended on her, or anything of the sort that English people so often said. It was absurd for them to say that when she knew how much Mr Hayward admired her or depended on her, much better than they could. 'It is so cold – would you come in for a moment? I'm afraid I must continue to prepare the ...' She waved at the piles of food in the kitchen.

'Well, just for a moment,' the lady said. 'Goodness, that smells delicious. We've just come to drop in Duncan's present and Ronnie's, too.'

'I go to school now,' the little girl said. 'I'm in the littlest class, but I can read and I'm very good at my times tables. My name's Celia. My best friend's name is—'

'I'm so sorry about my daughter,' the lady said. 'She never, ever shuts up. I wish I knew how it was done, having one of those children who never say a word.'

'That's lovely!' Annunziata said, meaning it. 'And you've brought some presents? You should have come when Mr Hayward is here – I don't know where he's left presents for you.'

'Oh, you know,' the lady said, 'I don't think we'd expect that at all – it was just a thought of Celia's, and they're really nothing, our presents.'

'I've done a picture,' Celia confided. 'I did a picture at school, in class, and everyone voted for it to be their favourite, and it got a gold star, and it's of Uncle Ronnie and Uncle Duncan and Mummy and me on Box Hill and the squirrel we saw, and that lorry on the way back. Whoosh, bang, smash. It's framed – Mummy got the man to frame it.'

'It's for my brother,' the lady said. 'I wouldn't dare to give Mr Hayward anything – I know how beautiful his house is – but my brother doesn't really mind about what goes on his walls, so I thought Celia's prize-winning picture. I got him –' she mouthed it speechlessly '– a *proper present*. And one for Ronnie too. I hope he likes it. Just a tie, though, and some hideous cufflinks that Celia identified, he doesn't have to wear them. *Now* we'll be off, Celia. No, Celia, don't start taking your coat off now – really, Celia, no, that's too bad. Button up – that's right – lovely to have met you, I've heard so much – and now *off* we go. Say goodbye, Celia.'

'Father Christmas isn't going to bring me a pony,' Celia said, turning round at the foot of the area steps, 'but I really don't mind, it's quite all right.'

Annunziata smiled to herself as she watched them go. And now it seemed to her that Mr Hayward's friend was quite all right. Because he had a sister and a niece in a beautiful sage-green coat with white piping. She remembered the day that Mr Hayward had gone to Box Hill: it had been in August,

461

and she had made up a picnic basket for them, including some food that a little girl would like, Mr Hayward had specified. She had not thought about it since, or wondered who the others on the picnic had been. And now it was nearly time for her to start thinking about her own Christmas. Like a letter written on tracing paper over another letter, she thought of her own preparations while her preparations for Mr Hayward were only just reaching their conclusion. Pina, her sister, was coming over to her house in Elephant and Castle from Palmers Green, with her two boys and her husband Massimo, and their brother Salvatore would be coming too; they would all be coming tonight, a real Sicilian Christmas, and there would be a beautiful big fish at the centre, because not everyone liked *anguilla*. What was *anguilla* in English? Annunziata smiled at the idea of giving it to Mr Hayward. And almond cakes and a great *sformato* of vegetables that Pina was already in her house making. And the boys would have Christmas crackers, since they were getting so English, and Salvo would smoke his cigar in the garden and tell them about life in Milton Keynes; and there would be games after dinner and present-opening, and then they would go to Mass together. Perhaps Graziana would play the piano, as she used to, so beautifully; there was a nice book of English Christmas carols, and everyone liked to hear Annunziata's daughter play so well. She did not think Graziana played the piano so very much these days, in the flat she shared with two other girls in Kentish Town.

It was so nice, them all being in England together; they would raise a glass in memory of Mamma and Papa, together again now, and Papa dead in his bed two years ago, twenty years after poor Mamma. Sometimes Annunziata wondered if she would ever see Acireale again, now that she had no family there apart from cousins; her Sicily was in Palmers Green and Milton Keynes now. Tomorrow, if Graziana did not play Christmas carols, Salvatore and Giuseppe, her husband, would sing a couple of songs; they would sing 'Volare' and they would sing 'Ciuri, ciuri, ciuri di tuttu l'annu'. Annunziata washed and dried her hands; she switched off the radio; she covered the dishes with clingfilm, leaving them on top of the work surface; she washed her hands again; she gave the sink a final wipe; she looked over the kitchen, and counted off her last few tasks on the fingers of her left hand. She took her Christmas card and her little present for Mr Hayward out of her handbag – the handbag had been Mr Hayward's present two years ago, now she thought of it. She put on her coat, set the alarm, and left the house, locking the door behind her. It was half past twelve, and plenty of time to get home and prepare her own Christmas feast. It was a shame that she had not seen Mr Hayward this morning. He was upstairs, asleep in bed, or not asleep, but in bed, and with his friend. But Mr Hayward was a nice man. He worked so hard most of the time that he was allowed to sleep in late, or to stay in bed late, even as late as this, to be with his friend, the owner of the bookshop. She had not known men of this sort before she had come to work for him, but now she would not mind it again, and if the younger of her sister Pina's two boys should indeed turn out to be such a man, she would not mind it, and her sister Pina would understand that it was not such a tragedy. She walked briskly towards Sloane Square and its Underground station. Two years ago, the younger of Pina's two boys had tried to join in with his uncle Salvatore's Sicilian song, and he had got it slightly wrong; he had sung what he always thought the words were, 'Ciuri, ciuri, ciuri dell'ortolano ...' Not flowers all year, but flowers from the greengrocer. They had laughed so much; the younger of Pina's two boys, Nicola, he had looked ashamed, and blushed and in the end had gone into the kitchen to console himself with leftovers. 'Ciuri, ciuri, ciuri dell'ortolano ...' Annunziata sang, under her breath; the song of her Christmas, and the song of the flowers in the greengrocer in Sicily made a cloud of her breath, there in the grey foreign city. But she was happy now. The green of the tiles in Sloane Square station was the green of her Sicilian Christmas, and the green of a garden, and the green of the greengrocer that was never in the song at all.

16.

The house in Chester Terrace was still being done up. The kitchen was finished first of all – Ronnie had said he wouldn't dare to do anything else: his Italian housekeeper Annunziata would look reproachfully at him if he decided he needed to take a bath, for instance, before she was able to cook for him. So the kitchen was done first, and then Ronnie hadn't seen why he shouldn't do it in a sensible, rational way, proceeding upwards from the ground floor, where the study and the dining room and the television room were, to the first floor, where the big drawing room was, and then to the second floor, where the two bedrooms and bathrooms were and then – well, the work had finished halfway through the second floor. Ronnie was still hanging his clothes in the two wardrobes he had taken from his parents' house. And the third floor Ronnie said he only needed for his hobby, so that hardly needed doing up. Duncan had been up there only two or three times, to express admiration and wonderment at Ronnie's hobby before coming back down again. Clearly, Ronnie had no expectation that Duncan would show the slightest interest or engagement in his hobby; there was no disappointment or engagement whatsoever with what Duncan had to say. Duncan had seen it, and was shown there was nothing whatsoever sinister about having a room devoted to your model railway, and that was that.

The model railway had been constructed over the last five years. Ronnie had made everything in it from scratch, apart from the wheels of the train, as you needed a lathe to make wheels. Around the track rose a town of Ronnie's design and construction, where the shops were named after Ronnie's family, friends and enemies. (There was a lurid sex shop called Pauline's, named after Ronnie's villainous colleague on the public-relations side at the bank, with a neatly painted sign, one inch high, advertising Anal Lubricants outside; it was next to the church, named St Katy's after Ronnie's best friend.) He had met Ronnie at the famous party to raise funds; he had gone out with him for dinner that night, and then home with him; they had met twice more before the existence of the model railway embarrassingly emerged. And Ronnie had already named a gay bookshop after him: Duncan's Gay Bookshop, there it was.

'That's a bit creepy,' Duncan said, not meaning it a bit.

'It's hard to get model books the right size,' Ronnie had said. 'You'll just have to imagine it.'

The whole village was called Franklin's Bottom, after Ronnie's awful-sounding Irish ex-boyfriend. 'Or at any rate the main point of his appeal,' Ronnie said.

'You liked him best when he was walking away,' Duncan said.

'Well, yes, I did,' Ronnie had said. 'Anyone would. Anyway, he never knew – I don't think he ever came up here after that first time. Shall we go down again?'

The curtains were so thick in Ronnie's house that it seemed dense night until you woke, and rose, and drew them. That had been the case even in the summer, when Duncan and Ronnie had met. Now, the day before Christmas, Ronnie was almost horrified to see how late it was. They had slept, and woken, and moved into each other's shapes and slept again, Duncan's chin against the back of Ronnie's neck with its nice warm morning smell. Sleep and sex alternated; coming out of the bathroom, naked, having thought it might be polite to brush his teeth before they started up again, Duncan picked up his watch and saw from the luminous dial that it was half past twelve. He had thought it might be after nine. They had slept for eleven hours, on and off. But it was nearly Christmas.

He gave Ronnie a kiss on his shoulder, and went next door into the absurdly over-glamorous bathroom – 'That'll be the first to go,' Ronnie had said, about its black tiles and eye-aching star's dressing-room lighting, the relic of the previous owners. But almost everything had been done, and the bathrooms on this floor had not been touched. He started to run the bath.

In a few moments, he felt Ronnie's arms around him from behind. It was nice to feel Ronnie's warm bare flesh and him being in Ronnie's nice-smelling white dressing-gown.

'I don't want to get up yet,' Ronnie said.

'Ah, you,' Duncan said. 'Do you know what time it is?'

'No idea,' Ronnie said, nibbling at Duncan's ear. 'What time is it?'

'Late enough,' Duncan said. 'Do you want to sleep some more?'

Ronnie made a humming, thoughtful noise, shaking his head in mild denial; a difficult gesture for him to make with Duncan's earlobe in his mouth.

'What are you thinking?' Ronnie said.

'What?'

'You look *all thoughtful*,' Ronnie said, dropping into stage Cockney. 'All thoughtful, you do.'

'I was just thinking if you don't do something about this bathroom soon,' Duncan said, 'you'll probably never do anything about it.'

'I'll get used to it,' Ronnie said, mumbling a little, 'and it'll just be what the bathroom looks like, and then I'll sort of forget what I wanted to do with it. I know.'

'Yes,' Duncan said. 'But what do you want to do with it?'

'What do you want to do with it?' Ronnie said, putting his hand up Duncan's dressing-gown.

'I'm going so grey,' Duncan said. 'Something avocado, perhaps.'

'With your hair?'

Duncan said, 'Or an aubergine suite with gold dolphin taps. That would be ever so nice.'

'With a peppermint bidet,' Ronnie said. 'For contrast. And your hair?'

'Avocado and peppermint, and those brown smoked mirrors all around,' Duncan said.

'I like your hair, really,' Ronnie said. 'I like your nice granny's hair, all grey and distinguished. You should go to a better place to get it cut, though.'

'The cheek of it,' Duncan said. 'But definitely gold dolphin taps, definitely.'

They liked being mildly snobbish to each other about the bathroom fittings that they hadn't got round to. Once Ronnie's terrifying mother had said to Duncan in quite a remote, neutral way, 'Yes, when I bought the house in Gloucestershire in 1974, the owners were awfully proud of having just installed a bathroom suite, as they called it, in nigger brown.' Duncan had wanted to run downstairs and tell Ronnie in the kitchen immediately. One of these days Duncan was going to catch Ronnie out and have a bathroom installed in aubergine, saying he'd thought Ronnie had meant it. One of these days: Duncan found himself thinking that. He hoped Ronnie thought the same thing from time to time.

Later, they were in the kitchen.

'Do you know,' Duncan said, 'I do believe that Dommie and Celia have been round. Those presents weren't there last night.'

'We must have been in bed still,' Ronnie said. 'How awful. But they're coming round on Boxing Day, aren't they?'

The ancient coffee percolator was popping and belching; they were on to their third slice of toast each. Duncan liked lime marmalade on his, and Ronnie liked Marmite. Sometimes, strangely, they both liked cottage cheese in the morning.

'I once had a boyfriend who was French,' Ronnie said, watching Duncan ladle cottage cheese onto his brown toast. 'He discovered crumpets for himself. But he thought they were a breakfast thing. He had them with apricot jam, first thing in the morning.'

'What did awful Franklin have first thing in the morning?'

'Cock,' Ronnie said. 'Only not mine, usually. Usually some stranger's in the public lavatory.'

'Not before breakfast, surely.'

'You'd be surprised.'

'The strangest thing I ever had for breakfast,' Duncan said, 'was in Sicily. That time I was there. In 'seventy-eight or 'seventy-nine. Good Lord, it's ten years since I was in Sicily.'

'That's very accurate of you,' Ronnie said.

'Well, I remember because it was immediately after that that my father died. I got called back because of it. And also because it was then – I was in Sicily – Mrs Thatcher got elected. I always remember because everyone used to ask me about it, and I used to say *e possibile, seconda lei, che l'Italia avrebbera ... avrebberai ...* Do you know, I've forgotten all the Italian I ever knew. I used to say to them, is it possible according to you that Italy will ever have a woman prime minister, and they would say *mai*, never, in horror.'

'They've got used to her by now,' Ronnie said.

'I suppose so,' Duncan said. 'But the strangest breakfast I ever had, it was there in the summer. A nice boy I picked up, he took me home and the next morning he went downstairs to the *gelateria* and got me a hot brioche with ice-cream in it, chocolate ice-cream. And the next time I picked up a boy, he asked me if I wanted breakfast, and I said brioche with watermelon granita, because I'd had that at a posh *gelateria* a couple of nights before. But that one stared because he'd only meant did I want a dry biscuit with my coffee.'

'The heart sinks,' Ronnie said. 'Ice-cream for breakfast.'

'Ah, you,' Duncan said. 'Only because it's so cold and it's so nice in here eating toast.'

'Did you ever talk to Annunziata about Sicily?' Ronnie said. 'I can't remember where she comes from.'

'Has she done all of this?' Duncan said.

'All what?' Ronnie said. Then he laughed, because all about them were dishes, jars, filled plates, and on the table between them was a special blue notebook with the words 'Christmas Instructions' written neatly in Annunziata's beautiful schoolroom hand. 'She's done everything. In there, I bet she's put a timetable down for what goes in where and when. There's no minute of the day between now and the twenty-eighth when there is the slightest risk of anything failing, or going wrong. We just have to follow every single instruction and she'll be back on the twenty-eighth and everything will be perfectly all right again.'

'We could have our Christmas dinner tonight,' Duncan said. 'We could just put the duck in the oven, and do all of that, and just get on with it, and Christmas itself would be nice and over with.'

'Oh, yes,' Ronnie said.

A thought came to Duncan. 'Did you actually like Christmas?'

Ronnie folded the last half of a slice of toast, and stuffed it whole into his mouth. 'When I was a kid?' he said eventually. 'Yes, of course I did. Everyone does. It's when you've got to do any of it for anyone else that you stop liking it.'

'I'm just glad that it's a week, almost, away from the shop and I don't need to think about it, unless someone smashes the window again.'

'As bad as that?'

'The smashing of windows I'm used to, frankly,' Duncan said. 'No one's done it since August. The worst year was 1982 – I think it was seven times we had the glaziers out. I'd rather not have to deal with it on Christmas Day, but apart from that, it's not the windows.'

'But a week off.'

'Oh, God,' Duncan said. 'It's just all so hopeless. I thought it would be OK after we saw off the court case. It was such a waste of everyone's time, that, but at the end of it – I don't know, looking at the books, we just lost so much income because of it, all the stock being confiscated. Some of it's coming back from the filth in dribs and drabs, but you couldn't sell it – it's all straight into the remainders pile.'

'The party, though, and the auction.'

'It seemed fantastic at the time. Seven thousand, nearly. It doesn't go far. Eleven hundred for that Hockney print, amazing. Nothing else came near it. It was really a bit embarrassing that no one wanted to pay more than ten pounds for some of those donations. Olivia Tempest, awful moment. I was going to pass Arthur a note to get him to bid, but that sort of destroyed the whole point of the evening, if we were going to have to bid for the lots ourselves. Did I tell you about the donation, just before Christmas? I got to the shop, and there was a brown envelope, no address on it, with a ten-pound note inside, and "With Best Wishes and Good Luck for the Future from One of Your Neighbours". I thought they all hated us. Well, they do, apart from maybe one closet case we didn't know about. Oh, God.'

'Seriously, as bad as that?'

'Terrible,' Duncan said. 'I'm going to have to ask Arthur if he'll mind going part-time – I can't afford to keep him on.'

'You can't do that,' Ronnie said. But his manner was mild and distracted; he gave a great yawn and a tousled grin.

Duncan stared. 'Well, I might really have to,' he said.

'Oh dear,' Ronnie said. Duncan looked at him in a quizzical way. 'Well,' Ronnie went on. 'It's been quite a while, hasn't it? There's absolutely no future for him in the bookshop – I mean, you're not going to have a chain of Big Gay Bookshops, are you? It's perfectly all right for you, but for him? He ought to start thinking about what he wants to do with his life.'

'Sometimes, Ronnie, I don't believe you think my bookshop is much of a success.'

'Well, I love your bookshop,' Ronnie said. 'But you just said yourself it's not making any money. Look. If you're really in need, if it's the difference between keeping going or not, I can put off doing the bathroom and get ten thousand pounds together.'

'As a loan.'

'Well, a loan of rather an unexiguous variety, let's say. I wouldn't expect to see it again until you felt that things were back to normal. Just think of it as me giving you backing.'

'Oh, God, Ronnie,' Duncan said. 'Spare me the innuendo.' He was not quite sure how he felt about becoming a rich man's plaything – that was how he put it to himself, pronouncing it in rather a Cockney way in his mind, *rich man's plaything*. He had never thought of himself as being poor until he'd met Ronnie, who knew people who were richer than Duncan had ever seriously envisaged. 'If it were just me I'd say no. But if it really comes to having to ask Arthur to work for less – I mean, that shithole he lives in already – I don't know that I could do it. Let me think about it. It really is very sweet of you. If you did—'

'Would I expect a say in things?' Ronnie said. 'Not much more than I do now. What do you suppose that brown liquid in the Evian bottle is? It looks truly sinister.'

'It's the orange sauce,' Duncan said. 'It's for the duck, which I suppose is in the fridge. What's she left us for our lunch? Or shall we go out for lunch?'

17.

It was nice, Christmas at Kevin's, once you didn't expect very much of it. This would be Arthur's sixth there. They followed the same path. You went down dutifully to Kevin's flat on the ground floor around twelve and had a glass of sparkling wine with anyone else who was around. There was a dubious smell of turkey in the air – Kevin said anyone was welcome to join his friend Adam and him for Christmas dinner, there would be plenty. But nobody ever did. Arthur had always been there, but the others varied – an Australian or a French lodger would go home; sometimes somebody who had been there the year before would have moved out or died. Tony sometimes stayed in London and Tim sometimes did. Otherwise they went off to their respective parents in Bradford and Guildford.

'It's lovely to see you again,' Kevin said, with a ghastly smile on his face and a Christmassy waistcoat on his body, ornamented with sequined swirls and splashes. His friend Adam was doing something in the kitchen. 'Another Christmas rolls round, regular as sin. Another year, another happy year, and Arthur's still with us and so are Tim and Tony. You're not eating Christmas dinner up there on your own, I hope? You must come down and join Adam and I, there's plenty of turkey – we'll be eating it until Tuesday week.'

'That's OK, Kevin,' Arthur said. 'I'll just have a drink and pop off if it's all the same to you.'

'Tim and I, we've booked at the Mumtaz in Upper Street,' Tony said. 'We thought we'd get away from it altogether.'

'Very unusual,' Kevin said. 'I know where you mean. That's an Indian restaurant, isn't it? I don't know that they'll have turkey. It'll be more like curry they'll be making, even today of all days, surely.'

'Tony and I,' Tim said, 'we thought about what we really like and what we'd like for ourselves – and the answer was chicken korma for him and meat dopiaza for me with extra poppadums. We're of an age to please ourselves.'

'Oh, we're all that age,' Kevin said. 'Just seems a bit funny, somehow, having curry on Christmas Day for Christmas dinner. And you, Arthur? Are you not tempted for once to go and see your family? Christmas, it's a time for family.'

'Never,' Arthur said firmly. 'The truth of matter is, you're my family.'

Kevin and Tony and Tim looked at each other; Adam was brought out of the kitchen, a laminated apron with a hairy hunk's body printed on it; he stared, a pair of mid-basting oven gloves on his hands.

'I'm not your fucking family, darling,' Adam said. 'What, I'm supposed to be your aunty Adam? What's Kevin – Grandma fucking Moses?'

'Cheeky cow,' Kevin said. 'I'm not your flaming family, Arthur love, either. I'm your landlord, remember, that you pay the rent to every month? There's a difference.'

'I only meant because I see Adam just once a year, on Christmas Day, and then within ten minutes I always remember I hate him,' Arthur said lightly.

'Oh, fuck off,' Adam said, going back into the kitchen.

'Poor old Arthur,' Tony said. 'You don't have any family at all, then. Just a lot of, I don't know, *customers*. Do they send you Christmas cards?'

'Some of them, wi' big kisses on the bottom and all,' Arthur said. 'It's my job to send the cards out in return. We cut right down this year, thank the Lord, one of Duncan's little economies.'

'And very sensible too,' Kevin said. 'I always tell everyone I don't want Christmas cards, and if I get one, don't you go thinking I'll be sending one in return, either. Now, a little top-up?'

Afterwards, Tony and Tim sat in the Mumtaz in Upper Street, and ordered everything they felt like, just because it was Christmas. It didn't quite work: Ali the owner had said he didn't celebrate Christmas himself and would be opening just the same, but when they got there, the place had been Christmassified, with tinsel hung over the hand-made paintings of the Taj Mahal, a tiger, a dancing girl, and a river with a tiger, a dancing girl and another view of the Taj Mahal, done on black velvet. Tony supposed that they served up Christmas like they served up beer and alcohol in general: not believing in it for themselves, but giving it to the customers. It was surprisingly full of older couples and two or three sad, solitary men. There were Christmas crackers on the table, which Tony and Tim left untouched until Ali came round and talked them into it. (He left the solitary diners alone, they noticed.) They sat with paper crowns on, a tin whistle and a tin powder compact on the table between them, and they read the jokes to each other.

'What do you call a man with a spade in his head,' Tony said.

'A corpse, or a seriously mutilated person who ought to be taken to hospital immediately,' Tim said.

'That's right,' Tony said.

'Why would you invite a mushroom to a Christmas party,' said Tim, looking over the top of his glasses at the slip of paper.

'Because you felt you had provided inadequate food and you wanted to give your guests something to eat, other than one measly bag of crisps, which considering that all your guests pay you rent for the rest of the year is really a bit of a cheek,' Tony said.

'That's right,' Tim said. 'I don't know why we're still living in that dump.'

'Oh, I know,' Tony said. 'It's cheap. That's the only thing. Where could we afford somewhere?'

'If we live together, we can afford Balham, I reckon,' Tim said. 'But no one's going to give us a mortgage. You have to fill in a form, you know, saying that you've never had sex with a man and you never would.'

'We could rent somewhere,' Tony said.

'We're renting now,' Tim said.

'Somewhere nicer,' Tony said. 'Where it's actually a flat, not my bedroom and your bedroom that we've turned into a sitting room but you've got to walk across the hall and the sofa's actually just your bed with a cover on it.'

'Oh, that,' Tim said. They had had this conversation before. 'Let's make 1988 the year when we actually move out of bloody Kevin's bloody house. I hate it there.'

'And here are your poppadums, sir,' Ali said, putting them down. 'And a very merry Christmas to you, sir.'

After the drink at Kevin's downstairs, Arthur went heavily up to his room. He'd tidied it up and he'd left a few Christmas cards on top of his shelf of books. This was his perfect Christmas. He had seen off Kevin and the lodgers, who could now argue with each other about small domestic matters, the festering objections of the rest of the year coming to the surface now. He had done his social duties and could go upstairs. He had got hold of an old book by Robert Liddell about the misery of being in a family, and was really looking forward to spending his afternoon with that. There was food to be got through, Arthur supposed. In celebration of the day, he'd got some bacon and eggs in, which he'd fry at one or so. Then in the evening he'd resort to his usual diet of baked beans on toast and Pot Noodle. He'd resisted the special Christmas flavour Pot Noodle. He thought that was depressing. Dommie had wondered, about once a month for the last nine years, that he didn't die of scurvy or some other deficiency, but he'd explained that he ate an apple every day and that seemed to see him all right. In the evening he'd go to the Edward IV, have a pint and pick up another sad case, he reckoned.

He put on both the bars of the electric fire and soon it was warm as toast up there, with Arthur tucked up under his duvet in the armchair and quickly absorbed in the travails of the two brothers.

Whether it was the book or the day, Arthur didn't know, but he found himself contemplating what had been his family, what they were up to. He supposed he was a missing person to them. He wondered what they were thinking about him, whether they imagined him living on the streets, addicted to heroin, drunk or dead. Maybe they thought about him on Christmas Day. There would be his stepfather and his mother, still in that house in Adalbert Street, and she'd have cooked the turkey all right and all the vegetables. There would be his stepfather's mother Maisie, that whiskery old bag smelling of wee and asking him if he was courting – no, she'd probably be dead by now. There'd be Arthur's sisters. Julie was bound to have married her Antony by now – they'd been going steady for five years when Arthur had cleared out. They probably had children of their own. He was an uncle! Karen, she'd have run away like him; she'd have dyed her hair or shaved her head. Or would she have stuck to it, become a teacher like she'd said she wanted to? Maybe one of these days he'd write to them, let them know he was all right and that. He thought about them all, in the house in Adalbert

Street, and for a moment felt a small pang. He reached for the big tin of Quality Street – it had been a sort of shamefaced present from Duncan, the first time it had ever happened, and Arthur reckoned it was because the shop had put both of them through too much this year. He rifled for a purple one, his favourite. Then he remembered that he could get on the train easily, get off when it stopped at Sheffield, get the number sixty-two bus that stopped at the end of Adalbert Street and go to number twenty-seven, knock the brass dolphin that was still the knocker on their door, still painted green. He could do that any time. But then they'd answer the door, and his stepfather would say, 'So you've come back, have you, Wayne,' and his mum would say, 'Why did you do it, Wayne.'

He popped another purple one into his mouth. Those were definitely the best. In the north, he remembered, nobody knew he was called Arthur, and nobody in the south knew he had ever been called anything else. That was why they hadn't found him, even if they'd been looking, and that was why he couldn't go back.

Some time in the afternoon, Arthur finished the book. It was so much almost his favourite book in the world. He wondered whether the two brothers in the book ever helped each other out when they were a bit older. He reckoned one of them wouldn't have minded and the other one would have wanted to but wouldn't have been able to say so. He didn't know whether Robert Liddell was still alive; he thought about writing him a nice long letter to ask him. He caught sight of the bacon on the shelf next to the Baby Belling, still in its plastic wrapper, the eggs in their open box next to it. My God, he said, like Duncan in his mind. I can't believe it. I haven't had my Christmas dinner. Arthur got up and stretched; he had been so absorbed in the book that his joints were sticking like an old man's. He gave the frying pan a wipe with the tea towel – it always needed a wipe, but there was no point in washing it unless you'd fried fish in it, for instance, which Arthur never had. Sometimes it tasted a little bit funny, but there was nothing that would kill you. He put six rashers of bacon in, cracked two eggs into the pan. While it heated, his hand crept towards the book that was sitting by the side of the Baby Belling. It was not properly a book: it was a bound proof of a new novel that the publisher had sent out and had said that Arthur would probably really enjoy. It was something about a swimming pool. Arthur started to read it, in a scoffing frame of mind, thinking of *The Garden King*. The watery hiss of bacon, a fierce spit of wet egg in bacon fat did not disturb him. He turned the page. Some time around six o'clock, Tony or Tim came up and knocked on the door. Tony or Tim called out that they wondered if Arthur wanted to go out for a drink this evening. Arthur said nothing. His right hand went from his face to a plate of chocolate digestives, next to the abandoned plate of his Christmas dinner, and back again. His left hand kept the book open as he went on reading. He hoped this book would last the evening, or he would just start reading it all over again.

18.

Wednesday was Andrew's day for the gay men's discussion group. His staff at Hoxton housing department knew that he liked to be off very sharp at five on Wednesdays. He also liked to be off very sharp at five on Tuesdays for the Friends of the Earth, and very sharp on Monday for the Spartacist League, and very sharp at five or even four on Friday because it was Friday.

The housing department was on the second layer of the piled-up terrapins behind the main town hall and offices; they had been placed there as a temporary measure some time in the mid-1970s to supplement the baroque 1930s splendour of the limestone town hall. The town hall was all idealistic mosaic and mahogany fixed furniture with polished brass fittings; it had been built by an architect whose name Andrew could never remember, but you knew it when you heard it. He rather approved of the lavish interiors of the town hall, where the population came to marry in a peach-coloured plush lounge, with lilies in a vase at the front, and register deaths in a little office off to one side of the main hall, behind an abstract blue and red stained-glass door. It was something for them to share and to make them feel part of something important, beyond themselves. But the functions of the town hall had long outgrown its size, and many of the offices were either in 1960s blocks in Ramsden Way and the newly renamed Bangabandhu Place or, like the housing department, in a series of temporary 1970s terrapins behind the town hall. You had to climb up an outside steel staircase to get to your office if it was on the first floor.

When Andrew had been promoted to head of the housing department, he had decided to make a break with old Wallis's pipe-and-half-moon-glasses style by moving his desk among the rest of his staff. The old office in the main building had been abandoned, and Andrew now sat among all his staff, however junior, and was available if they wanted to come up and ask him something. In practice, this did not happen because Andrew was so busy; Mohammed and Helena sat near by, and were experienced enough to deal with anyone's problems. Sometimes, too, a meeting needed to take place out of earshot of all the others, like the meeting when he and Mo and Helena had had to decide, today, who was going to get a promotion. (There had been going to be three, but now because of the budget cuts, there were going to be only two.) It was a shame, but there it was; and it was always a problem finding somewhere to sit and talk in confidence. Once or twice they'd gone out and sat in the new McDonald's on Old Street, at Mo's suggestion. If Helena had suggested it, Andrew would have refused; but you couldn't exactly tell Mohammed where he could or couldn't eat.

'Well, I think I'm going to leave that for the day,' Helena said, turning from her desk. Her personal noticeboard carried a post-card image of a kitten in a bowl of spaghetti, its mouth open and yowling. She got up with a sigh, brushing some biscuit crumbs from her bosom. She was a large woman, and the crocheted white cardigan she now lifted from the back of her swivel chair was on the scale of a bedspread. 'I feel that was a really useful day, and I'll be glad to settle for the evening in front of the telly.'

'Sounds like a good plan,' Andrew said, watching her put her purple coat on and wrap her scarf round her neck. 'It's cold out.'

'February,' Helena said, and theatrically shuddered. 'Are you off, too?'

'Yes,' Andrew said. 'It's my gay men's group on a Wednesday.'

Helena merely nodded at this. It was important to say where you were going without any embarrassment, or suggesting that you might like to conceal anything about it. At any rate, it was important to say this when Helena was around. Andrew thought it might be challenging or disrespectful to Mohammed to mention this, and perhaps raise some statement from him that, however understandable in terms of Mohammed's culture and heritage, would also be unfair and challenging to the gay members of staff within earshot, if any. (He wondered about that boy Ricky with the tribal tattoos on his biceps.)

They left the office together. In the fierce wind, Helena wrapped in her scarf and Andrew with his furry hat with earflaps, they did not speak; the bus for Marylebone was just pulling up as they got to the stop, and Andrew got on it muttering a kind of goodbye. He hoped someone would turn up tonight; the last few weeks there had been only four of them or, a couple of times, three. Behind him, an old person of indeterminate sex, wrapped up like a babushka, was fumbling in the depths of its outfit. The bus driver was getting irritated; he had shut the door against the cold, but was not moving off until the old person had shown that they had the money to pay for a ticket.

'Come on, darling,' the driver said. 'We ain't got all day, now.'

The figure went on rifling, a small sexless noise of indeterminate pitch escaping from the mass of cloth around the face.

There was a peculiar smell in the bus; it must come from this figure. Finally, a handful of coins was dropped on the driver's tray. He counted it. 'You're five pee short,' he said. There was a gesture of helplessness. 'Go on,' the driver said eventually. 'You can owe it to us. Don't do it again.'

The figure waddled on to the bus, devoid of gratitude, and took the seat in front of Andrew. The bus moved slowly forward. The figure unwrapped itself slowly, muttering. The smell coagulated; a curious, fishy, damp, cigarette-smelling odour; the gender of the person was no clearer – either a whiskery bald old woman or a femininely bulging old man of some sort. Andrew could not restrain himself. He leant forward.

'The bus is a public service,' he said, almost but not quite tapping the figure on their damp-looking shoulder. 'Someone's got to pay for it somehow. It's not much.'

The person turned round; it was the astonished face of someone to whom nobody habitually spoke, who was more used to strangers in buses removing themselves than beginning a conversation. 'I paid,' it said, in the astonished, ladylike tones of a dowager intruded upon in her private business. 'I paid. I was only fivepence short and he didn't mind, the driver.'

'But someone's got to pay that fivepence,' Andrew said. 'It's not a lot to ask.'

'I was only fivepence short,' the figure said complainingly. 'Are you an inspector? I was only fivepence short today. He's not an inspector. Only fivepence short.'

'Oh, leave the poor soul be,' a matronly woman in a cagoule and a woolly bobble hat said. 'She was only fivepence short. It won't bankrupt anyone.'

'I'm not a woman,' the person said. 'Don't call me she. I'm not she. Is he an inspector? I need to get home. I was only fivepence short.'

The person continued muttering all the way to Marylebone, where Andrew got off; *only fivepence short* and *not an inspector*; he saw how it would carry on muttering for miles, perhaps until the end of the route, its concerns preserved like the rituals of a class in society long after that class's functions and significance have departed from the world. If he were to die now, as he walked through the wind-blasted February streets, he would be preserved for a time in the misapprehensions of a stranger, *not an inspector* and *only fivepence short* keeping him in the ether as a tattered brain hung on to its momentary obsession before fading away. He entered Heatherwick Street. There was a new coffee shop at the corner, and a bookmaker's where the fishmonger had been until last summer. The bookshop was lit up, opposite the dark and closed-up sandwich shop run by Greeks. Inside, Arthur was leaning into the window display, and adding to a pile of copies of a blue marbled hardback book. Andrew observed him: as he drew upright, his face looked suddenly old and drawn under his mop of black hair, his expression mournful. What did his hair look like, underneath that ancient and much-renewed colour? It looked old, artificial, approximate in the shop's light. But then Duncan came forward, wearing a suit and tie for some reason, and Arthur's face burst into a smile at something he said. No – it wasn't Duncan in the suit and tie. It just looked like him. Andrew crossed the road and entered the shop with a tug and a ring on the shop-door bell. The man he had thought was Duncan was actually that millionaire Duncan was supposed to be going out with. Andrew couldn't remember his name – didn't want to remember his name.

'What's that you're putting in the window?' Andrew said.

'It's that new novel,' Arthur said. 'The swimming-pool one. We can't sell enough of it. We've re-ordered four times now.'

'Thank God,' the millionaire said. 'If it carries on like that, this'll save our bacon.'

Andrew noticed but did not comment on 'our' bacon. The millionaire was wearing a deep blue suit with some kind of red check in it, and a tie that had, what was it, horseshoes? The smell that came from the millionaire was some kind of luxury smell, of *gentlemen*; of *money*; of *toiletries*. In the middle of the bookshop, the smell transformed it, quite at once, into a place for the exchange of money for goods, for a profit.

'It's about rich people, isn't it?' Andrew said. 'Rich people fucking poor people. Charming.'

'It's fantastic,' Arthur said. 'Have you read it? Well, you should. Everyone's reading it. We keep quoting bits of it to each other. The big bookshops only ordered five copies each, if that, and they were caught on the hop, so everyone for a week had to come and get it from us if they wanted a copy. We've had all sorts in. They've come in for that and then they've said, I didn't know you were here, and they've wandered round and bought all sorts. It's been fantastic. We've never had such a fortnight. It's not just *poor* people, it's *poor black* people that get fucked in it, Andrew.'

'I must read it,' Andrew said. 'I simply can't wait. Is nobody here yet?'

'What for?' Arthur said. 'Oh, it's your group. No, nobody's here. Do you think—'

All at once he turned away and busied himself, as if it were not for him to finish the sentence, as if he had overstepped the mark. To begin with he stood at the round table at the front of the shop and squared copies of the books; but they were square, and in a moment to carry on busying himself, Arthur went to the counter and squared the stuffed pheasant. One eye was missing now, and had been for a year or two. Then he picked up the silver teapot – the one that just sat on the shelf at elbow level above the till, was never used and indeed looked fairly unusable. Andrew watched him levelly. His occupation was steady and his movements involved, but he had no doubt that Arthur was fluttering about with his hands so that he would seem busy and not have to talk to Andrew. The millionaire Duncan was going out with was more confident, however; he switched one leg over the other, standing cross-legged at the knee; he folded his arms and stood looking at Andrew without apparently feeling any need to address him. Like a squire. Andrew had been coming to this shop much longer than any millionaire. The shop had been in part his idea – he remembered those days at CHE when they had talked about how they could have a place to meet in, a neutral place to discuss and take the movement forward. It had been his idea and Nat's, and Simon's, and all those people's as well as Duncan's. A radical space. And here came the money-maker from the back of the shop, wearing – Christ, no – a bow-tie like a professional bookseller in an advert for toffees. His hair was different since last week, clipped neatly short and grey; he looked and, as he approached, smelt like the millionaire.

'Andrew,' Duncan said. There was something wrong: Duncan had a businesslike air.

'Hello, sweetie,' Andrew said, poisonously.

'It's so nice to see you,' Duncan said. 'Always so nice to see you. Are you here for your discussion group?'

'That's a nice tie you're wearing,' Andrew said. 'I don't remember seeing you in a bow-tie before.'

'You're here for your discussion group,' Duncan said again. Arthur was pretending, not very convincingly, to sort out the postcards in a pile by the till.

'Every Wednesday,' Andrew said.

'I don't think I can stay tonight,' Duncan said. 'We're going – Ronnie and I, we're going to the theatre.'

'Judi Dench,' the millionaire said, grinning.

'Oh, yes,' Andrew said. He waited.

'And actually Arthur said he can't stay either tonight, for once.'

'Actually Arthur said he doesn't want to stay tonight,' Arthur said, raising his head. 'Actually Arthur's sick to death of it, sticking around all evening listening to you.'

'It's not compulsory,' Andrew said. 'You don't have to stay.'

'Yes, well, someone's got to stay to lock up,' Duncan said. 'And tonight I don't think anyone can.'

'I'll lock up,' Andrew said. 'It's no bother.'

'No, I don't think so,' Duncan said resolutely. 'The thing is,

483

Andrew – is anyone else coming tonight? I mean, last week, who came?'

'It was that black boy from Leicester who sometimes comes,' Andrew said. 'He came.'

'No, that were week before,' Arthur said. 'Last week it were just you and me and Alan, and Alan said to me afterwards, that's last time he's coming, he's sick of listening to you and Trotsky, he's better off spending his evenings in Coleherne or even wi' his old mother. That's what he said to me, Andrew.'

'It's important—' Andrew began, but the millionaire interrupted.

'It's important – what?'

'I was going to say—' Andrew said, but the millionaire went on.

'It's important to have a discussion group, to have a safe radical space where you can plot your revolutions? The thing is—'

'Ronnie,' Duncan said. 'It's best if I talk, really. Let's be calm about this. The thing is, Andrew, the time for these discussion groups, it's over. There's nothing to stop you having your discussion group at home, or just round a table in a pub. But this – it can't go on. Every Wednesday we've got to make up numbers, we've got to stay and talk, or listen to you talking and lock up afterwards. This is just a bookshop. In the evenings, we might want to have readings every now and then, instead of your discussion group.'

'To a paying audience, I expect.'

'Yes,' Duncan said, not angrily, but perhaps even puzzled at the objection. 'Look—'

'What is this?' Andrew said. 'The Thatcherite revolution in action?'

'When was the last time you even paid anything towards group?' Arthur said, coming out from behind the till and walking with his shoulders back towards Andrew, who quailed: it was as if he were about to be hit, and hard. 'You never pay anything, and at end, you always just put a book in your bag when you think no one's looking.'

'That's not true,' Andrew said.

'Punchy little number,' the millionaire said, puzzlingly, and he and Duncan exchanged a look, a secret smile.

'Oh yes it is,' Arthur said. 'You always put a book in your bag. You wait until we're at door, talking to someone, then it comes out, your hand, and book's in bag. You've not paid for a book in this shop while 1984. Leave you in charge to lock up? It'd be like leaving Lady Isobel frigging Barnett in charge, you hairy thieving little shit. You say to yourself you're just benefiting from community resource, but you're in community and we're not benefiting from you. We're losing twenty pounds every bloody time you step over threshold. So frig off, you twat, and don't come back till you're prepared to spend some frigging money of your own.'

As Arthur had begun to shout in Andrew's face, Andrew took his hat and placed it firmly on his head. He paid no attention to Arthur's display, buttoning his coat with dignity, and turned without saying goodbye to any of them. He left the shop as Arthur shouted after him, turned and paused. He was trembling. From the shop there was a moment of silence, and then a single cheer – the millionaire's drawling voice made the huzzah. But then there was something worse: the noise of laughter from the three of them. One of them was shouting something in glee; it might have been *Punchy little number*, even. Over the road, a black man stood and looked at Andrew, bent over as if about to be sick. It was not the boy from Leicester. Andrew thought, as he straightened up, that it might be the man who worked in the sandwich shop opposite, the ones who hated the bookshop. He needed a drink.

19.

When Nat heard that Freddie Sempill had died, it struck him like news from a previous existence. It had been years since he had seen or heard of Freddie Sempill.

Christopher had rung him on the train. Nat now had eight

flats and had stopped using the expression 'property empire' – when he'd bought the last two last November, he'd done the sums and realized there was no point in working any more: he should just devote his whole time to what he owned. It was useful still to be in touch when he was out and about, talking to the builders who were doing up those last two. They were still working on them in June, and Nat was on the overground train to the Queenstown Road when his phone went. 'Sorry, sorry, sorry,' he said to the lady opposite, who had leapt up in a startled way, looking about her for where this ringing might be coming from. It was a hot day. Nat delved in his bag for the phone, not wearing a jacket to put it in. Around him, people craned to look, some with expressions already disapproving.

'I haven't heard from him for years,' he said to Christopher. 'To be honest, I thought he'd died years back. When did I last see him?'

He'd last seen him at that party to raise funds for Duncan's bookshop. That was more than three years ago. Nat remembered that was the evening when he'd got off with that double-bass player, and they'd gone round the corner to what had been then only his second flat; it was still being done up. It was impossible for the three of them, Nat and the double-bass player and the instrument, to get into the lift together. They'd had to take relays. Anyway. Was that the last time they'd seen Freddie Sempill? He'd fainted, that's right. Andrew Scott had come in a dress and was it then that Duncan had got off with Ronnie for the first time?

The woman sitting opposite Nat leant forward and tapped him on the knee. 'Is this conversation going to go on much longer?' she said sharply. 'Not everyone wants to listen to the details of your personal life.'

'Got to go, darling,' Nat said into the phone. 'People getting awfully cross. Speak later.' He hung up – hung up? Was that still what you said, or did you now say switched off, or something of that sort? Anyway, he stopped the phone call, and glared at the woman. 'I'm only going two stops,' he said. 'Honestly.'

The builders were, for once, hard at work when he arrived, and the flat looked close to completion: the windows were in, the paint dry, the floors sanded. With the first flat, he'd made the mistake of decorating it in a cool style, in grey with yellow details, and it had taken for ever to let. Ever since, he'd painted everything brilliant white, and nothing had taken more than a week to go. It was strange to think how, eight years ago, he'd been so worried about stretching himself that he'd constantly chivvied the builders and decorators at that first flat to get a move on. Now the cash flow was fine, and it didn't really worry him that the builders were a month behind schedule, that asbestos had been discovered two months before in the flat downstairs, that the whole thing was costing money and not bringing money in. The other six flats were doing just fine, bringing in a nice steady income from nice steady gay tenants, hand-picked by Nat. The whole thing was a pleasure to think of on a nice June morning with the sun shining through the windows, and Radio 1 singing out on a plaster-encrusted radio, and Nat, a property mogul now, in his shorts and sandals. He remembered Freddie Sempill was dead. Well, that was sad. But you couldn't say they hadn't had enough practice at early deaths.

'He looked absolutely terrible the last time I saw him,' Christopher said to Simon that night, as Simon was making dinner. They were both watching their weight these days, and there was a no-alcohol rule Monday to Friday for Simon, who was making what he called Complicated Salad, with prawns and hardboiled eggs. 'When did we last see him?'

'No idea,' Simon said. 'I thought he'd died years ago. I never really knew him.'

'He came to Paul's funeral, didn't he?'

'Did he? I don't remember. That was such years ago. With Donna Summer and *I Will Survive*. Ironic, really. Did he really come to Paul's? Was he friends with Paul?'

'Well, I think he came,' Christopher said. 'Nat thought he hadn't seen him since that party at Duncan's – you know, the one to raise funds.'

'Oh, God, yes,' Simon said, with a relishing, nostalgic, warm tone. 'I can't believe he's only just died. He looked weeks away from the end, then.'

'Oh, well,' Christopher said. 'He's gone now. I don't know how Duncan came to know about it. He phoned me at work – that over-zealous secretary of mine came into a meeting with the chancellor and passed me a note saying please phone Duncan Flannery AS SOON AS POSSIBLE, in capitals.'

'Are we going? Did we like him enough?'

'It's in Richmond, Duncan said.'

'Well, it's not far, at least.'

Simon stopped shelling the egg in his hand; with his saintly bald glow in the reflected light from the garden window and the hard white egg in his hand, he suddenly looked like a martyr in Piero della Francesca. 'No,' he said. 'Not Richmond upon Thames. Richmond in Yorkshire.'

'What's Freddie Sempill doing being buried in Richmond in Yorkshire? Is that where his people came from? I thought he was born in Simpson's menswear department on Piccadilly.'

'I believe you're right,' Simon said.

But it turned out that Freddie Sempill's people, as he always put it, came from Essex. They were in Shoeburyness, as they always had been. His father had worked for the Ministry of Defence there. Very hush-hush, Freddie Sempill had always said. After his retirement, they'd stayed there, liking it. Freddie Sempill had always lived in Fulham in an awful flat on the second floor of a converted semi, with a strange smell of disinfectant on the stairs. Then he'd moved to Richmond in Yorkshire.

Simon was telling all of this in Duncan's car as they were driving up. It was a bit of a squeeze. Alan, surprisingly, had said he wanted to come, and Nat too; and then some people had heard about the trip and about the funeral and said they might as well come, even though they had hardly known Freddie Sempill, or not known him one bit. Duncan's boyfriend Ronnie was driving another car, and his sister Dommie had been landed with Clive and Stephen. Christopher hadn't wanted to come, and it was in any case hard to get a whole day off from the Treasury. Arthur's friend Tim was minding the shop; Arthur was in with Ronnie and Dommie's ten-year-old daughter Celia, who loved funerals, anything like that.

'But I don't understand,' Alan said. 'Why Richmond?'

Simon said it had been either that or Catterick, apparently.

'Simon,' Nat said, 'Catterick is Richmond. The name of the camp is Catterick. The name of the town is Richmond. He did move to Catterick. Honestly.'

But Alan still didn't understand, and Nat had to explain that, at the end, Freddie Sempill had wanted to move to a town with a constant supply of squaddies. Catterick – the name of the army camp, as Nat explained – was the biggest camp in Britain. He had gone there on his own, and was being buried there this morning.

'Do you suppose there's going to be a salute of honour?' Duncan said, from the driving seat. 'From the squaddies he helped out with the odd twenty quid?'

They discussed it, and Freddie Sempill's appearance towards the end. It seemed unlikely that Freddie Sempill had been able, in his last years, to persuade anyone to do anything, with twenty pounds or ten times twenty. Yorkshire was quite a distance away. They began to talk about the funerals they had been to. There had been Andrew's, last year. But that didn't count; that had been suicide. The others?

'I loved Matthew's best,' Nat said simply. They agreed, Matthew's had been wonderful. Alan hadn't known Matthew – he had been a colleague of Nat's, when Nat still had a job, and had always been Nat's friend. Matthew had never been rich, but he had left two thousand pounds in his will to furnish the church with white flowers. It had made people cry, going into that little church in Putney on a grey March day, and finding it so blanched and fresh, and the smell so beautiful, too. You felt transformed, and then the vicar standing up in his white cassock, surrounded by lilies and white roses and branches of blossom, and his look of happiness to see his church like that. A look he composed before the service began, but there had been an air of happiness, improbably, over the whole ceremony. 'That was the first funeral I ever went to,' Nat said, 'with a woven willow casket instead of a coffin. That was so nice. You could imagine Matthew lying in it and not minding a bit.' And then there was Paul's. Everyone remembered Paul's – it had been a disco funeral with some bits of opera, and plumed black horses standing outside.

'What was it Paul used to say?' Nat said. 'When I go to bed with a man –'

'When I go to bed with a man,' Duncan said, concentrating on the road, 'I expect him to maintain ...'

He had started telling it as a funny remark, but he hadn't said it for years, and in a moment he had to say to the car, 'I'm sorry. I'd forgotten. I hadn't thought about Paul or about that for a while. I'll be all right in a moment.'

'He was so special,' Alan said.

But then there was that other one, where the gay vicar had got over-excited, and had taken a red rose from the bouquet at the end of his sermon, and had gone over to the grieving widow, handed it over and said, with a special deep, husky voice, 'For you.' Who had that been? No, they couldn't remember, but they all remembered the gay vicar. Hadn't he said, 'For you, Brian?' But who was Brian? 'I know I bought his boyfriend's books from him afterwards,' Duncan said, only a little tremulously. 'He wasn't a reader, Brian, or so he said. I think he lived in Barons Court. I could only give him sixty pounds, I remember.' There had been Kevin's funeral – that was another one with Verdi. Duncan explained to Alan that Kevin was the owner of the awful house Arthur used to live in. That had been two years ago. Never got over the shock of Mrs Thatcher being chucked out like that. Arthur was quite thrown – he had no idea where he was going to live when the house was sold out of the blue like that. Poor old Arthur, having to move in with his friends Tony and Tim for six months till they had had enough and told him to leave. No wonder they had all been crying at Kevin's funeral.

'They weren't really,' Nat said.

'I can't think what they're going to say about Freddie Sempill,' Simon said. 'He was so awful. I remember, years ago, he told me that he would phone up rent boys and get them to come round, and then he would say, in his pretend-Cockney voice, I'm sorry, mate – I ain't got no money. And then he said the rent boy would often have sex with you anyway. But sometimes he would hit you. But I quite enjoy that sometimes, too, Freddie Sempill used to say. I don't know why we're going to his funeral. I can't think of anything nice to say about him at all.'

And then there was that other funeral – Alan remembered a funeral where the boyfriend had broken his hip falling downstairs drunk and the mother was recovering from a stroke, and someone else, he couldn't remember, anyway, they were all in wheelchairs and pretending not to notice or to speak to each other because the family and the boyfriend didn't acknowledge each other. All wheeling around each other and pretending not to see. Nat had known one boy in a situation quite like that, a charming boy who had gone out with Patrick Dee, the old television presenter and closet case; had lived with him for years. And when Patrick Dee had died, the family had hired thugs and, during the funeral itself, this would have been, they went into the house they'd shared for years and took all of the boyfriend's possessions out and put them into black bin bags and left them outside on the pavement and changed the locks and everything. And then there had been that one two years ago—

'Has anyone got a phone in the other car?' Alan said.

'Ronnie has,' Nat said. 'Why? Do you want to speak to them?'

'I just want to pause for a moment,' Alan said. 'If there's a service station coming up. I'm awfully sorry, Duncan – just for a five-minute break.'

'It's fourteen miles,' Duncan said. 'Can you endure?'

20.

It was just after twelve as Richmond appeared. None of them had been there before. A square tower rose out of the mild stone town, set in green; the trees were dense with colour. They had rolled the windows down after leaving the motorway, and the scent of the country poured in in waves and gusts. Duncan turned down the music they had been playing, an old tape of *Dusty in Memphis*; they had stopped talking so exuberantly. Nat was reading out the directions from a piece of paper. The others sat quietly in the back of the car.

'It says third left,' Nat said. 'But it means – I tell you what, take this one. How could Freddie Sempill come here to live?'

Duncan turned left, and at the bottom of the hill there was the church. They were just in time, about ten minutes before the start, and the hearse was outside the church – an anonymous black Co-op car with a coffin inside it, and a single sour wreath of white flowers. They were on time, surely, but there was nobody much outside. Almost every funeral they could remember had been full, and the crowd outside before, like a busy, weeping wedding. It was the advantage of dying young: your friends outlived you, and came to your wedding. The other car had arrived before them, and Duncan parked his in the church car park. There was plenty of space.

'Has everyone gone in already?' Alan said. But they went in, and there was hardly anyone there. There was no leaflet on vellumed paper with a portrait of Freddie Sempill on the cover; only a sullen photocopied piece of paper with the words of a couple of hymns and 'TREVOR SEMPILL, 1943–1994' at the head of it.

'That's what he was called,' Nat murmured, as Duncan gave a small turn sideways. 'What he was christened, I mean. I would have thought – have we come to the right occasion? But he renamed himself when he came to London, Freddie with an *ie* on the end. Very *Brideshead Revisited*.' In the front row, there were two small elderly heads, both female; a mother and an aunt. Three rows behind, and again at the other side of the church, there were two men; one an older, shaved-head, fat man; the other conceivably one of Freddie's squaddies, with sharp-cut hair. And then towards the back, in two clumps, were the rest of them, travelled up from London. Dommie turned and, with Celia, gave Duncan a huge smile and a wave. She was wearing a curious black construction on her head, a substanceless design of stick and feather and ribbon patched onto a black saucer; Celia was wearing a black party shift with a white collar. They sat down. One of the two old ladies at the front turned round too, and inspected them with some vigour. Could she be Freddie Sempill's mother? She turned back and, with a few muttered words, made her companion turn round, too; and that, clearly, was Freddie Sempill's mother. She had the same disapproving pinhead air. They looked old, tired, bored; they did not inspect the other mourners in grief, but ready to express contempt. The younger of the two solitary men looked round too; he was pale and smooth, a once-a-week shaver, and he seemed to catch Duncan's eye before turning back again.

There had been a wreath over the coffin in the hearse, and there were two floral arrangements on either side of the altar. But they were generic arrangements, done by the church; there was nothing chosen or characteristic about them, and most of it was made up with carnations and greenery. The vicar came to the front and asked them to stand, and the organist started to play, too slowly, 'Sheep Will Safely Graze'. The coffin was borne in on the shoulders of the undertaker's men. Should they have volunteered to carry it? It was too late now. The coffin was set down and, slowly, to the vicar's half-smile, the organ performance came to a sticky end. The vicar, a porker with pink cheeks and a snub nose, welcomed them to this celebration of Trevor's life.

They sang a hymn, the sound of less than a dozen voices difficult to pull together into a congregation. It was a familiar choice, 'All Things Bright and Beautiful'. The heart moved painfully, reflecting the lack of engagement in the choice. Who had made it? Did Freddie Sempill have a favourite hymn? 'Eternal Father, Strong to Save' – that was the navy hymn, wasn't it? It would remind him of all those queens who had pretended to be in the navy for Freddie Sempill's benefit. This one had been chosen by someone who had remembered that Trevor as a little boy had liked it, as all children are supposed to like 'All Things Bright and Beautiful'. Or perhaps the vicar had suggested it, saying that everyone knew it.

The hymn came to its grisly conclusion. The vicar began to speak. He had a fluting, unctuous voice, as of a much older person, and gestured with both hands simultaneously, waving up and down, like a teacher quelling a noisy class.

'Although I never knew Trevor,' he began, 'or Freddie, as he liked to be called as an adult, I've had the pleasure of talking to Vera, Trevor's mother, about him in his early years, and to Sean and Keith, his two friends up here in Richmond where he spent his last years. We should probably remember Trevor in his best years. His last years were spent in suffering. The rare Chinese bone infection he picked up while travelling in the 1970s was something he bore bravely, with the support of Sean and Keith to help out in the house. But before his last years, we should think of him as he wanted to be remembered, as a jolly chap, you might say.

'Trevor Sempill was born in 1943, in London's East End. Before he was five, he and his mother and father, Vera and Martin, moved to Shoeburyness in Essex.'

The whole service was over in twenty-five minutes. Duncan cast a look over the aisle at Dommie as it came to an end with another singing of 'All Things Bright and Beautiful'. The organist had played 'Nimrod' from the *Enigma Variations* in between. There hadn't been a poem; that would have defeated old mother Sempill. Dommie cast a warning look back, and Duncan gave a consoling pat on the thigh to Nat. Vera, supported by her friend, came tottering up the aisle, followed at a safe distance by the two friends, going separately. The fat, bald one seemed a little upset. Vera was an upright, grey-faced woman of some height, her hair roughly brought into some sort of shape, her pinheaded face without makeup, her eyebrows left untrimmed, like a Soviet dictator's. Her friend, less bony but not much shorter, had made a little more of an effort, and an ugly orange slash of lipstick and two raw diagonals of blusher crossed her face. Vera stared straight ahead as she walked; the friend, walking by her but not supporting her, gave a direct look at Duncan's group – an accusing, cold, assessing look straight from the North Sea into the cold heart of Shoeburyness. Duncan looked back levelly. There was somebody, at any rate, who knew where Freddie Sempill had been when he said he'd been to China and picked up a rare bone disease there. Vera's friend knew where Freddie Sempill had been. He'd been to Earls Court.

'Come on,' Nat said. 'Let's go and introduce ourselves. Rare Chinese bone disease. Honestly.'

'I didn't know he was going to be such a silly old thing as all that,' Alan said, getting a helping hand from Dommie's daughter Celia. 'It's one of the best things in my life that I told Mother all about it – well, not all about it, but enough that she said she didn't really need to know the details. She wouldn't have said she loved me anyway. It wouldn't have occurred to her to say such a thing.'

'Alan,' Celia said. 'When you die, can I sing a solo?'

'Of course you can, my darling,' Alan said. 'Can I choose what it's going to be?'

'Well, you're not going to be there,' Celia said. 'But I'm going to be there, so why shouldn't I choose it?'

'Don't be pert, darling,' Dommie said, coming up behind and

putting sunglasses on. 'Alan knows lots of people who can sing whatever he wants to have sung. And I might point out that it's not going to be very soon, so your voice might very well have gone beyond its childish promise by then.'

'I don't mind,' Alan said. 'I never really mind what people sing. I don't really know about music. That hymn was nice, though, like the hymns you sing at school. Not like the difficult ones that some queens like to choose for their funerals, knowing that no one knows the tunes and you'll all be going Hurdy-hur-di-hur, gloria, gloria, hallelujah, not really knowing any of you what you're doing. No, I knew that tune, it was nice to have a good old sing-song.'

'Put on your sad face, dear,' Clive said to Simon. 'And stand by me. Stephen's ever so good at this sort of thing – it's being a barrister and having to speak in court all the time, he's never nervous. But I know the mother's going to make a beeline for me. I've only come for the day out. You've got to stand by me and do all the work.'

But when they came out, the vicar was standing helplessly on his own in his white cassock in the bright sunlight, blinking like a rabbit. Beyond the church gates, the mother and her friend were getting into a red minicab with a sign on top reading 1AAA RICHMOND CABS, the mother almost pushing the friend in. She hustled round to the other side, her haste making no concession to the occasion, and the car pulled out.

'Vera and Mrs Thompson had to make an early start back,' the vicar said helplessly. 'They came from Essex, and had a very early start. Were you friends of – of Freddie?'

'Thank you for the service,' Ronnie said smoothly. 'I thought it went very well.'

'I was sorry I had to call him Trevor all the way through,' the vicar said. 'It was what the family requested, you see. I know he didn't like to be called Trevor. Have you met Sean? And Keith? They were Freddie's friends up here. I'm sure they'd like to meet you.'

The vicar turned and went back into the church, perhaps hungry for his lunch. Sean turned out to be the fat, bald queen; Keith the squaddie, or he looked like a squaddie. He had a black earring in his left ear, which probably meant that he was another queen.

'Friends of his, were you?' Keith said. They agreed that they probably had been. 'Funny, he never mentioned you. From London, are you? Freddie always said it was the best thing he'd ever done, leaving London.'

'I only knew he'd moved when he died,' Duncan said. 'I'm sorry.'

'I was the only friend he had at the end,' the squaddie said.

'That's sad to hear,' Nat said. 'I'm sorry for that. But he had you, and Sean, isn't it?'

'Sean weren't his friend,' the squaddie said. 'Sean were –' he paused with scorn '– his *nurse*.'

They stood and watched the soldier-like figure disappear down the path.

'Oh dear,' Alan said. 'People so often get cross at funerals. I never know why. But there it is.'

The nurse, whose name was Sean, stood with them. 'That's Keith,' he said. 'He was hoping to be left the house, I've been told. Sorry about that. I'm Sean.'

'Rare Chinese bone disease?' Duncan said.

'Yes, well,' Sean said. 'That's what he wanted people to say. I don't know – I think he thought people might even believe it. I don't think anyone did, mind. Has the mother gone?'

21.

As there was nothing arranged back at the house, they went with Sean to a pub. It was at his suggestion, made without any reference to the fact that there was a ten-year-old girl in the party. But Dommie quietly said to Duncan and Ronnie that she and Celia would much rather have a walk round the town and play at ladies having lunch in a tea shop anyway. It was a pub that, as it were, all of them knew, but none of them had been to for years. It had a solitary alcoholic patron with a huge cardigan and an Alsatian at his feet; there were comedy paragraphs from the local newspaper stuck to the walls, with a chained-up charity box for a military cause, photographs of regulars with jocular additions, and, outside, a handwritten notice in upper-case italics announcing a *Night With The Stars – Andy McRae, The Heartthrob With The Voice of Gold*. 'I don't much fancy a night with Andy McRae, the Heartthrob With The Voice of Gold,' Arthur said, after inspecting the gruesome little photograph of a smile, being given by one unpractised in the art. Still, they trooped in and, in their black funeral suits and neat appearance, might have made a favourable impression on the landlord.

'I'm honestly envious of Dommie and Celia,' Alan was saying to Nat. 'These country towns, they're always full of treasures – you only have to know where to look. Those Staffordshire pugs on my mantelpiece, Mother and I found them in a strange little back-street in Taunton, twenty years ago. A house-clearer, really. Well, Mother always said to me, Alan, you're a little magpie, and you've got an eye for a bargain, but she knew when to keep schtum, and she went off and bothered herself in the back of the shop while I did the necessary. We were so gleeful and relieved when they were wrapped up – in newspaper – and safely in our hands. I was certain the man was going to drop one. They were seventy new pence for the two, believe it or not. I wish I could excuse myself and go with Dommie and Celia round the town.'

'It was always very important to Christopher,' Simon was saying to Duncan about something or other. 'Always, really, from day one.'

'Oh, God,' Stephen was saying to Ronnie, 'it just wouldn't work. It just wouldn't work at all, not one bit.'

'What are you two talking about?' Clive said.

'Shoes,' Ronnie said.

But then a pause in the conversation came, and over the pints of bitter, and lemonades for Alan and Nat, the man who had been Freddie Sempill's friend was suddenly talking over silence; he had been talking to Clive. 'I don't remember him mentioning you,' the man – his name was Sean – was saying. 'I don't remember your name at all. It's nice of you to come. There could have been more of a turn-out. His brother couldn't come, of course.'

'Freddie Sempill had a brother?' Duncan said. Sean gave him a hostile look, difficult to account for.

'Yes, Freddie had a brother,' Sean said. 'Didn't you know? He's in Kuwait at the moment, very hush-hush. He's a brigadier. Didn't you know?'

'No,' Duncan said. 'I had no idea. I don't remember him ever mentioning a brother.'

'Perhaps you weren't listening,' Sean said. He turned back to Clive. 'It's nice of you to come, though I don't remember him mentioning you. None of you ever came up to visit him when he was alive, I notice.'

'Probably because none of us knew he was living here,' Ronnie said drily.

'You could have found out,' Sean said, pulling savagely at his pint.

Nat and Arthur exchanged a glance in which amusement was not quite successfully concealed.

'How did you meet him?' Simon said.

'Oh, everyone knows everyone in this place,' Sean said. 'I looked after him, too, when he had a health crisis. Because of the way he looked – you know, with the growth on his face – everyone noticed him when he arrived. I think he'd got the wrong idea about Richmond. He used to say that he could have bought a mansion here for the price of his flat in London, and there might be some truth in that. He bought a nice house, a terrace, one of those in Almond Street, but not one worth the same as his place before. He said he'd come up here to splash it around a bit, have as much fun as he could. He used to say that to me a lot, even at the end. He liked soldiers, didn't he?'

'Rather known for it,' Ronnie said.

'Rather known for it,' Sean said, sneering in imitation. 'Yes, he was rather known for it. He'd go round the Fox and Hounds, because of the custom they get there, and he'd sit there, quite quietly with a pint, then another pint, then another one, then he'd go up to someone and buy them a drink, buy them another one, and then in half an hour he would say that he'd give them fifty pounds if they'd let him suck them off. He didn't have much luck, poor Freddie. He looked like that, you see. No one was going to put their doings in that face. You'd be afraid of catching something. You couldn't help it.

'Everyone knew him, to look at, but not many people passed the time of day with him. There was only Keith. You know Keith – he was the one who came just now.'

'The squaddie,' Duncan said.

Sean turned to Duncan in rage. 'Keith's not a squaddie,' he said. 'Course he's not a squaddie. He's like Freddie was. He'd moved here for the sake of the squaddies, and he cut his hair to look like one, and he dressed like one in civvies – in a white polo shirt and tight white trousers with a little belt on. And the first time Freddie saw him in the same pub, he went and offered him fifty quid if he'd come and wank off in his sitting room. "You don't have to look at me if you don't want to," Freddie said. He'd got humble like that. He'd taken to asking me if I'd wank off when I came to change his sheets. I were a nurse, though, I wasn't a squaddie, so he didn't ask me every time, only when he wasn't having such a good day. I don't suppose anyone had ever offered Keith money for sex before, or mistaken him for a serving soldier in Her Majesty's Forces. So he took the money and he went home with Freddie and he did what Freddie asked him to do. After that he'd go over to Freddie's once a week and take the money and do whatever Freddie wanted him to do.

That's why he was crying at the funeral. End of his income stream. I think Keith thought he was going to be left the house and Freddie's money, what was left of it after pouring most of it down his throat, Keith's throat. It's a nice street, Almond Street, I always think. But the mother's got it. There wasn't a will. I don't suppose he could think of who he wanted to leave anything to.

'I said to him once – this would have been after he went blind, and Keith had taken to coming over dressed any old how, not even pretending any more – I said to Freddie once, you do know Keith's not a soldier, he's nothing to do with the armed forces? And Freddie said, Course he is, he's on manoeuvres right now as we speak. I said to him, Some people call it manoeuvres, some people call it going to Cinderella's Nite Spot in Leeds of a Friday night. He said, Don't be daft, he can talk you through everything he's done, he could put a rifle together in front of you in thirty seconds. So I said, Fantasy, Freddie. Sheer fantasy. And he sort of smiled a little bit. I don't think he were under any illusions. I don't think he ever met anyone else up here, apart from me and Keith, who got paid fifty pounds a go.'

'That's a bit sad,' Duncan said.

'What would you know about it?' Sean said. His rage had been passing – most of his story he had been telling in the direction of Alan, who had been nodding and saying, 'I see,' and 'Really,' and 'Oh dear,' in encouragement. 'What would you know about it? You never made any effort with Freddie. He told me all about you. He was in at the beginning of your bookshop, doing all the hard work, the painting and the carpentry and everything, all the electricals, and doing it for nothing. Then he moves up to Richmond and you never try to reach him. There's not much gratitude there for everything Freddie did for you.'

'I see,' Duncan said. He wasn't going to say that it hadn't been quite like that.

'It's good to know that he had some gay friends,' Alan said

peaceably. 'I always think that helps enormously. Just to have two people to talk things over with, who'll understand what it's like, to be like this, all the little pleasures and the pains and everything, really. It's nice to have lots of gay friends, so that when you fall out and bicker, you've got someone else to rely on.' Nat started to giggle quietly: there was nobody less able to fall out and bicker with anyone than Alan, and Nat's giggle proved infectious. 'But even if you don't have a large social circle, if there's always two nice gay friends—'

'What are you talking about?' Sean said. 'I'm not gay. I'm not one of your gays. When he said to me, Sean, I want you to strip off and have a wank, I'll give you thirty pounds, I said, No, Freddie. I said no every time. I've got a wife at home. We're trying for a child. I'm very happy as I am, thank you very much. I've got to go now. I thought I'd be friendly to Freddie's friends, but I can see that he was right after all. You're none of you worth it.'

'Oh dear,' Nat said, as the man departed, slamming the door of the pub behind him. 'That was a bit unfortunate.'

'Closet case,' Arthur said.

'You are terrible,' Duncan said. 'Not everyone's gay, you know.'

'No, but he knew all about Cinderella's Nite Spot in Leeds, didn't he?' Arthur said. 'And Friday night there? Happens to be its only gay night. Very well informed, that Sean, I would say. Did you notice, too, he thought we knew everything he knew, what the best pub for picking up squaddies in Richmond were and what Almond Terrace were like? No idea about other people, that Sean.'

'You ought to be a novelist,' Simon said, drinking away – he was breaking his and Christopher's no-alcohol Monday to Friday regime, with some enjoyment. 'You've got excellent observational skills, as they say on the office away days.'

'Oh dear,' Alan said. 'Did we say something to offend that charming man?'

'Never you mind,' Nat said. 'I remember the day that Freddie Sempill went over and tried to paint the bookshop. It all had to be done again. He never did anything for anyone else, it was always for himself and because he might get a shag out of it with someone he'd never see again. He was trying to impress the electricians, as I remember. Honestly.'

'It's true,' Duncan said. 'I don't think he ever did anything. I don't know why I'm the villain of the piece. Oh, God.'

'Oh, we all feel like that sometimes,' Ronnie said. 'Don't you worry about it. Only an idiot would believe anything Freddie Sempill ever said to them about anything, or a mad old closet case.'

'They'll be reduced to each other now,' Stephen said cheerfully. 'One of them saying I've got to get back to wife and kids, and the other saying I've got to get back to barracks before sergeant major locks up for night, and then doing it with their eyes closed, thinking about someone else entirely. Poor old them.'

'Your Yorkshire accent is terrible,' Arthur said. 'I've never heard worse.'

22.

Hours and hours later – it took five hours to drive to Richmond in Yorkshire to witness the last rites of Trevor (Freddie) Sempill, deceased of a rare Chinese bone disease, and five hours back – Ronnie and Duncan were sitting in the kitchen of Ronnie's house, in the basement. Just for once, Duncan would quite have liked to phone out for a pizza, like a student, or something even worse. But Annunziata had left a delicious light supper with grapes at the end.

'What's up, honey?' Ronnie said, in an American accent.

'Oh, nothing,' Duncan said. 'Just tired. I don't want to go to any more funerals, that's all. I didn't even end up getting any books out of it for the second-hand corner.'

'Well, you won't have to tomorrow or the day after,' Ronnie

said. 'But you'll probably have to some time. They won't be as awful as that one, though.'

'It was just ...' Duncan paused. He didn't know if he should say what he wanted to say. 'It was just – he didn't do anything with his life. There was just nothing there. Not even old books.'

'Not everyone can do something,' Ronnie said, only slightly disapprovingly. 'Poor old queen.'

'No, it's just ...' Duncan said. 'It's just – oh, I don't know, Ronnie. It's not about making something or building a monument or running a Footsie 100 company.' (He realized as he said it that five years before he wouldn't have known to say Footsie 100 company with such confidence. Ronnie had brought some awful things into his conversation.) 'Do you – at school, do you remember there were those men, I can't remember, were they called Radley and Latimer? Ridley. I think.'

'Not at my school,' Ronnie said. 'Do you mean at school?'

'I mean in history,' Duncan said. 'In history lessons. And I can't remember what they were, or what they were supposed to have done, but they were burnt for it – this is back in the Tudors, we did them for O level. And one of them said to the other, "Be of good cheer, Master Latimer," or possibly Master Ridley, depending on who was talking, because, because—'

'"This day we light such a candle as in England shall never be put out,"' Ronnie said, surprisingly. 'I do know. How they know that one of them said it to the other as they were in flames, I don't know. We can't remember what they did or why they did it. But we remember what they're supposed to have said. You can't expect Freddie Sempill to die a martyr's death just to please you, you know.'

'Oh, you know what I mean,' Duncan said. 'He never lit a candle. He'd have put candles out if he had, whenever he'd noticed one. There was just nothing in Freddie Sempill's life that you'd want to copy. It was all just awful and empty and disapproving of everyone, and pretending that he wasn't gay in the hope that someone would shag him, just the once.'

'I wish I'd known him. I would have told him that was a strategy doomed to failure.'

'Once, in five years' time, someone will say to someone else, probably on their way to someone else's funeral, Do you remember Freddie Sempill, and the other person will say Oh, God, that one – I haven't thought of him in years. And that will be the very last time anyone will ever have any reason to think of Freddie Sempill. He didn't change anyone's life at all.'

'That queen will think of him, I dare say.'

'The nurse? Dead of a rare Chinese bone infection by then, I promise you. What was he called – Sean?'

'You've lit a candle,' Ronnie said suddenly. 'You have.'

'I've lit a fucking torch,' Duncan said. He felt warm and happy and secure, all at once. He wished they could be Victorian orphans, eating bread and milk from white bowls in the kitchen basement, wearing white nightgowns like angels. 'A fucking torch. That's what I've lit, darling.'

23.

It was at the end of September that Arthur found himself in the big bookshop near the university. It had always been a drab, academic sort of place, with, on the ground floor, only minimal piles of popular new books, and ascending towards still more austere and daunting material in the upper floors. Two days before, he had found himself in the bed of an Austrian, a student. There wasn't the age difference that might have been assumed. The Austrian had been a student for fourteen years now, and had ended up at one of the London colleges doing a dissertation on an aspect of an Indian language. He had explained which one, in the new bar on Old Compton Street. Then they had moved on together to another bar, another new one on Old Compton Street. And then they had moved on to a third. Old Compton Street was getting to be quite brazenly gay, and the new bars, unlike the old gay bars, had great sheets of windows rather than the blacked-out sheets of hardboard that had guarded the clientele of the Coleherne in Earls Court. Good luck with that, Arthur thought, remembering the number of their glazier without too much effort. But you could go on a short bar crawl now in Old Compton Street. Arthur had stayed the night with the Austrian, in his tiny rented flat in Bethnal Green, and in the morning had had breakfast with him – a hard-boiled egg, German black bread and a piece of apple cake. Interesting. The Austrian had turned out to be a great reader, with a wall full of books in English and German and, presumably, the Indian language. They looked like classics. Arthur said he hadn't read enough of the classics, Dickens and all that; he was ashamed of it but there it was. He knew he was missing out.

'And German books?' the Austrian said. 'Not even *Buddenbrooks?*'

Arthur just about knew that *Buddenbrooks* was by Thomas Mann. He'd read Mann's diaries and letters when they came out, and they stocked it in the bookshop – he'd enjoyed the moment when Mann couldn't get it up when his wife was lying next to him and had written afterwards that he'd be able to get it up soon enough if it were a man next to him. He told Ralf this.

'But the novels – you have not read the novels? The novels are why Mann is interesting to us in the first place!'

Ralf had insisted, asking him one by one about *The Magic Mountain* and *Joseph and His Brothers* and *Felix Krull* and *Doctor Faustus* and *Death in Venice* —

'Yes! I have read that one. I definitely have. I definitely saw the film, anyway. I don't know about the book. I'm sure I have. We definitely stock it. I'm so uneducated, I warn you.'

And something called *Lotte in Weimar* and *The Black Swan* and *Royal Highness* – Ralf was pretty genuinely enjoying himself here. He would see Arthur again when Arthur had read *Buddenbrooks* at least. *Buddenbrooks* was the book that everyone should read.

'But not until then,' Ralf said.

'I hope it's not a long book,' Arthur said. He was enjoying sitting there naked, at the naked Austrian's breakfast table, eating black bread and looking at his nice blond beard and the nice blond hair on his nice chubby chest, like a god. He would read *Buddenbrooks* and then he would phone Ralf and then they would go out again and talk about it, and then hopefully he would end up licking the salty sweat from Ralf's chest in his nice student bed again.

They didn't stock any Mann apart from the diaries, a biography and *Death in Venice*, so around twelve Arthur said he was going out, and got the bus to the big university bookshop – the ones on Oxford Street might have it, but he wanted to range freely over shelves and shelves of slightly different translations, snuffling in pseudo-expertise, like a pig after truffles. He found it easily – there was, after all, only one translation – and was about to go to the till to pay for it when he saw a mild, scholarly type of woman with spectacles, an uneven-hemmed browny-green dress. There was something calculated about her vague stance, a deliberate sort of who-me-Officer about the way she was peering at the shelves, and in a moment Arthur pinned it down: her expression was peaceful and half smiling, but her hands were moving restlessly, down at her side. In a moment, she picked a book off the shelf – no, two books, but held together. Arthur watched her closely. She brought both towards her face, shook her head in apparent disappointment and, by releasing her grip slightly, let one fall into her bag before returning the other to the shelf. If you hadn't been watching her closely, it would have seemed quite innocuous.

Like all shopkeepers, Arthur could not abide thieves. They came only behind bribe-hungry members of the Vice Squad and glass-smashers in his loathing. Most of all, he loathed them because he knew, somehow, that someone who stole a book from a bookshop would never lend it to a friend with the words 'You ought to read it – it's really good.' He didn't know whether the Big Gay Bookshop suffered more than most bookshops from thieves. In their case, it was always the potentially smutty books that were taken. Was it more embarrassing to pay for *The Nude Male* or to be discovered with it in your bag in front of a shopful of customers? The answer seemed obvious to Arthur, but not to the six or seven regulars that had to be watched constantly – one a vicary sort of fellow with half-mast trousers in Crimplene, and hair he cut himself, apparently. He was the reason that Arthur had noticed the woman with the hemline in the first place. She had seemed, to the expert eye, like a shoplifting type.

He followed her discreetly from the E–M bay to the N–Z, picking up and dawdling over a book as he went. She didn't appear to have noticed. In a moment she repeated the performance with, Arthur saw, two novels by Philip Roth. *The Great American Novel* went into the basket. It was impressive; Arthur realized with indignation that she had done this many times before to be so practised. She went into the next bay.

Arthur had intended, imprecisely, to follow her for a time, then priggishly warn the management. But in the next bay, after the end of fiction, there was something unexpected. It was a mixed bag of offerings, and his shoplifter gave one cursory glance to the categories and moved on to the richly glossy pickings of hardbacked biography. Arthur stayed where he was. There were nine cases in the bay, of social theory, politics and women's writings, and then, finally, over the ninth in chalk capitals the bookseller had written GAY AND LESBIAN. Arthur went over. The collection was meagre; there were about a hundred novels, he reckoned, most of which were classics, and some porn novels. On the bottom two shelves were books of photography. It wouldn't keep anyone curious busy for long.

But how long had this been here? Anyone wanting to read about people like them would have had to fossick through the whole shop for a reference or a single volume. You'd had to look, or to take a trip to the Big Gay Bookshop over in Marylebone. Now it was here. No one was looking at it. Soon every bookshop would have one. There would be glass windows in front of every gay bar, which would be full of gay people and heterosexual people mixing indifferently. People would say, 'Oh, are you gay?' casually, in the way that they said, 'Oh, are you left-handed?' Books would be about gay people and about straight people and everyone would know some of each and no one would care. You would be able to marry a man or a woman and all that was characteristic, that was deliberate, that was protective, that was shameful, that was unlike the normal would pass from human behaviour, then from human memory. There would be no need for gay people to have liberation groups; there would be no need for a bar for gay people; there would be no need for an area of a city to declare itself a gay place; there would be no need for a gay bookshop. Arthur knew that the work of the Big Gay Bookshop was done, or almost.

He left the bookshop and, instead of returning to Duncan's shop, he went home to the little flat in Streatham he now rented. There he packed his one suitcase with the things in his flat he really liked and the clothes he couldn't live without. He took his passport. That all went into one suitcase, not very big. Then he went out and caught the bus, then the tube, to the railway station at Paddington. He was glad he had saved, over the last fifteen years, ten thousand pounds. He didn't mind the expense, just this time, of the ticket he bought – to the airport on the fast new train, and at the airport, a flight abroad. It was just a one-off expense.

24.

Afterwards, when Duncan thought about the bookshop period of his life, he always thought of Arthur, who had come into it at the start and had stayed with it for most of its existence. And Arthur's appearance and disappearance were always a mystery to him. He had gone out one lunchtime saying he'd be back by two, and had never returned. Only after five days of phoning round the hospitals had a postcard arrived, from Berlin, saying that he'd moved there on the spur of the moment and he was sorry to have let Duncan down. Since then, nothing. Arthur: one of those tousle-haired angels in a fairy story, who arrives at the moment of the hero's greatest need, and teaches him three lessons before departing in a pillar of fire and smoke. Remember, Arthur's voice called from inside the vertical zip of fire, remember, Duncan …But what had the voice been telling Duncan to remember? What lessons had been learnt? He would have asked anyone else who had been around all through it, but so many of them were dead now. From the sky, or from Berlin, a thunderous tousled voice came, but so remote and so veiled with fire that Duncan, afterwards, could never hear it properly. As Arthur's nature revealed itself at the very last, and his quotidian shambling body and his way with the definite article were subtracted from Duncan, who had taken it all for granted, the purpose of the last fifteen years was concealed, hidden, made cryptic. The books had gone out into the world as, now, Arthur had. That was all that could be done.

BOOK 9
1927

1.1

The Variété Theatre in Dessau was an old institution, not painted or restored for years. When the upper balcony was full, and the whole of the front row leant on the brass rail in front of them better to admire some faded singer, reduced to appearing in Dessau, the customers in the back row could hear a terrible creaking and groaning behind them as the balcony began to part company with the wall of the auditorium. The whole frayed structure would, one day, come plummeting down onto the heads of the audience in the orchestra, there was no doubt. On stage, there was an Oriental dance, an aria from *La Dame Blanche*, a conjuror, two aged comedians practising back-talk, a strong man, a Russian ballet of five swans, another aria, some jugglers, and then the interval. In the uppermost balcony, the seats were three Rentenmarks. To Fritz, this seemed inexplicably much more than the billions and trillions of marks that had been demanded for cinema tickets a year earlier. It seemed more like money. Next week, at the Bauhaus, there would be a staging of a ballet of geometry and experiment that would change the notion of theatrical display for ever. Tonight, they were going to discover what theatrical display actually was.

In the pit there was a group of brass players, two violins, a clarinet and a solitary querulous bassoon. Now, an aged soprano was singing to their accompaniment with rouge painted on her cheeks and wrinkled bosom, pretending to be a country girl of no more than seventeen. Behind her was a backdrop of farmland, paint flaking off in patches. Her donkey, a trained animal with red-tipped ears, stood patiently while the hit of the 1870s ran its course. The audience were talking to each other while the waiters in white came up and down the aisles, carrying full beer mugs through the darkened auditorium. Onstage, by the side of the ancient singer, the band's best efforts were being supplemented by the jangling and thumping of an ancient piano, not tuned for many years; it was being played by the compère, who, as rouged as the singer, doubled his duties as accompanist. The band was leisurely; the singer was vague; the pianist was impatient; each phrase began at three quite different moments. Nobody in the audience was paying much attention.

Fritz sat in the upper balcony with five students. One was dressed as a pierrot. Fritz was at least ten years older than they were, and his style was that of the students of five years before. He wore a heavy blue jacket and trousers such as workmen wear; he had a knot of a red tie at the neck of his khaki shirt. He was paying intense attention to what was happening onstage. Through steadily narrowed eyes, he could perceive the essence of the space he was in. His perception then left out the trivialities, the rough red-painted surface of the walls with the plaster coming through, the holed seats of the chairs, the glare of a yellow spotlight shining out of the wings onto the unconvincing maquillage of woman and donkey. Instead, the whole scene was transformed into its essential truths. There were two large blocks of space, one cuboid and bright, the other rounded towards the back and dark. At their conjunction were three irregular dark shapes. The two large blocks met over a line of sound, buried deep in the ground. That was the orchestra. There was a smell in the larger rounded block, and there came another smell from the smaller, cuboid block. He opened his eyes more widely, and tried to see reality with the same intensity of perception. Beneath the scene – the auditorium, the stage, the singer and the donkey and the piano – were blocks of light and colour. Their nature was no longer concealed by the inessentials. He could see now how *The Euclidean Ballet* was going to reveal itself to its audience and performers.

With a trill, something that might have been a run of notes and a high sound, near a shriek, the singer finished and the pianist concluded with a few thumped chords. In her day, this last coda would never have been heard; applause would not have waited long after the last note. Now it waited, the audience talking over the pianist's last contribution indifferently. The donkey with its ears dyed red at the tip sneezed, shook its head. There was a spattering of applause and, from one of the students, an ecstatic *brava brava brava*, a leaping to the feet. Fritz found that he was looking at the inessentials again. The glimpse of the unreal, the ideal, the ungrasped truth had been brief, as it always was. He was not sure what the name of the enthusiastic student was. He was very young. Like the others, he was working on the design for *The Euclidean Ballet* and had followed eagerly when Fritz had suggested a trip to the theatre. In Dessau, that meant a trip to the Variété with its experimental-music orchestra and its superannuated turns expounding the taste of forty years ago.

The girl sitting next to him explained that Leoš came from a small village in Bohemia. German was his third language. Before he had come to study at the Bauhaus in Dessau, he had never been to any city but Brno, and had never been to the theatre in his life. For him, the girl explained, this was all too wonderful for words.

Her name was Stasia. She came from Berlin, of course, she felt the need to go on to remind Fritz. Another of the boys, a quiet one who looked at everything with a gleam of delight, was called Felix. He was said to be the son of one of the Masters.

The compère announced in his grating voice the last act of the first half. He retreated to the piano, and began to bang away at a circus polka. A small tuba in the pit marked the emphatic notes in the bass. A juggler came onstage and began to hurl two coloured balls into the air; then from his pocket a third; then a

515

fourth. A second juggler came on, and repeated the feat; then a third. They were dressed in jockeys' shirts of silk in different brilliant colours, spring green, electric pink and a comic orange. To the side, the compère, in his white tie and tails, continued to grin at the audience and to thump at the piano; with the end of each phrase, he hurled his hand upwards to his shoulders in a startled flourish. At a change of key, the jugglers turned smoothly to each other, and began to juggle not in solitude but tossing balls one to another. Fritz watched carefully. There was no need for him to narrow his eyes. Here was geometry revealed onstage. He waited for one of them to drop a ball, for the geometry to be broken and re-established. But it did not happen. The act came to an end; there was some applause; the lights in the auditorium were raised before the jugglers and the compère were all off the stage.

Fritz got up heavily and led his group out of the auditorium. The boy from near Brno came first behind him, applauding all the way and turning back towards the stage. The boy who was dressed as a pierrot followed in the rear. His costume was stained and dirty and his face paint was approximate. A waiter walking ahead of him with four *masskrugs* of beer turned and paused; he was an elderly man with a large, yellow, uneven moustache and heavily bagged eyes; he had, you might have thought, seen everything by now. But he stopped and stared, and the boy in the dirty pierrot costume made a floor-deep gesture of obeisance, almost a curtsy. He did not always wear the costume. He wore it mostly in the evenings. Nobody knew where he came from. When asked, he would say, 'From Bergamo, my homeland' – a theatrical line – in an affected, high, reedy voice with a fey gesture of the hand. During the day, he often wore a billowing white shirt and tight black jodhpurs with no makeup. His name was Egon.

'That was simply wonderful,' Leoš said, when they were out in the open air.

'It was as if nothing had changed since 1893,' Stasia said.

'I think the stage should be painted white and lit pink,' Fritz said. 'I am sure of it.'

'Like Bergamo, my homeland,' the pierrot called Egon whiffled. 'Like a great pink harvest moon over everything, and triangles and hexagons all dancing in the moonlight.'

1.2

In this weather, you wanted to leap out of bed and go to your window, to lean out dangerously over the curved railings to see as much of the building as you could. It was exciting to see other people doing exactly the same thing, however early you woke up. Today, with the sun shining through the thin drapes at the window, Ludo had been woken at six and had wanted to get up immediately. Those people in the big heavy buildings, with no windows, with stone and gargoyles and brick and ornament! How would they get up! How would they see the beauty of the blue-skied day and fling themselves into it!

The school was set in neat-trimmed lawns, and the road that ran alongside it was broad and empty. From his fourth-floor window, he could see brilliant white angles and a flash of window among the birch trees on the other side of the road. They were the Masters' Houses – cubes of chalk with bursts of interior colour, set among the birches like a prerequisite to thought. In there, great minds were already at work in the perfect diffused light of their private studios. Klee was preparing his knives and his pencils and his paper, and putting the contents of a just-finished dream onto a flat surface to dry. Or perhaps they were having their breakfast, ham and hard-boiled eggs and horseradish and nice black bread with their coffee, and feeding their children, who sat on their knees, from plain white plates with plain steel spoons. One day all families would be like that, in square white buildings, well lit, well constructed, without dragons or plaster gods at the door, without vine leaves on their knives and forks, without any attempt to make a plate into a flower or a teapot into a cabbage. Ludo opened the window and, bare-chested in his pyjama trousers, stretched out his arms and inflated his chest with the good summer air. There was a wonderful smell of grass and birch trees and summer. He smelt himself in this fresh summer air, raising his right arm and sniffing at his animal armpits with joy. Down there on the lawns, in exercise drawers and a vest, his friend Klaus was making great star jumps on the grass. 'Seven!' he shouted, as Ludo watched, and went on to make nine more star jumps before shouting, 'Eight!' He looked beautiful in his white vest and shorts, his skin burnt brown already by their lake expeditions and the sun of the last month. As he jumped, he looked like the last star of the night, blazing on into the morning.

Ludo splashed water on his face and hurried downstairs. He did not trouble to dress. Klaus was between exercises, and panting heavily; he gave Ludo a great smile and a hug that knocked the air out of Ludo's lungs. The animal pleasures of their joining bodies' smell, out there in the sunlight, were wonderful to Ludo.

'What is this!' he shouted. 'Lie in bed! Rise at noon! What is this thing called dawn!'

'It is so beautiful a day that I was woken and thought I would get up early for once,' Ludo said. It was not true. He was not a late riser. He liked to get up early and start work before nine. But Klaus was someone who got up early and cast himself into noisy exercise, and did not believe that anyone could match him in devotion or serious energy.

'Now – the running on the spot,' Klaus said. 'You are running on the spot now? Good. Not too fast at first. The air in the lungs! For me it is a rest, a warm relaxation between strenuous exercise. For you it is to pump blood into the muscles. Yes? Good. Today I reflected on something important, Ludo. On Tuesday it was the eighth time that you and I practised sodomy together. It was in my room. Do you remember?'

'I think it was the seventh time,' Ludo said.

'No,' Klaus said. 'I have kept a record and I am sure of my accuracy. This was the eighth time. It is good to give in to what you desire without consultation of the morality of the ornamental age on some occasions. Yes? We are in agreement? Now faster, like this – hup hup hup hup hup hup … And slower, hup, hup, hup, and down. Yes. Now, this giving in to the desire must be regular and agreed upon and not indulged without limit or structure, or we should be like monkeys in the trees.'

'Yes,' Ludo said. He had sometimes been ashamed of his desire to be like a monkey in a tree with Klaus. That once – Klaus shining naked by a lake, doing his star jumps and glistening with lake water and a shine of sweat, a question mark of lake weed on his dark and blond-hairy thigh, and from his face, the white blaze of his perfect teeth.

'That is good. Now we must set a date for the practice of desire next. I think it will be on the afternoon of next Tuesday, in four days' time. That will be the day after the first performance of the ballet, and we will have had a good deal of rigour and discipline, which needs to be given a counter. Is that a suitable day for you, Ludo?'

'Yes,' Ludo said, now joining in with Klaus's seamless move into more star jumps. He believed he was now fitter than he had been – at any rate he did not fall so quickly into breathlessness.

'Good. So, on Tuesday afternoon, we will practise sodomy on each other, first you on me and then me on you. That will be the ninth time.'

It filled Ludo with sadness that it would be only ten times, according to Klaus's timetable of behaviour, they would meet for this purpose. It was important to carry on the occasional practice of desire without reference to the morality of previous, ornamental ages. On the other hand this must have limits, or it would expand and become worthless, like a mark that once bought a loaf becoming mere paper in a pile of worthlessness.

For Klaus, the tenth occasion would be the monument at the end of possible lands, beyond which not an afternoon's desire but illusions like love and sentiment and ornament lay. So with the tenth occasion they would shake each other's hand and move on to the practice of desire with other friends. They were all agreed that this was a healthy and hygienic way to exercise an essential bodily and mental function. It was so sad. He thought that, with some organization, the tenth occasion could be delayed until September on their return from the summer, and then Klaus would feel that their meetings could continue a little longer.

'Hup, hup, hup,' Klaus said. 'And now – hup-hup-hup-hup-hup, yes, yes, at the double, and the knees up to the chest like – like – like—'

A citizen of Dessau walked past the building. There were two half-naked men doing violent exercises outside it and making too much noise when it was not even seven in the morning. Karl Richter, in his summer jacket and neat little trilby with a pheasant's feather in the band, irritably noticed a small stain of his breakfast egg on his lapel. He thought he would get used to the new school building. His wife said she never would. It gave her heartburn to look at it.

1.3

The musicians were having their last rehearsal before the dress rehearsal. In the ideal new spaces of the school, a room had been designated for their use. It had quickly filled up with detritus, with the large number of musical parts from different musical works needed to supply the accompaniment to *The Euclidean Ballet*, with the manuscript linking passages supplied by the composer, or a composer, with scraps of paper giving indications, with the performers' own annotations. As well as all of that, there were plates and cups that had never been removed and a garden fork that had been placed in the rehearsal room by a gardener, perhaps under the impression that this was now a lumber room.

The garden fork was not obviously a musical instrument. It would not be needed. The other objects in the room that were not obviously musical instruments would need to be gone through today. Over the previous six weeks, the three or four composers and dramaturges had introduced some strange and interesting objects for the sake of their sounds.

There was a neat little anvil and a shining little hammer. There was a typewriter. There was an aeroplane propeller. There was a pile of large white plates to be hurled and smashed. There was a crazy broken old violin and a phonograph with two records, Beethoven's *Calm Sea and Prosperous Voyage* on the turntable, and to one side in its brown envelope, a record of jazz music. It was called *Shufflin' Mose* and was performed by Eric Borchard. These two would be alternated throughout the performance, whatever the other musicians were playing. There was a wooden chair and a saw to cut it up. There was a crate of eggs, to be broken and beaten during the performance. This was not a waste of food: omelettes would be served after the performances to the audience, as they had been served during rehearsals to the hungry dancers. All these sounds, loud and quiet, curious and familiar, distinctive and mysterious, would be performed by Elsa Winteregger, the school's junior tutor in silversmithing, and one of her students. The student was here. Elsa had not yet arrived.

These sounds would alternate with the performance of music from the four proper musicians. An associate of one of the Masters, someone who taught art in a local school, turned out to be a good cellist, and he knew a clarinettist. The director of the ballet had insisted on there being a violinist of theatrical, tired appearance, and he had found one, a seventy-five-year-old veteran of the tea dances. They had worried about this musician, but nothing surprised Hans; he had, too, a foul mouth and a steady supply of obscene stories about his time in Paris in the seventies. Thomas was the pianist. He alone was supposed to know how everything would work.

'What now?' Hans said.

Thomas, from behind the piano, explained. At this point they would play the first four bars of Beethoven's *Pastoral* symphony sixteen times, while the aeroplane propeller was cranked up and Elsa Winteregger beat time by smashing the plates. When they were done with that, Thomas would signal –

'Oh, we can count to sixteen,' Hans said genially.

– and they would move on to the foxtrot written on sheet – on sheet – on sheet—

'I know it's here somewhere,' he said, rifling through his folder. 'The slow fox.'

'There are two foxtrots,' Christian the cellist said. 'There is one which is on a page I've labelled seven B and another on page nineteen. I don't know which one you mean. The one on page seven B is in D, the other one – let's see – no, that's in a strange key of your own invention, I believe. Two sharps, but F sharp and G sharp, yes?'

'It's the other one,' Thomas said. 'It should be labelled nineteen. Is that right? Everyone together? Yes? And then a small pause, while Fräulein Winteregger and Siggi break some eggs and pour water from a great height into the bathtub, and then the Strauss waltz, the first one hundred and twenty-seven bars exactly. It just breaks off. And then—'

'It is wonderful to me that we are still playing these shitty old tunes,' Hans said. 'At the tea dance, I understand. I remember playing that Strauss waltz, the *Emperor*, thirty years ago with a great orchestra, an orchestra of eighty. We still play it at the tea dance. There are just three of us: I, the pianist Frau Schmidt and her sister who plays the cello. The old people who come, they like the *Emperor Waltz*, they like to stand still in the introduction and catch their breath and perhaps to talk a little to their friends. And then they like to waltz, quite slowly, but as in the old days, some of the ladies with each other. I do not know how people who are so advanced as you came to know of the *Emperor Waltz* at all.'

'Times change,' Thomas said briefly, not really listening.

'Oh, I know that times change,' Hans said, smiling. 'I am not a shitty old fool like my brother Clemens, who says everything is gone wrong, that everything is falling to pieces, that people are worse than they used to be and that there are people, the Jews you know, who want to destroy Germany for ever. What is astonishing to me is that things sometimes stay the same, and it is astonishing to me that you want to play the *Pastoral* symphony and the *Emperor Waltz* at all. For myself, as I say, it is always nice to play the Strauss waltz, even the first hundred and twenty-seven bars ending in the middle of a phrase, even with Fräulein Winteregger imitating the pissing of a cow behind me.'

'What am I meant to be doing?' Elsa Winteregger said, bursting in. She was wearing an old and loose green man's shirt, frayed about the cuffs, and her short hair was wild about her head. 'I am so late for everything. I must be gone by half past ten. Tell me when it is half past ten. My sister was sick this morning, and her husband nowhere to be seen. You! Where were you? My sister said you left at dawn, leaving her alone with her sickness. I had to comfort her.'

They always forgot that Elsa Winteregger's sister was married to the suave cellist with the haunted look. The three of them, it was believed, actually lived together. It was hard to imagine Elsa Winteregger living on her own. The two of them mostly made a habit of not speaking to each other in rehearsals. The cellist muttered an apology to his sister-in-law, and Thomas brought them back to the rehearsal.

1.4

The dancers in *The Euclidean Ballet* were assembled and dressed. The costumes were an essential part of their movements, which were at root simple and straightforward. The dancers complained to each other about the chafing, sometimes to a state of being rubbed raw, that the costumes had brought about. They were brightly coloured and bulky, the costumes, and very heavy, being made out of frames of wood with dyed silk stretched over the top. There had been some talk about constructing the frames out of something light, like balsa wood, but at the first attempt, the balsa-wood frames were crushed and broken. Something stronger and more resistant was needed, and unfortunately those strong and resistant woods were painfully heavy to lug about the stage.

They had reached a pause in the rehearsal. They sat down as best they could. The pyramidal pink dancer balanced awkwardly on the base of her shape; the cuboid dancer simply rested squarely on the ground and withdrew her head into the yellow shape. Others were condemned to roll like barrels, rising from their rest periods dizzier than when they had sat down. The ones who had it easiest were those whose arms and legs, only, were encased in a series of small cubes or spheres. They could sit on their bottoms, like honest men and women. The principal dancers, who embodied single large shapes, whether pink pyramid, yellow cube, green sphere or blue egg, attempted to find a position where their stomachs were not rendered sore and the blistered side was given an easier position.

They were not proper dancers. Previous productions had relied on professional dancers, but nobody had been able to demonstrate that a professional dancer alone was capable of rising above the demands of his costume. They had the tendency, too, of complaining loudly about the impossibility of the ballet's requirements. All that was needed, even in the central unfulfilled love duet between the pyramid and the egg shape, was a slow and rhythmic walking about the stage without any falling over. The students who had been selected, and who were now pausing between actions, ought to have been at least as reliable as the professionals who had made such a hash of it in Berlin, two years before.

The director and the dramaturge had been talking at the back of the room while the dancers held their positions or sat down as best they could. Now the director came to the front of the room, and told them to get into positions for the final trio. Those not involved could remove their costumes, as this would take some time. The dancer who embodied the octagon, whose name was Klaus, got up and began to put on his heavy white costume over his black tights and tunic. There was no need for music as yet – that would come with the dress rehearsal. The principle of the ballet was that there should be no relationship between what was happening on stage and what music was being played, and the dancers had been instructed to remain quite indifferent to any sounds, musical or otherwise, that they should hear from the pit. How should they end at the same time, a little dancer had asked. The musicians in the pit would watch the dancers' moves, which were formalized and correct, and when the last dancer had reached his last position, the music would finish, even if there was theoretically more to play. It was not more important that music reach a final cadence than that the dancers should. Why, then, have even a dress rehearsal? Well, the director explained, it had been known for dancers to fail in that task of indifference, and begin to place their steps to the rhythm and tempo of what was being played. The dress rehearsal was to make sure that the lack of coincidence was absolute.

'At least the scenery is finished,' the egg shape murmured, taking the leather straps from his shoulder and delicately lowering the bright-covered frame. 'That's something at least.'

His friend the sphere ran her hands through her red hair; a strand stuck to her forehead with sweat. 'There was not much to it in the first place,' she said, stepping gracefully out and pulling her frame to the wings. The backdrop was a red square on a shade of just-grey white; at least, it seemed like a square at first glance, but as you looked at it more, it was clear that two of the sides of the square were slightly different in length, and the shape actually converged. It filled the backdrop; it was curiously disturbing.

The last exchange of the ballet began. 'Seventy-nine,' a deep, masculine voice began from the orchestra pit. 'Eighty. Eighty-one.' The pink pyramid was advancing from the back left quadrant of the stage towards the front right, revolving slowly as it moved.

'Stop, stop, stop,' the director said. 'Is that *three hundred* and seventy-nine?'

They agreed. The pink pyramid walked gracefully forward, one step slowly after another. When it reached the front right of the stage, it revolved one and a half times, and began to walk back across the same diagonal. At the same time as the pyramid's pause and turn, the yellow cube began to walk from the same starting point at the same speed. They met at the centre of the stage, and both moved to the other's left, walking around each other in a circle. After circling each other twice, a new shape emerged from the wings – a white octagon, as it was described. The white octagon moved to the centre of the stage, and after the pyramid and yellow cube had circled it twice more, they walked in tandem to the wings and exited, leaving the white octagon at the centre as the apotheosis of geometry. 'It's really very much like *The Nutcracker*,' the director had said, going on to add that in ballet and in art, rigour was a topic like any other, on which art could discourse but by which it was not necessarily limited. In this ballet, he said, the three of the pyramid and the four of the cube add up to the eight of the octagon. Or the four-sided and the six-sided add up to the – he would not count the number of sides on the octagon-based shape. Klaus, the dancer who embodied the octagon, was a strong fellow, but there was no possibility of his moving in anything resembling a dance. He would just walk to the centre of the stage and wait there until the ballet was finished, the object of all admiring or disgusted gazes from the audience.

But today the octagon had only just begun its journey to the centre of the stage when the doors to the auditorium were hurled open. It was the designer, Fritz, and his student assistants. The director recognized that one of them, the quietest, was Klee's son Felix. Fritz, the designer, was shouting for them to stop.

'We can't stop,' the director said reasonably. But it was too late. The three dancers on stage had interrupted themselves – they would never remember the point they had reached, and they would need to start again. The dancer who had been the sphere was sitting on a stool by the side of the stage, dabbing her flank where there was a little blood. She raised her head with interest.

'It's not right,' Fritz was saying. His associates were behind him, in enthusiastic and menacing postures. 'It's not right – it's –' he gestured to the stage, its red almost-square and its predominant off-white '– it's *sculpture*. Now, I've seen it in time to change it for the better. I saw yesterday at the theatre, the auditorium is one cube and the stage space another, harmonious and echoing. But not if there is clutter! There must be only a white space on the other side of the lights. We will start painting immediately to obliterate that –' he gestured contemptuously towards, it must be presumed, the red near-square '– *clutter*.'

'Impossible,' the director said. 'Not possible at all. Look – this is the apotheosis, where the octagon appears. We see the white octagon because of the red square!'

'Yes, yes, exactly,' a girl behind Fritz put in. 'The apotheosis disappears – it cannot be seen. That is perfect.'

'No,' the director said. 'Impossible.'

'We can redesign the costume,' Fritz said. He thrummed his fingers impatiently on the back of a chair in the stalls. 'Or make it a different colour.'

'No,' the dramaturge said. 'There is no time and the dancer needs his costume now.'

'Do we have a dancer in a black costume?' a boy with some sort of foreign accent said – perhaps Moravian or Bohemian. 'We could paint the space black.'

527

They thought. Perhaps it was not such a bad idea. 'The space on the stage is a representation of the darkened space in the auditorium, but not the same space,' Fritz said, in his oracular way.

'Their legs and arms are in black already,' the director said cautiously. He spread his hands, helplessly, in a kind of shrug. 'They would be invisible, or less conspicuous.'

'It will be done,' Fritz said. 'Stasia – Egon – you are to go to acquire some black scenery paint, plenty. We will do it immediately and it will be dry by morning.'

'When my dancers are finished,' the director said. 'And it must be finished in time for the dress rehearsal. Nothing must be delayed and the performance must start on time. The mayor of Dessau is coming, and almost every one of the Masters. The deputy mayor, I mean, of course.'

1.5

The deputy mayor of Dessau had, these days, a small official car when the mayor could spare it, and it was waiting outside the home of the deputy mayor and his wife. It was an ordinary villa, substantial in size and very comfortable, with solid wood gates and an English rock garden in the front. He had a statue of the Venus de Milo in the middle of the lawn to the back, and a range of interesting ericas in the rock garden. Some people, including his children and indeed his superior the mayor, thought the house old-fashioned, but it did not do to replace perfectly good furniture every five minutes. The children had laughed at the mahogany-framed sofa, and the goddesses holding up cabbages and pineapples that ornamented the structure of the sideboard, and even the well-made dining table with the pedestals representing the West Wind that they had bought in Dresden nearly forty years before. The mayor had said that it would benefit the deputy mayor to understand the future of civilization, by which he meant replace all his furniture.

The deputy mayor's wife plucked a fading peony out of the dragon-thick vase on the console table in the lobby – they were white and pink, and it was a pink one she disposed of. Her children would come to like all this, and nobody could say that the thickets of chairlegs and low flimsy tables among which they seemed to want to live were well made, or restful to look on. She thought of the evening ahead of her with dismay.

The deputy mayor of Dessau was coming down the stairs, in his dinner jacket with his silver-topped cane. As long as they had been married, she had been prompter than him to be ready to leave. She believed that was the secret of a happy marriage, never to keep your man waiting. Her evening wear did not take long to assemble. She wore a simple black silk shift dress with her hair neatly brushed back into a bun, and the gold and enamel brooch that the mayor had bought her after he had been recognized by the Emperor, the aquamarine and diamond pendant that his parents had given her on her wedding day, even though that was perhaps no longer the fashion. She wore a corset underneath, but it was not pulled tightly. After five children, all now grown-up with homes and families of their own, there was not much that could be done to give herself the physical shape of her youth.

'Ready?' the deputy mayor said, as he always had. He was a good man. 'You look beautiful. Is Adi waiting with the car? Good, good.'

'It is good of you to agree to come to see these people,' the deputy mayor's wife said as they left the house and got into the car. 'I don't understand why we have to have them in Dessau.'

'Well, they are here now,' the deputy mayor said. 'We voted for it, and the mayor says that it does us a great deal of virtue, to be shaken up like that. And it is true. People from all over the world come to our town now simply to look at it.'

'That building! It is beyond anything. Adi told me that

normally he drives in a completely different direction so as not to see it. How can anyone think that buildings should look like that? It has a flat roof! That is not – that is simply Oriental. It will do for Jews, but not for Germans.'

'My dear, we are their guests tonight.'

'The building is bad enough, but it is what goes on inside that so horrifies everyone. You know they were forced to leave Weimar. Free love. Anarchism. Communism. No one was safe in the streets. I do not know why they are in Germany, even.'

'My dear, we need only to go there once a year, and then you and Adi can forget all about it.'

'I had a low enough opinion of them based on their teapots. I can only imagine what their ballet is going to consist of. If we escape without open insult, that will be enough to be grateful for.'

'The Prince is coming tonight,' the deputy mayor said. 'Informally, very informally – he likes them. They will behave well enough, I am sure.'

'The Prince is coming? You know the sort of people who control what work they do, behind the scenes?'

'Put your normal, kind, happy face on. Remember that there is nothing in what they may or may not be doing that the wife of the deputy mayor of Dessau needs to notice. The Prince is coming, but you and I, we are the principal guests. Democracy, my dear, democracy.'

'There is a great deal in what Hannes was saying last week,' the wife of the deputy mayor of Dessau said. Her elder son had paid them a visit, and had stayed for dinner and overnight with his wife and their new baby. 'What happens in Berlin today will happen in Dessau tomorrow. When Hannes says the time has come to take the threat seriously, how can we endure such people in our midst?'

'It is only a fruit bowl,' the deputy mayor said, coming back to a previous topic of disagreement between the two of them. 'They meant well. Silver, too.'

'It was an insult. How could I possibly produce such a thing? That fruit bowl, silver or not, stays in the cupboard in the scullery. A silver bucket. I thought I would produce it when someone who knew about it and valued it came to dinner, afterwards, for dessert. But no. Never, never, never.'

'You must have whoever you want to dinner, in your own house. And here we are,' the deputy mayor of Dessau said peaceably, as the great white building came into view, curved like an ocean liner and flat on top, its square simple windows and curved railings, its single upper-case vertical stripe of a label saying BAUHAUS, the lawn in front, and a greeting committee of Masters, bold-haired, bow-tied, tweed-suited, came forward with the students behind. From inside, there came the noise of hammers striking, regularly and resonantly, metal and wooden, and a muted cheer. It was as if they were arriving at the monkey house at the zoo, and being greeted by the elder chimpanzees in tails. 'This is an evening of ballet, something everyone loves. Put on your best face, my dear, and hear nothing offensive. Adi, we are waiting.'

'That man is dressed as a pierrot!' the deputy mayor's wife said.

'He must be part of the entertainment,' the deputy mayor said. 'Do not worry. We will be home again before you know it.'

2.1

In a classroom in Dessau, on the ground floor, overlooking a dark stone square, an art class was beginning. The architects and the school administrators had not considered the matter very deeply when they had placed the art room here. It was dark inside – the birch trees grew thickly outside. There was no interesting view from the window to aid contemplation. It had been chosen because art was given very little importance at the

Dessau Gymnasium, and the room had been considered to offer sufficient space for the students, and had the largest cupboard attached. It was understood that the teaching of art required a good deal of storage space, to put both artistic efforts and the means of producing them away at the end of the school day.

A new master was taking a class of fifteen-year-olds. He was not a permanent member of staff; the pupils understood that he was not a permanent member of staff. He had been hired for six months at most. He was a fresh-faced man, prone to blushing when he had to speak to all of them. They faced the front, blank-faced, their expressions fixed on his in a way that was meant to disconcert.

'Do you have a sheet of paper in front of you? Everyone? Ah – does anyone have a piece of paper that they could lend Rottluff? Pencil? You all have a pencil, a good soft drawing pencil. Yes? Good. Now, I would like you to draw a line on your piece of paper. Yes?'

A boy had no pencil, and another wanted to know if his hard pencil would do. The junior master went into the stock cupboard, and extracted five soft pencils – he was just about experienced enough to understand that these two requests would be followed by others.

'Now. As I was saying, I would like you to draw a line on your piece of paper.'

There were now some genuinely puzzled expressions on the faces of the boys. One of them, the dreaded Rottluff, had raised his hand.

'Sir,' Rottluff said. 'If I may speak, sir. We do not understand. What sort of line are we to draw?'

'You may draw any kind of line you would like,' the master said. His name was Herr Vogt.

'A straight line, sir?'

'Any kind of line that you would like to draw,' Herr Vogt said.

'Please, sir, like this?' another boy said, holding up his sheet of paper on which a line had been drawn, no more than half the width of his fingernail. His name was Walliser.

'If that is the sort of line you feel like drawing, then that will do,' Herr Vogt said. 'Stop! Boys! No – not all of you. Don't draw a line exactly like the one that Walliser drew. Draw your own line. It doesn't matter whether it is like anyone else's line. But it should be a line that you have thought about. Walliser, think about the line, and then draw it.'

'How, sir?' a boy called Schmidt said. 'How can we think about a line? A line is just a line.'

'Ah, but is it?' Herr Vogt said. 'When does a line begin? If I place a pencil tip on a piece of paper but do not move it, is that a line?'

'No, sir,' Rottluff said. 'That would be a point, sir, which occupies no volume.'

'But if the point moves, Rottluff, then what does it become?'

'Sir,' Walliser said. 'May I ask a question? Are we to be tested and evaluated on this information and theory at the end of the year, or is this just your own ...' He trailed off. He had not necessarily meant it impertinently, but there was a smothered noise of laughter from the back of the classroom.

'Just draw a line,' Herr Vogt said. He made an expansive, generous gesture with his arms, a weighing of two imaginary weights at the arms' end, and gave a tentative smile. He was still blushing; his confidence was not very apparent. 'Draw a line of any sort in the next ten seconds. Let your pencil move, and demonstrate what it is thinking. Clear? Two, three, four, five ...'

He walked about the classroom, peering over the backs of the boys. They were drawing, most of them, but with an air of faint disgust. Almost all of them had drawn a straight line, a horizontal line in the middle of the paper, going from left to right. Three boys were doing something different: two, a diagonal line from one corner of the paper to another, the third a complicated, winding, sinuous line, which, as Christian watched, made a disappointing sort of doubling back to form a looping letter P – no doubt the initial of the boy, or of the boy's sweetheart, or something of that sort.

'Very good,' Christian said disconsolately. 'Now, I want you to draw a second line – no, stop, don't draw the second line immediately, listen to what I have to say – I want you to draw a second line that is completely and utterly unlike the first line. Do you understand? Spend a few moments thinking about it, and then draw it. What are the properties of your first line? That's quite a good place to start.'

'Sir,' a boy said, not troubling to put his hand in the air, 'are we supposed to do this on two sheets of paper or on one?'

'Sir,' another boy said, this one raising his hand and propping it up with the other, the elbow resting on the left-hand palm, the left elbow resting on the desk. 'Sir. Can I ask a question? It's a proper question. What my question is, is this. I'd like to ask – what is it for, what use is it for, this art? Last year it wasn't like this. We learnt about Michelangelo, and how to do crosshatching and how to put shadows in. Sir, what are your classes for? If there's a line then it should look like something. What are these lines going to look like? Sir, I just don't understand it at all. What do you mean, a line that's the opposite of the first one? I used to think I was good at art, but now I don't think I understand at all. It's not fair, sir.'

'Just do it, please,' Christian said, sitting down in the naval wooden-backed chair behind the desk at the front of the room. There was an easel there with a board placed on it, and a piece of paper pinned to the board. On the board were the beginnings of a seascape, performed for the benefit of the senior class, before, by one of the other masters. It stood as a reproach. 'Just think about drawing a second line that is the complete opposite in some way of the first line you drew. Can you do that, please?'

'Sir,' Rottluff said, not raising his hand. 'Can I ask a question, please? It's what Walliser asked. Are we going to be tested on any of this? It's an important question, sir.'

'No,' Christian Vogt said, defeated. 'You are not going to be tested on any of this, at any point in your school careers.'

Almost as one, the boys in the class drew their own single, simple, derisory line across the paper, and flung their pencils down. The boy at the front, with a military haircut and a blue ink stain on his white collar, turned to his neighbour and gave a contemptuous grin and a shake of the head. He was destined for greatness, in Christian Vogt's opinion, and this job was only to last for six months.

2.2

The boys left in a precise, silent way at the end of the lesson. They did not run off happily, making noise, but in a way intended to impress the masters with their diligence, discipline and silence. They must have known that a six-months art master would not expect or be impressed by military discipline. Christian took off his painting-room smock and, in the little mirror hanging on the wall, put on his soft red tie and his soft blue jacket. The jacket had been sponged and pressed a good many times, he saw; the ghost of a stain was on the right shoulder. The other jacket was in a worse state, and though Adele, when he had shown it to her, had clicked her teeth and said she would sponge and press it today, he felt that they had reached the point where both would have to be taken to the laundress. He left the art room, buttoning his jacket and brushing down the sleeves. For one moment he thought of an existence where you could consider that your jacket was old and tattered, make a joke about it and go and order another from your tailor. He thought of his child-hood.

Outside, the weather was beautiful; a late spring just turning into summer. It filled Christian with dread. The baby was to be born in the middle of August, three months away. It would be born, if the doctors were right, two weeks after his contract with the Gymnasium came to an end. He did not know what he and Adele and the baby were to live on. Adele was clever with money, and could make her sister's income as a young master feed all three of them. Elsa did not seem to care about money and, indeed, quite happily handed over her wages to Adele, with, almost, an air of relief that that was one responsibility gone. Still, Christian knew himself that it was not his money, and not Adele's; it was not much, and it was Elsa's. He did not like the idea of living on the small sum the Bauhaus paid his sister-in-law in the metal workshop.

In the square, a mother in a neat blue coat and dress held a white-clad toddler by a set of leather reins; together, they were feeding stale bread to the ducks in the pond in the middle of the square, with cries of wonder and delight. Above, in the lime trees shading the pond, a blackbird sang, as if sharing in the cries of wonder and delight. Christian went past the mother and child with a feeling of failure in his own child's life, even before it had begun. He went on in the direction of the town hall's spire, poking above the layers of solid, weary housing. The streets were full of houses, people living somehow in comfort and happiness, like his landlady in Weimar and her architect lover Neddermeyer. Was it just a question of being born at the right time, and muddling through somehow, that you ended up happily feeding waste bread to ducks in the afternoon with your happy son on reins in a knitted white cardigan?

The butcher's shop he used, the least good of the three in Dessau, was in a side-street. It was the only shop of its type in the street, which otherwise was taken up by junk shops, principally handlers of stolen goods. The street had an abandoned, desperate air, crowded with redundant furniture and gewgaws once thought to hold their value; the cast-aside atmosphere extended to the blood-soaked and dusty butcher's shop. It was very different from Haffener in the main street, with its gleaming brass rails and its gleaming purple livers and pink shining cuts of veal in the window; the butchers there wore striped blue-

and-white aprons which, if not immaculate, were clean on each morning and whose bloodstains were somehow fresh and even wholesome-looking. The butcher in the stolen-goods side-street – you felt that he acquired carcasses through other people's desperation, taking advantage of need. He had a villainous boy for an assistant, hacking away in the backroom at a purple carcass with an axe. Christian entered. Behind the counter, there was a small amount of inner organs in a pile, amid skin and detritus and old blood. Usually, the shop was empty, but today there was a middle-aged woman dealing with the butcher.

'Those ox hearts were delicious, Herr Lachenmann,' she said. 'My husband particularly commended them.'

'Only the very best from my shop for you, madam,' the butcher said. He was unshaven and red-eyed, a heavy drinker; his hands and fingers were fat, and scarred with blunders. 'And what can I do for you today?'

'Some nice kidneys,' the woman said thoughtfully, 'a brain, and I think another ox heart. We eat what other people's dogs eat, you see. We will end by eating lungs, I know.'

'Not the worst thing, lungs. And it's the healthiest food in the world, a brain,' the butcher said, with a gruesome smile. 'All that thinking, it stands to reason.'

There had been something familiar about the woman, and Christian realized, as she shook her head in tight, specific denial, that it was Frau Klee, the painter Klee's wife. What was there to object to in the idea that brains were healthy? She was eating them, after all – perhaps she wanted to impress the butcher with the idea that they ate brains and hearts for pleasure, not out of virtue. She loaded the weight of meat into her shopping basket, said goodbye to the butcher and smiled at Christian – was it a smile of recognition, or did she greet all strangers in Dessau shops like that? Christian was left with the butcher, whose smile had disappeared. There was a thwack and a cry of pain from the back room. The butcher paid no attention. 'What can I do for you,' he said. It was as if having Christian as a customer, with his stained jacket and need of a haircut, was a sign of his having come down in the world.

'Liver,' Christian said. 'Enough for two.' He had never mastered weights, and feared being cheated by butchers wanting to offload stock if he said how many people there really were to eat.

'Got some lovely pigs' liver,' the butcher said flatly.

'Very well,' Christian said in his best Berlin-lawyer's-son manner. 'Pigs' liver for two it is.'

'Nice romantic meal, is it? Nice romantic meal for two?' the butcher said, jeering somewhat. But Christian was now wondering how he was going to carry the bloodsoaked parcel home.

2.3

'It would be more useful in steel,' the Master said. He was turning Elsa's teapot over and over in his hands. The light in the metal workshop was beautiful at this time of day: indirect, though the windows were large, and dappled with the shadow of a large elm tree it had not been thought necessary to remove. Inside, the atmosphere could be oppressive and hot, and lit with sparks. But the students had left, and there were only the Master himself and Elsa, looking at Elsa's silver teapot. 'There is no need to use ebony for the handle, either, I believe.'

Elsa flushed with pride. If he were talking about whether you were allowed to use expensive materials like silver and ebony, then he had no objection to Elsa's teapot as a teapot. The silly old goat – he should have known it would work best with silver and ebony. What was she supposed to make it out of – tin and pinewood? The old Elsa rose up in indignation at the thought of it. She thought of tearing the teapot from the Master's hands and bashing him over the head with it! That would be what he deserved! Tin and pinewood! But then she breathed ten times, as Father always said she should, and she remembered that he had said nothing against the teapot itself.

'The silver is perfect,' she said. 'The shape is so pure that it needs a deeper metal, a softer one, to set it off.'

'Softer, how?' the Master said. 'If you wanted a softer metal, perhaps you should have used gold.'

But that was a sarcastic comment and Elsa paid no attention to it. 'No, softer on the eye,' she said. 'Not softer in the scale of hardness. It is softer to look at. Stainless steel is good, but it would hurt the eye here. Look!'

She took the teapot from the Master's hands and tugged him over towards the light. In the direct sunlight, it was so beautiful, so very beautiful. The surface of it shone, but there was something deep about its shine, like the shine of water on a deep lake. The shine of stainless steel was the shine of a wet pavement, not even a puddle. Elsa could not say any of this. The Master had a long-standing contempt for any talk of that kind. 'Look!' she said in the end, turning it over and over in the light.

'I know what silver looks like,' the Master said, taking the teapot back with a short smile. She knew that he liked her really. There had been some difficulty when he had refused her permission to use a sheet of silver for her teapot, the teapot she had woken up one morning seeing in her mind. She had sulked and thought about things, and tried to imagine her teapot in other metals. But it was no good. The teapot that was in her mind was a silver teapot with the curve of an ebony handle, and that was that. There was no discussing with it. It would be like asking a good friend if they would mind having hair of a different colour, and not dyeing it, but growing it out differently. Elsa remembered this thought, and sniggered.

'What is it, Fräulein Winteregger?' the Master said.

'Oh, nothing,' Elsa said. 'Nothing, nothing, nothing. Look! Look at it, just there!'

'Well,' the Master said eventually, setting the teapot down on the dark blue velvet cloth he used to inspect all finished pieces, 'well, I think it is a very good piece of work. The shape is good. It is fresh and pleasant to look at. You may be right – this teapot had to be made in silver. But I am very sorry that you felt you had to go over my head to the director of the Bauhaus to ask for permission to use silver, and very sorry that foolish students are now requesting permission to use silver in their turn. Which, naturally, I am refusing.'

The silly old goat, Elsa thought indignantly, but then made herself remember how he had managed not to be rude about the teapot. That meant he liked it. He was always rude about everything. And the teapot was wonderful, the best, the very best thing Elsa had ever made and the very best thing she had ever seen. Sometimes she had heard somebody at the Bauhaus say, 'One day, all plates,' or jugs or chairs or houses, 'will look like this one', 'this one' meaning the one they had just made. It was the highest thing you could say at the Bauhaus. But Elsa's teapot was not like that. One day someone would look at the teapot and say, 'No teapot ever, ever, ever, in the history of the whole world, has ever looked like that one, and there never, ever, ever will be one that looks like it. This is the only one, ever, ever, ever ...' She hugged herself in joy. The Master, when she opened her eyes, was looking at her strangely. Subdued, she lowered her head and picked up her beautiful teapot to go and place it in her work cupboard.

It was only ten steps from where they stood in the workshop to Elsa's work cupboard, but she felt full of electricity, holding the teapot. The shape was half a globe, flat-topped. The handle, inset with ebony, was the curve of a new moon, a slash in the air. It had taken such a long time to get that handle right, with its quality of being a shade too big. Elsa felt surreptitiously underneath the teapot, like the affectionate owner of an animal tickling their pet to see if there was anything wrong with its belly. Underneath, the teapot rested on two crossed sheets of silver, only a thumb's joint thick, and there she had allowed herself to solder it roughly, not polishing it into smoothness.

Everything about it was so nice! Before today, the favourite thing ever that she had made had been the fruit bowl out of hammered copper that she had done last November. That fruit bowl? She was glad she had given it away. This teapot – she put it back in its reverential, cleared-away space on the second shelf – this teapot, she would never let it go.

'And what are you thinking of making next, Fräulein Winteregger?' the Master said.

'A gold cup, a goblet,' Elsa said, unable to restrain herself. 'With chasing and dolphins and perhaps a jewelled inset.'

'Hm,' the Master said, looking at her with an assessing gaze. Outside, in the sunlit five and six o'clock, the sound of students at play with a bat and ball rose up, and a cry as one of them perhaps fell and lost a point. Elsa was so happy, and all at once the absurd idea for a gold goblet with jewels and a dolphin rose up in her mind. Oh, that would be so nice. A dolphin-like shape. But in gold like the light in the late afternoon, outside.

2.4

Christian turned the key in the lock. Adele would be home by now. The apartment was on the fourth floor of the back house, beyond the shabby courtyard in which nothing grew, which the concierge never swept. They had been lucky to find it; its door was not high and heavy and carved, like the doors in the flats below, but merely a solid varnished piece of wood. It was a flat for a widow, or the mother-in-law of a family living in a larger flat in the same building. In this flat lived Christian and Adele, Elsa, too, in the tiny second bedroom that was really a study or a sewing room. In this flat would live the baby when it was born. There was just room for a cradle by the side of the bed, if the wardrobe were moved. When the baby was a little older, they could move to somewhere larger. Christian did not know how.

There was a noise of women's laughter from the little salon.

Christian went across the hall and opened the door. Adele was sitting in the armchair, and on the sofa by the dining table, a wedding gift from Christian's father that cramped and shrank the already small room, sat a well-dressed woman and Adele's father. He, too, was well dressed, with a pair of lemon gloves in his lap and a yellow carnation in his buttonhole; his hair was *en brosse* and his lugubrious face was shaven, glowing with health.

Adele looked up as he entered. 'Look!' she said. 'Look, Christian! It is my father and Frau Steuer! What a lovely surprise! I was taking a small rest after luncheon, and thinking if I had the energy to walk down all those stairs to carry out some tasks, and then there was a knock at the door. I felt – oh, it is only Christian, home early, forgotten something as usual, and forgotten his keys as he so often does. But I levered myself up, and there were Father and Frau Steuer! And they brought such beautiful cakes, such lovely cakes, I am really ashamed of myself.'

'Good evening, Herr Vogt,' Frau Steuer said. They had paid a visit to her after their wedding; she was an old friend of the family and had attended, but it was not to be expected that Christian recalled her in the little crowd of old friends. She lived in a tall, sinuous house in Breitenberg full of gorgeous bibelots. She had hummed with pleasure as she turned the pages of the wedding album they had brought with them. She could barely be forty; today she was very elegantly dressed in a white wool coat with an explosion of white fur at the collar – one of what Adele called her Paris clothes. Christian remembered an old story about her giving Franz Winteregger a nutcracker in an attempt to woo him. She had succeeded in her aim at any rate, once Elsa and Adele were both out of the way. She and Franz were to marry before Christmas, when Adele and the baby were able to travel.

'What a pleasant surprise,' Christian said. 'I had no idea.'

'Well, Franz and I, we thought we would be migratory birds for once,' Frau Steuer said. 'We were planning a short trip for after the wedding, and I merely said one evening that it was a shame we could not take advantage of the weather. And before

I knew it, the workshop was closed, the hotels reserved, and Gunther informed us that he would be driving us about for ten days. My fiancé is so thoughtful and impetuous! And it would be a good opportunity to see Adele before Baby arrives. And Christian and Elsa too,' Frau Steuer continued, in an afterthought.

'Baby was so heavy today,' Adele said. 'Father and Frau Steuer came at just the right moment to divert me. And you will stay for dinner?' She gave a warning look at Christian.

'Oh, no,' Frau Steuer said. 'You will join us for dinner at our hotel – the Hotel Gansevoort, I think. It is perfectly pleasant. Gunther has gone ahead to settle us in there. In any case, is that your dinner in Christian's hand? I do not think that would be enough for five of us. You are eating properly, I hope, Adele?'

'Oh, yes,' Adele said. 'We eat so well.' She looked at the little brown-paper package in Christian's hand, soaked with blood. A tinge of the familiar contempt came into her voice. 'Of course, it is much easier when I can go to the market myself, but Christian does very well, all things considered.'

Franz, in his unfamiliar, elegant garb, had said nothing. But now he said, 'Good day to you, Christian,' in a quiet, friendly way, and smiled. There was always something secretive about him. Christian had hoped that he would give them a pair of puppets as a wedding present, but he had not; under instructions, perhaps, he had given them a set of dull, heavy, antique dinner plates with gold edging. Adele had greeted them with cries of joy, and promptly stacked them away in a cupboard, from which they had emerged twice in three years.

'Good afternoon, Franz,' Christian said, smiling. 'I thought Elsa would be home by now, too.'

'Oh, Elsa is home,' Adele said. 'She is in her room, arranging something. That reminds me ...'

Christian left the room. There were things in his wife's conversation that made him shudder: the expression 'that reminds me' strangely enough, and the use of the word 'Baby' as if it were somebody's name. He remembered Frau Steuer: had she caught

543

the usage from Adele, or had Adele picked it up from Frau Steuer or from somebody like her? He knew that Baby, when it arrived, would be exactly like Adele, neat and disapproving, and would gaze at him with contempt. She had measured him up, and had concluded that she was marrying the son of a rich Berlin lawyer, and had found only after the wedding that she was marrying a master in a school. The poor little nameless thing, too, had not asked to be born to such a pair. If only he had some money, but the pair of them had none, and Elsa had only the money from the Bauhaus. If he had money, he would be able to rent a flat in which he could get away from his wife.

'We thought it would be patriotic, as well as interesting,' Frau Steuer's voice came from the salon. 'A trip around this beautiful country of ours! And Franz has been to so little of it, I discover.'

'Things are so much better in Germany, now!' Adele's voice could be heard saying. 'I know not everyone agrees but, still, it is almost pleasant to hear from Christian's brother in London that troubles are visiting somewhere else, for a change. Now in Germany ...'

Christian knocked gently at the door of Elsa's room, and pushed. Behind it there was a pile of clothes of some sort, and it opened slowly, reluctantly. She was lying on the bed, with one shoe kicked off.

'Oh, it's you,' she said, without raising her head. 'What is it? Are they going out?'

'Didn't they mention it?' Christian said. 'Frau Steuer is inviting us all to dinner at the Hotel Gansevoort. I bought some pigs' liver, but it is hardly enough for five. I wish they had warned us they were coming.'

'I had such a beautiful day,' Elsa said. 'Here is Frau Steuer! I don't know why she wants to marry Papa. I would not.'

'Hush,' Christian said, closing the door behind him. 'Why was your day beautiful?'

'I finished my teapot,' Elsa said. 'My beautiful silver teapot. They would not let me have silver for it at first, but then they did! The Master of the metals looked at it, and he said I should not have used silver, but I did, and there it is.'

'Where is it?'

'In my cupboard, in the workshop,' Elsa said, lying on her back, her eyes closed, her hands behind her head. 'I am never going to let it go. It is just worth too much to me. It is the best thing I ever made.'

'I think they will want to go before too much longer,' Christian said. On the bedside table was Elsa's bag, a set of keys and a stub of pencil, much sharpened. There was also an empty orange-and-blue cup with the remains of coffee in it. He looked with concern and interest at Elsa's long brown skirt, full of stains; he wondered what she had to change into for the Hotel Gansevoort.

2.5

Today was a very good day. On the bed, neatly made by Adele, propped against the bolster, lay an unopened letter. Elsa must have brought it up. It was from Dolphus, from London. Dolphus was a good correspondent; but still sometimes weeks went by without a letter from him, then five or six at once. He hesitated for a moment, then opened it, using his finger as a paper knife. He sat down on the edge of the bed, nudging the empty cradle out of the way, and began to read.

63 Tregunter Road

Dear Christian,

As you can see, I have as threatened moved lodgings! My previous lodgings grew too inconvenient for me. So I packed up my bags and moved to a boarding house here, in Tregunter Road, which is in Fulham. The district has known better times, but it is very convenient for my studies. If I am feeling energetic and the weather is not too bad, I can walk to the university in forty minutes or so. There are not so very many German students at the university, and now that my English is better than it was a year ago, I am the target of much curiosity and many enquiries, some of them quite funny. I know that people are interested to hear what is happening in Germany, and anxious to put the past behind us.

That is not to say that there are not recent difficulties! A fellow student here, called Anthony, confided in me that his mother had to put down their dog, a *Dackel*, ten years ago when it was thought to be too German. I have heard, too, that the King here decided to change his surname, as it sounded too German, but I have not met anyone who knows what the surname of the King was before it was changed.

Now you will want to know what it is like in my boarding house! I was welcomed in by a strange lady, who is either the manager or the owner of the house. The first thing she wanted to impress on me was that I must not permit ladies of any sort to visit me in my bedroom. They may come and sit in the *drawing room*, as she called it, and sit and talk politely beneath the stuffed black parrot that sits on the cottage piano. There is always a bunch of carnations, too, at the tea table. I have not told her that these remind me of funerals.

Of course I was introduced to the house by another student! (I am answering the questions in your letter, though you have perhaps forgotten some of them.) You will be surprised and shocked to discover that I am such friends with an Indian student, whose name is Rahul. He is here to study engineering, and says that he hopes to transform his country when it gains independence from the British Empire. I was surprised, truly, to make friends with a person of his background, but we have become firm friends and talk for many hours about the independence of his nation, and with the leaders of the struggle in Calcutta. He has told strangers that he is the younger son of a maharajah, though he is in fact only the son of a lawyer, like you and me. He lives in a very tidy and clean way in the room opposite mine, on the second floor of the house in Tregunter Road, above the gentleman with the phonograph who is a permanent part of every English lodging house. He is a vegetarian – not for religious reasons, he informs me, but simply because his digestion is poor. I should perhaps say, too, that I am friends with an American Negro called Charles, also a student of engineering! He tells me very interesting things about the struggles in America for equal rights, and the different attitudes that exist in different places. I am almost proud, I may tell you, that I am often to be seen eating my dinner in the refectory in the company of an Indian and a Negro – as proud as other people might be if they were seen dining with a duke.

The letter stopped halfway down a page, and resumed on a new sheet in Dolphus's smooth, conventional hand.

The troubles of last year have passed by, it seems. There is no general strike this year. I must tell you of an exciting evening Rahul, Charles and I, along with other English fellows, spent routing objectionable political persons in Whitechapel. I have changed sheets of paper to write this anecdote, so that you can if you choose not show it to Adele! I know that she would not understand and, as you say, it creates difficulties between you if she knows what I am 'up to', as the English say. It was a Sunday afternoon, only ten days ago …

Christian read on, absorbedly. The German voices in the other room continued. He was in London with his brother Dolphus. When he had finished, it occurred to him that Elsa's silver teapot must be worth some money. She would give it to him if she knew what was needed in the house.

3.1

The Masters' Houses were in a grove of birch, set back deeply from the path and the road. There were seven of them. In the last lived Klee.

The house was white, and square-angled, and with a large dark window at its centre. It shone in the sunlight. There was no garden but a communal lawn that surrounded all the houses, and inside there was the sort of colour that Klee liked. Some of the other Masters had left the inside white, and others had painted it brilliant primary colours. But Klee liked the colours of earth and sand and mud as a background to his thoughts, with samovar and dark furniture. You could not fill these interiors with furniture. But you could give them warmth. In their house was a gym instructress, Lily and Felix, two cats and rooms of brown, undergrowth-colour, mustard, October and sand.

Today Klee had got up early and had gone to his studio. The light was beautiful, direct but filtered through the trees outside. In this warm cocoon, your thoughts were neutral, and the life of dreams continued seamlessly onto paper or canvas or wood or glass. He was in his studio because later today he would have to travel by train to Munich. He wanted the day to contain some work. Now he saw two beasts, one facing the other. Where were they? Was it in some forest, in the undergrowth, where the trees gave way to a glade? One was making so much noise! The other was like him. But the shouting beast would not know how important the occupation was! It would look childish and unimportant to them, and it would shout louder – Grow Up! Grow Up! Look At Everything That Is Wrong! Klee thought of drawing the beast on the oil-transfer stone directly and then printing it. But then he saw that the beast would be made up of lines that were too knotted and intricate. He needed to draw it on the paper, and he did so. Afterwards it could go through the oil-transfer process. There were only three lines: they went over and under each other. Then Klee took a deep breath. He got up. He walked to the window and let his spirit rise against the howling beast he had let into his studio. 'Here you are,' he said, under his breath, to the beast playing, its limbs writhing and twisted like a ball of wool. He hadn't known that the beast had gone until it came back. He came back, and drew it quickly.

The two beasts had nothing to do with each other. They were in the same picture, unconnected. Klee knew what the title of the picture was, but he would not write it just yet.

It was breakfast time. Klee went into the dining room, where Lily and Felix already sat. The gym instructress could be heard noisily washing herself in the upstairs bathroom with the window open; she would have been outside, exercising herself. There were dishes of eggs, and ham, and Swiss cheese, and fruit. Lily poured her husband a cup of tea. In a moment, the maid came in with Klee's breakfast dish. It was his favourite: it was a plate of plain-grilled rabbit kidneys. He lit upon it with joy; he loved the huge liver of an ox, but he loved also the tiny inner organs of the smaller animals, the heart of a chicken, the brain of a hare; and the sweetest of them all was the kidney of the rabbit, the size of Klee's smallest fingernail. There were forty of them, and Klee set about them with relish, explaining (as Lily and Felix averted their eyes) what he had made today.

He had no class to teach that morning, and after breakfast he returned to the studio to write the title of his painting underneath it, and to enter it in his catalogue. It was number 174 for the year. He thought about another painting, and began to draw it; this one was just a magic line, and he watched the pen move over the paper, doubling back, crossing over, making a being and only at the end being quite sure of what the line was creating. It was an unhappy boat. He smiled. The space in which the boat floated had been there all the time. And now it was time to take his train to Munich.

3.2

The train took Klee from Dessau to Leipzig. On the station platform, students observed him, and said, 'Klee,' to each other. The stationmaster saw him and recognized the man with the curious, puzzled, boyish face, not quite like anyone else. The stationmaster did not know who he was, but he raised his flag to an oncoming train, saying, 'The Chinese Emperor's on his travels again,' to himself. That was his name for Klee. Two men, catching the same train, did not see or observe Klee, but he saw them: the way that the one waiting on the platform fished his pocket watch out, not to see the time but to demonstrate from afar that he had been waiting, and the way that the one approaching spread his hands wide in apology. It was like a fishing expedition, with Time as the bait.

The train arrived, and Klee sat in his seat. He always took the same seat if at all possible. It was a good one for thinking in. He did not use the train journey to prepare his classes, or to draw, or to read. He used his train journeys to think. The students who had recognized him went past the compartment and observed him, already settled with his coat and gloves off, his hat placed neatly on the hook in the compartment, and looking out of the window with apparent absorption. A widow entered, and asked the gentleman if she could take a seat; he said yes, and she sat. He seemed a strange but benevolent gentleman to her. She watched the ways his hands moved, stained with paint though he did not seem like anything but a gentleman, moving the fingers like a musician practising in the air.

Presently the train arrived at Leipzig. Klee took down his small suitcase, and the suitcase of the widow. They left the train. There were eighteen minutes to change trains for Munich, and Klee took the opportunity to have a cup of coffee in the station buffet. Here, too, he was observed, by a Leipzig man who had seen an article about him in the newspaper, and a photograph too; the face was unmistakable. The man did not approach him: he thought Klee's work a disgrace. Klee prided himself on his familiarity with the trains, and arrived everywhere punctually, but not hours before. He left the buffet; he walked through the station; he handed his ticket to the inspector at the gates, and walked down the platform. He was observed by a man sitting in the train. Klee! he thought. Klee! Travelling from Dessau.

The man bent all his thoughts on persuading Klee to mount just where he sat, and to take a place opposite him. And after that, they would talk at great length and interestingly, and he would persuade Klee of his work. It was Itten. He had not seen him for several years. Itten asked the universe to unbend, and to instruct Klee to come to him. And Klee, with his broad smooth face under a Homburg, a beautiful grey coat, did what the universe requested. He mounted the train with a jaunty move-ment, and could be heard approaching along the corridor. But the universe failed, or fell short. Klee could be heard entering the compartment next door, and making a small muttering noise. Itten went next door. He accepted the failure, or near-success, of his request to the universe.

'Good morning, Klee,' he said. 'I thought it was you.'

'Oh, good morning,' Klee said. He seemed not quite irritable, but disappointed. It occurred to Itten that he might have made a request of his own, to the universe.

'It is I, Itten,' Itten explained.

'Oh, yes,' Klee said, as if reminded. But it was only three or four years before that they had been colleagues.

3.3

'Would you mind if I took this place?' Itten said, placing his coat on the hook and his bag in the net above the seats. 'It is a long journey, and it is pleasant to have a companion to talk to.'

Klee inclined his head. He had recognized Itten when he had entered, but had not quite known where he was from. He saw only a tall, innocent face with an expression not quite its own. In a moment, he remembered that the man used to go about with a shaved head. He remembered nothing about his art at all. What had his art been like? Was it – but, no, some kind of insubstantial quality presented itself to the memory, like a cloud made out of sugar, dissolving with its own attempts to rain. He used to go about with a shaved head, and had come to meetings in Weimar, and his name was Itten. Klee felt quite pleased with himself at remembering that.

'You are Itten,' Klee said. 'You were in Weimar, I recall.'

'But of course!' Itten said. 'Klee, we were colleagues – I so much admired what you were doing with the students, as well as your art, of course. There was a beautiful painting of yours, a painting of coloured squares ...'

Klee inclined his head. He detested specific praise. There was nothing to be done with it except enrol a disciple. And what was there to be done with a disciple of your own work, except introduce them to the principles of art?

Itten finished praising the painting of Klee, and waited with an eager, expectant face. He looked like a hungry puppy. But Klee had no memory of any work of art that Itten had produced, and he could not reciprocate, even if he had wanted to.

'You are in Dessau now, I believe,' Itten said, defeated.

'Yes, indeed,' Klee said. 'The school moved from Weimar two years ago.'

'Ah, yes,' Itten said. 'I think I recall reading about it at the time. It is a great success, I hear. Did you hear about my school?'

'No, I did not,' Klee said.

'You are so tucked away, there in Dessau! It must be so good for the spiritual development, not like Weimar, with its princes and its palaces. I truly found Weimar a struggle. Of course, someone like me can find spiritual solace in any place. I have ended in Berlin, at the Nollendorfplatz; it is no Himalayan summit, it is a busy place devoted to traffic and to commerce. But it is possible for me to close off the Nollendorfplatz and emerge into a realm of pure colour. You were interested in colour, I remember.'

'Yes,' Klee said.

'I left the Bauhaus, you remember,' Itten said. 'It was some years ago. I could not understand what the Masters were doing, and what the school was doing, and what the students were doing. I did my best. I brought light and colour into the lives of the students, and I asked them to study breathing. They thought me very odd, I dare say! And then there was the Mazdaznan, too. The students of mine who took up Mazdaznan, their spiritual growth and their artistic growth, it went hand in hand. They were achieving great things when I left. I planted a seed that had no need of me, and I needed to go somewhere else, to plant more seeds. Tell me, Klee – is there Mazdaznan thriving in Dessau?'

'I don't know,' Klee said. 'I don't know what that is.'

'It doesn't matter,' Itten said, laughing lightly. 'It passes into bodies and it lives there, no one knowing what it is, or how it changes things. No one understands it. Not even I understand it. It is like the working of the breath, or the movement of the blood as far as a primitive man, a tribesman, a caveman, a Neanderthal is concerned. He would see some of its effects, but he would not understand its workings. And so it is with the spiritual exercises of Mazdaznan.'

'I don't know,' Klee said. 'I think I remember now. It was the business with garlic. But it stopped a long time ago. I don't know whether anyone still does it.'

Itten paused, looked out of the window; smoothed his hands on his thighs. 'I have a school now,' he said. 'It was in Nollendorfplatz, and now it is in the Potsdamerstrasse. It teaches art with spirituality. I am travelling about the country to raise funds for it. There is a great friend of the movement here in Leipzig, Dr Immelmann. He is most interested in everything we are attempting, though he himself is too frail to visit our school. We are so fortunate in our friends! Dr Immelmann is an American, who returned here to the land of his ancestors five years ago, and is as blessed with worldly benefits as he is lacking in health. But his spirituality is strong, and he contemplates a sheet of colour, breathing deeply, for an hour each day. And after him I am travelling to Munich to meet with another friend and his wife. He has been of great help, and has introduced many of

553

my students to Indian strands of thought. It is so difficult to keep a school of art going when the main purpose of it is to connect spirituality with artistic understanding! So few people can see the point of that in the world where we live.'

'Excuse me,' Klee said, and got up. He went outside, along to the train's lavatory. A large pile of leather luggage was almost blocking the corridor, with a violin case on top. With professional interest, he looked into the compartment. In it was a very stout father, with the ruddy face of a baker, and the fat hands of a murderer resting on his knee. With him were four – no, five boys. He might be a schoolmaster or a widower, taking his five sons to stay with his mother. It was hard to know. The eldest son must be the violinist, Klee decided, the one with the broad and blank face that so often concealed pain in humans. He hoped he had not inherited his father's fat fingers, and thought about what it must be like to play the violin with fingers squeezing together so painfully. He would try to see on his way back what sort of hands the eldest boy had.

In the lavatory, he enjoyed pissing directly into the open hole, through which the swift movement of the tracks could be seen like the movement of a cinematograph, and almost regretted the brevity of the act. He made his way back to the compartment. He could not see whether the eldest boy in the widower's compartment had fat hands or not. The five boys reminded him of five sleeping puppies, or cats, or nameless creatures fitting their shapes to each other. He entered the compartment where the man he had been talking to was sitting. The man's name was Itten, he remembered.

'Is the first stop Jena, Itten?' Klee asked politely.

'I'm sorry?' Itten said.

'The next station,' Klee said. 'I think it must be Jena.'

'I don't know,' Itten said. 'I am not familiar with this route. I do not travel by train between Leipzig and Munich. I prefer to stay where I am, and not to move. That is the true route to understanding. It is a great sorrow to me to have to uproot myself and hurtle about the country, rewarding though it is to me to meet such wonderful people as Dr Immelmann and my friends in Munich.'

'I think it's Jena,' Klee said. 'I am almost sure it is Jena. Yes, it is.'

'Tell me, Klee,' Itten said. 'How do you begin with your students in Dessau?'

'That is an interesting question,' Klee said distractedly. The train was out in the open country now, and under a tree in a field near by, cows were crowding in the shade. Their squeezing together was like the five boys in the neighbouring compartment. Would it not be sensible for the cows to lessen their heat by standing apart from each other? It seemed to Klee to diminish the point of standing in the shade, to increase the heat by standing between the two hot bodies of different cattle. They were unlike the cows in Bavaria, the cows in Sachsen-Anhalt. He would ask somebody who knew about such things.

'Well,' Klee said in the end, 'I like to ask them to draw a line on a sheet of paper. That sometimes stumps them, you know.'

'I know!' Itten said excitedly. 'I ask them, too, to draw a line. I tell them that the idea of a line is one that I am putting into their heads, and that they should empty their heads and draw the line that I am thinking of. It stumps them to try to think of the line that I might be thinking of. But it proves the joining of minds, how it exists beyond a worldly plane. Sometimes, once or twice in a class, I see on the sheet of paper a line that is exactly the line I have thought of. I have reached that person. They have made a connection with me. It is so frail, that connection. The next time I ask them to do something, there will be no connection, it is just a light in the universe, being lit, once, and then extinguished, passing on into the darkness. But the connection is there.

'How to keep that connection! How to make the connection solid! How to give your message to the class and allow them to take it out into the world!

'Klee,' Itten said, with great solemnity. 'Sometimes I believe that I am nothing but a great failure.'

'Oh, surely,' Klee said. Out of the window, he could see hills approaching. Soon, the train would pass into a landscape of steep-sided hills; he saw in his mind's eye a woodcutter's cottage, smoke rising from the chimney, amid the forested slopes. He looked forward to that part of the journey.

3.4

'I do not know what to do,' Itten said. 'It is too obvious to me. I hate everything and everyone. I tell them what to do, I set them an example. And they do it while they are in the room and I am in the room. They are impressed. And then they leave the room.

'Nothing I do leaves the room. Nothing I do is carried away with them. And I look at my work. I do something and it seems wonderful, perfect, the best thing I ever did. And then I grow older and I change my mind, I start to do something different. What happens if you make a painting out of squares of colour? I say to myself, and I make a painting out of squares of colour. But I am so bored with filling in the spaces, long, long before it is finished. And then it is finished. I look at it and it seems that there is no reason why this should not be as wonderful and perfect and famous as the greatest works of art in the past. But I look at what I was doing three years before, and it seems pathetic, hateful, idiotic to me.

'There seems nothing of me in any of it. I have a truly original mind. I am not one for following trends. I start beliefs, and I spread a religion, and I explain to people a whole new way of thinking about colour, and about art. Sometimes I believe I am a saint, a modern saint, and the way that I cannot spread my word – it is my own martyrdom. People have told me this. Truly.'

'I wouldn't go about saying that, if I were you,' Klee said.

'But it is. For a saint, not to be listened to, it must be the worst torture. To feel that you are saying the truth, a truth that will change the lives of everyone who hears it – and for your truth to be listened to and forgotten. That is torture. That is martyrdom. I look at my work, and I look at myself, and every-thing seems empty and false. I pretend to be driven by love, and I am driven by contempt. I look at the world about me, and the faces rising up eagerly, the so few faces in my class at school, the faces of cranks and madmen and those ready for belief, and I put on my loving face, like a hat from the hatstand, and inside, I feel nothing of loving. And my art is just dead. It changes and changes, and then there is nothing of me inside it, nothing that anyone could want to have about them. How is it done? I can do anything with a pencil and a brush, anything. But I cannot do that. How is it done?'

'How is what done?' Klee said.

'What I am saying,' Itten said. He sank back, defeated.

Klee looked away, embarrassed. He was thinking about the G major violin sonata by Brahms. The first movement, so clean, like a good storyteller. But had Brahms been right to finish with the last movement? Klee often wondered about that.

'I want to achieve greatness,' Itten said, his voice lowered in a saintly way. 'I know I am not worthy, and I know I could never produce anything genuinely great, nothing compared to the great works of the past. But I want to paint a great painting, just one great painting, before I die. What I want to know is this. What does the first great brushstroke of a great painting look like? What is the great stroke of the pencil on canvas? Where does the greatness begin? You see, I do not know how to do it, how to make that great mark. I do not know how you begin with greatness. But you, Klee—'

'Yes?' Klee said.

'I am humble before you,' Itten said. 'I can see your work going out into the world. I know it will. I saw a painting of yours in a magazine that a student of mine was reading at the back of the classroom. It was not like any painting of yours I had seen before, and it was a poor photograph, in black-and-white, blurred, small, nothing in particular when I came to look at it. But I saw it from the front of the classroom, far away, and it was as if I had seen your face through a small square window, unmistakable. How is it done? How is greatness started? Tell me, Klee, tell me how you go out into the world.'

'I don't understand,' Klee said.

'Everyone goes out into the world,' Itten said. 'The brown-shirts, and the Communists, and the ideas and the designs and the paintings, they all go out into the world. But I stand and preach and I stand and make marks on canvas, and it all goes to the door, and turns, and will not go out. What is the first mark that you make on a canvas, Klee? Tell me! What is it?'

'I like to start with a line,' Klee said simply. 'This is Jena, I'm sure of it. Yes, it is. I very much like Jena, I must say.'

The train was slowing. Itten sank back in his seat. He closed his eyes. He seemed to be practising his breathing.

3.5

Itten waited until the rhythms of his breath were calm again, and opened his eyes. Klee was gone from the compartment, with his tranquil broad face and his restless, interested manner. When had he gone? It was not quite clear to Itten. He must have got up at some point as if to excuse himself, but now Itten paid attention, there was no sign of Klee left anywhere. He seemed to have departed. There had been no station; there had been no farewell. It could be that Klee was somewhere on the train and would return. Itten did not think so. His presence had been removed from the train; he could feel it. Or had there been a station? He was not sure. Outside, the flat sheets of field and agriculture were speeding up, rattling past, green, like the sea in a student drawing. One of Itten's favourite sights, the great monastery library, like the prow of a ship, was rising up remotely at the far horizon. He felt disquieted and not elevated by the sight. And now he looked there was a small boy in his compartment. When had he arrived? Had he been there all the time he had been talking to Klee? The small boy was fumbling with some wooden puzzle, some device or other. He was absorbed in his task to fit shapes together smoothly, and hardly seemed any more aware of Itten than Itten was of him. Was it strange that so small a boy was travelling on his own? He seemed perfectly tranquil. Itten looked at him benevolently. Or he tried to look at him benevolently; after speaking to Klee, it seemed to Itten that he was impersonating benevolence and putting on a kind general face. It seemed to Itten that next to Klee he hated the human race.

'Sir,' the train steward said, putting his head round the door of the compartment. 'Sir. You ordered a cup of coffee. It is here.'

'I don't think …' Itten said, but then for no particular reason he said, 'Thank you,' and took the cup of coffee. He placed the small white china jug of milk and the bowl of sugar cubes on the tiny wooden platform by the side of the seat. It had been paid for, apparently. The small boy seemed to have ignored the world around him until now, but as Itten held the cup of coffee firm, he looked up, with keen interest. With his fingers, Itten took the uppermost of the white sugar cubes. It was his one small vice; to drink coffee with the addition of a sugar cube. He had tried to rid himself of the addiction, and now he concluded that he need not stop it. It was only one cube of sugar, once a day, if that. Where had Klee gone?

Itten raised the cup of coffee to his mouth. But there was something rising to the surface as the cup met his lips. It was black and floating and spiked; it was – he saw, picking it out of the coffee – it was the black carved model of a spider. How had it got in there? It was bobbing and floating in the brown liquid. It must have been encased somehow in the cube of sugar. Itten plucked it out with distaste; he put it to one side. The small boy was entranced. His puzzle sat in his left hand as he waited to see what Itten would do.

'I see,' Itten said benevolently. 'It is some sort of humorous joke, I believe. I am an artist, young man. I do not know where this object comes from, but I have plenty of time, and now I have decided that I will draw this object. It seems most interesting to me.'

But the boy had raised his puzzle to his face. Itten could have examined the spider more closely. It seemed irreconcilable with the dignity of the universe, however. Shortly, Itten got up and opened the window. He threw the wooden spider out with a single, dignified flick of the wrist. It could not be hurled: it was made of too light a wood, and spun and bobbed as he threw it into the wake of the train. It would not do to make oneself ridiculous by complaining about an absurd attempt to make oneself ridiculous. Outside, the landscape of the country, of green fields and shining water, of dark woods and bright sky, continued to unfold under the regular rhythm of the train's wheels.

4.1

It was decided to hold an odyssey through the seas of alcohol; a long night's journey through the bars of Dessau. It had been decided in the introductory class that a Thursday night in November was perfect for this, and then somebody noticed that the date they had settled on was the eighth anniversary of the Armistice. The eleventh of November. It was so hard to pick on a meaningless date to go from one bar to another, and for a moment they considered altering it. But then someone said that Thursdays were perfect, as nobody expected anything much from students on a Friday, and in any case many people went away on Fridays, or found it a bourgeois sort of day to get drunk on. The eighteenth was impossible, and the twenty-fifth was too far away. So, in the end, there was found to be something rather splendid about the decision to go out and get drunk in twenty bars in Dessau on the day of the surrender, the Armistice, the stab in the back.

What a thrill! What a jaunt! What an outing! What a thing to dress up for!

Paul was a Marxist and despised the Bauhaus. 'The cube!' he said. 'The cube! One side blue, another red, a third yellow – a lovely toy for the Bauhaus collectors, the snobs! And the triangle must be yellow, and the circle must be blue, and the square must be red! Put a price on it and hand it to the collectors! The cube is trumps, and wins the game. And on the floor of the Masters' houses, what do you see? Woven. The interesting psychological complexes of young girls. Woven into interesting expensive carpets. No, we must strive to create art that everyone can own, that has no difference, that is made by factories in their millions, and the director of an art school drinks his tea from the same cup that an honest labourer works. And for that reason we are going to go out and drink in every drinking establishment in Dessau, and take a glimpse at society.'

Paul and Ludo together had a splendid idea, put into detailed execution by Egon, who had a solid knowledge of the structure of the town's drinking. The rule of the evening would be this: that every bar or pub or beerhall or *Kneipe* entered should be undeniably and objectively worse than the one before. The descent should be gently stepped and appalling in its final result. You see, Paul had said, it should be a demonstration of the suffering of the urban proletariat and the complacency, the emptiness, of the pleasures of the urban bourgeoisie, the rentiers with their little glasses and their little cherries in their drinks and their little diamonds about their wives' necks. 'Let's ask Max,' someone said daringly, and Max was asked (without offering Paul's detailed justification), and Max said it was a splendid idea and he would never forgive them if they didn't include him.

Would it not be better, Paul observed after this, if the bars grew better and better, as the voyagers grew more and more drunk and incapable? And if the last drinking establishment were unspeakably refined and ostentatious, and if it found itself hosting thirty drunk and violent Bauhäuslers on the verge of starting a fight?

It was an excellent idea, but the American Bar of the Hotel Gansevoort would, it was felt, happily refuse entry to thirty drunk and violent Bauhäuslers after midnight. It had to be conducted as Paul decreed, from good to bad, and his second thought was not put to Max at all. Paul led them into the American Bar of the Hotel Gansevoort. It was seven thirty on Thursday, the eleventh of November 1926. He wore his hair long on top, with a cursory parting in the middle; like many of the other boys, he shook his head and tossed it from his forehead regularly. The barmen and the three other parties in the bar looked at the Bauhaus contingent, ten of them in the end, with distrust. One of the other men was wearing a white blouse crossed with a leather strap, like a *moujik*; another made a habit of blackening the lower rim of his eyelids. They entered the bar, with the wainscoting in soft wood, the beaten brass fixtures and its warm chocolate glow.

'They are going to be more concerned about prostitutes than about us,' Thomas said to Klaus.

'What did you have for your dinner?' Klaus said.

'There were croquettes made out of turnip-tops,' Thomas said, and shuddered. 'And then a sort of shape that had been broached yesterday and turned up again today, tasting of almond soap. I am hoping for peanuts here at the American Bar.'

The drinks had been ordered by Max, the most respectable-looking of the men, who had come out in a brilliant white shirt with a scribble of a black string tie falling down the front. There was only one barman, a middle-aged and highly groomed individual in a white shirt that looked drab by the side of Max's, his black hair beautifully neat around a sharp white line of a parting. Max and Ingrid stood at the bar, Ingrid in a pair of enormous ear-rings like the ear-rings of savages. They discussed, at some length, the possibilities of American drinks with the barman, and finished by ordering brandy Alexanders for the women and dry martinis for the men.

'The bourgeoisie must be shot,' Klaus was saying to Karoline, a very young girl whose eyes were wide open with interest. She had arrived in Dessau only one month before; her parents were quite set against it, but it was all so rewarding and valuable. She was wearing a brilliant red skirt and yellow stockings, and a white blouse rather like the *moujik* one that Klaus wore; they looked like a peasant couple at the Russian Ballet. Karoline had been brought by Max. He had seduced her efficiently and hygienically after two weeks.

'There is no alternative,' Klaus said. 'They must all be shot.'

'Oh, but surely,' Karoline said, 'when you explain things as clearly and logically as you explain them – surely everyone would understand afterwards how things must be.'

Klaus gave a brief, harsh laugh, and plucked at the arm of the man who was wearing black makeup on his lower lids. 'Ludo, you must meet this comrade,' he said to the man. 'Here is a comrade who believes still in education.'

'I think I believe in education, Klaus,' Ludo said. 'There is always the possibility of education.'

'No, often there is no possibility of education,' Klaus said. 'There is no alternative but to take them outside and shoot them in the head. I am talking about the urban bourgeoisie.'

'What about the rural bourgeoisie?' Ingrid said, coming back from the bar. She had a charming inability to pronounce her *r*s, a plump girl with bloodthirsty views. 'What about them? Those of us who spring from the rural bourgeoisie – we would like to know their fate.'

'They,' Klaus said, accepting a dry martini from Ingrid and handing another to Ludo, a brandy Alexander to Karoline, 'they will be sealed up inside their vast palaces, and burnt alive, and the people's tribunes will line up and watch them burn. It will be a glorious spectacle.'

'Oh, good,' Ingrid said. 'I do hope I'm there when it happens to Mamma. Come on, Karoline – let's go and look at the mosaics in the bathroom.'

She had finished her drink so quickly, and Karoline, following instructions, too; they went out. Once in the lobby, Ingrid turned and called back into the bar, 'I say – *do* look at this,' and then the men, most of them, strolled out, their martini glasses in hand. The barman looked sceptical, but one boy remained at the bar. It was Ludo. They must have seemed pleasant and clean, though oddly dressed. But in a moment there was a blood-curdling scream from the lobby; the boy who had remained in the bar made a concerned face, and, leaving his glass on the bar, rushed out. The barman followed, more slowly, to find the last of the students piling out of the hotel and running for dear life, hurling their cocktail glasses behind them as they went.

The whole thing had been decided upon before they entered the American Bar at the Hotel Gansevoort. It was the best bar in Dessau, and by a long way the most expensive. The ten of them ran furiously, never having had any intention to pay for the drinks at the hall of the bourgeois predators.

At length they slowed down. Egon had led them through a complex series of side-streets, doubling back and crossing their route twice. Only when they turned into the Radegasterstrasse did they fall back into a walk, rather red-faced. Instantly Klaus began to talk about the revolution.

'Oh, I know,' Ludo said happily, at an inquisitive look from Egon. 'He looks forward so much to the future. I admire him so much.'

'What is your future?' Paul said. 'Your individual one, not the one that contains us all.'

'Did you not see Ludo's glass and felt piece?' Karoline said. 'It was all in shades of red, transparent and opaque, and the shades were identical but modified by whether it was glass or felt. There were polished aspects and raw aspects. It was—'

'But red is only red!' Max said. 'All that talk of associations – it is just like listening to my father talk about – about – about *anything*. We have grown out of all of that, surely.'

And then they turned into the second bar of the evening. It was another cocktail bar, but not quite so assured and elegant as the American Bar. The interior had been done in a hurry by someone recognizing a craze, and although its little wooden lights and its marble bar, the large golden mirrors behind the bar looked impressive through the window, there were already signs that it would settle down into a comfortably shabby exist-ence. The striped wallpaper, purple and cream with a thin line of gold between them, had been picked off at table level here and there; the glass ashtray at the table where they sat bore the name of the bar, but was chipped. Nevertheless, the drinks were said to be good, and gin fizzes, a curious mixture containing Curaçao and Chartreuse and a glass of sekt with a cube of brandy-soaked sugar were ordered. Here, it had been concluded, they would pay. The bar was called Bill's Bar, with a fashionable American apostrophe. A pianist played ragtime cheerfully on a small grand, perhaps too obtrusively for the middling-sized room; a single middle-aged man wearing an American suit, his crumpled hat on the table by his side, read the sporting news-paper with a glass of clear heavy liquid in front of him.

'Red is everything!' Ingrid came in. 'Nothing is only anything! You have not seen his piece. It was so much admired. Red is everything.'

'Oh, you mean it is blood, and passion, and Spain, and the Party, and more blood, and – associations, my dear Ingrid, associations,' Max said. 'The point is—'

'Those are such important associations,' Karoline said. 'We would not know what to do with red, or anything, without bringing our associations into it. When we see blue, there is the sea!'

'Oh, for Heaven's sake,' Max said. 'The sea is not blue! I have never seen the sea blue. The sea is grey, and sometimes a little greenish, and sometimes brown, and—'

'It is only blue in the pictures,' Egon said. 'The pictures that your grandfather painted and liked so much.'

They all burst out laughing. Karoline had perhaps thought that Max liked her for herself, that she had been brought along because Max thought her so special. But the others knew that Max brought many girls along, and would bring many more girls along, in the course of the year.

'The truth of the matter is …' Klaus said, but he found he was talking to no one. 'What are they talking about?'

'Red is only red,' Max said, 'as I say. It is for us to make our own associations, or to choose none. It is merely a vibration along a certain spectral line, an illusion, a range of shades that may remind you of blood and revolution and Spain, but which reminds me of a virgin's First Communion dress. There! And a wedding dress! And snow! That is what it reminds me of.'

'Oh, but that is absurd,' Willi said. 'No one gets married in a red dress. You always marry in white.'

It was tacitly agreed not to take any notice of this contribution. Willi's foolish contributions to any debate were familiar. He was a stocky boy with close-shaved head; his hair had been blond and glinted like the very beginnings of a mental insight, emerging. Whether he did not listen, or whether he listened and did not understand, his contributions more often led to an embarrassed changing of the subject than a continuation of it. He only made sense when he had a chisel in front of him and a block of cedarwood.

And then there was the Cairo, and then another bar, and there was the Rosebud, and then there was a healthy garden in which to drink, where they drank, though it was so cold and the weather was so brisk, in November, and then …

In the Karlsbad beerhall, the party had been going on for some time. The air was heavy with smoke. A waitress in bulging white blouse and Bavarian embroidered skirt indicated entry with a gesture of her head and neck; it was not much of a welcome from the best beerhall in Dessau, but her hands were full with six enormous *masskrug*s of beer. She looked too delicate to be carrying them all. Her cheerfulness was limited to the floral embroidery on bib and skirt; her face was weary, dismissive, had seen it all.

'One Gibson, two dry martinis, an Alexander and a gin fizz,' Egon said to her, when she had dumped the beers she was carrying and returned to them. Her fists were placed firmly on her sides.

'Don't know about that then,' she said, in a harsh Leipzig accent. 'Don't know about that. We're a beerhall, we are.'

'My God!' Egon said. 'My God! I thought this was a cocktail bar. What do we do? Do we order something called *beer*, then?'

'Order whatever you like,' the waitress said. She was flushing with the weight of the beer; she probably didn't care for Ingrid laughing behind her hand, or perhaps for Ingrid's green fingernails, green eyeshadow and green lipstick underneath her severely geometric black bob.

'Oh, well, if we can order whatever we like, we'll have a Gibson, a gin fizz, two dry martinis—'

'Ignore him, miss,' Klaus said. 'We'll all have beer. The wheat beer.'

'Dark or light?' she said, was answered and went off wearily.

'Oh, she's heard it all before,' Egon said. 'She didn't care. No – I know what you're going to say but we can tease each other, I believe. The thing is that the revolution will not be without humour!'

'Yes, and the working-class woman shall be the butt of your humour, unless she forms part of the detachment detailed to shoot fools like you,' Klaus said. 'Now – where did that come from?'

At the other end of the beerhall, somewhere behind a wall of smoke being put up by a line of middle-aged men with elaborate moustaches and immense yellow-ivory carved pipes, a noisy party of men was chanting something. Were they singing? Or was it just chanting, the sort of thing a group of men did to encourage one of their number to finish the last beer in as short a time as possible? There were words in it and a great thumping, as the *masskrugs* were brought down in unison on the table. There was something, behind the braying, about pulling the concubine out of the Prince's bed, about greasing the guillotine – no, it was gone behind a lot of cheering as a glass was shattered and one of the men wailed in disgust. One of the respectable drinkers was wearing a hat with a pheasant's feather in the brim. He picked at something, a stain or crusted food deposit, on his lapel, and said something contemptuous to his neighbour. Then they all fell silent again.

'My goodness, those fellows are drunk,' Willi said. 'Paul, can you hear? What an awful din they're making! Thomas, listen – they're singing some sort of song. It's not even ten o'clock! You're musical. Why are they making such an awful din?'

Thomas agreed to go and have a look on his way to take a piss. The waitress arrived with the many mugs of beer, dark and light.

'I think they must be part of your revolution,' Willi said to Klaus, in an amicable way. 'The thing I never understood, though –I never know about these things. I know we're not supposed to be for the princes, that goes without saying, but there aren't any princes any more. I'm a Communist, I know, and I want everyone to have the same things, and all that, but I always forget – what am I supposed to think about the Jews? You hear so many people saying things about them, and they all sound very convincing at the time, like people saying they're human beings, just like us, and you think, Oh, yes, that must be right, but then, a day or so later, you hear somebody in the street making a speech, and you think, Hmm, well, I don't know, that seems to make a lot of sense, really. So what I don't remember is—'

'They're all in some kind of uniform,' Thomas said, sitting down and taking a big slug of blond beer from his mug. 'They look as if they're pretending to be soldiers, but I don't think they are. A lot of them don't look at all fit, and some of the uniforms look as if they made them themselves. They look like insurance clerks pretending to be soldiers. Have you seen this great fat beast coming!'

And from the back a fat man, no more than twenty, reeled towards them. His uniform, crossed with a leather strap, was stained with most of a litre of beer. It had once been brown. He was holding up his hand, which somehow had been cut. Blood was running down the inside of his wrist. A cheering came from the back of the room, a hideous grunting: *Storm storm storm storm storm storm.*

'Students,' the man said. 'Students! Students!' A group of elderly beer drinkers, sitting in silence and observing his progress in a disapproving way, drew back and concentrated on their drinks. A waitress was standing back. Her arms were full of beer *krugs*, and she was waiting for him to pass. But he paused, wavering like a tree in a gale, back and forth, back and forth. 'More beer for us all,' he said, 'more beer, dark beer ...' and a flourish of inspiration hit him, and as he fell on the waitress, he managed to say, 'And Thuringian sausages, many Thuringian sausages,' before he brought her, too, to the floor, her beer glasses falling and smashing and pouring in a great flood over him, over her, over everything. Indignantly, she pushed him up, springing to her feet and leaving him where he lay. A man was quickly on the scene, a well-dressed and smooth man, with dark hair and glinting American glasses, just running to fat in his early forties, and explaining to the man that this could not continue, that he would have to leave if he and his friends could not contain themselves. 'It was the beer,' the man in the brown uniform was saying. 'It was the beer slipped on the floor – the beer spilt on the floor that made me slip and lose my stance and fall against your good waitress here. Let me pay for the beer

569

lost and the lost and broken mugs. Let me at any rate pay for that. Here are the marks to pay for that, my good sir, my good beerhall sir, and you and your lady wife, we would like to say to you, and to this wonderful lady, too ...'

Storm storm storm storm storm storm, the chanting went, from the back of the hall, a great tumult of banging, and then with a single voice, something was suddenly clear – *Judas seems to be winning the Empire* – and then cheering. The man in brown tried to reach out to shake the manager by the hand; the manager stared contemptuously at the hand, dripping with beer and blood.

'They'd be so shocked,' Willi said, 'if those people knew we were Communists, wouldn't they? I really think I'm going to come to one of Klaus's meetings and hear all about it.'

'Let's have some more beers,' Egon said. 'This is all very exciting.' Then, with a smooth, confident gesture, he stood up and walked over to where the man was still trying to detain the waitress. He took the man by the shoulders, turned him round forcibly and then, with a single blow, hit the drunk man hard in the face. The man fell heavily on the floor. Egon dusted his fists in a theatrical way, grinned like the hero of a movie, and came back to his seat. Was he expecting cheering?

'But what is all that achieving?' Karoline said to Paul, with the fervour of the just-arrived. She waved her arms about above her head as she spoke. 'Really, what is it achieving? Elsa Winteregger, she teaches in the metal workshops, she is trying to make a teapot. A teapot! What use is a teapot? And she is trying to make a teapot that is half a perfect sphere, sliced off with a flat surface, out of silver. Silver is no longer a good material for anyone to use. What we should be doing is making good, cheap, industrial products that anyone can own and anyone can make. Beauty! Who cares about beauty?'

'Yes, yes, that's right,' Klaus said. 'She is a reactionary, that old Winteregger, and crazy. Did you hear what she said to Ludo? He was telling her—'

Another man in a brown uniform was standing over them.

'Which of you did it?' he said. 'On this holy day? Which of you struck a German hero when he was in no condition to defend himself?'

'The truth is,' Paul said, 'that beauty was invented by nineteenth-century industrialists and linked from its beginning to the profit motive. What is beauty? There will be nothing of beauty –' he drew out the word in an ugly way '– in the new society. There will just be use. A silver teapot! What a dead, stupid, ugly object!'

'But if there is ugly there is beauty,' Egon just had time to say.

'Which of you was it?' the man said. 'This holy day of tragedy and betrayal? This day that Germany mourns, and you thought you would strike a German hero in the face?'

'Oh, do go away,' Ingrid said. 'You're boring us. You stupid, stupid bore. Sing another song. This one's too boring and dull and you don't know the tune, half of you. It will never, never catch on in the dance halls. Go. Away.'

'German womanhood!' the man said. 'A woman who should be bearing children, who should be caring for her husband, who should be modest and quiet and virtuous! Look at her! Thinking of nothing but green paint on her face, of shocking the decent, of whoring herself out, of bestial acts with black men, with jazz, making love to the Jews, of betraying your fathers. Listen to what Germany says, woman, and change your ways. It was him, wasn't it?'

'This is awfully exciting,' Willi said to Ludo. 'There's something in what they say, after all. I don't know, Ingrid, she should probably marry one fellow and have children. Women don't have for ever to settle down, after all.'

'You can't seriously think that, Willi,' Ludo said.

'Oh, well, perhaps not,' Willi said. 'Has he gone away? I hope he's not going to come back with lots of his awful friends.'

But before they could return and start a fight, Max had gathered their attention, and they left very quickly.

How had Max risen to be their leader, even when he appeared to be skulking at the back, joining in with an evening planned and executed by others? Why was it Max whose approval they sought and whose interest they tried to pique? When he was in the company, it was all a matter of asking Max to look at this, to tell them what he thought, to judge between them on matters of taste and opinion and politics. When he was not there, it was all deadly dull and posturing. One of them would say that he thought he would dress all in white for a year, and the others would nod; or that he believed the clergy were at the root of all evil and corruption, and should be lined up and shot, and whoever was listening would say, 'Very likely,' and go on to something else with a yawn. When no one could decisively judge, anyone could say anything, with a jut of the jaw and a widening of the eyes. It was all so impossible. But when Max was there – everything was decisive, and everything was a good idea, an exciting idea, or dull and flat, and everything could move forward under the beam of his judgement. Max was an architect's son from Düsseldorf, and had known all sorts of artists, politicians, writers from his cradle: his mother had been artistic, he said, giving the word a curious and perhaps ironic intonation of his own. She had liked to have famous people around. An actress had taken Max to bed during the long run of *Wibbel the Tailor* in Düsseldorf, some time in 1917 when Max was only thirteen; in 1919, when things looked bleak, the actor who had played the French general in *Wibbel the Tailor* had been brought round to their house and he, too, had seduced Max. Max had enjoyed both experiences. It was not always necessary to make a choice.

'Do you know the play,' Max had said, '*Wibbel the Tailor?*' But people did not – it was a Düsseldorf hit, and Max had been taken to see it many times, and afterwards had watched it from the wings of the theatre, courtesy of the French general or the heroine of the piece, or of a third encounter that neither of the first two knew about, the *soubrette* role. Well, during the Napoleonic wars, the French met their match – Max's eyes madly rolling – in a tailor of Düsseldorf, whose name was Wibbel. The merry scrapes that Wibbel got up to! For instance, one day there was a giant cheese in the market ...

Max's fantasy, drolly told, was enough to reduce the most sober of people to uncontrolled laughter.

They thought he would be in an artistic profession, and even encouraged him, Max's parents. But they thought he would grow up to be an architect, a builder of great houses and offices, as his father had been, and live like his father in a house that looked like the Ministry of the Suppression of Magic. 'First I photographed,' Max said. 'Then I drew. Then I drew naked people. They were always about the house! Those naughty naked people, sometimes five and six of them at a time, always forgetting something and having to pop down to the kitchen to ask the cook for coffee and cakes to keep going, pink and white and twinkling on the stairs. Cook was so shocked the first time it happened! Then the naked people were banned, and I made a tea bowl! Then I painted scenery for a drama, and the naked people came back and staged *Hedda Gabler* in the old folks' drawing room, for the old folks and their friends, like ministers and authors and painters and architects. I painted a great pink dragon on the backdrop! It was a symbol of everything that was wrong for Hedda. And nobody was naked during the production of *Hedda*. No – I tell a lie – that was not quite accurate. The actor who played George Tesman, he was naked all the way through. It was symbolic! Everything the play does is to strip him naked. So we thought we would have George Tesman walking naked through the play, and everyone else in crinolines and morning coats and everything, and a great pink dragon that I had painted behind everything.

'How the old folks did howl! And after that I was sent to the Bauhaus, as a punishment. Poor me.'

'Poor you,' Max's partner in conversation would say, entranced.

Tonight Karoline was the one under a sad delusion. She had been seduced by Max a very short time ago. She had not yet discovered that Max had taken more than one of them to his bed, efficiently and, usually, as a unique occasion – Ingrid, and Willi, and Paul, and Klaus, but not yet Ludo. She offered her approval as a support to Max. This was the spirit in which she now listened to Egon saying, as they walked beneath the tree-shaded stretch of the boulevard, that he knew an illegal bar, an anarchist bar, which took place in what had once been a piano showroom, and that perhaps the time had come to go there; in that spirit she heard Max saying, 'That sounds like an awfully good idea,' and piped up, 'I couldn't agree more.' The others were patient. Who among them could not say that the moment had come for them, too, when they realized that they were not at all special to Max, that he had only done what he had done in a moment of enthusiasm and speculation? She was the naked actor among them this evening, despite the care with which she had dressed.

Egon was saying some of this to Ludo as the door to the piano showroom, the nameless anarchist bar, was opened before them and they entered an unusual scene. The room was filled with the stock of the previous owner, who must have despaired of ever using the prices of his pianos to keep up with the cost of living. Abandoned, thirty pianos filled the room – upright cottage pianos at the side, but ten grand pianos intricately forming a kind of maze in the middle. The room was lit by candles, rudely stuck in saucers or just left to drip on the pianos, one Erard, another announcing itself as made by the Brothers Zimmermann of Leipzig. The crowd were recognizably Bauhaus and ruder folk. Against the far wall, there was a trestle table of drink, a beer barrel or two and twenty bottles of wine. The prices were chalked up on a board behind the scowling barman.

'Oh, I want to dance!' Ludo said impulsively. 'Look at all these pianos – and nobody playing them, and nobody dancing. Klaus – Klaus – dance with me. On top of a piano. Wouldn't that be marvellous?'

Klaus was talking about the revolution. His attention had to be brought. When he heard what Ludo was asking, he said, 'There is no music,' and turned back to Willi, who needed a good deal of education in this matter.

'Well, that is no problem,' Ludo said. 'Look – here is Thomas. You played the piano for *The Euclidean Ballet*, so I know you can play the piano. Play us a dance, and Klaus and I will dance on top of a piano for everyone. Klaus! Klaus! I want to dance!'

'There is no music,' Klaus said again, but just then the music started, almost before Thomas had sat down. It was something that Thomas had played during the ballet in the summer – some old-fashioned piece of music. But it was quite nice. Thomas was a surprisingly expert pianist, and a shock of amused quiet ran through the bar before chatter started again. 'No, Ludo,' Klaus said. 'I am not going to dance with you, even if there is music. We have decided that the practice of animal passions must now cease with each other. And the dance is also an animal passion. I have no objection if you want to dance alone, but it is against the spirit of our agreement for you to seek to dance with me.'

'But it is so nice!' Ludo said. There was some drink in his hand now – he was not quite sure who had put it there. 'Listen – Max – Karoline – listen, it is just so nice when Thomas plays it. Karoline, will you dance with me?'

'Not I,' Karoline said, almost indignant in her *moujik* red, shaking her head furiously. 'I cannot make a spectacle of myself.'

'Ludo,' Max said. The others had all quickly dispersed, to their separate friends, here and there in the anarchist bar. It had been open only six days, but this was the day, clearly, when the whole of the Bauhaus had decided to pay it a visit. 'Ludo! I'll dance with you, if you like. It would be my pleasure. Is this a Viennese waltz?'

'Well, you know, I rather think it is,' Ludo said, and as he and Max kicked off their shoes and clambered onto the top of the grand piano they were leaning against and took each other in their arms, he began to sing along with Thomas's fluid, trickling playing. The piano, despite being abandoned with all its fellows and sitting for a week in a drunken anarchist bar, was not too badly out of tune. It made, in fact, a lovely noise. 'Da-daaa-dit-daaa, da-da-da-daaa,' Thomas sang. 'I do adore this. It is just like my grandmother's favourite piece of music. I did love it when I was tiny. I don't know why – very well, let's concentrate. Look, Max, they're all looking. You start and I'll follow.'

'I do like you, Ludo,' Max said in his most purring voice, and Ludo looked very much as if he were going to laugh. Below, at the level of their knees, the crowd could not hear what Max was saying, murmuring bold suggestions into Ludo's ear, but they could see his pink, plump, pleased amusement as the pair of them waltzed. One of the people below was called Egon Rosenblatt, and in a few years he would pack his bags and go to America. He would live the rest of his life in America, teaching form and structure to blond and glowing children at a liberal arts college in Kentucky, and then at sixty-five, he would retire with his wife to Miami. All that lay before Egon that night. But for the rest of his life, in Dessau, in Kentucky, in Miami, at his deathbed, he would sometimes think of and sometimes talk about that wonderful sight.

They stood open-mouthed beneath Ludo and Max, or making a play of their uninterest, and in a moment, as the music continued beneath them, Max drew Ludo towards him and whispered in his ear. 'You are so nice, Ludo,' Max said. 'I so like you, Ludo. I like your little ears and I like your darling tiny neck and I like the lovely way you smell when you are a little bit sweaty.'

'I like you so much, Max,' Ludo said simply. 'I want to be with you tonight.'

'I don't know why that never happened before,' Max said. 'I want to be with you tonight and always.'

'Oh, Max,' Ludo said. 'Will you do sodomy with me tonight?'

'Oh, yes,' Max said. 'Yes, I will.'

'But, Max,' Ludo said. 'You won't stop doing it after ten

times, will you? I hate it when that happens, when it stops after ten times.'

'Oh, no,' Max said. 'I won't stop after ten times. I won't. I will go on doing it with you for ever.'

'That is so nice,' Ludo said. He thought with great happiness that Max must truly like him. Always, with everyone else, Max had done it just once or twice and then moved on. But when he had the chance of being with Ludo, he was definitely going to go on being with Ludo, and doing it with Ludo, for ever. That would be so nice, whatever Ludo had done to deserve it. 'Now dance with me some more,' Ludo said.

Beneath them, a drunk and bearded anarchist was plucking cigarette butts from a saucer that read *Hotel Gansevoort* in blue writing, and flicking them at Ludo and Max, now just swaying in each other's arms rather than trying to dance in a proper way. They paid no attention. They seemed hardly to notice. In a moment the drunk anarchist turned to Thomas, playing the piano; he flicked a cigarette butt into his face. Thomas blinked and shook his head as if the cigarette butt might have stuck in his hair; the drunk anarchist laughed, a coarse self-amused laugh, and flicked another. This one hit Thomas on his forehead, and a third hit his eyes. Efficiently, Thomas stopped playing, stood up, walked three paces to his left and tried to hit the drunk anarchist very hard in the face. The anarchist was prepared for this, and pushed the blow aside, hitting Thomas in return. A bottle broke, thrown against the wall of the piano showroom by some anarchist with a poor aim. Max jumped down from the piano onto the back of the anarchist, pulling him to the floor, and for a moment they rolled underneath the pianos. Ludo, more carefully, sat down and slid off.

'My goodness,' he said to Ingrid. 'What a very exciting night.'

'Oh, it's Armistice night,' Ingrid said. 'It's always going to be like this. Have you seen Karoline?'

'No,' Ludo said. 'What are we celebrating? Oh, yes, the November Criminals. We were undefeated in the field! That's what they say, isn't it? Which one is Karoline? Oh, the other girl, the other one apart from you. Is it you who is in love with Max or is it she?'

'It is she,' Ingrid said calmly. 'It is like a very bad play, with one person loving another and a third thinking that they are loved more and – shall they compete? What will happen? Where will the choice fall? I think Karoline was crying when she went off because of you embracing Max on top of a piano.'

'Is that a fact?' Ludo said, thrilled. 'Look, I think Max is winning.'

And here came Max, standing up, dusty about his jacket but smiling, and taking a beer from a boy they thought was called Siggi, a boy from the Bauhaus. 'Yes, I am winning for the moment,' Max said. 'But perhaps we should think about moving on. Where is a worse bar than this one? This seems like a very bad bar to me. Does Dessau present a worse drinking place than this one? Or does the game come to an end here? I could drink some more, I believe. Where is a worse drinking place?'

'Oh, Max,' Willi said. 'There are some drinking places worse than this. We have only been to the best beerhall in Dessau. There is another.'

'That is the second best beerhall in Dessau,' Paul said. 'Or, if you prefer, it is the worst. There are only two.'

'That is very bad,' Ingrid said. 'I am not sure if I would even be welcome there.'

'Oh, we make our own welcome,' Ludo said. He felt exhilarated with happiness. 'We make our own welcome with the gentlemen in brown shirts, and with anarchists who want to start fights, and we play the piano and we dance and we make love on the tables. Let us go to the worst beerhall in Dessau! And then –' he took an immense, celebratory swig of beer from a mug not his own '– and then perhaps somewhere else, a place in a cellar where they hardly ever wash the mugs up, and then finally I know a place that calls itself the Hundred Red Roses, where you can drink whatever you want. Only you must not fall asleep. Because once somebody, a soldier in a wheelchair, he fell asleep in the Hundred Red Roses and everyone thought he was quite all right, and then after two days of him sleeping in a corner, they thought to wake him up, and he was dead … It was so sad for the poor soldier … Oh, Max. Let's go to the Hundred Red Roses. We can dance there, and we won't fall asleep, not at all, we won't sleep. Max?'

But only some of what Ludo was saying made sense, he suddenly understood; the words were so difficult to make in his mouth, and the room was so hot and people coming towards him of different sizes and making threatening movements, and through the door now were coming, surely, a lot of men in brown and they were howling for something; there was the noise of something smashing, a window and glass falling; but it was all so much, and without meaning to, Ludo's stomach rose in protest. It was lucky that there was an open receptacle just there that he could be sick into, a good big receptacle. He raised his head, wiping his mouth. 'I'm so sorry,' he said. 'I didn't mean to.' He had been sick into an open grand piano. But no one was listening to him: they were all scrambling out of the way of the men with clubs, out of the way of the man with something glittering in his fist. Ludo thought he would just get underneath a piano and stay there until it was all over. Now that he had been sick, he would be quite all right.

5.1

Adele was still asleep when Christian left the flat, and Elsa, too. He had made a knack of dressing as quietly and as quickly as possible, in the dark, since Adele disliked being woken unnecessarily. He was aware that this inconvenience meant that sometimes he only discovered a stain on his jacket once he was outside in the courtyard. He was also used by now to doing without breakfast beyond a piece of bread and cold milk, since the noise of anything else disturbed Adele. It also saved money, and if he were known to be the first master always to arrive at the school, Christian believed that it would stand him in good stead for the offer of a further contract. He did not believe this strongly. He slung his large satchel over his shoulders and left the flat.

There was a figure in the courtyard of the house, examining the leaves of the solitary dusty lime tree that grew there. Surprisingly, it was Franz, Adele and Elsa's father. It was only a quarter to seven, though at this time of year the day was already well advanced.

'Good morning,' Christian said.

'Oh,' Franz said. 'Good morning, Christian.'

Christian waited, thinking that Franz might as well explain why he was there so early.

'It's a beautiful day,' Franz said. 'I'm always a very early riser.'

'I, too,' Christian said.

'In fact,' Franz said, 'I am too early and should have known it. Adele asked me to come today, before we left, but I don't think she meant as early as this. I have been waiting for twenty minutes or so. I thought you would have gone by now.'

'No,' Christian said. 'I normally leave about now. For work.'

'You are like me,' Franz said. 'I am in the workshop at six thirty, rain or shine, whether I have anything to do or not. And I always do have something to do, I must say. Would you mind so terribly if I walked with you a little? It would occupy the time before my daughter wakes up.'

'Not at all,' Christian said. 'I think Adele is usually awake and presentable by eight, or a little after. Please.'

They walked across the courtyard and into the street. As always when with his father-in-law, Christian felt very young. It was not that Franz was so very ancient, but he was small, neat and weather-beaten; he looked as if he had spent his life fending off disappointment in a forest workshop, and the life had been long and expert. His jacket was beautiful, traditional in cut and ornament, and his hat carried a sprightly badger's brush.

'I like a walk in the morning,' Franz said. 'Are you walking directly to your school?'

'The birds start up so early,' Christian said. He had a sinking feeling: Franz's company was going to prevent him from going on his true errand this morning. 'It is almost like being in the countryside here.'

'Tell me,' Franz said. 'How did you manage during the most difficult periods?'

'The most difficult periods?'

'The periods – the billions and trillions period. Before the Rentenmark.'

'Oh.' Christian was not surprised. Whenever he met Franz, there was some fairly direct probing into his capacity as an earning and managing individual. 'I don't know how I came through it. My brother Dolphus came to visit me in Weimar, and he could only come at the very beginning of the month, in the hour or two after my father had his monthly salary. If he had waited another day or two, the ticket would have cost more than a lawyer's monthly salary. If he'd waited three weeks—'

'It would have cost more than life itself,' Franz said, chuckling. 'It was so strange and interesting. Frau Steuer did very well out of it, you know. She had two thousand Swiss francs and even three hundred American dollars. I have no idea how she came by them – probably her late husband, somehow – and I have no idea how she had the luck not to think of changing them and spending them when the mark was good. But in the end she had five thousand Swiss francs and three hundred American dollars, and in the summer of 1923 she bought three large houses with all their contents, in the centre of Breitenberg.'

'That was useful,' Christian said, aghast.

'Yes, indeed,' Franz said. He paused under a boxwood tree with its black trunk, looking up into its leaves and listening to a blackbird, somewhere up there, singing. 'Some people might

581

say she was not the best person to talk about people profiteering from the misery of others. However. We don't know what happened to the three families who lived in the houses, so perhaps we should not condemn Frau Steuer and her five thousand Swiss francs. How did you manage?'

Christian saw that there was no point in being evasive. 'I was living in lodgings,' he said. 'My landlady supplied all the meals. Once there was crow and sometimes a lot of cheese with potato. We managed, I think.'

'But how did you pay your landlady?' Franz said. 'It is so interesting, how people managed.'

'Well,' Christian said, suppressing his impatience, 'my grandfather had a very good gold watch, and I think my father agreed with Frau Scherbatsky that the gold watch would cover a certain amount of time in her house. I know Adele and Elsa had difficulties when Adele was there. There was just no money.'

'Frau Steuer was really a genius in the way that she handled all of that,' Franz said peaceably. 'Do you know what she did with her stores of foreign currency? When the mark started to dwindle, shrink, dwindle, getting tinier and tinier and yet bigger and bigger at the same time … Frau Steuer had some Dutch money, some guilders, I think. There were only five hundred. But she saw that they could be useful, and she took them to the bank and offered some of them to the bank as security. She asked them for a short-term loan, only three months, and they took a hundred guilders as security and charged Frau Steuer a very large amount of interest on the loan, or so they thought. But at the end of the three months she could pay off the loan and the interest with the other loan she had taken out shortly afterwards using another hundred guilders, which of course was for an immensely larger number, and so on and so on. There was never any trouble about securing a loan and there was never any difficulty about using one loan to pay off another. And at the end of everything, when they introduced the Rentenmarks and a loaf of bread cost fifteen trillion old marks, Frau Steuer went from bank to bank, paying off the loans they had given her, and collecting, one after another, the hundred guilders she had left there as security. She still has the five hundred guilders, I expect. I cannot imagine why I am going to marry her.'

Christian wondered if he had heard quite correctly. 'Oh, surely,' he said.

'No,' Franz said. 'We depended on her so much during that time. It was dreadful. Has Adele never told you? No – I suppose she saw nothing so very wrong about it. Going round to Frau Steuer's house, eating Frau Steuer's food, closing up the workshop – I suppose you know she told me that she sees no reason for me to continue with the business after we marry. She wants me to be a gentleman of leisure, playing skat in the afternoons with her late husband's lawyer and her late husband's doctor. It was a terrible time. And what she demanded of me! Well, it is the way of women. And then to listen to her and her late husband's lawyer, explaining to each other how easy the Jews found it to destroy Germany, every night after dinner, and to listen to your daughter joining in with that – Christian, that was a terrible time. It still is a terrible time.'

'We live in terrible times,' Christian said blandly. 'But they are not so terrible as they were.'

'There was an apprentice called Rosenberg,' Franz said. 'Elias Rosenberg. His family had lived in Breitenberg for generations. He was an apprentice of mine. I got rid of him. I could not stand being questioned about him every day and what I had known about him when I had taken him on. He was the best carver – no, not the best carver, that was the boy Wilhelm who went off to the war with me and never came back, he was the best carver. But he was a very good carver, Elias Rosenberg. And he would not speak to me or say goodbye. I do not blame him. That was shameful, shameful, and I would have to do it again in exactly the same way. I have to marry Frau Steuer. There is no escape for me. But you! Christian! You!'

'Sir?'

'Christian, listen to me. You think you have obligations and duties. But you are in a town where nobody knows you. Your family have never been here except maybe on holiday. The Berlin lawyer! What is known about him? Nothing. I have seen him at your wedding with Adele and never again. Nothing is known about you in Dessau. You have no professional commitments. You have only a wife who is pregnant with your child and a sister-in-law whom we all love dearly, the poor sow. Leave them. Walk away and never look back. How many women have been left like that? Thousands. Let Adele come home to me and Frau Steuer with her child, and tell Breitenberg you died of the influenza. Let her tell her child that the Jews are to blame for everything, and let the women bring up Germany as they choose. You – you can walk away from it all and never see me, or Adele or Elsa, alas, bless her, or, please God, Frau Steuer ever again. Christian –' Franz turned and took Christian by the shoulders. His face was mad and blazing with belief, a natty prophet of the blazing future. 'Christian, just leave. Go to your brother in England. It has all failed for us here, in Dessau, in Breitenberg, in Berlin. It will only get worse for you, living with my daughter and her daughter, listening to that all day long, the rest of your life.'

'It may be a son,' Christian said, now suspecting for the first time that his father-in-law might be clinically insane.

'It is a daughter,' Franz said, shaking Christian's shoulders again.

'You don't like women,' Christian said.

'I once liked them,' Franz said. 'But I am clear of them now. If I could walk away from them for ever, I would. I feel about the women as Adele and Frau Steuer feel about the Jews. And I feel that the happiest time in my life was the time in the trenches when there were no women apart from the ones who wrote you letters and the ones in the nearby towns on leave whom you could— Ah, what is the use?'

'Thank you for the suggestion,' Christian said. 'However, I

love my wife and I am greatly looking forward to the exciting event of our baby together.'

'And here we are at the Hotel Gansevoort,' Franz said, striding forward and taking the hand of Frau Steuer, waiting impatiently at the front gate. 'Am I late, my angel?'

'I had no idea where you had disappeared to,' Frau Steuer said in her melodious, whistling Bavarian speech. 'I had no idea at all. I was so hoping to have a leisurely breakfast with my fiancé. Good morning to you, Herr Vogt! You would not care to join us for breakfast?'

'Alas, we busy working men,' Christian said. She was wearing a pretty floral dress, pink and blue and green, a touch of lace at the bodice, and was holding a white lace parasol. She seemed perfectly charming with, perhaps, a forgivable touch of lipstick at her mouth, but quite discreet. The madman went up the steps, leaving Christian behind, and kissed his fiancée on the cheek.

'What a delightful prospect,' Franz could be heard saying as they went back inside. 'A long, leisurely, hotel breakfast.' He seemed to have quite forgotten that he was to call on Adele once she had woken up. Christian looked up at the clock at the corner of the street. It was all right: he had, after all, plenty of time to go to the Bauhaus and commit his crime before the start of the school day. Christian walked on, wondering whether Franz had really been intending to intercept him all the time, the madman.

5.2

These were some of the things that Christian had prepared to say, if he were interrupted or discovered by staff or students at the Bauhaus in the middle of his crime.

'Oh, my sister-in-law asked me to come early, and lent me her key.'

'Oh, it's a surprise for my sister-in-law – a dealer from Berlin is coming, and I thought ...'

'It's of no concern – I myself was a student at the Bauhaus in Weimar days, and we were forever ...'

'It was only the little teapot I wanted to take – it is of no importance, only for the morning.'

'Well, I myself am a teacher of art, and I thought my boys would benefit from seeing an example of first-class work, of new and advanced first-class work ...'

'But I am Christian Vogt. Surely you know me.'

'I took the key and will be returning it tonight. I am sure Elsa, my sister-in-law, will not regard it as the slightest bit important, so I cannot imagine why ...'

'I am very poor and my wife is pregnant and I want to sell my sister-in-law's silver teapot and have a little, a very little, money of my own. Surely you can understand that.'

'This was all going to be an immense practical joke, and Elsa would be the first one to laugh when she discovers how she has been tricked.'

His mouth was moving silently as he took the five keys on a large brass ring from his pocket and, trying to prevent them from jangling, inserted the first in the lock of the metal work-shop, and turned. There was nobody about. He had walked through the grove of trees, and avoided the bold fronts of the building. He had come into the teaching school by the back entrance. The door opened, and Christian walked into the room, with its strange smell of sour fire, its unfamiliar and practical surfaces. He closed the door behind him. He knew, he thought, which the cupboard was where the Masters stored their work and the best of their student work: it was at the back of the long room. A line of metal lamps guarded the way, like soldiers at a wedding, each of them with an angled stem, poised in salute. He walked noiselessly to the cupboard at the back of the room. He tried the key, but it would not turn. He had a flush of panic before realizing, and almost laughed to realize, that somebody had actually forgotten to lock the cupboard the night before. He took a handkerchief from his pocket, not quite clean, and turned the doorknob while holding it. Inside, there were no more than a dozen pieces. Without turning the light on, he could not be sure, but none of them seemed to be gold. The teapot was unmistakable. Once, Christian would have described it as beautiful. But now he was not a member of the Bauhaus and it seemed ugly, absurd and, most of all, made out of solid silver. He picked it up, again with the handkerchief, and placed it in his large satchel. He locked the cupboard.

The whole sequence of events had taken only five minutes, from the moment Christian had entered the Bauhaus building, and he had had to use only one of the keys he had stolen. He was aware that he should feel remorse or shame. But he did not. He felt liberated, joyous, cock-a-hoop. He walked briskly across the grass and into the grove of trees behind the Bauhaus. He had seen nobody and nobody, he was sure, had seen him. In the afternoon, he would go directly to the street where the butcher nestled between the receivers of stolen goods, and ask them to receive and pay for some stolen goods.

In the event, he arrived at school at the same time as usual. 'Line up quietly, boys,' he said, to the small group already hard at work, scuffing the paintwork outside the art room. The weight of the silver teapot banged against his hip as he went in.

5.3

'It was quite dramatic,' Adele said, knitting quietly on the hard little sofa. In the other room, Elsa's room, the wailing and screaming had subsided, and the noise of fists being pounded into mattress, against walls, onto flesh. There was now merely a sobbing, rising and falling. 'First, Elsa came out of her room and said she was late. Then she looked about her for her keys, and could not find them. She said that she had had them, but I had not seen them, and I told her that she must have left them at the Bauhaus as she so often does.

'I am so annoyed. I had so hoped to go to that interesting-sounding meeting at the town hall about the political future tonight, the one that Frau Steuer somehow knew about. And now I must not go out because Elsa is so upset. And for what? For a teapot, and I am sure she could make another teapot, it is not the end of the world, after all. No, it is for me to stay inside and comfort my sister because she has lost something, and it is so unfair, since I have so little pleasure and am able to take so little interest after all in anything.'

'I would stay and make sure of Elsa,' Christian said uncomfortably. He was sitting at the little dining table, which was set for supper.

'And after all that,' Adele said, 'I told her that I had not seen the keys, that she should go to the Bauhaus and they would be there. Elsa, after all of that, was not sure at all that the keys had been where she thought she had left them, in the empty fruit bowl there on the shelf. So she went to the Bauhaus. But then only two hours later there was screaming at the door outside, the door to the flat, and I had been taking a rest but I levered myself up and there was Elsa, ringing to be let in, and I said to her, tired though I was, I said, "Elsa. Whatever is the matter? Whatever are you making such a din about?" And Elsa said – well, she told me the whole story, and she was truly almost hysterical. She was not herself, truly she was not. She told me that now she will not stay in this horrible country one day longer. That is what she called it, this horrible country. I am sorry. But it is not the end of the world, neither the theft of the teapot nor what my sister is saying. It does not signify, neither of them.

'Of course, now that the keys have gone missing, I suppose we will have to have a new set cut, and perhaps, since they seem to have fallen into the hands of a petty thief, to change the locks on the door to the flat. It really seems an awful waste of money, and just when we could do without spending anything much at all. I really do object to it, even though it does seem to be necessary. It really is too bad.'

Adele was jabbing at the air with a knitting needle, red in the face and hissing so that Elsa would not hear what she had to say. She was a little red face over a great belly, her legs and feet sticking out; she was in her going-out dress of black with red frills at the neck, the one she had made herself last month. When she gabbled like that, she grew breathless, her face sometimes pouring with sweat. Christian looked at his wife without letting an expression pass over his features.

'I don't know,' Christian said eventually, when the gabbling had died down. 'I am sure she has just misplaced the keys. They are probably behind the dining table or on the floor somewhere.'

'No, Christian, that is not possible,' Adele said. 'Because a strange person took the keys, and opened the cupboard in the art room, and stole Elsa's project. She cannot have misplaced them to be found again somewhere in the flat.'

'Oh, don't you believe it,' Christian said breezily. 'Everyone at the Bauhaus is always forgetting to lock things. I'm sure somebody forgot to lock the cupboard and forgot to lock up the workshop, and a hungry student waltzed in and took whatever he could find. Believe you me.'

The keys were, in fact, tucked safely away underneath the cushions of the sofa where Adele was sitting at the moment. Christian knew this because he had placed them there two hours earlier. Adele went on complaining about the obligations now being placed on her, knitting with a furious *clack-clack-clack-clack* in four-four time. In a moment Christian's mind wandered, and he was able to shut out both the noise of his wife's complaint, and the more measured and more disturbing sound of Elsa's distress, only a room away. He picked up the little metal fork from the table setting in front of him, and turned it over, as if checking to see that it was clean. The forks had a ceramic handle with the picture of an edelweiss on them; they had come from a cousin of Adele's as a wedding present, and she claimed to like them. Christian believed that, for their supper, there would probably be the same pigs' liver he had bought the day before from the bad butcher. They had not eaten it, having been taken out to dinner yesterday by Adele's father, who had left on his motoring holiday with Frau Steuer. His mind wandered on, and presently it came to the pleasant thought of the hundreds of Rentenmarks tied together tightly in the inside pocket of his jacket. What the money would go towards, he did not quite know. He expected it would go to defray many small expenses that he would rather Adele did not know about and her budgeting would have no control over. That was an agreeable thought, as she went on talking, her needles clicking.

'Oh, Adele,' he said, setting the fork down, and looking at her with his hands spread wide. 'I will never, ever leave you and the baby. I love you so much.'

Adele looked at him with amusement and surprise. 'Well, that is good to know,' she said. 'But I do not think I was in any doubt on the subject. When Elsa has calmed down a little, I shall go and start to cook some supper. It is only noodles and liver with onions, but I think I would like some supper. It is so bad! I was so looking forward to my evening out, hearing about what might be done to improve matters in Germany. I have so few pleasures now, with my belly the way it is. Baby was restless again today, Christian. Baby was so hot,' she said, caressing her stomach and smiling down at it as if the thing she was growing inside could hear and see and understand her. 'Baby was so hot and restless and tiresome today, I did not know what to do with Baby to give Mamma some nice rest. And now this.' Adele gestured towards the noise coming from the other room, the wailing.

Somewhere in the street where the stolen goods were received and the worst meats were despatched, in a back room sat Elsa's silver teapot, wrapped in newspaper as if it were nothing so very much. It waited for its purchaser, a gentleman of special interests and few scruples, to take it away and see what could be made of it. Christian expected that in the end it would be melted down and become something else entirely.

5.4

It was a good day. As sometimes happened, a letter from Dolphus arrived a day after a delayed one, the postal services, whether in England or in Germany, making up for their confusion by a prompt delivery of the next. It was propped up on their bed, like the one before, unannounced by Adele. Dolphus wrote weekly, and did not know about the irregular deliveries; he brought his brother up to date with what had been happening in his life. Christian skipped through the first page and a half, the better to have the pleasure of reading them properly later, on his second or third read.

A man called Norway, an engineer with Vickers, came to give a talk to a small supper club that a few of the fellows have here – an engineers' supper club. We are such jolly fellows, and build such bridges in the sky when we talk! Norway was a pugnacious fellow, who came straight to the point. He is working on a project of airships; he has been the calculator of stresses. But he says he is not excited by the project. There are too many problems with airships, too many things that the commercial requirements have asked him to overlook and neglect. He said that the future lies with the aeroplane, which will take such forms that we know not what they will become in our lifetimes, capable of hundreds of kilometres an hour, capable of flying at thousands of feet in the air. That is the issue, Norway said: how to pressurize the cabin, how to make it secure against the low air pressure outside, which will enable a plane to fly at many times the speed it is now capable of. The airship? It will be quite forgotten.

We were so excited to hear the views of the future expounded by one who truly understands. But after this exciting evening, I found myself disconsolate. In Germany, there is so much belief in the airship. And it seems to me that the future is here. Here is where the great ideas will spring from, and where change will happen. Nothing will happen in Germany, just an attempt to sit on the future and not allow it to happen. There will be nothing left in Germany from which to make anything new, just vast wobbling airships in the air, and in five years the Kaiser, or somebody like him, passing decrees in Berlin. Here is where the future is, Christian. I wish that you and Adele would see that, and come here. But I do not expect that Adele's mind can be changed in any respect. That makes me so sad. I have decided that after my degree I will go to work in aeronautics. It is where the future will be decided.

You will be interested to hear that I have finally met a woman of the opposite sex! However, you must not be excessively interested. The woman in question is merely a neighbour of my landlady's, here in Tregunter Road. She lives in a tall, thin house painted white, like all the other houses in Tregunter Road, and a house, like all the houses in Tregunter Road, that could benefit from being painted white again. I saw her standing outside the house remonstrating with a delivery man, a handsome old mahogany commode on the pavement. It was starting to rain. There was a small child by her side, holding her hand. The problem seemed to be that the delivery man and his mate would not carry the commode upstairs into the first-floor drawing room. Stairs, he said, would have been extra. The poor woman was beside herself. I think it did not occur to her that the men were merely asking for some extra payment, unofficially. I intervened and suggested that if she could manage to carry one side of the commode, I would very happily carry the other. She accepted with great alacrity and pleasure. 'You see,' she said, dismissing the delivery men, 'even a passing foreigner has more thought and consideration than you. I shall certainly be speaking to Mr Carrington about this. I have done a good deal of business with him over the years, but no longer. Come along, young man.'

She meant by 'young man' her little boy, not me, but I followed her in any case. It was no real effort, and she gave me a cup of tea. I could not understand where her husband was – whether he was absent, at work or perhaps even dead. She seemed very independent, but her most passionate interest was in her son, a small boy of four or five. At first I thought his name was de Sallen, or something of that sort, exotic though it appears. Later, I understood that he was called Alan, a much more ordinary name. She had introduced him by saying, 'Oh, he knows his antiques, he knows his stuff there, *does Alan*.' As they say in English, he was her *pride and joy*, and she entertained me with talk, quite improbable, of his gifts and abilities. 'Do you know,' she said, her eyes shining, 'even at his age, he can distinguish Wedgwood and Sheraton, at a glance? He has a real eye, he does. He knows the difference between Doric and Ionic in an old building. Oh, he knows his stuff, does Alan.' The little boy sat, beautifully dressed, looking at me as if trying to establish what my maker or hallmark might be. The child has an extraordinary sage, learned, knowing air, and is dressed in his best clothes by his doting mother. As he looked at me, I feared that he might want to turn me over and examine the marks on my bottom. Now I think about the encounter, I realize that I know what his name was, but not hers. So if she fulfils her promise to invite me to tea, when it will be properly carried out, she will have to remind me who she is when she drops the card in. She was very amused to hear where I live, and full of tales of the misbehaviour of previous inhabitants of the boarding house. I had thought that the street was an irregular one, but evidently those who live there cling to a belief in their own gentility. It was a small adventure but, as I indicated, it is almost the first occasion I have met a woman of any sort, so I thought it worth recording. I dare say that in several months, not to mention the years to come, you will be boasting about your own little Alan and his gifts in precisely the same way as my new friend. Take heed!

Christian went on reading, absorbedly. Outside, the smell of onions frying had begun, and the clatter of knives came from the kitchen. The sound of Elsa crying had begun to diminish. In his pocket were several hundred Rentenmarks. He was happy to think of it. He would stay with Adele for ever, and do his duty, and that would be his future, not Dolphus's in London. From somewhere in the building, the same and usual sounds of the neighbours were rising upwards: the first shouts of a row, laughter over something, the noise of a china plate being dropped on a hard floor, the front door being heavily slammed, the sound of a piano being practised, the same two or three difficult bars. It was agreeable to sit on the bed before dinner and read your brother's letter from London with its news of the future, and what the world might become. Through the window, the lights were coming on in the flat on the other side of the courtyard, and someone was washing the dishes from their dinner; the plump woman he often saw, her waist now being encircled by her plumper husband with the heavy moustache as she plunged the dishes into the sink. There was a faint delicate spatter of noise from the courtyard. He could not think what it was. It continued. Out there, it was beginning to rain, the drops falling singly on stone and roof.

EPILOGUE
2014/1933

1.

The young woman with the beautiful coat had walked over to the other side of the road several times to ring the bell at the apartment block opposite. She was Yusuf's only customer. It was a Tuesday afternoon, and the snow was starting to be quite heavy, but the café was not a success, and Yusuf doubted he would have had any other customers in any case. He was starting to believe that Steglitz was not ready for an elegant Turkish tearoom, with perfect tiny Turkish cakes. He had come here with Florian, away from all the Anatolians in Kreuzberg, and had been convinced that the ladies of the area would find the idea irresistible. They had made a lovely website, with beautiful photographs of the terracotta interior, the singing birds in the gilt cages, the elegant golden chairs and the antique photographs of Ottomans in golden frames. There were details of what cakes you could order, and smiling photographs of both blond Florian, who looked after the business, and dark Yusuf, who made the cakes. It had been a year now, and sometimes whole days passed with only one customer, or sometimes with none at all.

He did not think the woman today was Turkish, but there was something foreign about her. Her coat was expensive, a white waisted coat with a huge fur collar, and when she took off her white fur hat, like a Cossack's, her black bobbed hair was glossy and sharply cut. She had arrived out of the snow carrying a heavy parcel, saying, *guten Tag*, but that was the limit of her German. She must have arrived in a taxi, Yusuf thought, and rung the doorbell opposite before coming across the road to the café. She had coffee with a small cake; she ate it in tiny bites, her eyes fixed on the snowstorm. In ten minutes, she paid and left. She must have thought she had seen somebody entering the apartment block, but it was either a mistake or not the person she was looking for, because in a moment or two she came back, and asked for a glass of water. In a few minutes, she did exactly the same thing, sinking down with graceful tiredness.

Yusuf's English was not as good as Florian's, but he could make an effort and, after thinking for a moment, said, 'If you wish, I can keep your parcel when you want to go over the road.'

'Oh, thank you,' the woman said. 'I am waiting for a friend. He is not expecting me, however.'

'He is not— Ah, I see,' Yusuf said. 'I perhaps know him.'

'You know him?'

'Maybe I know him, I mean, if you say me who you are waiting for.'

'Oh, I see. It's a surprise, really. It's an old friend called Arthur. I think he lives there. I hope he lives there still. We heard from him five years ago and this was the address.'

'I think maybe he must be moved – in five years that is often what happens. I do not know anyone who is called that who lives there. What was the name you said, please?'

'Arthur. He doesn't move unless he has to, I don't think. He stays where he is. I thought it was worth a try. But you don't think he lives there.'

'No,' Yusuf said. 'There is only our friend Philip who lives there. He is English. He has lived there for many years now. Is it perhaps a friend of Philip's who you are looking for I think?'

'Perhaps,' the girl said, reflectively. 'I only have a number – it was flat number seven.'

'That is Philip's flat, I know,' Yusuf said. 'It seems strange, but perhaps he can help when he gets home. I can call him if you want it. He is not far from here.'

'Oh,' the girl said, and she broke out into a wonderful smile, the smile of a woman of thirty who has been given the gift of great kindness. 'Oh – would you? Would that be a great trouble to him or to you?'

'Oh, no,' Yusuf said. 'He works very near by. He is a waiter in a café – a big German café, a successful one, not like this one. I can call him and when he is busy then he will tell me over the phone what he knows.'

Yusuf went to the back of the shop and called Philip. When they had spoken for a while, he came back, smiling.

'You are certainly lucky,' he said. 'I asked him if he knew anyone called Arthur, that there is a young lady asking for an Arthur who lives in his flat, and Philip said to me that he will come straight away, and he sounded very excited and pleased. But he asked me what your name was and I did not know what to say.'

The young lady beamed, and began talking very fast in English. It defeated Yusuf, but he went on smiling. He thought of saying, in a joking way, that he hoped his friend Philip was not one of those people who are discovered to have imprisoned a young man in his flat for many years, but he thought it through, and he could not think of how to say 'imprisoned' in English, and could not think of another way to say it. So he smiled and nodded, and brought another cup of coffee to the lady, saying the phrase he had learnt, which was 'On the house.' And presently there was the form of Philip opening the door and shaking his umbrella and stamping his feet from the snow. He had come so quickly that he was still wearing his black waiter's apron.

The woman rose to her feet. She seemed to be scanning Philip for some sign of recognition, but was perhaps unsure.

'It's a long time since anyone's called me Arthur,' he said to Yusuf in German, looking the woman over in quite a friendly way. 'People used to call me Arthur in London.'

'Do you know Arthur?' the woman said to him. She had only

caught the name in what Philip had said. 'I've come looking for Arthur. Do you speak English?'

'I used to be called Arthur,' Philip said in English to the woman. 'And you?'

'I'm Celia,' the woman said. 'I've come to say hello.'

'Celia,' Philip said – Arthur said, rather – but in a warm, recognizing way. 'Celia. My God. Look at you.'

2.

They crossed the street in the falling snow, Arthur sheltering under Celia's umbrella, and into the apartment block. They kept casting sidelong glances at each other. Was the other what they remembered? Neither seemed sure. Arthur was stocky and muscular, his head shaved; at the cleavage of his white shirt the edge of a tattoo was apparent on his bulky chest. Celia had been a child before, but was there some essence there that had been preserved? Her colouring was dark, her face neat, her eyes big and her skin smooth and glowing. Mainly, she glowed; her face was so interesting to look at that you might forget to remark how lovely she was.

'I don't know how you found me,' Arthur said, opening his third-floor door with a key he fetched from his trouser pocket. 'I'm impressed. Excuse the mess.'

The flat was only a little chaotic, and what mess there was came from books, in piles in the hallway, on the worksurface in the kitchen, and on tables, on the dining table, on the sofa, on the floor. There were a few plates and mugs, unwashed, but no more than that. It could have done with a paint; in the hallway, there was a mark about the four-foot mark where Arthur had rested his head to take his shoes off, as he did now.

'You sent a postcard to Uncle Duncan, five years ago,' Celia said. She stood with her package, not taking her coat off, or her shoes; it was very cold in the room, almost as if a window were open somewhere in the flat. 'It had your address on it. My uncle said he hadn't known where you were until then. You just went away.'

'I told him I'd gone to Berlin,' Arthur said, sitting down and putting his stockinged feet up on the sofa. 'I didn't just disappear. I'd forgotten that – I sent him a postcard. I don't know why I did.'

'It was a good job you did,' Celia said. 'The bookshop was closing down. If you'd waited another month, your postcard would have arrived at a branch of Starbucks.'

'Oh, aye,' Arthur said, with the noncommittal quality that masks deep emotion. 'Is it cold in here?'

'Well, I do find it a little cold,' Celia said. 'But that's just me, I expect.'

'I expect it's not,' Arthur said. He went outside and turned a central-heating dial on. 'I can make you a cup of coffee, if you'd like,' he said, coming back in, 'or tea, even – I'm the only man in Steglitz who knows how to make a good cup of tea.'

'Yes, foreigners,' Celia said. 'They think a cup of warm water, delivered with a teabag in the saucer is good enough.'

'For you to dunk, hopefully,' Arthur said.

Celia shot him a grateful, surprised look. 'You used the word "hopefully" quite correctly there,' she said. 'It's unusual. I must be desensitized.'

'It's speaking German all day long that does it,' Arthur said. 'I remember you. I remember you very well. You used to come into the shop with your mother, and sit and chat with me. It used to surprise the customers, seeing a seven-year-old girl there, on the till, playing shopkeepers. I know why I sent the postcard. I heard about the shop closing one day when I was in Prinz Eisenherz. That's the gay bookshop here. They don't have a seven-year-old girl on the till playing shopkeepers, though, so it's obviously a bit rubbish.'

'I was such a very girly little girl, too, I expect,' Celia said. 'I think I will have that cup of tea. I've never been to Berlin

601

before. I just knew you were here, but I always thought … This is very respectable.'

'It was so cheap,' Arthur said. 'When I came here, the rents were so low. And now I can't move. I'm used to it here.'

'The Birkbuschstrasse,' Celia said. 'I've been practising saying it so that the taxi driver would understand. It's quite hard to pronounce, I must say.'

I don't know when the last time I saw you was,' Arthur said. 'I went all of a sudden and I never said goodbye to anyone, not even Duncan. Was he cross?'

'Well, I don't know,' Celia said, following Arthur into the narrow kitchen. 'I was only twelve. All I can remember is that I asked where you were one day, and my uncle said that you'd moved abroad. I think he might have felt a little let down. Nobody afterwards stayed as long as you did, and there was one girl who started stealing money from the till. Nobody could understand it – twenty pounds down, three or four days a week. There must have been a dozen new Arthurs, but nobody stayed long. And then in the end there was no money to pay anyone, and Ronnie just said—'

'Ronnie's still around, then?'

'Well, yes. Ronnie and my uncle, they moved. I'm supposed to say Uncle Ronnie too, but I'm very sorry to say the habit came too late to stick. They're living in Rome. Uncle Duncan speaks beautiful Italian nowadays. I don't know how Ronnie fills his days – I think he plays with his stocks and shares in the morning, goes to haggle with an antiques dealer or to visit a church or a painting and then has a very complicated sort of lunch that he's ordered from Annunziata. She went with them, she's very happy.'

'I don't remember Annunziata,' Arthur said. Some sort of chill had come into his manner as he fiddled with kettle and mugs. 'What's Duncan doing all day long? Is he happy? He must be sad about the bookshop.'

'Well, I suppose so,' Celia said. 'I think it was more of a relief in the end, what with the thieving lesbians, and the rent rising all the time, and no one buying books at all. He was just glad to be rid of it. He must be sad now, when he thinks about it. But living in that beautiful house, with the man he loves and more money than he knows what to do with – you should see the rent his flat in Notting Hill and Ronnie's house in Chester Terrace bring in. Mummy manages them. She's retired now, of course. So it worked out quite well for everyone. They never see anyone, I don't think – just a few Roman friends. None of them ever reads a book, as far as I could tell.'

'I wouldn't have thought that would happen,' Arthur said. 'Duncan going off into a bubble. I thought he wanted to— Oh, well, it doesn't matter. If I had the money, I'd never go out. I'd put up a big wall around myself – I'd never leave the house either.'

But Uncle Duncan, it seemed, left the house every day, and was very friendly with the local shopkeepers, the family in the café, the neighbours, such as the security guards and officials who worked downstairs in the *piano nobile* of the great historic palazzo where they lived. He had not put a big wall up around himself; everyone around knew them as the *gentiluomini inglesi*, and everyone loved them. 'I hate to say it,' Celia said, 'but they might love Ronnie a little bit more because his Italian is so bad. He sounds like an Englishman making quacking noises. *Mi scusi, signora, ma com'è il formaggio oggi?* They simply love it.'

'It sounds a lovely way to spend the rest of your life,' Arthur said, handing her a cup of tea.

'Well, he's writing his memoirs too,' Celia said, clutching it with white-gloved hands. 'Or it might be a novel. Nobody knows, really, not even Ronnie.'

'I see,' Arthur said. There were the beginnings of an undertone of hostility between the two of them; it was not the meeting that either of them would have wanted. What was it? The waiter looked at the frosted and furred dark woman, and she looked at him. She softened; she smiled.

'Let's go through,' she said. 'I've brought something for you.'

The parcel was heavy, and evidently some books. Arthur opened it, tearing at the brown paper with the end of his teaspoon.

'The German Customs made me open it when I came in,' Celia explained. 'I had to rewrap it afterwards in the hotel. I'm staying at the Adlon.'

'I was going to say,' Arthur said, 'you're very welcome to stay. You'd need to bring your own sheets and towels, though. But you've got a hotel you're staying in, that's nice.'

He pulled away the paper, and inside there were ten identical books; they were copies of *The Garden King*. They were old, but only a little faded. Arthur opened the top copy; it was signed on the title page with a confident gesture. He held the book and was young again. He had been there. Stuart Inkerville had come in, thin and exhausted, and had signed them all. It had taken so long. He, Arthur, had stood by him and opened one title page after another and, when Stuart had said, 'I think I could benefit from a short break,' had fetched him a cup of tea, a glass of water – what had it been? Whatever Stuart Inkerville had wanted. And then he had said he had no hope of writing anything else, and had gone. The signature on this copy had been in blue ink; it had once been fresh and dark and wet, as Arthur, at only eighteen, had looked as it had dried. He had shut this copy too quickly: the faded blue ink had made a mark on the opposite page, in reverse. He had been so careful about it, too, wanting to do the job properly. He remembered it well, and Duncan, who had a thousand and one things to do, just coming back and looking in a benevolent, encouraging way at his very first author, and it only sinking in slowly what a lot of copies of this book he'd ordered. It had been the slow progress of the signing that had done it. But here it was, and Arthur was glad of it.

'Thank you,' he said simply. 'I don't have a copy of it. Well, I do – I have a copy of the new paperback. I bought it when the film came out. I kept saying to people we knew about this book from the start, from the very first day. I said to people I'd met the author. But they didn't really believe me, I suppose, and I didn't really know anything about him. I just met him that once, and then he died. The film was—'

'It was wonderful,' Celia said. 'It was a wonderful film. Indescribable. I didn't think they made films as wonderful as that any more.'

'But the book,' Arthur said.

'Exactly,' Celia said. 'Uncle Duncan asked me to find you, and give you ten copies. He said you deserved it. The book in the end – you know, he put all the rest on eBay, and they went for a fortune. It turned out the publisher had only printed three hundred copies in the first instance. Most of the rest were in libraries. It was a sort of treasure trove no one knew about when the film came out. Of course, it's sold seven million since then, and then the translations, too. He had a sister. She worked for a travel agent, all her life. She's rich now.'

'I often wondered – how did he know the book? The director?'

'I don't know,' Celia said. 'He must have been a customer of the bookshop in the early days. You used to foist it on anyone who showed the slightest interest, my uncle said.'

'I did.'

'I bet you miss that, now.'

'Oh, I still do my fair share of foisting, even in the café. You'd be surprised how many opportunities there are to say to a lingering customer that they might like to try a different Joseph Roth next time. I live on my own, too. That seems to help wi' foisting.'

'Ronnie did say that the sister might have felt an obligation to give a donation of the royalties to the bookshop, since you and my uncle did so much to sell them in the first place. But of course the bookshop wasn't really open any more by then.'

'She could send her royalties to me, if she felt that guilty,' Arthur said.

'Well, feel free to sell them,' Celia said. 'It'll pay for a very good holiday, I would have thought.'

'I'll keep two,' Arthur said. 'One for reading, and one just to keep and look at and preserve. *The Garden King*. I knew people would come to it. Did Alan read it?'

'It was Alan's favourite book, at the end,' Celia said, with a crispness that indicated the subject could not be entered on; and Alan had been her favourite homosexual, Arthur remembered.

'I wondered why you'd come to see me,' Arthur said. 'To come all this way, just to bring a few books. That was so nice.'

Celia drank her tea. She looked in an assessing way at Arthur. 'There was something else,' she said.

3.

Not everyone had come in after the party last night. It had been in the basement of the former telephone factory in Birk-buschstrasse. They had been getting the building into teaching order, but there was no doubt that the Bauhaus had been in better condition in Dessau. The students who had come in were expecting the worst today, and sat about on the borrowed and stolen tables, talking about what it had been like in Dessau. What had happened to that building? The NSDAP had seized it, as it had seized all of Dessau, and it had become, what, a school, a medical institution? But the buildings would not do as they were, one architecture student told another. It had flat roofs. That was what Oriental, Jewish buildings looked like. Work was at hand to amend and improve the main building, and also what had been the Masters' Houses.

There was a little Master, a new one, who had been taken on only when all the old Masters moved to Switzerland, or America, or India, or England. He said he had been connected with the Bauhaus for such years – oh, such years, since he was a student and it had been in Weimar. And now they had taken him on in

Berlin. He heard the architecture student talking amusingly about the flat roofs of Dessau.

'The surprising thing,' the little Master said, 'the very surprising thing is that I myself grew up in Berlin in a house with dragons, plaster dragons ornamenting the portico. Dragons seem much more Oriental to me than flat roofs, but I don't know that the Party is thinking of tearing those down. I must ask my wife,' he finished, in a sort of mutter.

They were not quite sure what he was doing there. There did not seem to be any prospect of teaching happening today. It was a bright clear day in April; the light outside the shabby factory was making the eyes of some of the students hurt. It was always a surprise when one of the Masters remained, even a very little one. It was a pleasant game among the more ambitious students to name the people who had taught or studied at the Bauhaus, and then say, laughing, where they were now. Joseph Albers was somewhere else in America. Hannes Meyer was in the Soviet Union. Gunta Stölzl in Switzerland. Klee was back in safety in Switzerland. Someone else – Tel Aviv, was it called? Moholy-Nagy – England. Egon Rosenblatt was in Kentucky. Kandinsky – France. Elsa Winteregger – New York. Where had they gone? The place of the Bauhaus was here! The spirit still existed, but was it here, in the old telephone factory on the Birkbuschstrasse in Steglitz? All those people, sitting in their lonely rooms, starving amid the obscene riches of America, the cold, silent, urban fogs of England, they did not know what they were doing. The place of the Bauhaus was here, whatever the politicians decided.

The students sat in the dim room, perched on tables, their feet on the chairs, and presently one started passing a bottle to another. Another student remarked that the time was getting on, and they might have to go downstairs and start clearing up from the party. They might start by taking down the streamers in this classroom. But a girl laughed and laughed, holding the bottle. She said there was not much to be said for being closed down by stormtroopers. But one of the things in its advantage was that the school's last and best party would have to be cleared up by the stormtroopers. Look, she said. They are already outside, preparing for their task of cleaning. They all went to the windows. It didn't matter, a student remarked. He had himself rammed a broomhandle through the door handles, inside. Outside, there were hundreds of military officers, in black. Each had a truncheon, either in his fist or hanging from the waistband. At the front stood a major in, inexplicably, an American uniform. His men were waiting patiently, feet apart, for the order to begin the operation.

In the centre of the city, in a room high up in a heavy palazzo, the director of the Bauhaus stood and talked to a party official. He had said to others that he was not afraid before arriving. But now he was afraid.

'The Bauhaus is nothing to do with politics,' the director said. 'You have to understand – we are about craft and technology. It has a certain idea.'

'I, too, am an architect,' the party official said smoothly. 'I am from Riga.'

'We understand each other, then,' the director said.

'I think that will never happen,' the party official said. 'Whatever you expect me to do – that is not possible. Your Bauhaus is driven by forces that are enemies to our forces. This is one army against another, two spiritual armies.'

'I don't think it's like that,' the director said, helplessly.

'If you wanted to help yourself,' the party official said, 'you should have changed the name when you moved from Dessau to Berlin.'

'It is a wonderful name,' the director said. 'The Bauhaus. There is no better name.'

And then the party official seemed to speak in parables. He said, 'You can suspend something: you can cantilever something; but my feelings demand a support.'

'The support, too, can be cantilevered,' the director said.

'Yes, that is so,' the party official said. 'Tell me. What is it that you want to do at the Bauhaus?'

The director walked around the desk, with his heart in his mouth. He felt he could be shot at any moment. He pulled out the drawers of the official's desk and pushed them in again. He banged on the back of the official's chair. 'You are important. You are sitting here in an important position. And look at your writing table! Look at your shabby writing table! Seriously, do you like it? I would throw it out of the window. That is all we want to achieve. We want to have good objects that do not beg to be thrown out of the window.'

The official seemed cowed. He took his pen from the desk tidy and began to write something on a sheet of official paper. But it was not the letter that the director had hoped for. It was concerning something else entirely. The official cast a look upwards, and the director walked back to the other side of the desk.

'We will see what can be done for you,' the official said.

'Well, don't wait too long,' the director said. He left.

But now the factory was echoing with noise; the thunderous bang of shoulders being thrust against the door. The irruption could not be long delayed. There were only thirty or forty of them inside, and at the beginning of the noise, they instinctively slid off the tables and stood. At least one was regretting coming to the Bauhaus today. There was no point. It would be closed today, and everyone here would be severely beaten. But others were thinking that there was something glorious about being here at the very end. They were thinking this before the infliction of physical pain.

The noise continued, and a girl clambered awkwardly onto the scarred work table at the centre of the room. She was a girl with vivid red hair, tied back with a rubber band. Before she spoke, she gave a calm gesture of her hand over her hair, smoothing it down. 'Comrades!' she said, and a mild, half-suppressed jeer came from the room. 'Comrades, I say! This has been our story! And from now on, for us, the story continues outside the institution. It continues in the prisons, and in the schools, but it does not continue in the institution that made it. It continues in our hearts, and in our hands, and wherever a sheet of paper can be found! Think of that!'

There was some scattered applause from the group, but also a rude noise and a murmuring of dissent. The regular hammer of bodies against door continued. 'Comrades! Listen to me! What do we have? We have no guns and we have no clubs. We have no stones to throw. But we are stronger, in the end we are stronger, because we have a teapot! We have a tapestry! We have a carpet that we made ourselves! Comrades, I am serious! We have this above all. We have in our hands this wonderful thing. Look!'

She held it up, a heroic pose, and her face tilted upwards to hail the small thing. Some people actually laughed, a derisive, sharp laugh. Christian Vogt thought that this gesture was all very well, in its way, to fill the short minutes remaining to them, and to the Bauhaus. But he wondered if he would ever see his wife and daughter, his brother, again, or if he was about to die under the blows of a truncheon in a police cell. 'Look what we have!' she said. 'This is ours, and we know how to use it. Remember that they can smash our bodies, but they cannot smash our minds. They can smash one pencil, but they cannot destroy every pencil. Remember, too, that ...'

But the doors to the Bauhaus were now splintering and smashing, and there was the sound of heavy boots crashing towards them down the central corridor. The derisive laughter in the room died away, and the students faced the door. The red-haired girl on the table held her position for a moment. She felt like a statue of resistance, but nobody there was observing her. Still, as the thugs in uniform crashed into the room, their truncheons raised, she held her arm up; the small soft drawing pencil in her hand indicating the ceiling. With a nervous gesture, she smoothed her hair again, pulling it away from her neck. She was alone, indomitable, angry and, for a few last moments, free. Just before the end came, she caught a glimpse outside the room. In the corridor, as the thugs ran in, there stood, quite coolly, the major in the American uniform.

4.

'Say if you need to get back to work,' Celia said, clutching her second cup of tea in her gloved hands. 'You've been so kind. It's been wonderful seeing you.'

'There was something you wanted to ask me, you said,' Arthur said. 'Best just to come out with it.'

'Arthur,' Celia said. 'I can still call you Arthur, can't I? I was so much your friend as a little girl. It seems odd to call you anything else.'

'Arthur is fine,' Arthur said.

'When was it that you first knew me? I can remember being in the bookshop, very young, three or four. But you must have seen me before that.'

'I remember you later much better,' Arthur said. 'I remember you being there from start, though. Your mother coming in to say hello, and there was a big bulge, her tummy, you know, and I said to your uncle when she'd gone, she's surely not having a baby, your sister? He said, Oh, yes, didn't I mention it? There was a sort of pact between them not to tell anyone anything, much. You had to ask, or guess. And then when you were born, I remember your mother bringing you in when you were only three weeks old, a tiny thing, like a deflated balloon. A deflated balloon wi' hair on. I'm sorry if that sounds rude. And then I remember you coming in when you could walk, and going straight to a bookshelf. You were fascinated by books. Children are. They go to a bookshelf and pull one out and shake it as if they could shake all them words loose. So there was that stage. And then you remember rest, I dare say.'

'I wondered,' Celia said. 'You must have known Mummy quite well, I suppose.'

'Oh, yes,' Arthur said. 'Very well. I saw her every week, at least.'

'I wanted to ask ...' Celia began. 'Arthur, I wanted to ask. When you found that Mummy was going to have a baby, was going to have me, do you remember who it was that she said the father was? Do you know at all?'

'Is that it?' Arthur said, after a moment.

'Is that what?'

'Is that why you've come to find me?' Arthur said.

'I wanted to see you,' Celia said unconvincingly. 'But I wanted to know the answer, too. Is that really so surprising? Why did you think I would come?'

'I don't know,' Arthur said. 'I couldn't have guessed. You'd best ask your mother.'

'Mummy says she can't remember. But I don't believe it. How can that be true?'

'It's not for me to say anything,' Arthur said primly. He had never given the question a moment's thought.

'So you do know. Or you know something. I asked Uncle Duncan and he won't say, and Mummy won't. It's so terribly important to me. No one else is around. Mummy's friends – there were a pair called Katy and Bella, Uncle Duncan said, but they'd long disappeared by the time Mummy had me. And there were people she worked with, but she'd never have said anything to them. I never thought of Mummy as someone without friends, but there just doesn't seem to be anyone who would have known. It's so terribly important.'

'You haven't considered possibility that she's not hiding it from you. She maybe just can't remember. I never met your father. He wasn't important. I certainly never met him.'

'But you do know something, you do. Please. It's so terribly important to me. Wouldn't it be important to you?'

Arthur paused. 'Why is it important?'

'To know where you came from. To know what caused me. You can understand that.'

'I can understand people wanting to know what they've caused. But do you ever know what caused you? How would you know?'

'I would just know,' Celia said. They looked at each other, both curiously tranquil. Celia's face was firm with the determination not to express desperation; Arthur looked at the woman with interest. For the first time in years, he wondered what it must be like to feel like this. Where had he come from? What had caused him? The mother and father – dead now. His sisters; the books he had read. He looked at Celia, and for a fleeting moment saw not her dark father, but her mother, Dommie. He wanted, just for a second, to see Dommie again.

'He was Syrian,' Arthur said. 'He was a student. That's all I know. I don't think there is anything else to know. I don't suppose he even knows that you exist, or ever did know. Dommie wanted it that way. She's not keeping anything from you.'

'I see,' Celia said. She looked a little tearful. 'Look – it's been wonderful to see you. You were so much a part of – oh, I don't know. I had such a happy childhood. I just thought. Well, you've been really a help, I know. And now I'd better go. Do you think I can get a taxi on the street here?'

'The U-Bahn's just around the corner,' Arthur said. 'It's very safe. Are you sure you won't have another cup of tea? They aren't expecting me back at café just yet, I don't suppose.'

'No, I must go,' Celia said. 'You've been wonderful. I'll tell Mummy I've seen you – you'll send her your love, will you?'

'I will,' Arthur said.

It seemed as if the beautiful woman in the fur-collared coat was going to be Yusuf's only customer of the afternoon. The idea of an elegant Turkish tearoom was just not catching on. He went to the plate-glass front window and gazed out. The snow was thinning a little, and as he watched, the door of the apartment block opposite opened, and the woman stepped out. She turned about, to left and right, and, as if at a command, a yellow-brown taxi drew to a halt, and she stepped in. Yusuf reflected that she must have left her package of books with that nice English Philip opposite. Or perhaps, rather, with that nice English Arthur. It was interesting that he had, it seemed, changed his name at some point. Yusuf looked forward to Florian coming back, in order to tell him the interesting news. Florian always liked gossip, if there was any hint of the disgraceful about it. There was a veiled radiance in the air behind the snow, as if the sun were trying to break through before the snow had quite finished. Yusuf stepped out into the street to enjoy the quiet of snow falling under the bright-lit clouds. Somewhere, not so far away, someone was playing a CD with a window open, despite the snow. It was a familiar piece of music, the old-fashioned sound an orchestra might make for rich ladies and gentlemen to dance to, in the old-fashioned times. Yusuf knew it from some-where: he could not name it, however. He stood in the falling snow, and it fell onto his upheld face through the shine of light in the air. He was not quite sure where the music was coming from, from what bright direction.

Battersea-Charmilles-Murray Hill
August 2013

Final Note

There is, indeed, a London bookshop devoted to gay literature, which has been in existence for thirty-five years. I have been a customer of Gay's the Word in Marchmont Street all my adult life. Happily, unlike Duncan's shop, it is still going strong, and no one in this book bears any resemblance to anyone who works or who has worked in the real shop. I did not investigate its history, and this imaginary story only coincides with reality in the broadest outlines. The same is true of the Bauhaus sequence, where I have changed the order of events and happily combined real historical figures with imaginary ones. Where real people play a part in this novel, from St Perpetua to my friend Paul Bailey, they are always referred to by their real names.

> Diesseitig bin ich gar
> nicht fassbar
> denn ich wohne grad
> so gut bei den Toten
> wie bei
> den Ungeborenen
> etwas naher
> dem Herzen der Schöpfung
> als üblich
> und noch lange
> nicht nähe genug.